Darkflower

A Novel of the Scottish Borders

Book Four in the Spiral Pathways Series

Books in the Spiral Pathways Series

To Jennifer Rackow
Who taught me how to move like a goddess
under the moon

Table of Contents

The World of Darkflower

Characters

Saorsa Stuart's Family

Charles Edward Stuart*: Also known as Bonnie Prince Charlie. Stuart claimant to the thrones of England, Scotland, and Ireland.

Maria Stuart: Saorsa's mother and Charles Edward Stuart's older sister.

Saorsa Stuart *(Sur-shuh)*: Daughter of Maria Stuart and William MacDonald. Niece of Charles Edward Stuart. A Celtic witch.

William MacDonald: Saorsa's father.

Alexander Scott's Family

Adamina Scott: Conall's widow. Edan, Alexander, and Gilbride's mother. Knowledge seeker.

Alexander Scott: Son of Thomas and Adamina. A Jacobite rebel and a *leth dhia,* with human and Fae aspects.

Anne Scott: Killian's wife and Fia Elliott's older sister.

Conall Scott: Deceased Laird of Buccleuch. Adamina's former husband.

Edan Scott: Alexander's brother. Laird of Buccleuch.

Gilbride Scott: Alexander's brother.

Killian Scott: Anne's husband. Alexander's cousin and Fia Elliot's legal guardian.

Thomas Scott* *(also known as Michael Scot or the Magician)***:** Son of The Morrigan and King of the Deck of Crows in Faerie. Father of Alexander.

MacLeod Family

Duncan MacLeod: Vika's older brother. A Jacobite organizer and rebel.

The Aunties (Siùsaidh *(SOO-zed)* **and Beathag** *(BY-hek)***):** Vika and Duncan's aunts. Experts in magickal knowledge.

Vika MacLeod: Duncan's younger sister. Saorsa Stuart's mentor. A weapons specialist and trainer who trained Alexander Scott.

Other characters

Annag: Mother Agnes' apprentice. A Celtic witch masquerading as a nun.

Fia Elliot: Childhood friend of Edan and Alexander Scott. Practicing witch and engaged to Alexander Scott.

Mother Agnes: A powerful Celtic witch masquerading as a nun.

Caroline Frederick Scott*: Lieutenant Colonel. British officer who terrorized Highlanders after the Jacobite Rebellion. Same clan name but no close relation to the Scotts of Buccleuch.

Ciannat *(Chahn-ey-t)*: Diarmid's Fae companion and a henchman for the Violet Woman.

Diarmid: Knight of Hawks in Faerie. Claims to be distantly related to Saorsa Stuart.

Elen of the Ways: A Welsh goddess who guards and leads travelers between realms and worlds.

Laoise *(Lee-shuh)*: A half-Fae, half-human healer.

Macha *(Ma-ha)*: Saorsa's wolf familiar.

Malphas: A mysterious crow.

Rune MacAskill: Nordic pagan whose family has a close relationship with the MacLeods.

Svend: Married to Willow. Nordic pagan and friend of Rune MacAskill.

Tadhg *(Ti-gue)*: Diarmid's companion and a henchman for the Violet Woman.

The Morrigan: A Celtic goddess and member of the Tuatha Dé Danann. Associated with war, fate, death, and battle. Sits of the High Council of the Fae. Mother of Thomas Scott and grandmother of Alexander Scott.

The Valkyries (Fiona and Nola): Vika's childhood friends who help when needed.

The Violet Woman: A Fae with interest in the human world and Alexander Scott in particular.

Toran Armstrong: Vika MacLeod's former student and a weapons specialist. Fought with Duncan MacLeod.

William De Soulis*: Lord and former Scottish Border nobleman and practitioner of the dark arts.

Willow: Married to Svend. Energy healer, animal communicator, and herbalist.

Terminology

Faegod: A Fae with enough magickal power to be worshiped as a god. They then draw additional magickal power from being worshiped.

Jacobite: Supporter of Bonnie Prince Charlie.

Leth dhia: Half-god Fae creature that can split themselves in pieces. Warlike, charismatic, and highly intelligent, their existence is outlawed among the Fae.

Tuatha Dé Danann: The rulers in Faerie, once lived in the human realm.

Locations

Branxholme*: The castle seat of the Scott Clan of Buccleuch.

Buccleuch*: An older clan castle restored by Adamina Scott and used as her home.

Carlisle Castle*: A massive English stronghold not far from the English-Scottish Border.

Melrose*: An abbey that is mostly in ruins. Michael Scot's grave is at this location.

Morrigan's Cave: An old Celtic worship site now used as a hideout by Vika MacLeod and associates.

Ramsay House: Near Branxholme Castle, it is the residence of Killian and Anne Scott.

Wolfcroft: A site with meaning for Saorsa and Alexander.

*Based on historical figure or actual location

Carlisle Castle, England

The water seeped in under the door of his cell, and Duncan MacLeod was glad for it.

It had been raining for the last few hours. Enough that water was finding its way into Carlisle Castle unbidden. If it was here, it had most likely made its way into other cells, where it would keep other prisoners alive. The garrison commander at Carlisle, Caroline Frederick Scott, apparently didn't feel food or water was necessary for his prisoners. The men in Duncan's last cell, all Jacobites, had been left to lick their prison walls, hoping to survive off the dampness that sometimes clung to the stone.

They'd moved him to a cell of his own, away from the others, about two days ago. At least, he thought it was two days. It was hard to estimate the time when you couldn't see the sky. He didn't know the reason for the move, and he probably never would.

He'd been in a prison before. Not one as huge as Carlisle. This castle was the Crown's launching point for its operations in Scotland and looked the part. About a year ago, he'd been one of the attackers who took the castle for the Bonnie Prince during the uprising. He'd been impressed with the place from the beginning with its history as a Roman fort and where Mary, Queen of Scots, had been imprisoned.

He'd started off thinking they'd ship him to London. But as the days went on, he became convinced they'd try and hang him here. Well, they wouldn't actually *have* a trial. They'd fill out the paperwork and then simply hang him, like they had all the other Jacobite prisoners.

He thought of Vika. He knew she was out there. Probably stalking the southern road, hoping to spring him loose when they transferred him. He hadn't seen his sister in half a year. He prayed for her safety and the safety of the men who rode with her, occupying himself with childhood memories as he sat in the near-absolute blackness of his cell.

He wondered if Alex had made it west. He'd be headed this way once he got the message his mother was imprisoned here as well. If she still was. It made him feel better to know Alex and Vika might be out there in the woods together soon. They'd keep each other sane.

He heard a footfall outside the door and a creak as the door opened. He raised his hand and squinted against the brilliant light of the lantern one of the guards held. His eyes weren't used to it.

"Duncan MacLeod," said a man with a clipped English accent. "On your feet. Move."

Interesting, thought Duncan. *That's an educated accent. An officer, most likely. They wouldn't bother sending one simply to move me. Which means it's my turn to die.*

The highlander rose to his feet. *Let's get this over with, then.* His one regret was that he wasn't going to be taking at least some of these bastards with him. He thought of a night about eighteen months ago, sitting next to a late-night fire in an inn, drinking whisky with Alex and a few other friends.

"When they finally hang us," Mackie had said, "what will your last words be?"

He knew immediately. "*Alba gu bràth*," he'd responded.

Scotland forever. Alex had nodded, seconding the emotion, saying nothing. And Duncan had felt, once again, that his young protégé was as close to a brother as he'd ever get.

There were four guards in addition to the officer. They manacled his hands and led him up the stairs and into the courtyard, where the sun was just beginning to light the heavy gray sky to the east. *Dawn.* The rain had stopped. Duncan could hear the sounds of men as they began their day. Not long ago, it had sounded much the same when he'd been here with Alex. When they'd been focused on feeding and housing and supplying their own troops as the Uprising set its sights on London.

He looked up and saw the gallows. But there was no hangman there, as there should have been. And it was too early for much of a crowd from the town to assemble for the spectacle of a hanging.

His eyes roamed the towers and he saw her, up on one of the walkways near the front gates. Adamina Scott, accompanied by three guards and Caroline Frederick Scott. They shared a surname but were as different as day and night.

"Duncan!" Adamina cried. "Duncan!"

He smiled and nodded at her. Caroline Scott had no compassion for Highlanders; he certainly hadn't brought her out to be a friendly face at his execution. What the hell was going on?

The men were shoving him roughly toward the innermost gatehouse. And then...they took him *through.* His mind shifted into planning mode. *Something strange is happening. I'm through the first gatehouse.* An entirely different part of his mind jumped into action, pulling up memories of this part of the castle. *Maps. Resources. Exits.*

Maybe he wouldn't need those last words today after all. They were moving him toward the second gatehouse. *God Almighty, it's cold.* His mind turned to Vika. They'd been trying to catch her for years. Was this part of a plan to lure her in? Had they offered some sort of trade? *Vika'd never fall for that.*

Adamina and her escorts had crossed to a different area where she could see him better. He looked up, almost directly underneath her.

"Tha mi còmhla riut," he shouted up to his fellow prisoner. She'd understand. *I am with you.* He'd always been impressed with Adamina's unflagging devotion to the traditional and often endangered stories, language, and music of Scotland. He knew hearing Gaelic would boost her spirits. *So what if it's outlawed. They're either going to hang me or free me anyway.*

He saw Adamina's face light up. One of the guards shoved him hard.

"Innis dha mo mhic gu bheil gaol agam orra!" she shouted back. *Tell my sons I love them.*

I'm getting out, Duncan thought. Adamina clearly thought he'd be seeing Edan, Alex or Gil soon. *She knows. She's a part of this.*

But why release him, and not her? He turned to look up at her as they moved him under the overhang of the second gatehouse. Three of the guards left and went back inside.

There was a horse standing on the other side of the portcullis. A horse with full saddlebags and no rider. Just a groom, holding the reins. *They're releasing me. Holy shite, they're releasing me!* His mind spun. *And they're going to track me. They're hoping Vika's team pops up to assist me. How stupid do they think we are?*

He had to suppress a laugh. *Caroline Scott is convinced we're all idiots. It's one of the things that lets him hate us. Us Scots, we're lesser people in his eyes.* A small smile crept across his face. *Well, you know what the Crown isn't good at? Thinking on the fly.*
Garrisons don't pivot well.

The portcullis was open. His remaining guard and the officer with the clipped accent escorted him outside. The officer drew himself up to his full height and cleared his throat as the guard put the key in Duncan's shackles. *Oh shite, this motherfucker's going to make a speech.*

"Duncan MacLeod," began the officer with great ceremony, "Garrison Commander Scott...."

He made it no farther than the fifth word. Duncan pulled off his boots, ran right past the horse, and jumped over the side of the bridge into the freezing moat water below. Had he not been underwater, he would have heard the shouts from the bridge and gatehouses, and been treated to the sound of Caroline Scott cursing a blue streak at the top of his lungs.

It was cold. So very, very *cold.* Duncan struggled to stay conscious as he headed for the first checkpoint. He'd done this route before; he'd be able to do it again. He surfaced behind some debris from a fallen structure, gulped down some air, and disappeared underwater again. *Checkpoint one complete.*

They'd expected him to jump on the horse and lead them right to Vika. Screw them all. He was having trouble feeling his fingers and toes. *Nearly there. Nearly there.* Last time he'd done this he was well fed and in fine shape from riding and fighting. This time, he hadn't eaten anything in three days. *But this time was for real.*

He felt a rush of warm water. *The hot spring.* Checkpoint two was just a yard or so ahead. He'd bet those redcoat arseholes had no idea this spring was here. He surfaced again behind a large stone. *Checkpoint two complete.* He pictured Alex laughing as they'd surfaced last time, soaking wet and cracking jokes in Gaelic. Duncan inhaled a large lungful of air. The banks of this moat would be overrun with soldiers any second. This was the part where he'd have to go deep. He hoped nothing had changed in the last year.

He thanked God for Alex's overactive mind.

"I ken we hold it *now*," Alex had said to him once the Jacobite Army had taken the castle, "but that doesnae mean we always will. I'm going to plan a way out, just in case we ever need it." Alex grinned. "As many ways out as I can find. You or I could be a prisoner here one day, ye ken."

Alex had been the Jacobite army's quartermaster, and a damn fine one at that. He had a sobering habit of planning for the worst. And he loved, loved, *loved* a challenge. Thinking of ways out of Carlisle and then seeing if they would work had been *fun* for him. And he'd made Duncan try it.

Duncan went down and across the moat, toward a formidable iron grate that separated the moat from the underside of the town of Carlisle. The Romans had taken advantage of several hot springs in the area and had built a bathhouse for the original settlement here. The tunnels underneath the town had been expanded for defense and storage over the centuries; the current town was built on top of those ruins.

And Alex had discovered a sizable chunk of the iron grate was no longer intact. A sizable chunk *under* the surface. Any soldier looking at the grate from the banks would assume it extended all the way to the base of the moat. Not so.

It was hard to see, being as early as it was. But Duncan found the hole and made his way through, careful to avoid the jagged metal rusting on his left side. *Checkpoint three complete.* He surfaced, gasping for air. While the water was warm, the air was decidedly less so. And it was dark here, but they'd planned for that.

Duncan found the edge of the concrete landing and pulled himself up out of the water. He groped along in the dark until he found the left wall. *Alba gu bràth.* Eleven letters. Eleven steps. "So you dinnae forget, old man," Alex had teased him.

He took eleven steps forward and felt along the wall. On a recessed shelf he found fire starting supplies and two lamps with oil. A few strikes and one of the lamps was lit. He heard rats scurrying away in the darkness. He could move faster now and he knew what he was looking for. A wooden door on the right-hand wall. He grinned as he saw it. Alex found himself *very* amusing. He'd painted his initials "AS" in letters about a foot high on the front of the door.

Duncan shoved the door open. There was a large trunk inside. *Towels. Clothing.* Duncan dried himself off and changed his clothing rapidly, putting on the pair of boots they'd left in his size. *So much better. Warmer.* He pulled a wool jumper on over his shirts. *When I see that lad again, I'm going to make him an honorary MacLeod for thinking of this.*

He found a bag next to Alex's clothes containing a mirror and a razor. He returned to the hallway, found a crate to put his supplies on and shaved as best he could. They'd send soldiers to the town to look for him; any change in appearance was a good idea. He returned the supplies to the trunk and picked up a belt, a brown coat, and a black hat. There was a wool scarf and two of his old knives. He smiled. Paper and ink. He returned to the hall and used his crate as a desk to write five letters in code for the message drops.

He closed the trunk, leaving Alex's things. *I pray he never needs them. Checkpoint four complete.* He picked up the lantern and headed further down the hallway, through a room full of crumbling concrete and tile. Down another hallway full of disintegrating crates. And then, another door. *AS.*

Inside, two packs hung on the wall. Inside each was an empty canteen, a bedroll, a first aid kit, a comb, a fire-starting kit in a leather pouch, and a bag of coins. Duncan took one and slung it over his shoulder. *Checkpoint five complete.*

He took the stairs at the end of the hall and emerged through an old trap door in the storage room of a bakery. There were two men working at a counter in the next room. Duncan had long ago learned that if you just moved as though you were supposed to be in a place, people tended to give you the benefit of the doubt. Especially if you were tall, well-dressed, and armed. Which he now was. He walked through the room in plain sight behind them, and they didn't look up.

He was absolutely starving. He grabbed a loaf of bread that was cooling on one of the racks as he passed by without pausing. Through the back door and into the street. He took a sharp right and headed away from the town square. He'd need a horse, but not from here. Once he had one, he'd make it to the Aunties by tomorrow evening.

He ate the bread as he walked, filled his canteen from a pump near the farrier's, and bought two sausages from a street vendor, which he ate immediately. The soldiers scouring the town didn't even look at him. Ten minutes later he walked out of Carlisle, headed for the first message drop.

Morrigan's Cave, Scotland

The world felt different now. Saorsa MacDonald Stuart turned her back on the stone circle where the portal had been minutes before. She didn't know where the Fae beings who had disappeared through it had gone. All she knew for certain was that she had to find out.

There was a larger plan at work here. People she knew and loved were being collected and disappearing one by one; she'd yet to save any of them. She needed new tactics. A new plan. A bigger worldview. A wave of loneliness wracked her body. *Alex.* They'd taken him. The Fae had put their plan in motion right under her nose. She should have seen it coming. But regret and blame were not going to save Alex, her mother, Adamina, or Duncan.

She began walking back to Morrigan's Cave, trying to think what she should do next. *What would Vika do? After an attack, check on your team and handle any injuries. Get everyone to safety.*

She heard Fia walking behind her but was so angry she couldn't even look at her former friend right now. *Focus on your allies.* Fia was no longer one of those. Her most trusted confidant had become her enemy. Morrigan's Cave felt unsafe now. Their refuge had been invaded; their magick stolen and used against them.

Saorsa returned to the cave, fearing the worst. But the Aunties, Annag, Mother Agnes, Fiona, and Nola had been knocked unconscious, not killed. They were bruised and unhappy, but alive.

Saorsa was surprised that Fia followed her back inside the cave. She couldn't imagine doing what Fia had done. *If I had, though, I probably would have elected to flee. Not stay in the vicinity of those I'd betrayed.* But then, how Fia's mind worked was anyone's guess.

None of Saorsa's Circle companions remembered much. The portal that Elen and Saorsa used had reopened shortly after they had left, and the women thought Saorsa and Elen were returning. Instead, they had been stormed by enemies from Faerie. A dark-haired magick-user with a violet aura had come through first and raised her hands; it was the last thing any of them remembered before falling unconscious.

It was hard to tell them Alex had been taken. Almost as hard as watching it happen. Fia hung back, silent, and the others assumed it was due to grief and that she had been as incapacitated as they had been. Only Saorsa knew the truth.

They'd planned to sleep in the cave that night, but no one wanted to spend the night in the place where they'd just been assaulted. The Aunties invited the other six women to the house but, as exhausted as they were, sleep did not find them. It felt safer to stay together in the large, comfortable sitting room and talk. If they went off to sleep on their own, they'd be alone with their thoughts. The thoughts of where Alex was now, and what might be happening to him.

Duncan. Saorsa's thoughts were of him too. *Diarmid said that our deal stands. That he'd rescue Duncan if I got Alex to speak with him. I can't get to Carlisle in time to tell anyone that Duncan will be executed in the morning, or get a message to Vika about it. And even if I could get there, how would we get him out? Goddess, please let Diarmid keep his word. And please don't let him find out that I don't know where Alex is so I can't keep my side of the bargain.*

But Diarmid's two companions, Ciannat and Tadhg, had been in the cave with the Violet Woman. So whose side was Diarmid on?

Goddess, please watch over Duncan MacLeod. Lord of the Forest, watch over Alex for me. Please let them be alright. I cannot reach either one.

Saorsa struggled to converse with the other women in the room. *I want to tell them everything that happened in Faerie. But Fia is here. And Goddess only knows what she'd do with any information she hears.* There were also private moments from her visit to Faerie that Saorsa hadn't fully processed yet. And so the tale she told had to be edited. *Heavily* edited. She made no mention of the gray orb in her pocket.

The women finally drifted to sleep one by one on the chairs and sofas and stayed there until the morning's light. Saorsa was exhausted from the events of the last several days. She didn't want to sleep, but her body shut down anyway.

The women awoke at the same time, groggy and disoriented. But they pushed through and pushed on. "What do we do now?" Nola asked as she built up the fire. "What's the next move, ladies?"

Saorsa hadn't the slightest idea. The full moon had passed, and even if it hadn't, she knew Elen had been injured and couldn't be summoned a second time at present. "We need an ally. A *faerie* ally. We're in over our heads and I don't have the slightest idea where to begin."

They fell silent. After a moment, Mother Agnes cleared her throat. "Eildon Hills," she said, her voice hoarse. "There's supposed to be a gateway to Faerie there that the Rhymer used."

"What good is a way in if we have no guide?" Beathag pointed out. "Obviously we have enemies there that we didn't know we had. They know Faerie, and we don't."

The room went silent again. Saorsa found herself thinking of Edan. *I need to go to Branxholme and tell him what's happened. I wish Vika was here.* But Vika wasn't. And everyone in the room was watching Saorsa's face. Waiting to see what she would do.

For the first time in her life, she felt what being a leader was like, and her shoulders threatened to buckle under the load. *Before this, I wanted to learn to lead, but I didn't have to. I could always fall back and rely on Alex.*

It's all me now. I'm supposed to make the decisions. These women are willing to help in any way they can, but I'm the one who went into Faerie. I'm the one who swore to look out for Alex. This is my quest. Mine. And I don't know what to do.

She thought of the training Vika had given her. *Once you check on your team, gather information.* The person who had the most information about what had happened to Alex was Fia. She'd have to talk to her in private, though she didn't want to.

She took a long, deep breath. *Eyes up, like a queen.* "I need a little time to think," she said, "and everyone here needs to rest and to tend to themselves and their families. I can't thank you enough for everything you've done. But I think Mother Agnes, Fia, Annag, and I should head to the inn, and the rest of you have your lives to return to. And as soon as I think of a plan, I'll let you know." Everyone nodded, numb and tired.

And Saorsa had taken her first step on a new path. A journey where she made all the choices.

Near Carlisle Castle, England

Harris was checking the message drops again. It seemed pointless. Pretty much every trainer Vika had left in Scotland and anyone who worked with Duncan was camped with them now. Alex and Saorsa were expected any day, but they would most likely ride for the rendezvous point without bothering to message drop, knowing where everyone was already.

But Vika was thorough. *You never know.* So they checked. No one wanted to say it, but the fact that Adamina and Duncan hadn't been sent south to London by now did not bode well. Vika and her team had picked up coins and supplies from the carriages out of Carlisle and managed to interrogate an officer who had no idea who Adamina was but did confess that Duncan was still at Carlisle. That was it.

And it was freezing out here. Harris dismounted and hitched his horse to the remains of a fence outside of an abandoned schoolhouse that was missing most of its roof and walked inside. *We need a change,* he thought. *These long, cold days with no movement forward are grinding us down. We need Alex and Saorsa to show up with new information. Or for the redcoats to move Adamina or Duncan. We need....*

He stopped. *I'm pretty sure I put that stone on the hearth back in a different position yesterday.* He moved to the hearth and picked up the loose stone.

A message. *A new message.* Hands shaking from cold and eagerness, he unfolded it and worked out the code in his mind. *Holy shite.*

> Vika. I'm out. I'm well. They know you're there. Morrigan's Cave.
> -D

"YES!" Harris shouted as he replaced the stone. *He's out! But they know Vika is there.* That isn't good. *How the hell had Duncan gotten out?* Alex mentioned he'd looked for escape routes out of Carlisle, but that the three he'd found were not in normal prisoner areas and were extremely hard to reach. *So either Duncan had help or something unusual happened.* He'd think about it later. He headed for his horse and rode south as fast as he dared.

North of Morrigan's Cave, Scotland

Beathag seemed to have picked up on the fact that Saorsa and Fia weren't comforting each other. *Nothing gets past Beathag,* Saorsa thought with a smile. When Fia wasn't nearby, Beathag pulled Saorsa aside and spoke to her.

"Don't worry," she said. "Siùsaidh and I are going to keep looking for information. We sent letters to some of our book collector friends shortly after you left last time looking for more information on Michael Scot, Hermitage, dragon lines in this area, Carlisle, and a few other topics. That information should be arriving shortly. I also wanted to tell you, we heard from Lennox. He's well, and still headed west with your letters." Saorsa was grateful and told Beathag so. She needed all the help she could get.

Saorsa, Mother Agnes, Fia, and Annag said their goodbyes to the Aunties and the Valkyries and headed for the inn. The four women rented two rooms, one for Mother Agnes and Annag, the other for Saorsa and Fia. Minerva had a loose horseshoe and needed rest, so they'd left her with the Aunties. Once the shoe was repaired and she was rested, Auntie Siùsaidh's son would take Minerva to Ramsay House and drop off Alex's saddlebags at Branxholme on the way.

Saorsa took just five items from Alex's pack to add to hers. Three items were practical, and two were not. A bag of coins and two Highland knives, a mattucashlass and a sgian-dubh, would come in handy as she traveled. She found the tooled leather case Alex used to store small vials of essential oil mixtures and pocketed it. Then she found the velvet bag where he kept his rosary in the lining of one of the bags, and after a moment of hesitation she took that as well.

Saorsa had ridden Thor to the inn and Fia had taken Bridgit. Saorsa found riding Thor strangely comforting. The horse was such a huge part of Alex's life that she found herself thinking that being close to Thor meant Alex wasn't that far away. This made no logical sense, of course; but then, nothing did anymore.

It was nearly noon when Saorsa shut the door to the hall and found herself alone in the room with Fia and an incredibly awkward silence. Mother Agnes and Annag would hopefully be able to get some rest. But Saorsa had things to say before she closed her eyes.

"I'm sorry...," Fia began, trying to break the silence.

Saorsa held up her hand. "Don't. Let's make one thing very clear. The only reason I am sharing a room with you, or coming *anywhere* near you right now for that matter, is because there's a chance that the baby you're carrying is Alex's. *That's* who I'm protecting. *Not you."* Fia nodded and stared at the floor.

"Why you're still here I don't know. But since you are, here's how this is going to go. You are going to tell me everything you know. Who those beings were. When they approached you. What they promised you. I want names, dates, and locations, although Goddess knows if I should actually believe anything you say at this point. And then tomorrow, we are riding to Branxholme and telling Edan what you've done and about the baby. And then Edan will decide what he'll do. I am of the opinion that you should go back to Anne and Killian's."

Fia shook her head. "Alex said I could stay at Buccleuch."

"Yes, well," snarled Saorsa, "he's not exactly here to enforce that, *is he*, Fia?" Saorsa found herself pacing by the fireplace. "You can't marry someone you had kidnapped, can you?" She turned once she reached the mantle. "And apparently you've been keeping company with all sorts of beings from Faerie. For all I know, that baby might not even be Alex's!"

"It is!" Fia said, her voice insistent.

Saorsa advanced on Fia, a storm building on her face. "The truth, now! Did Alex take you to bed at Ramsay House? Because he doesn't remember that happening. Was that child conceived with him *in the room with you?"*

Fia seemed to shrink. There was a long pause. "No," she said in a small voice.

"Then explain to me *why* you keep saying the child is his! He's not the only male in his House, you know!"

"They...did this ritual. With my blood and his. They said...,"

Saorsa had to restrain herself from shaking Fia violently. She knew exactly what had happened. *The things the Keepers took from Alex's Faerie side and sold on the black market. Some of them had been used on Fia. Here.* "And you thought that was the right and moral thing to do, *why?*"

Fia stood up. "Look! Alex is miserable. He's got something possessing him, everything he was told about his family history is wrong, and he's constantly living in fear about who his other side in Faerie is. Admit it, Saorsa, he's not happy, and there was no real shot at rectifying the situation!"

"We were working on it!"

Fia raised her chin. "Oh yeah, and how's *that* been going? You ended your relationship because you were afraid of him and now he hates himself. We can't just wander aimlessly all over the Borders while he slowly turns into a monster, while you crack and fall to pieces! Someone had to *do* something!"

Saorsa was absolutely incensed. "So the thing you chose to do to make him happy was *drug him, lie to him, and give him to unknown Fae beings?*"

"They said," said Fia, "that Alex needed my help. That the only way he'd be happy was if his Faerie side and Human side were put back together. His Faerie side wants to do it. Once they were united again Alex would know who he was, understand his history, and be able to control his faerie traits. They said they could help him, but that the side of him here in Scotland would be too uninformed to participate willingly, even though it was what was best for him. They said they could heal what the Blade of the Dead did to you, too. And then we could all live in Faerie. Where it's safe."

Saorsa rubbed her temples. "Explain to me how the blood magick spell that resulted in a pregnancy was supposed to help?"

"They said when the two sides of Alex are rejoined that there might be side effects. That other *leth dhia* who have had parts merged back together sometimes can't reproduce. They said Alex's Faerie half sent them to see if I was willing to be a mother to his child since we're friends and I understand faeries. And I would love to have a baby. Someone of my own. So I said yes."

Saorsa could barely speak. *She thinks she understands faeries?* "That...is the biggest load of crap I've ever heard. *Tell me* you are making this up on the spot. Because if this is what *actually happened*, and you believed it, then you are *not* the smart woman I thought you were."

Fia shook her head. "It's the truth."

"So you are telling me...," Saorsa laughed incredulously, "that faeries showed up out of nowhere, volunteered to unite Alex's Faerie and Human side, offered to ensure he could have a child in case he became sterile, promised to heal me, and then said they'd let us all live in Faerie happily ever after *out of the goodness of their hearts*?"

"Not exactly," said Fia crossly. "Alex's father, Thomas, sent them."

"*What?*" Saorsa couldn't believe her ears.

"Yes. They're all House of Corvids. Thomas couldn't come, so he and Alex's Faerie side sent them to help Alex here."

"Fia, those Fae creatures were *not* all House of Corvids. I can tell you that with absolute certainty." She paused. "And why would Thomas participate in a plan to unite Alex when he's the one that split him into pieces *in the first place?* Also, none of the Fae talked to Alex's Faerie side about making you a mother because Alex's Faerie side is *in a prison* that they can't access. Or *was*."

Fia blinked in confusion.

"You didn't notice how panicked they were when they heard the *leth dhia* was loose? If they're friends with Alex's Faerie side, *why would they be running from him?*"

Fia just stared.

"I'll tell you what *I* think," Saorsa said, sitting down in a chair near Fia. "I think you wanted Alex to marry you. I think you're obsessed with him, and I think you wanted all the lovely trappings that come with being Alex's wife. Castles and connections and a big fat famous faerie sapphire. I think you were excited to marry further up the Scott chain than Anne did. You might even want a baby. But most importantly, you wanted *into Faerie*. So you were willing to do and believe *anything* to get it."

Fia shook her head. "I wanted to heal Alex."

Saorsa's eyes narrowed. "Not as much as you wanted a new life." She folded her arms. "You forgot the most important rule of witchcraft. 'An' it harm none, do what thou wilt.' You certainly did *what thou wilt,* all right. But you conveniently forgot to *harm none*."

A stubborn expression took up residence on Fia's features. "I told you. They said they were going to help him."

"When?" Saorsa fixed Fia with an icy gaze. "*When* did they approach you? When did this charade of yours begin?"

"Two days after you and Alex fought at Ramsay House," Fia confessed. "Right after you ended things, he was a mess. He left after arguing with you and went straight to talk to Edan. I saw him in the dining room. He grabbed two bottles of wine off the sideboard and looked at me. He was absolutely furious. Then he nodded toward his room and I followed him. Once inside he uncorked both bottles and handed me one. He wouldn't talk about you. He wouldn't talk about himself." She paused. "We fell into this pattern. He'd ask me a question and then would listen while I talked. He'd send me out for more to drink when we ran out. I hadn't slept well in days because of my nightmares. I'd get drunk and fall asleep on his bed, and it was the best sleep I'd had in months. He'd pace while I slept and help me when the nightmares came. The rest of the time he'd sit in the hall on the floor next to your door and just...do nothing." She looked away. "He was so devoted to you, even when you didn't want him. And I'd think, *why can't I find someone like that? Why can't he direct that longing toward me?* It's *so unfair*. And I'd drink more."

She sighed. "After a few days, I went back to my room to bathe and change and one of the Fae was there. Waiting for me." She took a deep breath. "I saw how awful Alex felt. And I felt awful too. And...it was a *faerie,* Saorsa! A real, honest to Goddess magickal being! Talking to *me!* With a way for all three of us to be whole again!"

"And when did you start drugging Alex?"

Fia looked away and swallowed. "Right after that. They would bring me bottles of things from Faerie. They had different amounts and kinds for me to give him at different times. They said it had to build up in his system. That it would keep him calm so he wouldn't fight them, and that it would start preparing his body to be together with his Faerie side." She took a deep breath. "They weren't always sure of the dosages. That's why it made him feel sick or knocked him out sometimes, or made it hard for him to think and communicate. I felt bad about that."

Saorsa snorted. "Oh, thank the Goddess you felt bad about that. That makes *everything* better."

Fia folded her arms. "How is your being nasty to me going to help Alex?"

Saorsa's eyes narrowed. "Please don't pretend his well-being is even a *remote* concern of yours."

Fia stood up. "Alright, look. *Yes,* I think life here on Earth is shite. I think most people are shite. I've never hidden that fact. And I do want to go Faerie. I've given up on this realm. And I won't deny that I found the idea of being Mrs. Alexander Scott very appealing. Hell, what woman wouldn't? When he's around, which would be *rarely,* he's sweet, funny, charming, generous and hands-down the best lay I've had in my entire life. And the other ninety percent of the time, when he'd be away, I'd run my own land and be one of about five women in Scotland who didn't have a man breathing down her neck and treating her like property." She walked toward the window. "But what you are leaving out of your assessment of me is that *I actually adore him.* And I actually adore *you.* I thought what I was doing would make things better. I genuinely wanted him to be *healed*, Saorsa." She turned and looked at Saorsa. "And I genuinely wanted you healed and to go to Faerie with you."

Saorsa didn't move.

"I've been desperate for a long time, Saorsa," Fia said quietly. "Long before Graeme. I've never felt I belonged anywhere. I've never felt really connected to anyone. Really loved. Maybe I was just born broken. Graeme was the closest I got. And then the fucking war took him." She put her hands on the back of a chair and Saorsa saw her hands turn white as she gripped the wood. "I wanted out. When the Fae came, I was willing to believe them because I needed things to change. As soon as I started doing what they asked, I was gifted *you.* And then Alex. And then the baby. All of these wonderful things happening seemed like signs that for once, I was doing *right.*" Her eyes clouded with tears. "I was never lying when I said I cared about you, Saorsa. *Never.* When you said you wanted to get over Alex, I tried to help you. To be your companion instead." Her breath caught. "I feel like...like you and I and Alex, we're almost a *family.*" A sob caught in her throat. "Please believe me. *Please.*"

Oh, my Goddess, Saorsa thought. *She lives in a fantasy world. She did this to us but thinks we're her family? She's not...she's not well. Her mind is all twisted up in knots.* "So we were running all over the place trying to find a way into Faerie, and you were talking to faerie creatures *the entire time,*" Saorsa said slowly. "If you really wanted to help, *why didn't you tell me?*"

Fia looked at the floor. "They said I needed to follow their instructions exactly. They said you couldn't know in case the thing that's been trying to capture you succeeded and found out their plan. They said...they said it was the safest thing for us."

Saorsa shook her head. "I guess it doesn't matter what the exact flavor of the lies they fed you was. Fia, here's the truth: I talked to Alex's other half in Faerie. He told me *nothing* about this plan. He said *nothing* about you being his child's mother. He hasn't seen Thomas and is worried about him. At least two of the Fae we saw at the cave are House of Raptors, *not* House of Corvids." A pause. "And the Violet Woman who tortures Alex? The one who works through him and makes him kill? The one who marked his arms? *She was the woman with the dark hair at the cave.*"

"No," Fia said, her voice sounding like a young girl's. "That can't be right. I've spoken to her. She's very kind. And she told me she was a relative of Alex's and that she loved him."

"Fia," said Saorsa, "if you keep insisting that your information is correct and mine isn't when *I'm* the one who went to Faerie, there is no point in us continuing to converse."

"But she has *wings,* Saorsa! They look almost like Alex's. But where his black feathers have that bluish tint, hers shine more than his and have purple. And hers are pointed more." She looked thoughtful for a moment. "Like a raven. A raven is a corvid."

Saorsa sighed. *Goddess, I'm exhausted, but I need this information.* "Fia, come here and sit down." She gestured to a chair near her and retrieved paper and ink from her bag. "Let's take this one step at a time. Two of those at the cave are named Tadhg and Ciannat. They are House of Raptors, Deck of Hawks, and claim to be related to the MacLeod Clan." She paused. "Then we have the Violet Woman. She says she's House of Corvids. I'll give you that one. She might be Deck of Ravens." She made a note. "Who else did you see, or speak with?"

Fia sat down. "There's another woman. Quiet. Once the Violet Woman came and spoke with me and she came as well. Has wings just like Alex's. And the same gray eyes, and red highlights in her hair. I mean, she looked like they were *definitely* related." Fia touched herself on the shoulder. "She had markings sort of like yours. Except...wolves on her shoulders. Ogham lines like bracelets on her forearms."

Saorsa's eyes widened. *Those markings sound like Alex's. The ones I saw on him in Faerie.* What had he said? *I have half-brothers and sisters, all older, all born long before Thomas met Adamina. They dinnae like me much.* Could the Violet Woman's companion be in the Deck of Crows?

"Alright," she said. "Fae number four. From House of Corvids, Deck of Crows." She looked at Fia. "Anyone else?"

Fia looked thoughtful. "I spoke to Tadhg mostly. The others would just deliver the bottles."

Saorsa could feel her mind wandering; she felt like she was going to collapse. She turned her head and suddenly she could see Alex standing by the bed, smiling at her.

"Ye need to lie down, *eun beag*," he grinned, his gray eyes twinkling. "Ye cannae fight without your rest, aye?" He nodded at the bed. "Time to sleep, sweet one. Come quick, an' I'll tuck ye in." He gave her a mischievous smile.

I'm hallucinating. He's not really there. I'm so tired and stressed I'm hallucinating. She stood up, and Alex disappeared.

"I'm going to sleep," Saorsa announced, and headed for the closest bed. She pulled back the covers and started stripping out of her clothing. Fia wandered off toward the other bed and followed suit.

Saorsa climbed into bed and turned her back toward Fia. Fia watched her from across the room, and after a moment sat down on the edge of her bed.

"Saorsa," she said softly. "Everything's going to be alright, isn't it?"

Saorsa didn't look at her. "I don't know, Fia," she answered. "I just don't know."

………

Saorsa dreamed Alex was in bed beside her. It felt real. Everything in her mind wanted to believe it was.

He was lying on his side, looking at her and smiling, his gray eyes sparkling with reflection from the firelight. They were close enough to the flames that she could see the red highlights in the dark waves of his hair, usually only evident in bright sunlight. She reached out her hand to run the backs of her fingers over the dark stubble on his jawline, and marveled for the millionth time at the perfect shape of his eyes.

"Come here, sweetheart," he said quietly to her, and she moved closer to the warmth of him under the quilts in the chilly room.

He put an arm around her waist and pulled her even closer, laughing as she let out a surprised squeak of happiness as she felt his chest against her breasts. He tucked her curls behind her ear, and her heart skipped a beat as she realized neither of them had any clothing on.

The world outside their bed seemed to disappear, and Saorsa nestled as close as she could to him as Alex pulled the covers up over her shoulders to keep her warm. She rubbed the arch of her foot along the side of his calf, following the contours of a body made strong from years and years of riding and working horses.

"There now, that's nice," she heard him sigh, and she lost herself in the timbre of his voice and the feeling of the rise and fall of his chest as he breathed. *Goddess, I love the scent of his skin. The feeling of his hands on me. I adore everything about him.*

"I love you, Alex," she told him. She felt him kiss her on the top of her head.

"An' I love ye too. *Tha thu an toiseach nam chridhe,*" he answered. *You are first in my heart.* She smiled as his large, strong hand found the base of her spine, and closed her eyes.

"It's time to rest, now," he told her, his hand making a repeated slow journey back and forth in an arc across her back. "I'm here with ye, an' all is well."

She realized their breathing had fallen into the same rhythm. *This is how I want to be, always.* She could hear his heartbeat slow in his chest as he drifted toward sleep. A part of her mind was still rooted in reality.

"Alex," she said quietly, "you're not really here with me, are you?"

There was a pause before he answered. "Ah, *eun beag,* I'm never as far from ye as ye think."

She held him tighter and tried to stay in the dream.

·········

Her eyes opened, and the world rushed in. It was late afternoon. Fia was still asleep. *What is the next step, Vika? Check on the team and handle physical injuries - done. Gather information - done. Next, take an inventory of your resources. What supplies and weapons do you have? How can you use them to move forward to get yourselves to a safe house and regroup?*

There was one resource she hadn't explored yet. She needed to do that now, while she had an experienced magick-user with her. She crawled out of bed and dressed quickly, putting the silver-gray orb she'd been given at the Court of the Morrigan in her pocket. She wrapped herself against the cold and slipped out the door.

She knocked lightly on Mother Agnes and Annag's door. Both were awake and greeted her with sympathetic smiles. "I was wondering if you might walk with me," Saorsa said to Mother Agnes. "I'd like some advice."

"Of course," said Mother Agnes before pulling on her cloak and mittens. "Lead the way."

Saorsa took a moment to reflect on the fact that just a few weeks ago, she'd never led anyone anywhere.

They set out into the woods. There were perhaps two hours before dusk. The days were short in Scotland this time of year. Mother Agnes broke the silence. "So, where do you want to begin? With the fact that you're furious with Fia? With how the revelation that she's pregnant made you feel? Or with what happened between you and Alexander the night we were all together at Melrose?" She raised an eyebrow. "Or perhaps the magickal object that's been riding around in your pocket since you've come back from Faerie would be a better place to begin."

Saorsa stopped and looked at her mentor, eyes wide, and Mother Agnes laughed. "Oh, *please,*" she exclaimed. "I *raised* you, Saorsa Stuart. You think I can't tell when you're angry or jealous?" She snorted. "And *him.* My Goddess, you go full turtle whenever Alexander is in the room."

Saorsa's eyes narrowed in confusion. "Full *turtle*?"

Mother Agnes kept walking with Saorsa beside her. "Aye. When you were a wee girl at Hermitage, I used to take you for a walk every morning after breakfast. We'd go through the gardens and the cemetery, and around the perimeter of the abbey grounds. One day at the fish pond, you spied a little turtle. A red-eared terrapin I think it was. Rather unusual; it must have come in with the fish when we stocked the pond. You'd never seen a turtle before; it's generally too cold for them here. You were about three years old. And you were *fascinated.*"

She smiled, remembering. "You were usually an agreeable and obedient child, but in this case you refused to leave the pond. You just sat and watched that turtle, eyes wide and lips parted in surprise, for over an hour. Whenever I suggested we leave you cried. I finally flagged down one of our sisters to fetch a bucket and we took the turtle back to the abbey. We found a very large metal basin in the shed and made a little place in your mother's room where the turtle paddled around and slept and did turtle things while you sat and watched. You didn't want to eat or do anything except watch that turtle. You'd sit and babble at him in Gaelic and sing to him. In the afternoon we found you sound asleep next to the basin with your little arm curled around it." She laughed.

"Whenever you were particularly passionate about something as you grew, some of the older members of our coven would wonder if you'd go *full turtle,* or in other words become delightedly obsessed to the point of losing your ability to function. When you were a teenager, painting the walls of your room put you in that state. And the moment Alexander Scott arrived outside the door of my study at Melrose, I saw it happen for the third time." She looked at Saorsa. "If he moves or speaks, you stare at him like he's that turtle. As though he's the most marvelous and unique creature to ever exist, and all you want to do with your life is sit and watch."

Saorsa blushed scarlet. "So, tell me" said Mother Agnes, "what are you going to do about Fia? And about him?"

"I'm in love with Alex," Saorsa said quietly, looking away. "And...he loves me back."

"Then...," Mother Agnes' brow furrowed, "where, exactly, did Fia's bairn come from?"

Saorsa sighed. "I have to confess I haven't told you everything. Part of it is because I didn't want Fia to know what happened in Faerie, and she's always around. And part of it is because I was confused and embarrassed."

Mother Agnes took Saorsa's hand. "I'm listening."

They sat on a fallen tree and Saorsa began. "Alex and I, we...were happy together. Things between us were just beginning. And then we found the knife and it changed him. And it was changing me, although you couldn't see it. I became overwhelmed and afraid. I felt like I was losing Alex and I couldn't stop it. So, something in my mind decided that it would be better to find an excuse to push him away than to stay close to him. To try and protect myself from hurting so much as he faded."

"And that excuse was Fia," Mother Agnes confirmed. "To be fair, your response was understandable. You've lost a lot in your life, Saorsa Stuart. Your mother. Your father. Your freedom. You were trying to protect yourself from losing more."

"I... suppose so. Alex told me there was nothing between Fia and him but...I didn't listen. I left him alone. I *failed* him. I didn't see...I now believe she forced her way in between us and pushed us further and further apart. Thomas the Rhymer told me to love, but all I could think to do was run." A tear escaped Saorsa's eye and ran down her cheek. "I told myself I didn't love him anymore and that I would just be his healer and his friend. And I was so caught up in the struggle between what my mind wanted to do and what my heart couldn't help but feel that I made a mess of things. And at Melrose, I just...gave in to my heart for a bit." She looked at the floor. "I let him take me to bed. I missed him *so much*. And then...I lied to you about it." She swallowed her tears. "I'm sorry."

Mother Agnes patted her hand. "I knew, Saorsa."

Saorsa wiped her eyes. "You... did?"

Mother Agnes laughed. "Do you remember how quickly Alexander went unconscious after that first dose? And how surprised I was? There was no way it should have taken hold that fast, and I became concerned that he had some sort of undiagnosed health issue. I was the first person to sit with him that night. After you left, I put a little spell on him to monitor his pulse, so that if his heartbeat became irregular at any time a bell in my room would ring and wake me. I was afraid the sedatives might accidentally kill him." She smiled. "Then I sat there and listened to him talk in his sleep for two hours. About *you*." She gestured in the air. "Sweet Nyx's stars, that young man has you on his mind. In two hours he must have said, 'Where's Saorsa?' more than fifty times. He'd ask if you were well in Gaelic, or say 'love you, *eun beag,*' which I assume is a pet name for you, again and again." She grinned. "Apparently he's *full turtle* for you as well."

Saorsa smiled, blushing.

"Interestingly, Fia's notes claim he only spoke about *her* when she was sitting with him. A bit hard to believe, after what I'd witnessed. And Annag...she recorded him talking about you and at times he became quite distressed. She said she felt very badly for him. Apparently at one point he said, "*Saorsa, thig air ais thugam, mas e do thoil e,*" and then just lay there silently weeping in his sleep for ten minutes. Annag wasn't sure if she should try to wake him, but eventually it passed."

Saorsa put her head in her hands. He'd said *Saorsa, come back to me, please.* She wanted to crawl inside the mostly hollow tree they were sitting on and curl up and die.

"And then," Mother Agnes grinned, eyes twinkling, "it was your turn in the room with him. And I was awakened by the little bell in my room at the end of the hall ringing and ringing. I jumped out of bed and ran down the hall, and...well, let's just say if the two of you intended to be quiet, you failed. I immediately could hear that the bell wasn't alerting me to a dramatically *decreasing* heart rate; rather, the pulse in question was *racing*. I shut the door, left, and deactivated the spell."

Saorsa was mortified. She now wanted to be dead in the hollow tree twice as much, and her face showed it. Mother Agnes burst out laughing. "There's no need to be embarrassed! He loves you and you love him. That's a sacred thing, Saorsa." She smiled again. "I've been to more than a few Beltane celebrations in my life. Trust me, I've witnessed a lot more than the happy sounds that came out of that room."

Saorsa sighed. "The reason the sedatives knocked him out is that Fia was drugging Alex without my knowledge. She helped the Fae take him."

Mother Agnes' eyes widened. "I thought something was up with that girl, but not *that*. Tell me everything. What happened with Elen? And what do you know about Fia?"

So Saorsa did. They walked while they talked in order to stay warm. And Saorsa was completely honest. She spoke of the Court of the Morrigan, of Elen's revelations about her parents, and about Diarmid. And about the Faerie side of Alex and his prison. And how they'd been together.

Mother Agnes took it all in. Saorsa could see her organizing the information in her mind as she listened. Her face changed when she heard Fia's confession that the baby had been conceived during a ritual. "Saorsa, I must stop you there. This is...not good. At all."

Saorsa took a deep breath. "I know. At first I thought maybe the Fae wanted Fia pregnant because then they could keep an eye on where Alex was. He'd always return to his wife and child." She shook her head. "But the Violet Woman can reach through Alex in Faerie whenever she wants. So that's not it. So the Fae must want that baby for a *reason*."

Mother Agnes lowered her voice. "I hate to say it, but if *leth dhia* blood and tears bring a high price on the Fae black market...well, imagine what his *offspring* might fetch."

Saorsa's eyes widened in horror. "You think...you think Fia's baby is a *specimen?*"

Mother Agnes nodded gravely. "It could be, Saorsa. You said they do experiments."

Saorsa stopped walking. "No," she said, gritting her teeth. "I won't let that happen!" She ran a gloved hand through her curls as another thought occurred to her. "Oh, Goddess! *Oona!*"

Mother Agnes put a steadying hand on Saorsa's arm. "Do you trust Donovan and Keena?"

Saorsa nodded. "Yes. And they're the sort to have wardings and protections on their house."

Mother Agnes nodded. "Then Oona's probably fairly safe from the Fae at the moment. But we do need to reach them and warn them. And if they're sending Oona west with people we don't know, that could put her in danger." She paused. "The children might also be bait, you realize. You said the Fae refused to take Fia with them because the *leth dhia* could sense his family's blood. If they want to draw him in, they now have three forms of bait; you, Fia and her unborn child, and Oona. They've learned you're difficult to catch and Oona may be protected. Which means manufacturing another offspring they can access whenever they want is in their interest."

Saorsa nodded. "Either side of Alex would do anything to rescue his child."

"Exactly."

Saorsa turned to Mother Agnes. "I don't like this. I don't like any of it." She looked at Mother Agnes. "Fia's child needs protection. Whether that baby is actually Alex's or not, he *thinks* it is. And if it is, I can't let the Fae...," she lost her breath for a moment, "I can't let them harm an innocent bairn!"

"Saorsa, I hate to add to your bad news, but there is something else you must be aware of," Mother Agnes said slowly. "If that child was indeed conceived through a blood magick ritual...." She looked away. "I don't know how to phrase this gently."

Saorsa steeled herself. "I'm fairly certain *gentleness* has left my life for a good while, Mother Agnes."

Mother Agnes sighed. "The child will likely be a daemon, Saorsa."

"What?"

"Elen told me that's one of the ways they're created. The most common way. As far as I understand, they are born of a cross between magickal and non-magickal beings in a blood ritual. That may be why they chose Fia. She's intuitive, but has no magick in her blood. Now, I know *nothing* about the rules for *leth dhia*. Fia may also have misunderstood or been lied to about what was happening. But you should be prepared. Fia's child may be daemonic or an entirely new species of Fae. One we don't know anything about."

Saorsa looked at the setting sun filtering through the bare tree limbs. "I'm going to need help. I can't protect one Fae child and one possibly daemonic child, find four captured adults, an escaped Faerie Alex, and a missing magician all at once." She shook her head. "And that's not counting tracking down my father."

"Saorsa," Mother Agnes said cautiously, "I know you said that Alex's Faerie aspect marked you as under his protection with the spell on your back. But what about the one on your neck and chest? Do you have *any* idea what that is for?

Saorsa shook her head. "No."

"You said that after you were together, you awakened feeling that a long time had passed. Certainly it was long enough for him to work a touchstone spell on the orb, and put marks on you without your knowledge. Are you certain...," Mother Agnes took a deep breath.

Saorsa's eyes narrowed. "Am I certain of what?"

"You said he told you *leth dhia* can consciously choose to impregnate someone, and that afterwards the woman sleeps for days. Are you *completely* certain that didn't happen?"

Saorsa stared at Mother Agnes. "He told me he wouldn't do that. It was our first time together! I slept a long time because I was exhausted. I'm also fairly sure he drew on the magickal energy we raised together to break out of his prison, and so there was an energy loss in my system as well. But he said he...," Saorsa stopped.

I'm NOT certain. When I woke up, it seemed like a long time had passed. But he turned away my questions about it. He didn't tell me he made the orb a touchstone. He didn't tell me he had marked me. He didn't tell me he had a way out of the prison and that he'd used the energy we raised together to that end. So what if he also didn't tell me...?

"Oh, Goddess," she said. "Oh, Mother Agnes, I *don't* know. I don't think he'd do that. But...I don't know for certain."

She thought of him when he spoke of Fia's bairn in Faerie. *I'm sad, though. I wanted this to be with...to be with you. God, I cannae tell ye how I hoped for that.* And she remembered telling him that she wanted to have his child when they were in bed together. And at one point he had said...he had said...*the Knight of Crows claims this woman for his consort. I give her my seed to make a child. I choose you. I choose you. I choose this.*

Saorsa closed her eyes. *Oh Goddess. It could be in my bloodstream, right now. Waiting until my body is ready. Which, because I have an irregular cycle, could be months.*

Or I could be pregnant already. Saorsa felt the blood drain from her face. *He wouldn't do that without my permission. But maybe he thought he had it. I did say I wanted to have his child.*

Saorsa put her hand to her forehead. Faerie Alex had been rather jealous of Alex here on Earth. What if he had done it to make his claim on her known? To show that she was *his*? She thought of having to tell Alex that she was pregnant with his Faerie aspect's baby while his other side watched and listened. *I'm going to pass out. I'm going to pass out.* She saw the edges of her vision go dark.

"Saorsa!" She felt Mother Agnes' steadying hand. "Deep breaths, my girl!"

"I...can't...," Saorsa gasped, "what if Alex has a *third child,* Mother Agnes? In *me?* Oona, Fia's baby, *and mine?*" She found herself staring at her abdomen. Her voice sounded far away, as if someone else were speaking. "If you cross a *leth dhia* with a witch born of The Lovers, *what kind of a creature do you get?*"

She felt her knees buckle, and Mother Agnes helped her to sit on a large, flat stone on the side of the path. The sky was growing dark. "Saorsa! We need to get you back to the inn," Mother Agnes said. "We've gone in a big circle; it's not far. Just rest for a few moments. We don't know for *certain* it happened."

"Melrose," moaned Saorsa. "I also stopped drinking the tea Vika gave me once I was at Ramsay House. For all I know I could have gotten pregnant when I went to bed with him at Melrose, too! I could be pregnant, and not know *which aspect of Alex is the father!*"

"Now, now, it does us no good to imagine problems," Mother Agnes scolded her gently. "Most likely everything is fine. It's just something to keep in the back of our minds."

"Back of our minds," Saorsa panted. "This magickal flower marking on my neck is *definitely* not a protection sigil for Faerie Alex's unborn child. Definitely not, right?"

Mother Agnes' brow creased with worry. "I'm...well, it could be *lots* of things."

I could be pregnant. Without Alex here. Either side of him. Saorsa felt a shiver race up her spine. *I want...I want to be with him. And have his child. But if I am pregnant, and the Fae want Oona and Fia's bairns...they'd come for mine as well. They'd come for mine first. A child born of two magicks. One of which is forbidden.*

Her hand brushed up against the orb in her pocket, and remembering it was there stopped her spiraling thoughts. *Breathe. Breathe. You have shite to do. No point in getting hysterical over something that might not even have happened.* She looked at Mother Agnes.

"Before we go back," she said, "I need to try something, and I need your help." She pulled the gray-tinted sphere from her pocket. "In Faerie, Alex said there was 'an old friend' in here, or something like that. And my instructions at the Court of the Morrigan were to deliver it to Alex on earth." Saorsa paused. "I've decided to go ahead and open it without him. Or try. It could be a resource that can help."

Mother Agnes nodded. "Go ahead. I'll stand ready to defend if something unpleasant comes out." She made a warding sign with her right hand and then moved back several paces, producing her wand from inside her cloak.

Saorsa looked around for a place to rest the orb and found an extra-large knothole in a nearby oak. "He said I should whisper to it." After gently placing the orb in the knothole, she bent close to it, and drew up power from the earth. "Ummm... open."

Nothing happened.

"Maybe in Irish, since it came from the Morrigan?" Mother Agnes suggested.

Saorsa nodded. "*Oscail, le do thoil!*" *Open, please.*

The orb just sat. "I'll try Scots Gaelic. Alex doesn't speak Irish, and it was supposed to be for him. *Fosgail suas!*" *Open up!*

"Try his name." Mother Agnes suggested.

"*Leth dhia!* Alex! Alexander William Thomas Scott! Knight of Crows!" Saorsa was growing frustrated. "Maybe only he can open it."

"Think, Saorsa. What *exactly* did he say?"

"He said to take it to the woods and whisper to it. That you could say any old...," she put her hand to her head. "I'm an idiot." She bent close to the sphere once more and cleared her throat. "Any old thing,*"* she whispered.

The orb began to glow. Saorsa took several steps backwards. The light in the orb grew increasingly bright, until Saorsa was forced to put up her hands to shield her eyes from the light. There was a loud hum, then the sound of breaking glass and the light faded.

The sphere was gone. In its place was something alive. It rolled forward out of the knothole, extending its limbs as it moved. By the time it reached the ground it was standing.

It was a crow, and a large one. It cocked its head to the side and looked curiously at Saorsa, then at Mother Agnes, and then back at Saorsa. It appeared to be waiting. It held a black slip of torn paper in its beak.

Saorsa crouched down and looked at the bird. "Hello," she said softly. "Do you have...is that paper for me?"

The crow looked around the clearing and flew up to land on a rather large boulder near Saorsa. She couldn't help but think the crow was waiting for someone else to appear.

"Alex isn't...he isn't here," Saorsa said to the bird as she rose. "He's been taken by some Fae. I need to rescue him. Can you help me? I'm Saorsa. Saorsa Stuart. I care for him very much."

Mother Agnes lowered her wand. "He doesn't seem aggressive."

Saorsa put out her hand tentatively and the crow didn't flee. When her hand was directly in front of him, the crow put one of his legs briefly on her fingers and dropped the slip of paper into her palm. Then he flew to a low nearby branch and watched her. Saorsa looked at the scrap. It was roughly textured and appeared to be made of linen. It had been dyed black, and there was one word written in silver ink on the paper.

Malphas.

Saorsa knew better than to utter anything that looked like a name aloud when it had been delivered by a magickal crow. She turned and passed the slip to Mother Agnes, who had walked forward to look.

"Oh," Mother Agnes said quietly. "Do you recognize the name?" Saorsa shook her head. Mother Agnes looked at the bird curiously.

"It's a daemon's name, Saorsa," she said, not taking her gaze from the corvid. "He's supposed to travel in the form of a crow. The good news is he only appears in daemonic form when it is requested. But whether this is the daemon himself or simply a crow is anyone's guess." She held her forearm parallel to the ground. "Alex said he is a friend. Let's try something." She looked at the ink-black bird. "If your name is Malphas, I invite you to perch here with me, and I welcome you."

The bird immediately took flight and landed on Mother Agnes' arm. "Ooh, you're a hefty one, aren't you?" Mother Agnes smiled. "My goodness, there's a tremendous amount of magickal energy coming off of you as well. And what a lovely bright blue aura you have."

Malphas took to the air again, landing once more on the boulder near Saorsa. He opened his beak and let out a startlingly loud *caw*.

"What else do you know about Malphas?" Saorsa asked Mother Agnes.

"Not much. There's a book, *Pseudomonarchia Daemonum*, that lists the major daemons and their characteristics. Malphas stood out to me because he supposedly builds things. I'd have to look at the book again to remember more. I have a copy at Melrose."

Suddenly Malphas took to the air and flew off, headed toward the inn. "Follow him!" Saorsa cried. "Come on!"

As they neared the inn, they could see Malphas circling in the early night sky above the inn, waiting for them. As they neared the back door, he suddenly dove, circled twice just a few feet above the ground, and landed on the sill outside Saorsa and Fia's room. He began tapping his beak on the shutters insistently.

"He wants in!" Mother Agnes exclaimed. "I'll go ask Fia to help me fetch dinner so she won't be in the room; you let him in and see what he wants."

Saorsa nodded and they hurried inside. They found Fia inside the room, building up the fire. "Fia," said Mother Agnes, "please come with me to the common room so we can place an order for our evening meal."

Fia nodded. "Of course. There's this strange tapping sound...."

"I'll see what it is," said Saorsa, pushing Fia into the hall and closing the door. She raced to the window, opened it, and then dove out of the way as Malphas soared into the room. She turned and watched him, uncaring of the cold air still coming in through the open window.

The big crow flew across the room to the bench where her still-packed saddlebags rested. He planted his feet firmly on the bags and let out a hoarse, insistent cry. "What? What is it?" Saorsa asked. Malphas responded by hopping up and down on the bags a few times, and then began tearing at the buckles with his beak.

"Hold on," Saorsa told him, unbuckling the bags and pulling out the contents. Malphas hopped up and down and made nearly human-sounding noises of appreciation in his throat. A few flaps of his wings and he was standing on the mounds of Saorsa's bundled clothes and belongings, rooting through them with his beak.

Saorsa's eyes widened as the corvid suddenly lunged at a pile and before she realized what was happening Malphas had yanked Alex's crystal rosary from its bag, planted one foot firmly on the center bead, and tore the silver crucifix and several links of chain and beads off from the rest of the rosary, leaving just the circle of decades behind.

"No!" shrieked Saorsa, diving for the bird, but he flew to Fia's footboard with his prize. "Give that back! It's Alex's! It's important to him!" *He must truly be a daemon, to destroy a sacred thing with so little care!*

Malphas looked at Saorsa, and she swore she saw him wink. And then he was winging his way across the room and disappeared out the window into the night sky.

"Malphas!" Saorsa cried, feeling tears in her eyes. "Come back!" But the crow was gone. Saorsa stared out the window at the waning moon, and then shut the window once more. *Hopeless. I can't even keep Alex's rosary safe.*

She sat down on the floor next to her spilled and scattered belongings and wept. All of the emotion she had bottled up since Alex had been taken came pouring out. *I miss him. I'm afraid for him. Is Duncan even still alive? Are any of them?* She cried and cried, trying to rid herself of the awful loneliness that sat on her chest like a scavenger waiting for a dying creature to expire. *How am I going to do this? How?*

She wiped her eyes with the back of her hand as she gasped for air through her tears, and slowly returned the violated rosary to its bag. *Why would the crow want part of Alex's rosary?*

The door opened a bit, and Mother Agnes slipped inside, shutting the door behind her. "Saorsa...oh my, what happened here?"

Saorsa looked up. "The crow came in and destroyed Alex's rosary! Tore the crucifix right off and flew out again! He's gone! I was carrying the rosary to...so I could have something of Alex's with me that was important to him, and now it's...," Saorsa looked forlornly at her things on the floor. "There's just...so much I don't understand."

Mother Agnes locked the door. "Fia's next door, eating with Annag. We have a little time." She sat down in a chair nearby. "Tell me."

"I opened the window, and the bird began biting the buckles on my saddle bag like he wanted them open. I started pulling out everything inside, and then he pulled the rosary out of its bag, snapped the chain, *winked at me,* and took off."

Mother Agnes' eyes lit up. "It was something of Alex's. Something he could carry." She looked intently at Saorsa. "Do you know where Alex got the rosary?"

"I think he said his mother gave it to him. But maybe I'm thinking of the pocket watch he carried. I *know* she gave him that."

"Where's the rest of the rosary?"

"Here." Saorsa handed Mother Agnes the bag, who tipped the contents into her palm.

"Oh...my," Mother Agnes breathed. "It...no. Can't be." She held the circle of beads and chain closer to the light of the lamp on the table, and her face lit up. "Saorsa. Come have a look at this."

Saorsa rose and moved toward the lamp. "What is it?"

"Look at the pater beads. The larger beads that are in between the groups of ten smaller beads." She held out her hand with the chain for Saorsa to see. "Notice anything?" Saorsa looked closer. *Something inside the beads was moving.* She looked up sharply at Mother Agnes.

"These beads look like moonstone or quartz at first glance, but they're *not,*" Mother Agnes said excitedly. "These stones...I've only ever seen some once before. The thing you see moving inside the beads? I think it's captured angel song!"

Saorsa stared at Mother Agnes. "Captured...*what?*"

"It's angel song, trapped in the beads! This rosary was made in an Angelic realm. There's no way Alex or Adamina would be able to procure this on their own! Someone had to have brought it here from another world."

"Thomas?" Saorsa looked at Mother Agnes. "Maybe he brought it for one of them."

Mother Agnes nodded enthusiastically. "That's my thought."

"But why would the bird take it?"

Mother Agnes gestured for Saorsa to pull up a chair. "Think about the gray orb that held the bird. Do you know how a touchstone works?"

Saorsa shook her head. "Not really."

"A touchstone is an object that a magickal being infuses with their energy. Sometimes if a touchstone is carried in or out of a forbidden area, the magickal being can connect with their essence in the touchstone to access that area. It's a very difficult sort of magick. Not something humans can do at all."

Saorsa nodded. "So, Faerie Alex infused the gray orb with his essence and when I carried it out of the prison, he connected with it and it helped him break out."

"Exactly. Essence can also build up in an item if it is of value to, or handled often by, a magickal creature."

Saorsa's eyes widened. "So...Alex's essence is *in that rosary*. He used to hold it all the time. He *prayed* with it."

"Most definitely. Although I doubt if Alex's human aspect has enough magick to make a touchstone work. But Thomas most likely has that kind of power. If Thomas owned it before Alex...."

Saorsa stood up, unable to keep still. "If Thomas is connected to it, he could use it to access a forbidden area if *Malphas carries it in for him!*"

Mother Agnes was now on her feet too. "Something's about to happen, Saorsa. I believe Malphas is delivering a touchstone somewhere here on earth. Most likely to allow Thomas in or out of somewhere." She put her hands on Saorsa's arms. "If we're right, this could be *good*. You've been wondering where Thomas is, and all the signs point to his arrival *in this realm*."

Saorsa threw her arms around Mother Agnes. *Malphas is an ally. An ally who might bring a potentially more powerful ally closer. There might be hope.*

"Do you think Malphas will return to us afterwards?" Saorsa asked.

"I don't know. If Alex is in this realm, Malphas may try to find him." Mother Agnes smiled. "Let's go and eat. Malphas is doing his part. We need to figure out ours, and be strong enough to see it through."

Carlisle Castle, England

Caroline Frederick Scott glowered at the portal that was slowly opening in the warden's apartment of Carlisle Castle. It had been a bad day; Duncan MacLeod had vanished and with him, most of his hopes for finally capturing Vika MacLeod. Word of this would spread, and he was not excited for the Duke of Cumberland to hear of it.

And now the goddamn portal was opening in this room again, which most likely meant a visit from Lord de Soulis. He detested the mage.

The portal made a strange sucking sound and Lord William de Soulis stepped out, the doorway behind him vanishing. He was wearing his green coat and a shit-eating grin, as always.

"Hello, Fred," de Soulis greeted him, looking around the room. "Trouble you for a chat?"

Caroline Frederick Scott didn't have a choice in the matter, and de Soulis knew it. He resented the fact that the mage acted casually about matters that weren't. "Of course." He turned and headed toward the whisky bottles and glasses that stood ready on a silver tray on a nearby table. "Drink?" *I sure as hell need one to deal with you.*

De Soulis removed his hat and waved it in his host's direction. "No thank you. I won't be here long." *Thank God for that.* Caroline Scott tossed down his first pour and refilled his glass.

De Soulis crossed to stand closer. "Bad day?"

"Yes." The second glass of whisky burned its way down.

De Soulis laughed. "It's only eleven in the morning. You've still got a good chunk of the day to go."

Scott turned and stared at him. "Why don't you say what you've come here to say?"

De Soulis raised an eyebrow, but his smile never disappeared. "There's been some complications on our end. Adjustments will need to be made on yours."

Scott slammed down his glass on the table. "These...*adjustments* of yours are growing tiresome, de Soulis."

De Soulis laughed. "Someone's a wee bit crabby about the MacLeod siblings, I see."

"No," Caroline Scott growled, "what I'm upset about is that every time *your* team fucks up, *I'm* left holding the bag!" He fixed de Soulis with an icy stare. "Instead of just taking Adamina Scott, you had to burn down half of Buccleuch Castle looking for that goddamn sapphire! And you *still* didn't get it! We nearly had another uprising start because of that incident! I had to evacuate a garrison! I lost scores of good men because you can't do *anything* with a subtle hand!" He pointed an accusatory finger at de Soulis. "And that fucking she-demon of yours is *out of control.* You said she had control of Alexander Scott, but apparently that's not true! Do you have any idea how many men the Crown has lost when she's conducted her experiments? *Do you?*"

De Soulis looked away and his smile faded a bit. "She's getting more control every day."

"Is she, though?" The Garrison Commander roared. "I was told Alexander Scott was headed out of the Borders, and now he seems to have fucking *turned around* and everywhere I look, he's there! Seven Hills. Buccleuch. Branxholme. Fucking *Hermitage!* And just recently a church up near Melrose! What's the point of us being on the same side if when your agent possesses him, she *murders my men?*"

De Soulis looked back. "Under the circumstances, these are acceptable casualties."

"Acceptable? *Acceptable?* If you all have so much control over him, drag him north and practice using him on Highlanders instead! You've made my job harder and made him a goddamn Scottish *hero!*" Scott started to pace. "I'm tired of having to come up with plans on the fly because of *complications* on your side. I want what I was *promised.*"

De Soulis' smile returned. "You'll have his body by the end of the week."

Scott stopped in his tracks. "What do you mean, *his body*?"

"Exactly what I said. His body. His soul won't be in it."

Scott didn't move. "And what am I supposed to do with *that?* How can I put a dead body on trial?"

De Soulis waved his hand. "It will have to be enough. Behead it, draw and quarter it, parade it through the streets of London, I don't care. But I am here to tell you Alexander Scott's body will be delivered to you within the week." De Soulis looked at his fingernails, ignoring the waves of seething rage radiating from Caroline Scott.

"And the girl?" he demanded. "I was told I'd have her by now as well!"

"We're working on that." De Soulis sighed.

Scott advanced on de Soulis. "May I remind you and your team that the Fae can't move around here without *my help*. You'd best get your act together and start respecting my wishes."

De Soulis rolled his eyes. "Oh *please*. You and I both know you're not going *anywhere*." He produced a large, heavy leather pouch and tossed it on the table next to the whisky bottle. "At this rate, you'll be able to buy the East India Company by year's end."

"We're supposed to be *partners*. I'm tired of being your lackey," Scott snapped. He went to the table and poured himself another whisky.

De Soulis sighed. "I need to go. You won't see me for some time. I have...some things to deal with." He looked at Caroline Scott closely. "The singing spell appears to be working, as far as we can tell. But make certain to keep an eye on Adamina Scott, just in case." He gestured to the north. "We want you to contact Edan Scott and offer to trade his mother for the sapphire. Maybe *he* knows where it is."

"Jesus Christ," Scott swore. "I'm *not* doing that. Find another way. That will go against *everything* the Crown wants done in that area." He shook his head. "May I remind you if I lose my position, *you also lose yours*."

"Do it," de Soulis said, his eyes narrowing. "You'll have Alexander Scott's body as soon as we're finished with it, and Saorsa Stuart once we're done with her as well." He raised his hand and the portal opened behind him. He stepped through just as an enraged Caroline Scott hurled his glass in frustration. The glass shattered in the air as the portal snapped shut on it.

Caroline Scott let out a bellow of rage. *De Soulis needs to learn. The Fae need to learn.* He stormed to the door of the room, threw it open, and shouted at the officer seated at the desk in the next room. "*Lieutenant!*"

The officer was on his feet at once, flustered at the state of his commanding officer's appearance. Caroline Scott looked hell-bent on murder. "Sir?"

"We're hanging Adamina Scott at noon tomorrow. I want the *entire fucking town* in attendance! Make damn certain Vika MacLeod hears about it. And find me a girl who looks like Saorsa Stuart. Someone no one will miss." He slammed his hand against the door. "The Borders are about to learn who their master is. Pull in the patrols and double our security. Alexander Scott's mother is going to die and after that, we're having a witch trial in London!"

………

Saorsa sighed and looked at the other three women in the room as everyone finished their dinner. They'd been making small talk for half an hour, but now plans needed to be made to move forward.

"Fia," Saorsa began, "Mother Agnes knows." Fia's eyes darted to Mother Agnes, and then she looked away.

"Knows *what?*" Annag asked. Mother Agnes patted Annag's hand. "I'll fill you in later."

"I'm going to need some help," Saorsa continued, looking at Mother Agnes and Annag. "Fia's child needs protection. Killian and Anne don't even know Faerie is real. So tomorrow we should ride for Branxholme. The four of us." She looked at Fia. "You need to stay at Branxholme with Edan until the bairn arrives. And Mother Agnes, Annag, if you could stay there with her to protect her from the Fae, I would greatly appreciate it."

Annag and Mother Agnes nodded. Saorsa looked at Fia. "This is my offer, then. If you stay at Branxholme and do as Mother Agnes and Edan ask, you'll be cared for and protected, and I will do what I can to make certain you and the child aren't separated. But if you fight them or continue your betrayals, I'm sending you back to Anne and Killian, and Edan and I will tell them everything. *Everything.* And you can be damn certain that I won't say a single word in your favor when Alex comes back." She pointed at the door. "You can also choose to run now, I suppose. But it will be tough going with no resources when the Fae seem to have left you behind. And if you think the King and the Knight of the Deck of Crows *aren't* going to take that child from you once they get wind of this, then you're even more insane than I thought."

Everyone looked at Fia. Annag looked completely lost, but remained silent. Fia looked at the floor. "Branxholme," Fia said quietly. "I won't fight." Saorsa nodded.

"Saorsa," Mother Agnes said, "I should tell you that when we went down to order dinner, I sent a note to Vika's Aunties asking for any information they might have on our new rosary-carrying friend. I imagine we should have something by morning."

"Rosary-carrying?" a clearly confused Annag cut in. "Are you talking about priests?"

"We're not," Mother Agnes said. "It may be a late night for us, Annag. There's a lot I have to tell you."

Annag nodded and turned her attention to Saorsa. "Where are you going to go after Branxholme?"

"To make a safe house," Saorsa answered. "My *own*. I need a base of operations. Somewhere with no portals, but a lot of magickal power." She looked at Fia. "And that's all I can say, for now."

·········

The crow had been winging his way south throughout the night, a broken rosary in its beak. He stopped to rest and drink and eat a little, but quickly took to the air again. There was much to do and Malphas was glad to be flying after so much time cooped up in that spell.

Carlisle Castle was on the horizon as the sun rose. Below him in the forests of the Borders a cacophony of bird song greeted the new day. It was quite nice. Not as nice as the rise of the Eternal Fire in the Underworld, but nice, nonetheless.

He could see the magickal shield over the castle, even at this distance. It would take a bit of time to find a flaw in the magick. Slow, but not impossible. All magick has flaws.

Unknown Location

Pain. Alexander Scott winced as his shoulder began to throb again and gasped as a wave of nausea tore through his stomach. *One of my limbs is bent the wrong way. And it's…inside me.*

He felt terribly ill and was certain his skin was on fire. There were voices around him, fading in and out. Frantic voices. Ones he didn't know. He tried to follow the words, but the twisting, pulsing pain in his body made it difficult. He felt dried out, as though all blood and moisture in his body had fled. *I'm dying, I know I am.*

A voice next to him suddenly, loud and angry. "He's a disaster! What the hell happened?"

Another voice, slightly distorted. "It's the drugs. The girl gave him too much."

"We could lose him! Why was he moved like this? We can't do the ritual like this!"

What are they talking about? Alex wondered. He felt like he was spinning. *Fire.* And then a cool hand on his arm. He tried to focus on the coolness of that touch and hang on.

A woman's voice. "I can do nothing with all of you crowded in here. You must do as I say or he has no chance to live."

Alex decided he trusted that voice. It reminded him of someone. Someone he missed. Someone who was far away and needed him. *My mother.* The woman's calm, kind tone reminded him of his mother. He felt a tear escape from his eye and trickle down his cheek. *Everything hurts. And it never stops.*

The hand on him moved away, and he missed it. *Homesick. I'm so fucking homesick.* He could no longer tell where the pain in his body stopped and the pain in his soul began.

………

His mind became obsessed with the return of her touch. That brief, calm, reassuring touch. When she put her hand on his arm it was the only place on his body that felt like it wasn't burning. A brief respite in a never-ending desert of agony.

He couldn't speak or open his eyes, for he had forgotten how. He felt so violently unwell that he was lost in it, fighting not to surrender himself entirely. Just when he was certain he would, the refreshing presence on his skin would return. A slight, steadying point he could focus on. A lifeline. A drink of cold water for a parched body.

He knew, without a doubt, that if that presence left, he would be no more.

It had gone quiet now. After a time, she spoke. "I'm a healer," he heard the woman say. Her voice was a balm, just like her touch. "I'm here to help." And then he felt a cold, wet cloth on his face, and collapsed inside in gratitude. *Water. I need water. I have none left, and it is what I am made of.*

He felt the cloth on his cheeks and his lips, on his forehead and eyelids. *Hope. There may be hope for me yet.* He felt his boots being removed, and a horrid pain shot through his ankle.

"I'm sorry," he heard her say. "I didn't know you were hurt here, too." He felt cool air and a cold cloth on his bare feet after the healer carefully removed his stockings, and was grateful down to his bones.

He could hear a new cloth being wrung out in the basin, and was thankful when he felt its chill over the flaming wound in his shoulder. "You're burning with fever," the healer's voice told him. "You were given a poison of some sort, which made your body too weak to fight off the infection. And then...there's the phantom remains of a wing. That will require treatment of a different sort."

He felt more like a person, hearing her speak to him, although he hadn't the strength to answer. "I will stay with you," said the voice. "Do not be afraid." She had no idea how much he needed to hear those words.

When Alex opened his eyes he saw his benevolent attendant for the first time. She was tall and willowy, with long, dark, smooth hair and an easy grace. But what put him at ease the most was the *smile*. A wide, authentic, unbridled greeting of a smile. He had not expected to see one of those in his current circumstances. *She is full of light. Like Saorsa is.* A pang of loneliness echoed in his heart.

"Well," said the healer, fixing him with her bright eyes and welcome, "this is good. Your eyes are open."

Despite his extreme discomfort, he couldn't help but smile back, although he couldn't seem to find his voice yet. *She is a caring soul. A strong soul, too, although she doesn't exert her power over others.* He had often sensed the same in Adamina. And in Saorsa.

"I'm Laoise," she said and gave him a happy little wave. It endeared her to him immediately. He watched as she used her slender, elegant fingers to tuck her hair behind her ear. And then he saw it. Her ear tapered up to a point. *She's of the Fae.* She saw him looking and nodded.

"Half, actually," she said, reading his thoughts. "Half Fae, half human." She patted him on the leg. "They said you were half, too? So we're much alike, you and I." She gestured in the air. "So, here's what's going on with you. You have been poisoned and from what I can tell, it's been going on for some time. I won't be able to assess the complete damage until you can move and talk. You also have a raging infection in your body and your ankle is in a bad way. And the wing...well, its physical form is long gone. Its spiritual form is still there and badly hurt, so we'll need to perform an energy healing to take care of that as I imagine it has long been giving you phantom pain. So, we have poison, infection, physical injuries in the form of the bullet wounds and the ankle, and then the residual wing to deal with. Was that a childhood injury? It's so hard to tell. Now, you're thinking, *how long until I am better?* The truth is, I don't know. Luckily, you're the patient type, yes? Get it? Patient? As in a doctor's patient *and* the ability to wait?" She grinned.

He got it. He marveled at her ability to carry on a complete conversation with someone who couldn't speak. And she was brave enough to show she had a sense of humor. Even if it was *the worst*.

"If we can get some fluids in you, you'll feel *much* better," Laoise told him, her voice carrying a note of laughter under her words. "So, I have some tea here, which should help with the pain *and* get some water in your body. Don't worry, it's cold."

He wondered if she knew who he was and *what* he was. She knew he was of mixed species parentage, like she was but what else had his captors told her? He wanted to ask her where he was and how long he'd been out. He thought he could trust her answers. *I'm a prisoner and she has to know that, doesn't she?*

"Coming at you with the tea," she said playfully, and moved to stand next to him. "Now, see if you can get your mouth open a little. That poison had a paralyzing effect, so if you can't do it, I can help." She patted his hand. "Don't worry if it spills. Just do your best." She was so kind that he found himself *wanting* to do his best. He wanted to make her happy so she'd keep speaking to him.

"Wonderful!" she smiled as she tipped the tea into his mouth, as though he'd done something spectacular. "Oh, this is so good! If you can drink, everything gets much easier and better." She raised her eyebrows. "And then eating could be right around the corner!"

They got the tea into his body, a little at a time. "That's the way healing goes," she sang, and he was once again reminded of Saorsa. "A little at a time. One sip, or one step, or one day at a time. If you try to look at the end in the beginning, you'll defeat yourself. It's all in the little victories. And you've just had one now!" She put down the cup on a nearby table. "All right," she said, "Now that *that's* done, we're going to get you really cleaned up. You've been sweating through these sheets for hours; it *can't* be comfortable. And you need to be as comfortable as possible to heal." She tapped him lightly on the knee. "I'm bringing in a few helpers since you can't move. We're going to get these clothes off you and have a nice sponge bath, then move you to an actual bed. Then, more tea. And a little bit of aura balancing on that wing so you can sleep better." She tipped her head slightly and smiled again. "Doesn't that all sound nice?"

He managed a smile again. *She's right. I shouldn't think of the ritual they mentioned, how I'm going to get out of here, or how I'll reach Saorsa, Fia, Duncan, Maria, or my mother. None of those things can happen until I can move. So, I'll focus on that step first. And pray about all the others.* Although, in truth, he wasn't certain to whom he was praying anymore. *The world - or worlds - are so different from the way I was raised. Is God even listening?*

Laoise moved closer to him and touched the back of his hand. He felt the coolness of her touch flow through him. "Sometimes," she said, growing more serious, "when things seem the most wrong, it's just a short walk to where things are the most *right*." She looked him in the eyes. "It's good when you're healing to find faith in whatever you can, and focus on that. It will help."

She's clairvoyant, Alex thought. *She has to be. At least a little.* He sighed. *Find faith in whatever you can.* What did he believe in with his whole heart? Saorsa. He believed in her. In her promises. In her love. In the fact that she had sworn to see this through to the end. He couldn't reach her now. He couldn't reach anyone. He would have to trust that somehow, Saorsa would find a way to be strong when he couldn't. *That is where I will put my faith.*

Laoise left his side and returned with three other women. "They are here to help us," she told Alex. "We'll work together and you'll leave this illness and pain behind."

He heard the women murmur their names to him, and listened to Laoise give them instructions. And then Laoise was smiling at him reassuringly as he looked up at her gentle brown eyes with gray ones full of gratitude.

Carlisle Castle, England

At eleven sharp the portcullis on the Carlisle Castle bridge rose, and the crowd flooded in. A hanging at Carlisle was a social, economic, and political event. Vendors from the town and surrounding villages could make a fortnight's worth of money in just a few hours keeping the crowd fed and full of drink, and an impromptu market sprang up on the other side of the moat to attract those heading home afterwards who needed a loaf of bread for supper or a new pair of mittens for the cold ride home. Those who wished to show themselves loyal subjects of the Crown would come to shout and jeer; those who wished to hobnob with their neighbors and local tradesmen would find plenty of people to speak with. And this was no ordinary hanging.

Everyone in the Borders knew who Adamina Scott was. A laird's wife, a defiant Catholic, and a Jacobite. Seeing soldiers hanged was one thing; seeing someone *famous* was something else. The pieces of the hangman's rope would fetch a high price after this event, to be sure.

And what of her vicious, redcoat-murdering son? Certainly Alexander Scott had heard of his mother's fate; the garrison had put up an announcement about the hanging at every crossroads and in every village square within a day's ride of Carlisle. Everyone's fingers were crossed that he would put in an appearance with the bandit Vika MacLeod at his side. Rumors were flying that Duncan MacLeod had escaped Carlisle just the day before. There hadn't been this much excitement in Carlisle since the Bonnie Prince had captured the castle. Everyone wanted to say *I was there when it happened.*

Debate broke out in the streets. Would Adamina Scott actually die today? Or would the Ghost of the Borderlands appear with Vika and her band of killers and wreak havoc on the Crown's plans once again? Money changed hands and bets were made. To which side would victory flow?

Vika had been one of the first through the portcullis. The last twenty-four hours had been a whiplash of emotions for her and her team. Yesterday morning Harris had arrived with Duncan's note from the message drop, and she had nearly collapsed with relief and gratitude. *Duncan was right to leave the area. We can't risk him being captured again, and there are a lot more troops in this area. This is England, not Scotland.* But just a few hours later Harris had brought more news: Adamina Scott was going to be hanged at noon tomorrow.

Where the hell are Alex and Saorsa? Vika had hoped the pair would have rendezvoused with her by now. *Something is wrong. I can feel it.* Vika was a woman of logic, but her intuition was rarely wrong. *We'll be going in without them, then.* At the very least Adamina wouldn't lose her life without a friendly face in the crowd. But Vika never aimed for the very least.

The crowd was extremely rowdy, pushing, shoving, and nearly trampling each other to get inside the castle walls, and Vika was glad for it. There were far too many people for the soldiers to be able to frisk everyone or even look at them carefully. The day was frigid; everyone was bundled up to their eyes and had on long woolen cloaks. It made it much, much easier for her companions to smuggle the explosives in.

Vika couldn't believe Caroline Scott was stupid enough to let this many people into Carlisle. It was well known that he had a nasty temper and could be impulsive, but something must have *really* gotten to him to allow an event like this to happen with less than a day's planning. Maybe it was Duncan's escape. *He overestimates the abilities of his guards. And he underestimates the ability of a crowd to suddenly go wild and cause chaos.*

She found a position to the side of the hanging platform, atop a stack of crates. Her crew would be able to see her up here and it was a near-perfect place to deliver signals to those watching. The crowd flowed in with the strength of a high tide. Vika slipped her hand under her cloak to double check her knives. *I don't know if we'll succeed at this, Adamina, but we sure as hell are going to try.*

She looked up at the castle walls and her observant eyes noticed something unusual. There were no birds inside the walls. Crows were rather populous in this area and could often be seen and heard all through the town. But none perched on the walls here or flew overhead. Not one.

She had never seen such a crowd at a hanging before. The entire place had the air of a festival, or a holiday. *What does it say about us humans that we make a spectacle of death?* Vika shook her head.

She saw several of her companions move toward their destinations along the walls. *I just need enough chaos to make this possible.* She took several deep breaths and watched as the hangman entered from behind the platform and mounted the stairs. The crowd cheered as they saw him ascend.

Vika was looking at the rope and the underside of the platform. The crowd suddenly surged forward, allowing her to pull something from under her cloak and toss it under the platform unnoticed. *I'm sorry, Adamina. This is going to be hard on you. But if we pull it off, you'll live.*

There was no room left, but spectators were still trying to push their way in. Vika noticed many of the guards who were on the ground couldn't move if they wanted to, boxed in by bodies on all sides.

Vika went over the plan in her mind. *They bring Adamina out. I wait until just before the door under her feet opens as the priest gives his speech. There should only be the priest and the hangman on the platform then. I give the signal. Explosives detonate in nine places, driving the crowd out of the gates and taking out the stairs from the upper levels. Malcolm takes out the hangman and goes onto the platform to open the trap door.*

My shuriken takes out the hemp rope, Malcolm pushes Adamina down through the opening into the straw below, and then follows. I get the hood off her head, get her into the cloak, and we disappear into the crowd. Past the gatehouses, across the bridge, into the church, and into the crypt to the other side of town and to the horses. While the explosives go off, Harris and his gang will be beating the shite out of the portcullis operator and jam the gate open. That portcullis cannot close, or we're all dead.

They should be bringing Adamina out soon. *Breathe. Breathe. Get ready. Be ready for anything.* She noticed a lone crow, soaring over the crowd toward Queen Mary's Tower.

The crowd was getting restless, anxious to begin. She could see Caroline Scott on a balcony nearby above the crowd with several of his aides. He took out a pocket watch, looked at it, then put it away. "Bring out the prisoner!" he bellowed, and the crowd went wild. *Bastard. He loves this.*

But a long moment passed and the prisoner did not appear. A low murmur began in the crowd. Vika saw Caroline Scott speak to one of his aides, and the man ran through a door and disappeared inside the castle. The crowd's murmurs grew louder. Vika heard an angry outburst to her left. *Something's gone wrong.* And then the shouting started. *There was something large swooping through the air!*

Vika MacLeod, who was almost never surprised, was surprised. *"What the hell IS that...?"*

It was large, square, about sixteen feet long and it moved and flapped like some sort of strange bird. The closest thing Vika had ever seen to it was a manta ray. But this didn't look alive, and it was moving too fast and was up too high to see details.

Vika heard the shrill sound of a woman screaming coming from the airborne shape, and the crowd below began screaming as well. The mob panicked and was pushing now, ducking and attempting to climb over each other, trying to find the exit. Unable to make sense of what they were seeing and feeling trapped in close quarters, terror quickly ignited in the throng and spread like wildfire. Vika heard a man yell *"Dragon!"* and another yell *"Ghost!"* A woman near Vika screeched, *"Witchcraft!"* and the entire area around her picked up the call and kept it going.

"Dark magic!" shouted the priest on the platform, turning and running to the stairs. "Satan is among us!"

"He's coming! He's coming for our souls!" bellowed another man nearby. "Let me through! Let me through!"

"Hermitage!" a woman cried. "We'll all be killed, just like at Hermitage!"

"Oh, I should never have come!" sobbed a woman to Vika's right. "He's brought a beast down upon us, in revenge for watching his mother hang!"

The crowd's imagination was running rampant as the thing in the air circled lower and lower, drawing ominously nearer. Vika realized many of those around her were now shouting about Alex punishing the crowd for attending the hanging. *We're going to end up with another bloody song because of this, aren't we?*

The strange shadow circled quickly over the crowd a few times and then suddenly dipped low and shot through the air just above their heads in the direction of the gatehouses like a horse running from a blazing barn. *Everyone* inside Carlisle's yard was screaming or shouting; the crowd had morphed into a mob and was losing its mind.

Vika grinned. She'd gotten a good look. There would be no hanging today. Carlisle Castle was in pandemonium; not only were the spectators slamming into each other in an attempt to flee, but it appeared a good many of the guards were being swept away in the crowd, helpless.

You know what? thought Vika. *I fucking hate this place. Let's give them a little something to remember us by before we go, shall we?* She pulled down her cloak's hood and looked up at the balcony just above her where the garrison commander stared at the bedlam below him, unable to believe his castle had descended into crazed madness. For a brief moment, he met her eyes, and she saw his widen as he recognized her. Vika raised her arms above her head and saluted him with the middle fingers of both hands.

"This is for the Highlands, you asshole," she shouted, even though there was no chance he would hear her. She'd given the signal. The explosions began.

....

Earlier at ten-thirty a.m., Caroline Scott had come to talk with his prisoner. He brought twelve armed guards with him. Adamina had been looking out the window, watching the crowd flow into the castle as the gates were opened to the public, when the men entered her chamber. The garrison commander was in fine humor.

"Good morning, Lady Scott," he grinned at her. "Wondering what the crowd is here for this morning, I presume?"

Adamina turned from the window and raised an eyebrow as she took in the sizable escort. "Do you really need twelve Englishmen with swords to protect you from one unarmed Scottish woman, Commander?" A small smile played on her lips, and her eyes flashed. "On second thought, that *does* sound about right."

Caroline Frederick Scott ignored her. This woman would be put in her place soon enough. "They're here for your hanging, my lady," he said to her with a grin. "I thought I'd do you the kindness of telling you at the last moment, so that you didn't worry about it during the night and lose your rest. We *do* want you to look your best as you mount the gallows."

He had expected her to faint, scream, or burst into tears. He had looked forward to this very moment. But she didn't do anything he expected. She simply fixed him with a stare, and replied, "Sadly, when you appear before the crowd, you'll look much the same as you do now."

He was thrown off guard and went quiet for a moment. Adamina raised her chin. *I'll be damned if I let this ghoul see me break.* "You've marched the Highlands with no regard for human dignity and a profound lack of compassion. Why should I expect anything different from you where I am concerned?"

For reasons Caroline Scott couldn't explain, he felt a pang of shame, as if he were a young boy being told he was a disappointment by his mother. It *enraged* him. He took a step forward, raising his hand to slap her, but instead of shrinking away she just laughed.

"You're no man, Caroline Frederick Scott," she said, baring her teeth at him, "you're a *disgrace*. Your Scottish ancestors *weep* when they look down from heaven and see what you've chosen to become. No honor, no morals, just a lapdog for the Duke of Cumberland and a common thug and thief. You may think you've brought Alba down, but *Scotland lives*."

The garrison commander attempted a laugh, but it was decidedly lacking in strength. The truth was he'd never been spoken to like this before in his life. By *anyone*. He didn't know how to process it and Adamina didn't relent. "I'm not frightened of you," she continued. "You may hang me today, but I know in my heart that peace and justice await me. There will be none of that for you, Caroline Scott. The only legacy you'll leave behind is one in which history frowns upon you and says, 'what a pathetic waste of a human being'."

Caroline Scott was suddenly very conscious of the twelve men in his vicinity. If Lady Scott was allowed to continue, he'd lose standing in their eyes. But if he struck her or killed her himself, they'd know she had gotten under his skin. *Bested by a woman. And a Jacobite, at that.* He settled for heading for the door, collecting his thoughts as he moved.

He turned at the door, determined to fire one last round in their conversation and make himself the victor. "You lost, Lady Scott. The Stuarts are no more. Your faith has been driven into the shadows. And today, I will take your life as well."

She didn't move. And then he was shocked by a small smile crossing her face, and he felt a chill run down his spine.

"He'll come for you, you know," she said, her voice calm, quiet, and cold. "The one they call the Ghost? He'll come. There's nowhere you can hide. He'll paint the walls with your blood, and he'll take it slowly, and the only regret I have in this life is that *I won't be there to see it.*"

There was something in her gaze that rooted him in place. He could sense the men that surrounded him were suddenly uncomfortable as well. For the first time in years, he felt actual *fear*. Her words seemed a curse, a prediction. He worried his emotions were showing on his face. He turned and hastened out of the room, and felt a haunting take up residence in his heart.

He heard the bar on the door of the apartment that had once held Mary, Queen of Scots, fall into place, and hurried away.

·········

As soon as they were gone, Adamina began to pace frantically. She had assumed that she'd be bartered for someone or sent to London, not hanged here in a garrison on the Border. She couldn't think clearly; her body wouldn't stop moving. She threw open the window and wished frantically for the gift of flight.

There has to be a way. There is always a way, isn't there? Scientifically, when you think you're at a dead end in the experiment, you start over and look for a different way. But all she could think of was her sons. And Thomas.

She hadn't seen Thomas in eighteen months. His last letter had been two months after that. She had long since resigned herself to the fact that something was wrong. She'd started researching portals, wanting to activate the one in Buccleuch Tower and try to find him. *I should have studied magick. I should have used this Bruce blood to become a witch.*

It was too late, now. The sun was climbing the sky, and the courtyard was filling fast. She could see the gallows and hear the rising noises of the crowd. *I'd rather kill myself than let them hang me. I'd rather go on my own terms.* She ran to the window and looked out. Nothing but stones below. *I'll throw myself out the window and deny these people their fun.*

But she couldn't. Not yet. She'd take that as a last resort. She still had perhaps a half hour or so to live. And she wanted to go peacefully. To prepare herself spiritually as best she could, so that she could die with dignity.

She wished for the rosary Thomas had given her. It always helped her pray.

A large black form streaked in the window, dropping something on the carpet by the foot of her bed. Adamina stared. *A crow.* The bird hopped back to the windowsill and looked at her curiously. Her eyes fell to the item on the carpet. *A rosary's crucifix. No...wait...MY crucifix!* She nearly tripped over her skirts in her haste to reach it. *What...what is...?*

"Alex?" she said. She'd given him the rosary to carry with him when he joined the Jacobite Army, as a talisman to keep him safe. It was his now. *How did it...?*

The crow let out a cry and swooped over to the writing desk on the other side of the bed. Adamina turned and saw the quill pen rise off the desktop *all by itself,* as if being moved by an unseen hand. Adamina let out a small shriek of surprise, and then the cork flew out of the inkwell and the pen dipped itself in the ink and began writing on a stack of papers there. She flew across the room and watched.

She had no idea what was going on, but read the following words: *Be ready. Stand back from the door!*

At that moment she turned as she heard the bar lifting on the outside of the door. *They were coming for her!* The door swung open and four guards and a young chaplain were there.

"Lady Scott," said the chaplain, "it is time to prepare yourself for your final moments. I am here to hear your confession...."

Adamina let out a startled yelp as the chair by the desk suddenly became mobile, flinging itself through the air and out the door, striking the chaplain and knocking him unconscious. The guards looked at each other for a moment, trying to figure out what they had just witnessed. Then they stepped over the chaplain's prone form and moved into the room toward Adamina.

The heavy mirror over the dressing table tore itself from its mounting and flew across the room, smashing into the guard closest to Adamina, breaking the mirror and knocking the man out. He crumpled to the floor, just as the floor-length mirror near the dresser vaulted itself up off the floor, knocking another soldier out the open window.

Adamina put her hands over her mouth to stifle a scream. One of the guards turned and ran, but a footstool hit the side of his head, and Adamina looked away as a letter opener found its mark through one of his eyes. The edge of the carpet suddenly lurched upwards, tripping the final soldier and knocking him to the floor. One of the bed curtains tore itself loose, and Adamina looked on in horror as it slithered around the man's throat and choked him until he lost consciousness.

The crow let out a cry from the windowsill, and Adamina watched the quill move across the room and out the open door into the hall, pausing as if waiting for her to catch up.

"Oh, my *God!*" she shrieked, and tore after the black quill. She stepped over the chaplain and watched as the quill took a sharp left and headed down the hall. *It's leading me somewhere!* She raced after it, terror-stricken that at any moment more guards would arrive. But it appeared that nearly the entire force of Carlisle was out in the courtyard; everything around her was silent, save for the muffled sounds of the crowd outside. She could hear her own heavy breathing as she followed the quill down a short flight of stairs, running as fast as she could; and every now and then she was aware of an involuntary whimper of fear escaping her throat.

The feather paused and swept around in a circle, as if to say *wait*. She heard voices in the hall ahead, and then saw the ax from a suit of armor in an alcove ahead free itself and speed around the corner and out of sight.

She threw herself against the wall and covered her ears, but the screams of the soldiers around the corner snaked their way into her brain. She heard the ax hitting wood and peered around the corner. *Two bodies.* The ax chopped its way through a door, went through, the feather followed, and finally Adamina.

It was a huge storage room, the shutters shut, full of darkness. *This is a dead end. Why bring me....* She looked closer at what was inside. Ornately framed oil paintings. Jewelry boxes. Stained glass lamps. Antique furniture. Adamina bristled. *These are all things Caroline Scott took from Highland families. All of this, stolen so he could sell it to the highest bidder in London.*

She saw a crate marked *Stuart*. And another. And another. And then more names. *Cameron. MacDonald. MacLean. Drummond. Fraser. MacLeod. Livingstone. MacGillivray. Munro.* On and on. He'd gone after the Jacobite commanders' clans and enriched himself. She wanted to tear Caroline Scott apart with her bare hands. This was his treasure room, where his spoils from the war awaited transport.

The ax cut the ropes on a rolled-up rug that had been set to the side of the room. She threw herself aside as the massive carpet began to unfurl at a high speed across the floor. She could hear shouting from somewhere in the castle. *They've discovered the men in my room and they're searching for me!* She turned to run into the hall, unable to control herself as fear gripped her once again.

But just then the heavy carpet rose swiftly from the floor, floating in the air and blocking her path. She stared at it, uncertain. A large, heavy velvet cushion flew across the room and hit her between the shoulder blades, knocking her forward onto the floating rug, and its edges curled up sharply under her thighs, sending her somersaulting forward into the middle. Before she could get her bearings, the sides of the stiff wool rug curled up around her, forming a tube with her inside and sped out the door.

She had nothing to hold onto and couldn't really see. The carpet bent for a moment as it rounded a corner, bending her with it, and then bent again in the other direction. It traveled down the passageways of the castle with her lying on her stomach, facing backwards, looking out the small circle of light at the end of the tube, barely able to see. She heard screams as the front of the carpet tube mowed down soldiers in its path, traveling at the same speed as a galloping horse; the front of the rigid tube caught man after man in the chest and knocked them to the ground before continuing on its way.

Adamina braced herself against the sides of the rug just as the carpet tilted sharply upwards at an angle, leaving her in the uncomfortable position of hanging nearly upside down. There was another crash as the carpet bowled through another obstacle, and then suddenly she was feeling the coolness of the open air.

Free of the constraints of the castle walls, the carpet unfurled itself again, and Adamina gasped as she realized she was *above Carlisle Castle*. The carpet rotated briefly in the air, so that Adamina was facing forward. She tried desperately to grip the carpet, but the fibers were too short. It paused for a moment, as if conscious of her plight, so she wiggled forward on her belly and reached out to grab the edge with both hands. And then it dove.

She screamed as she'd never screamed before. She desperately wished for the sides to curl back up over her and protect her; it felt like the bottom had dropped out of her stomach. She could actually feel her legs lose contact with the carpet as it plummeted, and was absolutely convinced that she was going to fall to her death.

She could hear screams below her now, but didn't dare look; she was too busy screaming herself. The wind had whipped her hair loose from its bun and it streamed out behind her as she held on for dear life.

The carpet suddenly changed direction and the degree of its descent, and Adamina found herself and the rug circling. She was going to be sick; her body was on a journey that humans weren't meant to take. Her fingers ached from the gripping the border of the tapestry; but she had no other choice than to hang on. She thought she saw the gallows for a brief moment, and then the tower where she had recently been imprisoned; and then she was aware of the presence of other humans below her, like a floor of bodies underneath the carpet on which she rode.

The carpet seemed to make an adjustment, and then rocketed forward. She could see a river of people running in front and below her, screaming and ducking; a shadow briefly crossed her as she flew through the arch of the inner gatehouse. A second later a second shadow was there; and then...and then.... The carpet gained altitude again, quickly, and the four sides curled up slightly toward her, as if trying to ensure she didn't fall. She turned her head and...*I'm out! Oh, sweet Lord, I'm OUT!*

Carlisle Castle was behind and below her, and she was no longer a prisoner. She let out a shout of joy, but her mind was too numb from fear, shock, and terror to do much more. She heard a church bell ringing below her in the town of Carlisle, and realized it was signaling high noon. High noon, when she was supposed to have died. She felt dizzy from the height, the relief, and the disbelief; she was shaking from cold and fright. Soon Carlisle itself was disappearing behind them as the bewitched carpet flew east, toward a destination unknown.

She rolled onto her back and tried to breathe. The carpet was steadier now, and had slowed somewhat, keeping a consistent speed as it soared over the English countryside. *What just happened? And where am I being delivered?*

She didn't have long to wonder. After a short time, the carpet began to gradually and gently lose altitude. Soon they were flying just above a forest of pines, and then they were descending into a meadow. She held on to the edge of the carpet again and braced herself for impact. *How does one land on a flying carpet?* She tried to remember the stories from *One Thousand and One Nights* she'd read to the boys when they were little at Thomas' behest; but she couldn't remember anything that told you how to sit or lie so that you weren't dragged mercilessly across the terrain when returning to earth.

In the end, it didn't matter. The carpet slowed and came to a stop, floating a foot off the ground, still. Adamina realized how incredibly cold she was. She couldn't feel her hands on the carpet's border.

She felt as though the carpet expected her to disembark, and then realized she had been thinking of the carpet as a sentient being. *This is insane. I am insane.* She tried to release her grip on the carpet's edge, but her hands had cramped and frozen in place. She saw the vapor of her breath billowing out in front of her. *I am going to have escaped Carlisle only to freeze to death in a field.* The adrenaline had disappeared; she felt nothing but exhaustion. *I don't know where I am. Am I in England? Or Scotland?*

"Ye can let go now," said a deep voice, and she startled and felt her body jolt off the hovering carpet. She was so overwhelmed by what had just happened she hadn't realized anyone was nearby. She turned her head slightly to the left. *Trousers. Black trousers and boots.* She looked up.

He was looking at her, concerned. "Are ye all right, *leannan?*" She couldn't see his face well; the sun was directly behind him, making him a silhouette. But she would know that voice anywhere.

It took several seconds for everything to register. *My brain feels like it's going to melt.* "T-Thomas?" she stuttered. "Is it...?"

He crouched down and smiled at her, the corners of his gray eyes crinkling, and held out his hand toward her.

Now she *did* let herself cry. She pushed herself up off the carpet, staggering to her feet as he rose and pulled her up by the hand after him, and threw herself into the warmth of his waiting arms. "*Thomas!*"

He pulled her to him, holding her tight. "You're safe now, Mina! Hold onto me." There was a desperation in his voice, and a moment later he kissed her, reassuring himself that she was whole.

I'm going to collapse. His hello kisses had always made her weak in the knees; but this time she was also trembling violently from the weather and her ordeal. She opened herself to the familiarity of him, her entire body welcoming his embrace; and he supported her and became her refuge from the world.

"Tha mi air do ionndrainn gu mòr," he whispered to her, looking into her eyes as she ran her hand through his dark hair, *"bha mi a 'miannachadh dhut a h-uile latha."*

I've missed you so much, he said. *I longed for you every day.*

"I missed you too," she said, before kissing him again. "Oh, I can't believe you're *here!*" There were too many questions for her to sort them into any kind of order. She put her arms around him and held him as tight as she could. He was here, solid and strong, and she could feel his arms locked around her, the motion of his breathing, and the sound of his words as he spoke reassuringly to her in Gaelic. *He had rescued her. Gotten her out of Carlisle. But how...?*

She realized it was late November. He was *never* here in November. Always at Beltane, often at Samhain, and sometimes at Lughnasadh or Yule. In all the years she'd known him he only appeared near old Celtic Sabbats, and only certain ones, staying short amounts of time. He'd been with her at precisely one Imbolc, and that was for his son Alexander's birth.

"What are you doing here?" she whispered into his shoulder. "Where have you been, my love?"

She felt the warmth of his breath on her ear. "I'm *so* glad to see ye, Mina, but we need to get ye inside," he told her. "It's freezin', and it isnae safe in the open."

She noticed a strange metallic smell on his clothing and a trace of smoke. And then she was letting him lead her to the carriage that waited on the nearby road. She looked for the flying carpet, but it was gone. The numbness that had occupied her mind began to recede. *There's his carriage. With the same driver and the same horses that he's had since I met him. But that was... almost thirty years ago now. And they look exactly the same.* She'd learned a lot about Thomas in the last thirty years. But there was still so much she *didn't* know.

Now he had the door open and she fumbled her way inside. He climbed in after her and shut the door. As soon as he was seated, the carriage began to move and he unbuttoned his coat and motioned for her to sit in his lap. "Come here, come here," he urged her, picking up a thick wool blanket next to him and wrapping it around her shoulders, holding her close so she could warm herself against him.

She didn't want to think. She didn't want to do anything but get warm in his arms. She sighed as he embraced her, and she settled herself in a comfortable position where she could rest her head on his shoulder. She felt him sigh as well, and it brought on the first moment of real happiness she'd had in a very long while. She closed her eyes, and felt herself start to relax.

The carriage pulled up behind a large estate twenty minutes later, and she climbed out of Thomas' lap, keeping the blanket around her for warmth. She followed him out of the carriage and held his hand as he walked her toward a rather grand and stately door and opened it for her.

"This is the home of a friend," he told her. "We should be quite safe here."

She walked into the room, and her eyes widened. The room was very large, with high ceilings and white marble pillars. The floor near the door was polished black marble and furnished as an entryway. To her left Adamina saw an area set up as a bedroom, with beautifully carved dressers and an enormous canopy bed with silk pillows and mounds of comforters. The dressing screen was oversized and painted with the same style and care that one might find on an Italian oil painting in a cathedral. There were two large fireplaces in the room, with gorgeous mantles sporting carved and painted Celtic beasts. One had a luxurious sitting area arranged around it, and the other had the biggest bathing tub Adamina had ever seen set into the floor, surrounded by a huge and very intricate mosaic. A dining room table and sideboard were set for dinner midway between the two fireplaces, with exquisite silver candelabras already lit on the table.

The entire room was decorated in blues and soft grays, and an assortment of mirrors decorated the walls, reflecting the firelight and the candles burning on various tables and in sculptured floor candelabras that were placed throughout the space. It was the loveliest, most sumptuous room Adamina had ever laid eyes on.

Thomas was hanging his black hat and coat on the coat rack near the door. He smiled as he watched her standing awestruck in the entrance to the room. "Mina," he said gently. "I have much to tell you. But you've just escaped a prison, so it can wait a bit." He walked to her, took the blanket from her and tossed it onto a nearby chair, putting his hands gently on her shoulders. "I ken you're half frozen; but other than that, are ye alright? Did they hurt you, *mo chreach?*"

"I'm fine," she answered him. *I nearly died today, but ....* "Well, to be truthful, I'm a bit in shock. But I will be fine soon. Especially now that you're here." She smiled hopefully at him. *Tell me you can stay. Tell me.*

He was looking closely at her face, and she got a good look at him for the first time. *He has a beard again. I love that.* She noticed a weariness in his eyes that wasn't usually there, and wondered at it. *Was he worried about me? About Alex? Where has he been?*

"Thomas," she said, placing her hands over his, "why didn't you come at Beltane? And where were your letters?"

He shook his head. "We should get you in a hot bath first, an' get you some decent food...."

She shook her head. "No. I need to know now, please." He let go of her and ran a hand over his head. She couldn't help but smile at that. *Alex is so like him.* She felt a stab of loneliness for her son. She wasn't prepared for what he said next.

"I've been at war, Mina."

She didn't understand. "What war? Where?"

He looked at her sadly. "I've tried not to tell ye too much, Mina. To keep ye safe. But I think the time has come to tell ye a bit more, now. So you can understand."

She moved to him and took his hand. "I'm listening."

He sighed. "Faerie has been at war for the last seventeen months. It's why I havenae written. I cannae get the letters here. I've been in different worlds."

She noticed the metallic smell on his clothing again. *Metal and ash.* "Did you...did you just come from there? From the war?"

He nodded. "I'm no supposed to be here right now, Mina. I had to steal the magick I needed to come and get ye out of Carlisle. All our resources are directed at protecting our borders and the borders of our allies. Magickal power is in short supply."

Adamina sat down on a blue velvet chair. "So...if they realize you're gone, you'll be arrested as a deserter?"

He smiled at her affectionately. "Ah, not quite. Mina, I'm one of the generals."

Her eyes widened. "You...what?"

He sat down on the large footstool in front of her. "I'm a Fae General, sweetheart. There are four of us. I command the armies of the..." he took a deep breath, "...the armies of the Dead. For the Great Queen. The Morrigan."

Adamina stared at him. "The Morrigan," she repeated. "*The*...Morrigan. As in, the Celtic Goddess of war, death, and fate." He nodded. "I knew you were a mage," Adamina said slowly, "and I knew you had your own realm there. But I didn't know you were so...so, your soldiers are *ghosts*?"

He nodded. "Ghosts, an'... more. But that is no so important; what I am tryin' to say is, I'm sorry I couldnae get here. I'm verra sorry I couldnae write. Do you forgive me, Mina?"

She nodded and took his hand. "Yes. *Of course.*" She paused. "Is it...very dangerous? Or is war there...different?"

He looked at her solemnly. "Aye, Mina, it's dangerous. It's an awful thing."

"And is...," Adamina felt her breath catch, "is Alex, the part that's in Faerie...does he have to go to war, too?"

Thomas shook his head. "No, Mina. They willnae send him." He looked away. "I've managed to see him a few times, when the...realm that he's in moves. But not lately. He may be worried by my absence. I didnae tell him about the war, Mina." *Just as I haven't told you he's in a prison there.*

Adamina breathed a sigh of relief.

"I tried to see him on the way here," Thomas told her, "But they had locked down the borders of Faerie an' the realm he's in. Didnae have time to wait and make it here as well." He gestured in the air. "An' timing was rather important in your case."

He took a deep breath and shook the tension from his shoulders. "But I dinnae want to talk about war, Mina. I'll need to go back when the sun is high tomorrow. But until then...," he smiled at her, "it will do me good to just be with ye, and speak of other things." He smiled at her and she felt a rush of love for him.

"Then that's what we'll do," she told him, patting his hand. "Everything that needs to be said will be said in time." She stood up, and glanced over at the bathing tub, which was easily big enough to bathe a horse. "I'd like to wash the filth of Carlisle off of me, and maybe you'd like to join me to get the scent of war off of you, too."

He stood and laughed; she remembered how much she loved that sound. "You're a vixen, Mina," he teased her. "We've been together not half a bell and you're already takin' my clothes off!"

She slipped her arms around his waist and moved close. "I don't want to waste a single one of the minutes you're here. We have so few."

He looked into her eyes and touched her cheek. "I love you," he said quietly, "an' I'm sorry I wasnae here sooner. When word reached me, I came at once." He shook his head. "I thought of tryin' to take ye from this realm to Faerie, Mina, but believe it or not, it's safer for ye here right now."

He left her, went to a door near the far wall and rang a bell on a blue silk cord. A moment later a man dressed as a steward came in through the door. Thomas spoke to him quietly, and the man nodded and left. A few moments later a group of servants entered quietly and began busying themselves with tasks around the room.

Thomas led Adamina to the sitting area as she saw a woman turn down the bed and several others moving and arranging things near the soaking tub. Another woman entered the room and began hanging clothes on a rack behind the dressing screen. Adamina saw shifts and dresses, and a beautiful gray silk dressing gown. Yet another attendant was placing ribbons and a comb and brush on the dressing table, along with small crystal bottles of perfume and various other items for a lady's toilette.

"Since you've no luggage with ye," Thomas said, his eyes sparkling, "I took the liberty of findin' ye some things. I had a bit of time until my...assistant flew in." He sat on the sofa, and she curled up next to him. "I hope you like them."

"You're wonderful," she told him. "You always choose the nicest things for me."

He took her hand again. "Have you seen our son lately? Here in Scotland?"

She shook her head. "Not in person since early September. One of the men who rides with Duncan said Alex is escorting someone important west. Alex is less known on sight outside the Borders; I imagine he'll be safer for a time." She looked at Thomas, and a shadow filled her eyes. "The Crown...they burned Buccleuch, Thomas. I got your message to flee, but they caught me anyway. That's how I ended up in Carlisle."

Thomas' face changed, sorrow and shock took up residence on his features. "They burned it? All you've built?"

Adamina looked away. "I don't know exactly how bad it is. The old halls may have survived. But the other side...." Tears came to her eyes. "Gone. I could see it as they drove me away in the carriage."

Thomas put his arms around her and held her quietly for a long moment. "We'll rebuild it, *mo ghràdh-sa*," he said quietly. "I'll give you all the help I can. Where is Edan? Is he at Branxholme?"

Adamina nodded. "I think so. I'm...a bit out of the loop. But Thomas, I must tell you what the garrison commander said...."

She stopped as he moved her gently away from him and gave her a look she knew well. *He has something to say. Something important.* She paused, and looked at him expectantly.

"Before ye continue," he said quietly, taking one of her hands in his, "there's somethin' I must tell you, Mina. I dinnae ken if you know already. But I think not." He took a deep breath. "When was the last time you saw your husband?"

And Adamina knew. *Caroline Scott had been telling the truth. Conall is dead.* A wave of conflicting feelings crashed through her, dashing themselves against the sea walls of her heart. *The men in the green coats. They came out of the walls at Buccleuch. Someone told them how to get in.* And the only two who knew all the passages in and out of Buccleuch besides herself were Alex and Conall.

Conall. He'd given her to Caroline Scott. "I think...I suspect Conall told the Crown how to attack Buccleuch, Thomas." She was enraged. But Conall had also been Edan and Gilbride's father. "He's dead, isn't he?" Adamina said slowly. "Caroline Scott said as much." She looked away. "He told me Alex killed Conall."

"No," Thomas said, squeezing her hand gently. "There are ghosts at Branxholme, Adamina. There's one verra strong one who I had tasked with watching over you and the boys. An' she was there in Conall's study when it happened, an' saw it. Alexander did no kill Conall." He paused. "Edan did to save Alexander's life. Conall disowned Alexander and meant to murder him. Conall found out about us."

Adamina's eyes widened, and for a moment she felt faint. *Edan.* Edan had always been a gentle, kind soul; she couldn't imagine what killing must have been like for him. And how, after all these years, had Conall discovered the truth?

"I owe Edan a great debt," Thomas continued. "He avenged Conall's betrayal of you at Buccleuch, and because of him our son still walks in this realm." He put a steadying hand on her shoulder. "But I am also sorry for your loss, Adamina. Conall gave ye two beautiful sons."

She looked up at him, and didn't know what to say. Conall had looked after her, been a solid business partner, and because of him Edan and Gilbride were in her life. But he had also burned her home, forsaken her to the Crown, and made a murderer of Edan. She looked at Thomas and thought of how strange their time together had been. *Only here for days at a time. But I love him immensely, in a way I never loved Conall Scott.*

She heard Thomas clear his throat and watched him rub his index finger with his thumb, as he often did when he was restless. "I wish we had more time, Mina. Time so that I could do things properly. But that is not the way it is for us. Our stars cross rarely, and at inopportune times. We must make the most of the moments we have when we have them."

He was suddenly wearing an emotion she'd never seen on him before. He looked slightly nervous. In all the years she'd known Thomas, she'd never seen anything from him but confidence. He could be cautious at times, but he always walked this world as though he'd done it countless times before. She couldn't imagine what he was about to say. She watched him curiously.

The servants disappeared through the door to the hall, and they were alone again. He took her hands in his, and she thought she felt them tremble a bit.

"Mina," he said to her quietly, "in all the lifetimes I have walked this earth, in all the ages I've been in other realms, I have never loved anyone as I've loved you." He went quiet for a moment, and Adamina let her eyes roam over his handsome features. "You've given me the two greatest gifts I could ever hope for: your love and our son. And ye did it despite havin' to live with my darkness and my secrets, with my absence and my edicts." He looked in her eyes, and all she saw was adoration. "No woman should have to tolerate what ye do with me. Yet, ye have. I have no right to ask what I'm about to ask. But I cannae help myself, even though I know it's profoundly selfish of me to put this to you."

She sat still, completely puzzled, and waited.

"I made a stupid mistake thirty years ago when we met," he said softly. "I...I didnae understand what this was to be, this bond between us. But now I've been afforded another chance." He let go of her hands, and she watched as his right hand executed a slight gesture, a pivot of the wrist and fingers.

"Mina," he said, his voice breaking a bit, "the truth is I cannae bear the thought of going away from you and thinking that when I return, you may once again be another man's wife." He moved off the sofa, and now he was kneeling on one knee in front of her. "You deserve more than me. I've always known that. But I'm asking anyway." His right hand moved again, and as his palm turned up toward the sky she saw that he had conjured something. *A ring.* "I understand all the reasons you should say no. But my God, Mina, *how I want you for my wife.*"

She sat, frozen, staring at the ring. It hadn't crossed her mind that Conall's death also meant she was now free from a loveless marriage. *Free. Free to choose, or not choose.* And here Thomas was. On one knee, ring in hand, doing what she'd dreamed of for three decades. She didn't care about anything else. *He was offering himself to her.*

"Yes," she said, without a second thought. "*Thomas,* yes!"

She threw her arms around him, and he laughed in relief and joy and did the same. His mouth found hers, and they ended up sitting on the floor slowly kissing each other, holding each other tightly, and losing themselves in each other's existence.

"I was a fool, Mina," Thomas whispered in her ear. "I shouldnae have let you marry Conall without a word. I fell for ye the first time we met, but I said nothing, because I thought I wasnae what you wanted in life." He squeezed her against him. "I was absolutely gutted when ye wed Conall, and have remained so all this time." He stroked her cheek. "I want ye to ken that I'm working on a way we can be together more. In another place." He looked down suddenly, a bemused smile on his face. "Ah...where'd the ring go, sweetheart? I was so busy kissin' ye I think I lost it, somehow."

Adamina started to laugh. "I think I might be sitting on it." She pulled herself closer to him with one hand and reached behind her to get the ring.

He laughed, delighted, and took it from her, holding it up for her to see. "It's a bit unusual, *mo tè àlainn*. This is a Fae gem, ye ken." He looked at her closely. "You'll have two rings soon. This one is our personal one, from me to you. The second will be a ring from the crown jewels, but you dinnae need to wear that one as much, if you dinnae wish." He grinned. "You'll be the Queen of the Deck of Crows, Mina."

She smiled and shook her head. "I don't know what *any* of that actually means, Thomas!"

He touched her cheek, his gaze full of tenderness. "You'll be a Queen of the Fae, *an tè as inntinniche*." He paused. "The Deck if Crows is perhaps the most powerful Deck in all the houses, my love. An' as I have armies to command, the people will look to you for decisions." His eyes searched her own. "I can think of no one better for that than you."

She raised her eyebrows. "From what you *have* told me, there will be those who will be quite unhappy with a human in that position."

He gave her a half-smile and nodded. "There's always someone unhappy with *everythin'*, my dearest. But none of them would dare say it to our faces." He slid one hand gently under the soft waves of her hair and around the back of her neck. "*I* will be happy with ye there. And hopefully, so will you."

She looked at the ring closely for the first time, and it took her breath away. Delicately etched into the outside of the band was a raven, wings outstretched in flight. A crow in the same position decorated the interior of the band, along with what looked like runes. There was a large dark jewel Adamina didn't recognize as the centerpiece of the ring, flanked by two stones that shone like diamonds.

She loved everything about it. She couldn't take her eyes from the center stone, which seemed both solid and a changeable, multi-hued pool of dark ink at the same time. "It's...so beautiful. What...what is that stone?"

Thomas pointed to various parts of the ring as she held it in her hand. "This raven here...."

"It looks like the one on your back."

He smiled. "Exactly. That's my banner, see? A symbol for me, bestowed on me in Faerie the day I was born. It shows my lineage, an ode to our House." He pointed to the inside of the band. "An' this...this is the symbol of our Deck. Alex has a crow as his banner as well, although his looks different from this one. It was given to him when I brought him to see the Great Queen, when he first arrived in Faerie." He smiled at her. "An' since he is grown now, he has his banner on his back like I have on mine. I dinnae think I ever told you."

"Thomas," she said quietly to him. "I understand that you did what you had to do to keep him safe. I don't know that I've ever thanked you properly for doing what needed to be done, even though it was hard. I fought you, and I'm sorry. I just...couldn't do anything else."

He touched his forehead gently to hers. "You have said similar things to me, Mina. Many times. An' I understood. There were also many times when *you* did what needed to be done, things that I am sorry you had to do. It is why we are good together; when one of us is weak, the other finds a way to be strong."

She kissed him gently, and he smiled at her and continued. "These runes here by the crow...they are protection symbols." He grinned. "I enchanted *the hell* out of this ring, my dearest one. Look here." He pointed to the two stones on either side of the large dark stone. "These two diamonds...they are linked to a third in my realm. Should anyone try to take you through a portal against your wishes or without your permission while you wear this, instead of going where they intend to take you, you will instead arrive inside the Castle of Crows. If you are ever lost and find a portal, you can announce your intention to return to the castle and it will perform the same service."

Adamina stared at the diamonds. "They'll...take me to your home in Faerie?"

"If you have a portal that leads to Faerie, yes." He wagged a playful finger at her. "Dinnae go skipping between worlds with this for fun. If it's not a Fae portal who kens where you'll end up?"

"And...this?" Adamina pointed at the center stone, afraid to touch it. It looked like moving liquid, reflecting light in its dark depths.

"Aye, now this took time," Thomas smiled. "This is called blackpool. Verra rare. But watch." He picked up a candle from the side table next to the sofa with his right hand and held the ring up next to his left eye with his left hand.

"Look close, now," he told her. He moved the candle close to his face, and Adamina noticed the reflection of the light on his pupil and the reflection of the light on the stone were identical. As Thomas' pupil contracted due to the light from the candle flame, the darkness in the blackpool stone contracted as well, leaving a gray ring around it that matched Thomas' gray iris exactly.

Thomas moved the candle away from his face, and both the dark area in the blackpool stone and Thomas' pupil expanded at the same time. He turned and put the candle back on the table.

"Your...eye," Adamina breathed. "I can see it in the stone!"

He beamed at her. "Aye. An' if I sleep, the stone turns bright blue."

"I can see if you're awake or asleep when you're not with me! I'll be able to see if you're alright!" Adamina was brimming with excitement. "Does it work *everywhere?* No matter how far away you are?"

He nodded. "It should." He lowered his voice. "An' if I die, Adamina, the stone will turn to blood. My blood. So, you never need to wonder if...," he put his hand on her arm, "if I'm alive or not. You'll ken."

She took hold of his hand and gripped it hard. "Don't say such things," she begged him. "Kings of the Fae live a long, long time."

"But we *can* be killed, Mina," he said to her quietly. "An' if it happens, I dinnae want ye bound by not knowing if I'm returning to you or no."

She desperately wanted to change the subject. "I love the ring, Thomas. It will help *so much.* When I miss you, I can...," she smiled, "see a little of you right on my finger!" She looked up at him hopefully. "When...when do you want to get married?" *I can't believe I'm saying this!*

He blushed. "I ken that you would like the boys to be there when we wed but...I was rather hoping for a short engagement." He ran his hand through his hair. "I was thinkin' if ye said yes, that...well, I dinnae want to go back to the front without bein' your husband, Adamina."

Her eyes widened. "That's...*tomorrow,* Thomas."

He nodded. "The man who owns this house, he's a bishop, *mo bhòidhchead.* He could marry us tonight." He gestured. "Unless ye want a Catholic officiant for certain, it'll take a bit longer to get one of those. This one owes me a favor."

She looked at him suspiciously. "What *kind* of a favor?"

He laughed. "How do ye think he got to be bishop?" He shrugged. "There's a fair number of holy men who dinnae mind sorcery so much when it directly benefits them."

"We're going to have to talk further about this, if I'm to be your wife," Adamina frowned, realizing she had no idea what the limits of his work in magick actually were.

"Marry me first," he grinned, "an' then ye can scold me all you like, as is right and proper for a wife." He moved closer so he could whisper in her ear. "I was thinkin'...a nice bath together, early dinner, get married, an' then tonight, I'll treat ye like a husband should treat his wife on her honeymoon."

Adamina's mind was reeling. *Almost get hanged by noon, consummate your new marriage by midnight.* She put a hand to her forehead.

"Say yes again, my lovely one," he said, kissing her on the cheek. "All ye have to do, ye ken, is say *yes.*"

"What am I going to tell Alex?" she said, turning to face him. "Aren't you forbidden from contacting the part of him in this realm? 'Hello, Alexander, I got married to your real father while you were away. And you can never meet him.'"

He smiled at her. "Mina, that's an *entirely* different problem, so." He ran his hand through her dark hair. "An' the sort of thing a husband and wife solve *together*. Once they're wed, ye see."

She gave him a playful push. "My God, Thomas, you don't stop, do you?"

He shook his head. "Never."

She took a deep breath. "You win. Bath, dinner, married."

He let out a whoop of happiness. She'd never seen him so celebratory. Thomas went back to the bell by the door, and the steward appeared again. There was a brief conversation, and then the man disappeared.

"Dinner in an hour or so," Thomas called to Adamina. "We'll see the bishop at seven, once his dinner guests leave." He walked over to the soaking tub and slid a small metal rectangle inside it sideways, and hot water flooded into the tub from a tank under the raised mosaic floor.

"What in the world?" Adamina said, leaving the ring on the table by the sofa and following him to the bath. "Don't the servants have to come in and heat the water?"

"No," he smiled. "This is somethin' I designed for the owner of the house. He has three here. The servants heat and pour the water into the end of an oddly shaped tank in another room, an' it stays warm in the tank, then when you push this here, it flows into the bath. So your guests can have their privacy without an army of staff heatin' buckets. An' it goes out through pipes to irrigate the garden when you're done." He shrugged. "It's basic science an' water pressure. Nothing the Romans didnae already do." He pulled off his boots and looked at her. "I've designed all sorts of things for this place over the years. An' the bishop, he has them all built."

Adamina smiled. She didn't understand Thomas' magickal enterprises, but she was intimately familiar with his scientific ones. He had adored engineering new devices the entire time she'd known him; to him, earth was a gigantic laboratory full of things to discover and build. She loved that about him. He had turned away from her and was stripping off his clothes now. *My God. I love this about him as well.*

He tossed his shirt aside, and she marveled once again at the way the tattoos on his arms and back defined his musculature and made him look like a living work of art. Every time he took his shirt off, she was reminded that he wasn't human; he was of the Fae, and a god as well, and the shape of his body showed it.

He looked over his shoulder at her and grinned, before pulling off his trousers and tossing them at her. She laughed and caught them, and her eyes drank in the sight of Thomas Scott's exceptionally well-muscled thighs and backside. *He's perfect. Perfect in every way.*

"Hurry up!" he chided her, and her heart raced as she watched him climb naked into the bath and settle into the water. "What are ye waitin' for? Oh, Great Dagda's Harp, this water feels *so good*."

I'm going to marry him, she thought, watching him smile up at her as he stretched out in the water, his eyes alight with happiness and anticipation of her joining him in the bath. *I'm going to marry him. Tonight. And...live in Faerie at some point with him. Maybe. He is the love of my life. I am so, so blessed.*

She began pulling off her clothes, not wanting to waste a moment of precious time with him.

Branxholme, Scotland

It was dark when they reached Branxholme. The castle looked different when they weren't trying to break into it. The garrison was gone, and instead of soldiers traipsing around the grounds, there was a quiet peace that stretched around the property. It felt strange to have a groom welcome them at the stables, and to have two of Edan's security men laugh and joke with them as they guided them to the front door, saddlebags thrown over their strong shoulders.

Edan met them in the front hall, a wide smile on his face, electric with anticipation. Saorsa saw his eyes quickly assess the group. "Where's Alex?" he said, looking at Saorsa. "Outside with the horses still?"

Saorsa shook her head. "No, Edan," she said, taking his hand. "Mother Agnes and I must speak with you. Right away." She took a deep breath. "We need your help."

Edan ushered them all up the stairs and moved them into a large, comfortable sitting room where Toran sat, reading a book. "Saorsa! Fia!" Toran said, waving at them. His leg was propped up on the sofa, healing well underway. "And...oh, I don't think we've met!" He grinned at Mother Agnes and Annag.

"Toran! How is the leg doing?" Saorsa crossed to him and bent to give him a hug. Fia kept her distance, staring guiltily at the floor.

"Better, much better," Toran answered.

"This is Mother Agnes and Annag. Would you mind entertaining Annag and Fia a bit while Mother Agnes and I speak with Edan?"

"Not at all! I'd be delighted." Toran closed his book. "Let me yodel for someone to bring in something for you to drink." He paused for a moment. "Alex is with you, right? Still out in the stable?" He watched a shadow cross Saorsa's face, and he became serious. "What's wrong, Saorsa?"

Edan met Toran's eyes, who nodded and changed course. "You can catch me up later, Saorsa. Please, Fia, and...Annag, is it? Have a seat, and warm yourselves." He watched Edan lead Mother Agnes and Saorsa to a door that opened into an adjoining study, his face cloudy with concern.

Edan held the door for the ladies to enter but didn't even have it closed before he began talking. "Is Alex in Carlisle? Tell me Caroline Scott doesn't have him! And what of Vika? And my mother? Duncan?"

"The Fae have Alex," Saorsa answered. "The knife has been returned to Faerie. I took it there myself."

"So, he's *not* a redcoat prisoner," Edan frowned. "I suppose that's something...."

"Edan, he *could* be. We don't know why the Fae took him, or where. These were not *friendly* Fae, Edan. It could be to pass him off to the redcoats." Saorsa paused. "Or, in this case, maybe the *green* coats. I saw a mage at Buccleuch who wore green. Or they could have taken Alex to Faerie. We're not sure why."

"Wait, wait," Edan said, putting up his hand. "I need to understand this. First...Madame, you are dressed as a nun, and you go by Mother Agnes. But am I correct in assuming you are ... ahm... the same...."

"Witch," Mother Agnes filled in pleasantly. "I'm a High Priestess. Trained in the Circle of Aradia in Italy, originally, although I was born here in Scotland." She smiled at Edan pleasantly as though they were meeting at a dinner party. "I'm also a midwife, a physician, an energy healer, a Mistress of Poisons, a Specialist Advisor in Exorcism and the Dark Magicks for the Pope, and an honorary Druid. In addition to my doctorates in medicine, I hold fourteen degrees in various ancient arts, four of which are from Cambridge, two from Oxford, five from Cologne, two from Cracow and one in ancient texts from dear old Sapienza." She smiled brightly at Edan and pointed at Saorsa. "And I'm her mentor, which I have enjoyed the most out of all of it."

"Aye," said Edan weakly, "so you're the same Mother Agnes Saorsa mentioned from her time at Hermitage Abbey." He swallowed. "And apparently, not a person to be trifled with."

"I'm not trying to be a braggart, Laird Scott," Mother Agnes continued. "I thought it best to let you know my qualifications, as it might inform the conversation."

"Edan," Saorsa said, "we need somewhere for Fia to stay. She's pregnant. The Fae want her child, and we need to make certain they can't take the bairn."

"What?" Edan's eyes widened. "*Fia's pregnant?"*

"Yes," Saorsa explained. "Her baby needs protection from the Fae when it's born, and maybe before. If she stays here with you, and Mother Agnes and Annag do as well, then everyone in Branxholme should be safe in case the Fae arrive. Mother Agnes can construct magickal barriers here at Branxholme."

Edan's mind was whirling. "Why would the Fae want Fia's child?"

Saorsa bit her lip. "Because," she said slowly, "the child is a half-Fae child. And we're pretty certain...that Alex is the father."

Edan sat down. "Fia...is pregnant...with Alex's child." He stared into space for a moment. "What the actual *hell,* Saorsa? Does Killian know? Does Anne?"

"Not yet," Saorsa said. "We need your advice on how to tell them."

"Does *Alex* know?"

"He does," replied Mother Agnes. "And he's proposed to Fia, of course. They're engaged."

"That's why he sent the Scott sapphire here," Saorsa said. "It's to be Fia's wedding ring."

"What are you talking about?" Edan stared at her. "That cursed thing's not here!"

Saorsa frowned. "Fia said Alex sent it here under guard here several days ago."

Edan stood up. "Nothing's arrived from Buccleuch, Saorsa." He looked sharply at the door. "Do you think those delivering it could have been attacked on the road?" He walked to a door on the opposite wall from the sitting room door and opened it. A guard was seated in the hall outside.

"We may be missing some people," Edan said. "Some items were being transferred here a few days ago from Buccleuch under my brother's orders. Rather valuable items. I need three men to ride there at once and verify that the shipment left, and if it did, attempt to track down what happened to our men. Make it happen, please, and report back." The guard stood at once and hastened down the hall, out of sight. Edan turned back to Saorsa. "When you say *the Fae took* Alex, what *exactly* happened?"

No sooner had Edan shut the door than they heard Toran's voice shouting in the sitting room. "Sweet Mother Mary, *what now?*" Edan exclaimed. He dashed to the sitting room door, with Saorsa and Mother Agnes behind him.

Standing just inside the doorway opposite Edan was...Duncan MacLeod. A rather shocked looking Duncan MacLeod.

"*Duncan?*" Edan gasped. "Where...*Duncan, is that you?*"

"Aye," said the Highlander, somewhat dazed. "Is Alex here?"

"That's the most popular question of the night!" shouted Toran. "How the hell did you *get here,* man?"

"Not...certain." Duncan looked around. "I was...tryin' to go somewhere else."

Saorsa shoved her way past Edan, ran to Duncan and threw her arms around him. "Duncan! *Duncan!* Oh, thank the Goddess, *you're alive!*"

Edan was so overwhelmed he just kept shouting. "Where's Vika? Where's my mother?"

Duncan looked down at the small female tornado of joy that was Saorsa Stuart and blinked. "Ah, you're... the lass Alex was escortin', aye?"

"Yes," Saorsa screeched, beside herself with relief. *Vika is going to be so happy! Alex is going to be so happy!*

"Everyone... EVERYONE, *stop shouting!*" Mother Agnes ordered. "We need to calm down!"

Another guard came racing at top speed into the room, all sense of decorum left behind in his haste. "Laird Scott! *Laird Scott!* We just received word that there was a jailbreak at Carlisle!"

"That was me!" Duncan declared, his arms still pinned to his sides under Saorsa's crushing embrace.

"No, *no!*" the man said, shaking his head. "The informant you sent, sir, the one inside Carlisle...he says Adamina Scott escaped just before her hanging!"

"*What hanging?*" Edan bellowed. "Where *is she?*"

"No one knows, sir!" gasped the guard, who had run all the way in from the bridge. "They're combing the countryside! There's no trace of her!"

"Vika? Alex? Did they do this?" Edan was waving his hands wildly in the air.

"Alex has been shot twice, poisoned, and cannae walk," Annag shouted, adding her voice to the din. "So most likely not him!"

"*Shot?*" Edan screeched.

Mother Agnes put her fingers to her mouth and let out a tremendous whistle. The room fell silent. "There now," Mother Agnes said calmly. "We need some *order here,* my friends." She looked at the guard who had escorted Duncan in and the winded man who had brought news of Adamina's escape. "I am Mother Agnes, Laird Scott's new personal advisor." The two men looked at Edan, who nodded. "Where is the man who brought news from Carlisle?"

"He's at the stables. Changed horses and rode straight through. Exhausted," said the guard, holding his side.

"Bring him here as soon as possible. And we need the castle steward at once," Mother Agnes instructed. "Thank you both for your dedicated service. On your way, now." She crossed the room and shut the door. "Everyone find a chair. Let's get on the same page."

There was a knock on the door and the castle steward entered and looked at Edan. "You called, sir?"

"Yes," Edan said, composing himself. "We need...," he took a quick headcount, "*six* guest rooms made up at once. Drawn baths in each in an hour, and dinner in each in an hour and a half."

"The riders have left for Buccleuch," the steward informed Edan. "Please let me know if I can be of further assistance to any of you." He nodded and smiled, closing the door behind him.

"Let's start with Duncan," Saorsa said, taking charge. "Are you hurt?"

"No," Duncan said, looking around. "I ken Toran and Edan, and you're...what's your name again, lassie?"

"Saorsa," Saorsa smiled at him. "Saorsa Stuart." She paused. "You don't know much about me, but I know *all about* you."

"They let me go from Carlisle at dawn yesterday," Duncan said. "They meant to track me to Vika, I think. But once they got me outside the gatehouse, I took a different route than they expected. Alex an' I, we set it up as an escape route during the uprising. I lost the guards. I saw Adamina with the garrison commander on my way out; I think she brokered my release, somehow."

"So, she was alive and well yesterday morning," Edan said quietly. "And then you came...here?"

"No!" said Duncan, raising his eyebrows. "That's just it! I *didnae*! I made it out, left messages for Vika at the drops, stole a horse an' headed for Morrigan's Cave! Was almost there, too, when...," he waved his hand in the air, "this pretentious *voice from nowhere* said, 'the Flower o' the West wants ye delivered, Duncan MacLeod.' An' then the horse was *gone,* and I was standin' in your back garden, Edan, up by the old passageway! An' I've...*no idea what happened!*"

Saorsa stifled a laugh. Duncan had gotten out of Carlisle without Diarmid's help, but the Fae still wanted to make good on his promise to deliver Duncan to Branxholme for her. So he had. He'd opened a portal and delivered Duncan here.

"When you were nearly at the cave and you...were transported," Saorsa asked, "were you on the road? Or had you stopped?"

"I was on a hilltop, takin' a breather an' havin' a look around," replied Duncan. "My horse was there one moment, maybe ten feet away, an' then...," he wiggled his fingers in the air, "poof! I was at Branxholme."

Saorsa grinned. "Did that hilltop have any faerie stones on it, by any chance?"

Duncan nodded. "What are ye gettin' at...?"

Saorsa sighed. *We'll have to tell Duncan. And Toran. Branwen's Braids, things are getting messy.* "A Fae creature named Diarmid took you through a portal and delivered you here, Duncan. He and I made a deal that he was to help you escape Carlisle."

Mother Agnes gasped. "You made a *deal?* With a f*aerie*?"

Duncan's eyes shifted from Saorsa to Edan with a look that said *the bonnie hen's a wee bit mad, aye?*

"Saorsa is telling you the truth," Edan said quietly. "I know this is hard to believe, gentlemen, but...faeries are real. And...we've had interactions with them recently."

Toran and Duncan both turned to stare at Edan. "What?" Toran said slowly.

Duncan laughed. "How much whisky did ye all have before I arrived?"

"I didn't believe it either," Edan protested, "until Vika convinced me."

"Wait...you say *Vika* believes this horseshite?" Toran exclaimed.

"She does," Saorsa said. "She's seen it for herself. As have I. As has Edan, Fia, Mother Agnes and Annag."

Duncan shook his head. "You're...you're all mad."

"Well," said Saorsa calmly, "you can choose to believe us or not. But I really hope you do because we could use your help. Because that's where Alex is, you see. He's...a prisoner of the Fae. They took him."

Duncan stared at Saorsa, incredulous. "You're tellin' me...that Alexander Scott... was kidnapped by *faeries*?"

Toran looked at Edan. "This isn't funny anymore, Edan."

"It's the truth," Edan said.

Fia, who hadn't said a word since arriving at Branxholme, suddenly felt a need to come clean and stood up. "It *is* the truth," she said. "Faeries are real. And I know because...," she twisted her rings and cleared her throat, "I helped them orchestrate Alex's capture."

"You *what?*" Edan thundered, moving aggressively toward Fia, and Mother Agnes and Saorsa moved quickly to block his path. "You *helped them?* You *betrayed Alex?* He's the *father of your child!* We've been friends since we were *children ourselves!*"

"I wanted to help him!" cried Fia, instinctively putting her hand in front of her belly to shield her child. "They said they could heal him!"

"Edan! *Edan!*" Saorsa shouted, putting her hands on Edan's chest to stop his forward motion. "Remember the baby, Edan! Don't hurt her!"

"What *baby?*" Toran was shouting again. "What the hell is going on?"

"Fia is pregnant with Alex's child," Annag blurted, "an' Fia poisoned Alex so the Fae could take him!"

"You're Alex's *wife?*" Duncan asked, incredulous.

"No," Annag answered, pointing at Fia, "*she* made the bairn through a blood magick spell without Alex's consent! Alex doesnae love her, he loves *her!*" Annag pointed at Saorsa. "An' it's all an awful mess, because Alex is half-Fae too, an' Conall Scott is dead because he found out Alex is a bastard, sired by a Fae mage!"

The energy in the room exploded into chaos. Duncan and Toran couldn't process all of the conversation, but what they *had* understood was that Alex wasn't here, he was in danger, and somehow Fia had betrayed him. Both of the men rose, Toran somewhat unsteadily, and began moving toward Fia as though they intended to join Edan in physically wrenching the truth from her.

"NOT HELPING, ANNAG!" shouted Mother Agnes as she and Saorsa now attempted to block three large, angry, confused men from reaching Fia. Everyone was shouting again.

"Separate rooms! Separate *rooms!*" yelled Saorsa, and she took Fia's arm, dragged her toward Edan's study, opened the door, and shoved her in. Mother Agnes followed suit with Annag, and then stood with Saorsa, their backs blocking the door to the study as their male companions loudly demanded answers.

There was a knock on the sitting room door, and everyone went immediately silent. "Come in," Edan said, and all the room's occupants turned to look at the door, masks of composure falling over their faces.

The steward was there, standing by a man who looked like he'd been awake too long and was dressed as a British soldier. "Lorcan is here, Laird Scott."

Edan gestured a bit awkwardly for the man to enter. "Please, Lorcan, come in and rest. These are my friends." The steward took his leave.

Lorcan looked at Duncan and his face lit up. "Good to see you well an' in one piece, Mister MacLeod. Ye caused quite a stir at Carlisle with that moat trick o' yours. The garrison commander was fair foamin' at the mouth."

Duncan smiled and nodded. "Thank you. What news of Lady Scott?"

Lorcan took a seat. "I tried to get free to send news of your escape here to Branxholme, sir, but they changed the duty roster an' I was stuck inside Carlisle for a bit. The plan was to follow ye to find Vika MacLeod, sir. When ye gave the hunters in position the slip, Caroline Scott was angry an' ordered Lady Scott's hanging for noon the next day."

"Good *God,*" exclaimed Edan.

"It didnae happen, though," Lorcan said quickly, holding up his hands. "Garrison commander wanted a big crowd. But the crowd was *too* big, an' filled up Carlisle so ye couldnae move. An' when they went to fetch the prisoner, they found her room open and guards on the floor. An' more chopped to pieces with an axe down the hall." He twisted his hat brim in his hands. "An' then it gets odd, ye see."

"Odd how?" Edan and the others all took a seat.

"A few minutes later, this *thing* comes flyin' out over the crowd in the courtyard. Circles around, an' people start screamin'. The crowd panics and begins to run. I was there, on an upper level. Then...," he gestured in the air, keeping his fingers together and his hand flat in imitation of the object, "the flyin' thing shoots over the crowd, with Adamina Scott on board, sir, flies out the gates, an' into the air over Carlisle Town, and then it was just *gone*. An' then...boom! All the staircases in Carlisle that lead to the courtyard just *explode*, sir. Carlisle's a mess; soldiers hurt, an' the mob went *crazy*, sir. People were jumpin' into the moat to get away, fighting' each other, and there was a stampede into the closest church. The crowd thought the devil was comin' for them. They say Lady Scott's a witch, an' that your brother Alexander was there and summoned a demon to get her out. They say it's another Hermitage, another Branxholme. They also say Vika MacLeod was seen in the crowd; some blame the explosions on her." He shook his head. "There's soldiers all over the Borders, sir, huntin' the MacLeod siblings, Adamina an' Alexander Scott. Adamina's a price on her head now, Duncan's capture amount has tripled, an' Vika MacLeod and Alexander Scott are just listed as 'shoot on sight', sir, for soldiers *and* civilians. They dinnae want those two for a fancy trial in London now; they just want 'em dead."

There was silence in the room for a moment. Edan broke it. "Did you see this flying thing?"

Lorcan twisted his hat again. "Aye, sir."

"And," Edan asked, "what do you think it was?"

Lorcan looked around the room. "Ye ken I was a good and loyal informant for your father these past ten years, Laird Scott. I didnae stop on the way here. I didnae tarry at an inn, or touch a drop, I swear."

Edan nodded. "Yes, I understand you're trustworthy and not drunk, Lorcan."

"Then...," Lorcan let out a long, slow breath. "It looked like...*a rug,* sir. A big wool carpet, like ye have in this room here. An'...Lady Scott was lyin' on it, holdin' on for dear life. An' *screamin'.*"

The room fell silent again. Edan rubbed his jaw for a moment with both hands. "You're saying...my mother escaped Carlisle aboard a *flying carpet*?"

Lorcan nodded. "I swear to ye, Laird Scott, *that's what I saw*. It went faster than any horse. It seemed like it was choosin' which way to go. But as God is my witness, sir, it looked to be a *parlor room rug*." No one said anything for a long while. Lorcan continued twisting his hat. "Am I...am I bein' released from your service, sir?"

Edan seemed to have briefly forgotten Lorcan was there. "Oh...ah, no, Lorcan. You've done very well. In fact, you'll be receiving a bonus for your trouble. If you step into the hall, there's a guard there who will show you to a guest room we have prepared for you. Please make yourself comfortable. Dinner should be up to your room shortly."

Lorcan stood, obviously relieved to have completed his task. "I thank ye, Laird Scott. I'll ask in the mornin' if ye have further need of me." He took his mangled hat and made haste to exit.

As soon as he was gone. Duncan put his head in his hands. "Maybe *I'm* goin' insane," he whispered. "Jesus and Mary and all the apostles, a *flyin' carpet*?"

No one said anything.

"If this is all true," Toran said cautiously, "what the hell are we supposed to do?" He shook his head. "I...just...*I'm havin' trouble believing this is all true.*"

"I have a feeling," Saorsa said, smoothing her skirts, "that we'll be hearing where Adamina is shortly. She may even turn up here."

Edan stood up. "Oh, Caroline Scott will have soldiers here to check for her and Alex by morning. Of that I have *no doubt*." He paused. "And the man had a *garrison* here. He knows this building back to front. It will be difficult to hide her if she arrives."

"Edan, if she comes here, you need to send her somewhere safe. Could she go to Paris with Gil? Or north, to stay with the Bruces?"

Edan nodded. "Let me think on this." He turned to Duncan. "Where do you think Vika will go next?"

"I told her Morrigan's Cave. She'll go there, looking for me." Duncan stood up. "I can head out before dawn and meet her and the team there. Regroup."

"Vika sent someone west to take your mother to Ireland, Duncan. I think she hoped you'd go too," Saorsa said.

Duncan shook his head. "Not while Alex is missing. I'll stay and help with that." He looked at Saorsa. "I...need some time to think on what's been said here. And ask questions. May I speak with you and Edan after dinner?"

"Of course!" Saorsa was thrilled. Duncan was slowly edging his way toward acceptance, despite the fact that the presentation of Faerie had been badly bungled.

"What about Fia?" Edan growled. "Saorsa, did she really sell Alex out?"

"Yes," Saorsa confirmed. "But before we knew, Alex found out she was pregnant and proposed to her, of course."

"So that she-devil is about to be my sister-in-law?" Edan said angrily. "I've no wish to have her under my roof."

"Please, Edan," Saorsa begged. "You don't have to talk to her, or even *look* at her. Confine her to a separate wing of the house. Mother Agnes and Annag will look after her. We just need the baby safe."

"And what am I supposed to tell Killian and Anne? They're just a few miles away!"

"She's not far along," Saorsa said. "I don't think they need to know yet. Maybe in a few weeks. Maybe Alex will be back by then."

"I can't imagine he'll marry her when he finds out what she's done," Edan said firmly. "But I don't know. If that bairn is his...."

"For right now, you and I can send a letter to Killian and Anne saying Alex had to head south, and that Fia's staying with me here, and that she's well. Don't mention the engagement, or the baby. Honestly, Edan, they didn't know what to do with her at Ramsay House. I don't think they'll have a problem with her staying here as long as they know she's safe. We can worry about the rest later."

"And you?" Toran broke in. "Fia, Annag, and Mother Agnes stay here, Duncan goes to find Vika...what are you going to do?"

Saorsa took a deep breath. "It's time for some different tactics. I have an ace up my sleeve, and I'm going to try and play it. I promise I'll share everything shortly. Just...it's safer for you all if you don't know yet. But I'm going to need an armed escort, some men I can trust, and a piece of land. A very *particular* piece of land." She looked at Edan. "Can you help me out with this?"

Edan looked at her curiously. "What are you up to, Saorsa Stuart?"

"The Violet Woman thinks she's winning," Saorsa smiled. "I'm about to give her a nasty surprise."

....

Mother Agnes was a wealth of magickal knowledge. While she didn't come out and offer to tutor Fia, she was always willing to answer questions and clear up things Fia didn't understand.

So that night, while they prepared for sleep, Fia asked, "Mother Agnes? What is the difference between a magickal and a non-magickal human? Because Lilias said I was non-magickal, but people say I'm good at divination and Saorsa said my spells feel powerful."

Mother Agnes had nodded. "It's a bit of a misnomer. Magickal humans have the blood of other magickal races in them. They both have a greater natural aptitude for magick, *and* they generate magickal energy of their own. A non-magickal human can practice magick, but only *human* magick, and does not generate as much magickal energy, as far as I know. You might be a brilliant human magick-user, but your abilities are very different from, say, a person who has faerie blood in them."

"So, I *could* develop strong magickal abilities as a human?"

Mother Agnes smiled. "Why not? I have." She folded her arms. "There is a tendency among humans who interact with the Fae to adopt the rather popular-in-Faerie viewpoint that the Fae are *more* and humans are *less* when it comes to magick. I believe that our magicks are simply *different*. They have their weaknesses, as do we." She gestured toward Fia. "Just because they seem to do certain things effortlessly does not mean we can't do them. Magick is *alive* in their culture, and nearly dead in much of ours, which slows our progress at times." She raised her eyebrows. "But in all my years of study I have never found an end. Something I couldn't learn or do."

Fia lay in bed that night and looked up at the canopy. *There was nothing Mother Agnes couldn't learn or do. Maybe I could be the same.* She rested a hand on her belly. *This baby...no one is certain what she might be. A leth dhia crossed with a human in a ritual. Her potential is limitless. I want mine to be, too.*

She hadn't tried to practice any magick since Saorsa left. She was fairly certain Mother Agnes would know right away if she did. But Mother Agnes hadn't said she *couldn't*. Maybe...something small. *She doesn't want me reaching outside of Branxholme. But as long as I stay in here....*

She took a deep breath and closed her eyes. She hadn't yet decided whose side she was on. She was furious with the Fae for leaving her behind, but on the other hand Saorsa seemed to have left her behind now too. Yes, Saorsa had her reasons, but knowing that logically did little to counter the horrible loneliness Fia felt. And the Fae had promised her a paradise, and might still come through.

But if she was powerful here...it might not be too late to have a *different* sort of paradise....

She took a slow, deep breath in. *I have power. The Fae still want to deal with me, and Saorsa wants me watched. This child gives me power too.* Fia smiled. *I'm going to be wanted, one way or another.* She let out a slow exhale. *Reach out. I'm going to let my energy reach out and explore this place. Open. Open.*

She imagined her body generating tendrils that unfurled and multiplied, reaching to the far corners of the room, and then out the door and down the hall. *This is an old castle. Adamina lived here. Alex lived here. There are probably ghosts. What magick might be in these halls? What might aid me in this place?*

She pictured the vines multiplying, multiplying. Curling around corners. Reaching down corridors. Hunting under the beds and behind the curtains. *The Magician's Lover spent thirty winters here. There must be something...*

She could sense Mother Agnes' magick whenever she neared an outer wall. A boundary she could not cross. *But I don't want to. I am not concerned with getting out. I want to know...what's already here.*

She sensed spirits and decided to avoid them for now. *But...oh, what is this? Passageways.* This castle had passageways between the walls, just like at Buccleuch. She sensed a movement inside one. Just a few rooms away. And a...*pool* of magick. Waiting. Fia's eyes flew open. Now she was curious. She got out of bed and pulled on her green dressing gown and slippers, and opened the door to the hall, candle in hand. *Not a sound. Not a soul.*

She crept down the hall to her right and slipped inside what looked to be a guest room. She opened her mind to the room. *There.* A set of drapes decorating the wall over the headboard. Made of silk, with embroidered flowers and stars and mythical beasts. Fia put the candle on the side table and climbed onto the bed, crawling toward the headboard.

She could *really* sense it now. She drew the curtains aside. Her eyes widened. Hidden behind the drapery was a large ornate mirror. Except the glass was *black,* and seemed to be moving, and the border around the glass was covered in symbols Fia had never seen before but which certainly looked magickal in nature. A humming energy radiated gently from the mirror's surface.

Fia's eyes flashed in victory, and a smile curled the edges of her mouth. "Hello," she said to the mirror, "what have we here?"

．．．．．．．．．

Mother Agnes sat bolt upright in bed. *Something is here!* She opened Annag's door "Come, Annag! *Quickly!"* The two witches were in the hallway moments later, candles and wands in their hands. Mother Agnes paused for a moment. "It's *inside the house.* Can you feel it?"

"Aye! This way," Annag replied, turning to their right. They turned down the next hall and stopped at Fia's door. Mother Agnes paused. "I don't like this. It's too close to her. Let me just make certain she's well."

Mother Agnes turned and opened Fia's door and was surprised to find Fia sitting on the floor in front of the fireplace, wide awake. "Fia! Why are you awake?" Mother Agnes asked.

"Something woke me," Fia lied. She manufactured a shiver. "Something feels different, Mother Agnes."

Mother Agnes frowned. Apparently Fia was sensitive enough that she'd felt the presence, too. This whole end of the guest wing was awash in a chaotic energy, as though something had *moved.* "Fia, I think it best if you come sleep in with Annag tonight."

Fia nodded, rose, and went to find her slippers. "Are we safe in here, Mother Agnes? They're not coming to...harm my baby, are they?"

Mother Agnes looked hard at Fia. *If the Fae did arrive, I think there's a good chance you might still welcome them with open arms.* "I don't think so, Fia. But it's better to be careful than sorry." She gestured at the young raven-haired woman. "Come along, then."

Fia followed them out of the room. The mirror's surface moved in the darkness as she left, hidden in its temporary home under the four-poster bed.

．．．．．．．．．

For the others, it was an exhausting but productive night at Branxholme. Bonds were forged and re-forged, and plans were made. Edan, Duncan, and Saorsa shared everything they knew and talked about what needed to be done. Free of looking after Fia, Saorsa began the first steps in her plan.

She spent hours talking to Duncan MacLeod. She'd only met him once, but spending time with Vika and Alex, listening to stories of him and seeing their love and respect had created a deep desire to get to know him better. Alex and Vika were family; she felt like Duncan should be, too.

They stayed up late, and when Saorsa finally went to bed she could feel that a friendship had begun. Talking to Duncan about Alex made her feel less lonely for him. And Duncan responded to her stories exactly as she had expected: with the kindness, wisdom, and consideration of an older family member. *I don't know what it's like to have an older brother, or an uncle. But I imagine it's a bit like talking to Duncan.*

Edan spent most of his night assembling a team for Saorsa and pulling together supplies and fretting about Alex and Adamina's whereabouts. He sent a messenger out to ride west to see about the location she had shown him on a map.

"Thank you," Saorsa said to him, and put her arms around him after he dispatched the messenger into the night.

"It's nothing," Edan said to her, patting her arm. "I will always help you if I can, Saorsa Stuart. Always." He sighed. "I need to go talk to Toran again. He thinks all of us have lost our minds, but hopefully he'll come around."

When Saorsa finally went to her bed, she dug Alex's case of essential oils out of her bag first. She put a drop of each of the oils on her pillow and climbed under the covers. It smelled like him in the bed now a bit. Cedar, rosemary, and pine. With her eyes closed, she could almost believe he was near.

But he wasn't. She let herself cry a little. "I'm going to find you and free you, Alexander Scott," she whispered into the dark. "Just hold on for me. I'm on my way." She fell asleep, and dreamed of him.

Unknown Location

"Good morning," said a quiet, cheerful voice next to him. "I hate to wake you, but there's no guard in the room, so it's a good time to talk."

Alex opened his eyes. It took him a moment to realize where he was. Laoise was sitting in a chair next to his bed. He didn't remember being *moved* to the bed. She was sunny and cheerful as always, clothed in a dark blue gown that wrapped around her sylphlike frame.

Laoise laughed. "Full disclosure. You looked *vastly* uncomfortable when four women began to undress you for your bath last night, so remember when I stopped them and gave you some more tea? I slipped a little something in it to knock you out, so that you didn't have to endure the embarrassment of it all." She patted his hand. "We got you cleaned up, moved into bed, and I did a lot of work on that wing. It's going to take a lot more, though."

She laughed again as she saw Alex blush. "It's *fine*. Trust me. Healers see men without their clothes on *all the time*." She looked at him curiously. "They told me you were half Fae, though, and I'm…a little confused. You don't have the ears, or any of the other characteristics of those of us that are halfsies. You *do* have a lot of magickal imprints on you, and you smell like cedar, and of course, it's obvious that you had at least one manifesting wing at some point, but I don't see *anything* else…." She moved a bit closer. "I can't figure out for the life of me what *kind* of Fae you are. It would help me heal you faster if I knew, but they won't tell me." She looked over her shoulder. "The guard by the door went down to get breakfast. Can you talk yet at all? Tell me your name, and…what exactly you are?"

He opened his mouth and tried to speak, only a hoarse whisper came out. Laoise got up from the chair and came back with some of the cold tea. "Try a little of this." Alex could swallow easier now; his mouth seemed to be much more under his control. Laoise was delighted. "Oh! You're coming along. Try again."

He took a deep breath. "I'm…Alex," he managed. His throat hurt like hell. "I'm…part of…," his eyes shifted toward the door as he heard the heavy door creak. "Crows," he gasped. His throat felt like it was full of sand. He was afraid to tell her the next part. What if she wouldn't heal him anymore if she knew? He'd never get out of here without her help.

"You're associated with the Deck of Crows?" Laoise said hurriedly. The guard was busy balancing his meal, his drink, and himself on a bench and wasn't paying attention. "Yes, but what *are* you?"

"Half-god," Alex rasped. "My father…he's a mage. I'm Alex Scott." Laoise looked over her shoulder at the guard again, and Alex was not sure she had understood.

"Good morning," Laoise called to the guard as she stood and smoothed her skirts. "I'm starting up here today; then I'll be needing access to the other patients on the lower two levels."

The guard nodded, and dipped his toast in his coffee, apparently in his own little world. Laoise began speaking to Alex and moved to the foot of his bed. "Now, then. I believe your fever has broken, which is *very* good. That last poison you were given burned your throat, so we're going to get as much cold on it today as we can. I'm going to keep dosing you on the antidote, and I'll be giving you something for the pain of the gunshot wounds and your ankle." Alex saw her eyes shift toward the guard. "Get as much sleep as you can today, because tonight the other healers and I will be doing a ritual to hopefully fix the wing injury, and you *definitely* won't be able to sleep during that. It shouldn't be painful, but you *will* feel it."

Alex frowned. They were going to do a *what?*

The guard spilled his coffee all over the timber floor. "Oh *shite*," he moaned. "Be right back." He lumbered out the door.

Laoise flew to Alex's bedside. "Are you telling me that you are part of the *Royal House of Crows?* But that would make you…you can't be…the *leth dhia?*" she hissed. She moved rapidly backwards and away from him, as if afraid he might hurt her. "Oh, my Goddess…!"

The guard wandered back in, a bucket and rags in his hand, and began mopping up the coffee.

Laoise immediately became casual again. "As I was saying, the swelling in your ankle is starting to go back down. I don't think it's broken, but badly sprained." She looked at Alex. "Do you think you might be able to eat something this morning?" She nodded her head subtly and widened her eyes as if to say, *don't talk, just nod.*

Alex nodded his head. "Wonderful!" Laoise beamed. "I'll send down for something cold, something that won't hurt your throat. Some cooled broth, maybe. Chilled milk, perhaps." Alex noticed a tremor in her voice.

The guard trundled out the door again with his bucket and empty coffee mug, and Laoise stood where she was, staring.

"You're *THE Alexander Scott*?" she said, "Knight of the Deck of Crows?"

"Aye," Alex rasped "But...I'm *human*. I *swear* I'm no an evil person! I think there's another part of me in Faerie. Those that keep me here...are they Fae? What will they do to me?"

"I don't know," Laoise said. "But do *you* know that your Faerie aspect just escaped his prison? They're hunting for him all through the worlds!"

"*Prison?*" Alex coughed, staring at her. "I dinnae ken...*anything* about Faerie...." He could taste blood in his throat now.

The guard re-entered with a full mug and sat down on the bench. "I'll go and ask them to send up something for you to drink that'll give you more strength than tea," Laoise told Alex, adopting her usual happy tone. "I'll be back in a bit." She patted him on the leg and left the room.

Alex lay in bed, stunned. *Prison? My other self was in a prison in Faerie? And now...a fugitive?* He sighed. *Out of prison in Faerie, into a prison here. Christ.*

He didn't remember the ritual at the cave. He didn't know where that cursed knife was, but he guessed it had been returned because his *leth dhia* traits were gone. Where was Saorsa? Here in Scotland, or in Faerie? And for that matter...was *he* even in Scotland?

He could see much better today. The room was square, with leaded windows that opened from the side on two adjacent walls, their panes detailed with the shape of diamonds. A long, low fireplace dominated one wall. The walls were white plaster over stone, and from what Alex could tell, looked as though they were ancient construction that had been repainted and replastered many times.

The floorboards were well maintained and highly polished. There was a rug on the floor, and an expensive one from the looks of it. His bed was beautiful, with a red square silk canopy and carved details on the posts and footboard. It looked to be made of cherry, as did the dresser, table, and chairs that stood elsewhere in the room.

A castle, Alex thought. *I think I'm in a castle.* He could see the color of the winter sky through the windows, and it was all one hue. *Up in the air, on a higher floor. Nothing but sky.*

There was an insistent tapping noise on the window next to Alex's bed suddenly, and Alex saw a darkness through the distortion of the elaborate glasswork. "Aw, shite, not again," grumbled the guard, and he stood, crossed the room, and swung the pane open on its hinges. "G'wan, *git!*" he shouted, and Alex heard the indignant croaking of a raven before the bird disappeared. "Bloody vermin," muttered the guard, closing the window as Alex breathed in the burst of fresh air. "They roost right near here, an' they fuckin' *tap tap tap* all the bloody time." He turned and made his way back to the bench.

Alex tested moving his legs a little. He was still in pain, but not nearly as bad as yesterday, and not being feverish went a long way toward feeling like himself. He was beside himself with curiosity. *I need to see what's outside that window.* He thought at first he was in Carlisle, but didn't remember seeing this room there – and he'd been all through the place. And while Laoise was half-Fae, this guard looked human, which made him doubt he was in Faerie. *Where the hell am I? Fort William, perhaps?* He'd been at Fort George and Fort Augustus; he'd never been inside Fort William, so it was a possibility. *But those windows are very fancy for a fort.*

Blackness Castle. That would make sense. Up on the Firth of Forth, it was a garrison for the Crown. He'd seen it, but never been inside. It had been a prison for ages. Often called "the ship that never sailed" due to its shape and position on the water, it had three famous towers. If he remembered correctly, they were called "Stem," "Stern," and "Main Mast." He could be in one of those.

A spark of hope ignited inside him. *Blackness.* If he could heal and get out, there'd be the water as an escape route and boats to hide in along the shore. Hell, he could probably swipe a rowboat and, as long as he didn't go far enough out to sea to knock himself out and end up on the shore again, he might make it a good distance from here. *Wait, there is a safe house at Midhope!* He could head east to it, and then continue east toward his mother's island once he was supplied, or head south again. *Of course. I lose my wings right when I need to escape from a tower. But this is doable.* If he remembered correctly, the garrison at Blackness wasn't terribly large. *Blackness is out of the way, and very secure. Not in the Borders, but not too far from them either, and securely in Crown hands. I bet this is Blackness Castle.*

He wanted to get up. He wanted to see if he could stand on his own and ascertain how weak he was. And he wanted to have a look out that window so he could start planning. *I need to orient myself. I need to have a look.*

As if on cue, the door to the room opened. "Smith!" a gruff voice said outside it, "Out here! I need to talk wit' ye!"

The guard on the bench gestured at Alex. "S'posed to keep an eye on him."

"We'll be right here! He's no goin' anywhere. Ye think he can fly? He cannae even walk!"

Smith grumbled and got to his feet, and stepped out the door onto the landing, letting the door shut behind him. Alex looked at the distance to the window. *Just a few steps.*
Getting up was *much* harder than he had anticipated. His whole body ached. But he made it to a sitting position on the side of the bed, his head pounding, his body shaking.

He realized Laoise and her assistants had put him in a nightshirt. *Sweet Mary, I must have been out like a light for them to get this on over my head and not wake me up.* Alex touched his feet to the floor. One good effort and he could hold onto the deep windowsill for support. He could hear the men arguing on the landing; they'd be occupied for some time.

He ran his hand over his head and steeled himself. His ankle was going to hurt, but it would be worth it. He put his left hand on the footboard for support and pushed himself up. *Shite. That ankle*...he stumbled forward, trying not to cry out in pain, and his hands found the windowsill. He was trembling all over as he threw the window open; he just needed a look at the Firth of Forth to begin his plan. He leaned heavily on his arms on the windowsill and took a deep breath as the cold air rushed in, trying to fight down the pain in his leg and shoulder.

But the Firth of Forth wasn't there. His eyes widened in horror. He could see the tower he was in was on the western corner of an enormous white building. He felt disoriented for a moment as memories of illustrations he'd seen fell into place, forming a complete picture. An understanding. As if he were now somehow outside the building, up in the air, looking in.

This building...he recognized it from countless books he'd read on the subject.

The White Tower.
The Execution Ground.
The Bloody Tower.
The Royal Armory.

He gasped and tried to keep from fainting.

The Moat.
Traitor's Gate.
The River Thames.

He should have known. He should have known from the raven. He wasn't in Blackness Castle. He wasn't even in Scotland. He looked at the masses of redcoat soldiers parading on the grounds below, and forgot to breathe.

He was in his worst nightmare. He was truly, truly unreachable now, beyond the grasp of everyone he loved.

The Tower. He was in the White Tower.

The Tower of London.

It was the last thought Alexander Scott had before he collapsed to the floor, unconscious.

The Bishop House, Northern England

Adamina couldn't remember the last time she'd been this relaxed. She was sitting in the warm bath, reclining against Thomas' bare chest, head tipped back on his shoulder, eyes closed. *This. This is heaven.* Thomas was holding her left hand in his under the surface of the water, and every now and then he'd raise his right hand to slide the cover on the opening to the hot water pipe back and let just enough hot water in to make the bath warm again.

She could feel him breathing behind her, and his deep voice was right by her ear when he spoke. When he wasn't letting more water in, he'd stroke the curve of her belly or her thigh with his thumb; and she loved feeling his legs outside of hers in the water.

"Are ye happy, my love?" he asked her.

"Yes," she said without opening her eyes. "I'm...in a state of bliss." She heard him laugh quietly.

"Mina," he said, after a moment, "how old do ye think I am?"

She smiled, eyes closed. "How old do you *look,* or how long ago were you born?"

He shifted slightly. "Both." He opened the cover, and more hot water flowed in. Adamina sighed and opened her eyes.

"Well," she said, "you looked to be in your thirties when we met. And because you're Fae, you age differently than I do. But every time you visit you've been making slight adjustments to your appearance so that you always look just a bit older than me. For example, there's more silver in your beard and hair tonight than I've seen before. I do notice, and I do appreciate it. If I looked decades older than you, I might feel...a bit self-conscious."

He closed the cover on the pipe. "You're always beautiful to me, *mo fhlùr,*" he said in her ear, and she could hear him smiling as he said it.

"Michael Scot was born in 1175. Five hundred and seventy-one years ago. And I'm guessing you existed in Faerie before that. So...why don't I say you're a nice round one thousand."

He laughed. "A good guess. Michael Scot wasnae my first visit here. Were you to look elsewhere on the globe, you'd find traces of me there, as well."

"Oh, I *have* looked. I have a few ideas. The language barriers make it a bit difficult, but that's never stopped me before. And I have one from right here in England that I'm nearly *certain* was you."

He was laughing now. "Please, do tell. I can't wait to hear your hypothesis." He tucked a damp curl of her hair behind her ear.

"You'll tell me if I'm right? Honestly?"

"Would I dare lie to my wife? Or...soon-to-be wife?"

Adamina sat up and turned around so she could look at him. His eyes were alight with merriment. "God, you're beautiful," he grinned, and she splashed some water in his direction.

"Alright," Adamina said, eager for answers, "my first guess is Appolonius of Tyana. Greek philosopher and miracle worker. Lived 15-100 A.D. Adored Pythagorus and the Occult, traveled the East. His influence is still evident today. In fact, there's been a resurgence of interest in him lately." Adamina raised an eyebrow. "You?"

He stared at her a moment, his face blank. Then he said, "They always get it wrong. It was 10 A.D., not 15. And I died in 97 A.D."

Adamina nearly burst out of the bath in excitement. "I got it right? *I got it RIGHT?*"

Thomas threw back his head and laughed. "YES, you got it right! What tipped you off?"

Adamina was so excited she was shaking her hands in the air. "I just had a *feeling*! I read everything I could on him and he just...sounded like you! The tone of his writings!" She let loose a squeal of delight. "Ha!"

Thomas grinned. "Who else? Give me your next guess."

"All right," Adamina said slowly. "Now, I'm not as certain on this one. I had to have everything on him translated, and you know things can be lost that way. So save me some trouble, and tell me if you were in China between 181 A.D. and 234 A.D.?"

Thomas started to laugh. "No, dear one, I was not Zhuge Liang." He wiggled his eyebrows at her. "But I did meet him. He was a mentor of mine."

Adamina's mouth fell open. "Are you serious?"

"I wasn't him, but I *was* there. So we'll give you partial credit on that one." He looked at her closely. "This is most impressive, I must say. Do you have any more?"

"Just one. Well, two that I can't decide between." She frowned. "They were alive at the same time, so you can't be both."

"Why not?"

Adamina looked at him. "I just...wait, do you *do* that? Live two lives here at once?"

He gave her a half-smile. "Sometimes. There have been a few times when I've been able to...wander more freely than I do now. I'll tell you a secret: I was someone else in Ireland while I was Michael Scot here. No the *entire* time. But they did overlap."

Adamina couldn't contain herself. *"Who?"*

"Ever heard of Ímar Ua Donnubáin?"

"Ivor O'Donovan? Of Loch Cluhir? YES!" Adamina started to giggle. "He had an enchanted ship! And there are the stories about the wolfhounds and the one about the snake! He was a famous navigator and magician!"

"An' he was *me,* my love!" Thomas boomed, making a grandiose gesture. "So, as ye can see, being two people at once is *not always* out of the question."

Adamina composed herself. "So, I'm just going to ask. Were you both Robert Fludd, Occult Philosopher, Astronomer, and Mathematician, 1574-1667, and also...," she looked at him and gave him a sheepish grin, "Sir Edward Kelley, born 1555, who claimed he could talk to angels?"

Thomas fixed her with a disbelieving stare. "Ye think I was Edward Kelley? Whom many people think was a *charlatan*? Please, Adamina, dinnae insult me!"

She looked at him carefully for a moment and came to a decision. "I call bullshite," she declared flatly. "You're having me on. You *were* Edward Kelley, weren't you?"

He held out for a full five seconds before an embarrassed smile crossed his face. "Yes, I was Edward Kelley."

"I *knew it!*" Adamina shrieked. "I saw a painting of him, and...well, I could just *feel* you in it! What were you *doing?*"

He grinned. "Havin' a bit of a laugh, most of the time. But I wasnae lying *all* the time; I *do* speak with angelic beings on a regular basis."

"And Robert Fludd? I'm right, aren't I?" He gave her a smile and nodded slowly. "YES!"

"Don't get *too* proud of yourself! There's a lot of time between 100 A.D. and 1175 that you havnae guessed yet, and it took you thirty years to get these!"

"Oh, I *am* proud of myself," laughed Adamina. "I got you, Thomas Scott! Got you, got you, GOT YOU!"

He held out his arms to her, and she moved in close. "An' I'm verra happy to be caught by you, Mina. Truly." He gave her a kiss on the nose. "Ready to get out and have some dinner?"

They toweled off and Adamina put on a lovely new shift and the gray silk dressing gown. Thomas made himself comfortable in a pair of black loose trousers and a dark pull-over linen shirt.

"Can I get married in my dressing gown?" Adamina teased. "It's so lovely!"

Thomas grinned and shrugged. "Why not?" He caught her around the waist and pulled her close. "Just wear *somethin'*. Otherwise I'll be so distracted I willnae be able to say my vows."

Adamina put her arms around his neck and gave Thomas a gentle, loving kiss. "Why did you ask me about how old you were?"

He pressed his cheek against hers and closed his eyes, and she smiled as she took in the feeling of his beard on her cheekbone. "Ah, because I was leadin' up to somethin' I have to tell ye, so."

She moved her head back and looked up at him. "Thomas?"

He looked into her eyes. "You're human, Adamina, which means ye age much faster than I do. An' humans die much, much sooner. I dinnae want us to be apart, Mina. So...after we're wed tonight, there's a...a ritual I have. One that will allow you to age like the Fae. If you wish it, we'll do it. But if ye want to live a human life, and age like those ye love here, well...that will be your choice." He hugged her. "I will have ye with me for any time I can, an' be grateful for it."

She looked at him sharply. "So, this ritual...what does it do?"

"It will return ye to the age ye were when we first met, Adamina. An' preserve ye there, until you come to Faerie. Once you're in Faerie, ye will stay the same, an' the effects of the ritual will wear off. Once it does, though, anytime ye come to earth you'll begin to age again if ye stay more than a short while."

Adamina frowned. "And...do I have to decide *tonight?*"

He looked at her, concerned. "Well...the ingredients I use, there are a few that must be fresh. I have them with me. An'...they were verra hard to get, Mina." He sighed. "As in, next to impossible."

"Why are they so hard to get?"

Thomas ran a hand through his hair. "They're outlawed in Faerie, Adamina. The whole *ritual* is outlawed. The Fae dinnae want me doin' what I'm about to do with you." He touched her cheek. "High Fae an' human, especially magickal humans, we're not supposed to mix like you an' I do."

"Or you get *leth dhia.*"

He nodded sadly. "Yes. Among other things." He paused. "An' the ritual is also outlawed among the Fae because...it's blood magick, Adamina."

Her eyes widened. "*What?*"

"Just a wee bit, now." Thomas put his hands on her arms.

"A *wee bit of* blood magick? What does *that* mean? You're going to...make me a *vampire?*"

He waved his hands. "No, no, no. It's no what you think, Adamina. Those are just *stories.*" He shook his head. "No one is gettin' their neck bit."

"Thomas, you said you commanded the Army of the Dead. How about the *undead?* Do vampires exist?"

His eyes shifted to the side, and back again. "Yes and no."

She pushed him away from her and put her hands on her hips. "What kind of an answer is that?"

He held out his arms to her, wanting to be close again. "Ye can animate a dead thing, or possess it. But it isnae *undead*. It doesnae walk around on its own an' make choices. Dead is dead, Mina. Well, unless ye stuff a soul back in, but I am one of the *verra* few who can do *that*. But there *is* such a thing as blood frenzy, an' beings can experience it for numerous reasons, which is the closest to what you're thinkin' of."

He ran his hand over his hair again. "This will involve some fresh blood. The blood of the living. I'm living, Adamina. You'll drink some of my blood in a potion, and take on Fae characteristics, for a time. The Fae dinnae like that; they like Fae an' human to be *separate*." He shook his head. "No monsters. Just chalices mostly, sweetheart, an' just *once*. I swear."

Adamina wrapped her arms around herself. "It's been...quite a day, Thomas. I was nearly hanged, then you rescued me on a flying carpet, then you proposed, and now you want me to do a blood magick ritual? All in *one day?*"

He gave her a crooked smile. "An' I want to consummate the marriage too, please dinnae forget *that*."

Adamina frowned at him. "Don't try to be charming, Thomas Michael Andrew Scott. It won't make me forget the words *blood* and *magick* and *outlawed*."

There was a knock on the door, and Thomas moved to answer it. "Ah! Dinner's here," he said, opening the door. Several members of the house's staff entered and began setting covered dishes on the sideboard near the dining table. Thomas took Adamina's hand and led her out of the way.

"You can say no," he said to her quietly, his hands on her shoulders. "But will ye think on it? Over dinner? For me?"

She looked up into his gray eyes. "I'll think on it." *My goodness, can you imagine? How would I explain this to people? Alex and Edan would come to visit and we'd look the same age!*

She wasn't sure she could do it. She liked who she was, and how she looked. *What would it be like to look nearly thirty years younger than I am? Suddenly? Who would take me seriously? I'd...it would be freakish.*

But Thomas. *Thomas.* He wanted them to be together. For centuries. Did she want the aches and pains, the failing eyesight, the dodgy memory, the creaky joints of being older when her husband was an eternal and robust thirty-three?

And...he'd know that he'd have to watch her fade and die. If she chose her human timeline, he'd know that they wouldn't have their golden years together. Because the Fae didn't *have* golden years.

She wasn't prepared to live for centuries. Her entire life had been on this mortal human timeline. Did she want to outlive Edan and Gil? Outlive their children, and their children's children? Live among the Fae, who didn't understand what it was to be human at all?

And what about Alex? Would his human half die before she did? She had no idea. She had accepted Thomas' proposal without thinking about these things.

"Adamina?" His low, rich voice brought her back to the present. He was looking at her, concerned. "I...maybe I shouldnae have said anything."

She looked at his face. There was a need there. An aching desire for her, for her affection, for her acceptance. He was worried that he'd asked too much, and ruined things. She put her arms around him, and he immediately pulled her close. "I just need to think about it," she told him. "But no matter what, thank you for giving me this option, Thomas."

She felt him breathe a sigh of relief. "I will always love you, Mina. Whichever way this goes."

She gave him a kiss and held him tight. "And I will always love you, Thomas."

………

After dinner, they curled up on the bed together, wanting to be close again.

"Och, *God,* that was good," Thomas groaned, putting his hands behind his head. "The bishop has someone in that kitchen who knows what they're doin'."

Adamina put her cheek on Thomas' chest, and absentmindedly ran her hand slowly back and forth over his muscular stomach. "Can you see the clock behind me?" she asked.

"Aye."

"How long until we get married?"

She loved how she could hear the echo of his voice in his chest. "Around two hours, so."

Adamina moved her hand down to stroke his thigh and snuggled closer.

"Ah, Mina," Thomas sighed, "I cannae tell ye how many nights we've been apart that I have dreamed of lyin' just like this with ye." He moved his right arm to put it around her and kissed the top of her head.

"Two hours is a good length of time," Adamina murmured, and let her hand wander to the center of his waistband, and then down over the front of his trousers. She felt his body respond immediately to her touch, and smiled.

"Oh *God,*" she heard him breathe. "Touch me like that again, Mina." She felt his arm tighten around her. "I've missed ye so."

Adamina felt a strong spike of arousal shoot up her spine, so strong that it caused her to move her hips toward his body. *Eighteen months. It's been eighteen months since we've made love.* She stroked him again, applying a bit more pressure and intensity to her touch. *I know just what you like, Thomas. I may not know everything about you, but I know this. A few more touches, and you'll be happily lost in me.*

She was rewarded with a soft moan and saw him shift his pelvis slightly forward, and felt an electricity appear in her blood. *I want to hear him like this. I want more of him. I love that he doesn't hold back with me. He may have gone by many names, but he's always his authentic self when we're alone.*

She was surprised when she felt his large, strong hand circle her wrist, and relocate her hand away from where she'd been touching him to his chest. He placed his hand over hers, firmly but gently, to keep it in place.

"Thomas?" she said, concerned. "Did I do something wrong?"

"No, *mo ghràidh,*" he said to her quietly. "Just...we shouldnae do that yet."

She propped herself up on her elbow and looked at his face. "Why not?"

He reached up his hand to stroke her cheek with the backs of his fingers. "I want ye too, sweetheart. *So much.* But we must save that energy in case you tell me *yes* about the ritual."

She looked at him, confused. "Thomas...let's pretend that I don't do blood magick regularly. Could you...*explain* a bit?"

He sighed and smiled at her, running his fingers lazily through her long dark hair. "If you decide ye want the ritual, *leannan,* it is a...more difficult sort of magick. It will require a lot of power, a lot of energy. Mostly from me, because as a human, you cannae generate but so much. I have a greater capacity for it, as Fae, as a mage, and as a god." He took her hand and raised it to his lips and kissed the back of it. "If this wasnae illegal, and a rather intimate sort of ceremony, I'd normally bring in another energy source. Another magickal being to help. But there's only you an' me here, an' I'm not even supposed to be in this realm, so that's out of the question."

She looked at him intently as she caught on. "You...plan on powering the spell with our lovemaking." She paused. "So this...would be a blood magick *sex* ritual."

He nodded as though she hadn't just said something that sounded positively horrific. "Aye. We havenae been together for a year and a half, an' we'll have just gotten married, Mina. That should drive me quite high. An'...I have two other ways of raising the power higher. Between those four accelerants, I *should* raise enough energy for the spell to work. You will have to do parts of the ritual, though. But just a few simple things, an' I'll show ye how." He looked away for a moment, and then back. Mina was momentarily lost in the gray sparks in his eyes. "I tried to alter anything I could that ye wouldnae approve of in the ritual, Mina. So ye dinnae feel that you're doin' somethin'...immoral. So that when it happens, it happens as naturally as possible." He patted her hand. "But I cannae use my energy with ye now until I have your answer."

It's so strange how he speaks of our passion for each other as if it's a resource, or a sort of fuel. He's so matter of fact about it. And yet, in the throes of it, he isn't at all. He's a bigger romantic than I am. Thomas never failed to amaze her in his capacity to be swept away by emotion while simultaneously observing himself doing that from a distance and making scientific notes. His desire to harness power tonight was nearly as strong as his desire for her.

She nodded. "Thomas...I've read enough to guess that mages don't perform magick as part of a practice of faith, like a hedge witch might. And as far as I know, most witches have rules about harming others. But...with magicians, it doesn't seem linked to faith, but is more about exerting *will*. Am I correct? And...are there any rules for you? Things you won't do?"

He shifted in the bed and took her in his arms. "The magick I practice is more like...*science,* Adamina. My faith is something separate. Scientists must decide for themselves what to bring into being, and what *no* to bring into being. A scientist might create a weapon that has the power to both protect and destroy, and it is up to them to decide if they are going against what is right and good in that creation. You are right in that I dinnae do my work with a god or goddess. I *am* a god, myself. I use the tools of the ritual to exert my will, but I would like to think I dinnae do so from a place of evil. I dinnae pray to someone when I do magick, Mina. I am my own." He touched her cheek. "I wish...I wish you could know how much your love has changed me, Mina. *You* are the goddess in my life, in my morality. Your love rules the halls where my faith rests. Before you, it wasnae so. Now I think, 'how would Mina feel about this?' and it alters my will. I willnae go so far as before, perhaps."

"But what we might do tonight...would it...I mean, if the bishop knew, would he think it might...damn someone?"

Thomas laughed. "Mina, my sweet, I'm afraid it's a wee bit late for that. If the Church is deciding, you were damned at that Beltane celebration with me thirty years ago." He grinned. "And most likely before that, in truth." He gathered her closer in his arms. "Mina, I've *been* to the sort of hell you speak of. It's not a fixed location; it's in many places, and many realms. It's in people's *minds,* at times. You're no goin' into it for this I dinnae think, sweetest one." His face grew serious. "You are no marryin' an evil man tonight, Mina. At least, I dinnae think so. An' if I *am* evil in some eyes, I've been made a lot less so by your love."

She couldn't help but kiss him. She felt his hands on her backside as her tongue touched his, and then he was pulling her roughly against his body. Her entire core flamed into anticipation as she recognized the familiar topography of him, and they began moving against each other, their kisses slow and deep and full of the promises of things to come.

Thomas suddenly shifted himself on the bed, and she found herself underneath him and felt his mouth on her neck. She shivered violently with want, and then his hands were on her hips, his fingers searching out her bones, caressing her in the same way she'd remembered every night since he'd been gone.

I want him. She loved the way he was moving against her, the way he touched her, and the feeling of his weight on top of her body. *I have so little time with him. I want him, and I want him now. He's the most beautiful being in all the worlds, and he's mine.*

She felt her mind and body suddenly merge into a deep flowing river of desire for him. She couldn't think straight and didn't want to; she felt him pulling her shift up with his hand as he kissed her, and a space opened inside her body to receive him. She was turning to liquid longing; she was compelled to merge with him.

"Thomas," she whispered to him. "I want you to take me. Make love to me, Thomas, *please*. I love you. I want you. I need the sight and sound of you in my bed. I need the feeling of you storming my body. It's been far too long."

Suddenly he was moving away and gone, on his feet next to the bed, running his hand through his hair, a look akin to profound pain on his features. "Macha's Red Wolves, I cannae keep myself from you! That bishop needs to finish his damn dinner an' marry us!" Thomas began pacing near the bed and wouldn't look at Adamina.

"I'm sorry!" Adamina cried, sitting up on the bed. "I shouldn't have encouraged you!"

He stood a short distance away, his back to her, and she watched as he clenched and unclenched both hands several times. *He's trying to control himself. He wants to touch me.* She tried to get her own breathing under control.

"I need...," he said to her, his voice strained, "a moment or so, please, *leannan*." He laughed. "You're a hard woman to resist, Adamina."

Adamina looked at the clock. "Not long now. Maybe the bishop and his guests will skip dessert." She swung her feet over the side of the bed. *There are so many questions he's never answered, so many things he's avoided telling me. But he seems willing to talk tonight, so I'm going to make the most of it.* "Thomas, can you explain to me...how does one become a god?" Her question to him had two purposes: one, she honestly didn't know; and two, she knew that explaining things to her would make the time go faster and be a welcome distraction for both of them. "Not all Fae are gods, so why are *you?*"

He laughed and turned back to her. "That's easy. You're a god when they start to worship ye as such."

"So...someone worshiped you once? Here? On earth?"

He smiled. "It doesnae have to be on earth, Mina. Just somewhere. An' it has to be a collective of beings. No just one."

"So, when people, or beings, started worshiping you, you became a god?"

He nodded. "It's a bit more than that. You must have a much higher capacity for magick to be a god or goddess. Otherwise, no one knows you exist in order *to* worship ye. They must be able to *feel* you. When followers can connect with you from far away, then they can start to follow you, my love. An' of course, ye must make yourself known to them from time to time, even across realms."

"So you were a Fae born with a gift for magick, and then you were worshiped. And then...you studied to become a magician?"

He nodded enthusiastically. "Aye, *mo nighean tuigseach,* now ye understand."

"If they stop worshiping you, are you still a god?"

He nodded. "Aye. Once a god, always a god." He gestured to his side. "When ye are born Fae, they teach ye to use your Fae gifts. Once they see your magickal abilities, there are those who can train ye higher. Then, if you are worshiped, the devotion of your followers builds in still more magick. An' once I had that, then I went out to learn the magick of other worlds, to grow my capacity further an' become an archmage." He sat down next to her on the bed. "That's how it is among the Fae. Other races an' worlds, it could be a different path."

"So...Thomas, what do the Fae call you?"

"*An Draíochta* is what they call me. *An Draoidh* in Scots. The Magician."

"But that's not your *name*."

He laughed. "It is to them, now." He touched her cheek gently. "The only name I care for anymore, Mina, is what *you* call me."

She touched the rough texture of his cheek, and saw love reflected back to her through his eyes. "So...does that mean there was once a Temple of Thomas out there, somewhere?"

He laughed. "Not *was, òran mo chridhe. Is.*"

Her eyes widened. "*Now?* You have worshippers, *right now?*"

He gave her a wry smile. "I do." He grinned. "Is no called the 'Temple of Thomas' obviously, though."

She felt him shifting away from the topic. "You're done talking about this now, aren't you?"

He laughed again. "Ye ken me verra well."

She smiled at him and playfully ruffled his hair. "You know, I worship you too, Thomas."

He pretended to be cross with her. "No more flirtin' Mina! I told ye, I *cannae take it.*"

There was a knock on the door. "Thank *God,*" he exclaimed, heading across the room.

Adamina pulled on her dressing gown over her shift. "I think it's adorable that you curse like a human does."

He shot her a look. "Ye pick up a lot of things when ye spend time here on earth that they dinnae have in Faerie. Casual cursin' is one of the best of the lot." As if to illustrate, he let loose a stream of happy, loud obscenities. "*Hell! Fuck! Arsehole! Goddamn!*" He opened the door to reveal the bishop's steward.

The man gave Thomas a little bow. "The bishop invites you to join him in the chapel in fifteen minutes," he told Thomas. Adamina brushed her hair and put it back in a loose braid, and then put on a pair of velvet slippers that had been delivered with the dressing gown. *I'm going to get married in my nightclothes!* She let out a laugh. In thirty years, she and Thomas had never done things the way they were supposed to be done, and she thoroughly enjoyed it.

Thomas had returned to stand behind her now, and circled her waist with his arms, suddenly sentimental and serious. "I am glad we are finally doin' this tonight, even if it is no verra traditional," he whispered to her. "Because, *mo bhean-bainnse gu bhi*, my heart has been yours since the Tower of Stars."

My bride to be. He had called her *my bride to be.* She couldn't get over it. She turned and looked up into his eyes. "And I have been yours, Thomas Scott," she said, "since the first moment you stepped through my door."

·········

As they left the room, Adamina stopped at the threshold for a moment. "Hold on a moment." Adamina smiled, making a show of stepping out the door with her right foot first. Thomas tipped his head and looked at her, questioning.

"It's an old Scottish tradition," Adamina explained. "When a woman leaves her home and goes off to be wed, she's supposed to step out of her old house right foot first. For luck." She looked at where he stood a pace or two ahead. "You've probably done tons of wedding traditions from all over the world in the past thousand or so years, yes? Carrying brides over the threshold? Burying your sword in front of a door?"

He just looked at her, his eyes soft. "I've no been married before, Mina."

She looked at him closely. "But...you told me you have children. Other than Alex, I mean. In Faerie. I just assumed...."

He shook his head. "I've children in Faerie, yes, but I didnae wed their mothers. Or even love them. It's different among the High Fae, dearest. An' on earth, Alexander is the only child I've had."

"But..." Adamina protested, "some of the people you were...in other times, here...they had wives and children, didn't they?" Her eyes widened. "Or, when people asked, you *told* them you did."

He smiled and nodded. "Easier to fit in, at times."

She thought of her other two marriages. The first to Phineas, the second to Conall. Both had been lavish, public affairs, more for the clans and community than for her personally. She'd never looked forward to a wedding night before. She'd never said *I do* with a heart already full of love.

Thomas looked at the floor for a moment. "You've done this before," he said quietly. "Would you show me how, my love?"

She was overcome with feelings of tenderness for him. Thomas, who always seemed to know *everything,* who was a king of the Fae, a god, a general, and a magick practitioner so powerful that his own people simply referred to him as *The Magician*, had the wedding jitters.

She moved to him and took his hands in hers. "It's my first time, too," she said to him. "I mean, I was married before. But I never went to the altar holding the hand of someone I love." She raised his hand to her mouth and pressed her lips to the back of it. "We'll discover this together." He smiled at her, and it was everything she could do not to drag him back to their room and cover him with kisses.

He led her across the dimly lit front hall and down a smaller hallway of polished marble. The bishop clearly spared no expense when it came to his house. Thomas pushed open a beautiful relief-carved door and the chapel was revealed before them, illuminated by candles.

Flowers. There were flowers *everywhere.* And it was the end of November. Adamina hadn't seen blooms like these since last summer at Buccleuch. She stopped and stared, and then realized they *were* the same types of flowers she grew at Buccleuch. But these were twice as big, and the colors were so vibrant they seemed almost unreal. She looked up at Thomas. "Where...it's almost Christmas time, Thomas. Where did these come from?"

He was obviously quite pleased with his surprise and her wonder and astonishment. "Well, I ken very well what your favorites are. So, every time ye planted something at Buccleuch, I had the same planted at the Castle of Crows. So when I couldnae be with ye, I could...wander among them, and think of you, Adamina." He smiled and gestured at a vase of roses with blooms bigger than Adamina's head. "But the soil and air and suns are different in Faerie, so I couldnae make them exactly."

Adamina reached out to touch an enormous eight-petaled mountain aven. "These were grown in Faerie? At your home?"

He nodded. "Aye, *màthair mo leinibh.* There wasnae time to find ye a dress ye liked, nor bring your children here to honor ye at a feast on your wedding day. So I thought, at the very least, I could bring ye these."

She threw her arms around him, and realized she was on the verge of tears. *I don't usually cry. But...oh, the day I've had. And he makes me so happy.* "They're beautiful, Thomas," she said, wiping a tear with the back of her hand. "I shall never ever forget them."

He put his arms around her and held her tight. "When I can bring ye home with me," he said quietly, "your garden will be waiting for ye there, so. Maybe...maybe it will make it so ye won't miss Buccleuch as much." He kissed the top of her head.

They heard the bishop enter through a door at the other end. The chapel was easily the size of a small church, and Adamina counted at least ten complete rows of pews on either side as Thomas walked her up the aisle. She couldn't help but compare this trip down the aisle to the others she'd made. *I'm not on the arm of someone giving me away, nor walking on my own, surrounded by pomp and ceremony. I'm just walking hand in hand with someone I love, going toward the same future, as we will walk together from now on.*

Adamina noticed that as they walked, it was becoming significantly brighter. The candles here had mirrors behind them, reflecting the light. Floating in the air above the altar and on both sides of the space in front of it were hundreds of tiny, faceted glass globes, reflecting the light from the candles hundreds of thousands of times and splitting it into millions of tiny rainbows. She had no idea how they were suspended there, and then realized they *weren't;* they bobbed slowly in place, each one independent of the others.

Magick. I'm seeing magick. She looked up higher at the steep incline of the chapel's roof, but instead of ending in shadows there was something else there. *The sky.* Adamina blinked. *The dark blue velvet of the night sky. And stars.* She looked at Thomas, uncomprehending.

"I may have saved a wee bit of magick for this," he said, taking both of her hands in his. "It's a sky you've seen before, my dearest one. This is what the sky looked like the night ye first took me to your bed, an' felt the Goddess rise in ye at Beltane. The night we conceived our son."

Adamina's eyes widened and she looked up again. She knew her constellations, and saw a spring sky over Scotland, not one about to plunge into the depths of winter. She *did* cry now. She was overcome with adoration and love for this man. He held every moment that they had been together close to his heart and guarded it carefully. She looked up at the sparkling ornaments catching the light all around them, and felt like she was back in her library, where they'd first fallen in love.

"My tower," she said quietly, weeping. "It...looks like my tower."

He nodded and pulled her close. "Thank you for saying yes when I asked ye to marry me, Adamina," he smiled. "I dinnae have the words for the feelings in my heart."

Adamina suddenly realized the bishop was standing there. She let out an embarrassed laugh, wondering how long he'd been standing there watching her cry. Thomas produced a handkerchief from his pocket and handed it to her, and she took it gratefully. "Adamina, this is Bishop Jamieson," he said, gesturing to the man. "An old friend, and luckily a man who doesnae mind performing a rather unusual wedding ceremony."

Adamina almost never saw Thomas standing next to people, and was struck once again at how he towered over the man next to him. He seemed to take up more energy, more attention, more space than a normal man without trying to; and standing next to a man like Bishop Jamieson, a well-respected person of stature in his own domain, it was glaringly evident that Thomas was something more than human.

The elderly bishop put out his hand and grasped Adamina's in his own. "Welcome, Adamina. You shall want for nothing while you are under my roof." He let her hand go and turned to Thomas. "I...ahm...took the words you gave me and put them together with the traditional words from the Common Book of Prayer." He raised his eyebrows. "I shall do my best, Thomas, with the...ah, rather *pagan* pieces."

Thomas nodded. Adamina looked up at the stars overhead, the candles, the reflecting light, and the flowers all around. It was the most beautiful wedding she'd ever had, and she was getting married in her shift and robe.

The bishop cleared his throat, and the silence that followed blanketed the three of them, pulling them into a place that seemed to belong to another realm.

"Let us begin," Bishop Jamieson said quietly. "We are here tonight to join together this man and this woman in holy matrimony...," he paused and looked at Thomas, as if he wasn't certain if Thomas would mind being described as a human man or not. Thomas looked back at him calmly, and the bishop continued.

Adamina lost the thread of the words. She was staring at Thomas, her heart bursting with love for him, and as her eyes traced the shape of his features, she completely forgot that Bishop Jamieson even existed. She'd heard these words before and participated in this ceremony twice before; but it was not the words she wanted etched in her memory tonight. She wanted Thomas, the way he moved and spoke and looked at her; Thomas, who was willing to do anything, no matter how difficult, to love her forever.

Adamina came to a decision. She pulled on Thomas' hands, drawing him closer. "I'll do it," she whispered to Thomas, as the bishop continued to speak next to them. "I'll do the ritual with you after we're wed. I want to be with you forever, Thomas. Just...teach me how."

She saw a flash in Thomas' eyes as his joy ignited; and then he was pulling her to him, taking her in his arms and kissing her, overcome with relief and adoration and a hunger that had been burning for a long, long time.

The bishop cleared his throat and adjusted his glasses, unused to this behavior in the middle of the vows. "Ah. Again, Adamina... wilt thou have this man to be thy wedded husband, to live together after God's ordinance, in the holy estate of matrimony? Wilt thou obey him, serve him, love, honor and keep him in sickness and in health, and forsaking all other, keep thee only unto him, so long as ye both shall live?"

Thomas looked sharply at Bishop Jamieson. "Adamina obeys and serves none. She is her own."

"Oh, yes," said the bishop, a bit flustered. "So sorry, that *is* crossed out. Eyesight isn't what it used to be. Wilt thou love, honor and keep him in sickness and in health, and forsaking all other, keep thee only unto him, so long as ye both shall live?"

Adamina wasn't moving away from Thomas. He had his arms around her, and she was happy there; this is how she would stay. "I will," she answered the bishop.

"And," the older man said, continuing the ceremony, a bit thrown off by the fact that the bride was already nestled close to the groom's body while the groom held her with a ferocity that made the bishop nervous just looking at it, "do...ah, do you, Thomas...."

But Thomas was already speaking to Adamina. *"Tha mi gad iarraidh mar nach robh mi a-riamh ag iarraidh dad,"* he murmured. *"Rè na h-uile bliadhna a tha agam agus a choisicheas mi an saoghal, cha robh ann ach thusa."*

I want you like I've never wanted anything before, he had said. *In all the years I have walked and will walk the worlds, there has only ever been you.*

He kissed her again, and she was clutching at him, desperate to be closer. *I'm going to do it. I'm going to do the ritual,* she thought.

"I'll...take that as a yes," said Bishop Jamieson.

"I will," said Thomas quickly to the officiant, before kissing the back of both of Adamina's hands.

The bishop shook his head. "Thomas. The ring, please."

But Thomas was lost in his bride's eyes, and she in his. "Gods above and below, *how I love you,*" Thomas breathed. Adamina felt him trembling with emotion.

The bishop couldn't continue without participation, and it was clear that trying to get Thomas' attention was becoming less possible by the second. He looked beseechingly at Adamina, who put her hand on Thomas' chest. "The ring, Thomas. He's asking for the ring."

"Yes," said Thomas, handing the bishop the ring without looking at him. The bishop rolled his eyes.

Adamina laughed. "*You're* supposed to put it on my hand now, Thomas."

Thomas remembered himself and became all smiles and laughed. "Oh, *aye. The ring.*" He took it back from the bishop and seemed to suddenly remember the clergyman was there. "My apologies."

Bishop Jamieson waved him off. "Just keep going, Thomas."

Thomas nodded, and Adamina held out her hand so he could slip the ring on her finger. "With this ring, I thee wed," Thomas said quietly, looking into her eyes. "With my body I thee worship, and...." Adamina felt suddenly dizzy with desire as she heard him speak those words. *Is a wedding ceremony supposed to sound so erotic? It never had before.* She could feel her pulse racing.

But now the words from the Book of Common Prayer were being left behind. They had completed the part of the ceremony that belonged to the Church, and to this earthly realm; but there were other things still to be said.

The bishop brought out a silver cord. *A handfasting cord,* Adamina thought. A Celtic ceremony in which the cord would be looped around her and Thomas' wrists in the symbol of eternity, and then slipped off and held above their heads and tightened, creating a knot. Adamina had seen the tradition at country weddings before; it was believed that as long as the knot stayed tied, the marriage would be strong. She'd never done this at her previous weddings, but thought it a lovely tradition.

She put her right hand next to Thomas' left, and the bishop wound the cord, tying their lives together, and murmuring an old invocation in Gaelic. He slipped the cord off their hands, held it up before them, and pulled on the two ends. "*Cheangail mi an snaidhm,*" he intoned, and set the evidence of what could arguably be called a pagan spell on the table to his left.

But the ceremony wasn't over yet. Thomas took Adamina's hands in his. He began speaking entirely in Gaelic, and Adamina listened intently to the words. He was taking a vow of the Fae, and Adamina felt a strange and twisting power surge up from the ground under her feet and begin to climb inside her body. She had never watched him work magick save for quick conjurings and opening gateways before, and she watched with fascination as he raised his gray eyes up toward the stars. Reality shifted slightly before her eyes, and then her Thomas seemed to become an entirely different being in that moment, one possessed of a tremendous amount of power and with a personality that was a mystery to her. *"Banrigh na h-uachdranachd,"* he began, his voice echoing off the cut stone walls of the chapel as he began extending his hands out to the side of his waist, *"Banrigh na Taibhse, Banrigh na Fàisne...."*

Queen of Sovereignty, Queen of Phantoms, Queen of Fate, Thomas called, *open the doors to our most beloved House. Let the wings of night bless this woman, may the red wolves run by her side, may the dead fall to their knees in her presence and rise to defend at her word. I swear to her my loyalty undying, my protection unending, and my devotion everlasting, and I seal that vow with the promise of bone, blood, and flesh. Hers will be the singular name that I cry out in the night; hers will be the name that I utter with my last breath. Open your arms and embrace my choice, O Great Goddess of War and Rebirth, of Destruction and Change, of Darkness and Revelation, for I bring you this night the Queen of the Deck of Crows!*

A sudden and tremendous tremor rocked the entire house, accompanied by aftershocks and a crash of thunder so loud that Adamina and the bishop both jumped and nearly fell. For a full six seconds every candle and globe in the room burned with an eerie, blue-black flame. The chapel windows were suddenly lit from the *outside,* as though a momentary, brilliant-blue sun had appeared in the night, and the silhouettes of hundreds of crows taking flight appeared outside of the windows, accompanied by the sound of their beating wings and a chorus of discordant cries. Adamina had never seen Thomas do *anything* like this before; he seemed in communication with an omnipotent power she couldn't begin to fathom, and one that was dark in nature. As the lights in the chapel winked back to white, Adamina's eyes widened in shock as she noticed every flower in the chapel had changed color and was either now blood red or black as pitch.

The bishop was crossing himself repeatedly, terrified, but Thomas was smiling. He pulled Adamina roughly to him, and she felt the power that had moved into her body recognize the same power in his. The two energy flows seemed to click into place when they touched, like a key fitting a lock. He was looking at her hungrily, and then he kissed her as though he meant his soul to devour hers. The surge of magickal power into their two bodies had severed something in him that had been restraining a part of him until now; his desire to conform to human protocols was quickly falling away.

"Here, my Queen," he growled in her ear, his hands roaming over Adamina's body, "I mean to mate with you *here.*" He was starting to touch her in ways that were generally reserved for their bedroom, and Adamina knew the point at which the increasing passion would switch to a hurricane was but a moment or two away. Thomas generally conducted himself within the boundaries of human emotions and social norms rather well, but at times the overpowering *will* of the Fae and his godhood would emerge, and he refused to be denied. Adamina worried he'd soon be thinking of creative and highly inappropriate uses for the surfaces of this lovely chapel as he gave into his desire for her.

The ritual. He needs to show me how to do the ritual. I need to calm him down, to interrupt this flow of energy between us. She fought to untangle herself from his embrace and staggered backwards, breaking the magickal connection between them that had been generated by the invocation to the House of Corvids. Adamina held up her hand, showing him she wanted space.

"Thomas!" she cried, holding on the end of a pew for support, "the ceremony isn't finished yet, my love! Let the bishop finish!"

The bishop, who looked very much as though he wished to immediately leave and lie down somewhere, looked at her with apprehension. "Oh no, my dear lady, I'm *quite* done. As a matter of fact, I'm not entirely certain I shouldn't begin an exorcism!"

"No, no," Adamina said to him, widening the distance between her and an extremely amorous Fae king with a tremendous amount of power pulsing in his veins, "you...you haven't said we can kiss! *That's* the end of a wedding. And you haven't done it!"

Bishop Jamieson looked at Thomas with more than a hint of terror in his eyes. "It's fine. *Really.* He kissed you straight through the vows basically, anyway."

Thomas turned to look at the bishop and appeared to be himself again. The break in contact and the conversation had allowed the magick to dissipate somewhat. He cleared his throat. "Ah, she's right. Wouldnae feel like we were wed until ye say it, Bishop."

The fact that Thomas was conversing normally drew a sigh of relief from the clergyman. He just had to say two sentences, and then he could head to his study for a shot of whisky. Or eight. "Very well, then. Ah, join hands, please." He looked cautiously over at a wall of darkened windows. "The, ah...the birds are done and gone, yes?"

Thomas just looked at the bishop and smiled before politely taking Adamina's hands in his.

"Right," the officiant muttered, wiping his brow. "I now pronounce you man and wife. Or...King and Queen. Whatever keeps things calm in here. Thomas, you may kiss your bride. *Again.*"

Thomas was gentle with Adamina now. His face lit up with a smile so big he could barely kiss her at first; he just stood there beaming at her and grinning. Adamina marveled at how quickly his entire being could change; a few moments before he had been a thundering force of nature and now he was a love-struck newlywed, tender and sweetly affectionate. "I love you, *mo Bhan-righ*," he said, and the rich, low tone of his voice took Adamina's breath away.

She was smiling at him too, as she told him she loved him, and then they had their first kiss as man and wife. She could feel happiness radiating off of him and was certain he could feel the same from her. *I want to hold him and whisper to him. Hold him in my arms and just be with him, forever.*

"We are joined now, Adamina," Thomas murmured in her ear. "I am yours, and you are mine, not just in each other's eyes, but in the eyes of all. The Great Queen has made her favor known this night."

She touched his cheek. "Let's go to our room," she said to him, as she heard the bishop quickly exit, "and take the final step to make this forever."

Adamina picked up the handfasting cord on the way out. They had tied the knot.

………

He carried her across the threshold to their room, another first for Adamina. *Everything about the way he moves is imbued with a strong grace. Like watching a stag run in the forest.* He kissed her again and laughed, and then set about his preparations.

Adamina watched him move a small table so that it stood by the side of the bed, and then he began pulling items out of a leather satchel he had placed on a nearby chair. She took note of the fact that he didn't ask if she'd changed her mind, or if she was certain of her decision. He trusted that when she'd said yes, she had meant it – and forged ahead under that direction without question.

It was one of the things she loved about him. Her entire life men had been asking her, "are you certain?" whenever she'd informed them of her decisions. She'd thought to herself on those occasions, *if I wasn't certain, I wouldn't have said it.* She noticed men never asked other men if *they* were certain of their decisions; it seemed a subtle way of doubting a woman's strength and convictions when it was said.

Thomas didn't do that. She thought of the wedding ceremony they'd just completed; *Adamina obeys and serves none. She is her own,* he had said. He had always treated her that way. If she gave an answer, he respected it; if she said *go* he went at once. This ritual would be no different.

"Thomas," she asked, watching him dig through his bag, "in the chapel, if you're not supposed to be here...well, it seems like you told *someone* in Faerie that you were."

He stopped and looked at her and nodded, a half-smile on his face. "Correct," he answered. "The Great Queen. She needed to bless your entry into the family, my love. An' she *heartily* approved." He raised his dark, arched eyebrows. "That doesnae mean she willnae give me hell for how I went about it. I'll have to go to court once I leave here and she'll...have a word with me." He shrugged. "But she's kin, so she willnae turn me in to the Council for it."

Adamina crossed her arms. "You know, after thirty years I still don't have a clear explanation from you of *exactly* how things work in Faerie."

He smiled and resumed his work. "Plenty of time for that once the ritual is done, *mo bhean ghrinn.*" He sighed and shook his head. "It's actually a blessin' *not* to know, trust me."

Adamina smiled. He'd called her *my sweet wife.* Thomas always had been a master at using an endearment to gently change the subject away from things he didn't feel like talking about. *He's sweet-talked me out of one topic and into another a thousand times. It's amazing how he always makes me feel he's sharing all of himself while simultaneously hiding so much.*

It was a habit Alex had as well, although he wasn't as skilled at it. Trying to get details out of Alex as a teenager had been *maddening*. Alex would often just go silent and look away to exit a conversation. At least Thomas always made you feel you were being kissed on his way out the conversational door. She thought of what Caroline Scott had said to her about Alex. Alexander's got himself a little girlfriend! And even better, she's a Stuart. The Prince's niece, no less. Everywhere Alexander is spotted she shows up too. *Was it true? Caroline Scott had been honest about Conall's death. She smiled and shook her head. If it is true, I hope the dear girl has more luck getting information out of Alexander than I have getting it out of Thomas.*

Adamina watched Thomas half-fill two chalices with water from the crystal decanter on the sideboard and set them on the bedside table; an assortment of vials and small leather pouches full of herbs were set on the table next. He tied a red ribbon around the stem of one of the chalices and pointed it out to her.

"This one is yours," he said seriously. "Dinnae get them mixed up, please. The one with the ribbon is *yours*."

"The one with the ribbon is mine," she repeated. "I understand. What happens if I were to get them reversed?"

He stopped what he was doing and looked at her solemnly. "Bad things," he answered. "*Verra* bad things."

She swallowed hard. "How bad?"

He put his hand on her shoulder. "You'd put me in a blood frenzy, Mina."

"You mentioned that before. Help me understand, please."

"Everyone in this house would have their throats torn out by me, including you and the nice bishop who just married us. And after that, I'd keep hunting. In my true Fae form, Mina. An' I have *wings* in my Fae form."

"So...you could fly somewhere else and kill everyone there too. And then keep going."

"Aye. An' since I have no leave to be on this plane currently, and I'd be in the throes of a forbidden spell, my House would have no choice but to dispatch soldiers from Faerie to take me down. An' trust me, they'd lose men doin' so. An' if I die, there's no one to speak for Alexander among the Fae."

Adamina took a deep breath. "Right. Thank you. I will not mix up the chalices."

He patted her hand. "Mina, you're no doing this alone. I'll be *inches* from ye. I'll be...a bit beside myself, but I'm certain I willnae let ye feed me the *wrong damn potion*." He began crumbling various herbs into the chalices and adding drops from the vials. He paused for a moment with one of the vials over Adamina's chalice, and looked at her for a moment, assessing. Then he added four drops.

"So, we need to raise energy," Adamina said, trying to shake off her nervousness about the blood frenzy. "How do we know if we have enough?"

He produced a metallic gray cube, about six inches on a side, from the bag. "This."

"It looks like hematite."

He grinned. "There's hematite in it. An' other things." The cube suddenly changed color in Thomas' grasp and began to glow a bright green. "This is an energy monitor. It changes color based on the amount of magickal energy in its local vicinity. It's white when it's off, gray when it is calculating. Purple is low energy, like a magickal human. Blue is higher, then green, an' so on an' so on up the spectrum." He rubbed it with his finger. "It's been attuned to me, so although I give off a lot of magickal energy, if I'm just sittin' around it should be white."

"Then why is it green? It should be purple because it's just picking up on me, correct?"

He gave her a knowing smile. "Because I am no just *sittin' around,* Mina. My energy is high because I just married ye, an' we're about to do the ritual, an'...he looked back at the table, "because I'm anticipatin' bein' in your bed, *leannan.*"

"Oh," Adamina smiled, and felt herself blush uncharacteristically. *That cube will change color based on how badly he wants me.* "What color do we need to get to?"

"Gold," he answered. "After red, it will go pitch black, an' then gold."

"Five more levels."

"Aye. An' the amount of energy needed to reach the next one is a bit more each time."

"That's a lot of energy, Thomas."

He laughed. "It is. But I have two ways to help boost it, an' we're already solidly at green."

"Are there colors after gold?" Adamina was fascinated.

"Yes. But ye cannae see them. The Fae, remember, can see more colors than humans. It would just look gray to you." He reached into the satchel again, and took out a silver teaspoon, and a small dagger.

Adamina frowned. "What's the dagger for, Thomas?"

He was watching her face. "It will just be one small wound, Adamina. Over my heart."

"WHAT?" she said, her mouth falling open in disbelief. "You said it was just *chalices!"*

"I said chalices *mostly,* dear one," he smiled. "It willnae hurt me but just for a moment or two. An' ye dinnae have to worry; I heal *verra* quickly."

Adamina's eyes widened. "Wait...you want *me* to cut you over your heart?"

He nodded. "I willnae be able to do it myself."

Adamina shook her head again. "I don't...I don't know that I can do that, Thomas. Hurt you like that."

He put his hands on her shoulders. "If you cannae do it, I understand. But I cannae take it out of the ritual. Two small cuts, that's all it will be. That's all that stands in the way of us being together for many, many years to come." He fell silent, awaiting her response.

Two small cuts. She took a deep breath. "Of course. I...was just surprised." He smiled at her and continued.

"Here is how it will go, Mina," he said. "In a few moments, I will release a spell out of a box. It's the start of a miracle, Mina. It will cause a miracle to happen elsewhere among a large group of those who worship me. They will then offer prayers and begin to focus on me, which will deliver a large amount of magickal energy back to me in a short while. That should boost us up a few colors."

She took his hand. "Where are they, Thomas? Those who will see the spell?"

He looked at her for a long moment. "In realms of the dead, Mina. And the dead...they tend toward religious fervor, so the spell should help."

She didn't want to ask where the realms of the dead were. She probably didn't want to know right now.

"Next," said Thomas, "you and I...well, we can be together, Mina. But the state I'm in...I'll raise energy too quickly." He laughed. "I'll be done before the energy from my followers arrives." He put his hands on either side of her face and looked into her eyes. "So, to slow things down, an' generate more magickal power, I'm goin' to restrict myself. I'll be in restraints."

Adamina raised her eyebrows.

"You need to have power over me in this ritual, Adamina," he told her. "You alone will have the power to free me from my bonds. Love me, but love me slowly. When the cube turns gold, take the dagger and make two small cuts over my heart. Use the spoon to take some of the blood and add it to your chalice alone. Then help me drink mine, and you drink yours." She saw lust swirling in his eyes. "An' then, take your pleasure from me, Mina. Dominate me. Make me submit. You'll absorb all the magickal energy I give off. Your body will feed on my desire for you. I must not be in control or the spell willnae work. I'm supposed to be your victim. An' when I cannae hold myself from you anymore, release me at your whim."

She stared at him, lips parted in shock. "How am I...how am I supposed to control an archmage of the Fae?"

He looked deep into her eyes, and she had the feeling that he was showing her something written on his soul. "I want it, Mina," he whispered to her. "It willnae be difficult, because at the core of myself, I want this from you." His eyes searched hers. "I may beg ye to release me, Adamina. I may fight ye. I'm...used to havin' my way. But pay that no mind, for *I want this*."

She felt herself tear in two, suddenly. Her mind and the tender part of her heart, the part that loved watching him sleep and holding his hand and listening to him as he read to her, was of the vehement opinion that she should flee the room *immediately. This is too dark. Too dangerous. There is no nurturing in what he is asking me to do to him. He wants me to make him my prisoner and submit to my will until he begs.*

But another section of her heart and her instinct in her belly wanted the *opposite. He wants this. It's a different form of love. A type of love he's never asked for before, and you've never experienced. He has a darkness in him, and he is asking you to see that darkness. These are his secrets. They are a part of him too.*

But do I have the courage to tend to his whole being without reservations?

She took three deep breaths. What was it Lilias had told her about magick once? She could see Lilias sitting in the garden at Buccleuch, in late summer after Alex was born, bouncing the little gray-eyed, laughing bairn on her knee during one of her visits.

"Ye ken that he is a magick-user, aye?" Lilias had said, after she'd told him a story about Thomas. "The One Who Speaks says he is powerful, known throughout the realms."

Adamina had looked up from where she was deadheading flowers. "I don't know how to feel about that, Lilias. How do I know he isn't a practitioner of dark magick?"

Lilias had shrugged and wiggled her fingers in the air. "The witches, they have a saying," she had answered. "'An' it harm none, do what thou wilt.' Ye cannae choose the path of Thomas' soul for him. But ye *can* choose the path of your own. So if he asks ye for somethin', an' it harms none, then you're on a right path most likely, aye?"

Right now. What he's asking me to do right now, it's intimidating, but does it hurt anyone? Adamina paused. *Only if I mix up the chalices. And he was careful to tell me how important that is and says it won't happen. And I trust him.*

He was stroking her hair now and kissed her on the cheek. She heard the cube hum, and the green glow intensified. *He's thinking of it. Of what it will feel like for me to rule him.*

She closed her eyes for a long moment and then opened them, trying to get her bearings. *Science, Adamina. Go through the steps of the procedure and see how it sounds.* "So, you release the miracle. Then we...go to bed. You'll be restrained, and the bonds only come free if I will it. Wait until the cube on the table glows gold. Two cuts over your heart with the dagger, spoon the blood into the ribboned chalice only, help you drink your chalice and then drink mine, and then build as much energy as we can until the end to make the spell take effect." She paused and put up her finger. "Safety note; you are not to drink from the ribboned chalice." She paused. "Other safety note: if something goes horribly wrong, probably only you can do anything about it. So just be aware that if either of us looks like we are in actual danger I'm releasing those bonds."

He nodded. "Understood. But not just because I ask, Mina. Not until after gold, an' the chalices."

She nodded and took a deep breath. "I'm ready when you are." *I can do this. I can do this.* She thought about what it would be like to wake up with Thomas every morning, one day after another, forever. *I've been so lonely for him most of the time. For nearly thirty years.*

He nodded and made a gesture with his right hand. The candles in the enormous room immediately went out, save for the ones near the bed. He uncorked two small wax-sealed vials, and poured one into each chalice, and murmured something under his breath. Both chalices immediately began to steam, creating a billowing cloud of vapor that quickly disappeared. "They're ready," he said quietly. He made certain the chalices, knife, spoon, and cube would be within easy reach of the bed and put away all the other supplies. Then he reached inside the bag once more and took out a black bog-oak box with a carved crow on the lid. "Back in a moment," he said to her, and walked off into a dark corner of the room.

She heard him speaking in a different language a few moments later, but did not know the words. *He's speaking a Fae language, I think.* She saw a strange, reflective vapor followed by a white cloud in the darkness near him, and thought she heard the flap of wings. He left the empty box on a table near where he stood and returned to her.

"It's done," he said. "Magick should be arriving soon."

They stood close to each other in the candle-lit space, and Thomas took her hands in his. He could tell Adamina was extremely nervous.

"It will be fine, Mina," he said, looking down at her. "You are my Queen. My consort. My goddess. My *wife*. I ken that you love me dearly, but I wish you to exert your will over me this night. I go to this bed your willing servant." He let her hands go and touched her neck gently. "This spell requires an imbalance of power. Drive me before you. Make my desire go as high as ye can, even if I try and change my mind about bein' in control. Make me call out in desperation for want of you, and then together we will triumph over time and death." He kissed her softly on the forehead. "And now," he said, lowering himself to his knees on the carpet before her and looking up with longing in his silver eyes, "what is your bidding, my Mistress of Crows?"

She looked down at him and thought of the enormous power he embodied. Legions moved to war at his command; he was known throughout worlds as an archmage and King, and there were beings who *worshiped* him. He was placing all that before her now. Asking for her to control him.

But to her, he was just *Thomas*. Her research partner. Her rescuer. Her son's father. He'd been her healer, supporter, and friend. Her beloved. The keeper of her secrets and a thousand private jokes. The one she trusted with her body, soul, and her entire heart.

"Tell me why," she said softly, brushing his dark hair back from his face with her fingertips. "I know it's for the ritual, but you are glad of that requirement because you *want* to submit. Tell me why, my love."

He was opening his heart to her, and it showed on his face. "There are those who have no power, and pray for power and standing," he said quietly. "But there are also those who *have* power, and pray for a brief respite from it." Something in his eyes changed, and she saw the weariness she had noticed earlier return. "Sometimes gods and generals grow tired of being gods and generals. But there is no running from it." He took her hand, beseeching. "For a brief time, here with you in this room, I wish to be free from control. From thinking. From who everyone expects me to be, Mina. I want to explore what it is to *surrender*. Completely. To be the one who receives. An' I trust, with all my heart, that you will still love me if I do." He squeezed her hand.

She understood. *Now* she understood. She nodded, and reached inside herself for a different voice. A different way of being with him. A way that, for a time, even as she bound him, might also set him free.

"Take off your shirt," she said to him. "Lie on the bed in nothing but your trousers."

He nodded and rose; she watched as he pulled off his shirt over his head. He looked decidedly more pagan and wild now that she could see the Fae tattoos on his arms and shoulders, and her first sight of him disrobing next to her bed momentarily took her aback, as it always did.

No matter how hard she tried, she could never remember all the details of him when he went away. It was as though her mind was too full of love to be able to preserve the shape of his shoulder and chest muscles, the rays of his collarbones, the strength evident in his arms. And so every time he returned, she discovered his body all over again, and was astonished by the beauty of it.

He tossed his shirt onto the back of the chair without speaking, and Adamina realized that just about every time they'd been intimate together, he'd initiated the encounter. She'd grown accustomed to this over the years, and the two of them had fallen into particular roles without being aware of it. *He initiates action and I receive. When I do initiate, like earlier tonight, it's often quiet or hesitant on my part, and then I wait for him to assert control. But that's not...fair, is it? For either of us?*

She was determined to break that pattern now. *This will be an exploration. An experiment.* She found her mind igniting with the fire of curiosity at the same time her body began to burn with arousal at the thought of exploring this new path before her. *What might we learn about each other, and ourselves, tonight?* She watched him climb into the enormous bed and stack a few pillows where his head would go, and then he settled himself obediently on his back and waited.

He's so quiet. Adamina looked at him thoughtfully. *Well, if you don't want him quiet, direct him not to be. Tell him what you want. What DO I want?*

There was nothing but possibilities here. Her heart fluttered with excitement as she thought of the *choices. I have all the choices. And I can be selfish, if I want to. What would it feel like to be selfish?*

As a wife and mother she always tried to put the needs of others before her own. *I did it as a hostess. And as a benefactor of the Church. And as a Laird's wife. Perhaps now, I will try something different. Without fear of being judged for it.*

"Thomas," she said, her voice firm, "look at me." He turned his head toward her. "You may watch," she said to him, "but you may not touch. Understand?"

He nodded. She saw his breathing rate increase in anticipation, and the cube turned from a leaf green to lime. *Climbing. Good.*

"Do you remember," she said to him, moving to stand next to the bed, "when you first came to stay with me? You could see my window in the library alcove from your room."

He nodded. "Aye. I could."

She moved closer, her body against the side of the bed, looking down at him. "One night," she said softly, "I saw you at your window. And I...turned my back toward you, so that I was facing the alcove bed. And..." she turned now, facing away from where Thomas lay, and recreated her actions from three decades before. "I took off my nightclothes." Adamina let her gray robe fall to the floor, and then shifted the straps of her silk shift off her shoulders, letting it follow the robe to the carpet. She heard Thomas draw in his breath sharply behind her on the bed as she was suddenly unclothed before him.

She didn't look back at him. "I always wondered," she continued, her voice low and sultry, "if you saw me do it or not. I've never asked." She reached back and unfastened her braid, letting her dark hair flow loose in waves over her bare back.

She turned slowly and looked at him over her shoulder. "Did you?" she asked. "Did you watch me from your window?" She looked away again. "Did you look at me, naked before you, and think of what you might do to me?" She saw the cube turn a dark ochre. He was remembering. She knew the answer.

"Aye," he said, his voice husky behind her, "I saw you. An'...I imagined."

She turned back to him, and watched as his eyes lingered over her face, traced her elegant neck and shoulders, and slid down to the round firmness of her breasts. "What did you imagine?" she said to him. "Tell me."

His breathing was rapid now, his pulse increasing. "I want to touch you right now, Mina."

"No," she said flatly. "You may look only. *Tell me.*"

He closed his eyes for a moment, and she saw a new emotion on his face. *Delight.* He opened his eyes again. "I thought," he began, and then to her astonishment she saw him *blush. Thomas is blushing. Have I seen that before?*

"I thought," he continued, "that I could...climb the stairs to the library, an' none of the staff would mind, for they would think we were workin'. And then I could...I could...." He paused for a moment.

"Tell me," Adamina commanded. "What did you want to do?"

"I wanted to touch ye, so," he breathed. "I wanted to be with ye in that little room of yours." She watched him rub his thumbs against his index fingers on both hands, full of an energy he could do nothing with.

"More," she demanded. "Tell me more."

"I wondered," he confessed, "well, I knew that because Phineas couldnae walk...I wondered if you and he...."

"You wondered if I was a virgin," she finished.

He nodded and looked away. "Aye."

"And what did you want to do?" she reached out and stroked his muscular shoulder with two fingers. "What did you want to do to the young widow you were visiting?"

"Let me touch ye, *please,*" he said, beginning to sit upright in the bed. "*Please,* Mina. You're *so* lovely, an' it's been *so* long. Just a little. Then I'll be good, an' we can start the spell *then,* I swear."

She put her hand on his shoulder and stopped him from rising further. "Do as I say," she said, her voice icy, "or I'll get dressed and walk out that door and ask the bishop to let me sleep in a different room for the night."

The cube hummed, and turned the color of canary feathers. Adamina picked up the cube and moved it to the nightstand where she could see it, but Thomas couldn't. *I don't want him distracted. I want him thoroughly engrossed in his emotions.*

He didn't say anything about it. Instead, he answered her. "I thought about you all night, Mina," he confessed to her. "Over and over again. Of what ye might do if I came up there to your study, and that bedroom of yours by the window. I pictured all the ways it might happen. I wanted...well, if you'd never had a lover before, I wanted to...to show you. To guide you. To instruct you in how men are made. To be your first, to watch you discover it all, and take you in ways you'd never forget." He took a deep, shuddering breath. "I couldnae sleep because of the wanting, Mina. I wanted to kiss my way down your spine. I wanted to watch your face as ye felt what it was like havin' a man inside ye for the first time. I wanted to hold you down an' make you cry out my name. God, how I wanted you to *want me*! An' I exhausted myself, thinkin' of you." He looked up at her, hungry for her. "I answered your question. May I have a kiss, please?"

She bent over him slowly, and she saw his eyes light with anticipation. But Adamina stopped just two inches from his lips, and instead of kissing him whispered, "Bind yourself. With the bindings only I can release."

His face changed from joy to disbelief, and he looked at her forlornly. "But..."

"You heard me. Do it. Immediately."

He swallowed and looked at her desperately, "Ah, Mina, just...just one kiss first?"

She put her hand on his throat and squeezed gently, showing him who was in control. "Three. Two. One...."

Two rents appeared on the mattress, and two gold ropes snaked their way up and out of their own accord. The ends of the ropes looped themselves three times around Thomas' wrists where they lay at his sides, and then disappeared back through the mattress top, holding his hands firmly in place.

She could see his breathing was irregular now. She reached over and ran her fingertips lightly down the center of his well-muscled abdomen. "Tell me how you feel," she said to him.

"I'm...," he looked up at the ceiling, taking stock of his emotions. "*Nervous*," he said, a note of incredulity in his voice. "I'm...nervous, I think. It's new for me. I'm used to controlling what comes next. An' it's makin' my wanting *worse*." He looked up at her in amazement. "I dinnae ken what to do if I cannae...*do things*." He moved his wrists against the ropes, testing their strength, and then looked up at her. "What are ye goin' to do to me?"

Adamina climbed onto the bed and straddled him, sitting down on his hips. He pulled on the ropes and groaned with pleasure. "I'm not going to tell you what I'm going to do," she said, stroking him lightly on the chest. "But you are going to be good for me, aren't you?" She leaned forward, placing her hands next to his shoulders. *"Aren't you?"*

"Yes," he whispered, "I'll be good."

Adamina bent over him and kissed him on the cheek. He turned his head, hoping the next kiss would be on the mouth, but she grasped him on the jaw and turned his head away. "Stay," she whispered in his ear. "This is not about *your* wanting. I will take from you what I please."

He moaned. "Oh, Mina...!"

She took her time. *Love me slowly,* he had said. She ran her fingers through his hair and stroked his beard, nibbled her way down his neck, and let him hear her voice whisper quietly in his ear. *Drive him higher. What can I say to drive him higher?*

"You belong to me, Thomas," she told him, pressing her naked breasts against the heat of his chest. "No one else shall have you. I will do with you as I please. You are mine to toy with, and you *will* satisfy me. Tell me."

"You will do with me as you please," he whispered back. "I am here only for your desires. You have all the power and I have none."

But he didn't truly understand the depths of what he was professing. Not yet. She kissed her way down his chest, and bit him lightly just under his collarbone, and listened to him gasp. She kissed his arms, and then he watched as she moved lower.

"Ahhh, *yes,*" he sighed as she began stroking his abdomen and caressing the muscles there with her lips. His breathing was becoming irregular, and he shifted his hips forward. "Lower. Lower, my love. I like that. Oh...I want you to take my clothes off, Mina. Take my clothes off and touch me."

She moved backward and he spread his legs so she could lie on her belly between them. Adamina kept her face straight, but it was hard not to smile. He was telling her what he wanted, and clearly thought she was going to deliver; she'd let him believe that for a few moments more. *Then he'll start to see what a loss of control really feels like.*

She looked up at him and made eye contact. He was pulling against the ropes; he wanted to touch her, and the anticipation of her taking off the rest of his clothes was building. She could see clearly from the shape of him under his trousers that he was already extremely aroused, and ran her fingers gently over the long, pronounced bulge in the fabric.

"Yes," he said, moving his hips again. "Touch me. *Touch me.* Oh, *take me out of my clothes.* Oh God, I'm achin' for you! I want your mouth on me there, *please*, sweetheart."

She went agonizingly slow, looking him right in the eyes as she undid one button at a time. He was shifting his hips again and again, unable to stay still.

"Eighteen months since we've last been together," she said to him quietly, watching his labored breathing. "Eighteen months. Did you imagine me, Thomas? Did you imagine what I'm about to do to you? Did you imagine my mouth on you, and how willingly I'd come to you? Did you imagine putting your fingers in my hair and holding me where you wanted me? Did you imagine what it would feel like?"

"Yes, *yes*," he responded. "*Every night.* I'd picture you…I want to watch you…oh, *please*.…"

She moved her head toward his erection, and he held his breath, straining against the ropes to move closer. "*Please, Adamina.…*"

But his lover was getting up off the bed without touching him.

"NO!" Thomas cried. "*What…what the hell are you doing*?" She pulled his trousers to his knees and then took hold of them by the ankles and pulled them slowly off, leaving him naked and beside himself on the bed before her.

"You seem to be laboring under the impression that you are allowed to *ask for things*," said Adamina calmly, rising to her role. "You *aren't*. It seems I need to make you understand that."

The cube on the table turned a fluorescent yellow, so bright it was hard to look at. *Good.*

"What are you going to do?" Thomas asked as she walked over to the dresser.

Since she'd had no luggage with her, Thomas had provided not only her nightclothes but an entire wardrobe for her to travel with. She opened the top drawer of the dresser and removed two beautiful silk scarves she'd seen earlier. *He might tear them to pieces. But I don't think he will.* She turned back to the bed and began tethering his left ankle to the footboard with one of the scarves.

"This isnae what I planned," Thomas protested, his voice tight. "The ropes on my hands are enough."

She finished with one ankle and moved to tie the other. "You said to restrain you. You don't get to tell me how."

"Oh Adamina," he said, his voice sounding tortured, "come back in the bed, dearest. I'm...I'm *begging you*. I want ye so!"

She ignored him and walked away into the darkness of the room. He didn't know what she was doing, which completely unnerved him. "Mina? *Mina?*" He pulled on the ropes and felt a loss of control and a moment of panic. He wasn't used to feeling these emotions and hadn't methods in place for dealing with them. Adamina emerged out of the darkness a moment later, holding a silver candy dish she'd filled with something.

"How nice," she said pleasantly, as though they'd been discussing the weather, "the servants must have visited the icehouse for us again while we were out with the bishop." She placed the dish on the dresser and retrieved a final scarf from the dresser. "Now, I know from experience you're very perceptive with a blindfold on, Thomas. But I wonder if you'll be less so if you're distracted. Let's find out."

The cube hummed and switched to a deep orange as Adamina tied the scarf over Thomas' eyes while he protested. When she was done, she bent and gave him a long, deep kiss. Adamina noticed he couldn't stay still *at all* now. He was moving against his restraints and even tried to shake the blindfold off, and Adamina smiled as she watched him. *I'll have you out of orange and into red before you know it, Thomas.*

She realized with a start that she was enjoying herself. *Really* enjoying herself. Seeing Thomas tied to the bed and blindfolded lit a strange fire in her body, one she couldn't explain. She thought back once again to those first days they'd known each other, when they'd blindfolded each other for an aura experiment in her Tower. *I'm not a power-hungry person, but my God, seeing him like this again is arousing!*

He couldn't sense her due to the chaotic wanting in his body. She stood next to the bed, silent, enjoying the sight of him bound and blindfolded and rapidly losing his ever-present composure.

"Mina? *Mina?*" he called. There was frustration in his voice, and also desperation.

She took the large piece of ice out of the candy dish and placed it on the table next to the dagger, looking at the small amount of ice-cold water it had left behind in the dish. *Perfect.* She raised the dish in the air over Thomas and tipped it slowly to let several drops of the water fall onto the insides of his warm, muscular thighs.

He let out a roar of surprise and strained against his bonds; the cube hummed louder. Adamina bent over him and used the warmth of her tongue to lick the tiny streams of water off the inside of his legs, and stroked the most intimate parts of his body gently with her hands.

"PLEASE!" Thomas cried out to her. "Oh, *God*, I want, I want, *I want!*" He was losing his ability to form coherent, reasoned thoughts. He tried to get the blindfold off again by pressing his head hard against the pillow to trap the scarf in place and then moving his head quickly to slip it off, all to no avail.

Adamina had never seen him like this. She was breaking him down, reaching a new part of him; and it was so thrilling it was making it hard to think straight. She took the ice chunk and ran it slowly over his lips, and then down the inside of one of his arms and watched him jump in surprise. Then she touched the ice to her own lips for several seconds and kissed him low on the belly with an ice-cold mouth.

"Please, please, *please*," he begged, writhing as she climbed onto the bed again. "I want ye so *badly*, Mina! I cannae...I cannae hold back much longer...you're going to make me...I'll lose control...*oh, please*...."

Adamina ran the ice slowly along the length of his rigid phallus, and listened to him issue a strangled cry of desire, and then followed the path of the ice with her warm tongue. He began begging in Gaelic. *Gabh mi, gabh mi, gabh mi! A Dhia, tha e cho dian! Take me, take me, take me! Oh God, it's so intense!*

Red. The cube had turned a pale red. Just up a little more to black and then gold. Adamina put the ice on the table, climbed onto the bed, straddled Thomas on her hands and knees, and bent to give him a kiss. His entire body tried to levitate away from the mattress toward her. She laughed. *My God, seeing him like this has me excited.* She smiled at him, but he couldn't see it; he was shivering with a passionate madness.

"Do you want to make love to me, Thomas?" she said playfully, twisting the knife.

"Yes!" he said, his voice sounding tortured. "Oh, the need...I *need*...I want to put myself inside you! *I have to do it!*"

She moved her body down so he could feel the soft heat and dampness of her aroused sex against his engorged member. "Why *don't you then?*"

"FUCK!" he bellowed, baring his teeth and thrusting his hips repeatedly, trying in vain to enter her. "Let me! *Let me! LET ME NOW!"*

He was unused to having his will denied, and his frustration only increased his desire. The cube turned a bright, flaming red. And then Adamina heard the sound of *wings*.

She looked up. The room was full of crows, flying straight toward the bed. Adamina shrieked and instinctively covered her head, but as the crows drew near, they came apart and dissolved mid-air, and the black mist they left behind was pulled toward Thomas' body at an incredible speed and disappeared into his skin.

The miracle. The magick was here. The devotion of Thomas' worshippers flapped and soared through the room, wave after wave, hundreds and hundreds of phantom corvids disintegrating into magickal power and being pulled into his body the same way the moon pulls the tide. The birds emerged out of the darkness like ghosts.

Thomas hadn't been able to see them coming and had been too distracted to sense their energy, and they took him completely by surprise. There was a sudden, unexpected, powerful wave of magick drowning him and he became disoriented from the onslaught, but the rush of power also heightened his desire into the realm of frenzy. The cube flickered briefly black, and then shone a bright, sunny gold.

That's it! Adamina reached forward, pulled off the blindfold, and lunged for the dagger. Thomas was repeating something over and over under his breath in a language of the Fae, his eyes wild as he fought to stay sane. Adamina didn't dare wait; the cube was gold, but might not be so in another few moments. The last of the crows had gone, and she had no idea how long the magick they had delivered would stay.

She took a deep breath and held the razor-sharp dagger over his heart. She looked up at him; he was yanking against his restraints and howling for her to end his torment, seemingly oblivious of the dagger. *It's now or never!*

"Be still!" she commanded him, and he froze, letting out a soft sound akin to a whimper. She traced the blade gently against his chest, and was surprised to see it neatly slice into him. Blood immediately flowed onto his skin. She was shocked that instead of a shout of pain, he let out a deep, satisfied moan of pleasure that seemed to rise from a hidden place in his spirit, as though she'd just done something incredibly sexually gratifying to him. "*More,*" Thomas breathed. "Oh, yes, MORE! Dominate me! Subjugate me! *Bend me to your will, Mistress!*"

He's no longer himself. All rationality has left him. I think I might be on my own, Adamina thought. *It seems like no matter what I do to him, he'll want it!*

I have to make two cuts. He specifically said two. She adjusted her wrist and quickly executed the second cut, leaving a bloody X on his flesh. Thomas shivered, threw back his head, and let out a shaking cry of near-climactic bliss and wanting. Blood trickled down his chest in vivid red streams.

Red-ribboned chalice. Just the one with the ribbon. Adamina reached for the spoon and the correct chalice, and used the spoon to collect some of the blood at the wound and mix it into the liquid.

She tossed the spoon back on the table and put down the chalice, grabbing the one without the ribbon. *No blood in this one. Help him drink.* The cube was still gold.

"Thomas! *Thomas!* I want you to drink this!" She held the cup to his lips. "Look at me! Drink! *Now!*"

He opened his mouth willingly and she tipped in the contents, and he swallowed it down, eager to follow her commands.

And now, mine. She put the empty chalice back on the table and picked up the one with the ribbon. *Here goes.*

He was staring straight at her. "You're so beautiful, my dark Queen," he rasped, his voice breaking. "I want to take you so hard. Be in you *so deep.* Use me as you will, and let that be my reward!"

She kissed him hard. "*Slàinte*," she whispered, and then gulped the potion down.

The first swallow was *awful*. She could taste the blood and the musky, waterlogged herbs. It tasted like iron and sand. It tasted like a brackish, stagnant pool. But on the second swallow, it sweetened, and became smooth. And after that...*ambrosia*. Honey and spices and the essence of Thomas' thirst for her. She gulped it down greedily. It seemed the most refreshing, delicious thing she'd ever tasted.

Adamina flung the empty chalice aside. *Drive the energy higher for the spell. Take your pleasure,* he had said. The potion was spinning in her body, shooting off sparks that lit every sense she had aflame and made her want to...*consume him*.

There is nothing in the world but him. Him, and my desire. She let out a desperate sound that was unlike her own voice, and reached down to grasp him and join their bodies together. He let out a rapturous cry as she allowed him to thrust himself into her, and began moving up into her as hard as he could as she rode his hips. "Mina! Ah, *yes! YES! Dinnae stop!*" he called to her, feeling her body surrounding and rhythmically stroking him, and his lover undulating her pelvis over him, chasing the satisfaction her body craved.

And that was when Thomas realized he'd misjudged one of the potion amounts.

His eyes widened and the shock of seeing what he was seeing provided him with a few moments of clear thinking as he looked up at Adamina's face. Her beautiful, beloved face, eyes closed as she focused on the feeling of him inside her. Mouth slightly open, breathing hard. Open far enough that he could see *the fangs*.

She was oblivious to it. She didn't notice her teeth, or the fact that her ears were reshaping themselves to taper gracefully at the top, or the forked, black tongue he saw briefly flick against her lips.

He had known Adamina was a Bruce. That there was magick in her blood. But he had mistakenly assumed that all magickal humans had about the *same* magickal capacity. He'd assumed that Alex's glowing eyes, black tongue, and fangs were recessive, rare, and long-buried traits from *his* side of the family, revealed in his son only because of Alex's unique magickal composition as a *leth-dhia*.

But he was wrong. Alex had gotten them from his *mother*. Which meant Adamina was carrying pure Fae traits from an ancient tribe that most of those among the Fae, himself included, had thought were on the razor's edge of extinction.

And to pass on those traits, Adamina had to have a fairly large capacity for magick. And he hadn't dosed her that way. And he was still bound.

The potion was bringing those characteristics to the surface. The traits of the Fae of the East, one of the four original tribes that had merged to form the Tuatha Dé Danann.

Blood frenzy. This means she's capable of it. The thought rolled through Thomas' mind as the liquid he'd just been fed started to take effect. He'd put both a powerful aphrodisiac and a logic dampening potion in his chalice to ensure she'd have domination over him once the spell was triggered; now there was no motivation in the vast majority of his brain for him to do anything but mate with her. *Blood frenzy. There's a chance she might turn.* He hadn't thought Adamina had the magickal capacity for it to be a possibility; but now it was too late.

"Release me!" he cried. A small part of his brain was shouting at him to get out of his bonds if he wanted to live. But the potion he'd drunk was now making the rest of his mind dive back into the fog of lust where he just wanted to *take her.*

She opened her eyes. They began to emit a soft, white glow. She was crying his name, over and over, grinding herself against him without a thought or care for how he felt or what he wanted, hunting her own exquisite sensations in the depths of her body. To see her wild and hungry like this struck a chord deep in his heart and in his sex; he was nearly transcendent with erotic fulfillment.

"Yes!" he shouted, encouraging her. "Oh, Goddess, *use me! USE ME!*"

"No release for you!" she shrieked, as his entire body throbbed with a fierce lust, "Not until I say! I take my pleasure *FIRST!*"

This further restriction made him dizzy. "I cannae stand against you! Oh, release me! *Unbind my hands!*"

"NO!" she moaned, throwing back her head. "Mine! *Mine! I POSSESS YOU! You only exist to serve ME!*"

The erroneously mixed potion caused all her latent Fae characteristics to burst to the surface now, burying the human attributes in her personality. She looked and sounded Fae, and her capacity for different sorts of emotion and movement was on full display. She was transforming into an ancient form of Fae in the throes of madness as the potion worked its intended effects and the years began to melt from her body. Her skin was tightening, her joints strengthening, and her heart skipped as Thomas' faerie blood, which had been absorbed into her bloodstream before it had even made it down her throat, rocketed through the chambers of her heart and unwound the clock that had been ticking on her mortality.

And then suddenly, she caught what she had been pursuing with her whole being. She let out a gasp and began to shake and vocalize the intensity of her climax, and Thomas watched her and couldn't take the stimulation anymore. He lost control wholly and completely and against his will, submitting to the demands of her body and his, and he felt something in his mind crack open.

"No!" he gasped. "I cannae...I cannae hold back...*oh, Goddess, RUIN ME!*"

He was crying as his body, which never did *anything* without his permission, ignored his will and flooded itself into her, each spasm of release deeper and more essential than the last. He had no more words now; she had driven him over an edge he had feared but craved, and he had no choice but to fall. He heard her shout, and then suddenly his hands were free, and he was bruising her hips as he tried to drag himself further into her. She was beauty, she was tyranny, and he was *hers*. Willingly, completely, and forever. He felt happily broken. Destroyed, become dust. Wracked by a rare and exquisite sweetness. He existed only *for her*. He thrilled at the idea that both his blood and semen were inside her body now; he would willingly give her his life now should she desire it.

He felt her hands putting a firm pressure on him, just above his pubic bone, and for some reason this set off another round of marvelous, near-orgasmic sensation in his lower body as he started to surface from his soul-wrenching climax. He arched his hips upwards and sobbed, closing his eyes as she gradually slowed the motion of her body atop him.

"There, there now," she whispered to him, leaning closer and brushing the dark waves of his hair back from his face. "That's right. Oh, you've done *well*. You have serviced your mistress admirably. Even if you *did* disobey me at the end."

Thomas opened his eyes. He watched Adamina look at the blood on his chest and lick her lips. Her eyes glowed a soft white; her delicate fangs were still on display. She was lovely in an otherworldly and disturbing way, and the part of Thomas' brain that understood warning signs began to assume more control.

Blood frenzy. She may be capable of it, but she is also unaware of her Fae characteristics right now. Perhaps if I give her time to settle, both the danger and the physical changes will fade. He smiled at her and traced the curve of her left breast with his fingertip. He felt a tide of incredible fatigue threaten to sweep all of his thinking away. He was physically and emotionally spent, and he'd drugged himself to be under her power. Yet through the haze of exhaustion he could hear a voice in his head warning him. *Be careful. Very careful, here.*

He reached up to stroke her cheek. Every drop of magick in the vicinity was now inside her body, working. He didn't even have the bit it would take to untie his feet or heal the wound over his heart. "I love you, Mina," he said to her, his voice and eyes soft. "The spell will take time to work. Will you untie me, so I can turn on my side an' hold you, my dear?" He watched her face carefully. She was fixated on the blood on his chest. She stared at it, panting.

"Oh, Thomas," she said after a moment, unable to tear her eyes away, "I'm so...*thirsty*."

Thomas swallowed hard. *Not good. Not good.* His only recourse at that moment would be to attempt to knock her out, and the thought of hitting his new bride made his blood turn to ice. He managed a casual laugh. "Mina, sweetheart, untie my legs and I'll go fetch ye whatever ye like."

She tilted her head to the side, unblinking. Her eyes glowed as she stared at his chest. *"Thirsty,"* she sighed.

"Oh, *whoa*, hold on, then," Thomas said sharply, and sat bolt upright in the bed. He pulled her roughly to him, so that their chests were touching and she couldn't see the blood. He looked past her at the scarves binding his ankles. *Too far to reach, and tightly tied.* He felt weak and dizzy, and he reached out with his mind for any magick lingering in nearby spaces. *Maybe someone in the house is praying. Maybe there are remnants in the chapel. Maybe one of the servants has a poppet tucked in a drawer, or a Saint Brigid's cross stuck behind the corner of a door frame.* But he'd pulled everything in the area into the spell; there was none to be had. *And I did this during a waning moon, when energy is harder to raise. Fuck.*

He rubbed her back, trying to settle her. She was wrapped around him, holding him tightly, her head on his shoulder. *She's tired too. If I can just get her to go to sleep, and keep the blood out of her mouth....*

He thought about what made humans sleep and slowed his breathing. Within a few breaths she had matched the tempo of her breathing to his. *Good.* He faked a yawn, and felt her yawn in response. Despite the danger, he had to smile. *I bet she doesn't know that the Fae don't yawn.* He did it again, and felt her body respond the same way.

"Ye need to rest, my Mina," he said, running his fingers through her hair to relax her. "You did so well, an' now it's time to sleep. Let the spell do its work, an' when ye wake we'll talk more, aye?" He kissed her cheek. "Just climb off me, dear one, an' lie right here on the pillow. I'll fetch ye some water."

He began shifting her away from him before she could protest. He could see her eyes were heavy with fatigue, and that she had begun to relax. The fangs and ears and tongue were all still evident, but her eyes had lost their glow. *Good. Keep her away from blood and mirrors. Blood and mirrors, for just a little more time.* Once she was off his lap, he quickly undid the restraints on his ankles, and then hastened out of the bed and headed across the room, not wanting her to be out of his sight. *She has my blood on her chest now. If she tastes it...*

If he'd gone into a blood frenzy, the fact that he had wings would have made it worse as he'd have been harder to catch. Adamina didn't have wings, but he suspected she *did* have a different trait: the ability to flash forward at an incredible speed, so quickly that she briefly became invisible. The Fae called it *striking*. He'd seen Alex do it many times. If Adamina could do it, she'd be hell to take down as well.

He splashed some water from a pitcher into a glass, and then grabbed a napkin from the sideboard and dunked it in the pitcher. He hurriedly scrubbed blood from his chest and stomach; the wound itself was nearly dried now. He tossed the napkin onto the table and grabbed a second and soaked it as well, poured her a glass of water, and headed back to the bed.

Adamina lay quietly, observing him as he returned. He felt a lump in his throat as he realized he wasn't certain if she was lying comfortably or lying in wait to attack him, but pushed the thought away. It wasn't being attacked that bothered him; it was the concept that he would have to hurt her to stop her, which he wasn't sure he had it in him to do. The worst day he'd ever had was the day he'd had to restrain her so that he could perform the ritual that would split Alex and save his life; the thought of having to actually become *violent* with her now, even to save lives, made him physically ill.

"Here, my love," he said, handing her the glass. "Drink this, and I'll get you cleaned up." Adamina took the glass and drank quickly and eagerly, and he used the damp napkin to clean his blood from her body. He took the glass back from her and she sighed and sank back onto the pillow, watching him.

"Can I look yet?" she asked him. "Do I look any different? Did the spell work?"

Oh, it's working, he thought. *Just...not quite as predicted.* "It's starting to work, Mina. It just needs more time." He looked at her ears and fangs, and saw her black tongue flick across her lips. *Keep her away from the mirror.* "If ye dinnae think ye can sleep just yet - you've a lot of magick runnin' in your system - why don't we have another bath an' see if that relaxes ye a bit?"

"That sounds lovely, Thomas," she said, and started to rise. He saw immediately the path she'd take, and it led straight past the mirror on the dressing table. *Shite.* He put himself in her path and picked her up in his arms, pivoting her away from the mirror. "Come on, then," he said playfully as she laughed in surprise. "I'll give you a lift over there." *Walk past the mirror quickly. Don't let her see.*

"We should bandage your chest," Adamina protested.

"Ah, I'll be healed in a few minutes," he said to her. "Dinnae give it another thought." He was still feeling very tired and somewhat weak, but his worry about the possibility of a blood frenzy occurring pushed those concerns to the back of his mind. *Get her in the bath. Get her relaxed, and hopefully the traits will fade.* He deposited her next to the bath and opened the cover on the hot water pipe, beginning the flow of water, and climbed into the tub. *Get her sitting with her back to you like before, so she can't see the blood and you are in a position to restrain her, if necessary.* He climbed in, positioning himself where he'd sat earlier in the evening. "Come in and sit with me." The water started to rise.

Adamina climbed in and sat with her back against his chest and let out a contented sigh. After a few minutes she laughed. "Look, Thomas! The spell must be working. The skin on my legs looks...brighter and my scars are fading." She sounded positively delighted.

He put his arm around her and kissed the back of her neck. "It *is* working. Ye did well, Mina. I knew ye could do it." He noted that her ears were still pointed. *Give it time.*

"You're all right, though?" she said quietly, interlacing the fingers of her right hand with those of his left. "I wasn't...too hard on you?"

He smiled and nuzzled her neck. "You were *perfect,* my beauty," he whispered. "Perhaps...we can try somethin' like that again sometime. *Without* the spell."

Adamina reached for a washcloth sitting at the edge of the tub and a bar of goat's milk soap scented with roses, and began lathering her chest and arms. "It was...rather liberating," she smiled. "I was surprised."

He laughed. "It's always good to experiment a wee bit, aye?" He took the soap and cloth from her and began washing her back. He could see her body changing right before his eyes, and made subtle adjustments to his own appearance as well.

She sighed as the warm water cascaded down her spine. "I can't believe...I just can't believe that I was at Carlisle this morning. And now...we're *married,* Thomas! And I'm...," he heard her voice catch, "so *happy.*"

"I'm happy too, *leannan,*" he told her, shifting slightly in the bath and scrubbing himself off with the cloth and soap. *The wound on my chest is closing. Good.* "Do ye think ye could sleep now, Mina? I'm a bit worn out myself."

She nodded and stood up. "The water did wonders. Let's go to bed." She climbed out of the tub and began toweling herself off. "Oh, good! You're healing up!" she said when she saw his chest. "I'm so glad!"

One more trip past the mirror, he thought, climbing out of the bath. *One more and then she'll sleep, and hopefully the traits will fade while she does.* He toweled himself off quickly and grinned. "It will be nice to get in a warm bed wit' ye."

"Ooh, it's cold outside the bath," Adamina smiled, and gave a little shiver. "Race you to the...."

And then she disappeared, appearing less than a second later next to the four–poster bed across the room, a look of confusion on her features. "Thomas...?"

He closed his eyes. *Shite.* She'd just used her faerie blood to strike. And now she was bewildered and, even worse, standing right next to the mirror.

"Thomas?" she said again, her voice plaintive, "How...did I get over here...?"

He moved quickly toward her. "Adamina!"

But she had turned toward the mirror already. He watched her eyes widen in horror as she saw her ears and her teeth. She gasped, and then saw her tongue. She went completely pale and began to shake. "What's...what's...oh *God, what's happening to me?*"

He put his hands on her shoulders and turned her roughly away from the mirror to face him. "Adamina, it's temporary, it should fade...."

"Should? *Should?* Oh my GOD, Thomas, am I a *monster?*" She was having trouble breathing, moving quickly into hysteria. "Why didn't you *say* anything? Oh, God, *what have you done to me?*" She pushed him away, attempting to turn back toward the mirror. "My *ears!* I have...I have *fangs!*" She began to cry. "I'm a vampire, aren't I? *Aren't I?*"

He shook his head. "No, dear one. You're no a vampire. Those are *faerie* traits. Because ye have my blood in ye now."

"But *you don't look like this!* You don't...," she saw her tongue again and wailed.

"Adamina."

"Can you make it stop? Can you *make it stop?*"

"Adamina," he said from behind her, "turn around." She did. What she saw struck her speechless.

Thomas had always been careful to assume a wholly human form in her presence. She knew he had a different one in Faerie, but had never seen it. Until now. The King of the Deck of Crows stood a short distance from her in the middle of the room, wings extended. The wings were *huge,* black and gray with edges of a brilliant blue, shot through with gold, arcing up toward the ceiling and so far out to the sides that they more than filled Adamina's field of vision. Thomas' ears pointed upwards at the top, just like her own, and because he was unclothed she could see that he had many, many more tattoos on his skin than she'd seen before. In addition to his arms and back the spells covered his thighs and hips and outer legs as well. The whites of his eyes had disappeared along with the gray of the irises, and so he appeared to be looking at her with nothing but a liquid black ink in his eye sockets. And his hands...his hands looked somehow *stretched,* longer and more articulated, almost as if his human hands had been crossed with the shape of a bird's foot. Adamina shivered. And if that wasn't enough, Thomas now appeared to be over eight feet tall.

She had always known he was of the Fae. But now she *understood*, right down to the bone. If Adamina had ever doubted Thomas when he claimed there were beings who worshiped him, those doubts would have been washed away at this moment. He looked every inch the supernatural deity that he was. A raw *power* radiated from him as he stood quietly, looking at her. For a brief moment his black eyes turned completely red, and then the effect was gone, and they were full of the void again.

"Thomas," she breathed, forgetting about herself for a moment, "is this...what you...*oh, my God.*"

She saw him smile. "This is what I look like, my beloved. In my Faerie form. Do ye see? Our ears are the same. Ye just have some different traits than I do. That's all."

"But *why* do I have them, Thomas?" Adamina felt weak in the knees. His presence alone made her want to fall to the floor before him. "Why do I...?" Her thoughts were getting lost as she stood before him. *I'm looking at an angel. Or a monster. I don't know which.* She couldn't wrap her head around the fact that this was *Thomas.*

His huge wings folded slowly and gracefully behind him and disappeared, and the next time she blinked he was walking toward her, looking like himself. He held out his hands to her, a look of regret on his face. "I made a wee bit of a mistake in the spell, my love. I am so, so sorry. I can explain if you will let me, and it should all be correctable."

Adamina was still trying to absorb what she'd just seen. She looked up at him, stunned. He took a careful step toward her and when she didn't move, put his arms around her. "It's just me, dear one, I swear," he whispered to her. "Come to bed with me an' let me hold you, and then I'll explain." She let him lead her to the bed and watched as he pulled back the covers, and she climbed in beside him, dazed.

"Rest, now," he said to her, as she nestled close and put her head on his chest, "an' just listen. All will be well, my Mina. All *is* well, ye just dinnae ken it yet." He wrapped his arms around her, pulled her closer against him, and kissed her forehead. *She's exhausted. It would be best if I can get her to sleep before we talk. She'll be able to follow it better.* The natural tide of magick on earth was beginning to seep into the room again, and Thomas was aware of two additional, small sources from somewhere in the castle: someone was singing a lullaby in the servants' quarters, and somewhere above in the east wing, two people were beginning to make love.

Enough to calm her. He pulled the song magick toward him and began to sing the same lullaby to Adamina in Gaelic. The air around his body began to vibrate, creating a soft purring sound. He directed the vibration through his touch as well as he stroked her back, and felt her heart rate and breathing gentle. He'd never used this particular skill on her before, as he didn't like bending her will to his whim; but in this case he needed her to have a good, deep sleep so that her body could finish processing the spell and hide her faerie traits. He was also exhausted himself, and could barely keep his eyes open to supervise her anymore.

"Oh, *Thomas*," Adamina sighed. "What are you doing? It feels so *nice*. So...*soothing*."

"Is called 'trilling', my love," he responded, kissing her head. "It is a Fae trait of mine to calm, to relax someone." He smiled. "The *Rugadh Dùthchasach* - or native-borns - of my house do it to calm their bairns, or to help with healing."

"Isn't everyone in your house native-born?" Thomas noticed Adamina's eyes were closing.

"Oh, not at all. There are those in the bloodline of the Great Queen, but then others ask to join the house. Other gods and goddesses, who may not be Fae at all. If they are accepted, we treat them like family, to a point." He ran his fingers through her hair. "Those in the bloodline, they can all sense each other's blood if we can get close enough. Find each other. Those that join, we cannot."

"So," said Adamina slowly and sleepily, "you can find Alex if you need to?"

"If I'm in the vicinity. Unless he wears a spell to intentionally mask himself, yes." Thomas sighed. "Family, as you know, is complicated. The most on-demand item on the Fae black market is an amulet made in the Field of Reeds that masks your blood from those in your family. Verra expensive. An' I see them all over Faerie. Must be attuned to a specific individual's blood, though. I...." He looked down and realized Adamina was sound asleep.

Thank the Goddess. He allowed himself to relax, to let the vibrations around her fade. He closed his eyes and sighed. Perhaps a day would come when he could fall asleep with her like this every night. It was the last thought he had before he, too, was asleep, and the wedding ring on Adamina's finger began to glow a soft blue.

-December 1, 1746-

Waning Moon

Branxholme, Scotland

The Laird of Branxholme and his guests were up before dawn. They had two wanted persons in their midst, and it was best to get them on the road before any representatives of Caroline Scott arrived. They had breakfast quickly and a short time later the party was headed outside, saying their goodbyes. Before they left the front hall, Edan had Saorsa look over the letter he intended to send to Killian and Anne as soon as the sun rose.

"It's perfect, Edan," she said, hugging him. "I'll be back as soon as I can. Thank you for everything." She hugged Toran as well, being careful of his crutches, and he wished her well. She gave Duncan a long hug goodbye, and then gave him one more. "That one is for Vika."

He smiled at her. *You can tell he's a good man by the way he smiles,* Saorsa thought. The smile reached everything from his bushy salt-and-pepper eyebrows down to his bearded chin, and his brown eyes almost disappeared when he grinned. "Your uncle would like ye very much, Saorsa Stuart," he said to her. "As do I."

Annag gave Saorsa a hug goodbye. "Merry meet, merry part, an' merry meet again," she whispered in Saorsa's ear. "Take care of yourself, friend."

Saorsa nodded. "You too, Annag."

"Saorsa," Mother Agnes said quietly, slipping her a bag, "Fia's been around, so I had no time to tell you before. The Aunties sent back information on Malphas just before we left the inn, and a few other things. And I gathered the items you asked me for. It's all in here." She patted Saorsa's hand. "Annag and I began building protections here last night. We'll keep working and look after Fia. Perhaps...perhaps there's something salvageable in her. Take good care of yourself, my girl." Saorsa gave her a hug and put the cross-body bag over her head and shoulder.

And then there was Fia, standing there, staring at the ground and twisting her rings. This wasn't what she and Alex had wanted for Fia. She thought of the night the three of them had done the bonding ritual at Ramsay House. "I'm doing my best," Fia had told them when they asked if there was anything they should know about her.

What if she is doing her best? And was? What if she really thought Faerie was her best chance at survival, and her decisions had been made from a place of desperation? What if Fia is actually deranged? If she can't help the way she is, does it mean she isn't deserving of compassion?

Fia had done damage. She had lied. She had betrayed. But she had also helped, and Saorsa wasn't sure how she would have made it this far without Fia's intervention. *She made me feel cared for when I needed it most.* She was a complex person, Fia. It was hard to tell if she was broken, or just pretended to be broken so her manipulations could be successful. *Does she care for me, in her own way? Does she care for Alex?*

Saorsa remembered what Alex had said about Fia. *Do you think I dinnae ken what it looks like when Fia's in love with someone?* She'd never asked Fia about it. If Fia was in love with her. She'd been too afraid. *Thomas the Rhymer told me to love. The Stones have told me to love. I am supposed to be the Flower of the West. West is the direction of love and emotion. Not everyone is easy to love, but I'm going to try.*

Saorsa took a deep breath. She thought of what Fia had said at the inn: *I genuinely wanted you healed and to go to Faerie with you.* Truth, or manipulation? *You won't be seeing Fia for a while,* she told herself. *So in this moment, just pretend that it was the truth. It's the loving thing to do. She can't hurt you any more right now.*

"Fia," she said, "Take care of yourself. Take care of the bairn. I *am* angry at you. I'm not going to pretend I'm not. But that doesn't mean I think you can't redeem yourself." She took Fia's hands in hers. "You are a smart and vibrant woman, Fia. I look forward to hearing from Mother Agnes that you have conducted yourself as an ally when I return." She gave Fia's hands a little shake. "Move toward the light, Fia Grace."

It was the best she could do, given the circumstances. Fia lit up like a bonfire on a Midsummer's night. "Saorsa," she said, "I *will.* I'll do as they say. I'll...move toward the light." She looked like she wanted to embrace Saorsa, or kiss her on the cheek, but then thought better of it. "I'll...I'll be working spells in your favor. Be safe."

Saorsa let her go and turned to Duncan. "Let's head out." There were two horses, saddled and ready on the cobblestones a few feet away.

"Head for the bridge," Edan said to Saorsa. "Your team is waiting for you there."

"That's Thor!" Duncan said, grinning, as he saw Saorsa's mount. He looked at Saorsa. "You're takin' *Thor* with ye?"

Saorsa nodded. "The team has my horse Bridgit with them. She'll be one of our pack horses until we get where we're going." She patted Thor on the neck. "When I find Alex, I want him to be able to ride Thor back here. He'll like that."

Duncan smiled. He admired this girl's unrelenting optimism. It reminded him of the Bonnie Prince. He could see why Alex was smitten with her. "Isn't Thor a wee bit big for ye though, lass?"

Saorsa led Thor to a mounting block and awkwardly scaled the tall horse with gusto. The onlookers couldn't help but smile at her determination. "Where I'm going, Duncan," Saorsa grinned once she was in the saddle, "*nothing's* too big for me." She watched Duncan mount a tall black stallion Edan had gifted him and settle into the saddle.

Saorsa had one more thing she wanted to do. "Here's where we part ways, friends," Saorsa called merrily to the assembled group. "Watch the drops and watch each other's backs. Long may you ride, and *biodh bhur sgeanan beannaichte.*"

"*Biodh bhur sgeanan beannaichte!*" Torin, Edan, and Duncan responded enthusiastically, surprised and delighted. *May your knives be blessed.* It was what Vika said to her team when they parted ways.

"Followin' in my sister's footsteps, eh, Stuart?" Duncan called. "She'll be pleased as punch when I tell her." He pivoted the stallion around to head in the opposite direction from Saorsa. "But do you ken the *other* ritual she has when she and a certain friend of ours go *their* separate ways?"

"That I do!" Saorsa called to him, turning Thor toward the path to the bridge.

Duncan looked over his shoulder. "Then...*na bi a' smaoineachadh cus*, Stuart!" he shouted playfully at Saorsa. *Don't think too much, Stuart.*

Saorsa giggled and saluted him with her middle finger. "Fuck you, MacLeod!" she yelled cheerfully. Duncan threw back his head and laughed, and they rode off in separate directions, leaving the safety of Branxholme behind them.

………

Edan had done well, especially considering how little time he'd had. After Mother Agnes, Fia, and Annag had retired to their beds the previous evening, Edan had walked into the sitting room where Saorsa and Duncan were talking.

"I'm sorry to interrupt," he smiled at them wearily, "but if the two of you could come into the study for a moment, I would like to introduce Saorsa to the leader of the team that will be heading west with her." Saorsa and Duncan followed Edan into the study.

There was a man there, sitting with his boots propped up on a stool with his soles in their direction. Upon seeing them enter, he quickly put his feet on the floor and stood up to greet them. But not fast enough that Saorsa didn't notice the man's boots had runes and symbols painted in white on the soles; Saorsa thought some looked familiar. *He's pagan. I'd bet my amulet on it.*

"MacAsgaill!" Duncan roared joyfully, recognizing an old friend. He moved quickly forward and embraced the man, wrapping him in an enthusiastic bear hug before pounding him several times on the back. Edan let them finish their rambunctious greeting before continuing.

Edan smiled. "Saorsa, this is Rune MacAsgaill. He's been an advisor and guard for the Scotts for many years, as well as a good friend. He was Adamina's escort of choice on many of her journeys and Clan MacAsgaill has a long and storied friendship with Clan MacLeod. I can think of no one better to lead your team on your journey."

Saorsa looked up at the broad-shouldered man. He was Edan's age and very fit, with strawberry-blond hair that was shaved very short on the sides and braided back in the center. He was bearded and blue-eyed, with tattoos on his neck and the back of his hands. He was taller than both Duncan and Edan, most likely matching Alex for height; and Saorsa could tell from the way he stood that he was made of solid muscle. *A Viking. He looks like something from a book on Vikings. Or, rather, people who WENT Viking.* And based on the symbols on his hands and the bottoms of his boots, he most likely worshiped like one as well. Saorsa inclined her head toward him and smiled.

"Rune, this is Miss Saorsa Stuart." Edan continued. "Although, it may be best to use a different surname as you travel, for obvious reasons."

"I'm most pleased to meet you, Miss Stuart," Rune said, giving her a quick bow. Saorsa was surprised; she had expected from his stature and the way he greeted Duncan that he would be a loud and boisterous man. Instead, his voice, while it had a rough, gravely tone to it, was pitched low and soft. *Either he is adjusting himself so he doesn't bowl me over, which is good, or he's the sort of man who doesn't need to be loud to be listened to, which is also good.* Saorsa thought of Alex; Rune's demeanor echoed a similar quiet alertness. She liked him.

Everyone was taking a seat, so Saorsa did as well. "Rune is...ah, not a Christian," Edan said, gesturing. "I thought having one of your own along might make you more comfortable, considering the circumstances."

Saorsa smiled. She was pretty certain Edan didn't know the difference between one type of pagan and another; Rune most likely worked in the Norse tradition, which Saorsa didn't know overly much about besides what few things she'd read in books. But they would understand each other; Edan had done just fine.

"I have assembled a group of four to travel with us, who practice as I do," Rune said, smiling at her. "Edan had informed me that we will need to watch for both physical enemies and those that may wish to harm us in a...more spiritual way."

"Yes," said Saorsa, and felt her stomach flip over. *What is that feeling? Why do I suddenly feel ill?* She paused for a moment and took a breath, and it came to her what it was: *I'm headed west. To get Oona. And I'm being escorted by a man who isn't Alex.*

The stomach flip turned into a wave of nausea. *Where is he? Is Alex in pain? Oh, Goddess, watch over him.* She could feel the blood rush from her face; she could see that all three men were suddenly sitting a bit forward in their seats, concerned.

"Saorsa? Are you alright?" Edan said gently.

"Excuse me for a moment. I...I feel a bit unwell." Saorsa stood up, and the room seemed to tip. She staggered forward and found herself being held upright by a man who looked like an earth-bound version of one of the inhabitants of Asgard.

"Stødig, stødig der," Rune said calmly in Norwegian. Saorsa didn't understand him but inferred that he was telling her *steady*. She found herself looking at the piercing blue of his eyes, so blue they were almost unnatural. And then her feet went completely out from under her as he picked her up, and the next thing she knew he was carrying her as Edan and Duncan directed him to a nearby bedroom.

"I'm fine," Saorsa mumbled, but in truth she wasn't. *I haven't had a rejuvenating night's sleep in a very long time. And I don't know when I'll ever have one again.*

She felt Rune pivot her so that her feet wouldn't hit the doorframe as they entered the bedroom. A moment later she was looking at the underside of a canopy as her bearer placed her gently on the bed. "Edan, I'm *fine*," she called as she saw Edan leave the room. He went to see if Mother Agnes was still awake and could help.

"I'll get ye some water, lass," Duncan offered, and she saw him leave the room as well. And now she was lying on a bed alone with a man who looked like a woodcut of a Norse god. To her surprise he pulled a chair up to her bedside and sat down. He leaned forward and looked at her intently, one elbow on the sculpted oak arm of the chair. She looked back at him, wide-eyed, as he collected his thoughts quietly for a moment. *We've just met, and now I'm unwell. What could he possibly have to say to me?*

"Miss Saorsa," he said quietly. "Forgive me, I am a stranger to you, but I am also a very direct man." Saorsa tried to place his accent; it seemed slightly Scottish, but something else as well. *As though English might be his third or fourth language, and he is working to enunciate the English correctly.* "I think I may understand a bit of your trouble, and perhaps I can help."

Saorsa looked at him out of the side of her eye, skeptical but also curious. *I have said exactly one word to him, and he's going to diagnose me? What is this?*

Rune looked at her seriously. "Edan has told me how you were traveling west with his brother. I have not had the pleasure of meeting Alexander, as he was away in France when I began my tenure with the Scotts. Then he went to war, and became an outlaw. But I have heard much of him from Lady Scott and Edan, and from Duncan as well." He shifted slightly in the chair. "Edan has told me we are going to collect a child that means very much to you and Alexander. That you had hoped to be making this journey *with* Alexander, but now things have changed. You must be worried for him, *Min Dame*, and saddened that he will not be with you to retrieve the child." He sighed. "I pledge to do everything I can to alleviate as many of your worries as possible on this trip, Miss Saorsa. And I recognize your grief, and grieve with you. I will make an offering to Allfather for the safe return of your loved one." He smiled apologetically at her. "I think maybe you have something similar in your tradition. Maybe Dagda? Or Cernunnos, The Green Man, eh?"

Saorsa stared. She could feel her nausea receding.

"My team and I," Rune continued, "we know we are a poor replacement for the one who is family in your heart. And to make it worse for you, we are but five men. That is why on the way to Fenwick, I have asked Edan's permission to visit someone who has ridden with us many times. She and her husband are powerful healers, *Min Dame*. If I tell them of your quest, I believe she will agree to accompany us for some time and help you." He smiled warmly at her. "Then there will be a wise woman along, for your company."

Saorsa suddenly was much more focused. *A female healer? Coming along to help?* Saorsa felt a burst of happiness, and then a moment's hesitation. The last woman she had counted on for help had gotten Alex kidnapped. But she took a deep breath. *Let her be more of a Vika then a Fia.* "What's her name?" Saorsa asked.

Rune's smile grew. "She goes by Willow, *Min Dame*," he told her. "And she carries a light most bright."

Saorsa looked up and realized that Edan, Mother Agnes, and Duncan were standing quietly and patiently by the foot of the bed. She'd been so engrossed in what Rune was saying - and his shockingly accurate appraisal of what ailed her - that she hadn't heard them come in. Duncan moved up on the opposite side of the bed from Rune to hand her a glass of water.

Saorsa sat up and gratefully took the glass from Duncan. "I'm...sorry," she said to those gathered around her. "I just...I think I'm just overwhelmed, a bit." She drank some of the water, and Duncan took the glass and placed it on the bedside table.

Duncan sat down on the bed next to her and to her surprise, took her hand in his. She heard him clear his throat. "Saorsa," he said to her kindly, "I want ye to ken...well, I'm sure *all* of us want ye to ken...that you're not doin' this alone. Alex is a brother to Edan, an' like a brother to me as well. An' he's a friend to Mother Agnes now too. An' Vika, well, she'll be up here soon, along with Alex's brothers in arms. So we dinnae want ye thinkin' that you're goin' into this journey alone. It isnae just your fight. It belongs to all of us, so even when ye cannae see us standin' beside ye, *we still are*."

Saorsa took a deep breath. "I miss him, Duncan. And I feel responsible for what happened to him. If only I'd listened, if only I'd *seen*...."

Duncan waved away her declaration of guilt. "Saorsa, ye cannae think that way. I could say that if I'd never recruited Alex for the uprisin' that he wouldn't be a wanted man right now."

"I also didn't see Fia for what she was, and perhaps I should have," Mother Agnes added.

"There are a thousand things I could've done differently," Edan said, shaking his head, "and perhaps any one of them would have resulted in a better outcome. I could've told Anne and Killian that I had doubts about Fia riding out with you. But I didn't."

"Regret does us no good, ye see," Duncan said, patting Saorsa's hand. "But havin' family *does*. That's what Alex, Adamina, Edan, an' Rune are to me and Vika, an' so you are too. Mother Agnes raised ye, an' so she's with ye, in your heart. Ye dinnae ken your father, or much of your mother; but blood is not all that makes family, ye ken. So dinnae ride out tomorrow thinkin' you're alone." Saorsa bit her lip, trying to contain her tears.

"We're goin' to find him, an' your mother, an' get them back," Duncan said. "I got out. Adamina got out. Maria Stuart and Alex, they will too."

………

Once she'd recovered her energy, they left, riding west to get Oona. *Duncan was right. Faerie might have powerful houses, but here on Earth I am building one of my own. Alex. Mother Agnes. Annag. Duncan. Vika. Toran. Edan. Father Andrew.* She looked over at Rune, who smiled at her from atop his horse. *Maybe him too. And maybe a woman called Willow.*

They had about three and a half days of riding in front of them. The rest of Rune's team included Aeric, Olav, Trig, and Eske. They were efficient, smiling, and courteous men, if somewhat quiet. Like Rune, each sported an extremely tall and broad physique; they looked as though they spent most of their time carrying tree trunks around for fun. Eske in particular was *huge*; Saorsa felt like a doll next to him. The men all spoke English in her presence save for Trig, who appeared to speak only Norwegian and French.

"Aeric's my cousin," Rune had explained. "Olav, he's my brother-in-law, but we were friends before he married my sister. Trig's from Norway and is a friend of Olav's, and…" he grinned and pointed to Eske, "I met Eske at a pagan gathering on Skye fifteen years ago. Came up to me, roaring drunk after winning a stone-lifting contest. He said, and I quote, "A thunder-bear told me to drink with you." I decided it was in my best interests not to piss him off and it turned into one of the best conversations of my life. He doesn't look like a philosopher, but he is. And he's ridden with me ever since. People call him *Veggan* when we go to Norway. It means 'The Wall'."

All of the men were enthusiastic when Saorsa explained that the horse she was riding was named Thor. Saorsa was fascinated by Eske's mount, who was even bigger than Thor.

"He's called Fjell," Rune explained, gesturing to the enormous white horse with four black stockings and gray mane. "The name means 'mountain'. He's part draft horse, we think." He laughed. "He's a big lover is what he is. When Eske takes him into a town, all the ladies gather around to pet him." He grinned. "That's how Eske gets all his girlfriends." He laughed again. "It takes a brave woman to bed Eske. One wrong move and you get a crushed bone." Eske, who had been listening, grinned and thumped himself on the chest.

Rune didn't mind talking as they rode, something Saorsa was unused to after riding with Alex. He kept up a pleasant stream of conversation whenever she showed interest in it, and Saorsa found herself learning much from him.

"Can you tell me about the Uprising?" she asked him after lunch on the first day, when she realized he possessed an in-depth knowledge of politics and history. "I…well, I missed it." She paused. "And since my family was at the heart of it, I should probably understand what happened." She shook her head. "Alex told me some, but there are a lot of holes."

Rune nodded and smiled. "What many don't understand is that the uprising was not just a Scottish versus English dispute. The Dutch, French, Spanish, Prussians…all the royal houses of Europe were involved. It was not just Scots fighting the English at Culloden. There were Scots and English on *both sides*. The Uprising had causes and effects all over Europe, and in America too. And, I fear, it may be the death of the Highland culture."

For the next hours Rune explained politics among the royal houses of Europe, and Saorsa listened, fascinated, asking questions as they went. When Alex talked about the Uprising, she saw his pain talking about it; it was too close, too personal for him. With Rune she didn't have that worry, and he seemed glad to be talking.

That night they stayed at a large, one-room cabin that Duncan sometimes used as a safe house. Saorsa was glad to get out of the cold, and before long Rune's team not only had the horses stabled and the fires built up, but had performed a ritual of protection on the property and set up a watch schedule. The men gave Saorsa the one large bed in the cabin and moved the dressing screen to its foot so she could have some privacy; they settled themselves on straw mattresses on the floor against the opposite wall. It turned out that Trig was a marvelous cook, and Saorsa filled her belly with bannocks with melted cheese and herbs, a thick smoked ham and potato stew, and a bottle of sweet cider. The men sat up talking, but Saorsa was exhausted, said her good nights and retreated behind the dressing screen to bed.

But she couldn't sleep. When she'd traveled with Vika and her crew, she'd often fallen asleep where she could hear men talking as she dozed, but her ears had always been focused on finding Alex's voice in the conversation. Now her mind continually searched for the low tones of his voice or the sound of his quiet laughter, and the absence of them twisted her awake time and time again.

Where is he right now? Is he in pain? Is he lonely? The lack of him felt like a living beast, breathing down her neck, taking up space in her mind. *Is he thinking of me? Of how I failed him? And his Faerie half? The leth dhia is out, they had said. Where has he gone? And why didn't he tell me he could free himself?* Saorsa stared at the ceiling. *Lost. I've lost them both.*

She must have fallen asleep eventually, for she dreamed. She was standing in an empty room. She recognized it as the room where they'd found the ceremonial circle at Buccleuch. In Thomas' tower.

Adamina Scott stood to her right. "Thirty years," she said to Saorsa sadly. "Thirty years I've waited for him, seeing him just a day or two at a time." She turned to Saorsa, her eyes full of anguish. "But Thomas could never stay. And I've been so, so alone."

Saorsa heard someone behind her and turned. *My mother. Maria.* She was weeping. "William thinks I'm dead, doesn't he? Is that why he didn't ever come for me? I waited. I'm *still* waiting."

Saorsa didn't know what to say. "You're doomed, just like us," Adamina whispered. "Thomas split my baby boy in pieces and took parts of him away! Took him away! We're doomed to love just *parts* of men!"

"Memories and shadows!" moaned Fia, who suddenly appeared in front of Saorsa. "My first husband is dead! And my next may be too! And the faeries...they'll come! They'll come for my bairn, and there's no one to help me when they do!"

Saorsa was terrified. "No!" she shouted at the women. "No! I'm not going to lose Alex! I'm going to find my mother and my father!"

"Cuimhneachain agus faileas! Cuimhneachain agus faileas!" came a chorus of wailing, keening voices from all sides. *Memories and shadows! Memories and shadows!* Saorsa blinked, and now the tower was filled with sobbing women, tearing at their clothes and pressing in from all sides. "My son! My husband! My brother! *All dead on the moors!*"

"Leave me alone!" shrieked Saorsa, trying to push her way out of the mob. "Thomas! William! Alex, *where are you?*" She was screaming now as the women's hands began clutching at her. "Alex! *Alex!* Help me! Come back, *come back!*" She somehow broke free, shoved her way through the crowd and raced through the doorway and up the stairs to the top of the tower. The women pursued her, shouting. Saorsa tore up the stairs, stumbling on her skirts as she ran, and burst onto the roof.

Bedlam. There was the sound of armies clashing in the air. Saorsa ran to the railing and looked at the ground below. Every inch of the landscape was covered with men fighting, and she stared in horror as men died right in front of her. The battle stretched to the horizon in all directions. She screamed again and covered her eyes.

And then she was on the ground among them, in the thick of battle. She had never experienced anything like this before. It was...senseless. It went against everything she knew to be human. Men cutting down men, and then moving on without pause. "Stop!" she bellowed, but no one would listen.

And then she saw him. Alex. Moving to meet a red-coated opponent and she watched as he dispatched that first opponent, and then a second, and a third. He was fast and graceful, and as far as Saorsa could see, the only thing that looked like balance and order among the chaos. She ran toward him.

But then a bullet tore through his shoulder, and then a second hit him in the hip. He gasped in pain and dropped his sword and fell, and the rest of the combatants vanished.
Then she was back in that wood from just a few nights ago, and he was lying on the frozen ground, a mangled wing extended out to the side, torn and bruised and bleeding. And as she called for him, reached for him, she felt the agony of it all again.

She was crying now, just like the women in the Tower. Desperate. Afraid. Lonely. Frantic. All she wanted was to reach him, to touch him. To somehow bring him back. But as she took her final steps toward his lifeless form, she felt a pair of hands grab her shoulders and restrain her. She fought them with all her might.

"Min Dame! Wake up!" she heard a voice say. "You're in a night-haunting, come away from that place! Come back to us here!" She was sitting on her bed in the cabin, and Rune was there, shaking her gently awake while his companions stood back, concerned looks on their faces.

"I have to get to him!" Saorsa cried, her face wet with tears. "I have to...," she stopped as she finally remembered where she was. She must have awakened every man in the room. "Oh," she said, wiping her eyes. "I'm...I'm *so* sorry." *But Alex is still not here.* Her weeping began anew.

Rune pulled her toward him and wrapped his arms around her. "I am so, so sorry for your loss, Saorsa," he whispered, patting her on the back. "The dream, it is over now. And it is clear we must do more to protect you." He looked up at Olav. "Some incense, the salt, and the chalk, brother. We must shield this bed where she sleeps."

Rune stayed with Saorsa, his arms around her, letting her cry herself out, feeling her shake as the emotions she'd been carrying ran rampant through her body. She saw the men starting what she assumed was a warding ritual in the Old Norse way, inscribing runes on the wood floor and drawing a circle around her bed. And although their tradition was different from hers, she recognized the elements of it, and felt a profound gratitude for these men, who understood that not all enemies come from the outside.

The Bishop's House, Northern England

Thomas felt Adamina stir next to him and opened his eyes. It was not yet morning, and the room was dark, save for coals smoldering in the two fireplaces. He moved closer to her warmth under the covers and reached up to gently tuck her hair behind her left ear.

Fae. She still showed Fae characteristics. He was willing to bet her pointed teeth and tongue were still there as well. *This should have faded. How could I have been so wrong?* Well, in the first place, he'd never actually performed this spell before. And in the second...Adamina was *clearly* a rarity in terms of the way magick affected her.

And three. There's only one half-blood Fae from the eastern tribe left in existence. And few get close enough to glimpse her, let alone study her. He suppressed a groan. He was going to have to explain a lot to Adamina, and all of it things humans were not allowed to know. And he was going to have to be very, very honest about it.

Thomas could tell his new bride had opened her eyes because of the soft glow they emitted. "Thomas?" she said in the dark, "Are you ok?"

He pulled her close. "More than that, I'm with you."

She turned toward him. "I...fell asleep before we could talk." She reached up in the dark. "It's all...still there, Thomas. My teeth. And my ears...."

He sighed. "I know, my love. I can give you a charm to cover it, so no one sees it until it fades."

"But it *will* fade, won't it?"

He was quiet for a moment. "It should. But to be honest, I *could* be wrong." She said nothing. "I'm so sorry, Adamina."

She went very still for a moment, and then seemed to arrive at a decision. "Well...as long as you don't think I'm monstrous...?"

He pulled her close. "Oh, Adamina, *of course no.* If I may be honest, I...I dinnae mind seein' ye like this. At all. Ye look...Fae to me. An' that's beautiful too, in my eyes."

"Well, then," she said, adding a note of resolution to her tone, "it won't worry me either."

He grinned. *God how I love this woman! She always just carries on. I don't deserve the grace she gives me.* He took her hand and kissed the back of it.

"But I do want to know," she said softly, "*why* I have them."

He found her hand in the bed and squeezed it, letting out a long sigh. "Of course." He looked at her eyes glowing in the darkness next to him. "Long, long ago, when Ireland and this island were one with the continent, there lived four tribes. A tribe in the north, one in the east, another in the south, and one in the west. After they discovered each other, they traded together but each kept their unique ways and traditions. As time went on and the tribes grew in numbers, conflicts arose. The people wanted to draw borders between their lands, and soon war threatened."

Adamina moved closer, and he let go of her hand and rested his hand on her hip. "The leaders of the tribes wished for peace, not war. The wise folk knew that they all had had common ancestors once." He reached up and stroked Adamina's ear gently. "A meeting was called, and it was decided the wise men and women would rule together, uniting the tribes. They called this new nation the *Tuath Dé*, or Tribe of the Gods. Later, they would be driven from earth to live in a new realm and would be referred to as the Fae, but that is a separate story." Thomas took a deep breath.

"The original four tribes had similarities, such as the shape of their ears and the fact that their languages seemed to stem from the same root, but they also had different physical characteristics and abilities. The Tribe of the North, the Earthworkers, were skilled craftsman and farmers, and tamed beasts and wild things, and brought forth new species of plants to nourish and heal. The Tribe of the West, the Soulworkers, created unparalleled artists and musicians, who could sway emotion and access the World of Dreams. They were seers, mystics, and spirit guides." Adamina was listening intently.

"The Tribe of the South," Thomas continued, "had incredible magickal aptitude, and the ability to learn the magicks of other races. They were skilled in languages and communication. They could move energies at will. It is from this tribe that I am descended." He paused. "Traits of the southern tribe include wings and hands that can move and sense energies. Their houses are often named after birds. They are mages and magick users who use their lives to seek out rare knowledge. They were called the Dragonworkers, or sometimes Those Who Ride the Flame."

"They worked with the energy pathways that run between the worlds," Adamina asked, "didn't they? You told me to look into dragons and dragon lines when we first met."

Thomas grinned. "I was *tryin'* to give ye a hint about who I was, as I couldnae tell you," he said, ruffling her hair playfully, "but it took ye *four years* to even begin!"

"That's not fair!" Adamina protested. "The only thing I found on dragon lines was *in Chinese*. And I had to get it sent from China!"

"Excuses, excuses," he teased. She gave him a light, playful slap on the arm. "But ye are correct. We work with the dragons. More on that later." A long pause. "The traits you are seeing in yourself tonight are from the Eastern Tribe. The Galeworkers. They were the scientists. They created new inventions and pushed the boundaries of philosophy and thought. Exceedingly skilled at logic. The teeth, the tongue, the glowing eyes, the ability to strike forward at high speeds...these are all eastern traits. Their houses are often named after reptiles. House of Asps, for example." Another pause. "When the new peoples came and threatened the *Tuath Dé,* it became apparent that the inventions of the Tribe of the East were going to allow the *Tuath Dé* to prevail. So the newcomers did the unthinkable: they found a way to poison the strain of magick used by the Tribe of the East. And those with Eastern blood began dying by the thousands."

"Oh," Adamina breathed. "How...exactly does that work?"

"There are many, many different types of magick," Thomas explained. "Imagine that each one...is like a lake. And many are connected to each other by tiny creeks. But the lakes are all made of the same thing. The Men Who Came found and polluted the lake of the east. And once that worked, they did the same to the lake of the south. And those who worked my sort of magick, we began to die as well."

Thomas shifted his position in the bed. "Magick is in the blood of the Fae, Mina. It makes up an enormous part of who we are. The interlopers had some small capacity for magick, but it was different from ours. With our scientists dead and the poison spreading into the magickal reservoir of the mages, the *Tuath Dé* had only one choice: to flee earth. We went to a different world, the Otherworld, which is now called Faerie by those here. And the majority of the magick here became weakened, corrupted, or destroyed. The Fae cannae stay here for long or we weaken as well; our resources here are limited. As far as I know, only one of the original offspring of the eastern tribe survives to this day, and she is...well, not as she once was."

"Were you there when this happened?" Adamina asked. "When the Fae left the earth? And...were you ill? If you are from the southern tribe?"

Thomas smiled. "I was young. I remember the great magians, or you say magicians, dying by the score. My mother, an unparalleled magick-user, was able to save herself and several members of our house. It is one of the reasons why we are so strong now; we are some of the very few who survived, and we kept the archaic knowledge alive with us. But not enough of us survived to be able to keep the *Tuath Dé* safe here."

"So," said Adamina slowly, "The Men Who Came were not strong magick users, but they had armies. And they managed to poison the magickal sources for both the eastern and southern tribes. How did they figure out how to do that?"

"They had help," Thomas said quietly. "From a being we thought was an ally of ours. Who saw this as a means to his own ends and betrayed us." He shook his head. "It is why so many Fae dislike humans, Mina. They feel that this world belonged to the Fae, and that your ancestors drove us from it and took it for themselves."

"If my ancestors murdered your people and took your world," Adamina said slowly, "why don't *you* hate me, Thomas?"

He touched her cheek. "I used to dislike humans. *Immensely*. I willnae lie and say I havenae killed many myself. But over time, I became...more at peace. And then, *curious*. Humans are *fascinating*. And then, I couldnae help myself: I began befriending them. And loving them." He shifted in the bed. "It wasnae *you* who caused my people injury. You didnae even know about it. But many Fae feel differently." He paused. "There are strict, *verra* strict rules for interacting with humans, and the Fae that come here are censored and greatly weakened while we are here. It is why I can only come at certain times and am only able to stay for such a short while. I am...*perpetually* scrutinized for my visits here. Were I not my mother's son, and the mage that I am, you would never see me in this world." He shook his head. "The only way I am able to tell you all this tonight is I went to great lengths to shield us while we were doing the ritual. It broke the bonds on the censorship spells as well. But my work will soon fade, Mina, and then I'll no be able to speak freely with you again."

Adamina sat up in bed. "At Beltane...that first night we were together," she said, her eyes widening, "you made me say that I knew who you were three times! And you said...that if you'd been able to kiss me before, *you would have*. Was that because of another rule from the Fae?"

He nodded. "Aye. It had been noticed how...*attached* I was growin' to you. The Council didnae like it. I had broken the rules and come to see you without permission. Eventually they let me come, but only if I made a deal not to become physical with you." He laughed. "An' ye can see how well *that* worked out for them. Now the Deck of Crows has a human queen!"

"So, you found a way around their restriction?"

"Correct." He chuckled. "They know a lot of magick, but I may know *more*."

Adamina was quiet for a moment. "Thomas...if the eastern tribe is extinct, how do I have their traits?"

Thomas put his hands behind his head. "That's a verra good question, Mina. It means that at some point, someone from the eastern tribe had a child with a human. An' I was no aware that had happened. The blood of the south is in the Scott family, and the blood of the west has shown up strongest in the MacLeods and the MacDonalds. We've seen the blood of the north in the Bruces and then the Stuarts. But...I wasnae aware of the blood of the east bein' in this world once we left. *Ever*." He paused. "An' you have it *strong*, Mina. It came from somewhere, an' I intend to find out where."

"Thomas, you said there's a child of the eastern tribe still alive." He stayed silent. "Thomas?" She saw him rise from the bed, pull on a pair of trousers and run his hand through his hair. *He doesn't want to tell me*. She sat up in bed. "Thomas, what's wrong?"

He lit a candle on the dressing table and looked at her. "I just...I just need a moment."

Adamina was rapidly growing alarmed. She climbed out of bed and moved toward him, but he walked away and headed for the wash stand, splashing water on his face before vigorously drying himself with a towel. Adamina watched him as she pulled on her shift. *He's bracing himself for something. This is...a secret. A dark, dark secret.*

He turned to her as she walked up behind him. "Just tell me," she said quietly. "It will be alright, Thomas. It will." He was looking at her face, carefully watching her expression. He set the towel aside.

"Yes. There is one still alive. She's...no a pure Fae. But the closest there is. Her father was eastern Fae and a god, an' her mother was a human. It was a forbidden act." He shook his head. "But I am certain, *certain,* she has no had a child. So your blood must have gotten here another way."

"But we could still be related. I mean, *distantly,* but still related, yes? She could be an ancestor of mine. The same tribe...."

Thomas looked pale. "She's mad, Adamina. She's cursed. I am one of a handful of people who have sought her out in the last thousand or so years. An' Mina...I'm also the only one to see her who's survived."

Adamina had to know now. She *had* to. She sensed that Thomas' next words would be ones she needed to understand. To understand something fundamental about her story, about who she was. But that didn't mean she was prepared for it.

"Thomas, my love," she said, taking each of his hands in hers and interlacing their fingers, "tell me. I need to know." She looked up at him, her eyes casting a soft glow in the darkness of the room. "Be open with me, while there's still time, I beg you. What do you know of her?"

He looked away, and then at her hands in his, and took a deep breath.

"Medusa," he said quietly. "They call her Medusa."

Wild Willow Ridge, Scotland

Up. The horses were still headed up. The trail seemed to go on forever, and Saorsa bemoaned the fact that magick-users and soul-healers always felt the need to locate themselves in the most difficult places to reach.

She knew she was on the brink of collapse. She'd awoken this morning to find Rune and his men sleeping on the floor in a circle around her bed, and the floor and walls of the cabin in her vicinity covered with chalk symbols and various runes. They'd put every protection they knew, including their own bodies, around her. Saorsa felt grateful for their attention and care. But she'd still only managed about four hours of sleep, and after so many days of movement and grief and unrest she could feel her body starting to shut down.

If I'm going to do what I have planned, I need healing first. Alex had been her haven. She was going to have to find a way to create one without him. *And that right there may be the most difficult magick I have to do.*

She didn't remember finally reaching the top of the hill and rode right past the stone circle there without noticing it, too numb to commune with its energy. *I need a place to hide. To lick my wounds, and....*

"Whoa!" Rune shouted, dismounting quickly and running to Thor's side as Saorsa started pitching sideways in the saddle. "Saorsa!" The other men were there in an instant, helping him to untangle her feet from the stirrups and lower her gently to the ground.

She came to for a moment, looking up at him and blinking. "What happened?"

Rune shook his head. "You're not well. You are in desperate need of sleep." He looked over his shoulder and spoke to the men behind him. "Svend and Willow, their house is just ahead. She can ride with me." A few moments later Saorsa felt herself being lifted by Eske and put in Rune's arms. "Let's get her to the cabin, friend Thor," he said to the big horse. "There will be healing for her there."

Saorsa was grateful for Rune's support. She couldn't keep her eyes open any more, and she felt herself slumping back against him. *It's strange to be on Thor with him like this,* she thought. *As though Alex has been...suddenly replaced by Rune.* A moment later she was asleep, and barely stirred when Thor came to a halt a short time later. Eske lifted her from the horse and she heard the men speaking, but they seemed far away. She felt Eske put her down on something soft, and then she heard a woman's voice say, "He'll be saddened that he missed you," and then all went silent. *We're at the healers' house. We made it.*

She lay on the bed, three-quarters asleep, but one section of her mind still would not let her sink into oblivion. *You must be vigilant! They could take those you love at any moment, or harm the ones they've taken! You cannot rest! You cannot....* She heard a door open, and footsteps.

She managed to open her eyes, her vision blurring for a moment. A woman was there. Saorsa could only see her silhouette in the dim room. She was short of stature but energy poured forth from her in *waves*. Had Saorsa not been lying down, she was certain she might have been pushed backwards by the gentle force of it. It rolled toward her like a tide, lifting her, floating her, bearing her along. Washing away all the things she tortured herself with for a time, so that she could just *be*.

The woman lowered her hands. "Oh. I'm sorry. I thought you were asleep."

But Saorsa was desperate for the flow to continue. *I can think clearly with her moving that energy!* Saorsa cleared her throat. She needed help, and this woman had it. "No, *please*," Saorsa choked. "What you were sending...what you were letting come through...I need it, please. It's...clearing the smoke away."

The woman looked at Saorsa again for a long moment, and then nodded. She raised her hands in Saorsa's direction once more and the flow began again. "I'm just clearing the space around you," she heard the woman say kindly. "There's...magickal energies all over you. Symbols and banners and deep fissures. Remnants of past magicks. The fingerprints of ghosts. It's like...many different beings are trying to claim you, and they are all at war." Saorsa lay there, trying to find her breath the way she'd been trying to find it since she left Alex in Faerie. And, shockingly, *she could.*

"I can *breathe!*" she blurted. "Oh, Goddess, *there I am!*" The woman who stood at the foot of the bed laughed softly. Saorsa couldn't see her clearly; it was like she was looking at her underwater. But what she could sense was *light*. A star in the darkest of nights. A spark of hope that maybe, just maybe, Saorsa could surface from this exhaustion with her help.

"Close your eyes," she heard the woman say gently. "Keep breathing. I am going to keep clearing all I can away, and hopefully you can sleep. We can meet properly once you've rested." She said it all with sunshine in her voice. A strong warmth that sank into Saorsa's mind and nestled there. "This should keep away nightmares for a time."

Saorsa felt like each of her bones was disintegrating into fine sand, one at a time, and sinking into the quilt below her. *Release. Freedom. Space.* She sighed and became nothing but her slow breath. *I am open again. I have room to receive.* She fell asleep and the woman named Willow covered her with a quilt and crept quietly out the door.

Realm of The Morrigan, Among the Fae

Thomas was distracted as he moved through the portal into the Ways of Faerie. Morning had come too soon, and his hours with Adamina had fallen away, like sand through his fingers. They'd talked until the sun rose, and then had fallen asleep in each other's arms, exhausted. When they'd awakened it was nearly ten a.m. and there was much to do.

Adamina's Fae traits were still present. He had needed to enchant a medallion for her to hide them, and then he'd had to get her to Branxholme before heading back to Faerie himself. Once he arrived he would need an audience with The Morrigan, which would take time, and then he needed to look in on Alex before heading to the front once more. But all he wanted to do was sleep next to Adamina for about twelve more hours and then wake up and make love to her again.

"It's too bad you don't have more time," she had whispered in his ear once they'd awakened and he'd groaned upon seeing the clock. "Because, Thomas, if you set my body back to the day we met...well, doesn't that mean that physically I'm a virgin again? We could have...," she laughed, "given you the honor of being *my first*."

He'd knocked her gently backwards in the bed when she'd said that and pounced on her, kissing her neck and tickling her while she squealed and giggled.

"Next time," he said grinning, looking into her eyes and holding her close. "Next time I'm here, I promise, we'll make your *last* first time nothing but a distant memory."

Her beautiful countenance had become suddenly serious then, and she had put one hand on either side of his face.

"I don't want you to go, Thomas," she whispered. "I *never* want you to go, but this time is just...harder, somehow."

"Of course it is. We're just wed," Thomas smiled at her. "But think on this. You'll see Edan tonight. And maybe, soon you'll see Alexander too." He kissed her forehead. "I'll find a way to not be gone so long this time, Mina. I will."

She tightened her embrace, trying to remember exactly how he felt in her arms. "I love you so much, Thomas," she had said, her voice breaking. "Please, *please be safe*."

Leaving her outside the portal at Branxholme hours later had been gut-wrenching. A fierce wind had whipped her skirts as he put his arms around her one last time, pulling her into his embrace. She'd put on a brave face, as had he. They'd become accustomed to doing that over the years. But this time he was heading back to war.

"You stay safe," he had said to her, locking her in an iron embrace. "Tell Edan to send you to stay with your sister and Gil in France. Or head toward your island and take a ship to Norway or Ireland. Just get out of the Borders, my love. You're no safe here any longer." He paused. "And if Edan can get Alexander out somehow with you, so much the better." He shook his head. "The turning point has been reached. This cannae be your home right now."

"When you see our son in Faerie," Adamina had cried, "tell him I love him."

Thomas was crying now too. "I will. I always do." He rocked her against him. "An' you look after him here as best you can."

They had spotted the riders coming out of the back gate of Branxholme, headed their way. Thomas had smiled. *Someone in that castle had sensed their arrival.* He squinted at the castle proper and was surprised to see the subtle swirling magick of multiple layers of protection spells. *Human witchcraft. Edan has a human magick-user on his side.* This made him curious; as far as he knew, Edan didn't even know magick existed. Yet Edan was home; he could sense his presence inside the building, in a state of calm. *All is well in the house. Yet...something has changed.*

Edan's magick-user wished to keep the Fae out, obviously. Thomas was glad of it; he found Adamina's capture by the Crown highly suspect and sensed a Fae hand behind it all. *Good lad, Edan. This will help keep your mother safe.* He'd have to investigate this further upon his return; time was too short now.

The riders had passed the bridge. They'd be here in the old gardens shortly to escort Adamina safely inside. Thomas and Adamina were beyond words now, beyond *I'll miss you* and *I love you*. All he could do was hold her tight and pray she could understand what she meant to him. And then he'd gone through the portal. He sighed. *Back amongst the Fae.* Faerie no longer felt like his home; only Adamina did.

He noted that all the surrounding realms seemed to still be locked down tight. *What was going on?* Well, he'd made himself a shortcut to his rooms in The Morrigan's palace a long time ago. He walked forwards ten steps, raised his left hand, and focused. *There.* A section of the darkness on the ground in front of him receded, and a set of steps appeared, leading down. He followed them and at the base of the staircase, put his hands in front of him and pushed. A door swung away, and he stepped into his room. The passage and steps behind him dissolved.

No one ever came to his rooms except his familiar, who was elsewhere right now. He sighed as he took in the peaceful silence of the dark, orderly, luxurious chambers, and snapped the fingers of his left hand. Fires roared to life in the various fireplaces and all the candles sparked to life.

He didn't need to tell the Queen he was here. She would know. But before he spoke with her, he needed rest. A clear head would be important when making his case. He began stripping off his clothing, headed for a bath and bed. He had no idea of the chaos that had happened at the prison.

The Tower of London, London, England

"What *exactly* did you think you were doing?" demanded a hushed female voice. "I'm telling them you can't get out of bed yet to slow things down until we can talk more, and then as soon as I leave you make a liar out of me by *going and getting out of bed!*"

It was Laoise, and her usual sunny bedside manner had been replaced with that of a mother scolding a toddler. Alex could feel his ankle throbbing. He opened one eye and looked up at his nurse. She pursed her lips and cocked her head slightly and was giving him a look he'd seen on his own mother's face many, many times. He was back in the bed, somehow; he had no recollection of traveling there.

"I needed to see," he whispered back. "I have to get out of here."

"If you keep walking on that foot, you'll only make it *worse.*" Laoise pushed a small bag of ice carefully up against Alex's ankle, and he sighed as the coolness hit his skin. "Now, I am doing my best to gather information for the both of us, but you are only getting it if you *do as I say when it comes to your health.*"

Both of Alex's eyes were open now and he perked up. "What sort of information?" He looked around. "Wait, where's the guard?"

"I may have put," Laoise confessed, "a strong herbal laxative in his coffee. He's spending most of his time running up and down the stairs to relieve himself. If he comes in, *hush.*"

Alex grinned and nodded. "Dinnae mess with the healer."

"*Never* mess with the healer. A bit of advice you would be wise to follow yourself." Laoise crossed her arms. "The longer I work for this group the more suspicious I get of their motives. And for some inexplicable reason, I feel sorry for you, even though you are an aspect of what is arguably one of the most *terrifying* creatures I have ever heard of. So, you tell me why I should be on your side over theirs. If you convince me, you have yourself an ally."

She was the only potential friend he had. The door opened and the guard came in, took about four steps, cursed a blue streak, and raced back out the door. Alex smiled. Apparently she *had* dosed the guard so they could talk. But he honestly didn't know what to say.

"As I said before, I dinnae ken why they want me," Alex said. "I dinnae ken anything about *leth dhia* other than what they look like, an' that no one likes my Faerie half. My father, whose name is Thomas but has also gone by Michael Scott an' the White Wizard, is from Faerie, an' he did a ritual to split me into pieces when I was young. He works with the dead and is part of a clan called the Deck of Crows. An' I know my mother Adamina Scott was taken by the Crown for seemingly magickal purposes, an' that the Fae have tried to take...," he paused. He missed her so much it hurt to say her name.

"Who?" Laoise prompted him.

Alex paused for a moment, hesitant to reveal too much. *She knows more about the situation than I do, though. I'm in LONDON. I'm going to have to tell her some things in order to get more information.*

"Saorsa," he managed. "Saorsa Stuart. Charles Edward Stuart's niece. She's a witch. They tried to take her too. An' she has parts of a magickal amulet embedded in her skin...."

Laoise stood up so fast she knocked over the stool she was sitting on. "Say that last part again?"

"Saorsa. She an' her mother were imprisoned in Hermitage Abbey, an' Saorsa's mother is missing, an' both of them have parts of a magickal amulet in their skin that we think the Fae want...," he trailed off as he saw the look on Laoise's face. *"What?"*

Laoise grabbed Alex by both shoulders in a completely un-nurselike manner. "You said Saorsa's mother has the amulet in her skin too? *What does she look like?"*

"A wee thing. Long, blonde, curly hair an' blue eyes. Verra fair. In her late forties, I think," Alex said, confused. "Why?" Laoise let Alex go, and took a step back from the bed, her eyes wide. Alex pushed himself painfully up to a sitting position. "Tell me!"

"Downstairs," Laoise said, looking stricken. "Her body is *downstairs*. As in, one level down, *right underneath this room.*" She stared at Alex. "She's...not awake. It's like her soul isn't there. They've been having me do small surgeries to try to retrieve parts of the amulet from her skin. They told me a completely different story and said I was saving her life!"

"Oh, Christ!" Alex tried to get up out of the bed, but Laoise gave him a sharp shove that pushed him back down. "Are you sayin' *Maria's been here the whole time I have?"*

They heard boots on the stone landing just outside the door, and Laoise looked at Alex and hissed. "Asleep! *Now!"*

Alex went limp and shut his eyes as the door opened. The guard stumbled in, looking spent. "What's the matter with you?" Laoise demanded of the guard. "Why do you keep leaving your post?"

"Oh, mistress," the man moaned, "everythin' I ate the last few days is comin' out of me all at once!"

Laoise stepped back and feigned horror. "Oh *no*. We need to get a replacement here *immediately*. There's been cases of the bloody flux among the soldiers. Three that I know of died this week." She pointed to his coffee mug. "And you eat the same food and bunk with them."

The man shook his head frantically. "Oh *no,* what came out...it wasnae bloody!"

"Doesn't have to be. *Yet*. Could just be full of mucus, which you might not have noticed. Do you feel feverish? Have cramps?"

The man had run up and down the stairs so many times that he *did* imagine he felt feverish. "Well...yes." His eyes widened.

"I'm the healer here. I think you have the bloody flux." Laoise paused. "You don't have much time. You need to go see the barracks physician *immediately*. Don't stop for anything; I'll arrange to have another guard sent up." She raised an eyebrow. "Godspeed. I hope you survive."

"Thank you, mistress! *Thank you!*" the man shouted and dashed out the door.

Laoise sighed and shut the door behind him. "It will take them at least an hour to realize he's not up here and another guard needs to be sent." She turned around to find Alex sitting on the edge of the bed. "*What* are you doing?"

"I need to see her," Alex explained, panting in pain. "Maria. I need to see her."

"No. *Out of the question.*" Laoise put her hands on her hips. "You've been shot twice, poisoned, and have one working foot, to say nothing of magickal damage to a phantom wing. You're not *thinking straight*."

"I have to get her out of here," said Alex. "For Saorsa. I need to get us *both* out of here."

Laoise crossed to the bed and sat down on the bed next to him. "Listen," she said. "We don't have any plan. You're a broken body trying to move another broken body. And to *where?* Even if you got Maria out of here somehow, *you are in the center of London*." She put her hand on his arm. "I understand you are upset. But you need to think more before you do anything."

Alex laughed. He wished Vika had heard Laoise say that. He looked at Laoise's face and his eyes narrowed. "What do *you* ken about the situation?"

Laoise looked away. "Less and less, it seems. My employers claim to be associated with a powerful healing center in Faerie. They said the people I heal here must be kept here because the magick they've encountered is too corrupted to take into Faerie. I'm supposed to pull out the magick out to be studied and heal them, or heal them to the point where a more experienced magick-user can take a look." She looked at him closely. "They said you were someone *completely* different, and that your mind isn't right. But you seem...sane enough to me." Her eyes went to the door. "They don't know we've spoken. They claim the guard is in here to make sure you don't attack me. They said *nothing* about *leth dhia*. If they had, I probably would have headed for the hills. You realize you're the story parents in Faerie use to get their children to be good. Do as you're told or the *leth dhia* will get you."

"Tell me," said Alex, "what ye *do* ken about *leth dhia*."

Laoise shook her head. "Not much. Just stories."

"I want to hear them."

She sighed. "This place has more magickal shields on it than The Morrigan's throne room, so I imagine no one in Faerie can hear me telling you this. The Fae are at war. And they have been for about a year and a half." She paused. "And some say we're *losing,* Alex." He watched her, listening intently.

"The Council who rules us tells us everything is in hand. That our generals cannot be beaten, that sort of thing. But some who actually return from the front say differently. They say our allies are falling, and we'll be next. That we may lose Faerie the same way we lost this world. The vast majority think everything is fine. We've been in wars before. But others, some of whom have highly-ranked loved ones at the front and are perhaps in a position to know, think differently." She paused. "And they are looking for a solution."

"Which is?" Alex said slowly.

Laoise stood up and began to pace nervously. "My uncle, he's a highly-placed Fae commander. He told me this. You are part of a creature called a *leth dhia*. There have only been two who survived into adulthood and *both* started wars, splitting themselves into pieces to command *all fronts* of the war at once. They were hell-bent on domination and *extremely* powerful, and as they could communicate instantly across worlds there was no matching them. Their armies moved like one giant creature. The Fae barely defeated them both times. So *leth dhia* are outlawed. They're not allowed to live. For the good of all."

Alex looked at her intently. "How do they do it?"

"How does what do what?"

"The *leth dhia*. How did they split themselves into pieces?"

Laoise shook her head. "I don't know. And even if I *did* know, me telling you how to do what literally *everyone* in Faerie doesn't want you to do is probably a very poor idea. Alex, the only reason you're alive is because you've been prevented from operating like the other *leth dhia* did."

Alex stared at her, incredulous. "But I was allowed to. Live, that is. Why?"

Laoise nodded. "You are...different. Instead of killing you, you were split, and your parts separated from each other. I think it was because your house is so powerful. An exception was made. I was a healer in one of the royal courts not long ago, and I heard confirmation of my uncle's story. Your parts have been separated so that they cannot communicate. Because of this, you are allowed to live."

"My Fae aspect was in a prison," Alex said. "But now he's not."

"About that. There's a rumor one of my assistants told me this morning. Some say that your Fae aspect did not *break out,* but rather was *broken* out. That you couldn't have escaped the prison on your own. That the reason you were broken out was to be used as a weapon. To create a whole *leth dhia* again. One that could be used to command armies and win the war." She shook her head. "The Council would *never* allow that. They say *leth dhia* are uncontrollable. That you can *never* be joined, because once you are, you'll be chaos. You wouldn't fight for the Fae; you'd only fight for *yourself.* If someone did break your Fae part out, it's most likely a general gone rogue. One who thinks the Council isn't listening and is desperate to win the war."

"So you...," Alex swallowed hard, "your job is to...heal me so I can be joined with the rest of me, an' go to war? An' those who brought me here are working for someone at the front who's stopped following the Council's orders?"

"They want you for *something*," Laoise gestured, "and they said you need to be strong. So...I don't know for certain. But it's all I can think of that would explain why you're here and why they want you healed."

"Anything else?"

"Something you said before. It reminded me of a prophecy."

Alex shifted on the bed. "*What* prophecy?"

Laoise ceased her pacing, righted the stool, and sat on it to face Alex. "In the past year or so, a cult has formed in Faerie. As some of the Fae began worrying about the war, they started looking for saviors and signs, of course. That's what Fae *do*. And they are horrible, horrible gossips. Now, as I said, the vast majority are mostly unconcerned about the war. But some...," she sighed. "There are these two humans called The Lovers. They were blessed by a Fae queen eons ago, and they are reborn on earth, over and over again, always seeking each other out, their love undying through each incarnation. And sometimes, they have a child. There have been two children who lived, and both were incredibly powerful magick users who changed the course of human history for the better."

"Saviors," Alex said. "Aye?"

"Yes." Laoise. "Saviors. And they had a third child just over twenty years ago. Who was imprisoned but survived. Most Fae are aware of her. They call her the Darkflower." Laoise looked at Alex. "And...this cult claims she's going to save all of Faerie. There is a renowned seer who made a prophecy just a few months ago. It seems to allude to the Darkflower and claims she will save both domains, Faerie *and* human."

Alex frowned. "I dinnae see what that has to do with me bein' here. Or Maria Stuart."

"The prophecy *also* seems to suggest," Laoise continued, "that the Darkflower could command a united *leth dhia*. That he will become her...familiar. Or slave. It's a prophecy, so that bit is...unclear."

"So there's also a chance," said Alex, "that you're working for this cult, an' I'm bein' kept to give to this Darkflower." He shuddered. *The Violet Woman. She controls me at times. It must be her they speak of.*

"Yes," sighed Laoise. "There's a chance, but I don't think that's the case...."

Alex cut her off. "So, either way, I'm doomed. Go to war as a weapon, or be enslaved and be some sorceress' familiar." His jaw set. "If you think you're working' for *either* of these two groups, this isn't good."

Laoise overlooked his frustrated outburst. "My uncle, who is the smartest Fae I know, says the Darkflower is called that for a *reason,* Alex. The children of The Lovers all hold the title of 'Flower'. Flower of the East, Flower of the South. The Darkflower is the Flower of the West. The direction of *love.*" She looked at the fire in the grate. "My uncle reads the prophecy as saying the Darkflower doesn't *control* the *leth-dhia,* but loves him. That she takes on his darkness and redeems him. And so he listens to her *willingly.* And then his abilities can be used constructively."

"That's verra romantic and all," growled Alex. "But what proof do ye have?"

"Because of something you said earlier," Laoise said simply. "The Darkflower has an earthly name as well. Someone you obviously already care for. And her name is Saorsa Stuart."

Alex stared at her as he tried to absorb all this information. "So, do *you* believe this?" he said slowly to Laoise. "You believe that...the prophecy, where Saorsa - *my Saorsa* - becomes some sort of faerie savior? That she ends the war?"

Laoise took a deep breath. "I *want* to believe it. I like the hopeful way the prophecy can be read. The one where it's not so...dark. And you care for her, don't you? Saorsa Stuart? So isn't that evidence it could come true?" She paused. "But what we do know for certain is that those people downstairs have been lying to me. And the fact that the woman downstairs is Saorsa's mother, and you are sitting here, *cannot* be a coincidence. We need to figure out what is going on. These Fae are not here in London because you have corrupted magick. They're probably here to prevent anyone in Faerie from seeing what they are up to."

"Laoise," Alex said quietly, "I need to tell you somethin'. There's this woman - or Fae or daemon - what she is I dinnae ken exactly, but she takes control of me here on earth at times. Kills people. I wake up an' everyone around me is dead, and I dinnae remember doin' it." He looked away. "So, whatever ye think about Saorsa...someone else already has a hold on me. Is already using me as a weapon."

Laoise looked horrified. "But...you're just one aspect."

"Apparently it's enough." He looked up at her, distressed. "If I'm this deadly now...well, when I had Fae traits a short while ago, the Violet Woman used me to kill a hundred armed men. *By myself.*"

Laoise held up her hand. "What do you mean, *when you had Fae traits a short while ago?*"

Alex rubbed his temples. "There was this knife. From Faerie. When it was near me, I had wings and fangs, could walk in an' out of graves, an' could move energy. Saorsa was tryin' to take it back to Faerie. It was changin' me, an' it was changin' her too. Activating the amulet shards in her skin."

"No. *Impossible.*" Laoise shook her head. "You were *completely separated.* You can't hear or see or feel each other. Everyone knows that. And you should be completely *human* in this aspect. That's what those who rule in Faerie believe."

"Well, they've got it *wrong,*" Alex argued, "because you can see for yourself *I had wings recently.* That injury was no from bein' separated as a child, Laoise; that's from having' *actual fuckin' wings* a week ago!" Laoise stared at him, aghast.

"An', *furthermore,*" Alex continued, "the Fae need to find my father Thomas Scott or Michael Scot or whatever damn name he calls himself now and ask him, if he told the Fae I was in two pieces, *why did he separate me into three?*"

"Three?" Laoise said, dumbfounded. "How...why do you think that?"

"Found his spell book with the ritual in it. An' it says he was goin' to cut my soul *in three,* no two!"

Laoise was in shock. "That doesn't...there's *another* aspect?" She put her hands to her face. "All right. We need *help* here." She started to pace. "We need to reach someone in Faerie who can help. *Immediately.*" She stopped pacing for a moment. "You're *certain* the ritual said three?" Alex nodded.

"Because Alex...if I tell the Council this, and they bring your father in for questioning, and I'm *wrong,* my life is over. *Over.* He's...," her voice trailed off. "He's a god, Alex. And perhaps the most powerful practicing magician in Faerie. Certainly the most famous. They just call him *The* Magician." She paused. "And...he's a Fae general."

"You said before," Alex said quietly, "that the people downstairs may be working for a general who thinks the Council isn't listening. What if it's *him?* What if Thomas broke me out in Faerie, and arranged for my capture here, and works with the Violet Woman to learn how to control me? An' since he's the only one who knows about the third aspect, isn't he the only one who could put me back together?"

"Maybe he thinks once you're united again, you'd listen to him because you're his son," Laoise whispered. "Oh, clouds and stars, this makes *sense.* He broke you, so he knows how to put you back together. And once he does...well, if you don't listen, he can have the Violet Woman control you for him. And she's been practicing doing that, *right here on this island.*"

"He's just kept that third part secret, all along, in case he ever needed a weapon for himself," Alex spat. "For all we know he might use me not to protect Faerie, *but to rule it.*"

Their eyes met. Laoise wasn't sure what to believe. *Were her employers the enemy? Or was this leth dhia aspect in front of her trying to gain her trust so he could escape as his other aspect had?*

"No healing ceremony for the wing tonight," Laoise said. "I'll stall them. Tell them you've taken a turn for the worse so we have time to figure things out." She took a deep breath. "We're both stuck in this tower. If what you say is true, I need to figure out how to get word to Faerie." *They'll tell me not to believe him. That he is devious and deadly and will say anything to get loose.*

Alex's mind had already been at work during the last half of the conversation. "I'm findin' myself a bit tired, now," he said to her, wanting to be alone. "Do you mind if I say goodnight?"

………

Alexander Scott was alone in his room. The parade grounds at the base of the tower were finally quiet, and light from the waning moon created a glowing abstract shape on the floorboards near his bed. He'd tried to eat and relax in the evening, wanting to be well-rested in case he was successful.

There was no guard in the room. Laoise had complained that the constant in-and-out of the guards was disturbing Alex's rest and slowing his recovery. The new guard was assigned to stay outside on the landing.

Alex sat on the bed, staring at the moonlight on the floor. *Leth dhia.* Laoise had said they could split themselves into pieces to command armies. *Well, it takes more than three people to run an army. Which means there's a good chance three isn't the highest number of leth dhia aspects you can have alive at once.*

His father had split him when he was two years old. But if his father hadn't... *well, it stands to reason I would have discovered how to split myself, correct? No one teaches a leth dhia how to duplicate themselves. There's probably never been more than one alive at a time, which means they figure it out on their own. Which means I can figure it out on MY own.*

If he could do it successfully - make a *fourth* Alexander Scott - then perhaps that one would be able to escape. To reach Saorsa. To find a way to rescue Maria downstairs. Hell, what if he could make *several* of himself? All of whom could communicate without speaking. Who all knew how to fight as he did and could work together seamlessly?

Would it matter then if he died here, if another aspect of him lived on? Wouldn't they all know what he knew, and act as he did? Would anyone even be able to tell it wasn't... him?

He shifted his gaze to the fire, watching the flames consume the logs. But this idea...it had him nearly paralyzed with fear. He'd never been anyone but *himself* before; he couldn't fathom it. *If there's more than one of me...which one holds my soul? Or do any of them?*

Perhaps this had been the problem all along. He'd failed at becoming a priest. He'd failed at starting a family with Morag. He'd murdered men - hundreds of men - and been possessed by a creature who found death *amusing.*

And Saorsa. He'd bedded her out of wedlock. Put her in harm's way. And before her, had committed all sorts of carnal sins with others that he had then *lied* to her about. He'd *tried* to be good, but now he felt most at home with people who followed a decidedly un-Christian path. And all those prayers - years and years of prayers - just felt *unanswered.*

His sire was a necromancer. His mother had committed adultery to bear him. So now he was certain he understood. *I've had no soul all along*. His prayers weren't answered because he was *unsavable*. A creature beyond redemption.

He put his head in his hands. Nothing he had tried to do for the advancement of his soul had been successful because he didn't have one. That had to be it, didn't it? And then, shockingly, a new emotion: *relief*. Things finally made sense. *Leth dhia are damned. So I can just...give up that worry now. Stop worrying about sin because it's just in my nature.*

I can just do what I want instead of what I'm supposed to do. I cannot help but burn. But what do I want? Saorsa. He wanted her protected and to be with her. *And answers.* He wanted to know what was happening. And if Saorsa had made it into Faerie, she'd have those answers. *And freedom.* He was so tired of looking over his shoulder. And he sure as hell didn't want to be a mindless weapon or someone's familiar. *Power.* Enough to protect Saorsa and the others he loved.

So he was going to attempt it, then. Try to stop worrying about his soul and find a way to get *some* part of himself to Saorsa, by any means necessary. *But how?* He'd never heard a story of anyone doing this. *Think, Alex. Figure it out.*

What would Saorsa do? He pictured her sitting at the foot of the bed, her blonde curls framing her face as she smiled at him. He could see her resting there, beaming up at him in her shift and blue dressing gown, getting ready for bed. "So Alex, let's just walk through this. *Leth dhia* have faerie blood, correct? So this is an act of *magick*."

He shook his head. "Saorsa, I dinnae ken how to do magick."

She gave him a playful, exaggerated frown. "Yes, you do. You watch me do it *all the time*." She cocked her head and gave him a grin. "Remember when we saw you in the sphere at Buccleuch? When you were two? You disappeared from your mother's arms and appeared in your father's! That was *magick,* Alex! So...you've done it before. You've just forgotten."

He carefully stood next to the bed, gripping the footboard, and made his way painfully to his knees on the floor. Once he was down, he crawled over to the patch of moonlight.

"That's right," Alex's memory of Saorsa said cheerfully, following him to the floor. "When I cast a spell, what do I do first?"

"Ah...," he said aloud, "well, you told Fia that if ye dinnae have a knife, just to use your hands." He couldn't believe he was about to do what he was about to do: *perform an act of witchcraft by himself.*

"You're not by yourself, Alex, you know that," came Saorsa's reassuringly sunny voice from where he imagined her next to him. "What do I do next?"

"You...," he swallowed hard, "you greet the four compass points. North for earth. East for air. South for fire. West for water." He paused. "An' ye ask for protection."

"Go ahead," he heard her voice say softly. "I'm right here if you need me."

Alex knew where he was in relation to the Thames and used it to re-orient himself so that he was facing north. He tried to quiet the part of his mind that was shouting at him that he was going to hell. "Who do I talk to, Saorsa?" he asked her. "Once I cast this circle, who will be there to hear me?" His hands were shaking.

"Your ancestors," Saorsa breathed next to him.

"And...who *is that,* exactly?" He ran a hand over his head. "Who are my ancestors, *when there's almost none like me?*" It hit him like a bolt of lightning. He'd just answered his own question. *Half-gods are still...part-gods.* So...couldn't you call on them?

His ancestors were the other *leth dhia.* He had the old Fae gods on his father's side, and the Bruce clan on his mother's side - those were his ancestors too, but the ones he *really* needed right now were the *leth dhia* who had come before him. It was they who might guide him, and help him accomplish this task. *Are they still out there, somewhere?*

Trembling, he raised his hands and looked to the North. "Spirits of the North," he whispered, trying to remember what he'd seen Saorsa do, "aid me this night as I seek to walk this earth in a new way." He looked at where his memory of Saorsa sat, and she nodded encouragingly. He turned, "Ah...Spirits of the East, I ask for your help in finding and communicating with Saorsa Stuart, wherever she might be." *Oh, what am I doing?*

He shifted, aware of how bright the moonlight was. He raised his hands in front of him again. "Spirits of the South, may this magick I am attempting harm none." *Saorsa says that often.* He turned to his right. "An'...Spirits of the West, protect me an' those I love during this...whatever this is...an' keep us from harm." He shifted back around to face north. *I don't know what I'm doing. This is never going to work.*

He could see Saorsa sitting cross-legged on the floor a little way away. "Very good," she encouraged him. "You're doing fine."

"No, Saorsa," he sighed. "I'm about to...."

"Don't think too much, Scott," she grinned. "Just do it. Or, rather, *feel* it. Imagine power coming up through the floor and down from the moon. You are a rare and powerful magickal creature, Alex. *Act like it.*"

He took a deep breath and closed his eyes. *Believe. I have to believe.* "I call on the spirits of the half-gods who came before me. My ancestors. *Leth dhia*, if you are there, show me my birthright. Show me the knowledge that has been stolen from me." The words were flowing from him quickly now, as though they'd already been written, and he had been waiting his whole life to read them. "Guide me to the same power you once possessed. I wish to be here an' elsewhere, to make my own choices. Teach me to be what I was born to be, a creature of many realms at once!"

He felt a tingling in his fingers, and then a terrific power surged up from the floor, arcing the floorboards up and pushing him several inches into the air, as though a strong wave had risen under the wood. And then he became terrifically dizzy and closed his eyes as he felt bile rise in his throat before tasting blood in his mouth. The world went momentarily dark.

But now…he was *standing*. Standing pain-free, his ankle solid, his gunshot wounds healed. He looked down and… *what in the name of everything holy?* He had to suppress a scream. He was looking down at *himself,* lying unconscious on the floor. *I'm dead. Oh, God, I've killed myself.*

He crouched down for a look. He thought he detected a slight rise and fall of the chest on the body he'd left behind. *I'm…breathing, I think.* He couldn't tell for certain, and the idea of touching another version of himself made him nauseous. *Am I…still in there, too?* He had a frightening thought. *If I'm not in there…because I'm here…can some other spirit come along and use that body? Animate it?*

He was overcome with a desire to undo what he had just done. *I want to be one again! This isn't safe! I want to be….*

Something caught his eye. He turned, and saw a glowing portal to his right by the window. It didn't look like the one he'd seen Elen come through at the cave; this one was red and appeared to be made of flames. But it was a portal.

Saorsa. This could be a way out of here, which meant a way *to* her. If he went back in his body, he'd be no better off than when he started. He took a step toward the portal. *I'm whole. I can walk.* And then he was through, hoping he had made the right choice.

Wild Willow Ridge, Scotland

Willow had come back from her walk in the woods to find a crowd of familiar men and horses outside of her cabin. *Rune and his men. It's been too long since we've seen each other!* As Willow drew closer to them, however, she was hit with a wall of energy the likes of which she'd never felt before.

Chaos. Multiple energies, some ancient, some new, were slamming into each other in the space in front of her. *Something is wrong.* The energies were moving so fast she could recognize *none* of them. Before she could voice her questions, she saw Eske turn. He was holding a woman, either asleep or unconscious, in his arms.

Her, Willow thought. *It's all coming off her!* She'd had to pause then and clear the space around her so she could think straight. *That poor woman! To be the center of all of that…lack of balance!*

"She needs help," Rune said after greeting her when she reached them. "We are traveling and cannot stay but a short while, but she needs you. Her name is Saorsa. There's…well, more at work here than I can explain easily now."

"Bring her inside," Willow said, opening the door and gesturing for them to follow. "You all are most welcome here. Svend is away and will be for several days; he'll be saddened that he missed you."

Eske and Rune followed Willow inside as the other men began unloading the bags from the horses. Willow led them across the main room to a bedroom on the right side of the cabin. "In here." Eske deposited Saorsa on the bed, and Rune unhooked her traveling cloak and removed it, pulling off her boots a moment later. Saorsa did not move.

"Rune, she...," Willow paused a moment to try and sort out her thoughts. The energy coming off of Saorsa was growing again. "She is *coated* in conflicting magickal energy. I've never seen *anything* like this. What happened to her?"

"Exhausted," Rune said quietly. "And plagued by nightmares. In the past few weeks, from what I understand, she journeyed into Faerie, has had multiple encounters with spirits, and was exposed to a powerful magickal object from another realm for an extended period of time." He looked up at Willow. "And...she has had the shards of a magickal amulet of unknown origin embedded in her body since the womb." He paused. "And we believe she's being *pursued*."

"And she's a magick user herself," Willow said. "I'm sensing...a lot of earth energy here. And also...a lot of water." She looked up at Rune, who was nearly a foot taller than she. "Bruce? Stuart? MacDonald? MacLeod?"

"Stuart," Rune confirmed.

Willow shook her head. "As if she needed the trouble of that on top of everything else. Do you know what path she walks?"

"Hun følger gudinnen," Rune responded. *She follows the Goddess.* *"En heks."* *A witch.*

The rate at which the chaotic energy was building again was concerning Willow greatly. "Do you think she would mind if I tried to dispel some of this? Keep the level of it from overwhelming her?"

Rune shook his head. "She's desperate for help, my friend. She would be most grateful if you did."

Willow put her hand gently on Saorsa's shoulder. Her patient did not move. "Come out to the hall with me, Rune. I'm going to fetch some stones I think might help keep that energy at bay, and then I will come in here and attempt to move some of this off of her." She looked at the woman lying on the bed in front of her. *I am here to help you, Saorsa. I will do all I can.*

"Thank you, my friend," Rune said quietly. "There are many who wish to conquer this woman, I fear. And she has a great mountain ahead of her to climb."

Willow came in to check on Saorsa three times more and to clear away the foreign energies she found swirling in the room. And each time Willow came in, she found more questions than answers. *There's a huge mark on her neck – a symmetrical flower. Another on her back in the shape of a crow. Blue swirling spirals on her arms...those spells I have seen, those I recognize. But...there are cracks and fissures and a flowing energy as well, and the residue of attempted possession. The scent of ghosts. The amulet at her neck has its own energy. As does...that's a high priestess ring she's wearing. And then....*

Willow stepped even closer, reaching out with her mind. Sensing. *There's been a daemon near her. Recently.* Willow's eyes widened. *There's something in her bloodstream, I think. A more subtle energy. Attempting to work on her. And portals...my goodness, she's traveled in and out of multiple portals, and some of them were protected and left their own damage.* Willow shook her head. *Who IS this woman?*

The last time Willow went into the room the cat darted in, jumped up near Saorsa's shoulder on the bed, and made herself comfortable. Willow smiled. The animals always liked to be around when she was doing energy work. She decided to leave the cat in the room with the door cracked open when she left; the calm, steady presence of little Dreki would be good for Saorsa. The cat would keep Saorsa company and provide a bit of warm solidness in a world that was obviously anything but calm and warm for her.

"Goodnight, Saorsa," she whispered as she left her guest in Dreki's care, "sleep well. We will find out all about you tomorrow." She shut the door most of the way and returned to Rune and the others by the fire. She missed what was about to happen by mere seconds.

The little gray cat raised her head and stared. There was a shimmer in the corner of the room near the dresser, and then for a few seconds the air there seemed to be burning, the flames dancing around the opening of an invisible door. Startled, Dreki stood up and decided to make a hasty exit, running straight across Saorsa's stomach as she headed for the hall, jolting Saorsa awake.

Saorsa turned over, opening her eyes for a moment before closing them again. And then her mind processed what her eyes had just witnessed, and her eyes flew open again, staring at the silent inferno hanging in the air nearby. Someone stepped out of the burning portal, and it disappeared.

Saorsa sat up slowly, unable to believe her eyes. "Oh. *Oh, my Goddess!*" She had to be dreaming, or so tired she was hallucinating. This...there was no explanation for this. Alexander William Thomas Scott was standing six feet from where she lay, blinking as his eyes adjusted to the darkness of the room. He clearly couldn't see her yet. Saorsa threw back the quilt and leapt to her feet, her voice catching in her throat. "Alex?"

He acted as though he hadn't heard her. But then he turned, and his eyes widened, and she saw the smile she knew so well. The one he'd given her when he'd come to get her from Vika's. The one he'd given her after finding her in the woods after Seven Hills. He was smiling the way he'd smiled when she'd awakened after Hermitage. The smile that said *I love you* and *I've missed you so* and *I'm relieved you are in one piece.*

"Alex!" Saorsa gasped and raced toward him. But as her hand found his arm it passed straight through; she could see him, but there was no way to touch. They both stopped, shocked, and stared at her hand, which was only half-visible as the rest of it had disappeared inside his arm. They looked up at each other, confused and distressed.

"Are you...are you really here?" Saorsa asked him quietly. He pointed at his ear, and she could see his mouth moving, but no sound came out. He was here and yet...he wasn't. She could see him, just as solid as she remembered him, but sight seemed to be all they had. Saorsa smiled up at him, and his handsome face lit up again.

*We can't touch and we can't hear each other. But...we can use Vika's signs! The words are limited, but...*Saorsa moved to stand as close to Alex as she could, and he looked down at her, his eyes filled with longing. She raised her hands and signed. *Where?*

But he had had the exact same idea and was signing at the same time. *You-safe?* He was worried about her. She didn't know how much time they had, and it occurred to her that she wasn't completely sure *which* Alex was standing in front of her right now. *I think this is my Alex. I mean, my Earthly Alex. But it could be my Fae Alex as well. Or Fae Alex looking through Earthly Alex.* She realized she had a million things to tell him, and to ask. But first things first. *Yes. Safe. You-safe?*

He looked off to the side and made a face as though he wasn't sure. He signed back quickly. *Safe. Now. Heal. Friend.*

He has a healer friend, I think. And he's not in danger at the moment, but that could change. Saorsa nodded enthusiastically. *Where?* She mouthed "where" as she signed it.

The sign language Vika used during raids wasn't extensive, but it was enough. Alex made several signs. *South-south-English.* Then he made the shape of an L with his thumb and index finger.

Far South. England. L. Saorsa looked up sharply. *"London?"* she gasped and he nodded, seeing she had understood. "Oh, *Alex!*" She tried to put her hands on his chest without thinking. He looked down sadly as he was reminded of their inability to touch, but then conjured a smile for her. *Fine,* he signed.

This *was* her Human Alex, and he was trying to reassure her. And she realized she had information that could reassure him. *You-man!* She signed frantically, trying to figure out how to say what she needed to say. She'd never been on a raid with Duncan; she didn't know if there was a sign for him. Alex shook his head. He didn't understand. Saorsa tried again. *Vika-man-no-English-hold!*

Alex's eyebrows went up. *"Duncan?"* He mouthed, and shaped his hand into a lower-case D. Saorsa nodded. She put her thumbs together and, using the rest of her fingers as wings, mimed a bird flying away. *Free!*

Alex's face lit up, and she saw him close his eyes for a moment in gratitude. His shoulders dropped slightly in relief. *You-see-D-where?* he signed.

Saorsa didn't know the sign for Branxholme, so she did her best. She mimed having deer antlers, hoping he'd understand she was trying to be the deer on the Scott family crest. *Deer-base-safe.* Alex burst out laughing at her pantomime but he understood. *"Branxholme"* he said slowly, exaggerating the pronunciation. Saorsa nodded so hard her curls bounced.

He laughed again, and then he looked at her intently. He pointed to himself, and then made the sign for woman. *He's asking about his mother.* Saorsa nodded again. *You-woman-no-English-hold!* She repeated the flying bird pantomime. *Free!*

Alex's eyebrows shot up in surprise. *You-see?*

Saorsa shook her head. *Friend-see.* Alex nodded. Someone had seen Adamina escape. She saw Alex look away for a moment, and then back. *He knows something, but not sure if he should say it yet.* She went to put her hand on his arm and stopped herself. *What?* she signed.

He looked at her, his gray eyes searching her expression, and she let herself take in the shape of his face for a moment. *Every time I see him, I fall in love all over again.* But she needed to pay attention to his signs. *You-woman-love. With-me.*

Saorsa's eyes widened. "My mother?" she whispered. "She's in *London?* With you?" He was signing again. *No-see. Me-hear.*

Now he was making another set of signs. *Where-weapon?* Saorsa caught on. *The knife. He's asking about the knife.* She smiled encouragingly. *Gone.* He put his hand to his chest and mimed letting out a huge breath, and she laughed.

He signed again. *Vika-safe?* Saorsa wasn't sure, but she nodded. The next question felt like a punch to the gut.

You-friend-woman-baby-safe? He was asking about Fia. Fia and the baby. He had no idea that he was where he was because of Fia. That she'd betrayed him. And she didn't have the signs to explain. So she swallowed and nodded.

But now he was signing again, and it wasn't about Fia. *Love-you,* he signed. She could see his eyes were glassy with tears, and could tell from the heat in her eyes that hers looked the same. He was telling her he missed her, and it was all she could do to keep from crying. *Love-you,* she signed back.

He put his hand to his face now, covering his eyes. She wanted to reach for him, to throw her arms around him, but it would only serve as a grim reminder that they could not touch. Telling him about Duncan and Adamina definitely took a load off of Alex's mind, but there was so much more to say.

She signed *travel,* pretended she was rocking a baby, and mouthed the name "Oona." She didn't have a sign for where she was going after that. He nodded.

She asked, *How-you-here-now?* He held up his two index fingers and put them side by side, then split them apart abruptly, watching her face. Saorsa frowned. He repeated the action, trying to make her understand. And then she did. "You've...been *split?*" she sputtered, disbelieving. *Oh, Goddess! The Fae split him again!* But how? Her hands shook as she signed. *You-four-now?*

He nodded. Saorsa bit her lip. *Who-do?* A little smile formed on his lips, and he pointed to himself. Saorsa shook her head. No, he had to have misunderstood. Alex nodded and signed *me.*

How? Saorsa signed, dumbfounded. He shrugged, and then she saw something she never thought she'd see in her lifetime, Alexander Scott folding his fingers into the sign for the Horned Lord of the Forest and inscribing a five-pointed star in the air in front of him, the beginning of a spell.

Is he saying...? No. She stared at him, mouth open, and he threw back his head and laughed, delighted. *He's not telling me he performed witchcraft!* But now he was nodding enthusiastically and mimed swirling a wand in the air. Saorsa knew he couldn't hear her but couldn't stop the words from coming. "You...*YOU*...performed a spell? And...it WORKED?"

He'd been desperate to reach her. But if the spell had worked once, when he had no idea what he was doing, maybe it could work again! *What-you-do?* she demanded. *What-you-do?* He made the sign she'd made twice before. *Me. Free.* And Saorsa knew he was working on a plan.

The fire portal suddenly burst to life again next to the fireplace, and they both turned to face it. He had to go back. She couldn't help herself. She wanted to be brave for him. But he was in London, the very place he'd told her they'd execute him if he were ever caught. Tears began to roll down her face. "Can you come back, Alex?" she cried, even though he couldn't hear her. 'Don't go! Oh Goddess, *I miss you so much!*"

He was standing close to her now, looking down at her face, trying to remember everything about her. And then he kissed his fingers and pretended to place it on her forehead, trying to comfort her.

"I love you!" she sobbed, trying to sign. "I love you!" He nodded, and then signed back. *Love. You. Little. Bird.* And then the flames of the portal reached out toward him with a fire so bright she had to shield her eyes, and when she looked up again, both he and the portal were gone.

The Tower of London, London, England

Alex stood in the tower, looking down at his own body and shaking. He'd seen her. Found Saorsa and *seen* her. And learned Duncan and his mother were free and Fia safe. The relief he felt was not just mental but a profound physical one as well. Exhaustion did not begin to describe what he was experiencing. And then, on top of it, moving through the portals seemed to have sapped his energy as well. He could barely stand, and barely keep his eyes open. But he couldn't rest yet. He was still *two*. He needed to figure out how to join with himself again, then he could collapse.

He sat down heavily on the floor beside himself. Every muscle in his body was sore, as though he'd been through sustained strenuous physical exertion. He was having trouble thinking straight. *How do I get back into my body, Saorsa? And what just happened...that was all real, wasn't it?*

And then he laughed. He knew what she would do, what she'd showed Fia back at the inn at Melrose. The spell to ground someone in their body. It was worth a try. He took a deep breath.

"Ancestors," he said quietly, "I thank you for this gift you have given me tonight. It is time for this part of my journey to end. And so...," he looked down at the body in front of him on the floor, "the...the soul resides in three places. The head, the heart, and the belly."

He was going to have to touch his other self. Saorsa said you had to touch to do the spell, to bring someone back into their body. A wave of fear washed over him, and he couldn't explain why. *Perhaps once leth dhia separate, they aren't meant to be joined again. Maybe that's why I have a natural aversion to it.*

But he was out of energy. It was either move forward or collapse on the floor, leaving *two* bodies for the Fae to discover and imprison. He reached out to touch his own forehead. *Pain.* He wasn't sure if he cried out or not. A tremendous, searing pain in his head, worse than any headache he'd ever had. It felt like his brain had swollen and was being squeezed inside his skull. He gasped for air and then he *did* scream.

The door to the room flew open and the guard ran in. Footsteps outside the room and voices a few moments later. The pain was ebbing away now, but his whole body was trembling from exhaustion. He felt hands lifting him, and there was a ringing in his ears, then he thought he heard a voice he knew. He couldn't manage a complete thought. His skull felt shattered.

".... found him on the floor," the guard was saying. "He was screamin' like someone was *murderin'* 'im!"

Alex's mind emerged from the haze of hurt, his head still throbbing. *He only speaks of one of me! I must be....* Alex tried to open his eyes, but the light from the fire and the guard's candle was so intense that he was nearly nauseous looking at it. He squeezed his eyes shut, and then felt a cloth being put to his face. *They're trying to drug me! Knock me out!* Eyes still closed, he attempted to shove whoever was touching him away, thrashing violently.

"Whoa! *Whoa!*" he heard a man's voice say. "Hold him down!"

"Your nose is bleeding!" he heard a female voice say. "I'm trying to help you! Don't fight me!" *Laoise.* Alex stopped moving and felt her hand on his arm. "Easy, now," he heard her voice say as she tried to soothe him. "It will be fine, I'm here." He felt her hand pat his shoulder. "Steady now...you have a nosebleed, and your ear is bleeding too."

Alex swallowed and tasted blood. He was glad for Laoise's hand on him, for he wasn't entirely certain that he wasn't about to die. He couldn't open his eyes because any light made his headache worse. He heard her shooing away the other occupants of the room. "Can you open your eyes?" she said to him quietly.

"Hurts," he moaned, and felt something running from his eye that didn't feel like tears. *Oh, God, I think my eye is bleeding too.* "The light hurts."

"Move the dressing screen to block the light from the fire," he heard her direct someone. "And I need more cloths, a bucket, and some fresh water." Alex felt Laoise's hand on his chest. "What did you *do* to yourself?" she whispered.

Now his eyes were stinging as tears began to flow. "I'm tired," he choked, weeping. "Oh, God, *let me be.*" The fatigue in his body took over. He couldn't follow what Laoise was saying. Her voice sounded further and further away, and then it was gone altogether, as his conscious mind shut down and he passed out cold.

Wild Willow Ridge, Scotland

Saorsa stared at the space where Alex had just been. He'd been here. Actually here. And he had indicated that somehow things *she* had taught him had made it possible. *But London...oh, Goddess, he's in London.*

A little voice rose inside Saorsa's heart. *But alive. Alive! And...here, on this plane!* She recognized the hopeful thought and held onto it with all her might. *Hope!*

She wasn't certain what to do. Run out into the main room and tell everyone what she'd seen? Or...wait until morning? What if Alex could do it again? What if he learned from this experiment and could do it *better*.... Maybe they'd be able to hear each other next time. Saorsa took a deep breath. *This is good. Good. But you are on the brink of collapse. If Alex were here, he'd tell you to sleep, not try to communicate when you're exhausted.*

She climbed under the covers and turned on her left side, smiling as she remembered the way he used to hold her before they fell asleep. *Perhaps all is not lost. Perhaps we'll be together again.*

Branxholme, Scotland

Edan Scott found Mother Agnes in the study near her room. "May I have a word with you?" he asked, shutting the door behind him.

"Of course." Mother Agnes pushed aside some books that had been sent to her by Vika's Aunties. "What can I help you with, Edan?"

Edan didn't sit, too full of energy to relax. "Do you remember the messenger I sent to Buccleuch? To look into the shipment with the Scott sapphire? Well, I got an answer."

Mother Agnes folded her hands. "And?"

Edan began to pace. "I'm not sure what this means. When my messenger arrived at Buccleuch the staff working on the restoration had no idea what he was talking about. None of them remembered any shipment being sent to Branxholme by Alex. But after more questioning they tracked down a man named Collin who'd spoken with Alex. Collin was there to hear Alex tell Fia he'd send word of their engagement to her mother and send the sapphire here to Branxholme. But then after Fia left the room, Alex pulled Collin aside, pocketed Fia's letter, ordered the sapphire sent elsewhere, and instructed him to mention it to no one until after Alex and Fia had left." He shook his head. "What the hell was Alex doing?"

"Where was it sent?" Mother Agnes sat forward in her chair.

"That's the thing," Edan said, fishing a paper from his pocket and passing it to Mother Agnes. "This is Alex's writing, but I have no idea where this place is. And Alex asked for it to be delivered there by a very specific person. Gave Collin a sealed envelope, the sapphire, and a great deal of money to pass on, which he did."

Mother Agnes looked at the paper. "Do you have a map of the Western Isles?"

Edan nodded, headed to the bookcases on the wall, and returned with an oversize book of bound maps. "Have *you* heard of it?"

"I want to double check my memory." Mother Agnes stood and began flipping through pages. She paused, putting on her glasses, and peered closely at the page. "Here," she said, pointing at the map.

"Isay Island." Edan looked up, confused. "Off the north-west coast of Skye?"

"In Loch Dunvegan," Mother Agnes nodded. "It's also called Porpoise Island. There are two smaller islands with it, Mingay and Clett. Clett, of course, just meaning "rock" in Old Norse. These islands aren't big, Edan. Isay is uninhabited. Only seals live there."

He put his hand to his forehead. "*Someone* must live there! Why in the world would Alex pass off an insanely valuable family heirloom to someone to deliver to an island inhabited *only by seals?*"

Mother Agnes grinned. "My guess is your brother wasn't as taken in by Fia as she'd hoped. That gem has a faerie story attached to it. Perhaps as a partial Fae himself, he was suspicious of why she was so eager to get her hands on it and wanted to put it out of reach for a while." She looked back down at the map. "Say nothing about this to Fia. I wish Saorsa were here to look at this. If anyone understands the way your brother's mind works, it's her." She looked up at Edan. "Could we send a message to Saorsa? I think this is very, very important, Edan."

Edan nodded. "What do *you* think Alex was doing?"

Mother Agnes tapped the map. "This is MacLeod territory. Other than Vika and Duncan, has your family had any dealings with the MacLeods?" She shook her head. "This is no small journey for someone to make. There's a reason he sent it to that spot." Edan could see her mind working. "Isay. *Isay.* Didn't Olaf the Black live there in the 13th century? And Roderick MacLeod of Lewis' massacre was there, yes? Or was that somewhere else?" She looked at the map again. "I'm forgetting something. Isay is a decent size, about a hundred and fifty acres, if I remember correctly. There *could* be someone living there, I suppose. And there's probably some ruins. But...," her eyes wandered over the other islands. "Saorsa told me Adamina's mother had been from the Western Isles. Could he be sending it to a relative of yours?"

Edan shook his head. "My grandmother's long gone, and as far as I know, we've had no contact with anyone else from that branch since before I was born."

Mother Agnes looked at the fire. "If not Adamina, let's think about Thomas." She tapped the book. "Where would Alex have gotten the idea that Isay was a safe place for a faerie gem? We have to think like him, Edan. Had Alex shown great interest in this sapphire before?"

Edan shook his head. "Not that I know of."

"That green-coated mage...they burned Buccleuch looking for *something*," Mother Agnes stated. "What if Alex thought it might be the gem? But why would they want it now, after it's been here for so long and no one seemed to care? What are the Fae trying to do?" She looked at Edan. "Do you mind if I bring Annag in on this? She may remember something I don't."

"By all means," he nodded, and Mother Agnes headed through a door into the adjoining music room, where Annag was reading. "Annag. We need your mind in here, please."

They brought Annag up to speed, and she squinted down at the map. "I dinnae ken if this is anything important," the younger witch began, "but although I've never heard of Isay, I *have* heard of Mingay."

"From whom?" Mother Agnes demanded.

"Sister Elen. Well, I guess she's Elen of the Ways now. When she was first at the abbey, she told Saorsa and me a story about it. I was feeling' poorly and Saorsa came with Elen to my room to cheer me up. The three of us sat on my bed an' Elen spoke of Mingay. Said there were caves there that were enchanted. That the great Celtic warriors of old were trained by priestesses in them. Said there were more caves like them in Ireland, but that these were the only ones in Scotland."

Mother Agnes stared at Annag. "Are you certain?"

Annag shrugged. "As certain as I can be about bedtime stories from twenty years ago. Saorsa might remember. Elen told us several tales in the nights after too, an' always started with, 'As it was in Oweynagat.' I remember, Saorsa thought the word was funny, 'the great warriors were made in the caves of Mingay...' she shook her head. "But I think Mingay is just an' old English word for 'stone', so there's probably other islands named that. I could have the wrong one."

Mother Agnes looked up at Edan, triumphant. "No, dear Annag, I'm sure you're remembering right." She put her finger down on the tiny island of Mingay on the map. "We know where that gem is headed, I think."

"A cave on Mingay?" Edan asked. "How can you be sure?"

"Because," Mother Agnes beamed, "if the cave on Mingay was used the same way Oweynagat is used in Ireland, then it's most likely dedicated to the same Goddess."

"And who would that be?" Edan said cautiously.

"The Queen of Battle and Fate," Mother Agnes answered. "And ravens and crows. And Alex said his family in Faerie is from the Deck of Crows." She gave Annag a smile. "Alex has sent that gem to The Morrigan."

"But there's *no one there*!" Edan protested. "Is Alex's courier just going to leave it in the cave? Bury it?"

"Saorsa said they found Thomas' letters to Adamina at Buccleuch. *Volumes* of them. I can't imagine Alex wasn't tempted to have a look. Maybe Thomas said something about it being a safe place."

Edan's face suddenly changed as he remembered something. "Wait," he said. "Our inheritance. When my mother passes on, there's this strange property...."

There was a knock on the door to the hall, and Edan turned. "Come in," he called wearily. The door opened, and Edan's valet Henry was standing there, a stunned look on his face. He seemed at a loss for words.

"What is it, Henry?" Edan asked.

"Laird Scott, those bells Mother Agnes rigged up...well, the one for the back garden started to ring, an' so we sent some riders up to take a look."

"*And?*" said Mother Agnes. The bells were set to ring if magickal energy was detected in various areas of the castle grounds.

"I think, sir," said Henry, looking unsettled, "that your mother, Lady Scott, is downstairs in the front hall." There was a pause, and then all three inhabitants of the study nearly ran over Henry in their haste to reach the staircase.

....

Fia had been trying to get the mirror to work, but had no luck. She'd tried raising as much power as she dared with Mother Agnes and Annag in the castle, but there hadn't been any response. The surface moved like the dark water of a midnight lake, but nothing beyond that appeared.

She tried singing to it, talking to it. Nothing. *There must be a password or a spell.* She assumed the mirror was Adamina's, kept here in secret so she could speak to Thomas when he was away, and so she tried to think of passwords he and Adamina might have chosen together. "Thomas," she whispered to the mirror. "Adamina Scott. Michael Scot. Alex. Alexander. Alexander William Thomas Scott. House of Corvids. Deck of Crows."

She was engaged in yet another round of *Guess the Magickal Password* one morning when she heard excited voices and running footsteps in the hall outside her room. She tossed a blanket over the mirror where it lay on her bed, and ran into the hall, just before two of the staff disappeared around the corner.

"Wait!" Fia called, and they paused. "What's the commotion about?"

One of the chambermaids was bouncing up and down in excitement. "She's returned, Mistress Fia! They say Lady Scott has escaped Carlisle *and she's downstairs!*" The two young women turned and raced off again, eager to be part of a story that was certain to be on everyone's lips soon. *Adamina Scott had escaped from Caroline Scott's prison and had returned home!*

"Oh, *shite!*" Fia hissed to herself, and spun around, headed for the mirror. *If it's hers and she goes to it and finds it missing, they'll have my head!* She uncovered the mirror and began awkwardly navigating it back down the hall to the room and onto its hook behind the curtain. *Please don't let anyone come in!*

The wire on the back of the mirror finally caught as Fia held it close against her, struggling to get it into position, and Fia breathed a huge sigh of relief. Her breath fogged the strange, slightly moving glassy surface of the mirror, and then her exhale disappeared into its surface. And the color of the surface began to change.

Fia almost didn't see it at first. She was so eager to pull the curtain to cover the glass that she barely looked at the mirror itself. But then, there it was. A violet wave, followed by a silver one, rippling across the dark surface. And then, the entire surface came *to life.*

Fia moved away from the mirror, staring. *I breathed on it. And it's working!* She ran across the room and shut the door. They'd realize shortly she wasn't downstairs and come looking for her, but she just needed a minute or so. She returned to the mirror and blew across its surface twice more; the violet and silver waves multiplied and an image came into focus.

And Fia forgot how to breathe. Forgot how to speak. For the face and presence on the other side of the mirror struck every chord in the instrument of her soul. She would never forget this moment. It was the moment she understood what it was to *worship.* Fia scrabbled at the frame of the mirror, desperate to see more, to be closer. *This...this is a goddess. I can feel her! She is...everything I need right now, and more!*

The woman in the mirror looked at Fia and blinked slowly. She had long, silver hair, which draped smoothly over her shoulders and was accented with tiny braids throughout. Her irises were silver and her eyes looked out from under dark gray, highly arched brows. She was pale, and her lips were of a similar silver hue to her irises. Fia had never seen coloring like this on a human before. But then, this alluring creature wasn't human; her ears tapered up to a point.

Her visage was so disconcerting that Fia expected a forceful voice and personality to accompany it. *She's going to strike me down. And if she does, that moment of her attention will be the best thing that ever happened to me.*

But the voice that came through the mirror was soft and gentle. And the being *smiled.* That smile struck Fia speechless and motionless. "You figured it out," the woman said. She laughed, and Fia felt the sunshine of the woman's favor warm her to the bone. "I was wondering if you would."

"You...you *heard* me? Or...saw me?" Fia managed to gasp.

The woman nodded. *She reminds me of a star,* Fia thought. "Oh yes. Your side was working fine. But I believe you may have moved the device from the location where someone on *this* side could speak to *you.*"

It was hanging here for a reason, Fia thought, putting her palm to her head. *And when I moved it, I broke the connection.* She suddenly remembered what was happening downstairs, and how little time she had. "Goddess," she cried, "I cannot stay. But...I would give anything, *anything,* to look upon your face again!"

The beauty in the mirror raised her eyebrows slightly. "Where are you, dearest one?"

Dearest one. Those two simple words of affection nearly undid Fia. She was dying for affection, for attention, to belong; but every attempt she'd made down that path only seemed to wound her and everyone around her further. *Dearest one.* She knew logically that she couldn't be dear to this woman yet, for they'd only just met; but the possibility that she *might be* one day made her forget every safety protocol she knew about magick and the Fae in her eagerness to please.

"In Branxholme Castle," she blurted out. "In Scotland. Scott territory. My name is Fia and I'm...I'm a witch."

The woman in the mirror's eyes widened slightly, and then she smiled again. "Come back tonight, Fia of Alba," she said in her musical, soft tone. "Never fear, I will be waiting."

....

Edan came down the stairs to the front hall so quickly he nearly fell down them, with Annag and Mother Agnes right behind. The staff who had been alerted to her presence and those who had escorted Adamina in quickly retired to adjoining rooms to give the family their privacy and corral the younger staff members who might be inclined to eavesdrop and gawk.

Adamina stood quietly in the center of the hall, the hood on her cloak still raised, which cast shadows on her face on this cloudy day. Edan slowed as he approached her; this behavior was not typical of his mother at all.

When she didn't move or speak when he was just a few steps from her, he halted, wary. "Mum? Is...it really you?"

Mother Agnes' hand tightened around her wand. *Something is wrong.* She met Annag's eyes with her own, and Annag nodded and raised her hands slightly. *Be ready.*

"It's...me, Edan," Adamina said in a shaky, uncertain voice, which put Edan completely on alert. "Just...something has happened, and I don't want you to see my face just yet."

It *was* her voice, though. Edan turned and looked at Mother Agnes. Mother Agnes cleared her throat. "Lady Scott, my name is Mother Agnes, and I am assisting the Laird in magickal protections for this residence. You appear to have a glamor spell currently at work on your person, which I believe is being generated by an amulet around your neck. There are also very strong spells on your ring finger. If you *are* in fact Lady Scott, please make yourself known to your son in such a way that your identity is not in question."

Edan took a step back, and held his breath. Adamina reached up with both hands and lowered the hood of her cloak. *It was her.* Edan stared, alarmed. This woman looked just like his mother, but this woman was...*younger than he was.*

"It's me, Edan," she said, looking at him desperately. "I swear it. There's...I have to tell you...."

"Does this have something to do with Thomas Scott?" Edan said flatly, cutting her off. "He's...made you over to his liking, hasn't he?"

Adamina's eyes widened. "How do you...what do you know of Thomas?"

"Everything, Mum!" Edan cried, stepping forward and putting his hands on her arms. He looked as though he might shake her, but didn't. "Da is *dead,* mum! Because I had to...I had to...," he looked away, his voice full of anguish. "I'm so glad, so relieved you're alive, but *how could you lie to me that way?* Did you think I wouldn't love you? I knew you and Da weren't in love with each other anymore but...," he let her go and put his hand to his eyes, trying to stop the tears from falling.

Adamina threw her arms around him and pulled him close. "I'm sorry, Edan," she whispered, and although he didn't return the embrace, he also didn't push her away. "I didn't... I didn't know what to do. I'm in love with him. Thomas."

"Faeries are *real,*" Edan said, putting his arms around her. "Magick is *real.* And witches. And *monsters.* And ghosts, Mum. You raised us to believe something and left out *all the other things you knew.* And I love you but...I'm so, so *angry!* I dinnae like being like this, Mum! If you ever lie to me about these things again...," and now his relief at having her home broke through, and mother and son were sobbing as they held each other tightly, "I dinnae know *what I'll do.* You need to swear to me, on the Scott family name, on your love for *him* if you have to, that you'll never, *ever* lie to me again!"

"I won't," Adamina sobbed, holding her son as tight as she could. "*I won't!* I'll tell you everything. All of it! And when we're done, if you can forgive me, I need help finding Alex. I need to confess it all to *him.*"

"Oh, Mum," said Edan sadly, as he held on to a younger version of his beloved mother, "it's far, far too late for that. Alex already knows."

Wild Willow Ridge, Scotland

Light crept in through the frost on the window, and Saorsa opened her eyes. She felt different now. Despite all that had happened, she felt *positive*. Upbeat. *Alex had been here. Alex found me!*

She washed her face and changed her shift and clothing. Brushing her hair and cleaning up a bit felt wonderful. *I feel like I'm slowly emerging from a dark despair in which I was trapped.* After slipping on her stockings, she tucked her amulet under her clothes and headed for the common room. *There is much to do.*

She found Rune and the others gathered around the table and fireplace, sipping coffee and finishing breakfast. Among all the tall, muscular bodies, a much smaller one drew Saorsa's attention. And then she felt her breath being knocked out of her. All she could think of was the word *doorway*.

Willow was there, beaming up at her male friends and sending her welcoming energy toward all. But beyond that...a tremendous amount of additional power seemed to radiate from her like the vibrant colors of the first flower of spring on a sunny day. It was like walking past a stone circle, except that the magick was coming from a *person*. Saorsa had never experienced anything like this before. *Mother Agnes is incredibly powerful. Elen radiated magick. Alex hums with a certain captivating energy all the time for me. But this is...different.*

Saorsa stopped dead in her tracks as she picked up on the *something* flowing through Willow. *It's good. It's peaceful. But also...wild. Like parts of nature itself flow through her.* Mother Agnes' energy was like a strong, constant wind. Elen's energy was like a crackling flame. Alex...like a wolf running, or a crow's beating wings as it took flight. *And Willow...she's a rainbow. It's her, but it's also...other beings.*

When she'd first met Fia she had been in awe of her. *And to be honest, self-conscious. If I am being totally honest, there was also a certain...attraction, I suppose.* But with Willow, it was different. *Sisterhood.*

Willow put down a cutting board on the end of the table and turned. Saorsa's eyes lit up. *Look at...oh, look at her hair!* Willow's hair was fashioned the way Saorsa had seen in a book at the abbey, in a story about an Irish high priestess. Her long brown hair was knotted and twisted into wild ropes, the long locs adorned with bits of brightly colored wool. *Spells. There are spells woven into her hair!* Saorsa had dreamed of having hair like this ever since she'd seen the book. *I have them in dreams, sometimes. When I do self-portraits, I often add them.*

Willow had adorned herself in a way Saorsa had admired for *years. And...look at her clothes!* Willow was the only other woman besides Vika she'd seen wearing trousers like she did. But whereas Saorsa's were cut-off men's breeks found in various supply drops, Willow's were *beautiful.* She'd added ruffles to the bottom of hers and embroidered vines and moons and symbols and stars into the fabric. *And words...I think it's poetry. She's wearing poetry on her body!* The idea struck Saorsa with a thunderbolt of inspiration. *I miss my painting so much. But...I could decorate MYSELF. And not just decorate. PROTECT. I can work protection spells into ALL my clothes, not just my knitting!*

Willow looked up at Saorsa from across the room and wrinkled her delicately freckled nose playfully at Saorsa, her eyes alive with merriment. "What are you waiting for, silly?" she teased, talking to Saorsa as if they'd known each other forever. "Come get some breakfast before they eat it all!" Saorsa heard Rune and the others chuckling and making jokes back at Willow, a spirit of brotherly camaraderie amongst them.

Saorsa found herself not just walking, but *running* toward Willow. *Safe. She's safe!* A new day had begun.

The Tower of London, London, England

"I've pushed it off *again*," Laoise sighed, looking at Alex's bloodshot eyes. "We'll have to try to heal that wing issue another night. You're in no shape to have such intense magick worked on you." She crossed her arms and looked intently at him.

It had been sixteen hours since the guard had found Alex on the floor in agony, blood coming from his ears and nose and eyes. He'd slept nearly the entire time since, then eaten a bit, but refused to tell her specifically what had happened. "I learned somethin'," is all he would say, and then he'd look away.

Laoise was a keen observer, and an excellent judge of character. From her time tending to Alexander Scott, she'd come to several conclusions. One, he was *incredibly* stubborn. Two, his mind was working on something, and once he'd figured out a plan nothing would prevent him from attempting it, even if it might kill him. And three, he was desperately lonely for Saorsa Stuart. He spoke her name often in his sleep.

Whatever he did to himself, it most likely will kill him next time, or damage him to the point that he can't hope to heal from it. She needed to find out what he was up to, and what those who held him here were planning. *And I know where to start.*

The Fae who had hired her had an office at the base of the tower. She'd seen a human magick-user in a green coat go in and out of that office, as well as two redcoat officers of high rank. There were Fae using living quarters in the tower who went in and out as well, and the guards reported there at the beginning and end of their shifts. She'd been in the office once before on her first day here and had seen a redcoat set down a stack of books and scrolls on the desk. *The redcoats keep records.* She knew next to nothing about the Stuarts and only rumors about the *leth dhia*'s human side. If she could get into that office and see what the orders were for Maria Stuart and Alexander Scott, she'd know once and for all which side she'd be standing on, and perhaps more about Alex, too.

Her patient was staring at the window now, lost in thought. The only part of him moving was his hands. He had terribly restless hands most of the time, and not much to do with them.

"Alex," she said softly to him. "Will you tell me about Saorsa?" She reached into her apron pocket and produced a coin. "Here." She'd guessed right. A moment later the coin was traveling back and forth over the backs of his fingers, and it seemed to help keep his attention in the here and now. He gave her a small smile, and Laoise thought his eyes were improving. *Such a startling color, those eyes. Like silver mist on a winter's morning.* She pulled up a chair. She had a few minutes before she needed to be elsewhere.

She noticed again the blue markings braceleting his arms. *He'd made some powerful Fae angry.* She didn't recognize the symbols at the termination of the lines but knew the practice. *A warning to other Fae to be wary. This one violates the rules.*

"Tell me about Saorsa," she urged him. "I haven't been in the earth realm long, and it's just been in this tower. So, who is she? Is she your wife?"

Alex's eyes met hers briefly. "No," he said quietly. "I'm engaged to someone else. But Saorsa, she's...," he seemed to struggle to find the words, "verra important to me."

"You're engaged to someone else?" Laoise said, interested. "I haven't heard you mention anyone else."

"Aye. Fia." Alex's eyes darted away, and Laoise could see there was a lot there he wasn't going to reveal.

"Do you have children here in Scotland? I mean, I know the *leth dhia* in Faerie isn't allowed offspring, but maybe you are?"

He shook his head, and she watched the coin continue its journey. *Flip. Flip. Flip.* "No yet." He stopped talking.

"So...*Saorsa*," Laoise said, trying to keep the conversation targeted. "How did you meet?"

This got a smile. "She was runnin' away from someone. She was a prisoner, got loose, an' rode right into our camp. Was thrown from her horse an' then just kept *goin'*. No matter how hurt she gets, she finds a way to just keep movin'." He laughed. "I caught her an' tried to stop her, an'...we got on."

We got on. Laoise smiled. She could see from his face that Saorsa was everything to him. But he didn't like sharing too much of her with other people. "And then?"

The coin stopped, and he ran a hand through his hair. "She needed to go west to find her father, an' so I took her."

"Just the two of you?"

He had that far-away look again, and his voice softened. "Aye. Just the two of us."

She decided to try once more. "Alex," she said, shifting in her chair, "what happened last night, when you were hurt. Does it have something to do with seeing Saorsa?"

It was a guess. The magickal energy he'd left behind in the room last night was like nothing she'd sensed before. And now she could tell immediately by the way his eyes moved away that she'd guessed correctly. The coin resumed its journey, but over his left hand this time.

"You didn't...," Laoise began, before lowering her voice to a whisper, "find a way to summon her, did you?" She knew this wasn't the case; she knew what sort of energy summoning left behind, and what he'd done wasn't it. Besides, there was no way to summon in this tower without a device like a scrying mirror or a crystal, and Alex had neither.

Shockingly, he answered her. "No," he said.

"But *did you see her?*" He met her eyes. *That's a yes. He wants to tell me, but is worried what I'll do with the information.*

"Alex," she said, pulling her chair closer, "I'm not asking so I can rat you out. I'm wanting to know what sort of magick you used because if you try it again, it might cause you more harm. And if I know the magick I can help *heal you from it.*" He stayed silent. "Because I'm right, aren't I? If you found a way to see Saorsa, *you're going to do it again.* And I don't want you to die from it, Alex."

He used his thumb to flick the coin into the air and caught it on the back of his right ring finger, and the journey continued. *Flip. Flip. Flip.* "It's all right, Laoise," he said to her quietly. "I dinnae think if I die it's the worst thing."

Laoise eyes widened. "How can you *say* that?"

Now he was looking right at her, and the coin was still. "They're goin' to kill me, Laoise. Soon, too. I'll be hanged in the city square if they dinnae kill me doin' something' magick with me in here. An' I cannae walk well, or swing a sword well with these wounds, an' I'm in *the center of London.*" He raised his eyebrows. "I'm thinkin' it's just time to let this body *go.*"

And Laoise suddenly understood. "If you didn't bring Saorsa *here,*" she said, thunderstruck, "it means *you got out to see her.*" She shook her head. "That's *impossible.* This tower...no portals get in; no portals get out. Especially not *human* magick." She swallowed hard, her mind racing. "And...let THIS body go...oh, sweet Borvo's springs, Alex, are you saying you *made a duplicate of yourself?*"

His expression gave her nothing, but his hands did. *Flip. Flip. Flip.*

Laoise reached out and snatched the coin back. "Alexander Scott, *look at me,*" she ordered him, and he did. "Whatever you did to yourself last night *nearly killed you.* If you try it again tonight, *you are going to die or damage your brain.*" She paused. "It's not worth it. We can heal this body, but we have to work *together.* I'm one hundred percent sure you are not proficient at the magick you attempted, which means you also don't know for certain what happens if your primary body here *dies.* For all you know, that could kill any other aspects you make as well!"

"Then I'll just *haunt* Saorsa," Alex snapped back. "At least I can see and be with her that way!"

Laoise generally didn't lose patience with her patients, but found that she was losing it now. "You stubborn bastard," she said to him. "You're *determined* to make things worse for yourself, aren't you? If you could just stop single-mindedly following the course you've already decided on and just *let someone help you* for a while, I think you will find your outcomes can be *much better than ending up brain-dead!*"

She could see her plan was working. She wanted to get him upset and emotional, so that she had *some* chance of breaking through the walls he'd built up to protect himself. Unfortunately, all his frustration with the situation came out directed at her as well. "Oh, who's going to help me? *You?*" he spat. "You dinnae even know *which side you're on!* You *work for them,* Laoise! Diggin' amulets out of Maria and healin' me up so that they can turn me into some sort of faerie weapon! If you've a better plan for lettin' me see Saorsa or gettin' me an' Maria the hell out of here, I'd love to hear it instead of listenin' to ye *scold* me all evenin'!"

There we go! Laoise had to suppress a smile. His temper was up, but he was *listening.* Listening meant connection, and that was what she needed. It was the most fire she'd seen in him since he'd arrived. "As a matter of fact, I *do* have a plan, you obstinate Scottish arsehole," she snapped, trying to keep him engaged in the argument she'd purposefully created. "Let me stay in here with you when you go see Saorsa tonight, so I can watch over your body and maybe see something that will help you learn to perform this magick without *bleeding out of your eyes?*" She paused. "And then, what if I break into the office downstairs tonight and see what I can find about Maria, Saorsa, and their plans for the *leth dhia?* And what about if in trade for me helping you, *you actually do as I say* for once so I don't lose my job, which means you will lose the only ally you have, and you actually *focus* on healing so that you *can* fight your way out when the time comes? What about *that* plan?" She folded her arms and glared at him.

He paused and looked at her suspiciously. "How do I ken ye won't tell them everything?"

"You don't. And I'll be honest with you. I'm not completely certain you're *not* some horrible monster. The stories about *leth dhia* are *not* good. If I go down into that office and discover you *are* the bad guy, all bets are off. But either way, you still get to see Saorsa first, with the possibility of *surviving* it."

He was watching her face carefully. "So...you'll help me see Saorsa, an' after that, you'll go to the office, an' then tell me which side you are takin'?"

Laoise nodded. "Correct. If they are trying to save the world from you, then I'll tell you our partnership is over. But if they are up to something that goes against the Fae High Council, or traffics in any sort of dark magick, you've got yourself an ally. I *want* to believe in you, Alex. I *want* to do what's right. But before I let a *second leth dhia* aspect loose from a Fae prison, I need to make damn sure I know what I'm doing." She looked at him closely. "Does that sound fair?"

He smiled at her now. "Aye. That's fair." He looked at the ground. "Thank ye, Laoise." He cleared his throat. "So...ah, what do ye want me to do?"

Finally. "I'm going to make my rounds to the others here in the tower," she said to him, pulling the covers up to cover him as he sat back against the pillows. "By the time I come back, this tea here and this water on the table need to be in your body. Stay off your foot. Get some rest. We need your eyes to heal, so no reading right now. Understood?"

He nodded. "Coin," she said, and tossed it back to him. He caught it in his left hand. "Be good, Alex. I'll be back in about an hour." She smiled at him. "And then we'll get you to Saorsa."

"Aye. *Saorsa.*" He smiled, and Laoise left him behind.

Wild Willow Ridge, Scotland

They would be riding out in the morning. Saorsa had spent the day resting and talking to Rune and Willow. She had summarized everything that had happened since she'd escaped from the Burn Clan, leaving out the more personal revelations. To their credit, they seemed to believe her, and Willow held her hand through much of it. Saorsa had no words for how glad she was for that. Rune and Willow had asked questions at times, but mostly Saorsa had done the talking. A light snow had fallen outside as they spoke, and soon the daylight was fading.

"Where's your husband?" Saorsa had asked Willow at lunch. "If you don't mind my asking. Rune and the others speak so highly of him. I was hoping to meet him."

Willow had smiled. "Away for a few days. He's looking into something. You mentioned dragon lines in your tale earlier. Svend is somewhat of a specialist in them. He studies them and has been able to commune with the forces that generate them."

Saorsa had become terribly excited. "He *can?* It's so rare to find someone who even knows the term, let alone someone who studies them! I have *so* many questions about them!"

Willow had laughed, and Saorsa thought how much she loved that sound. "Well, I'm sure he'd be happy to share. After talking to you and Rune today, I'd like to accompany you for a while on your journey and help, if you agree. I can leave a message here with our caretaker for Svend to catch up with us once he returns."

Saorsa was thrilled. "You'll really come and help?" She couldn't stop smiling. "You have no idea what that would mean to me!"

Willow grinned. "It's partly selfish on my part, to be honest. There are so many opportunities to learn in this situation, and I can't wait to get started. I mean, I work with all sorts of beings and forces, but rarely cross paths with the Fae. And you have actual Fae entities interacting with you! How could I possibly pass up this chance?"

Saorsa smiled. "You're also just a terribly nice person, I think," she added. "I feel so *comfortable* with you. And...I think I have a lot to learn from you too. You're just so full of *light*."

Willow reached out and squeezed Saorsa's hand. "I think we recognize each other. I was thinking you are full of light, too." She gestured at Saorsa. "We just have to get some of these magickal fingerprints from other beings off of you, and then you'll feel better. We are going to clear off all the energy that's not yours that we can, and replace it with protection spells of your own making."

"It might seem a silly thing to think about in the middle of all this, but...would you consider," said Saorsa, suddenly feeling shy, "helping me do my hair like yours? We could...put protection spells in the knots. I've wanted to do it for years, but the time never seemed right."

"Of *course*!" Willow laughed, and Saorsa let out a squeal of glee.

"And," said Saorsa, "I like how you've altered and embroidered your clothes. I was thinking maybe you might teach me that too? I love how you look...," she smiled at Willow, "like a woodland faerie. Your clothes look magickal, but you can still travel in them. They look like they are part of who you are. Like Vika looks in her clothes. Like she knows who she is."

Willow nodded. "When you were talking about your friend Vika today," she said, "I was enthralled. I'd very much like to meet her."

"She showed me how to start discovering *myself,*" Saorsa said. "But lately...well, ever since the knife and the ghosts came at Hermitage, I haven't felt as much like myself."

"You can't raise power if there's no *you* left to raise it," Willow agreed. "And to make matters worse, the person who is most important to you, Alex, has been undergoing a major identity crisis as well. We need to get you grounded back in yourself, Saorsa, so you can be stable and strong for him and move through the world in a way that you are happy with."

"How do I do that?"

"You say you've wanted your hair done like mine for years. What are other dreams you've had? Other desires? Other things that you've wanted to explore? The more of those things we make time for, the more you will feel like yourself. And the more authentic you are, the more power will be drawn to you." Willow gestured. "When you feel like yourself, you will feel energetic and comfortable, and what you call magick will *flow*. Taking time to be yourself isn't selfish, Saorsa. It's essential. It's the groundwork upon which everything else you do will be built."

Saorsa had never thought of that before. "How do I begin? I've been so lost lately."

"For you? The basics. Good rest. Good food. Good company." Willow grinned. "And after that, let's get into your wishes and dreams. We can start your hair tomorrow when we camp. What else brings joy to your life?"

"I used to paint," said Saorsa. "I miss it. And I miss the simple tasks that used to fill my days. Baking bread and singing. Making a basket. Knitting. There's never time for that now."

"We'll *make* time," Willow assured her. "Each of those pastimes, they are part of what it is to be a human being. Humans have painted and made bread and woven baskets since the beginning of time. If we forget those things, we lose our humanity." She took Saorsa's hand again. "You said Alex was losing that part of him these last few weeks. That had to be *terrifying*. Let's make certain you don't feel you are losing yours, too."

Saorsa thought back over everything Willow had said to her as she lay in bed that night. *She's right. I need to keep discovering who I am. That will give me the energy I need to help Alex and take on the Fae.* She felt terribly excited, like she had at the beginning of her training with Vika. *I am going to reclaim myself. The ghosts, the Fae...they all wanted to control me. But I'm going to find my own power again. And make it sustainable.* She fell asleep on her back, gazing upwards, and dreamed of who she might become.

....

The fire was dying down, and a mostly-asleep Saorsa tried to pull the quilt up higher. But it wouldn't move. She tried again. Then she tried to roll onto her left side and discovered she couldn't do that either. And then she heard a contented sigh, one that most definitely had *not* come from her. She opened her eyes and looked down at her blankets.

Alex was there, sound asleep on top of the covers, his head on her belly, his arms wrapped tightly around her thighs. Her eyes widened as the realization hit her: *He's come back through the portal again! Wait! I can feel him lying on me! We can touch this time! Goddess, how long has he been here?*

She moved her hand toward his shoulder, intending to wake him, but found she couldn't bring herself to do so. She rarely saw him asleep and loved to watch him when the opportunity presented itself. *He's at ease. Comfortable. When was the last time he was either of those things?*

She just looked at him sleeping peacefully and felt a pang of longing for a different path. *If we weren't wanted by the Crown and important to the Fae, what would our lives be like? Imagine if we had a simple life, one where we woke up together and fell asleep together and just did the work of our days in between. What if I could feel him next to me like this every night, without the fear that someone is about to steal him away?*

She wondered if he would be able to hear her on this visit too. She reached down, and ran her fingers through the thick, dark waves of his hair, joyful down to her core to be able to touch him. He nestled closer and gave a happy murmur. *The fire is low. He's probably a bit cold.*

"Alexander," she whispered. "Come here and get warm, my love." He stirred and raised his head. *Oh, I think he can hear me!* But she didn't want to ruin this moment with too many questions, too many words. She just wanted to be near him. To hold him. To feel him breathing next to her and to know, just for a few moments, that he was with her.

She pulled back the covers and moved aside, making room for him. He looked at her and smiled, his startling light gray eyes crinkling at the corners as he looked at her, and she felt a flutter of excitement in her stomach. He climbed under the thick layers of down comforter and hand-stitched quilts to join her in the warm, private space she had created, and she tucked in the covers around him.

He lay his head on her pillow, and for a moment they just looked at each other. And then his hand found hers under the blankets, and next their fingers were interlaced for a moment, and then Saorsa was climbing into his arms.

Touch. She wanted this touch so very, very much. She felt her eyes sting with tears of relief as his arms went around her, and then everything was familiar and right. *The shape of him. The scent and heat of his skin. The way he spreads out his fingers as he cradles the back of my head when we embrace. The way he kisses my forehead.*

Home. She started to cry a little. "You're really here," she choked. "Or...a part of you is? Did you split yourself again?" She felt him nod. And the floodgates of Saorsa's heart opened.

She was sorry, sorry for everything that had happened between them in the last few weeks. *I didn't believe him. I pushed him away out of fear. I let Fia come between us. I went to bed with his other aspect in Faerie.*

She realized Alex was crying too. Holding her as tight as he could, overcome with emotion, and then she heard his voice. *Goddess, it feels like a blessing to hear him speak!*

"I'm verra sorry, Saorsa," he whispered, and Saorsa realized that although she'd seen him wipe away an errant tear before, she'd never seen him let himself *weep*. But he was doing it now, holding on to her tightly, his breathing disordered and his voice full of regret. "I'm so sorry! I didnae tell you...I should have been honest with you from the start. I should have told ye about Fia. An' Saorsa...there are others I should have told ye about as well. I should have told ye about *all of them*...I just, I didnae ken *how*." She felt him tremble a little from the force of his emotions. "I was stupid, I was selfish, an' all I could think of was how to *keep* you, *eun beag*. An' then...oh God, the things I've put you through since then! I didnae treat ye well at Melrose, I didnae treat ye well at Buccleuch, I've been nothin' but a self-centered bastard."

It's the first time we've been able to talk since the knife has been gone. Everything's going to come out now. "No, stop, please," Saorsa said, gently pushing him away so she could see his face. "It wasn't just *you*, Alex. You *told* me you didn't bed Fia, and I wouldn't listen! I'd push you away and pull you back, so that you didn't know what to expect! I replaced you with Fia and made you watch while I had someone, and you had *no one*."

"No, *no*," he protested. "What I've done...how I treated you...you were right to push me away. I didnae act with honor. I didnae treat you with respect. I *frightened you*, Saorsa. It pains me to think of it!"

"Alex, *the knife was making things worse*. Yes, I *really* wish you'd told me about Fia. But that shouldn't have been enough to drive us apart! I didn't trust. I didn't listen. We were both affected by that knife. Don't try to bear the responsibility for everything that happened! Please? The knife was causing us to act out of character!"

He tried to take a deep breath. "Saorsa...I *wanted* to tell you about the others I've been with. I did. I just couldnae find the words. God, I dinnae even ken how to explain some of them to *myself*." Another deep breath. "I've learned the lesson now. I swear I'll be honest with ye about it, Saorsa. I need to tell ye, I've been with a lot of people. I need ye to understand, it's *a lot* of them. The things I've done, they're no for a lady to hear. But I'm ready to confess them all to you. To lay them at your feet. But I want ye to know I didnae *love* them! I just wanted to...distract myself. To not goddamn *think* for a while!"

She thought about what his Faerie aspect had told her. *Faerie communication is three things: speech, music, and touch. The side of me that's more human in Scotland, he only has speech, mostly.* Saorsa paused, *I wonder if the reason for the long chain of ex-lovers in his past is due to some attempt to express himself through touch as the Fae do.* "I understand, Alex. Really," she said, brushing his hair gently back from his eyes. "It's harder for you to communicate than it is for me. You get...lost in your head."

He nodded, wiped away a tear with the back of his hand, and frowned. "I just need to find a way to be better, so I can be worthy of you." His silver-gray eyes found hers. "I'll tell ye whatever ye want to know." He put his hand on her cheek. "They'll be no more half-truths from me. When I speak, ye can count on the whole truth. No more walls between us, aye?"

No more walls between us. Saorsa took a deep breath. "I agree Alex," she said slowly, "And I have something I need to confess to you too."

He took her hand under the covers and looked at her intently. "I'm listening."

"I went into Faerie. The knife is back where it belongs. And...in trade for returning it, I was allowed to meet your Faerie side."

He went perfectly still, holding his breath. *"And?"*

"He's just like you, Alex. An identical twin. He moves like you; he sounds like you. He knows everything you know, because when he's asleep he dreams what you are living. He can hear your thoughts." Alex said nothing, trying to process what she had said.

"He's *exactly* like you. He...IS you. Smart and sweet and charming and...in love with me. Because *you* are." She paused. "And...well...." Now it was Saorsa's turn to cry. "I couldn't help but love him the way I love you. And you and I here, we were apart, and I missed you. I'd just found out about the baby, and you had just gotten engaged to Fia, and I...." Saorsa was crying harder now. It didn't make it any easier to know Alex's Faerie side might be listening too, *right then.* "I thought I'd never get to make love to you again, Alex. You'd become Fia's, even if you loved me. I was never going to get to have a home with you, or have a child with you, and so I...." She looked him right in the eyes. "I went to bed with him, Alex. You, but in Faerie. Which is...going to bed with *you,* isn't it? It's just...the part of you no one else but me can touch." She stopped then, wanting to give him time to speak, and because saying more felt like making excuses.

He looked away, a line appearing between his brows as he tried to digest this information. "You...you went *to bed with him*? In Faerie?"

"Yes. But...he's *you*. He's in a prison, miserable and all alone. I wanted to comfort him and then...I just wanted to be with him. He was the only *you* I still had."

He looked back at her, his eyes cloudy. "I think if he was *me*, Saorsa, then I'd remember the tryst, aye?" His voice held a hint of bitterness. *Jealousy.* He held her gaze, giving her nowhere to run to, letting her know he was hurt.

"Alex, I *missed you*."

He moved slightly away. "But...you could've had me anytime you wanted me. I told you in that tower at Buccleuch I still loved you! I tried to get you to come back to me at Ramsay House *and* at Melrose!"

Saorsa was having trouble finding the words for this situation. "Alex, with the knife here, *you weren't you*! And when I got there...he *was*. He was you as you were before the knife. Before everything that went wrong! I just...oh Goddess, Alex, I just wanted to be with the man I loved one more time before he was gone from me forever. And then...." Saorsa sat up and put her head in her hands, "I got back here, and found Fia had betrayed *both* of us! That she'd been poisoning you all along so she could give you to the Fae! And that *you hadn't slept with her at Ramsay House at all!*"

Alex was on his feet next to the bed now. *"What?"* he gasped. "She did *what?* Are ye sayin'...," he ran his hands through his hair, "that I'm in prison in London *because of her?* That Fia's bairn's *no mine?*"

"It is *but it isn't*," Saorsa moaned. "The Fae...the Violet Woman...they keep your Fae side imprisoned and take blood, tears, feathers, skin and other things from him by force. To use in magick, since *leth dhia* are so powerful. They impregnated Fia in a *ritual,* Alex. Using parts of your Faerie side. So...using parts of *you*. Without your permission or participation."

She hadn't wanted it to come out like this. *I just blurted out that he's been violated. Or part of him has.* And on top of that, she was now certain that the Alex standing here in her room was a fourth aspect of the *leth dhia.* He didn't seem to have any injuries. She wasn't sure which parts of him could hear what, or how the aspects were connected. If there were two Human Alex Scotts here on earth, could Faerie Alex hear and see through *both* sets of their eyes and ears? Now there were *three* of them she had direct dealings with. When this Alex went back through the portal, would Alex in London know everything she'd just said? Or did they operate independently? Would they keep information from each other? *Oh God, they seem...jealous of each other. What might that cause them to do?*

Alex was pacing now and rubbed his face with his hands as though trying to wake himself up from a bad dream. "So...to clarify. Fia had been workin' for the Fae since *when?*"

Saorsa took a deep breath. *How much time do we have? I don't even know how long he's been here. And if he's split himself...are there any differences between the two earthly Alexes?* "Ramsay House."

"An'...her job was?"

"The Fae promised her she could live in Faerie if she helped them. They fed her a pile of bullshite that barely makes sense. She believed it, though. She thought your father was trying to help you...."

Alex held up a finger. "Wait, please. I need the facts first. What was she supposed to *do?*"

"Weaken you so you couldn't fight back. You said you were sick from something other than the knife, and you were right. She was drugging you over time so the Fae would be able to take you. And apparently she was supposed to keep us far enough apart that I couldn't catch on."

He stopped pacing and looked at her. *"Well, that fuckin' worked."* Saorsa looked at the ground. "And the bairn?"

"Apparently she agreed to carry the baby as well. We don't know why the Fae want this baby in existence." Saorsa sighed. "Mother Agnes, Annag, Edan, and Toran all know. They're keeping Fia safe at Branxholme. But Edan is *furious* with Fia." *Should I tell him Mother Agnes said the child could be a daemon? No, that's not a known fact. Later.*

"And...," Alex started pacing again, "at the cave, ye went into Faerie with Elen."

"And I returned the knife. In trade the House of Corvids let me into the prison where the *leth dhia* is kept. It looks like a palace. But he's all alone there. The only joy he has is seeing this world through your eyes. He's with you all the time, Alex."

Alex was silent for a long moment. "An' ye...invited him into your bed." Alex's voice was dull. "I know that from your perspective I shouldnae be upset, Saorsa. But I still...it just feels...," he fell silent, and Saorsa could tell he didn't know how to proceed.

Saorsa couldn't help herself. "You just begged my forgiveness for all of your lovers, but you can't get past the *one* I've had, even when he's *you?"*

He looked at her silently for a moment, his jaw set. "Mine were all before I met you, Saorsa. Yours was a different thing entirely. You let him have his way with you while I was lyin' unconscious an' sick in a haunted fuckin' cave after bein' *shot!"*

Alex started to pace again. "An' what about what ye said at the inn while Fia was sewin' me up? Ye told me at that inn you loved me, an' ONLY me! That was *the same day* you let him take you to bed!" He shook his head and pointed an accusatory finger at her. "Maybe ye just bedded him to get back at me for screwin' Fia at Ramsay House, which ye now know *I didnae do!"*

"You said we were *through!"* Saorsa cried. "You said you didn't even want to be alone in a room with me ever again! You *proposed to someone else!"*

"Saorsa," Alex said, moving toward her angrily, "dinnae pretend ye didnae ken that I wanted you! I *told you* I loved you! You ken very well that that proposal was for the bairn, *no for Fia!"*

"*Did I* know that?" Saorsa countered. "You've slept with her before! Maybe you still have feelings for her! Maybe a little part of you was secretly happy things worked out that way!" *Oh, my Goddess, the knife isn't even here anymore and we're still fighting!*

Alex put both of his palms on his forehead in frustration. "I told you I loved you *five minutes* before the proposal! An' *you wouldnae send Fia away!"* He started to pace. *"God, I fuckin' hate this!"*

Saorsa walked over to Alex, determined to help him see her side of the argument. "Alex, where are you right now?"

Her question took him aback, and he scowled. "Standin' here with *you.*"

"Are you? Or are you in London? I mean, the Alex currently in London is the one I went to Holy Cross with and the one who first said 'I love you' to me. So, if I were to hold your hand right now," she took his hands in hers, "and if I were to kiss you, would that make me unfaithful to him?"

"He's *asleep,*" Alex spat, "an' I'm *awake.*"

"When I was in Faerie, *that* Alex was awake, while the part here in Scotland – you - was asleep," Saorsa stated. "What if the Alex in London were to die, but *you* could still be with me? Would you still be the same Alexander Scott I fell in love with?"

"Yes!" he blurted out. "Or...no! No, it's...," Alex let her go and started to pace again. "I just cannae help but feel ye took another man to your bed, Saorsa! He and I have led separate lives for over *twenty-five years!"*

"Alex," Saorsa said, slightly exasperated, "there are *four* of you now. Three of whom are *interacting with me.* If you keep duplicating at this rate, by spring we'll have enough of you to form our own shinty team!" She put her hands in her hair. "What am I supposed to *do?* Not touch *any* of you? Touch *all* of you? Only the human ones? Only the ones not engaged to other people? How am I supposed to navigate this if you don't know how to either?"

He looked at her, crestfallen. "I...I dinnae have an answer for ye, Saorsa." He looked at the fire. "I just know that *I'm here now."*

He could leave at any minute. Saorsa moved toward him and stood close. He didn't move away. "I didn't want to hurt you," she said softly to him. "I'm in love with you, Alex. *All* of you. No matter where you are. No matter how many of you there are. And most of the time, I'm worried it's the last time I'll ever have a chance to be with you. So I want to be with you however and whenever I can. Whatever I can get. Because I don't ever, *ever,* want to miss an opportunity to know you and love you."

He stood very still. Saorsa reached up to touch his chest. "Alex," she said, her voice breaking, "I want to be with you so much. Watching you propose to Fia...I felt like a huge part of me died." She looked up at him. "I understand if you feel betrayed. I might feel the same way in your place." She paused for a moment. "I wish we could make the last few weeks disappear and be back on the same side together. A team. Like we were when we were headed west."

He looked down at her face as if searching for something. Then she saw his eyes change to the color of smoke, and he turned away. "Saorsa," he said softly, "even if we forgive each other...the past few weeks *did* happen. An'... we both got hurt."

"I know," she said. "I don't know what to do."

He ran a hand over his head. "We need some time, Saorsa. Time to try an' build trust in each other again. An' what ye told me tonight...about you, Fia, an' the part of me in Faerie...it's a lot to take in, *eun beag*. It changes everythin'. I need to give this all thought so I'm fair to ye, and so I'm comfortable with my choices." He fell silent.

Saorsa felt like she was losing him. *Is he saying he might decide he doesn't love me?* She suddenly felt desperate to be physically close to him. She took his hand and tried to pull him toward the bed. *Please, please be with me!* "Alex, can we try to be...like we used to be? Can you please come to bed with me? Make love to me? I...*I need you*." She was crying again.

He stopped, a pained expression on his handsome features. "Saorsa. Oh, sweetheart, I cannae do that right now. Not with...all of this such a mess. I'm so sorry." Saorsa began to shake. *I'm losing him. Or I already have.*

He stepped forward and took her gently by the shoulders. "It is no fair to either of us to just jump into bed, pretendin' nothin' happened. It willnae go the way you think. I want to do things *right*. I want us to...," he paused, "to think things through. To really ken what we want. We both need to really trust each other again before we're close like that."

Saorsa looked up at him. "You still think I have unresolved feelings for Fia, don't you?" she asked. "Or...you think of your Faerie self as separate, and you think I have feelings for *him*."

Alex sighed. "Aye. I'm no goin' to lie. I do." He looked away. "An' Saorsa...if I do get free...well, the bairn still needs a father."

Saorsa's jaw dropped. "You're still going to marry Fia? After what she's done? She *ruined our lives, Alex!*" Saorsa pulled away from him. "I can't believe this!"

"Saorsa, *I didnae say that*," Alex said quietly. "But we cannae punish the mother without punishin' the child, it seems. All I said was I need time to figure this out." He gestured vaguely in the air. "My body is broken an' in a prison. I just found out I have a child conceived in some sort of ritual an' that the mother, whom I considered a friend, has been *poisonin'* me. An' I *also* found out that my counterpart in Faerie was bein' tortured an' is miserable, an' that the love of my life *slept with him*." He tried to shake the tension from his hands. "That's a lot to take in, *eun beag*."

Ever since they'd started to travel together, Saorsa had always tried to help Alex when he was anxious or overwhelmed by using touch. She moved toward him, certain if she could put her arms around him that everything would be solved. He didn't resist as she placed her arms around his waist now, and Saorsa felt a spark of hope that things could be repaired. The spark grew into a flame as his arms circled her back and he pulled her close. *There he is. We're where we belong. With each other.* She felt him take a deep breath.

"Alex," she whispered, her voice shaking, "do you still love me?"

"Aye, sweet one," he answered quietly as he began stroking her back. "It's why I'm here now, so."

She pressed herself closer to him. *Goddess, he feels so good.* She ran her hands over his lower back and let one hand drift around to his side to touch him on his hip, adding just a bit of pressure as she circled her hand there. She felt his body respond, his arms tightening around her and his hips shifting slightly forward. Feeling him move against her started a blaze in her belly. *I burn for this man. I will always burn for him.*

One of his hands moved lower, taking hold of her backside firmly, and his other hand was tangled in her curls. *I think he wants me. And I want him.*

"Saorsa," she heard him say softly, "I miss holdin' ye *so much.*"

"And I miss you," she responded, pressing her cheek against his chest and letting her left hand wander down to stroke his thigh. "I miss your voice and your kisses and your touch. I miss the silly songs you sing to me and the way you smile. I want to make you laugh again, Alex. I want to make you *happy.*"

He was stroking her side now, letting his fingers graze the side of her breast. "*Tha thu a' faireachdainn cho math,*" he crooned to her. *You feel so good.*

Saorsa felt her pulse begin to race. They were in a *very* different place now than they were a few minutes ago. One where they were enjoying each other and forgetting to think. *One where,* Saorsa thought, *if we can just stay here a little longer, we might become lovers again.*

The thought sent a lightning bolt of pleasure through her body, and she gave a little shiver. And felt his breathing rate increase in response. *I want to touch him.* She turned her head and kissed him gently on the chest, and then snaked her hand up under the hem of his shirt and traced the crescent moon-shaped scar on his back with her fingertips. She heard him give a short, shallow gasp as her fingers found his warm skin. And now he had *both* hands on her backside, and she heard him give a murmur of appreciation and happiness. Saorsa felt as if someone had released butterflies in her pelvis. *I want him. I want him. And when he stops thinking and just lets himself be with me, he wants me too.*

"I love the way you touch me, Alex," she told him as she slipped a second hand under his shirt and began stroking his back. "Do you like the way I'm touching you?"

"*Aye,*" he breathed. "Oh, sweetheart, you're makin' it hard to think."

Good. Saorsa slipped her fingertips under the waistband of his trousers. *Kiss me, Alex. And then take me to bed. Let's remember what it feels like to be together.* She was already picturing him getting undressed, and what it would feel like to have him over her and inside her again. *I want it a little rough, but slow. I want him to gently bite me and then kiss it better afterwards.* She took her hand from his waistband and let it wander over the front of his trousers. *Do you want me yet, Alex?*

She heard him inhale sharply at her touch, but she didn't move her hand. She could feel him now. She stroked him slowly through his clothes, and he let out a soft moan. *I think he'll listen to me now.* "Alex," she said quietly, "please come back to bed with me. Think about how good it would feel. Let me love you. Let me make everything stop hurting for a while." She looked up at him, meeting his gaze. "Don't you want to feel me moving with you again? Don't you want to make me cry out your name while you hold me down? I want to wrap my legs around you and take you deep. After I...," she added a little pressure to her touch as she caressed him, "put my mouth right *here.*"

She could tell from the way he was holding her and looking at her that he wanted to take her. *Very* much. But his mind was still engaged and determined to keep the rest of him in check. He closed his eyes and shook his head slowly as he let her go, and then opened his eyes to look at her with an expression of profound regret.

"This isnae what we should be doin' right now, Saorsa," he said, unable to tear his eyes from her. "I want to lose myself in you. But I cannae let myself do this tonight."

Since they'd begun sleeping together, he'd never told her *no* when she'd wanted to be intimate, and now he'd told her twice. Saorsa felt the rejection like a blow to the stomach. "I've lost you," she whimpered, feeling lost herself as the tears started to come. "Oh, Goddess, *I've lost you.*"

He pulled her close again. "Saorsa Stuart," he said, a note of gentle scolding in his tone as he held her against him, "just because I dinnae think takin' ye to bed tonight is wise doesnae mean we are done. You and I, we're *more* than that together. *Much* more. Going' to bed together...it's an expression of love, sweetheart, *not the whole love itself.* Ye ken that, aye?"

Saorsa sighed. "I know that," she answered, wiping away a tear. "But when we're in bed together, and you shelter me with your body, I feel...I feel so *safe.*"

"Aye. I understand." He gave her a gentle smile. "Of course you want to feel safe with all that's happened. But Saorsa, afterwards you'd think, 'Oh God, now I've been with *three* of them.' You said yourself that that isnae a good thing. Let's get things sorted before we make it worse, aye?" She nodded, and he rubbed her arm affectionately.

"You told me the truth, sweet one. I'm verra glad for it. That was a hard thing to do. I ken that, because I've often failed to do it myself. You were verra brave. Things are complicated but we will figure out how things should work between us." He put his hands on her shoulders and moved her gently back to look at her tear-stained face. "You're still my home, Saorsa. Dinnae *ever* forget that." He held her hands in his and ran his thumbs lightly back and forth over the backs of her hands, trying to soothe her. "An' I'm goin' to fight like hell to get back to you so we can find our path forward."

The portal opened then, flaming to life behind him. *We have so much more to say! He can't go!* Saorsa held his hands tightly. "Can you come back?" she cried.

Alex smiled at her. "I dinnae ken. But I love you, Saorsa Stuart. An'...just ken that I'm on my way." The flames seemed to fill the room, and when Saorsa opened her eyes, she was alone again.

The Tower of London, London, England

The sun had gone to its rest just after four, and Laoise had made her way to Alex's room at the top of the tower. Alex had done the ritual while sitting on the bed while she had stood behind the dressing screen so he wouldn't be self-conscious. When she'd heard him call her name quietly, she had emerged to find her patient slumped on the bed asleep and a second Alexander Scott standing next to him.

"Whoa," was all Laoise could think of to say. While she was an experienced practitioner of magick, she'd never seen two of someone before. She swallowed hard. "How do you feel?"

"Better than last time," Alex responded. "I can talk this time. Last time I couldnae do that." He reached out and touched her arm. "Huh. I'm solid this time too."

Suddenly the flaming portal burst into existence, startling Laoise so that she jumped and put her hand to her chest as she gasped for breath. "Ravens and crows, Alex, that scared me!"

Alex grinned. "I guess 'no portals in, no portals out' isnae accurate anymore."

"I guess half-god portals are the exception." She gestured at the portal. "That goes to Saorsa?"

He turned toward it. "I hope so. Only one way to find out."

"Could you carry your sleeping self through, and just escape altogether?"

Alex shook his head. "I dinnae think so. Last time just touchin' myself made my head start to bleed."

"Could someone else carry you through? Or maybe drag you on a blanket or something? Use this as a way out?" Laoise walked up to the portal and gingerly reached out her hand to touch it. Her hand appeared on the other side as if the portal didn't exist. "Oh. I guess it's...just for you, then."

Alex had smiled at her. "It was worth a try." He moved toward the portal.

"I'll be here," Laoise said. "Good luck." He had nodded, and then he and the portal were both gone, leaving Laoise with time to kill. She checked the body Alex had left behind on the bed. He appeared to be breathing just fine, and his coloring was good. She tucked the blankets in around him and looked at him for a long moment. *What am I going to find out about you when I get into that room downstairs later tonight? Am I going to regret helping you, or the things I've done here the last few weeks?* She had a feeling she already knew.

She spent a few minutes preparing for Alex's return. *Last time he was bleeding and light bothered him.* She moved the dressing screen to block the view of the fire from the bed and moved some candles further away. *Cloths. A bucket. Potions for pain.* There was nothing to do now but wait. Laoise sat down by the fire with a book and decided to check on her patient in the bed every fifteen minutes.

Nine-thirty p.m. Breathing normally.

Nine-forty-five p.m. Same position, breathing rate the same.

At three minutes to ten, she sat up straight in her chair and set her book aside. *Something feels...off. Like I'm being...*she raised her eyes. *Like I'm being watched.*

Alex was standing next to the dressing screen, motionless. The portal had made a sound when it had opened before he left; it must have opened again for his return and she hadn't heard it, but that seemed strange considering the silence in the room.

He remained motionless, staring at her, and something about his gaze made her skin crawl. She cleared her throat. "I didn't hear you come back. That was fast." He still said nothing and remained still. Laoise stood up. *Something is wrong.* "Alex?"

A faint white glow began to emanate from his eyes in the darkened room. And then Laoise heard a strange sound. *Like a cat, purring.*

As a healer, Laoise was used to keeping calm in situations that sent most beings into a panic. She looked around the room. *What if he attacks me? Do I have anything to fight him off with?* But of course there was nothing, Alex's jailers had made very certain there were no weapons inside his cell.

She watched as he opened his mouth to speak and noticed another change. *Fangs. Lady of the Streams and Waters, he has fangs!* She took a step backwards and looked to her left behind the dressing screen quickly. The body on the bed was gone. *He didn't come back through the portal. The part that was on the bed is awake!*

Alex spoke, but his voice didn't sound like his own. "Where is my mistress?" he demanded, his pronunciation dwelling on the *s* sounds to create a hiss. "I can feel her."

Laoise watched him look around the room, searching. She had the distinct impression that it wasn't Alex doing the talking, at least not the Alex she knew. Another entity was speaking through the man she'd grown fond of, animating his body as it did so. Laoise took a deep breath. *Don't panic, now. He hasn't become aggressive. Perhaps you can even find out something useful.* "Who are you?" she said, trying to keep her voice steady.

"I am the *leth dhia*," said the voice from elsewhere. "He of many worlds and many swords. Why am I being *moved*?"

Laoise had no idea what that meant. *Mistress. He'd said mistress. Did he mean Saorsa? Or the one Alex called the Violet Woman?* She answered his question with one of her own. "Where are you?" *Maybe I'm hearing the escaped leth dhia in Faerie!*

"In the Blue," he answered. "Where is my mistress? I await her command." He blinked several times, and Laoise noted he looked right at the door and blinked several times, but made no motion to move toward it. *I'm not certain he can see very well.*

She tentatively raised a hand and waved at him. No reaction. He took a step toward her, and then looked down at his injured ankle, as though surprised that it was causing him pain. *He wasn't expecting an injured body. He doesn't know what's going on at all!*

"I want to help you," said Laoise, hoping to find out more information. "This body you are in, it is badly hurt. I am a healer your mistress has employed to care for you."

"*Why?*" he hissed. "Why does she save this body, when there are others*?*"

"How *many* others?" Laoise asked. "How many pieces are you in, *leth dhia?*"

He squinted again and stumbled. Laoise moved forward to support him entirely out of habit, as she would have for any patient. She reached out and pulled a chair closer, and carefully helped him to sit. He looked at her, blinking, the glow softening somewhat.

"Why," he said softly, "why do the children of Rhamnousia not come?" And then he collapsed, falling into unconsciousness in the chair, as Laoise tried to position him so he wouldn't fall out of it. The fangs disappeared after a moment and his skin turned pale, reminding Laoise of a corpse.

She stood and brushed her long, dark hair back from her face. She wanted to get him back into bed, but he'd be a dead weight. *In the Blue? What is that?* The *leth dhia* in Faerie was *out* of his prison and most likely free, and she assumed the duplicate Alex who had gone through the portal was with Saorsa somewhere in Scotland. And if this body was one of the original three... Could she have just spoken to the missing third aspect that the Magician had created when Alex was a child?

She had a feeling the commanding 'mistress' was the Violet Woman. *And this leth dhia aspect seemed totally in her thrall.* And who are the 'children of Rhamnousia?' Whatever was going on, she certainly had a lot to tell Alex when he returned. *If* he returned. She checked his breathing. Normal. The color was returning to his cheeks. She sat down across from the body in the chair and thought about breaking into the office at the base of the tower.

....

Laoise heard the portal open and rounded the dressing screen just in time to see Alex pitch forward from the flames and fall to the floor. The fire vanished in the air behind him. "Oh, my God, are you hurt?" Laoise cried, dropping down onto her knees on the floor behind him. "Are you in pain?"

"Christ, I feel awful," Alex groaned into the floorboards. "Goin' from here wears ye out some, but comin' back...I feel like I cannae get up." He sighed.

"Maybe you're not meant to come back," Laoise hypothesized, getting hastily to her feet and going to the bed to retrieve a pillow and a blanket for him. "Maybe *leth dhia* are supposed to stay separated after they split, and the aspects aren't supposed to rejoin."

"Then why does the damn portal keep suckin' me back here?" Alex asked. "I'd be verra happy not to come back at all."

"Here," said Laoise, putting the pillow on the floor. "Can you roll over and we'll make you more comfortable? Until you have enough energy to stand?" Alex nodded and slowly shifted position on the floor, while Laoise attempted to cover him with the blanket.

The shift in position allowed Alex to see his other self, unconscious in the chair near the fire. "Laoise," he said cautiously after thanking her for the blanket, "I thought I left myself in the bed. How did my body get over there?"

Laoise sighed. "You walked. And you talked to me, Alex. But...it wasn't you."

Alex let his head fall back and closed his eyes. "*Sweet Christ,*" he muttered. "It's one damn thing after another."

"And," said Laoise, "not only was your body mobile, but it *spoke*. Had a hissy sort of voice. Quite intimidating."

"The Fae side of me, eh?" Alex said, his eyes narrowing. "I'm sorry I missed him. I'd like to cut the bastard's throat."

Laoise looked at Alex strangely but decided not to ask. The hour was late, and they still needed to get Alex back into one body before she broke into the downstairs office. "I'm...not certain it was the Fae part of you, Alex. This one said he was 'in the Blue' and asked why he was being moved. He didn't sound free, which your Fae self is, supposedly. He was looking for his mistress and said something strange about the 'children of Rhamnousia'. I don't think he could see well. And he had fangs and glowing eyes."

"Sounds like the fuckin' Fae," Alex spat, and Laoise wondered where this new anger at his Fae aspect had come from. She was even more curious and became slightly unsettled when Alex started muttering to himself as though he was talking to an unseen entity. "Ye can hear me sayin' all this, can't ye? With me all the time, she says. Seein' everythin' through my eyes. Well, I dinnae want ye here! I dinnae want ye even *lookin' at her!* Fuckin' come near her again an' I swear I'll carve your heart out slowly, whether we're connected or no."

He's losing his mind. Laoise had heard stories about the *leth dhia* of old: while they often appeared rational and, according to witnesses, seemed in possession of rather brilliant minds, behind the facade raged an unhinged madman. *How could any creature keep their sanity once they started splitting themselves in pieces?*

"Alex," Laoise said calmly, attempting to get his attention by putting her hand on his arm, "I'm not sure who you are talking to right now, but I think getting you back in one body soon is a good idea."

He looked up at her sharply as though he'd forgotten she was there. "Och, *Laoise*...I'm just so *tired*. An' I'd like to not hurt for a time."

Laoise looked at his other aspect in the chair. "Alex, if I'm going to get into that room downstairs I need to get moving. And I can't leave two of you up here like this. You're both disasters."

Alex looked at his other self with a worried expression. "It just...hurts so much to be joined."

"Tell me *exactly* what you did last time."

He sighed. "Saorsa...she has this spell to bring someone into their body. I started it, an' touched myself on the head an' then the pain started."

"And the pain was all in your head?"

"Aye."

Louise thought for a moment. "So you started to raise power, and then the place you touched experienced pain. So, let's try *not* raising power. No spell at all. And let's pick a place that if it hurts, it doesn't kill you. Like a hand, or a foot. No head, no chest. Stay away from vital organs."

Alex nodded. "Ye think it can be a simple as that? That I just touch my own hand?"

"Why not? *Leth dhias* are designed to split. Think about lizards."

Alex frowned at her. "What?"

"If a predator grabs a lizard's tail, it just falls off and the lizard escapes. There are *lots* of animals with the ability to self-amputate. They don't need to raise power to do it, it just happens. What if you're designed to merge just as easily? What if you just need to touch to pop back together again?"

He stared at her for a long moment. "Laoise, I've had a bad night," he closed his eyes, overcome with fatigue. "Is there any way I can talk ye into just killin' *both* of my bodies here right now so I dinnae have to think about any of this shite any longer?"

"Come *on*," Laoise said, standing up. "Enough bellyaching! Marshall your energy, get up, and come touch your hand. If it works, you *get to go to bed*." She whipped the blanket off him and offered him her hand. "Up."

She helped him stand, and he leaned on her heavily for the short walk toward the fire. They came to a stop in front of the inert body of his original form. "Just...touch his hand," Laoise encouraged him softly. "I'm right here. You can do this, Alex."

"It's no goin' to work," he said nervously.

"Then we'll think of something else," Laoise said with more confidence than she felt.

Alex reached out and touched the back of his sleeping aspect's wrist with one finger. Laoise felt like she'd run full tilt into a brick wall. She flew backwards across the room, landing on the floor next to the bed, dazed and overwhelmed by a throbbing energy in her limbs. *What the hell?*

"Laoise! *Laoise?*" She could hear Alex's voice, but couldn't focus her eyes on anything yet. "Are ye all right?"

Slowly, her blurred vision resolved itself. He was hobbling toward her, favoring his hurt ankle. *Just one of him. I was right!* She gave herself a quick check for blood or broken bones. *I'm in one piece. But I need to remember not to touch him when he joins himself again!*

"I'm so sorry," Alex apologized, looking down at her with a worried expression. "Can ye get up, *mo charaid?*"

My friend. It was the first time he'd called her that. Laoise nodded and reached out cautiously for the hand he offered her. "Don't shoot me across the room again, Alex."

"Sorry about that." He helped her to her feet while holding onto the footboard of the bed to stabilize himself. "You were right, though. I just needed a touch. No blood or pain, this time. Just...a bolt of energy." He grinned. "An' a flyin' healer."

Laoise sat down on the bed and attempted to smooth out her clothes and hair. "This is pretty incredible, Alex. You can split yourself, put yourself together, and send one of you out through a portal from a place that's supposed to prevent portals from opening." Alex nodded, smiling, and sat down on the bed next to her. "Did you find Saorsa?"

She noticed his eyes flick away briefly. *Something's bothering him.* "Aye. I saw her."

"I bet she was thrilled to see you."

Laoise saw his expression soften, and his gray eyes tinted slightly green, the color of ocean waves during a storm. "She didnae want me to go," he said quietly. "An' I didnae want to leave." He raised his eyes up to meet Laoise's, and there was such a fierce beauty in his expression that for the first time Laoise recognized him as not just as one of her patients but for what he was: an aspect of a half-god of tremendous power among the Fae. "I'm done with this place, Laoise. I've bided my time long enough. I think I know enough now to try and make it out of here. I'm done waitin'."

"But you can't walk well," Laoise protested. "You still have two gunshot wounds, and that wing injury is sapping your strength!"

He looked at her for a long moment as if deciding if he should trust her, and then nodded. "Aye, you're right. But I have this." He opened his hand. He was holding a lady's hair pin in his hand.

Laoise shook her head. "A hair pin? I'm not following you, Alex."

He held it up for her to see. "It's Saorsa's. Took it out of her hair while I was visitin'. It's metal." He grinned. "If I carried a metal object with me through the portal with no problems, I should be able to bring back *another* metal object next time. A bigger one."

"A weapon," Laoise said slowly. "You can arm yourself now."

"And," Alex continued, "then I can get out."

"But you're *injured,*" Laoise reminded him.

Alex rolled his eyes. "Laoise, I'm no takin' *this* body. I bring back knives, kill the guard an' take his clothes, murder myself, an' walk out the door. The broken, dead body stays here in the bed, so they willnae think anything is wrong for a time. Meanwhile I find myself a horse and make my way to Scotland."

Laoise eyes widened. "*Murder* yourself? Alex, what if that kills *both* of you?"

He shook his head. "Dinnae think it will. If the *leth dhia* commanders could all be killed by takin' down just one, they wouldnae have been such a problem, aye?"

Laoise stared. Alex looked pleased. "It'll work, aye?" There was a flash of excitement in his eyes. "Once I'm out, I can be in Branxholme, where my brother Edan is, in a little over a fortnight if the weather is good and I've a strong horse. Edan will ken where Saorsa is, an' Duncan, then I can track down my mother." There was a note of hope in his voice. "I can split myself again to come visit you later, so that I can figure out how to get Maria out too, so." He grinned. "I read the first man to escape the Tower of London was Lieutenant General John Middleton in the 1650s. A Scot. Left dressed in women's clothes he had smuggled in. If he got out, I can do it with a guard's uniform, a dirk, an' a doppelganger *for certain.*"

Laoise noticed he was weaving a bit as he sat next to her. *His balance is off. He's exhausted, about to fall over.* She stood up to make room for him and pulled back the covers. "Here, lie down before you end up back on the floor."

Alex crawled up to settle himself on the pillows, still talking. "The first time I went, Saorsa could no hear or touch me. This time, rested an' a bit stronger, was much better. As soon as I've slept, I can try splittin' an' going to one of our supply drops." He seemed to be talking mostly to himself now. "I dinnae ken if goin' farther wears me out more or no. I suppose I could just visit Branxholme now. Or even try to find Vika an' Duncan."

Laoise tucked in the blankets around him, and then watched as he wiggled his feet to free them from the cocoon she'd made. "I'm going to see what I can find out downstairs now," she told him, blowing out the candle. "I'll visit you in the morning."

She stopped to put out several more candles on a table halfway across the room. As she was returning the candle snuffer to the table, she heard Alex's voice in the shadows behind her. "Thank you, Laoise," he said quietly. "You've helped me more than I can say, an' I'm grateful."

She smiled. "I haven't been downstairs yet, Mr. Scott. Who knows which side I'm on?"

"I do," he said softly. "An' I'm in your debt."

....

Laoise found the door to the office open, with a red-coated man inside, seated at the desk. She'd seen him before but didn't know his name; she took her orders directly from Tadhg, one of the Fae. *This one is from the human side of the team.*

"Ah, my good Lady Healer," he smiled when he saw her in the doorway. "If you are looking for Tadhg, I'm afraid he's retired."

"I was hoping to use the library, if it won't disturb you," Laoise lied, gesturing to a door in the wall behind him. "I have a patient with an unusual reaction to one of the potions and I need to figure out why."

He waved her toward the door. "Of course, of course. You won't bother me at all." He returned to the rather untidy piles of papers on his desk.

Laoise nodded and walked past him into the library. The Fae kept a small magickal library here, and she could search for information while she waited for the man to leave.
She looked around the room. There were also human books here on science, metaphysics, and mythology. She pulled a few books from the mythology section out and sat down at a table. *Children of Rhamnousia*. This was important: she could sense it.

In the third book she found it. Rhamnousia, also called Nemesis, was a goddess venerated in ancient Greece who enacted retribution against those who succumbed to hubris, or arrogance before the gods. She was the daughter of Nyx and Erebus and portrayed as holding a whip or a dagger. With Tartaros, the Spirit of the Great Pit Beneath the Earth, she parented the Telkhines.

In the second century A.D., the poet Mesomedes wrote a hymn to Nemesis where he addressed her as:

Nemesis, winged balancer of life,
dark-faced goddess,
daughter of Justice

"Wonderful," Laoise said to herself. "Alex's third aspect awaits the Children of Retribution, who was herself parented by the union of Night and Darkness. How incredibly cheerful." She flipped back to the glossary.

The Telkhines were the original inhabitants of the island of Rhodes in Greek mythology, and some stories say they were entrusted with the upbringing of Zeus. They could create poisons, control the weather, shapeshift, and were skilled in metalwork and crafted items for various gods. They were eventually killed when they began using their abilities for evil rather than good. These magickal beings are often described as lacking feet and having the physical characteristics of a fish, while other sources describe them as having the heads of dogs. Still other sources claim that they were, in fact, daemons.

Laoise pushed the book and her candle away. *Why was her visitor earlier tonight asking about shape-shifting, metalworking Greek fish daemons?* This made absolutely no sense. Unless "children of Rhamnousia" didn't literally mean offspring but instead meant *followers*. In which case, Alex's possible third aspect was actually waiting for servants of the goddess herself, Nemesis.

She shivered. She had heard of Nemesis before, but had no idea what house in Faerie, if any, she might have associated herself with. But there was one thing she *did* know: *Nyx is House of Corvids*. At least, she used to be. Might her possible daughter be the same?
There had been rumors that Nyx and the Magician had had some sort of relationship once. But whether it was as allies or as mentor and student or as lovers, Laoise didn't know.

Nyx and Nemesis. They were tied to one of Alex's aspects, somehow. Could one of them be the mistress he had spoken of? Could one of them be Alex's Violet Woman? She didn't know much about either, but resolved to find out. It was a lead, at the very least.

Erebus. The human mythology book referred to Erebus as an entity. Then why did she feel she'd heard it used as a *title* before in Faerie? That it was an honorary title bestowed on someone? She flipped to the glossary, and then back through the book. Erebus, born of Chaos, he is a primordial deity and the personification of darkness.

She had just decided to return the books to the shelves when she heard a commotion in the front room. A woman had stormed in the door to the office and was raising hell, her voice echoing clearly off the stone walls. "Do I have to do *everything* myself here? Where's Tadhg? Get him here *now!*"

She heard the man in the front room stutter out a nervous protest of sorts, which was immediately answered by the sound of something shattering against the wall. *"NOW!"* the incensed woman bellowed, and the human went scurrying from the room. Laoise rose and crept toward the door. There was a large, ornate mirror hanging near the library door, and in its reflection she could see a good portion of the front room.

The woman was tall, with long, dark hair styled in black twisted locs and braids that fell to her waist. She was a Fae and dressed all in black, save for silver layers of silk that sometimes emerged from underneath various hemlines when she moved, like moonlight illuminating a figure in the dark. Her belt was of a deep violet leather, and she was shockingly, distractingly beautiful. *A goddess,* Laoise thought. *At least, she looks like one. And has the air of one who is always obeyed.*

The woman was pacing. She looked up at one point, and for a moment Laoise thought the woman had sensed her or seen her in the mirror. But then the woman just kept moving, and Laoise realized that the woman's irises were *purple.* And such a bright, scalding violet that Laoise had noticed them when the woman was over ten feet from her.

She's familiar, she thought. *I've seen her before, but I don't think her eyes were like that last time.* And then Laoise realized with a start *why* the woman felt familiar. The shape of her eyes, and eyebrows. The color of her dark hair, shot through with red highlights that shone as she neared the fireplace. The woman reminded her of *Alex.* She could be his sister, maybe even his twin. The bone structure, the facial expressions, the mannerisms were all there. *They have to be related. They have to be!*

The room was now filling with both Fae and humans, many of whom had clearly been dragged from their beds. And every single one of them looked vastly uncomfortable to be in the same room with their newly arrived superior.

"Tell me," hissed the woman at the group, "what is happening with my *leth dhia* upstairs."

Tadhg stepped forward, the most composed of the group. "Things are progressing. The Human aspect was in much worse physical condition than we originally thought. Our healer had to delay the work on his wing, but things *are* moving forward."

"Oh, *are they?*" the dark-haired woman said with a mocking tone. "Then perhaps you'd care to tell me why there's *a fucking leth dhia separation signature* radiating off the top of this tower!" Everyone in the group widened their eyes in surprise, almost in unison.

"Yes, *you idiots,*" she continued, "your 'too sick' *leth dhia* has been *separating* himself upstairs, while you waltz around down here with your *heads up your asses!* I could *literally see the energy* from his magick *clear across London!*"

"That...can't be," Tadhg said, looking much less sure of himself than he had a few moments before. "The rooms in this tower were warded by the best. No portals in or out. No summoning. No spells of any...." He stopped as the woman in silver and black advanced on him, taking a step backwards as she invaded his space.

"Are you telling me I'm *wrong?*" she seethed.

He looked at the floor. "No, my Lady," he said quietly. "Perhaps...perhaps the mage who did the warding is not as well versed in *leth dhia* magick as I had thought."

The dark woman began pacing again. "And *tell me,*" she said, her voice deadly, "*tell me* you weren't stupid enough to leave Maria Stuart's body in the *same tower* that holds Alexander Scott." She watched as several in the group exchanged worried glances. *"Tell me that."*

"We were worried about the amulet," Tadhg explained. "Most of the shards are nearly out, and they give off a tremendous amount of magick. We thought this was the safest place because we didn't want to draw the attention of...," he trailed off as the goddess stared at him.

"Are you aware," she said in a sweet, deadly tone, "that the Faerie *leth dhia* aspect has escaped?"

Tadhg nodded. "Of course, my Lady."

"And you never stopped to think that he might try and come *here,* to find his other half? I mean, if *you* were looking for Alexander Scott on this island and knew the Crown was involved in his abduction, *where would you look?*" Everyone in the group was silent, like mice hoping an owl wouldn't notice them.

"And we *know* he's friendly with Maria Stuart," the silver and black-garbed woman continued. "So...imagine how *delighted* he'll be when he arrives, and it turns out Maria's missing body is *conveniently placed in the same tower as his Human aspect!*" Laoise was fairly certain no one in the group was breathing now.

"I'm taking over now," said the goddess, slamming her fist onto a pile of books on the desk, "or you'll undo *everything* we've done. First, take this to the cellar." She handed Tadhg something Laoise couldn't see. "You're lucky I don't kill you where you stand," she growled at him as he took the object. "You know where it goes."

Tadhg's eyes widened. "Is this?"

"Yes," the woman said, cutting him off. "Kerr finished it before I killed him. But it took a while to...develop." She looked at the assembled party. "This *will* hold him. And as for Maria Stuart, I'm sending her north to Glasgow at once."

Laoise felt her breath leave her. *They were going to move Maria!* The woman was still talking. "Once she's there, we'll finish with the amulet, and then she and her daughter can be executed together. I am *so* looking forward to ending this particular chapter of our story."

Tadhg looked at his commander. "We have Saorsa Stuart now? At Glasgow?"

The woman laughed. "The Stuarts will be executed in Scotland once the amulet shards are all out, and Alexander Scott will be executed here. After too many delays, our Crown allies *will* be happy." She grinned. "Old man Kerr invented some *fine* devices, and they are about to serve us well. The Crown gets the bodies, we get the souls!"

She clapped her hands. "Get the carriage ready! Team One, you'll be escorting Maria Stuart to Glasgow. And the rest of you," she turned, striding toward the door, "come with me. It's time to pay my troublesome little champion a visit upstairs!"

Laoise was momentarily paralyzed with fear. *They were moving Alex! And Maria! And Saorsa had either just been captured or was about to be.* She didn't know what to do. *She* was technically part of Team One, which meant they'd be looking for her to escort Maria. *And Alex! I have to tell him about Saorsa! I have to....*

She spun around, shaking. She'd seen another door out of the library that led to a back stair; perhaps if she ran... A ghostly figure loomed out of the darkness, eyes wide, disheveled and pale. Laoise tried to scream but no sound came out. And then the figure grabbed her, sobbing and babbling, and Laoise was as terrified as she'd ever been.

"Help me," the apparition cried, "I don't know where I am, oh God, *help me!*"

Laoise saw stitches in the woman's pale, nearly glowing skin, and realized with a jolt that they were *her* stitches. *This is Maria! Maria is...walking and speaking!*

Laoise knew she had but seconds. She could hear shouts in the stairwell as Alexander Scott's human and Fae captors attempted to drag him down the tower stairs toward the cellar. Injured or not, he was putting up a hell of a fight. The goddess had activated the spells on his arms so that his wrists were bound together, but he was still giving his captors a lot of trouble. He managed to knock one man over backwards with a well-placed kick, and the man tumbled down the stone spiral stairs and lay still, unconscious.

I can get Maria out. There was no time to waste. Every tower guard was running toward the spiral staircase where Alex had just broken a man's arm and sent another man to the landing below, howling in pain after Alex had smashed his foot into the man's testicles.

"Knock him *out!*" shrieked the Fae with violet eyes, as Tadhg attempted to get Alex in a choke hold only to receive a violent blow to the stomach. The goddess activated the second set of bracelets on Alex's arms and his vision blurred, making it harder for him to land blows. The tower's spell-dampening powers were causing the spells on his arms to behave unpredictably, and for a moment Alex's wrists were completely free, and he took the opportunity to take a wild swing at Tadhg, who was trying to choke him out.

The violet-eyed woman tried her magick again, just as Alex managed to get away from Tadhg and dive toward her. In the close space of the stairwell, Alexander Scott was simply lashing out at everyone in his vicinity like a wounded wild animal, thrashing and howling, utterly convinced that if they got him to the bottom of the stairs they'd turn him into a mindless thrall or a weapon of war. He managed to sink his teeth into the goddess' left arm, and jerked his head sideways, tearing at her flesh.

She howled in pain and outrage as blood began flowing freely from the wound, hauled back her hand and hit Alex hard across the jaw with a closed fist. His head slammed sideways into the stones, and Tadhg saw the opening he needed. He grabbed Alex and forced his head forward, applying pressure to both sides of his neck and restricting blood flow to his brain. Alex tried to tear Tadhg's arm away, but the room was spinning, his vision was blurry and his gunshot wounds were causing him immense pain. Seconds later he slumped forward, a dead weight in Tadhg's arms.

"What a fucking *daemon,*" Tadhg panted, dropping Alex's body to the floor. The stones of the stairwell were splattered with blood, and several bodies lay unconscious and broken on the steps. More guards had arrived to clear away the injured, and Tadhg supervised the guards as they carried the Human *leth dhia* aspect carefully down the stairs.

Tadhg turned to his goddess, whose eyes were now the color of rubies. She was holding her arm, full of barely contained rage. "Find me that Healer," she seethed. "Apparently her reports of his weakness were lies."

………

Laoise dragged a barefoot and barely clothed Maria across the freezing grounds of the Tower of London toward the remains of Wardrobe Tower. It had fallen into disrepair in recent years, and she knew it to be uninhabited and unguarded. She hoped its shadows would give her a hiding spot for a few moments until she planned where to go next.

She pulled Maria in through a dark archway at the base of the tower. *They'll find her gone at any moment, and then this entire place is going to come awake as they hunt for us.* She put her hands on the shivering woman's shoulders. *We have no cloaks, no shoes for her, and nothing to trade with. And even worse, I've never been outside the White Tower. What is the human world like?*

"Maria," Laoise said, trying to stay calm. "My name is Laoise. You're inside a prison. I'm going to get you out." *Why is she awake at all? She's been completely unresponsive since she arrived!*

Maria blinked, confused. "No," she said weakly, "I *was* in a prison. Alexander got me out. And then...I was in my body. Here. Where is *here?*"

"*London,*" Laoise whispered, confused. *"We're in the Tower of London."*

"Oh, my Goddess!" Maria cried. Laoise noticed Maria's legs were shaky. *She's very weak.*

"Maria," said Laoise. "We can do this. I know you're sick and cold, but if you can follow me quickly, just for a time, everything will be fine. Just hold my hand, and don't make *any* sounds." Maria nodded. Laoise tried to remember the layout of the grounds from what she had seen out of the White Tower's windows. *Lanthorn Tower is at the end of the green. Then Cradle Tower. That's part of the outer wall; the Thames is past that.*

Laoise thought she heard raised voices coming from the direction of the White Tower. *They may have discovered we're gone.* She grabbed Maria's hand and ran in the direction of Lanthorn. *Airmid, Goddess of Healing, your devoted servant needs you. Give Maria the strength to follow. If she stops moving, both of us are done for.*

What had Alex said earlier tonight? People had escaped the tower in disguise. *Hiding in plain sight. We need clothes.* Laoise hoped the lateness of the hour would be an asset. She stopped briefly as they approached Lanthorn Tower and scanned the area for a guard. No one. She raced off again, thankful for every step that Maria was able to follow.

She flung open a service door at the base of the tower and pulled Maria in. This tower had royal apartments in it, and where there were apartments, there should be servants. *And servants have cloaks we could steal.* Despite the apartments being ready for use at all times, they were rarely occupied. That suited Laoise just fine. *There will likely be few persons about. And a chance of supplies to choose from.*

But it was pitch black inside of the round tower. No fire. No light. "Stay here," she whispered to Maria. There was a table in the center of the room; she found candles on it and was heading for the fireplace with one in hand to search for fire starting supplies when she heard voices outside. *Coming this way. Coming this way!*

She put the candle back on the table and took Maria's hand once more, pulling her through the room in the dark, crashing into furniture in her haste. *We have to get out!* The door out the other side of the tower was locked, and Laoise fumbled hastily with the locks in the dark. Her heart was racing; panic threatened to overtake her.

She felt Maria touch her gently on the back. "Breathe," Maria said softly. "Breathe."

Laoise did and suddenly the locks came open, and they were running again. And at that moment, she could hear bells begin ringing from every tower in the vicinity. They were now, without question, being hunted.

Maria stumbled as they headed for Cradle Tower. Laoise knew they had to slow; Maria was on the brink of collapse. Even though Laoise had given her potions to try and preserve muscle tone, Maria's body hadn't walked on its own in weeks, and her muscles had atrophied. She was moving by willpower alone, and she was already exhausted. Laoise slowed to a walk and put her arm around Maria's shaking body. *She's so thin and frail.*

"Almost there," she whispered, and then she found the servants' entrance and they were inside. *Cloaks! We need cloaks!* She found a chair for Maria and locked the door behind them. A quick glance out the bevel-paned window revealed torchlight and men moving; it wouldn't be long until someone came in.

She felt a sick feeling in her stomach as she thought of Alex again. *Not now, Laoise. Don't lose focus. Get Maria out. It's what he wanted done.*

She heard Maria whisper in the dark. "What did you say, Maria?"

"She wants to help."

Laoise turned to look at Maria, pale and small in the chair. "What?"

"Anne Askew," Maria said dreamily. "She says her name is Anne Askew. We're supposed to go upstairs."

"Who the hell is Anne Askew?" Laoise hissed, becoming frustrated. *There's nothing here we can use. Nothing to help us against the cold.* She'd been hoping for a tablecloth or something to wrap around Maria for warmth, or perhaps a ceremonial dagger on the wall to take with them as some sort of defense. Laoise was a healer; she'd never used a weapon before but it seemed like a good idea. *Anything to help us once we get out.*

"They burned her," Maria answered, matter-of-fact. "They kept her here before she died."

Laoise was becoming desperate. She yanked open drawers looking for anything in the way of supplies or clothing. *I'm going to have to pull down the curtains and wrap one around her...*and then she saw Maria rise and walk out of the room. "Maria!"

She raced after her charge to find Maria climbing the stairs. "This way. Anne says this way." Laoise was shocked Maria *could* climb the stairs. She followed her up, uncertain of what else to do. Maria drifted down the hall, whispering. "Oh, thank you, Anne! You're very kind." Maria passed two locked doors and turned toward a third. "In here? Yes, yes, *thank you.* Poetry, you say? Why yes, I *am* rather fond of it myself."

Either she's insane or talking to a ghost. But if it IS help of some sort, I'm not going to turn it down. Laoise had never seen or spoken to a ghost before. She knew there were entities in Faerie that claimed to have done so, and the House of Corvids claimed to have whole *armies* of them under the rule of the Magician. But she'd never seen one, nor met anyone else that had. *I didn't know humans could talk to spirits!*

She heard sounds downstairs. Men's voices, shouting. *They were coming inside!* She looked up just as Maria touched a carved angel on the fireplace mantle on the left wing. "I know what you mean dear," she murmured to someone unseen. "I've very recently been out of my body *myself.*" A panel in the wall paneling swung open.

Laoise stared. *Did...did Maria's spirit companion just give them a place to hide?* Maria was already moving into the space behind the paneling. "Oh, darling, I think it's...maybe 1747 here now? 1746? I'm not certain how long I was gone. No, the Tudors are no longer on the throne, dearest. Henry the Eighth is *long gone.*" She paused. "Me? Well, I'm a Stuart." Maria paused again. "Scotland, my dear."

Laoise dove into the space behind the wall and Maria reached up and pulled a lever on the wall. The paneling swung shut behind them. Laoise moved backwards and felt something up against her body. Something...*soft*. It was very dark in the space, but it was also quite sizable. Maria had fallen silent. "Are you alright?" she whispered to Maria.

"I'm resting down here," sighed Maria from the floor. "Oh, Anne, I have a funny story for you...," her voice trailed off into silence. Laoise kept exploring, her hands outstretched. *A wall here. And fabric.* The fabric moved under her touch, and a sliver of light found its way in. *Curtain. It's a curtain!* Laoise pushed it a few inches to the side, and the light from the moon lit what looked like a hidden dressing room.

Laoise sank to the ground. *Clothes.* They were surrounded by *clothes*. Capes and skirts and shawls and blouses. Boots and bags and dresses and hats. There was a dressing table in here, too. *Jewelry. Maybe there was jewelry to trade!* All around them hung velvet and silks and furs and leather. Not just clothing...*royal* clothing. Forgotten from another time. Another set of monarchs, who no longer held power here.

Laoise thought she might cry with relief. As long as no one knew about this room, they had a real chance. They could bundle themselves up and stuff silk scarves in a bag and trade them in town. She rose and went over to the dressing table and pulled the drawers open. Cosmetics, turned to dust. Silver hairbrushes and combs. And a large, ornate box.

Laoise took it to the window, opened it, and lost the ability to breathe for a moment. *Jewelry.* Huge, faceted rings. Delicately carved cameos. Bracelets. Pendants. Earrings. Hair clips that glittered in the soft light from the window. Gemstones, reflecting the light. *Emeralds. Rubies. Diamonds. Jet and sapphires, jade and pearls.* The sort of tokens a king might bestow on his wife.

"Yes, yes," she heard Maria whisper. "I suppose once Henry had a new wife, he just forgot about the things that belonged to the one before." She let out a sigh. "You're right, Anne. We women must look out for each other."

....

The chamber in the base of the Tower of London was full of activity, all surrounding an unconscious figure on a bed at the center: Alexander Scott.

The woman who led the team was furious. Furious, and for the first time in many centuries, a bit surprised. Maria Stuart had disappeared *while she'd been here.* Apparently assisted by a healer she herself had engaged. *When I find Laoise, I'll kill her.* They'd be found soon. All of the exits had been shut down, and soldiers were moving from building to building searching for them, leaving no stone unturned. At least they had all the amulet pieces out of Maria.

The Violet Woman moved to stand next to Alex and brushed his hair back from his face with her fingertips almost tenderly. "Here we are at the end, then, My Champion," she purred to him. "I won't pretend you haven't been my favorite plaything in a long time. This aspect of you isn't needed anymore. But I have learned so, so much. You've been a sweet little pet."

She turned to two healers that stood nearby and handed them several potions from her belt. "Plan B. These should heal him up. Bloody hard to get. Rub them over his wounds and on the shoulder blade where the wing was. Shouldn't take more than two days." The healers took the vials and began removing Alex's shirt. She gestured to Tadhg, who crossed the room to speak with her. "It's working?"

Tadhg nodded. "Where the hell did you *get* that thing? This field generator is *incredibly* strong. Is it from the prison? And if so, how did you get the plans?"

The Violet Woman smiled. "The Council isn't the only party interested in containing the *leth-dhia*. We had the initial work stolen, and then Kerr was able to work out the rest."

"Stolen from *who?*"

The Violet Woman met his eyes. "Why, the Magician, of course. You really think he's had access to a *leth dhia* for twenty-seven years and didn't come up with plans for how to contain and use this creature to his advantage? And then *this,*" she said, withdrawing a large gem on a chain from inside her neckline and reveling a bit in her success, "is where this aspect's *soul* goes when the Crown kills him."

"The soul? It will just...go in?"

"That's the idea. It's attuned to him. He needs to be strong to survive the transfer, or he'll simply die, so we're healing him up first. Three days from now, Alexander Scott will be killed on Tower Hill, where all of London can enjoy it. It's going to be quite an event; they're setting up already. I'll be next to him at the gallows and when his neck snaps, the human half of his soul will take up residence here." She touched the gem again carefully. "The Crown can behead the body, draw and quarter him, I don't really care. Then it's on to Glasgow to execute Saorsa Stuart. Caroline Scott wanted it done in London, but his superiors want the Stuarts killed in Scotland...as a reminder to the Scots to obey."

She walked back toward where her captive lay at the room's center. "You think you are smarter than me, don't you, Alexander Scott? Well, you're not. And just as a reminder...." The Violet Woman moved her right index finger and a third set of blue bracelet tattoos seared themselves into his arms. "Pity you aren't awake to really enjoy the pain of that set."

She turned and raised her voice to those around her. "After we leave here, *no one* is to enter this chamber. His keepers can manage everything from the outside. Do *not* speak with him. And no one, and I mean *no one,* touches him on execution day but me. Do so and I'll kill you where you stand." She turned to look at Alex, lying inert on the bed. "You can try to learn to split yourself all you want in here, darling. But one thing's for certain; you won't get out." She gave him the same smile a wolf might give a cornered sheep before moving in for the kill, then she and her attendants left.

An eerie glow filled the dark stone room once they had gone, covering the floor, ceiling, and walls with bars of light. An incredibly powerful and specialized magick ran along them. Magick designed to keep the rarest of magickal creatures in.

Alex opened his eyes. *Glasgow.* They had plans to take Saorsa, if they hadn't already, and move her to Glasgow. And he was *here,* in England, in a prison he had no way to portal out of. He stood up from the bed, pulled off the top sheet, and tore off a long section of it, which he rolled tightly into a strong rope. He tied it back on itself in a sliding knot, put the makeshift noose around his neck, lay back down on the bed and began to think.

………

Laoise and Maria were ready to get out of the tower grounds. After dressing themselves in the plainest clothing they could find and stuffing their pockets with jewelry, they had made their way back down the stairs, cloaked and booted. The search appeared to be over and the ghost of Anne Askew was still with them, and still helpful.

"Anne says there are barges," Maria whispered. "They drop off supplies at Traitor's Gate. The servants here sometimes ride in and out on the barges to go to the nearby village. If we can get below to the gate, we might get out that way."

Laoise couldn't believe how resilient Maria was proving to be. She knew Maria was supposed to be one of The Lovers, but her physiology was entirely human; her body had been riddled with amulet shards and she'd been comatose for days and days before suddenly awakening. There was no reason why she should be moving as well as she did, or reasoning as well as she did, but here she was, supplying Laoise with a possible way out. Traitor's Gate wasn't far; just a short walk along the wall. With advice from Anne on when to leave so that they were walking in between guards passing by on patrol, they hurried along the wall toward the water gate. Apparently Anne's ghost wasn't confined to any one building within the Tower of London; she kept advising Maria as they stumbled along in the cold, and Maria kept up a steady stream of whispered conversation with her.

"Why, thank you, Anne. Stairs down just ahead? Which side? Oh my, it *is* terribly dark out here. What would we do without you?"

Down the stone stairs in the darkness. And then…not one, but *two* barges. One was being unloaded and seemed to be drawing the attention of the three guards on duty. One was moving toward the open water gate, the area behind its cabin full of old barrels and tarps, and crowded with shadows.

"Go!" Laoise gasped, pushing Maria ahead of her. The only light down here was from the lamps on the barges, and two torches on the wall set on the far side of the waterway near the guards. The guards and the men on the barge were arguing about something; if she and Maria were quick, they might just get by unseen and make it on to the departing watercraft in time. *But Maria's been unconscious for a week, at least. Can she…?*

But Maria was moving, and Laoise followed suit. There was no time to worry that the guards might hear footsteps, no time to worry about making the jump from the stone sides of the canal onto the boat. They made a decision and there was no time to waste. Laoise could hardly believe her eyes when she saw Maria suddenly put on a burst of speed and fling herself over the watery gap and land sprawling on the barge's back deck.

Laoise ran as fast as she could. The barge was picking up speed; the front of it was already near the archway that led to the Thames. For a brief moment she wasn't sure she was going to make it. And then she did. The impact knocked the wind out of her, and a heavy crate toppled onto her. But Maria was there, moving the crate aside, and Laoise sat up, head spinning, blood pouring down her shin from where the corner of the crate had hit her. She saw one of the guards behind them by the second barge raise up his lantern and stare in their direction. Laoise froze.

But Maria waved. *Waved* at the guard and *laughed*, laughed loudly as though the commotion they'd made was just a stupid error. And, shockingly, Laoise watched the guard wave back, and turn back to his duties.

"Are you alright?" Maria whispered, sinking down on the deck next to Laoise. "Are you hurt?"

Laoise was already using the inside of her cloak to staunch the bleeding. "I'm alright." She looked up and saw the archway to the Thames had passed overhead. She froze for a moment as she heard a man's footsteps coming toward them. It was one of the barge crew with his pole, readying himself for the turn onto the Thames.

Once again, Maria stepped in. She gave the man a little wave and he nodded, before returning to his task and ignoring both women completely. *Maria's just acting like she's supposed to be here. I will do the same.* She adjusted her cloak to be certain her ears were covered.

The barge turned and passed outside the walls of the Tower of London. Laoise thought of Alex. *I wish I could help you. But maybe you'll find a way out too.*

Maria sighed. "I think...I think I'll need a place to lie down soon. And...I could use some food."

"We'll find it," Laoise said reassuringly. *I don't care where this barge goes, as long as it doesn't turn around.* "We'll find an inn or something. Hire a carriage, once we can sell what we found." *I have never been anywhere on earth but the Tower. What will this place be like?*

"They're going to keep looking for us," Maria said quietly. She paused. "I need to find my daughter if I can. And...William. But I don't know England."

That makes two of us, thought Laoise. *I don't know much about earth geography. But I think...* "Maria. Is Scotland north of England?"

"Why, yes."

"Have you ever heard of a place called Branxholme?" *Alex's brother is there. Maybe he can help us.*

Maria patted Laoise on the arm. "It sounds familiar. But then, I'm not a reliable source right now. My soul just got back into my body again, and *everything* sounds like a possibility!" And Laoise had to laugh. *Possibilities are good things.*

....

"They're going to come looking for you here, Mum," Edan said, pacing in front of the fire. "We need to get you out of the country and somewhere safe." He frowned. "If Thomas Scott brought you *here*, why didn't he just drop you in France, where you'd be out if the Crown's reach?"

"I don't think," Adamina said, smoothing her skirts, "that you and I entirely understand the situation with Thomas. He wasn't supposed to be here, Edan, and he said something about magickal resources being in short supply. I think he thought the best place for me given the circumstances was here. With you."

"We don't really understand *any* of his situation, though, do we, Mum?" Edan paused. "I'm not trying to make things more difficult. *Truly,* I'm not. But I have to say that you seem ready to accept whatever bits of information Thomas deigns to give you as *fact*. We have no way of verifying *any* of what he says. I know you love him, but...how can you just be so accepting of everything he says and does without proof? You're a scientist, Mum. We've been talking for nearly three hours here and I can't help but think that..." he gestured toward Adamina, "that his side of the story is a bit *sparse*. Thomas comes and goes when he pleases. He doles out information when it serves his purpose. And all the while...."
Edan shook his head, "Alex is watching himself turn into a *monster,* Mum! I had to watch it, Saorsa had to watch it, and so did Mother Agnes! Alex gets... wings and fangs and he loses his ability to control his emotions. To be *himself,* Mum! And all the while this supposed father of his makes the excuse that he's not allowed to be there. Not allowed to help. While Alex and everyone around him *lose their damn minds!* "He gestured in the direction of Branxholme's Tower, and his voice dropped to a whisper. "I killed my own father up in that tower. I committed *patricide*. Against the *chief of our clan*. To save Alex. And don't get me wrong, I'd do it again if I had to. *But I shouldn't have had to*. If Alex had known his situation, he could've stayed away. He could've...," Edan fell silent.

Adamina stayed quiet, listening to her son.

Edan found his voice again. "You," he said, his voice shaking, "are the most brilliant person I've ever met. I grew up surrounded by your inventions and your experiments. Your books and your notes. Your theories and your lectures. I am, and have always been, in *awe* of you, Mum. Of your...*boundless* curiosity. And so I can't understand, I *don't* understand, how you can go thirty years without applying that same curiosity to the truths behind Thomas Scott!"

Mother Agnes, who was seated in a chair near the door, watched Adamina rise from her seat.

"Now just a minute there, Edan Scott," Adamina said, moving a step closer to him. "You don't know *anything* about my relationship with Thomas. Or, my relationship with your father, for that matter. You think I'm letting Thomas lead me around by the nose, do you? Well, it's not true! I may not know much about Faerie, but I know *him*. And let me tell you...let me tell you..." and in that moment, Mother Agnes saw something inside of Adamina *break*. "I know you've been hurt, and Alex has been hurt, and I never wanted *any* of that to happen! *Of course* I didn't want it to happen! I love both of you!" She took a deep breath.

"Do you have *any idea* what it's like to be an educated woman in this country? For over *thirty years* I watched men give credit for *my work* to Conall Scott. Do you realize that the books I published and the patents I received had to be written under a *man's pen name?* That was *me* in those pages! ME! For three decades I did the work, I created the plans, I chose the investments, *I ran the fucking businesses,* Edan, while someone else took the credit. I wasn't *allowed* to be smart because I'm a woman. After Phineas died, there was *one person* in all that time, *one man,* who treated me like an equal. Who saw me as worthy. Who cherishes me and trusts me enough to run an entire kingdom, if need be! And that man is *Thomas Scott*. The scraps of time I've had with him on this earth have sustained me through all the other bullshit that goes on here. Yes, he could be lying to me. Yes, he could be using me, but for what I certainly don't know. He is at once the greatest puzzle and the greatest prize of my life. He is...the one thing that is just *mine*."

She paused and took a step back. "I understand you are furious. I can't even imagine what will happen when I see Alex again. But I don't think Thomas is the villain here. He and I...we've been doing our best. We've been doing the only thing we *can* do. And I don't know why everything went wrong." Her voice grew quiet. "He adores you, Edan. Has loved you since you were a baby. Please don't blame everything on him." She looked away. "Alex was never, *ever* supposed to suspect he wasn't fully human. Was only supposed to be human. And I've thought about this since he was born. I don't see that telling him would've improved things much."

"It would've been the *truth*," Edan countered.

"Edan," Adamina said evenly, "*think about that*. The truth might have been better for you, but would it have been better for Alex? The Fae would have killed him for knowing what he was. And if they didn't...I think he just might have killed himself."

Edan stared. "Alex would never do that." Adamina looked at Edan sadly.

Mother Agnes cleared her throat. "May I...say something?"

Her voice seemed to relax Edan and Adamina somewhat, and they both turned away from each other. "Of course," Edan said quietly.

"Edan, have you ever had a conversation with a cat?"

Edan frowned and blinked at Mother Agnes. *"What?"*

"A cat. You know, one of the mousers down in the cellars."

"Why are you asking me this?"

"Trust me."

Edan folded his arms. "Well, of course not. It's a *cat*. That would be pointless."

Mother Agnes smiled. "Do you think cats can talk to each other? Are they capable of love and affection?"

Edan looked a bit exasperated. "I suppose so. They...seem to greet each other and such. They're fond of certain humans, sometimes."

"What I think is important to remember in this discussion," Mother Agnes said gently, "is that, just like cats, the Fae are entirely different from humans. They may look similar to us, and some - Elen, for example - are exceptionally gifted at *passing* as human. But they most definitely *are not*. The Fae, like cats, have a different lifespan than we do. A different culture. Different instincts. Different perspectives. Different physiology, too. The Fae interact with all manner of creatures that we don't - angels and daemons, elementals and spirits. I mean, Thomas Scott's most constant companion is supposed to be a *Formorian*...."

"A *what?*" Edan interrupted.

"His familiar. A chaos being with the head of a goat and the body of a man. What I'm trying to say is, both of you are making a case for or against listening to a being whose perspectives and motives and cultural rules are much, much, *much* more difficult to comprehend than how difficult it would be to fully understand the common cat. An animal that resides here in your home with you, and whose perspectives you *still* know nothing about." She tipped her head slightly to look at her companions. "Adamina, have you ever been to Faerie?"

"No." Adamina sighed. "I haven't."

"How do you imagine it to be?"

Adamina frowned. "Well...I imagine it would be like visiting a different country. Like...going to China, or Egypt. A different culture, I suppose, but *more* so." She smiled. "I'm guessing from your face that you think I'm way off."

Mother Agnes nodded. "Vika's Aunties sent me information on Thomas Scott while we were at the inn. It may or may not be true, of course, but some of it came from writings of Thomas the Rhymer. He claims that the Magician is several thousand years old and that there is an actual *religion* in other realms built around him, among other things. Various gods in other cultures were actually all *him*. For example, Thomas the Rhymer claims that Thomas Scott held a title in ancient Greece, Erebus - the personification of Darkness." She paused. "What I'm trying to say is this. It does the two of you no good to argue about whether or not Thomas has led Adamina astray because his motives are *unknowable*. He is an ancient god with an eternal lifespan who apparently can raise the dead at will. He is Darkness personified. He comes from a political and social culture we cannot hope to grasp, and a world where, from what I understand, even physical science operates differently. His companions are creatures we cannot even fathom. All we know about him for certain, if we consider Adamina a reliable observer, is that he appears to love you both, and Alex as well."

Edan sat down in a chair by the fire. "I suppose that makes sense." He sighed. "But...he appears to be part of our lives, now. How do you deal with the *unknowable?*"

Mother Agnes laughed. "You already deal with it every day. What happens when we die? Why were we created? Why are some things funny and others aren't? What is the definition of art? Attempting to know the unknowable is what humans *do*. I imagine it is what first attracted Adamina to Thomas in the first place. So, what I would say is this: Thomas is in your life and he has love for you, Edan. Do you think you can forgive him his unknowable-ness and try to love him back? Embrace the fact that neither of you will probably ever completely understand him? There's just as much of a possibility that the things he's done were done from a place of love as from a place of malice."

Edan looked away. "Edan," Adamina said softly, "*please*. He's...he's my husband."

Edan was on his feet now. "He's...*what?*"

Adamina looked down at her ring finger. "I married him, Edan. After he got me out of Carlisle."

"And what does that *mean?*" Edan looked completely overwhelmed.

"I'm...married here on earth to Thomas Scott. A bishop did the vows. And...in Faerie, Thomas' mother gave approval."

Edan put his head in his hands. "Do I know who his mother is?"

"According to the Aunties, it's The Morrigan," Mother Agnes said conversationally. "I've mentioned her before."

Edan moaned. "Remind me which one she is, again?"

"The original 'Washer at the Ford'. Her story led to the tales of the *bean nighe,* or banshee in English and Irish. A Celtic battle goddess of war and fate. Bringer of the omens of death." Mother Agnes paused. "Although *Morrigan* may be a title for the group of goddesses known as...."

"That's enough, thanks," said Edan weakly. "I got it."

"I'm...technically a queen in Faerie now, Edan. Of something called the Deck of Crows." Adamina sighed. "I'm sorry. That's why I look like this. Thomas and I did a spell on our wedding night so we could age the same way. So...we could be together."

Edan looked at his mother, his eyes red. "So are you a Faerie, now?"

Adamina smiled at him. "No. I'm...just me." She managed a weak smile. "A scientist who became curious and fell in love with a certain very mysterious being, who is full of endless adventures for my mind."

Edan Scott got to his feet and walked to stand in front of his mother, who now looked like his younger sister. He looked at her for a long time, as if he was wrestling with something inside. Finally, he seemed to come to a decision. "I'm just glad you're safe," he sighed, and held out his arms to her. "And human or Fae, I'm going to try and keep you that way."

Adamina put her arms around him. "I love you, my son."

They stood quietly for a few moments. Mother Agnes smiled. Edan was trying. He let go of Adamina. "Our problem still stands, however. We need to get you out of here and somewhere safe. I think you should go to France and stay with Gib."

"Who is Gib, please?" Mother Agnes asked.

"Gilbride. Some days he's Gib, some he's Gil, depending on who's doin' the talking. My younger brother. Well...Alex's younger brother too. Half-brother now, I suppose."

"He's in France?"

Adamina nodded. "He's much younger than Edan and Alex. He's still a child. When he was born, he...well, we realized he couldn't hear. My youngest sister Mary is married to an art professor, Artair Armstrong. They live in Paris where Artair teaches. And there's a school there for children like Gil, where they learn to speak with hand signs. And Gilbride has a great gift for art, which my sister and her husband nurture. He's been living in Paris since he was five. He comes home here in summers, and I go there frequently. He...has much more of a future there than he would here in Scotland. He has friends at school. I'd be there all the time if I didn't have the businesses to run."

Mother Agnes could hear the undercurrent of pain in Adamina's voice.

"Mum was in Paris nearly constantly the first two years Gib was there." Edan turned to Adamina. "Gib would be thrilled to have you come stay, as would Mary and Artair. The Crown will be looking for you, of course. But I dare say we have enough friends in the shipping world to smuggle you out, especially because you now look much younger than Adamina Scott is supposed to be. But I think we might want to send you on a circuitous route, just to be sure. Perhaps go north, head to Norway, switch ships, and then go down. Or over to Ireland first."

Adamina shook her head. "I'm not leaving while Alex is missing. There has to be something I can do to help." She took a step away from Edan and looked at him closely. "Do you know where Saorsa Stuart is?"

"No, no, *no*, Mum!" Edan protested. "We need to send you to *France*. Stay in the Borders and you'll end up right back in Carlisle!"

"Edan, I can't sit in France and paint watercolors and eat macarons while Alex suffers," Adamina said firmly. "I don't know much about Faerie, but I probably know more than any of you. I've had a Fae god in my life for *thirty years*. I may be the best current resource you have."

Edan was shaking his head. "Mum, Alex would be *beside himself*. He wanted you out of Carlisle so badly! Now you're out and...well, *he'd* want you on a ship to France, too!"

Adamina folded her arms. "Well, he's not here to vote now, is he?"

Edan put his hands on his hips. "Mum, you're being unreasonable! It's my job as Laird to protect this clan now, and I must *insist* that you leave for France *at once*!"

Adamina raised an eyebrow. "Oh, you're getting *dangerously* close to pulling rank on your own mother. Do you really want to go down this road?"

Edan met her gaze. "Dear God in Heaven, it's obvious where Alex gets his stubborn streak from. If you continue to make choices against your own welfare, Lady Scott, you will give me no recourse except to *forcibly* put you on a ship with an armed escort."

Adamina laughed. "Oh, *good luck with that,* Laird Scott. Who the hell do you think hired every ship's captain we have in our employ? You might force me on board somewhere, but I'll have that ship going anywhere I want it to five minutes after it leaves port!"

Edan was becoming frustrated again. "You're *determined* to get yourself hanged! Have you thought about how that would make Alex and Gib feel? How about me? Do you want your faerie lover to come back and discover he pulled you out of Carlisle for nothing? How many flying carpets does the man have?"

"And how will everyone feel if *Alex* turns up dead because I *didn't* help?" Adamina countered. "Who does Saorsa have helping her right now? Who?"

"I sent Rune with her. And his team. And they might have a healer named Willow with them."

"So, she's trying to interact with Faerie with only human knowledge on her side," Adamina stated. "I'm a Fae *Queen,* Edan. The Morrigan *knows who I am.* I'm married to her son, a Fae general. You don't think that might help bring your brother home in one piece?"

Edan stared at the ground. Adamina lowered her voice. "You said it yourself about an hour ago. Alex needs help. Saorsa needs help. And Alex's father can't be here. It's my responsibility, Edan. I owe it to Alex to help him, especially since a secret I helped keep created the situation." She took a deep breath. "If there's a choice here between Alex's safety and mine, I choose his." She moved closer to her son, and took his hands in hers. "I love you, Edan. But I'm going to do this. I'm going to do everything in my power to help bring your brother home." She took a deep breath. "So...please. Take me to Saorsa Stuart."

Edan nodded and sighed. "I'll get men ready to ride." Mother Agnes smiled.

. . . .

"What are you going to do?" Mother Agnes was sitting in Edan's study alone with him.

"Send her to Saorsa, I suppose. The only problem is Rune and his team are already there, and the only other people I'd trust to get her there are Vika and Duncan." Edan shook his head. "I could send a messenger to the Aunties to see if they're still there and bring them back, but it would take a few days, and they might not even still be there. Meanwhile, Mum's sitting here when the Crown comes knocking." He sighed.

"Who else might take her?"

"She needs mortal *and* magickal protection. You need to be here to watch over Fia. *I* need to be here to deal with the Crown. Toran could go, but I can't send him alone." He looked at Mother Agnes. "Could Annag fend off an attack if needed?"

Mother Agnes smiled. "Annag is stronger than she looks. I think that's a fine idea. Toran and Annag then." She sighed. "I wish there was at least one more in the party for safety. But sometimes we must trust the Goddess that things will be as they should."

………

It was midnight, and everyone at Branxholme except the guards were asleep. And Fia Grace Elizabeth Douglas Elliot.

She'd watched all day. No one had made a move toward the guest room where the enchanted mirror hung. Fia knew that Adamina was in the building, but Lady Scott hadn't appeared in the hall at all, either to see Fia or to go in the room with the mirror. *They've told her what I did, and she doesn't want to see me,* Fia had mused.

Mother Agnes had Fia's dinner sent up to her room that night. "Lady Scott has returned," Mother Agnes had informed her. "She'll be leaving in the morning, and all will be as it was." She hadn't offered any information on where Adamina Scott was headed, and Fia didn't ask. *They all have their own plans now. And I have mine.*

She thought about the baby. It didn't feel quite real yet. She'd seen evidence that the child was there, magickal evidence, but her body didn't look or feel any different. *Perhaps Fae bairns are different in the womb.* And thinking about the baby made her think about Alex.

She wished the baby hadn't been conceived through a ritual. *There was no fun in that. And oh, what fun it could have been!* She closed her eyes and thought of Alex, her memories of him as crisp and clear as if they'd happened yesterday. *God, those kisses of his!* And that *voice.* She could still hear him whispering to her, feel his hands on her, even though a decade had passed. *Fia Grace, you feel so good to me. Yes, just like that, my lovely one. Oh, Fia, dinnae stop now. Put your mouth right there. Please. Please.* Maybe once the bairn was born he'd find his way to her like that again.

What *could* still be fun, she imagined, would be walking around pregnant in front of everyone. Especially in front of all the women in the area that she'd known all her life. She'd be in a shop in town, and then...*Oh, hello! Why yes, I'm due next summer. Alexander can hardly wait.* She'd watch their faces flush crimson with jealousy at the evidence of his desire for her. Fia smiled. By having Alex's baby, she'd instantly become the center of gossip in the Borders. She'd get that air of mystery that came with being an outlaw's lady. Tall, dark, and handsome Alexander Scott had been an occupant of young women's minds in this area for years, whether they were married or not. *And I'm the one that caught him. Even if he doesn't marry me, with a big round belly it will be obvious how he must have wanted me, and it will be SO scandalous!* A delicious shiver went up Fia's spine.

Fia had grown up feeling that she was living in her sister Anne's shadow. Everything was always about tall, elegant, talented Anne, and her perfect love with tall, elegant, talented Killian. Their parents had doted on Anne. Anne seemed to take all the attention in the room. *No more. Now I'll be the one on everyone's 'must invite' list.* She pictured the conversations she'd have, and the mystique she'd cultivate in the social circles of the Borders. *There's Fia Elliot. They say she's pregnant with Alexander Scott's child! And not married yet! They say Alexander just couldn't keep his hands off her. I hear she'll be staying at Drumlanrig Castle after the baby's born while they renovate her new home. Why, I imagine with Alexander gone all the time, she'll rule that area like a queen. Another Adamina Scott, that one.* Fia let out an involuntary squeal of glee.

And now there was the mirror, too. Mother Agnes was keeping out any of her former Fae allies who might try and see her. But that didn't mean *new* bonds couldn't be forged. There was more than one way into Faerie, right? She decided now was the time. She crept down the hall to the room where the mirror waited. She shut the door quietly behind her and placed her candle on the bedside table. *All right. Here goes.* She shook the tension out of her hands, climbed onto the bed, and pulled the curtain aside. Then she leaned forward, and breathed on the mirror.

A disturbance, like a stone being thrown into a still pool formed and Fia sat back and waited. Then...there she was. The same hypnotically beautiful woman who had appeared before was back. Smiling. Her eyes were enchanting, but different this time. Her pupils were jet black, her irises no longer silver but instead a deep, deep blue, but full of tiny specks of light. *Like stars.* Fia wanted to stare into those eyes for a long, long time.

The woman's hair was silver. Not a white or gray that comes with age, but a vibrant, shining silver. Thick and healthy with tiny braids worked in places, unbound at the bottom. Her lips had a slightly bluish cast to them this time, as did the tint of her cheeks on her alabaster skin. Fia found her rare, and tantalizing.

"What's your name?" Fia breathed, forgetting how to begin a conversation with a greeting. *She's gorgeous.* She felt a flame of attraction growing in her heart. The woman appeared to be about her age, perhaps a few years older. *But she's Fae, so that means nothing.*

The vision laughed. "Oh, it's way too early for *that,* my darling. We don't give names in Faerie until we trust each other."

"I trust you," Fia blurted. "I mean, I *want to.* You're the loveliest thing I've ever seen."

The Fae in the mirror gave a soft smile. "Honest, I see. I like that." Fia's face lit up. "Tell me, little raven-hair, have you any Fae blood in you? You didn't say last time."

"No...no," Fia stuttered. "But...I'm going to have a baby. And the bairn has Fae blood."

"Oh," said the Faerie with the galaxies in her eyes, "a Fae lover, then. You have one. Too bad." Her eyes were alight with a sparkling merriment. "Better luck for me next time."

Fia's mouth fell open in surprise. Was this beautiful creature *flirting* with her? It couldn't be. Her shock showed on her face, and the goddess in the mirror laughed. "Oh, you're *delightful.*"

"Why are you talking to me?" Fia managed to get her mind in motion again. "Fae don't just talk to humans all the time. What is it you...well, just...why?"

"Curiosity, mostly," mused the silver-haired woman. "I've come to visit with someone, but they're not here. I kept hearing a voice in my room and found this mirror hidden in the back of the wardrobe. I could hear you talking to it, trying to make a connection. And I became...curious." She raised her eyebrows. "You obviously don't know what you're doing, but your attempts were *quite* amusing. You must want to speak to someone here quite badly."

Fia blushed. "I...well, I wanted to see if I could make it work. I'm rather curious myself."

"Well, here I am," said the woman. "What is it you want to know, you pretty little thing?"

Fia was taken aback again at the intimacy of this woman's tone. Every encounter she'd had with the Fae, apart from Alex, had been quite formal. "Are you...a goddess?"

The woman nodded. "Yes. And an Elemental, as well."

Fia shifted closer to the mirror. "I...don't know what that means."

A small smile formed at the corner of the woman's mouth. "It's a type of Fae, dearest."

"If I can't know your name, what shall I call you?"

The starry-eyed woman looked up and away. "You can call me what the Greeks called me, I suppose. Mother of Doom, Sleep, Blame, and Distress. Daughter of Chaos, Consort of Darkness." She laughed. "Or Nyx, for short."

Fia moved slightly away from the mirror. "You're...joking," she spluttered. "You're...*Nyx*. The Mother of Hecate?"

Nyx shook her head. "No, no, the Greeks got that wrong. They adopted Hecate from the east and just shoved her into their pantheon. I know Hecate, but we're *not* of the same house." She waved a graceful hand. "Humans alter history to serve their purposes *much* more than they should."

"What...house are you from?" Fia was captivated. *Am I really speaking with Nyx? The actual goddess?*

"Elementals...are outside the regular structure of things a bit," said Nyx slowly. "I've allied myself with different houses at different times." She ran a hand through her moonlight-colored hair. "To give you an idea, though, I am currently sitting in a guest suite at the Castle of Crows."

Fia felt a surge in her blood. "The Castle of Crows?" she repeated. "My...the father of my child is from that Deck!"

"Is he, now?" Nyx suddenly looked deeply interested. "I could say the same!"

"*You* have children in the Deck of Crows?" Fia said, eyes wide. "*Who?*"

"Oh, *quite a few*," Nyx laughed. "And some in the Deck of Ravens, as well. I don't see them often. We Elementals live somewhat....*apart*."

"Could you teach me how to be a mother?" Fia said, feeling slightly out of breath. "I understand that Fae bairns...well, they are a bit different from human ones. I've heard the children of the Deck of Crows sometimes need...special music. Songs. And that animals treat them differently, and that they sometimes move around in space."

Nyx tilted her head slowly and looked at Fia curiously. "Why isn't the father of your child teaching you these things? Does he not know about the child? Not want it?"

"No, it's just...," Fia paused. Something in her belly told her not to bring up Alex, or the *leth-dhia*. "He's...dead. And I'm here all alone with no one to guide me." The lie flew from her mouth as easily as if she had breathed it. "I don't know any other Fae. Just one came and delivered a message that my beloved...was gone."

"Did he die in the war?" Nyx asked gently.

"Yes," Fia nodded enthusiastically. "He did." She had no idea what she was talking about, but she could see sympathy on Nyx's face. *She might take me under her wing. Teach me. She has to be powerful!* Fia could feel excitement rising in her chest. *I just need to ensure she wants to talk to me again! And if she feels bad for me....*

"Oh, you poor, beautiful little creature," Nyx breathed. "All alone on Earth with a Faeling on the way, and no help."

"Yes," Fia said, conjuring up a face of pure tragedy. "I'm...worried what will happen when the bairn is born. It's my first. And my lover, he said that the Magician might be interested in our child...."

Nyx's dark gray eyebrows went straight up. "What has *An Draíochta* to do with this?" she said, her eyes narrowing.

Fia's mind raced. "The father of my child. He...he couldn't tell me a lot. Said it was forbidden, that he shouldn't even be here on earth with me in the first place. But he *did* say that the Magician might come and want to take my child." And Fia could see immediately that something she'd just said had struck a chord.

Nyx's eyes turned pure white. "*An Draíochta* thinks he can take your child, does he?" she snarled. "We'll see about *that*." Her irises reappeared as she composed herself, turning silver as they'd been the first time Fia saw her. "Tell me your whole name, darling."

"Fia Grace Elizabeth Douglas Elliot," Fia said. *She's interested in me!*

"I must go," Nyx said, looking at Fia intently. "Put your hand to the glass, dear."

Fia pressed her left palm gently against the mirror's surface, and watched Nyx do the same. She felt something move against her palm, and when she pulled her hand back she discovered that in her hand was a deep blue stone with streaks of purple and flashes of white moving in its depths.

"Put this under your pillow when you sleep in three nights," Nyx commanded, "and we will talk again." Her voice softened. "Goodnight, Fia Grace, most cherished one. I must admit, I find you...a marvel." The mirror turned black.

Fia stared at the stone in her hand, and a slow smile spread across her face.

………

East of London, England

Laoise looked down at Maria's sleeping form as she put the tray on the table near the fire. She'd grown quite fond of her in the short time they had been together; they had traded whispered stories while hiding in the forgotten royal closet, waiting for the search for them to die down. Laoise now knew Maria's story, and Maria Laoise's. It was clear that hope and adrenaline had been responsible for Maria's ability to endure her escape from the Tower of London; shortly after they had been underway on the barge, she had fallen deeply asleep. They'd ridden the barge past three small towns and at the fourth Laoise awakened Maria, thanked the crew, and disembarked.

They're going to be looking for us, Laoise thought. She felt inside the pocket of the apron she was still wearing. *Still there.* But whether her little bag of secrets would save them or allow them to be found by the Fae, only time would tell.

Dawn was breaking in the east as they walked south from the river into the village. Half-frozen and confused, Laoise could barely think straight. "We need a place to stay," she whispered to Maria. "I don't...I don't know anything about human towns. Do you see anywhere that looks good?"

Maria took Laoise by the hand. "Come," she said. "I'll find us something." Maria wandered along the waterfront for a few minutes, and then took a large road into the town proper, where a market was just beginning to set up on the square.

"Excuse me," Maria said cheerfully to a man setting up a display of large baskets under a tent, "can you direct us to the inn, please?" The man nodded and gave them directions, Maria smiled sweetly and thanked him, and then they were off again.

Two more blocks and then through a door under a sign that said *The Red Deer Tavern*. Maria never hesitated. She chatted up the man stacking plates on the sideboard and told him a complete lie about them losing their purse on the journey. "Might you be willing to trade room and board for a few days for...this?" She gave him a winning smile and opened her palm to reveal a dainty pearl bracelet they'd brought from their hidden closet at the Tower. "We'd be most grateful. If you're uncomfortable, though, we can just sit in the common room and enjoy breakfast until the jeweler's opens...."

It turned out that the innkeeper wasn't uncomfortable with this trade in the slightest. His eyes widened and took the bracelet from Maria quickly, and promised them room and board for two weeks, with a hot bath and a bottle of wine every night.

"Thank the Fates," Laoise had breathed as she unlocked their room. She and Maria had collapsed into bed and slept, barely removing their cloaks and boots first. Laoise awakened around noon and went to fetch food and hot coffee.

"Maria," she said softly upon her return, "Wake up. We need to eat and then I need to go out for a bit. And there's hot baths to be had, my friend." Maria had awakened, smiling, and they had quickly devoured the boiled eggs, bacon, and bread Laoise had brought.

"I have an idea," Laoise said. "But I need a map of England and of Scotland. And a picture of Branxholme Castle." She paused. "And I need to know everything about that amulet I've been removing from your skin."

"There isn't much to tell," Maria said, wrapping her hands around her stoneware mug. "My grandmother was a witch, a High Priestess, and she thought it was important and needed to be kept safe. After she died, I came to Scotland to look for it, and a book of hers. I found them with the help of...well, William and I were given a rather mysterious key after I attempted a rather haphazard summoning of someone named Michael Scot. And the key opened a compartment in my grandmother's tombstone. Both the book and the stone were there but as I ran to find William at the port, I ran through a stone circle and the amulet burst and embedded itself in my skin. And I was...taken away."

Laoise looked at Maria, thoughtful. "So the amulet has enough magickal energy to open a portal, if you take it to a place of power with a portal in it."

"I...suppose. Is that what happened? It opened a portal?"

"I think so. But I don't know why it exploded."

"When it was in me, I couldn't keep my consciousness in this world, as I told you. I'm so glad most of it is out."

"Do you think most of it was in you? Or in your daughter?"

"Oh, me, I think. Otherwise I imagine Saorsa would have been affected in a similar way."

Laoise fell silent. "What are you thinking?" Maria asked.

"From what you've said, Scotland is a long way away. And that's where Branxholme is. Alex thought it was a safe place. But they will be looking for us, so we need a shortcut."

"A ship, maybe?"

"I thought of that. But the Fae might have the Crown looking for us at the ports." She paused. "I was thinking of trying to use a portal. Portals are easier to open if they've been used recently. When I came here with the Fae, we came through a portal about three day's ride to the northeast of London. My employers kept calling the portal we came through 'King's Men'." She paused. "They probably took Alex out of a portal in Scotland. If we can find the portal at King's Men, we can hopefully re-use the portal in Scotland as well, which would put us significantly closer to Branxholme. The only problem is, you're human and I'm half-human, so we don't have enough energy ourselves to open one."

"You are thinking if we had the amulet shards you took out of me, we would." Maria sighed.

"We *do* have them." Laoise pointed to a small leather bag hanging from her belt. "I...well, I stole them. Once I started talking to Alex, I became worried about who my employers actually were, and I switched the shards with broken glass. What they have locked up in your surgery is a box with a smashed apothecary bottle in it, and I have the amulet pieces."

Maria stared at her. "My goodness, you're a naughty thing," she said, her face breaking into a grin.

"Believe me when I say I've never stolen anything before *in my life*. And now I've stolen this," she said, gesturing at her belt, "and *you*. And a lot of antique royal clothing and jewelry. All in twenty-four hours!" She shook her head. "But part of the amulet is in Saorsa, and there are still fragments in you. I don't know if it can power a portal opening in pieces like this and without being whole."

"We have to try," Maria said.

Laoise frowned. "We have no idea where the portal Alex was taken through in Scotland *is*. It could be inside a Fae hideout, or a fort and we might end up putting ourselves right on our enemy's doorstep." She sighed. "There could also be other portals in Scotland that have been used recently. Although with the war, there's supposed to be very limited interaction between Faerie and here. But...we could see."

"This is going to work. It *has* to," Maria said excitedly. "We've made it this far! What do we need to do next?"

"We need money for maps, horses, and accommodations. Maybe a carriage would be better. And we need new clothes. The innkeeper was willing to take pearls, but the next person might assume we stole what we're offering and turn us in. So I need to head to a jeweler and see what we can sell." Laoise put her head in her hands. "What is English money called?"

"I'll go," said Maria.

"No, you won't." Laoise argued. "I can hide my ears, but you'd have to hide your entire *face*. Charles Edward Stuart is persona non grata here, remember? And you need rest. You were in a coma *yesterday*."

"The shards," Maria said, changing the subject, "do they give off magickal energy all the time? Could the Fae see that and find us?"

"I'm not sure," Laoise confessed. "They are definitely giving off *something* right now. Whether or not it's enough to make us stand out, I don't know. I don't know what other sources of magick are here. I don't know *anything*, it feels like."

Maria patted her hand. "Laoise, you've done so much for me. You've healed me, freed me, and gotten us food and shelter. I can't thank you enough."

Laoise smiled at her. "Let's hope that portal opens," she said, finishing her coffee, "and that the portal on the other side is a good one."

………

Laoise had been successful at selling a fair amount of jewelry, and had procured good travel clothing for both herself and Maria, as well as other basic supplies that went a long way to making them feel less like recent escapees. Toothbrushes and tooth powder, combs, rosewater, travel bags, and new nightclothes.

But she was worried. She wanted to be moving. She wanted to hire a carriage, and sleep on the way to the portal. *We could cut our time in half if we have someone to drive us. But we also have to find a trustworthy someone.* She also worried about Maria. Maria had managed to escape, running mostly on adrenaline, but she was weak and tired now. But every minute she let Maria rest was another minute she felt like a target.

She paused for a moment. *Maybe I'm thinking about this wrong. This amulet must have a lot of power. I was planning on using King's Men Circle because I know roughly where it is, and because it's been used recently, which means it will be easier to open. But what if the amulet we have is powerful enough that I don't need a recently opened portal? What if I just need ANY portal?*

London was an ancient town. She'd read about it before coming here. *It was founded by a group called the Romans. Not long ago in faerie time, but a long time for humans.* She shook her head. There had to be a portal closer than three days from here.

She remembered reading that humans in this area now built places of worship called *churches. I remember hearing that many of these church things are built on top of older magickal sites. Well, then. I need a powerful church. Something that has survived centuries and has a lot of human activity in it.* She unrolled a map of London she'd purchased. *A holy site.* Her eyes were drawn to a label near the Thames. *Thorney Island.*

Except, the area didn't *look* like an island. *Maybe it was once, long ago, and the waterway silted up, or was built over. But islands are powerful places.* She moved the candle closer to the map and looked closer. *Something called...Westminster Abbey.* She paused. This abbey was big enough that it was featured on the map. And it was right next to something called the Palace of Westminster. It sounded like a powerful place. She needed to find out more.

She left a note for Maria, bundled herself once again in her outerwear and left the room. Down the stairs she went, double-checking that her hat covered her ears. In the common room, she went up to one of the serving girls, who was preparing the room for the influx of patrons who would come in for dinner. "Excuse me," she said to the young woman. "Can you tell me...where is the closest church?"

The woman nodded at the door. "Two streets over, toward the river. Has a massive steeple on it. Can't miss it." Laoise thanked her and hurried out the door into the cold. A short time later was walking in the door of the church in the fading evening light. She'd never been inside of a church before. It was *fascinating*. There was some sort of service going on, and Laoise crept quietly in and took a seat in an empty pew in the back.

The candles gave the entire room an otherworldly feel. And then the small congregation stood and began to sing. Laoise's face lit up. *Listen to that. Magick being created.* The service was finishing up, and Laoise stayed seated as the devotees filed out of the church. Soon she was the only person still seated in the pews.

"Can I help you, my child?" An elderly, gentle-voiced priest stood at the end of the row. "Or would you prefer solitude?"

"Oh...yes, I could use help, actually," Laoise said, standing. "My mother and I are traveling to London. We're on our way to...Westminster Abbey? My sister is a priestess there."

The priest frowned. "I assume you mean a *nun?*"

Laoise nodded enthusiastically. "Oh, yes. That's what I meant." She paused. "We haven't seen her in some time. And I've never been there. I was wondering if maybe you had a sacred bard or a ritual crone who might educate me on the practices of the Westminsterites of Thorn Island so that when I arrive, I am prepared to participate in any customs they require on the sacred grounds."

The priest looked at her with an odd look on his face. It made Laoise nervous, and she began to talk faster. "At home, there's this nomadic Druid who is well versed in the practices of all the local temples, and he'll mentor you for a small fee," Laoise said, smiling. "Can you direct me to someone like that?"

The priest looked very confused. "I'm not certain I...."

"Perhaps I can help," said a voice from behind Laoise. "I'm Mother Enid. It sounds as though you might be looking for a *religious historian?*"

The priest looked relieved. Laoise turned and standing before her was a woman a good six inches shorter than she was, with a kind, inquisitive face and gentle eyes. Her voice, however, contained a strong note of authority. "Yes," Laoise said, nodding quickly. "A historian would be wonderful."

"Father, I'm happy to help, if you don't mind," said Mother Enid, but the priest was already leaving the conversation, heading quickly back up the aisle toward the altar. She turned to Laoise. "Come with me, my dear. I believe I may be able to help you." She patted Laoise gently on the arm as she led her toward the doors of the church. "And for Goddess' sake, until we get where we're going, don't use the terms *ritual crone* or *nomadic Druid* in front of anyone," she whispered. "I don't know what circle you're from, but they should have told you to be *careful* here."

The Borders, Scotland

Willow, Rune, Saorsa, and the others set out the next morning, headed west. The day was clear and bright, and the wind was low. A good day for riding. A good day for a fresh start.

Saorsa felt immensely better. She'd confided in Rune and Willow, and seen Alex twice. He was alive and determined to free himself. *And we're going to give him all the help we can. And once I'm with him again, we'll work everything out. I am choosing to believe we can.* The only thing Saorsa hadn't shared with her new companions was her exact plan for interacting with Faerie.

"I hope you don't mind," Saorsa said, "but in light of all that has happened, I think it's safer for everyone if I keep a few things to myself for the time being. I'll share more with you once we're established. I promise."

Rune and Willow had been incredibly understanding. "We can wait," said Willow, "until you're ready to speak."

Saorsa and Willow conversed nonstop while they rode. Rune was a few lengths ahead of them, watching the road, but dropped back to answer questions or offer his opinion from time to time. Between the three of them, a plan began to form.

"I need a place of power," Saorsa told them. "A place we can work from, and retreat to. Somewhere to act as a home base for us. One where we can ground ourselves and build a defense." She paused. "One that the *leth dhia* Alex is drawn to, because I'm going to try and communicate with his aspects. And I happen to have just the place."

They had stopped to water the horses, and Saorsa spread out a map Edan had given her on a large, flat stone. "Here."

Rune squinted at the map. "There's nothing there but forest. What is it?"

"It's called Wolfcroft," Saorsa explained. "Alex and I camped here once. There's the remains of an old farm. But it has a working well and some shelter. And most importantly, *wolves*."

Willow looked up at Saorsa and gave her a cautious half-smile. "Saorsa...I've never seen a wild wolf in Scotland."

"Hunted to extinction on this island," added Rune mournfully.

"Not yet. We saw them. A whole pack." Saorsa put her gloved finger over the circled area on the map. "Right in this area."

Rune and Willow stared at Saorsa a moment. "You're...serious," Willow said slowly.

"Dead serious. I think this place is special. And Alex had a real connection to it. I've rarely seen him so happy. And The Morrigan, the Queen of the Wolves among the Fae, is Alex's grandmother. There's something *here,* I just know it. I think if we build here, I'll be able to connect with the power that flows through Alex's family. I think it will make it easier to contact him, and ...perhaps other parties."

"You think this place is like Morrigan's Cave," Rune said. "Vika took me there once. It's...closer to Faerie, somehow."

"Exactly. I thought to go there, but the Fae who took Alex have used that portal and worked magick there. They know it too well. It feels…too close to them. Not defensible. But Wolfcroft, I think it might give us some incredible results with the added bonus that the energies and spirits there will have only worked with *us*." Saorsa looked up at her traveling companions. "What do you think?"

"You mentioned *other parties*," Willow said, twisting her brightly twined tendrils of hair up and out of the way. "Other than Alex, who else are you hoping to talk to?"

"Well," said Saorsa, looking at her new friend, "the wolves, for one." She smiled at Willow. "You mentioned earlier having done healing for animals and speaking with the wild spirits of the wood. Do you think you might teach me to talk to the wolves, if we can find them? And…the crows?"

Willow grinned. "We can try. What sort of plan are you forming, my friend?"

Saorsa squeezed her hand. "One full of magick."

Wolfcroft, Scotland

They made it to Wolfcroft. Willow's face lit up as they drew near. "Saorsa," she breathed. "You're right. The energy here is...different. And very strong."

Saorsa grinned. "Now we just need to turn it into something." It was both wonderful and strange for Saorsa to see Wolfcroft again. *I'll never forget being here with Alex. And I'm excited to establish a safe place here. Something of my own. And yet, everything I set eyes on makes me miss him.*

Aeric, Olav, and Trig immediately began establishing a camp upon arrival, with Rune and Eske walking the perimeter of the old farm to get the lay of the land. They were looking around for firewood when they heard a sharp whistle from the woods, and a minute later Rune and Eske appeared.

"What is it?" Willow asked.

Rune was laughing. "Come and see." The others followed him up to Eske, who led the way higher into the woods.

"I guess you didn't come up here on your last trip through, Saorsa" Rune grinned. "Apparently your Wolfcroft wasn't just a farm. Take a look!"

At first, Saorsa didn't see what he was talking about. And then her eyes widened as she did. It was almost completely covered with tangled vines, but it was there: the outline of a tower among the towering Scotch pines.

"It's a broch," Willow said, amazed. "And it looks...intact!"

"It has a roof and everything," Rune smiled. "It's not the original, obviously. This has had substantial repairs. But it will make better protection against the elements than tents will, that's for certain." He looked at his companions. "We came right back when we saw it, but I think there's more here. Aeric, can you, Olaf, and Trig bring the horses and supplies up? The rest of us will have a look around."

The trio headed down for the horses, while the others inspected the broch more closely and then fanned out to peer into the dim, dense undergrowth of the forest. Saorsa's heart was pounding. *A broch! Like Vika's at Wyldwood!* Vika had told her brochs were rare in the Borders. *And there's one here! At Wolfcroft!* She could hardly wait to tell Alex.

She heard Eske shout and headed in the direction of his voice. He'd found a burn, flowing clear and strong, invisible under the tangled winter remains of plants. Saorsa heard another excited shout from Rune, and they found Rune standing with a hand on his head, staring in disbelief.

"Oh...my...Goddess," Saorsa stopped short when she looked in the direction of his gaze. "It *can't be!*" There was a clearing in the woods. And inside it, what appeared to be a stable and a large stone cottage, complete with a woodshed. The buildings looked as though it had been abandoned for some time, but they appeared intact.

"Wait here," Rune cautioned Saorsa and Willow. "Eske and I, we'll go make certain no one's around." He put his hand on his dirk.

Saorsa highly doubted anyone was. The forest had tried to reclaim these structures: the cottage and barn were completely overgrown, and the open-sided woodshed little more than a gigantic clump of dead plants. *If we'd come in summer, we might never have seen these at all,* Saorsa thought. She watched as Eske and Rune went into the barn, and then emerged and headed toward the cottage.

She heard Willow's voice behind her. "Saorsa. Come and see." The burn wound its way near the cottage, and Willow was exploring its tangled banks. She pointed to a muddy area near a shallow crossing. "Look what I found!" It was a track. A huge canine track, sunk into the mud.

"They *are* here," Willow whispered. "They really are!" She looked at Saorsa, unable to contain her excitement. "You were right!"

"All clear!" Rune called. "Come have a look. There is...one sad thing, though." Willow and Saorsa hastened toward the cottage, where Eske stood in the doorway with Rune, who led them inside.

"I think...whomever lived here left for the Uprising and never came back," Rune said quietly. "Look what Eske found."

The cottage was simply furnished, and a wooden box sat on the table near the cold fireplace. Spiders had worked their magick in all the corners, and a layer of dust and grime had settled over everything. Rune nodded to Saorsa. "Open the box."

Inside was a bible, well-worn, with a family tree drawn inside the front cover. A large, heavy Catholic crucifix was also in the box, along with a marriage certificate and several papers that seemed to commemorate baptisms. And under those, a locket with a picture of the Bonnie Prince, along with several small reproduction paintings of Charles Edward Stuart and James Frances Edward Stuart. The inhabitants of the cottage had been Jacobites. Saorsa held the locket in her hand.

"There's no clothes here, so I don't think they were arrested after the Uprising. They took things with them." Rune looked around the room. "All the vegetation has had time to grow. I think they left to follow the Prince and never returned." He gestured at the walls. "Well made, this. There's even a large loft upstairs. The stable's in good condition. This will be even better than camping in the broch."

Saorsa looked closely at the family tree. "Maxwell. They were Clan Maxwell." Saorsa sighed. "Do you think...do you think maybe they just left? Went somewhere else?"

"Edan sent a man to look into the property," Rune reminded her. "He's to meet us here once he finds something. I left him a message at that message drop this morning, telling him we'd arrived." He smiled at Saorsa. "No matter what, I imagine they would be fine with us staying here. You are, after all, the Bonnie Prince's niece."

Willow put her hand gently on Saorsa's arm. "We can reach out tonight, and see what we can feel of them," she said. "Send light in their direction, wherever they may be."

Saorsa felt gratitude ring out in her heart. She was so glad for the fact that Willow seemed to understand what was in her heart without her having to express it. *Willow is not a witch, but we understand the same energies. And hers is good and calm and full of light.* She took Willow's hand and squeezed.

Eske headed out to intercept the others at the broch and lead them to the stable. "This is going to take some work," Rune said with a smile, "but this is *much* better than what I expected. Shelter for us and the horses, firewood, good water, and very private. There may be more to discover here that we can use, as well."

"And," Willow chimed in, "with this cottage, we have a place to bring Oona back to. If we set to work on this cottage today, maybe we can head for Fenwick to fetch her soon!"

Saorsa's spirit soared. *She had a place to bring Oona!* Alex would be overjoyed. *I've missed her. I can't wait to have her with me!* She'd thought of the little girl so many times since they'd parted. *Maybe if Alex can come through the portal again to visit, he could see Oona!* Saorsa felt hope roar into her soul like a fire catching tinder in a fireplace. *We've wandered for so long! This could be a chance at something like a home!*

"Rune, do you think the property Alex and I camped at down below and this one belong to the same family?"

Rune dusted off a chair and sat. "I think it's the same. The buildings below are older and smaller. I'm of the mind that the croft you and Alex found was the original homestead, and then they built this later. I have a feeling if we walk around a bit more, we might find more outbuildings and a fence line."

Saorsa and Willow pulled up chairs. "You're running the show here, Saorsa," Rune nodded. "How would you like us to begin?"

Saorsa hesitated a moment. Her first instinct was to defer to him, to say *you have much more experience in the world than I do.* But then she heard Vika's voice in the back of her mind: *eyes up, Saorsa. You've seen safe houses before. You know what to do. This one's yours.* How would she ever learn to lead if she didn't try?

"I think," said Saorsa, "that we put Aeric and Trig on the stable. Start clearing it out and get the horses settled. Olav can help me bring in water and clean things so we can cook and function in a clean space. Let's put Eske on security. He can draw up a watch schedule and walk the perimeter to see what we need to keep an eye on...if there are nearby roads or signs of any neighbors. Rune, I would like you to start by taking a walk with Willow. I'd like you to place any magickal safeguards you know on our boundaries and keep your eyes open for more buildings as you go. And Willow," she turned and smiled at her friend, "if you could go out and get to know the woods, that would be wonderful. Get a feel for the energies here. See what wildlife is in the area." Saorsa's smile widened. "Talk to this place and let it know why we want to be here and ask the plants and animals for their permission to dwell with them."

Saorsa was nearly vibrating with excitement. *We can do this! I'm going to take everything I've learned and use it here.* She'd work protection and blessing spells on this place while she cleaned. *I'm going to ground myself here. Center myself.* She felt welcomed by this place. As soon as everyone headed out, she'd spend a few minutes in conversation with it herself.

"I have paper and ink in my bag," Saorsa said. "I'll leave it on this table. Anything you find we need, put it on the list. When we go to fetch Oona, we can get more supplies." The team set to work. Olav headed out to get water and Saorsa found herself alone.

She pulled a chair over to the empty hearth and sat down to rest. She let her mind settle and took a few minutes to take in the space. She could hear the sporadic gusts of wind outside, and a brief, bright birdsong in the woods. And underneath it all, the soft music of *magick*.

It was moving up toward the soles of her feet, rising up from the earth and through the wide, smooth floor planks, penetrating her boots with its energy. It flowed up her legs and bubbled in her blood, moving its way in a twisting path around the topography of her bones. *We are here. We are the ancient voices of the earth. We are your companions now, child.*

The magick here was different from other places. Its voices were more intimate and personal, and had a dark, sultry, more *textured* feeling. It was difficult for Saorsa to describe. *It is as if...all the places I've been until now spoke in the bright, clear voice of a mother singing to her child on a sunny day. But here...* It came to her.

Here, it's like being whispered to by your lover. Elements of heat and danger. It's...deeper, somehow. And I am drawn to it. Saorsa took a deep breath. *This place, this house, is welcoming me. It's putting its arms around me and drawing me close. Watching over me even as it suggests something new and, until now, hidden. It feels like...Alex.*

She closed her eyes for a moment, and vivid images flashed in her mind. *Wolves. A crow in flight. A blood-colored moon. Bones.*

Saorsa knew, in that moment, that she was starting down a new path. One that would leave her forever changed. One in which she would move toward a sort of magick she had never fully understood or used before, but that was part of the whole.

She thought of what Fia had said back at Ramsay House. *Goddesses like The Morrigan, isn't her domain part of life too? Being a woman isn't just all nurturing, Saorsa. The Morrigan is the battle Goddess. Don't you need help in battles you have to fight? Isn't part of motherhood protecting your clan?* About this...Fia had been *right*. She could learn a different sort of magick here, if she was brave enough to open herself to it.

Come to us, Saorsa, the house whispered. *We are here to receive and support you. Listen to us and find your calling. Find yourself, your balance, and your rightful place. Lead your clan. Don't be afraid. Come to us. Darkness is not evil; it is the balance to light and both are needed.*

The volume of the voices around Saorsa increased, and now there were many, many of them, their invitations overlapping as they beckoned. *We can teach you,* they said. *We can show you the way! Come to us, Darkflower, and find your power!*

A fire roared to life in the fireplace, despite the fact that there was nothing there but ash. *Open your eyes, Darkflower! Claim your title! Step into your own, and fear the Dead no more!*

Saorsa gripped the arms of the chair. "I can't be afraid anymore," she said to the voices. "I don't want to live in fear! I want to be who I was meant to be!"

The fire suddenly doubled in size and there was a strong gust of wind, then the door flew open. Something with wings was suddenly in the room. It moved quickly, and Saorsa stood up in surprise and turned toward it, trying to track it. And then she heard the sound of something hitting the seat of her chair.

She looked down. *Alex's broken rosary.* Her eyes widened as a shadow came to rest on the mantle.

He had returned. *Malphas.* He opened his beak and let out a cry of greeting, and then soared back out the door to land on a broken post just outside the door. *He brought it back! He brought Alex's crucifix back!*

Saorsa smiled up at the roof of the house. "I'm listening," she said softly, as the flames in the fireplace disappeared. "I'm ready to begin. I place myself in your hands."

………

Dusk fell at Wolfcroft. They'd made tremendous progress that day. The stable was in working order, and the horses were resting comfortably. The woodshed and a path to the burn had been cleared. Willow and Rune had found additional outbuildings and gardens nearby, but no roads or other settlements close.

"This is a safe place," he'd declared, as they returned from their walk, all smiles. "A good place. No one around for miles, as far as I can see, and there's no reason for anyone to come here." Snow had started to fall shortly after their return, which cheered Rune and his crew even further. "No one will want to be out riding in this. And any tracks we made will quickly be covered. I think we can settle in tonight without much worry."

None of you are wanted, thought Saorsa. She was so used to traveling with Alex and Vika that the thought of a safe house without a rotating watch schedule seemed strange. *But it's just me the Crown wants now. And I'm more worried about Fae than humans.*

The cabin had been turned into a comfortable space. The loft had been swept and scrubbed, and Olav, Aeric, and Trig had created sleeping spaces for themselves there. Downstairs, there were two smaller bedrooms and what appeared to be a pantry and workroom off the main room. Saorsa and Willow each took a smaller room and had beds to themselves; Eske and Rune set up sleeping spaces in the main hall near the fire. The huge fireplace was open on both sides, providing warmth and light to the main room and to Saorsa and Willow's rooms through smaller fireplaces set in the corners of their rooms, which were divided by a stone wall.

They'd scrubbed, swept, washed, and dusted; flipped the mattresses, brought in boxes of kindling, rinsed the dishes, and unpacked their supplies. They'd found a large cupboard full of sheets, blankets, and towels in the pantry, and another full of dishes and pots. Willow had brought supplies with her to make a smoked salmon and potato stew for their dinner, and Saorsa had found a large mixing bowl in the pantry and set about making bread dough to rise on the hearth as soon as she'd had a dust-free space to work. They would need supplies soon, but for tonight they had plenty.

As night fell, the team sat down at the table and on chairs near the hearth to enjoy bowls of hot stew, crusty rosemary bread, and hot tea. The snow had covered everything in white, and everyone began to relax a bit, feeling that a foundation for their work in this place had been established.

Saorsa sat back in her chair, a quilt over her knees, and let her mind wander. The low conversation of her companions was a balm for her soul; they were good people, and she was happy to be among them. But she was also missing those who weren't here. She missed Vika, Edan, Mother Agnes, and Annag. She missed Toran and Duncan, too. She thought of the evenings at Morrigan's Cave, and at Deadwater, Melrose, and Wyldwood. *And Father Andrew. I miss my friends at Holy Cross.*

And, she had to admit, she missed Fia. *I don't know how I feel about Fia. I am so angry at her. And...hurt.* But she also thought of all the times she'd laughed at Fia's bawdy jokes and held her hand at night when she was lonely, and how nice it was to talk about things like divination and casting and have Fia *understand.* She missed Fia's grand plans and intimate stories and the way Fia had *looked* at her. Like she was special. *Like I was wise.*

And, of course, she missed Alex. She could picture him here, in this room, right now. There he was, standing near her by the fireplace, with little Oona in his arms. The child kicked her tiny feet and giggled, and Alex gave Oona a smile, said something softly to her in Gaelic, and tickled her on the chin affectionately with his finger before turning his attention to Saorsa.

Saorsa remembered how the firelight would play with his silhouette, revealing and then hiding his features. His height, and the shape of his broad shoulders, and the red highlights in his dark hair where it curled. She remembered the sparks in his gray eyes when he looked at her. The arch of his brows. The angle of his jaw. The way he stood, and the position of his hips and the contours of the muscles of his thighs in his breeks, dusty from the road. The way he smiled at her with his eyes first, and then his mouth. The way his eyes creased at the outer corners when he was happy.

"You're tired, my Saorsa, eh?" he said to her, his voice low. "What do ye say we put the wee one in her bed, an' then turn in ourselves?" He took a step closer to her, and raised his eyebrows, a playful suggestion on his lips. "I'd verra much like to be abed with ye on such a cold night, *mo bhòidhchead le fuil teth.*"

My hot-blooded beauty. She smiled. The last time he'd called her that she'd given him a little smack on the arm. "Am I nothing but a walking bed-warmer to you, Alexander Scott?" she'd huffed, not angry in the least.

He'd grinned and tickled her before pulling her into his embrace while she pretended to protest. "Ah, *ean beag,* dinnae be cross with me," he'd whispered in her ear, rocking her against him. "I was thinkin' we could make heat *together,* so."

And she had *melted.* His voice made her bones turn molten, made her heart jump, made her breath falter. His touch seemed to transform her into another creature entirely, one with less reasoning ability and an unstoppable need to join with him. His presence created a *craving.* An obsession. A beautiful, dark, tyrannical madness. He was sweetness and poison all at once, drawing her in and killing off any rational, logical thoughts she might have possessed a moment earlier.

She shook her head, clearing the fantasy from her mind and endeavoring to bring herself back to the here and now. *I would do anything for you, Alexander Scott. Anything. Including what I plan on doing tomorrow night. Even though I'm terrified.*

"Saorsa." Willow moved her chair closer and Saorsa's vision of Alex faded. "Are you alright?"

Saorsa shook herself back to reality. "Oh...aye. I'm fine. Maybe...a little tired." Willow smiled. *I'm glad she's here,* Saorsa thought. *I think we're going to become great friends. She's the sort of woman I want to be. She has a quiet strength.*

"You know," Willow said, raising her eyebrows, "if you'd like, I could start on your hair now. It's going to take hours. But we could get your hair washed tonight, and begin the spells, and then start twisting when it's dry."

Saorsa sat up, immediately awake. "Really?"

Willow nodded. "Your hair needs to be really clean to get started. And based on the invasive magick I've been fighting to keep off of you the last few days, I think the sooner we can get protection spells worked into your hair, the better."

Saorsa's heart jumped in excitement. "How do we start?"

Willow gestured at the fire. "I started an extra kettle of water warming. I brought some peppermint and soap with me from home that will raise energy in your skin. I can wash your hair and then rinse it with rosemary and basil infused water for protection. I'll clear any energies that I can while I do it. The water should help balance your energy as well." She patted Saorsa's curls. "You realize once we knot your hair, you're going to lose some length, aye?"

Saorsa nodded. "I'm not worried. My hair grows incredibly fast. I cut it in September and it's already almost three inches longer." She looked at Willow and for a moment felt a bit shy. "I know it's a silly thing but...I'm so excited to do this, I've wanted to for *years*."

Willow sat forward in her chair. "I don't think it's silly at all, Saorsa. Until just a few months ago, you were kept from the world. Isolated. You weren't allowed to bloom the way the rest of us were." She patted Saorsa's hand. "Now the lovely rose you are is starting to unfurl her petals. What sane person would deny you the chance to finally show the world your colors? It's part of human nature to adorn ourselves, Saorsa. To manifest ourselves. To tell you that desire was a silly thing would be to deny you your humanity."

Lovely rose. That statement reminded Saorsa of Alex again. She was transported back to when the two of them had discovered Wolfcroft together. The morning after they'd seen the wolf pack, he'd awakened her by gently drawing her into his arms just after the sun had broken the surface of the horizon. "Open your eyes, *mo ròs Albannach fiadhaich*," he had whispered into her neck, wrapping himself around her warmth. "The road is callin' to us. Can ye hear it?" *My wild Scottish rose.* Of all the nicknames Alex had bestowed in her, it was one of her favorites.

She stood and they moved to a chair next to a low cabinet with a removable metal basin set into the top, most likely used at one point for bathing a baby or washing up. Saorsa took off her wrap and looked in the mirror hanging on the wall nearby. *I'm going to start to transform now. To unfurl. To manifest as the woman I've dreamed of being.*

Willow sang to Saorsa as she rinsed and gathered her hair, moving and balancing energy with the sound of her voice. Saorsa closed her eyes and relaxed her neck onto the rolled towel Willow had set on the edge of the basin, and took deep, cleansing breaths as she felt the warm water flow through her hair. *All the ghosts that touched me, all the fears that have haunted me, all the entities that tried to capture me and make me your own. I banish your energies from my body! I breathe in cool, bracing air to make space between my bones! I am my own, and none shall claim me! I call in light, love, hope, optimism, and peace!*

Willow's song continued.

Ancestors, I ask for your protection. May the Great Queen look my way. Saorsa took a deep breath. *This place, Wolfcroft, is a place of power for The Morrigan. I feel it. And so I will call on her, for the first time.*

Saorsa paused. Willow was protecting her, moving energy as she cleansed her hair. The proximity of such a benevolent woman gave Saorsa courage.

Goddess of sovereignty, Saorsa thought, opening her heart to a new aspect of feminine energy, *help me to reclaim my own boundaries from those who have tried to imprison and invade. Help me to find the strength to build here. To learn new magick. To grow. To rise. To find the path toward who I am meant to be. For in doing so, I will do the work of love. Work that will benefit the children of your House. You intervened to let Alex live. Let me be strong so I can save him, and guard and defend in your name.*

She said none of this out loud. But something subtle in the room changed as she finished. She noticed the tune Willow was humming altered dramatically. It had settled into a rhythm. Like the prelude of a composition. It was becoming a presence.

Then Aeric and Trig began whispering something in unison across the room, like a drumbeat coming in to layer itself with Willow's tune. It took Saorsa a moment to hear it. But when she did, she sat up abruptly and stared. Eske and Olav were now singing, and a moment later Rune's voice chimed in. But Rune's part seemed to be a sort of prayer.

Something was singing to Saorsa through the voices of her friends. Compelling them to add their music. Aeric and Trig were chanting the same thing over and over again, their words acting as the root of the hymn.

> *Blood, blood, like petals on the snow*
> *Blood, blood, like petals on the snow*

Eske and Olav's deep voices were layered over that, their words providing a tune, singing in a round.

> *She is coming for you*
> *She is coming to you*
> *Wings of pitch and eyes of night*
> *She is coming for you*
> *She is coming to you*
> *The Blackbird has begun her flight*

Saorsa noticed that everyone's eyes had turned white, as though their irises and pupils had disappeared. Her companions didn't seem distressed, in fact, quite the opposite. Their voices were beautiful, raised in praise. Their bodies seemed relaxed. And now Willow's part had transformed again.

Her crystal-clear bell of a voice rang out, singing in something that sounded *close* to Irish, but not quite. *It sounds like...like the language Alex used when he bewitched me at Melrose. A Fae language. She's singing a song of worship. Like a priestess might.*

Willow's voice wove itself in and out of the sounds the men were providing. It was arrestingly beautiful, full of emotion and passion. A song of praise. Of rapture at the beauty of the world. Saorsa's brain was screaming - *they are being possessed!* - and yet, her instinct in her belly told her to sit. *This is a welcoming. A welcoming to what I am destined to be. And this is the way whoever it is can reach through to this realm. When Fae Alex reached through, it was terrifying at first. But it wasn't meant to be. And neither is this. It has an otherworldly beauty to it.*

And there was Rune's voice now, strong and powerful, adding yet another dimension.

> *O Phantom Queen*
> *We raise our voices in song*
> *Consecrate this place once more for your children*
> *Build us a sanctuary of sacred bone*
>
> *O Queen of Battle*
> *Make us swift and strong*
> *Teach us not to fear the cauldron of birth and death*
> *To which we must all one day return*

The music composed of voices repeated, played and dipped, with all five singers working in perfect harmony with each other. And then, as suddenly as it has started, each of the living instruments returned to themselves, with Aeric and Trig whispering alone as the song faded.

> *Blood, blood, like petals on the snow*
> *Blood, blood, like petals on the snow*

Small rivers of water ran from Saorsa's curls onto her clothes. As the voices died out, she saw five men and one female healer staring back at her, looking just as they had before.

There was a moment of silence in the room. "What," said a normally extremely composed Rune, his voice tight, "*what in the name of the Allfather just happened?*"

No one replied for a moment. Then Eske cleared his throat. "We...sang." He gestured at Willow. "With *her*."

"I...," Willow began, "I was just letting energy come through. And then, the words just appeared."

"What *language* was she singing in?" Aeric asked. "Was it Irish? I... *where did those words come from?*"

"I think," said Rune slowly, "that we were visited. That Saorsa is right. This *is* a place of power. Sacred to an auld one." He raised his eyebrows. "And she's not been stopped by any of my wards, not at all."

"Because she was already *here*," Saorsa whispered. "This is *her place.*"

"Saorsa," Willow said, putting her hand on Saorsa's shoulder, "the energy that was on you. Other than the spells on your arms and the two spells that were placed on you by Alex in Faerie, everything else is gone."

"You helped her find me," Saorsa whispered excitedly. "Willow, you helped her energy *find me and heal me*. She was...welcoming me, I think."

Malphas, who had been sleeping on a tall perch Rune had constructed for him near the fireplace in Saorsa's room, suddenly let out a loud caw of approval and flew into the main room to settle himself on the arm of Saorsa's chair.

"You think your Morrigan has noticed us, eh?" Rune asked.

Saorsa raised a finger to stroke Malphas' feathered breast. "Aye," she said. "I think she has."

The Tower of London, London, England

The day of Alexander William Thomas Scott's execution by the Crown dawned clear and bright. Tower Hill had been packed since well before dawn, with the inhabitants of London jockeying for the best locations near the gallows. The tales and songs of the Ghost of the Borderlands had permeated every inn and public house in England and Wales as well as Scotland, and after Adamina Scott's escape from Carlisle the legend had increased tenfold.

He can shapeshift, the crowd murmured. *He's a demon in human form. He's a wizard with a hundred witches to please him and do his bidding. He can summon ravens. Branxholme. Buccleuch Church. Seven Hills. Carlisle. Hermitage. He leaves men hanging from trees upside down. He's the Devil himself. And he's a Jacobite.*

The soldiers were in fine spirits this morning. *Jacobite traitor. Murderer. What sort of perverted, twisted psychopath arranges dead bodies on a hill? Well, that all ends today. And that Stuart bitch he runs with and her mother will be next. It's only a matter of time until we get the MacLeods, too.*

There were those in the crowd who were saddened that they wouldn't have their own opportunity to inflict harm on Alexander Scott before his hanging. *Remember the stories about Wallace? They dragged his body from the tower behind horses, and that crowd got their turn with him. This one's no better; why do they keep him from us?*

But the Violet Woman had been very specific with the Crown. *We delivered him, and so you will listen. Until the moment he hangs, no one touches him but me. After I have the soul, you can let the crowd shred the body to ribbons if you like.*

There was an underground passageway from near the Tower of London to Tower Hill, mostly used by dignitaries who wanted to make it to the execution site without having to expose themselves to the commoners. Today it was being used to transport the prisoner. One who seemed resigned. And subdued.

The healing ointments had done their work. They'd been stolen as well, and there was a good chance the owners in Faerie would discover them missing and launch an investigation, one that might draw attention to the Violet Woman's enterprise. But she'd had no choice. They were wildly behind schedule on the original plan, and having a healthy *leth dhia* aspect was essential. And in less than half a bell, this part of the scheme would be done.

Alexander Scott sat quietly in the back of the wagon drawn by a black horse. He looked neither left nor right and said nothing. The Violet Woman had come to see him that morning, and he hadn't fought her. "We thought you should look your best for your last moments on earth," she crowed, bringing him a set of exquisitely tailored black clothing and depositing it on the bed. She stood by while he bathed and she shaved him herself, a twinkle in her eye as she did so. "Wouldn't want the blade to slip, now, and deny the crowd their fun," she crooned to him.

They'd led him out of the cell a short time later, scrubbed, dressed, with his dark hair tied back, a striking and elegant figure in his long dark coat. "Oh, this will be hard for the ladies near the gallows, won't it?" the Violet Woman whispered to Alex. "So handsome, but also *such* a villain. They won't be able to decide if they want to dismember you or take you to their beds!" Alex's gray eyes had shifted away.

The first two sets of spells on his wrists had been activated once they were outside the tower, immobilizing his wrists and blurring Alex's vision. They added a thick pair of manacles to his hands and another set to his ankles once he was seated on the back of the cart.

No fewer than a hundred redcoats fell in behind the wagon, escorting Alexander Scott to his doom. When the cart emerged from the tunnel behind the gallows, some of the crowd caught sight of the prisoner arriving. A moment later, as word traveled, the crowd let out a roar.

"No one touches him but me," the goddess hissed as one of the hangman's lackeys moved toward the cart. She removed the irons from Alex's feet and ordered him out of the cart. The way to the stairs behind the gallows was crowded with soldiers who had come through the tunnel, pushing their way around the huge platform to try and steal a space at the front of the crowd; after what this monster had done to their brothers-in-arms they were damn well going to get a good spot to watch him swing.

The Violet Woman had hold of Alex's bicep, steering him toward the stairs. He raised his head only slightly to look around him. Tadhg was just a few steps ahead, moving people out of the way so they could ascend.

The noise from the crowd became deafening once the prisoner stepped onto the platform. A wall of sound, composed of screaming, jeers, and accusation. It held a dark, evil magick all its own. A magick designed to reject, to push away. A magick born of *fear. We will raise our voices against you,* said the crowd. *And in doing so, we will create a divide between us. You are not of us anymore. We cannot show care or empathy for you, for it would put us on the same side. And on your side stands death.*

Alex could barely comprehend the enormity of the mass of the throng before him. If you'd taken every person he'd met in his entire life and assembled them in one place, this crowd would dwarf that group in size. It didn't even seem to be composed of people anymore, but was instead some massive mythological beast that lurked at the base of the realm of nightmare, frothing and gnashing its teeth. And then he turned his head to the right and couldn't believe his eyes.

There was a stand of dignitaries there in a special box to watch the proceedings, no more than fifteen feet from where he stood. One man in the box was staring right at him. A face Alex had seen in paintings. King George the Second of Britain.

The King stared at Alex with a sullen expression full of disdain. He knew he'd most likely never get his hands on Charles Edward Stuart, and from what he understood Alexander Scott was a big part of the reason. The quantity of resources and men he had spent trying to bring this impudent Scotsman in had been astronomical. He'd assumed that the Alexander Scott he'd been told about was some sort of seasoned, wily statesman, pulling the strings of a web he'd woven based on years of military experience. He was disgusted to discover this morning from his advisors that prior to the uprising, Alex had had no military experience at all and was just twenty-seven years old.

And Alex stared back. He was determined not to waver and not to blink. And as he saw the King's brow furrow, Alex lifted his chin an inch higher as if to say, *I'm not afraid of you.* Duncan had once told Alex that if he were ever caught, his last words before execution would be *Alba gu bràth* - Scotland forever. Alex was giving his own final political salvo at this moment. He was looking the King of Britain in the eye defiantly. *I am not of you; I make my own choices.*

Without a word having been spoken, King George understood. Understood, and was *incensed.* He snarled at Alex and, without taking his eyes from him, motioned over an attendant and whispered something. And the attendant turned and raced out of the royal seating box, only to appear a few moments later next to the Royal Executioner. Alex could hear the entire conversation.

"His Majesty says," panted the attendant, "that after the execution the hangman's rope is *not to be sold.*"

"What?" howled the Executioner. "We already have a bid of eight thousand for the damn thing!"

"His Majesty wishes the traitor's rope for his personal collection," the attendant continued.

"He's never done that before!" The Executioner was clearly not happy.

"His Majesty says," the royal attendant continued, "that it is a *personal matter.*"

The Executioner swore and nodded, and the attendant disappeared back down the steps.

"Oh, *my, Alexander,*" purred the Violet Woman in Alex's ear, "it appears you made a friend!"

Another few moments of chaos, and then there was the sound of a bell ringing from the Tower of London, and the crowd fell silent. It was time to begin.

The gem around the Violet Woman's neck had been energized by the raw emotion of the crowd, as she had anticipated. It hummed against the skin between her breasts, sending out small, invisible tendrils of magick to search for its intended victim. It found him, standing just a few feet away. The stone adjusted itself slightly, its teardrop shape focusing its main facet in Alex's direction.

The list of charges against Alexander Scott was being read to the crowd, and it was comically long. "Alexander William Thomas Scott of Buccleuch, Scotland, you have been convicted of the crimes of High Treason. Mass Murder. Murder of Agents of the Crown. Murder of Military Officers. Attempted Murder of His Majesty's Appointed Judges. Arson. Arson of Government Buildings. Possession of Illegal Firearms. Failure to Follow the Direction of an Agent of the Crown. Trespassing on Crown Property. Theft of His Majesty's..."

The crowd waited.

"...Robbery. Robbery of a Government Establishment. Highway Robbery. Amoral Behavior. Aiding and Abetting the Known Criminals Oliver Selby, Vika MacLeod, Duncan MacLeod, Adamina Scott, Toran Armstrong, Saorsa Stuart, Charles Edward Stuart..."

A vicious roar went up from the crowd when the Bonnie Prince was named.

"...Destruction of His Majesty's Property. Impersonating an Agent of the Crown..." The man reading the charges had to stop and take a breath. "Larceny. Breaking and Entering at a Royal Residence. Breaking and Entering at a Government Building. Breaking and Entering a Garrison Prison. Obstruction of His Majesty's Roadways. Manufacturing Illegal Explosives. Utilization of Illegal Explosives. Maritime Theft. Commandeering a Royal Vessel. Destruction of a Royal Vessel. Impersonation of a Naval Officer. Kidnapping an Agent of the Crown. Smuggling of Stolen Property. Smuggling of Illegal Items. Trespassing on Garrison Grounds. Horse Theft. Impersonating a Religious Official. Moral Corruption. Moral Corruption of a Female. Contributing to the Moral Corruption of a Female. Theft of Official Documents. Falsification of Official Documents. Unsanctioned Redirection of Crown Resources. Attempted Assassination of His Majesty's..."

The Violet Woman was trying not to smile.

"...and the Murder of Lord Burn of Hermitage, Scotland. The Murder of Lord Conall Scott of Buccleuch, Scotland. The Crime of Patricide. Inciting Riot. Poisoning a Government Official. Poisoning a Military Officer. Intimidation of Agents of the Crown. Sheep theft. Destruction of Church Property. Assault. Cattle Raiding. Impeding Government Proceedings. Robbery of a Tax Official. Espionage. Assault on His Majesty's...

The Violet Woman raised her eyebrows. Even she was impressed.

"...Organizing an Illegal Assembly. Organizing an Illegal Religious Assembly. Harboring A Known Criminal. Harassment of an Agent of the Crown. Vandalization of Crown Property. Battery of an Agent of the Crown. Conspiracy. Illegal Transport of Stolen Goods. Infliction of Grievous Bodily Harm on an Agent of..."

The Violet Woman rolled her eyes.

"... Piracy. And..." the man reading the charges took one last breath, "...Witchcraft." He paused. "You are sentenced to hang from the neck until dead. You will then be drawn and quartered, and...."

Alex didn't hear the rest. The crowd was impatient and starting to shout, and the Violet Woman shoved Alex forward toward where the noose hung. The Executioner moved toward the lever for the trap door.

The Violet Woman pulled out her keys and undid the manacles on Alex's wrists. They were iron, and iron sometimes impeded the flow of magick; she didn't want anything to prevent the gem around her neck from trapping Alex's soul.

The Executioner's assistant brought forward the burlap sack with which to cover the prisoner's head. But now the King was standing in his box and ranting, waving off the assistant with the bag, and frothing at everyone around him.

"I want to see his face when he goes!" howled the King like a deranged madman. "I want to see this traitor's eyes *burst out of his head!*"

A thirst for blood seemed to rise up first in the royal box, and then spread to the military men just below the platform, and then the crowd at large. A chant had started, and all the men and women in the vicinity, regardless of class, were shouting it in unison. They seemed in that moment to completely forget that Scotland was part of Great Britain and contained many loyal Crown subjects. Alex, as a Scottish citizen, had turned Scotland into *them,* and so all of *them* were no longer acceptable. *Kill the Scot! Kill the Scot!*

"Goodbye, Alexander," purred the Violet Woman, shoving his head through the noose and tightening it, "it's been positively *delightful* to spend this time with you!"

Kill the Scot! Kill the Scot!

Alex turned and looked the Violet Woman right in the eyes. "Is no tight enough," he said calmly. "The noose. A bit tighter, please."

The Violet Woman looked at him as if he were insane, but then threw back her head and laughed. "*Happy to oblige.*" She reached up and pulled the noose uncomfortably tight.

Kill the Scot! Kill the Scot!

The Violet Woman stepped back, the amulet shaking against her, once more drawing power from the crowd. It was ready.

Alex closed his eyes slowly, and thought of Saorsa.

"Do it!" screamed the King at the immobile, dark elegant figure of Alexander Scott. "*Do it now!*"

The crowd was in a frenzy. The Executioner reached down, and yanked the lever to the trap door open, and looked up to see Alex's black boots kick the air once. And then....

The entire crowd was struck silent, as though an unseen hand had torn away their common voice. For a moment, everyone stared. Stared, and blinked. Because...no one's eyes seemed to be working correctly.

For on the hanging platform there were now six Alexander Scotts. And none of them were hanging from the noose.

And while everyone else on the platform and in the royal box had to take a beat to process this information, Alex didn't.

Three days. For three days he'd been in the *leth dhia* cage under the tower, completely alone save for thrice-daily visits lasting less than five minutes each where food was shoved through a space near the floor and his vital signs were monitored from outside the cage by either Tadhg or Ciannat. In that time, he'd had nothing to do but experiment. He couldn't open a portal out, but the cage gave off enough residual magickal energy that he *could* split himself. And he had made several discoveries.

The first discovery was that he could keep his original body conscious during and after the process of splitting if he made himself slightly uncomfortable. Perhaps by lying in an awkward position, or pinching himself, or...making the practice noose he'd made for himself out of his sheet a bit too tight.

He also discovered that whenever he did split himself in two, there seemed to be a moment where his original body became *incorporeal,* and in that moment he could actually move. Soon he was slipping out the practice noose every time he split.

Laoise had been correct about being able to unite two of his bodies just by touching. He wondered if it was possible to split without an entire ritual too. He began editing what he'd been doing down, cutting out pieces, and soon realized that the *will* to split was tied mostly to one thing: the thought of seeing Saorsa again. When he thought of her face, and felt his need to see her rise again, he discovered that *that* moment, that thought, contained all the power he needed. Just the memory of her lovely, smiling, heart-shaped face.

By the middle of day two, he was duplicating himself with one thought in an instant while simultaneously slipping sideways out of the practice noose, leaving himself and a duplicate both conscious.

It was terrifying, the first time he opened his eyes and saw another of himself sitting next to him. He could hear a low hum in his mind, a background noise of his duplicate's thoughts. But...it wasn't overwhelming. In fact, his thoughts felt more ordered and calm then they usually did. As though the mind that had been overactive his entire life had finally found its purpose and the correct way to occupy itself. It had been waiting for these other streams of information to flow.

The two Alexes sat for a long time and simply looked at each other and listened. And then Alex tried...*promoting* one of his thoughts. Trying to push it higher in his consciousness, as if he was about to speak to his doppelganger.

Are you afraid?

And he heard an answer immediately, like a whisper. *Fuckin' terrified. You?*

They both laughed. Alex tried to speak to himself in his mind again. *Do you think we can make a third, somehow?*

His second stood up and grinned. *Worth a try.* And then there were *three*, as his second split once more.

Incredibly, while going through portals exhausted him, simply being in multiple bodies didn't. With each additional split there was more noise in his head, more background thoughts. But it wasn't yet unmanageable. He began playing little games with his other selves, each sitting in a separate corner of the spacious cell. *Guess the word I am thinking. Six letters.* The word would always be there, of course, if he dove far enough into the white noise of their common thoughts. But he was getting better at tuning out the static of the low-level thoughts and just listening to the ones that were promoted.

The games never lasted very long, though, because he knew himself too well. *Six letters? S-A-O-R-S-A.* His other selves laughed. *We're all fuckin' obsessed.*

His jailors didn't seem to have any idea what he was doing. It seemed that not only was the cage effective at containing him, but it kept in any evidence of the magick he was working as well.

Soon they'd made a fourth, and Alex attempted to coordinate physical activity. *Twenty press-ups. Jump three times. Ten roundhouse kicks.* Four Alexander Scotts executed these commands with no noticeable delay between them. *Do your own thing. Return.* His other selves could make their own choices, have their own agendas, but once one promoted a thought everyone listened, and it became the focus.

Alex joined them back to himself, and split. Joined and split. At one point he had eight other Alexes in addition to himself. *I'm starting to not be able to hear everything. This is probably the limit for now.*

He didn't enjoy being in two places at once. It made him disconcerted, like having a body part suddenly start to move without your brain telling it to. These exercises had helped him find out the answer to Saorsa's questions, however. *What am I supposed to do?* she had said. *Not touch any of you? Touch all of you? Only the human ones? Only the ones not engaged to other people? How am I supposed to navigate this if you don't know how to either?*

He knew how he felt about his duplicates. They were part of him, like a hand or his eyes. But they weren't *him*. Those bodies hadn't ridden all over the Borders of Scotland; hadn't marched with Charles' army, hadn't been possessed by the Violet Woman. Hadn't made love with Saorsa Stuart.

Yes, he was more than just his body. But *this* body had been at Culloden. Had carried a girl out of Seven Hills. Had sat by Saorsa's bedside after Hermitage. *This one* had longed to hold Morag's child, played music with his friends, and had taken Saorsa dancing the night she fell in love with him. This one had earned the scars, manifested the healing, patted Thor on the nose, and hugged his brother. This one had endured. It was his home. Where he was whole.

His other half in Faerie was more Fae than human, just as he was more human than Fae. Their histories were different. Their culture. Their abilities. He considered the Fae half a separate being. There was only one *him*.

And so he was going to do everything in his power to get his primary Human aspect back to Saorsa alive. And tell her that while he understood her confusion, *he* was no longer confused. In his heart, he felt she'd taken another man to her bed.

Now he stood on the hanging platform, with five of his duplicates, and promoted a thought. A whispered battle cry.

The Scotts are out.

And chaos came to visit Tower Hill.

Alex's duplicates moved to attack the main threats. One on Tadhg. One on the Executioner. One on the Executioner's Assistant. Two were already clearing the guards on the stairway and arming themselves with swords from the belts of the guards behind the platform.

And the principal Alexander Scott whirled in place, tipped neatly to the side, and lashed out with his leg, the side of his boot striking the Violet Woman directly in the jaw.

She reeled, hands flailing. Alex's boot came up again, smashing into her nose. Blood poured from her face as she attempted to fend off another attack. Alex grabbed hold of her by the shirt, lifted her a foot in the air, and ran forward until her back crashed into the post from which the noose was suspended. She let out an anguished wail.

Alex was in her face now, beside himself. "I'll teach ye to make a slave o' me, ye spooky haunted bitch!" he snarled. He didn't know her name, but he knew damn well who she was: his torturer. The creature that had made a mindless killer out of him.

He could hear his other aspects promoting thoughts. *Move! Clear the platform!*

He could listen, or he could lose himself here. Stay and finish things with her and lose this body. Or go, and maybe, just maybe, make it back to Saorsa. The thought of Saorsa made him able to breathe.

His hand violently scratched at the Violet Woman's chest, until it closed around what he was looking for: the gem she'd meant for his soul. He yanked it forward, breaking the chain and the Violet Woman let loose a chilling howl.

He saw it then, on her hip. *A weapon.* A violet whip made from the finest leather, coiled neatly on her belt under her cloak. He dropped her to her feet on the platform and grabbed it, and she hissed and spat and then...there were ravens where she had just been standing, bursting into flight.

Alex nearly fell backwards as the screaming corvids took to the air, the whip in one hand, the gem on a broken chain in the other. In another step he was lunging for the open trap door in the platform, and landing in the hay below.

One of his duplicates had spawned two more, and there were five now in front of him, finishing up on the guards between the platform and the tunnel's entrance, leaving piles of unconscious and damaged bodies in their wake. Alex heard commotion above him and looked up to see two more of him making the leap from the platform to the royal box. Screams pierced the air as the King and his attendants rushed from the box, afraid for their lives, while their bodyguards raced to put themselves between the two black-clad attackers and their charges. The bodyguards were at a disadvantage going into the fight, pausing as their minds tried to understand why they were being confronted by two identical men who *clearly* had been hanged less than a minute ago.

The hesitation was all Alexander Scott, aspects three and five, needed. Armed with knives they'd lifted from Tadhg's weapons belt and a headsman's ax they'd found on a rack behind the executioner, they made short work of the first row of bodyguards and then touched hands, morphing back into one being right in front of the second line of defenders who, unable to believe their eyes, simply turned and ran. The remaining Alex dropped the ax, turned, and vaulted out of the box into the back of the horse cart below.

The soldiers at the base of the platform were trying to push their way through, but the quarters were too tight. Soon stacks of the injured and dying were blocking each of the possible paths around the platform, impeding any soldiers from moving toward the tunnel; and now the occupants of the royal box were adding to the bedlam by trying to push their way to the tunnel as well.

The crowd was so big that most couldn't see what had happened at the execution site. They were instead relying on what they were hearing. It was clear that the execution hadn't gone as planned, and that some sort of battle was underway, but most of the crowd at the back seemed to be laboring under the impression that order would be restored momentarily, and the execution resumed. But the crowd in *front* had a better view, saw the panic ensuing in the royal box, and heard the sharp voices of red-coated officers as they tried desperately to maintain order. This much more informed part of the crowd had seen enough, especially once they considered Alexander Scott's reputation. *Hermitage. Branxholme. Carlisle. Buccleuch Church. Seven Hills.* In each of these places, the Crown had been bested. They decided to retreat from the area immediately.

But the back of the crowd was unmoving as the front tried to leave. Pushing turned to shoves, and then voices began to be raised. Feeling trapped, those in front began to cry out. *Let me out! Let me through!*

There were guard towers at three different points on the hill, and the occupants of each were well aware that things were spiraling out of control. The closest to the Tower of London itself signaled someone in the bell tower, and an alarm bell began to sound across the Tower grounds: *escaped prisoner! Escaped prisoner!* And that started the stampede.

The occupants of Tower Hill began attempting to move, but by this point fistfights were beginning to break out in the crowd. The perimeter wasn't expanding fast enough for those caught down front; people were abandoning possessions and beginning to climb over one another.

Alexander Scott barreled down the tunnel toward the Tower of London on foot, surrounded by his other aspects. Most had swords and several knives as well, and Alex had a tight hold on the Violet Woman's whip. They raced around the bend in the tunnel, only to meet twelve soldiers on horseback coming through the tunnel. The men on horseback reined in, and for a moment the two sides stared at each other, as the mounted men tried to understand what the hell they were looking at. The Alexes had been joining and splitting during the battle as they saw fit, and there were currently nineteen of them, each one identical to the rest.

"What the...?" began the officer in front, and then he saw a whip unfurl.

The tunnel was soon full of rearing, shrieking horses, as The Violet Woman's whip came alive in Alexander Scott's hand. A regular whip wouldn't have been an issue for the mounted soldiers, but this was no regular whip.

The Scourge of Nemesis was ancient. It exhibited signs of possessing its own sentience. When coiled, it appeared to be but one lash; but when in motion, it became a cross between a very long whip and a scourge and multiplied its length eight times over. Nine separate lashes coiled and struck in various directions throughout the air, cracking independently, leaving a trail of fire wherever they struck. It was a weapon designed to punish the gods themselves.

And, unfortunately for the riders of the horses, it made an additional, rather unpleasant sound. For the moving Scourge carried with it the cries of a certain creature not native to London, England. The whip was screaming like a gryphon.

As Alex raised the whip, a tremendous, ear-splitting screech shook the tunnel. Seven of the riders were unseated immediately; the fire lashing through the air took down another two; and in the smoke that billowed in the Scourge's vicinity caused the remaining riders to lose sight of which direction they were headed. The terrified mounts wheeled and bucked and began running into each other and trampling the soldiers already on the ground; and the nineteen Alexander Scotts quickly reduced themselves down to seven and began trying to capture the fleeing horses for themselves. Alex stared at the whip in his hand, mystified. He wasn't even moving his hand, and this beast of a weapon was striking out in front of him, over and over, causing bedlam.

Alex wasn't sure how to stop the whip. By now four of his aspects had managed to catch horses and were attempting to assist the other four. Alex pulled the whip handle toward his right hip, as though wishing to put it away, and was delighted to find it immediately coiled itself up into a neat set of loops and went still, anchored against his hip bone with nothing to secure it.

The seven Alexes had made themselves five, and after one put his hand down to help the original up onto the back of a horse, those two merged as well. Four Alexes came rocketing out of the smoke- filled tunnel onto the grounds of the Tower of London and turned their mounts at top speed in the direction of the Thames and the Tower Wharf.

People were fleeing Tower Hill in droves; it was impossible for anyone to make their way against the tide toward the execution platform and the tunnel. The air was full of the voices of the hysterical, many of whom, as they had at Carlisle, were now cursing the curiosity that made them want to see a member of the Scott Clan hang. The soldiers on site were trying to prevent people from being run over and trying to ensure the safety of the royals as well; trying to find Alexander Scott in this epic mess seemed to be falling further and further down the priority list as they fought not to be pulled underfoot themselves.

There'd been precious few people besides prisoners inside the Tower of London who hadn't gone to the hanging, meaning there was almost no one there to witness the four Alexander Scotts thunder across the parade grounds on horseback, heading for the exit by Cradle Tower. Almost no one to hear one of his aspects let out a whoop of freedom as the horses nearly trampled the two shocked guards facing the wrong direction at the gate. Nearly no one to hear the hooves of the horses on the boards of the wharf, headed for the road.

Nearly no one to see the group take a sharp right on the banks of the Thames and then swing left to cross London Bridge. And Alexander William Thomas Scott disappeared into the smog and din of the streets of Greater London, like the Ghost of the Borderlands that he was.

·········

It was wet in the streets of London, the rain freezing as soon as it hit the cobblestones. And Alexander Scott was tired.

He'd split up the group as soon as he and his copies had cut across the Thames, and then each had traveled a mile or so separately before crossing the Thames again further north. Alex found a quiet back alley as a rendezvous point for himself and his other selves, and as each arrived he quickly reduced himself to one person. He took two knives off the last of his duplicates before touching hands and watching his remaining other self disappear. Now he was one man standing in a London alley off Fleet Street with four stolen horses.

I need to find myself a safe house, he thought. *If I can get somewhere safe, I can open a portal and find Saorsa. Then, send another self through to Edan, and get my hands on enough money to outfit myself here for the trip north.*

He just needed a room, an empty room. Surely there had to be one of those nearby. He didn't dare try to sell these horses; each of them displayed a brand that identified them as property of the Royal Cavalry. They had no saddlebags, nor any supplies he could readily use, so he simply drove them out onto the street to wander loose.

He ducked out of the alley and started walking as the rain fell faster, chilling him to the bone. He wished like hell he had his hat. His eyes flicked across the signs hanging outside of the varied businesses on the street. He wanted someplace out of the way and quiet. This area was positively crawling with inns, but he needed to avoid crowds of any kind. No inns. No public houses.

He heard a church bell toll. His execution had been planned for noon; it was now two-thirty. It felt like evening, with the weak December sun hidden by heavy clouds. His mind, exhausted from his near-execution and subsequent escape, began to wander, looking for a place of comfort. He thought of the first evening at Deadwater, with everyone beginning to gather around the fire after dinner, talking. Vika was there, and Edan, Toran, and the others, laughing and passing around a bottle of decent French wine they'd found in Duncan's supply cache. And Saorsa had walked over to where he had sat and smiled.

She'd leaned over and spoken quietly, so she didn't interrupt the conversation around her. "It appears we're out of chairs," she said, raising her eyebrows. "Can I...do you mind if I sit on your lap?"

He remembered the way the firelight made her hair shine. Her hair had been a light, soft brown when he met her; weeks of riding in the sun had made it turn a sunny blonde. Her eyes were a dazzling green, the color of spring grass. Every time she walked up to him all he could think about was being alone with her again, with her little warm, round body pressed against him. He found himself once again under her spell, and it had nothing to do with witchcraft.

At a loss for words, he'd simply nodded and patted his thigh, and she perched herself there and beamed at him. *I wonder if she knows,* he'd thought to himself. *I wonder if she knows that most of the time when I don't answer her it's because I'm too captivated to speak.*

She draped her arm around his shoulders and snuggled up against him. He tried to follow the amiable conversation flowing all around him, but instead became fixated on the movement of her breasts slowly rising and falling as she breathed, and the feeling of her touch as she absentmindedly played with his hair. She smelled of roses and sunshine, of lavender soap and the wool hap she had gathered around her shoulders. And even more miraculous than the fact that she brought light and sweetness and humor everywhere she went was the fact that she wanted to bring it to sit with *him.* He'd sat in that chair and wondered if he'd ever be happier than he was in that moment.

He shook his head, back in London. *Focus.* He was soaked through. And then he saw a possibility.

A bakery. A *closed* bakery, all the lights off. He approached it and saw a note in the window. *Closing early today due to a family matter. Back tomorrow.*

He squinted up at the second story, where the baker most likely lived. No smoke coming from the chimney. No candles lit that he could see. No motion.

He went around to the back of the building. Stairs there, and another door. Locked. The rain was coming down in buckets now. He wished he had his lockpicks with him. He looked around for something to make a lockpick out of and spied a cellar door buried under a stack of crates. In a few moments he'd moved the crates aside. The lock on the wooden door looked none too strong, and the door itself was quite old; he took a chance and tried smashing his foot against the lock. Three good efforts and the wood supporting the lock splintered and gave way; another few well-placed kicks and he was through. He went down the stone steps, pulling the door shut behind him.

It was pitch dark in the cellar. He felt his way along the wall, brushing his dripping hair out of his eyes with the back of his hand. There was no sound of anyone moving about, and no voices. His hand brushed along something that felt like a mantle, and a little further on he found what felt like a door. He opened the door to reveal a set of steps going up. He was surrounded by barrels of flour and salt.

He made his way halfway up the steps to the bakery, listening. Still no sounds. All was quiet. The shop windows were large, though, and looked out on the street, so he didn't want to tarry here although in the rain few were about. He took the stairs quickly and emerged into a room that smelled strongly of yeast.

He hadn't realized how hungry he was until that moment. He spied another set of stairs and moved quickly to them, then saw a basket full of fresh baps on the counter. He grabbed three as he sped by, and had one in his mouth before he'd made it halfway up the stairs.

Empty. All the rooms on the top two floors were empty. Satisfied that no one was home for the time being, he set to work. He found supplies on the mantle to start a fire and lit a fire in the fireplace. He hoped the baker and his family's "family matter" was far from home.

He lit a candle and headed for the wardrobe and the dresser. The good news was that the baker was nearly as tall as he was; the bad news was that the baker was apparently a product of his occupation, meaning he ate a lot of flour, sugar, and lard. Alex tried on a pair of the man's trousers which were comically large on him at the waist; Alex took the candle and went searching in the wardrobes of the other bedrooms.

After two wardrobes full of dresses, he discovered a dresser that had to belong to the only other male in the house, perhaps the baker's son. While the trousers were a few inches short, they were nearly a perfect fit at the waist. Desperate to be warm and dry, Alex pilfered the man's breeks, shirt, stockings and vest, and was delighted to find a belt as well. Boots back on with hair towel-dried and combed a few minutes later, Alex set about looking for a few other supplies. He found a rucksack in one of the wardrobes and stuffed his wet clothes inside to take with him.

The kitchen yielded butter, jam, and some cold sausages, which Alex ate with the remaining baps so fast he barely tasted them. He discovered a dark brown tricorn hat on the chair in the parlor, and a rather lovely black wool scarf sitting on a desk. He found a wooden candle box that made him quite happy. It contained a variety of hair ribbons and a brooch, and underneath that...coins. One pound thirty-six shillings, to be exact. He realized it was the baker's wife's treasure, and Alex stared at it for a moment. It would have taken the poor woman quite a bit of time to squirrel that much away, and he felt just awful taking it. So he didn't take it all. He pocketed the thirty-six shillings and left the pound. She'd be sad, but not completely devastated. And thirty-six shillings could keep him fed and dry for quite some time. A very nice meal at an inn was around three shillings, and that included whisky. *If I get through to Edan I'll send repayment.*

He calculated how far it was to Glasgow. *Probably eighteen days, but only if I switch horses.* He hoped it didn't snow. Well then. He was dressed, fed, had a good bit of coin, and was armed. All he needed was a horse, and it wasn't as if he hadn't stolen one before. He missed Thor. He didn't have to tell Thor to do anything; Thor just *knew.*

He put the whip under his still-damp coat and once again, it took its place at his hip as if attached. He wrapped the scarf around his neck, put the hat on his head, and headed back down to the cellar, saying aloud a few words of thanks to the baker and his wife as he extinguished the fire. They were going to be mighty surprised when they returned home. He wished them well.

He wanted to be by the back door before he tried splitting and opening a portal so he could make a quick escape if someone came home. He was so excited at the prospect of seeing Saorsa again, even if she was in danger, that he could barely stand it. *I got out. I escaped the Tower of London. It worked.* He hadn't been certain it would. As a matter of fact, he'd been utterly convinced that some unforeseen circumstance was going to prevent his plan from working. *I should be dead right now. I can't believe I'm not.*

Back in the cellar once more with his candle, he took a quick look around. In addition to barrels of baking supplies there was an assortment of stored furniture. Alex chose an old sofa, sat down, split himself in two, and waited for a portal to open.

But it didn't. He frowned. He wasn't in the cell anymore; where was the portal?

Both he and his duplicate looked down at their wrists at the same time. Three sets of bracelets now. Alex had felt the first set of marks tingle when the Violet Woman had restricted his hands and had felt the second set ache just before his vision had become blurred both in the stairwell and on the way to the gallows. And now, when he expected to see a portal to Saorsa open in front of him, the third set had begun to throb. *Fuck.* He absorbed his duplicate and tried again. *Split. Try for Branxholme. To see my brother.*

Again, no portal. Again, a pulsing under the third set of bracelets. Alex frowned, frustrated. *I can't make a portal. I'm stuck.* A stabbing loneliness took up residence in his gut; he was absolutely crushed that he wouldn't get to see Saorsa. *Do they have her already? What will they do to her?*

His sorrow deepened. *Maria.* He'd had to leave her behind. *Did they know Laoise was helping me? Have they imprisoned her, as well?*

Dark thoughts started to cascade as his mind kicked into high gear. Even worse, he could hear the thoughts of the duplicate next to him doing the same. He was on a slide toward being inconsolable; tired, lonely, guilty, and desperate. He put out his hand and his duplicate vanished.

And his memory of Saorsa appeared next to him on the sofa. "Hey, cheer up," she said, tucking her legs underneath her and clapping her hands. "That's enough of that, Alexander. If you're going to get through this you need to look on *the bright side,* my love."

He could see her sitting there, willing him out of his misery. Could see her so clearly he began speaking out loud to her. She was barefoot, wearing a pair of turmeric-colored velvet pants Vika had given her that were cropped on Vika but full-length on Saorsa. On top of that she had on a soft dark green wool jumper, long enough in the arms that she'd cuffed the sleeves and it still came down to her knuckles, layered over a faded and fraying bright blue linen shirt she'd found at one of the safe houses. Alex shook his head. This woman of his was so wee that even the smallest of men's clothing looked enormous on her. He entertained a fantasy, once again, of being able to take her somewhere to shop where the clothing wasn't fifth or sixth hand. *She deserves that. She deserves to be treated like the lady she is. What is she doing with the likes of me?*

"Alex, I can practically hear you *doing it again,*" imaginary Saorsa piped up. "You're thinking about the bad. But you should be thinking about the good! You *escaped the Tower of London* today! You looked old stinky King George in the eye and made him *run for his life!* I'm so *proud* of you!"

"Saorsa," he said quietly, "the portal doesnae work. How are we supposed to build things again between us, *eun beag,* if I cannae see you? The Violet Woman, she's won today. Kept us apart."

Saorsa laughed. "Alex, she has a broken nose, a fat lip, and a failed execution on her plate. She's probably spitting out her teeth, too. And you *stole her whip.* And that gem of hers, too! It doesn't sound like she's winning to me!"

Alex managed a half-smile. "Wish I'd killed her, though. There wasnae time. An'...there was somethin' else strange, but we can talk about later." He sighed. "Nearly *three weeks* to Glasgow now. I dinnae ken if you are all right or no."

"Well, it's a good thing you are already ready to go, then," Saorsa grinned. "Look at how well you've done! You're armed, have some money for food and expenses, and have decent traveling clothes. *And* you know where to head next. That's a lot better than being drawn and quartered, which is where you were headed a few hours ago, mister." She stood up and motioned to him. "Come on, break's over. Get a horse, get the hell out of this town, and come see me!"

Alex stood up as Saorsa faded. *Right. I'll feel better once I'm moving.* He opened the cellar door and looked around. The steady rain was not letting up. But out on Fleet Street there were now rows of carriages, hoping to pick up wealthy patrons from the taverns who didn't wish to walk home in the rain. He climbed quickly into the first empty one he saw, pulling his scarf up to hide his face, and directed the driver to head for Seven Sisters in north London. There was an inn and pub there, the Wolf's Moon Tavern, that Vika had mentioned during a particularly outrageous drunken storytelling session. The name had stuck with Alex, and it would hopefully be much less crowded than anything in central London. He'd get a room and try to get some sleep. And then tomorrow morning Seven Sisters would find itself unexpectedly short one horse.

He settled back in the carriage, watched London pass by outside, and smiled. *I may not like you much, my other half in Faerie. But we're both out of prison now, and that seems a mighty good thing. Or at least, a problem for the Violet Woman, I think.* He patted the whip at his waist, and wondered.

Seven Sisters, England

Alex found the Wolf's Moon Tavern, secured a room, ate a hearty dinner and was right on the edge of sleep when he noticed the framed map on the wall over the mantle. He got up off the bed and went over for a closer look.

England's Rivers. He raised his eyebrows. On a sailing barge he could go *much* faster than on horseback. And since they were inland, hopefully he wouldn't get magickally dumped back on shore, which had happened whenever he'd tried to leave Scotland by sea. He looked closer at the map. He needed rivers that ran north to south. *Derwent River.* He estimated it to be about a hundred and fifty miles long. *If I made it to the Derwent, and followed it to the end on a sailing barge, I could cover nearly six days of riding in about a day and a half or so.* He looked closer, his eyes moving north on the map and west. *Then to the end of the Aire and onto other rivers, that would be close to one hundred miles. Another three days saved, maybe.* He drew in his breath. *I could cut a lot of time to Glasgow. I might make it there in about half the time.*

He was starting to get excited now. *Once I cross the border, there's a short river trip of about fifteen miles, but it would take an hour to do what would take a horse half a day. Then take another horse or carriage to the Clyde and sail right into Glasgow. Might make it to Saorsa in just about a week if the weather is good.*

He'd avoided traveling by river in Scotland, mostly because ports were always crowded and full of wanted posters. But in this case, time was the major factor to consider. *It's a much higher risk of being spotted. On the other hand, if they've already got hold of Saorsa, getting there in just over one week instead of three is worth it.* He grinned. His worst-case scenario of being caught and hanged in London had already come to pass. *I'm not as worried about humans quite as much anymore, although being arrested would slow me down. I also don't want this body to be hurt. It's the Fae I have to be the wariest of.*

He'd have to steal horses between rivers, starting right here in North London. And he was going to need coin for fares, and there was always the problem of getting too far from shore on wider rivers. *But this is the best possible way to go.* He thought that sailing barges on a good day could cover what a horse covered in a day in around two hours. *And they don't tire. Or have to be fed and watered.*

He climbed back under the bed clothes and stared at the ceiling. *Haggs Castle.* He didn't know anything about it. *Maria and Saorsa would be inside.* He paused. *Perhaps Laoise, as well.* He sighed. He'd have possibly three people to get out, in a building most likely swarming with Fae. *And Maria would be unconscious.* He thought about the amulet. They'd want the shards out of Saorsa, too. Would she be conscious when he found her, or might he have *two* unconscious women to move?

He could split himself, but even so this whole thing seemed daunting. Once he got Saorsa and Maria out, he didn't have anywhere to take them. *Moving bodies is a slow business.* And the Fae would be right after him, and he couldn't open his portals. *I need help.*

He wondered where Duncan might have gone to rendezvous with Vika. *Morrigan's Cave, most likely. The Aunties are there.* But once Duncan had found Vika, then where? Head west to Ireland? He doubted it. He prayed they hadn't headed south to try and help him, a suicide mission for certain. *They would probably head for Saorsa, wherever they thought she was.* He wondered if they'd check message drops. *Vika probably would.*

He could try it. Message drop up near the Border, on the off chance that Duncan and Vika saw it. God, it would be good to see them both again. And he needed people with clearer heads before he went tearing into Haggs Castle alone with a screaming supernatural whip and no plan whatsoever. He rolled onto his left side and closed his eyes. It might be the last chance for a decent night sleep until Scotland.

London, England

Mother Enid had been a lucky find. She had bustled Laoise off to a quiet chamber in the parish offices across the street from the church before she could make further errors in conversation that might arouse curiosity. Being an accomplished magick-user herself, Mother Enid had sensed the power radiating from the amulet shards in the pouch on Laoise's belt and felt the need to investigate at once. She suspected the young woman was much more than she seemed, but at the very least she could tell Laoise was acquainted with magick and needed assistance.

"So. What is it about Westminster Abbey that you want to know?" Mother Enid asked, offering Laoise a chair and putting on the tea kettle.

"I...was wondering if there might be...," Laoise hesitated and fell silent.

"My dear," Mother Enid said, "let me lay my cards on the table for you. I can sense that you are carrying something that generates a *tremendous* amount of magickal energy on your belt. So much power, in fact, that I am of the opinion that you may not hail from this world. I also am rather skilled at reading energies and auras, and I find you to be a profoundly gentle soul. A healer of some sort, if I had to guess. If there is something I can do that will help you get where you need to go, I am only too happy to help. I imagine I'll learn a little something from the experience, which would make me rather happy."

Laoise couldn't help but smile. She felt a goodness in this woman's being as well. "Well, then...I was wondering if Westminster might have been built on an older pagan site."

"You're looking for a portal," Mother Enid declared flatly. "Aren't you?"

Laoise couldn't hide her surprise. "Well...perhaps."

Mother Enid let out a laugh. "I'm guessing the reason you keep fiddling with your hat is to be certain you are covering a certain Fae characteristic, isn't it? Oh, how lovely! You see," she lowered her voice conspiratorially, "I have a friend among the Fae myself. She's visited me about once every two years since I was a child. She's quite curious about humans. And while she picks and chooses what she reveals, I've learned quite a bit about Faerie myself." She tossed a spoonful of leaves into the tea kettle. "Westminster is a good guess for a portal location. There *are* some pagan remnants there. The door to the Pyx chamber is constructed from the trees of a pagan holy grove. There are remnants of a ceremonial circle under the Cloister Garth. And an old sacred spring still runs through a corner of the undercroft. But any portal that might have been there has most likely been out of use for a very long time, if there's one at all."

"Oh," Laoise said sadly. "So...there's no way out of London there."

"There might be," said Mother Enid kindly, "but if it's so, I don't know about it. But luckily for you...," she smiled, "my Fae visitor has one near it that *she* uses. Right between the Queen Anne statue and the western front of Saint Paul's Cathedral."

"Is it...," Laoise was starting to get excited, "is it far?"

Mother Enid laughed. "Saint Paul's is a bit closer to us than Westminster by a few miles." She began pouring the tea into two salt-glazed ceramic mugs. "I don't know much about portals, but I do know they require less power to activate if they've been used recently. And my friend was just here at Samhain." She handed Laoise a mug. "I can take you, if you like. The parish has a barge we use to carry supplies and we often take it into London."

"How soon could we go?" Laoise was almost on her feet in excitement. "Could we go tonight?" She tried to collect herself. "If you could take me, I could make a sizable donation to your group. Or, to you." Laoise pulled a small bag of gems she'd taken from the jewelry box at the Tower of London from her belt and poured them onto the table. "Would these suffice?"

Mother Eric's eyes widened. "Rhiannon's fourth-favorite pony, *are those real?*" She carefully picked up a ruby. "My goodness, these are *huge!*"

"Take them," Laoise blurted. "If you can get us to that portal tonight, they're yours!"

"Well, I won't keep them for myself personally," Mother Enid explained, "but this could go a long way toward helping shelter, feed, and educate a lot of Children of the Stones." She smiled at Laoise. "You really don't need them?"

"No, I just need to get my friend and I through that portal," Laoise explained. "We need to get to Scotland."

"Hold these until you return," Mother Enid said, putting the gems back in the bag and handing it back, "and fetch your friend and meet me at the docks in an hour. There's a little sculpture of a mermaid right by the warehouse. Ask anyone, they'll know where it is. I'll be waiting." Laoise expressed her gratitude and hurried off into the night. *Please let our luck hold.*

Branxholme, Scotland

It snowed for two nights and a day before it stopped, and the world seemed frozen in time. Adamina's departure had been delayed, but no representatives of the Crown had arrived to hunt for her yet. Edan felt as if he was living every day with a vat of acid churning nervously in his stomach, waiting for the next unexpected thing.

They'd figured out some potential hiding places for Adamina, just in case. But Edan didn't know how familiar Caroline Scott was with Branxholme's secret passageways. *My father may have shown Caroline Scott and his commanders everything here. I just don't know.*

Edan was sitting at the breakfast table with Toran, Mother Agnes, Adamina, and Annag when conversation was suddenly cut short by one of Edan's guards rushing into the room. "Laird Scott! Those bells are going off again!"

"The portal!" Mother Agnes whispered to Edan. "Someone's activating the portal on the hill behind the castle!"

Annag leapt to her feet, and Adamina and Toran did the same. "We need to hide you!" Annag cried, taking hold of Adamina's arm, and the two women rushed from the room.

"Is it the Fae? Can you tell?" Edan was on his feet now, looking at Mother Agnes. He noticed poor Toran looked white as a sheet.

"Not from here," said Mother Agnes. "The spell just senses the change in energy that happens when the portal opens. The bells that ring here are sort of metaphysical wind chimes, if that makes any sense."

"How do we know if this is an attack?" Edan asked.

"Can you get some men up there? Like when Adamina came through? It could be Thomas. Or Alex. Or Elen."

"Or that Violet Woman, or that green-coated mage Saorsa told us about," Edan countered. "Hell, it could be Caroline Scott!" Edan looked at Toran. "Let's have our swords at the ready. I told our men to head up there whenever the bells rang, but in this snow it's going to take them a bit to get up there." Edan led the others to a window on the top floor where the back approach to Branxholme was visible.

"Well, it doesn't look like hordes of winged monsters are descending on us," Toran joked, his voice tight. "On the other hand, maybe they're on the roof already."

"I've got a different spell on the roof and walls," Mother Agnes informed him. "And I don't hear the alarm from that."

"What does that one sound like?" Edan asked.

"Roosters."

"So, the way we'll know if a faerie's on the roof is if we hear roosters," Toran said. "That makes perfect sense."

Mother Agnes grinned. "If something tries to come down a chimney, you'll hear an *extremely* loud bullfrog -- multiple times."

"Well, that goes without saying," Toran said sarcastically, his hand on his sword. They watched Edan's men plow their way uphill through the drifting snow on horseback. They'd cleared part of a pathway to the bridge that morning, but it was still very slow going.

"This is going to take a while," Edan said. "It seems like a visitor, not an attack. Still, let's keep my mother hidden for a bit, just in case." They saw the horses coming down again sometime later, and Edan breathed a sigh of relief as he looked out the window through a spyglass.

"Six horses went up, and six are coming down," he said. "Looks like they've picked up two additional people. But who the hell are they?"

"I think it's safe to have Adamina join us again," Mother Agnes reasoned. "Two people don't seem to be much of a threat."

They were all waiting in the hallway when the bodyguards came in, wet and cold, leading two women in cloaks. Edan and Mother Agnes approached them at once. "I'm Edan Scott, Laird of these lands," Edan stated. "What are you doing here?"

Laoise carefully removed her hood, making certain that her hat covered her ears. "My name is Laoise. I'm a healer. I was told this was a safe place by Alexander Scott. I was told...this is Branxholme, yes?"

Her explanation was cut off when Maria Stuart removed her hood and everyone saw her face. Mother Agnes gasped. "Maria," she breathed. "Dear Goddess, *is that you?*"

·········

Edan Scott was staring at the wall in his office. He'd been uncomfortable sending his mother to Saorsa with just Toran, Annag, and regular guards along; and now he needed to send Maria Stuart and a half-Fae healer with no fighting experience as well. Toran was adjusting to this new faerie-inclusive reality, but it was still hard for him; he'd taken one look at Laoise's pointed ears and had suddenly felt the need to sit down. *If a whole group of Fae pop up in front of Toran he may just pass out cold.*

Edan grinned. He'd done the same when meeting Thomas the Rhymer. He'd have to take the group to Saorsa himself. Mother Agnes could stay here with Fia. It was the only way he wouldn't be beside himself with worry while they were on the road.

There and back. Probably a week. Mother Agnes can handle Fia and any Crown representatives that arrive for a week. I can send a letter to Killian to keep an eye on things in the area for a bit. Tell him I have shipping company business to handle. Hopefully he won't actually come here to discover Fia is here, but Saorsa and Alex aren't. Mother Agnes would have a devil of a time talking her way out of that one.

He rose and went to the door to call his steward. *What I wouldn't give for one peaceful day.*

Wolfcroft, Scotland

The day was unseasonably warm and Saorsa took it as a good sign. She, Eske, and Rune were headed to see Oona. Saorsa was so excited and relieved that at times she felt close to tears. But before they headed out, she needed to talk to everyone.

"I have something to share with all of you," Saorsa said to the others at the end of breakfast. "You all have been so patient with me, and I thank you for that. It's time for me to tell you some of what I've learned, so that we can all prepare ourselves for what's to come."

Saorsa disappeared into her room and came back with a stack of papers. "Vika's Aunties have been hunting down information on the Fae that they thought might help us. Mother Agnes gave it to me when we left Branxholme. Some of the writings are very old, some more recent. Apparently, the Fae are often cautious about speaking with humans, and there are rules in place about what they can and cannot say, so there are some holes. And, of course, we should probably take everything with a grain of salt. But some of these writings are from Thomas the Rhymer, whom I have met and who is generally accepted to be a trustworthy fellow." She smiled. "I mean, he has no choice. He's famously compelled to tell the truth by a faerie spell."

She put the papers on the table. "Some of these are from persons who had Fae lovers or claim to have gone to Faerie themselves. Even though these accounts are from different times and places, and the persons in question didn't know each other, what stood out was their similarity. And I, of course, have been to Faerie myself, and I must say that some of these things seem to ring true. We're lucky the Aunties are quite well-known for their metaphysical knowledge. It has given us access to information I could never hope to obtain on my own."

"There is a lot here, but here is what I think would serve you best to know. There are several types of Fae, and not all the creatures who live in Faerie are Fae. Just like we have travelers in Scotland who hail from elsewhere, they have that too. But it appears that the beings who attacked us at the cave and took Alex are all Fae, based on what Fia told me."

Rune nodded. "Understood."

Saorsa continued. "Most Fae are just that: common Fae, like we have commoners here. They have some basic magickal abilities and live in various realms, going about their day-to-day business. But *some* Fae are much more powerful, and are not only Fae, but gods and goddesses here on earth and in other worlds."

Willow asked, "Could we have an example, please?"

Saorsa nodded. "It's said that the Fae once resided here on earth. Something happened, the scholars argue over what exactly it was, but they were forced to leave. They went to Faerie and set up shop there, leaving earth to the humans. Faerie is one world. There are apparently other worlds out there that hold all manner of races, but we're just focusing on Faerie for now."

"Because that's where our problem is comin' from," Eske noted.

"Exactly. These writings seem to agree that the world of Faerie is ruled by a Main Council of some sort, composed of various powerful beings, many of whom were once gods or goddesses here on Earth or in other worlds, and still might be today. So, to give Willow her example, let's take The Morrigan. She is a Fae and we know she was a Celtic goddess as well. Some of the scholars call these more powerful Fae *faegods*."

"How many are there?" Aeric asked.

"We don't know for certain. But what we *do* have, from more than one scholar, is the theory that there might not be as many as we think. The faegods can draw magickal power from being worshiped. And so they appear from time to time here on earth in order to get followers. And they don't stop with just one group. This particular scholar," she pointed to a sheet of paper, "a man by the name of Albero, posits that if a god or goddess notices their popularity waning with a particular group, they might pop up elsewhere in the world and try to generate a new following."

"So, wait," said Rune. "He thinks that a faegod might show up as Loki in Norway, but he might also be Lugh in Ireland, or...."

"Or as Anansi in western Africa," Willow said, eyes wide. "But they are, in fact, all the same person. I mean, Fae."

"Exactly," Saorsa said. "And we have information that Alex's father Thomas might do the same thing. He comes to earth repeatedly, in different times and places, sometimes as a god and sometimes walking among humans on a quest for knowledge. He might have been called one thing in Scotland, another in Greece, another in China or the Middle East, but they're all *him*."

"And I am guessing you are telling us this," said Rune, "because we are not going to be dealing with common Fae."

"No. The beings interacting with us are what the scholars call High Fae. They have strong capacities for magick. They are used to being worshiped by humans and other creatures. They are ancient beings. They have their own politics. And they are, in our human view, basically *eternal*."

Willow laughed. "So, we call our gods and goddesses different names from culture to culture, but we're all interacting with the same beings."

Saorsa nodded. "If Albero is right, *yes*."

Rune sat back in his chair. "If this is true...well, this changes everything. About...how I see the world. How I worship."

"It doesn't have to, though," Saorsa cautioned him. "We don't know which gods are which. We don't know the level of power they have. Odin may be *exactly* as you imagine him. We just don't know. The only ones we really are learning anything about are the one we call 'Thomas' and his family."

Rune nodded thoughtfully and Saorsa continued. "Lucky for us, we have some information from A.L. Garcia in Barcelona, who claims to have spoken at length with one *Thomas Scott*."

Willow sat forward. "Alex's father?"

Saorsa smiled. "The same. This was around thirty years ago. Garcia was a Celtic linguistics professor and metaphysics scholar who claims to have had a series of conversations in which Thomas Scott *told him directly* he was Fae. The two were friends who ended up in a rather drunken argument one evening about the nature of light. And apparently Thomas forgot himself and started spouting something about waves and measurements and declared that he knew this from work he'd done in Faerie and that, and I quote, 'I should know about light as I am Darkness itself, *tú scríobhaí dara ráta aineolach*.' For those of you who don't speak Irish, that translates to *you ignorant second-rate scribe*." Willow stifled a laugh.

"The good news is when Garcia questioned Thomas about it the next day, which is impressive because he must have been nursing a terrific hangover, Thomas Scott not only confessed he was Fae *again* but also said he was pining for a particular human woman from Scotland. Which we *know to be true*. And then during subsequent meetings Thomas, who was apparently in the grips of a loneliness that made him more loquacious than normal, confessed all manner of things. That he was not only Fae, but a god. That he had been worshiped here on earth by various groups. He also declared that he had *changed over time*. So, the Fae are not stagnant. Garcia apparently asked him why he had a Scottish accent if he had existed in many cultures, to which Thomas answered, "It's the best one.""

This drew a round of laughter from the room. "Well, he certainly has a Scottish temperament," Rune grinned. "It sounds like he has a certain fondness for us here."

"So, wait, *wait a moment,*" Willow said, holding up her hands. "Doesn't it seem like Thomas is breaking an awful lot of rules? He tells people he's Fae, has a child with a human, and, if he got Adamina out of Carlisle, he meddles in human affairs. I thought the Fae weren't supposed to do things like that."

"It's interesting," Saorsa answered. "If you look at all the old faerie stories we have in these islands, Tam Lin, Thomas the Rhymer, and so on, you notice that the Fae who appear nearly *always* identify themselves as 'The Faerie Queen' or 'The Faerie King'. It's never, 'hello, I'm a Fae blacksmith'. Apparently High Fae have the magick necessary to open portals and travel here. Regular Fae don't. I've been told opening a portal takes a lot of power." She raised her eyebrows. "And, apparently, some have the political clout or simply the confidence to break the rules at times."

Saorsa unfolded a large piece of paper that looked like a map. "As for the political structure of Faerie itself, we have accounts of Fae describing *houses* and *Decks*. And Alex's Fae half described the same thing. The ruling families, most of which are related to someone on the High or Ruling Council, are organized into these houses and Decks. And each is ruled by a King, a Queen, or both, I suppose. Alex told me his father Thomas was the King of the Deck of Crows, and that his grandmother, The Morrigan, is Queen of her House." She paused. "But sometimes gods and goddesses switch Decks, depending on who they want to align themselves with. Between Fia and myself, we have met members of the Deck of Crows, the Deck of Ravens, and the Deck of Hawks. These Fae all seem to have wings, and particular abilities and characteristics. Other writings describe encounters with the House of Hounds, the Deck of Owls, the House of Cats, and the House of Whales. The Fae encounters on earth seem to lean *heavily* toward Fae with wings. There seems to be something about them that makes them particularly earth-curious. Or perhaps it's just ease of transportation. It's probably hard to travel here if you are House of Whales." She pointed to her paper. "Take a look at this. I think it's the most interesting thing here."

Drawn on the paper was a large land mass, surrounded by water. "This, according to the Aunties, is a map that was drawn by a man who worked for one William de Soule in the 1300s, right here in the Borders of Scotland. William de Soule was a practitioner of the dark arts - they claim he had a particularly vicious familiar, and the story says that he was taught his magick by *Michael Scot*."

"That's Thomas again, right?" Eske asked.

Saorsa nodded. "De Soule described five types of magick at work among the Fae, and I'm guessing he learned this from Michael Scot himself. De Soule claims that when the Fae were here on earth, *all* the land was in one big mass and magick flowed easily. There were four tribes, or first peoples, living on the big island. A Tribe of the North, one of the South, one of the East, and one of the West. Each had particular characteristics and talents, although they were all types of Fae."

"That's only *four*," Rune pointed out. "You said he described *five*."

"De Soule claims there was a fifth type of magick, which he describes as *Elemental* or *Chaotic*. This is one of those things we know next to nothing about. But here is the interesting part: look at the writing on the map, where de Soule describes the tribes in each area."

Willow moved the candle closer and read aloud to the group. "North: earth and stone work. Plants and animals. West: soul work. Emotion. Art. Dreams and seers. South: Magicians. Dragon. Language. And East...," Willow looked up from the paper, "it says, 'Science. Thought extinct.'" She took a step backward. "What's going on, here?"

"We don't know where exactly the tribes were located relative to today, because the land, according to de Soule, *split apart and moved*," Saorsa said. "But down here in the corner, there's more writing: 'Tribes unite to become *Tuath Dé*.' We know the story of the *Tuath Dé;* they were the Fae, who left earth and went to Faerie."

"Four tribes, four magicks, became one nation," Rune said. "And apparently, that Tribe of the East is no more."

"That's what de Soule seems to be saying."

"And the royal families of these tribes, the High Fae, came back to earth after the Fae left, becoming part of our faiths and stories," Willow said. "But if that's true, then...Zeus could know Osiris, who could know the Dagda!"

"Or they could even be one entity," Rune added.

"If all this is true, then all of our stories...none of them make sense now," Eske said, shaking his head. "None of them are true."

Saorsa smiled. "I think, Eske that they *are*. For a story to endure, it *must* have a current of truth in it. A heartbeat that the listener can hear and wants to keep alive. The details of our stories vary from region to region, from bard to book. But the core of them, their *truths,* stay the same. Think of all the great legends and stories. The reason we know the ancient tales is that the truth in them speaks to us, so we pass it on to let it live. Whether it's Odin trading his eye for knowledge or Hercules enduring his labors or Medusa being cursed, each of these stories tells an essential truth about what it is to live and be human.

Here's the proof: every writing we have about The Morrigan, *every last one,* was written down not by the Celtic tribes but by *Christian monks*. There was something about her so compelling that they felt the need to preserve her stories, even though it was in direct conflict with their own faith. So yes, we may have the details wrong. But the core of these stories stays the same. They are something alive, and they help *us* live." She nodded at Willow. "The other day Willow told me that adorning ourselves is a human trait. Telling stories is, too. It's how we teach each other and bond with each other. Without them, our civilization dies."

There was a moment of silence in the room. And then Saorsa looked at Willow and grinned. "Notice anything *else* about the map?"

Willow looked for a moment and blinked. "Wait...oh! Yes!" She laughed. "The four Tribes correspond to the four Directions in your magick!"

"Got it!" Saorsa grinned. "When I do spells, I use symbols to mark the four directions of my circle. In the north, something representing earth, perhaps a stone. In the west, something representative of water and emotion. In the south, I use a symbol for fire, a wand, like a magician might use. And in the east, a sword representative of air and thought."

"The symbols we use in magick here are based on these tribes," Rune said. "Every time you cast, you're recreating that map."

"Yes," Saorsa said. "It's the origin of my tradition of witchcraft. It came right from how the four Tribes were organized before they became the *Tuath Dé*."

There was a long pause. Then Aeric sighed and said, "So, in short, you think we may be fighting gods soon, and ones who invented the very magick we are trying to use to keep them at bay."

Saorsa nodded. "That's the long and short of it, yes."

Willow elected to stay behind at Wolfcroft. "There's so much to be done, and I can make certain everything is ready for Oona when you return tomorrow," she smiled, detailing her plans over breakfast. "Olav found an old wooden infant bed in the loft in the stable, but it needs repairs. We're going to work on that this morning, and I'd also like to spend some time getting to know the animals in the area." She raised her eyebrows. "And see if I can find more traces of the wolves." She put a bit of bread onto the bench beside her, and Malphas hopped up and gobbled it down. "I hope you don't mind. I asked Malphas if he might help me. I think it would go a long way toward making some friends here."

Saorsa readily agreed. After the events of last evening, she had half expected at least one of her companions to express some discomfort in staying in this place. After all, The Morrigan's reputation in most stories was quite ghastly. But instead of shying away, each of them seemed to become even more dedicated to unlocking the secrets of this place. *And if I can use it the way I hope to, I will gain enough power to make the Fae notice and listen.*

Rune and Eske would take Saorsa to Keena and Donovan, and then head off to buy supplies. Aeric was intending to spend the morning repairing a chicken house they'd discovered; with luck, they'd have fresh eggs for cooking soon if they could find chickens for sale today.

Willow walked out to the stable to see them off. She tousled Saorsa's hair playfully. "These first few spells I worked in under the rest of your hair in the back here are staying in nicely. I can do some more tonight. How do they feel?"

Saorsa laughed. "Bumpy. And a little bit tight. But I am *thrilled*. I can't wait until they're all in!"

Willow grinned. "Being on the road will be good for them. Sunshine and wind to set the tangles. I added extra salt to the supply list; washing your hair in salt water will help them set." She patted Bridgit's nose. "Too bad we're not near the sea in summer. When I had mine done, I just ran around on the shore and swam in the water for a fortnight. They locked up nice and tight." Willow smiled. "My husband did them for me. I said I looked like a savage thing." She laughed. *She misses him*, Saorsa thought.

Suddenly Willow looked up and to her left, toward the stall where Thor was waiting to be saddled. She moved down to the big horse, murmuring to him quietly. Thor stretched out his neck to put his head next to Willow's and closed his eyes. And Saorsa realized they were *communicating* with each other.

Willow seemed to forget about everything around her for a few minutes, her eyes closed, her body listening. When her eyes opened after a time, she looked pained. "Oh, my friend," she whispered to Thor. "I'm sorry."

"What is it?" Saorsa walked closer, concerned. She'd never seen someone commune with an animal this way. Thor had recognized that Willow could hear him in a way most humans never thought of.

Willow turned to Saorsa. "Thor is upset. Confused. He wants to know why we're leaving again without Alex."

Guilt hit Saorsa with a sharp, swift blow. Alex and Thor had a special bond; they'd been each other's constant companions for years. And now both she and Rune had been riding him, with no explanation as to what had happened to Alex. *The last Thor saw him, Alex couldn't walk. He might think Alex is dead. Alex used to spend hours with him in the stable talking to him, and I haven't told him anything.* She hadn't thought to. She was mortified by her behavior.

"I'm a terrible person, Willow. Can you...beg his forgiveness for me? Tell him I'm trying to get Alex back?"

Willow gave Saorsa a gentle smile. "Would you like to tell him? He knows you much better than me. You're his herd. His family."

I am his family. Saorsa realized how true that was. Thor, Bridgit, Alex...they were *all* her family, and had been for months. But she hadn't ever tried talking to the non-human ones. She took a step closer. "I don't know how, Willow. What do I do?"

"Talk to him. Put your hands on him and look into his eyes, if you feel that he wants that. Make yourself as open as you can. Clear your mind. And...listen." She paused. "Ground yourself. Imagine the wind blowing away your human thoughts. Slow yourself way, way down."

Malphas swooped into the stable and perched on a saddle, watching. "It's not that it's complicated," Willow said. "It's just that for most humans, it never crosses their minds to *try.* And the more you do it, the easier it is. Like learning a language."

Saorsa moved to stand in front of Thor. *He's going to be angry with me, isn't he?* She took a deep breath. *I will beg his forgiveness. I will learn.*

She reached up to touch Thor's face, half expecting him to toss his head and snort and move away. But he didn't. Instead, he lowered his head, pressing the space between his eyes gently to her forehead. *The same way Alex likes to touch his forehead to mine when he holds me. A light, gentle touch. A receiving.*

She felt the energy of the earth rise up into her feet, and let her thoughts fly away. *Listen. Listen. Be present.* And...suddenly *she could hear Thor.* Or...feel him. Some of both. Thor was glad, *so glad,* that she was here and she was trying. Her eyes began to brim with tears.

Glad, Thor said to her. *Glad for you.*

I'm glad for you too, Saorsa thought. *And sorry. I didn't know we could do this.*

She felt Thor's hot, gentle breath on her shirt. *Where is he? Is he hurt?*

Saorsa sighed. Thor was thinking of Alex. *He's in a prison, my friend. I am trying to help him so he can come back to us. I miss him too.*

Thor shifted a little, and nuzzled her neck. *I help. I help him too.*

Saorsa tangled her fingers in his mane. *Do you remember the baby, Thor? You and Alex carried her a few weeks ago.*

Important, Thor said. *Young one is important. His.*

Yes, Saorsa thought. *He loves her. We are going to get her today to bring her here and keep her safe. Will you help?*

Thor nickered and bobbed his head. An enthusiastic yes. *What else? I guard. I help.*

Can you tell the other horses that we are making a home here? Saorsa thought. *Can you ask them for help?*

Yes. Thor pressed his cheek against Saorsa's head. *That crow is not a crow.*

I know, Saorsa grinned. *What other animals have you seen?*

Dogs. Thor sighed. *Dogs are here. I smell them. Careful.*

Saorsa's eyes widened. *Have you smelled them before?*

Yes. When he was here. With you.

He was talking about the wolves. They must have come close last night. She'd have to tell Willow. *You and I, we can talk again. Every day if you want.*

Yes, Thor thought. *I help. He will come home.*

Saorsa kissed Thor on the nose, and the connection faded. She turned to Willow. "He says the wolves were near last night. And to be careful." She paused. "Thank you."

Willow grinned. "Let's get you two on the road to fetch that baby."

Fenwick, Scotland

The temperature was beginning to drop again. It felt like years since Saorsa had last knocked on Keena and Donovan's door instead of just a few weeks. *So much has changed.*

Rune and Eske hung back several paces with the horses, wanting to give Saorsa the space to greet her friends alone. They tended to look a bit intimidating if you didn't know them, and thought it best to be introduced by her. Saorsa heard footsteps inside the house, and a moment later she let out the breath of anticipation she'd been holding as Donovan opened the door.

Saorsa was grateful for Donovan's delighted, excited smile, and even more grateful when he enveloped her in a familial bear hug. "Saorsa! Oh, thank the Ancestors!" As he let her go, she saw his eyes dart up to Rune and Eske, and his face grew concerned. "Where's Alex?"

"He's not with me," Saorsa said quietly, having difficulty getting the words out. "A lot has happened. He's a prisoner in London, Donovan. These are my friends Eske and Rune; they work for Edan Scott. I...I need your help."

"Of course, *of course,*" Donovan said, hugging her again. "Come in. All of you." He nodded toward her companions. "Do they know we're...."

"They're pagan too. They follow the Allfather," Saorsa whispered.

Donovan called back over his shoulder into the house. "Keena! Saorsa's here, with friends!" He gestured at Rune and Eske. "Please, come inside. You are most welcome here."

The men shook hands and introduced themselves, and Rune grinned at the Norse sign carved by the door. "We are most welcome here indeed," he nodded to Donovan as Keena appeared in the doorway.

"Saorsa! Oh, Saorsa!" Keena laughed, enveloping her friend in her arms. "How did things go?" She took in Rune and Eske while Donovan leaned in close and whispered something in his wife's ear. *He's telling her about Alex so I don't have to say it out loud again,* thought Saorsa. It was the sort of caring, considerate attention to detail that made Saorsa feel so at home with this couple.

The travelers made their way into the spacious kitchen and were soon warming themselves by the fire with glasses of hot spiced wine. "Oona's sleeping," Keena told Saorsa as she took her cloak. "She should be up soon. She's moving around so much! Crawling already! And...," Keena's eyes darted to Donovan. "Well, I'll just come out and say it. Some strange things have happened while you've been away. We've had a few instances where Oona moves...in *other* ways than crawling." She looked at Saorsa, worried, waiting for a response.

Saorsa sighed. "I'm...not surprised. I don't know how to start telling you all this. Oona has Fae blood in her. We didn't know it when we left her here. And...," she gestured vaguely in front of her, "there's a very good chance she is related to Alex in some way. Because, umm...well, Alex has Fae blood in him too."

Donovan sat down rather quickly on the bench behind him, and Keena put her hand over her heart to steady herself. "Oona is...*a faerie?*" She went very still for a moment. "*And Alex is too?*"

"Not...quite," Saorsa said slowly. "Alex is...complicated. And Oona could be either half-Fae or...less than that." She put her hand to her head. "Depending on if Alex is her father or not, and then *which* Alex is her father."

Donovan's eyebrows went straight up. "What do you mean, *which Alex?*"

Rune cleared his throat. "Is this house warded, my friends?"

Keena nodded. "Yes. With everything we know how to do." Her eyes narrowed. "*Why?*"

Saorsa spoke up. "There's a very high chance that some among the Fae would like to take Oona away with them."

Donovan was suddenly on his feet again, his hand instinctively reaching for a sword in a weapons belt he wasn't wearing, and Keena momentarily touched her pregnant belly protectively before she turned and raced down the hall to where Oona was sleeping in her room.

"The three of you need time to talk," Rune said. "Donovan, we have what we believe is a safe place for Oona. We've established a croft a few hours' ride from here. But we need supplies. Eske and I can go fetch those while Saorsa shares what she knows, if you can direct us."

"Of course," Donovan said, a slight tremor in his voice. "And for the love of the Lord and Lady, if the two of you have anything protective in the way of spells you can layer on this house, I would be overjoyed if you did."

Rune looked at Eske, who nodded. "We will be happy to. Take heart in the fact that the Fae have not yet come here. They have difficulty moving in this realm. But keep in mind, we believe they have human agents who are working to assist them. Keep Oona close until we return."

Keena returned just then, a sleepy Oona bundled in a blanket in her arms. "Should we call everyone in? We have people helping on the property," Donovan asked Rune.

Rune shook his head. "I would not spread alarm at this point. There is no evidence that the Fae are planning to come here *now*. Eske and I will put up what wards we can. The fewer people who know what is happening, the better." He paused for a moment. "And if you permit us to take the child, then once we leave, the Fae will no longer be concerned with you." Donovan nodded.

Saorsa felt terrible causing her friends such distress. But they seemed to be moving past it now, with Donovan giving directions to Rune and Keena protecting Oona in her arms.

"We have a cart you can take," Donovan offered. "I've two fresh horses, to give yours a rest while you're gone. Take the cart with you to your croft. I won't need it again until next week." He smiled at them. "And you are all welcome to stay here with us tonight. It sounds as though you've had a challenging road behind you, and more troubles coming up."

They readily accepted and Donovan headed outside to show them around and help hitch the wagon, while Keena moved toward Saorsa. "Here she is," she said softly, pulling the blanket back from Oona's head. "I won't pretend I haven't fallen in love with her while she was here. Donovan and I...well, if you didn't return by year's end, we were discussing keeping her ourselves. We love all the children who come through but...we've never thought of keeping one before."

Saorsa watched the blanket fall back and a shock of dark hair appear. *Dark with the same red highlights as Alex's.* And then Oona turned her head to look at Saorsa, and Saorsa gasped. *Oona's eyes had changed color.* No longer blue, they were now a pale, startling gray.

"It started about a week ago," Keena said, understanding what Saorsa was seeing. "The blue faded. And...now they're silver." She shifted Oona in her arms. "And Saorsa...she makes these expressions. Ones she shouldn't have the muscle control to make." Saorsa watched as Oona suddenly arched one eyebrow by itself, followed by a half-smile that reminded her of Alex so much that it took Saorsa's breath away.

"She looks like him," Keena whispered. "You think she's his, don't you? But...he didn't know?"

Saorsa's arms were already moving toward the child. She wanted to hold Oona desperately, and reached out to the little girl. *I need to keep her safe!* Keena handed the child to her, and Saorsa wondered for a split second if Oona remembered anything about her at all. *Will she let me hold her? Will she cry for Keena?*

Oona stared at Saorsa for along moment once she was in her arms, and Saorsa waited, slightly tense. And then the baby let out a delighted giggle and clapped her hands together before nestling close to Saorsa and holding on to Saorsa's shirt with all the strength in her tiny fists.

"She remembers you, it seems." Saorsa saw Keena wipe away a tear. "That's so good. I'm...sorry. Just the thought of having to say goodbye...."

"This won't be goodbye," Saorsa said firmly. "Keena, you and Donovan *rescued* her. Took her in when she had nowhere else to go. Protected her and loved her." Saorsa listened to Oona coo, and then realized it was transitioning into another sound. *A purr.* There was no doubt in Saorsa's mind that this child belonged to Alex's House. She looked up at Keena. "The Christians have a tradition of giving children godparents."

Keena nodded. "They're responsible for watching over the child's religious upbringing. And if something happens to the parents...."

Saorsa smiled at Keena. "We can have that, too. Mother Agnes raised me when my mother couldn't, and watched over my education. I don't know who Oona's mother and father are, exactly, but until such time as we discover that, I think you, Donovan, Alex, and I should declare ourselves her...," she grinned. "Co-God and Goddess-parents." Oona babbled her approval. "She can be Clan Kerr-Scott-Scott-Stuart."

Keena wiped away another tear and laughed. "I'd like that," she nodded.

"I'm just taking her where she'll be safer, and *you'll* be safer, for a time." Saorsa shifted Oona in her arms. "I don't know how everything is going to play out, Keena. You may end up with her back here sooner than we think."

Donovan came in and put his coat up on the wall. "All right, Saorsa," he said quietly. "Tell us, please. What the hell is going on?"

England

The horse was sure-footed and strong, with unusual coloring that Alex found intriguing. The gelding was a red dun, with dark-tipped ears, a dorsal stripe, striping over the withers, and, most notably, striping on the legs. Alex had walked up to the inn stable where the horse had been tacked and hitched to a post, waiting for his rider. And Alex had simply taken the reins, swung into the saddle in the quiet early morning hours when the groom wasn't looking, and galloped away.

He had a habit of talking to his horse and couldn't do that without giving the beast a name, so he decided to call the horse Tam, after a knight from a Border tale his mother used to tell to Edan and him when they were little. He'd have this horse longer than any other on this journey, as his first waterway north wasn't for several days.

But he was going to need more coin for the journey. *Get well away from London first, into the wilds.* And he knew exactly what he'd do then. Something he hadn't done since before meeting Saorsa. He was going to commit highway robbery on the King's roadways. And although he was doing it alone, he also *wasn't;* he could split himself and have an entire team, all of whom possessed the same knowledge and skills he had. And he was really, really looking forward to it.

"So now, Tam," he said, patting the horse, "we're on the lookout for a good target. A tax man would be ideal. A supply wagon for the army is also nice. But we willnae turn down a noble with a heavy purse an' a few fat rings on his fingers."

He was nearing Saint Alban's when he saw the carriage he wanted ahead of him on the road. Alex trailed it for a while, hanging back and blending in with the other riders and wagons heading into town. The carriage took the turn to bypass the town and continued on its way north. One carriage, and two guards on horseback. And a Crown seal painted on the doors on the sides.

Alex left the road, moved his horse to a canter, and passed the carriage, hidden by the trees. He needed to find a good place to take it down.

He couldn't get the smile off his face. *I missed this.* There was nothing quite like the challenge of executing a plan to bring him into alignment. When he had a robbery underway, he didn't think about anything else; didn't worry, didn't fret, just *handled things.* And even better, he was good at it. He loved the rush of energy, the flow of movement, and the satisfaction he felt afterwards. *You were born to do this,* Duncan used to say. *You'd have been a restless, distracted crofter or tradesman, but you do make a fine highwayman.*

He saw the spot he wanted. He moved Tam well off the road and split himself in three. *Any more and it will be too easy.* He could barely contain his happy anticipation. His mind dropped into the calm place that was reserved for these sorts of activities. For a brief moment, he wondered if the Violet Woman would appear. *Can she possess me without access to my Fae half? If she could, why didn't she do so to stop me from escaping?* He didn't know what the rules were. He wondered if Saorsa did.

He could hear the carriage well down the road and got into position. Well, *positions*, plural. He watched one of his aspects flag down the guards who were riding in front of the carriage and call out to them, asking for help. "There's a man down in the road ahead. Hurt, I think. Was walking home an' came upon him."

He watched one of the guards leave the carriage on his horse and move forward to where aspect Three lay in the road, apparently unconscious. The guard dismounted, and took Three by the shoulder, rolling him onto his back to look at his face. A moment of shock as the guard realized the man who had flagged him down and the man he was touching were *identical.* And then Alex smiled, and moved toward the carriage.

The second guard moved his horse forward away from the carriage, trying to help the first guard who now lay unconscious and disarmed in the road. He didn't last long. He made the mistake of stopping to aim his pistol at one aspect and found himself with a knife in his shoulder a moment later, and then he was being pulled from his horse to the ground. Each of Alex's aspects was doing their own work, their thoughts a quiet background hum while he went through his own steps in his head.

Step one: Mount the carriage and disarm the driver. Knock him unconscious with the butt of his own pistol.

Step two: Over the carriage roof and to the ground behind the carriage. He could see the aspects who had handled the guards were now moving toward the carriage horses to make certain they didn't bolt. *This is too, too easy.*

Step three: Take a look in the back. Two men. A guard and one other. He saw the guard reach toward his belt for a weapon, and threw open the carriage door, grabbed the man's arm, and yanked him forward out of the carriage. He twisted the man's arm violently behind him as he fell, and heard a sickening snap as the man howled in pain. A second later Alex had the pistol out of the man's belt and tossed it a good way off into the dirt before kicking the man in the head. He slumped onto the road, unconscious.

Step four: Neutralize any remaining threats. He looked at the men lying motionless in the dirt. *Well, that's done.* The other man in the carriage was talking non-stop, jabbering away frantically and holding his hands in the air in an attempt to convince Alex to spare him. Alex simply pointed to the road, and the man climbed obediently out, and a short time later joined his companions in a state of unconsciousness.

Alex smiled. His two aspects were busying themselves dragging the guards off to the side of the road. There were quite a lot of cases and bags to go through inside this carriage, so he'd ride along for a time and have a look. The belts and coats of the five men yielded a tidy sum of money, and a short time later the three Alexes were on the road again. One Alex rode Tam and led the two guards' horses behind him, one drove the carriage, and the original Alexander Scott made himself comfortable inside the rather luxurious government vehicle and began opening cases, a satisfied smile on his features.

Fenwick, Scotland

Saorsa lay in her room that night, restless in the dark. She was all talked out. Keena and Donovan had been wonderful, listening to everything that had transpired without seeming to doubt a single word. Every time Saorsa told her story, she was aware of how insane it sounded. *But people believe me. Even when I can't believe it myself.*

She'd slept in this room before with Alex and Oona the last time she'd been here. Now Oona was down the hall, and Alex was.... *Think on happier times. You must believe you'll have what you need to help him soon.* Getting to Wolfcroft and setting up a safe house had been part one in the plan; getting Oona was part two. *And part three, that's tomorrow night. And the one that scares the crap out of me.* But if she was successful, she was fairly certain she'd be able to draw in the other players in this game. And deal with them on her own terms.

I'm going to get him back. She rolled on her side and closed her eyes. And let her mind wander back to Deadwater Tower, and the second time she and Alex had been together.

"Get over here, Alex Scott," she had said to him. "I want to be in your arms again." The hour was late, and the fire was low. He had moved closer in the bed, and she had caught the scent of cedar, leather, and soap, and underneath it, the familiar scent of his skin. And he was smiling, and then she was feeling his lips on her cheek, a soft, gentle kiss.

Everything else in the world fell away as he pulled her close and kissed her on the mouth. And then he was tasting her tongue, her lips, finding the shape of her, moving inside her space. And she *wanted* him. Wanted him so badly her insides ached that he wasn't there already, wanted him so badly that she wanted to completely occupy the same space he did in this world. She felt the fingers of his right hand interlace strongly with the fingers of her left, and now he was moving that hand slowly back onto the pillow near her head, and he was holding her down.

"Oh *yes*," she gasped, in between kisses, wrapping her right arm around him. "I want you, I want you," she whimpered quietly, and he kissed her gently on the forehead.

She looked up at him in the rapidly darkening room. She wanted to remember everything about him right now: the pressure of his body on hers. The heat of him. The storm of excitement he was generating in her body. The shape of his eyes as he looked at her, full of wonder and need.

He was beautiful. But not just because his face and body had all the components of ideal attractiveness: the high cheekbones, square jaw, piercing eyes, and exceptionally well-muscled body that would make any woman in her right mind swoon. He was beautiful because of how he cared for her, tended to her, and spoke to her. It revealed the heart of a man of worth, a man of compassion, a man of honor. And he had declared himself *hers*.

"I want to make ye happy tonight, Saorsa," he whispered, pulling up her shift under the covers. "I want to make ye cry out in joy. I want to be your servant, to give ye everythin', to tend to your every wish. Will you let me, *mo bhòidhchead?* Will ye tell me what you wish for?"

His words were making her dizzy. She was sitting up now and wasn't quite certain how she'd gotten in this position; she was so busy listening to him and being dazzled by his proximity that she barely noticed him pulling her shift off over her head. But then his nightshirt was up and off and tossed away as well, and she was sitting in bed next to the unclothed form of the most stunning, sensuous man in the world, and she was naked herself. *Oh, Goddess, here we are again. He wants to make love to me. It wasn't just once. It wasn't just once! He wants me again!*

"Lie down, my dearest one," he whispered to her. "Let me love you, Saorsa." She took a deep breath and lay back on the pillows. And she watched him, her entire body tingling in anticipation, as he bent and kissed her on the stomach, and then moved lower to press his lips to her trembling thighs. He looked up at her and gave her such a devilish, knowing smile that she momentarily forgot to breathe, and then she knew without a doubt what he intended to do to her. She wasn't sure she could take it without fully and completely losing her mind; she'd been aching for him every single moment since Hermitage, and now that she had him, the length of time since they'd last been intimate seemed to magnify every sensation.

He was stroking her hips now. She let out a muffled sob of extreme excitement. She could hear the merriment in his voice. He was thoroughly enjoying her unbridled expressions of want. "Saorsa," he sang, teasing, "move your knees apart for me, sweet one."

"I *can't*," she moaned, laughing, her hands covering her face. "If you kiss me there, I'm going to *cry*. You're just too wonderful, Alex! I can't...," she dissolved into giggles, "I can't let you be that *good*."

He climbed back up to lie next to her body and kissed the back of her hands as they covered her eyes. "Look at me, Saorsa," he said, his voice low and smoky, and Saorsa felt her heart flip completely over. "Please?"

She moved her hands and gazed up into his handsome face. *My Goddess. Those beautiful silver eyes of his!* "You let me kiss you there before, at Hermitage," he said, raising his eyebrows slightly. "You dinnae like it anymore?"

She was holding his hand again. "No, it's not that," she said shyly. "I like *everything* you do to me. It just seems like...like I'm being..." her eyes darted away, "...*selfish*."

Alex frowned. "How is letting' me do somethin' *I* want to do selfish on your part?"

Saorsa blinked. "Well, I'm not...*doing* anything."

Alex smiled at her and ran his hand through her curls. "Why do ye think you have to be doin' somethin' all the time?"

Saorsa put her hand on his cheek. "Well...I could be doing something *you* like."

He looked at her, puzzled. "I *do* like it, *eun beag*. That's why I'm *doin'* it."

Saorsa shook her head. "No, you're just doing it to make me feel good. You don't...actually enjoy it, do you? I mean, nothing's *happening* to you."

He looked at her in wonder for a moment. "Oh, Saorsa," he whispered to her, "you've got it all wrong. It's somethin' I dream about, sweetheart."

"It is?" Saorsa asked weakly. "Why?"

He shifted his weight slightly and propped up his head on his arm. "Well...it means ye trust me, *eun beag*. It means ye let me see an' touch the most tender, intimate parts of you. An' the sounds you made at Hermitage when I kissed you there, ye dinnae make them any other time, an' I want to hear them again. I love the way you feel under my mouth, under my hands, and the way you move your hips an' the way I can see your body respondin' to me...it's like no other feelin' *in the world*, sweet one. You cannae hide anythin' from me when ye let me adore ye like that." His eyes searched hers. "An' I *crave* bein' with you that way."

She stared at him in disbelief. "You *do?*"

He nodded. "Mmm. Aye." He moved his head to kiss her cheek. "An' ye taste good, too."

Saorsa stared at him, horrified. "I do not!"

He laughed and laughed. "Aye, ye do." He raised his eyebrows at her twice, playfully. "Why will ye no believe good things about yourself, sweet one? I love *everythin'* about you, *eun beag*." She blushed.

"So, how about it then, eh?" She watched as he moved down on the bed and kissed her belly once more. "I was thinkin' about doin' this on the way home tonight. Be kind to me, Saorsa. Dinnae make your man beg." He arched an eyebrow and looked up at her, expectant. "Please? Just for a time?" He kissed her high on the front of her left thigh, teasing her. "I'm *thirstin'* for ye, Saorsa. I want to get drunk on your sweet spiced wine." He grinned at her and winked.

She pretended to debate for a moment, which made him chuckle. "Well, *alright,*" she said dramatically, rolling her eyes, "I *suppose.*"

But all traces of humor left her voice a moment later when she felt his mouth on the inside of her thigh. "Oh...*Alex,*" she breathed, her hands gripping the sheets. "Oh..."

"Saorsa," she heard him whisper, "you're so beautiful, *mo ghràdh*. Oh, God, *yes,* I can see your body *wanting*." And she felt the touch of his tongue.

She tilted her chin up and shut her eyes. She could feel him, *feel him,* his tongue moving against her with a strong, increasing rhythm, his hands stroking and caressing her thighs and hips and buttocks. He was driving her higher and higher; and now her back was arching and she wanted nothing more in life but to be closer to him. She wanted to *rise*.

"Oh!" Saorsa wailed, every muscle in her body tensing. "Oh...oh my *Goddess*...oh, don't stop, *please don't stop,* I'm...I can't...I'm going to..." and a tremendous, crashing, chaotic wave of pleasure manifested in the core of her body and drove her senseless. *Lightning. I'm being struck by a beautiful lighting.* "Oh, Alex," she sobbed, "come here! Please, please, *please* come hold me!"

And then he was next to her, kissing her again. "God, I want you so much right now," he whispered. He kissed her as he rolled her on her side towards him and put himself slowly inside her, holding her tight, and then he was moving with long, luxurious, strong strokes, riding the aftershocks at the end of her orgasm. "Yes!" she cried, burying her face in his neck. "I want to be close. I want to be close! Hold onto me!"

"I've got you, sweetheart," he crooned in her ear as he moved into her. "I'm here. Oh, Christ Almighty, Saorsa, you feel *so good*." He kissed her, slow and deep. "God, you have me excited. I want to be like this with ye *forever*."

"Look at me," she said to him as she felt the urgency in his body increasing. "Look at me, Alex." She put her hand gently on the side of his face as he looked into her eyes. "Don't look away," she said softly. "*Please*. I love you. *I love you.* And I want to watch you."

He looked deep into her eyes and held her gaze. 'I love *you*," he gasped, and she realized his breath was coming quick and chaotic as the tension in his body mounted. "Oh, my beautiful Saorsa..."

He was trying to stay focused on her eyes, but his eyes kept blinking or briefly closing as he was transported closer to bliss. The gray of his irises was clouding with his approaching ecstasy; she heard him give a soft, involuntary cry of rapture. "I...I...*oh, love...*"

And then he shared it with her. Shared holding each other close; shared his most vulnerable, intimate, and personal moment. Shared every ragged breath, and every quake of release. He showed her something no one else in his life was allowed to witness, and let her hear what no one else in his life heard. He *trusted* her. Trusted her with his body, and the most private act he had. And he was so beautiful in those moments that Saorsa fought not to weep with gratitude. *I don't want to miss a moment of you, Alexander Scott. I don't want to miss a moment of this gift that you give me when we are together. The gift of yourself.*

He had held her tightly afterwards, with her curled up against him, her head on his chest, and she smiled as his breathing slowed. "I never want us to be apart," he said, kissing the top of her head. "Ever. Saorsa Stuart, you're in my soul now."

Saorsa rolled over alone in the bed in Donovan and Keena's house. *You're in my soul too, Alex. Hang on.*

Wolfcroft, Scotland

They had returned to Wolfcroft with Oona, a full wagon, and two pack horses of supplies, to find Edan's man, Edward Bruce, waiting for them. The return was a joyful event. Those who had stayed at Wolfcroft were excited to see the wagon and so many supplies and eager to meet Oona, as well as brimming with news of their own. In their absence Willow had found more wolf tracks that had led to a cave entrance. A cave entrance that showed evidence of old carvings in the stonework underneath the vines that had covered it.

Everyone pitched in to unload the wagons and help get the supplies safely stored away. The horses were tended and the wagon safely stowed, and then everyone went inside to pull chairs and benches near the fire and listen to what Mr. Bruce had to say.

Saorsa sat on a chair by the fire. Willow spread a quilt over the rug and sat down on the floor to help Oona with a set of blocks Keena and Donovan had sent along. It had been hard for them to let her go, very hard; but they knew she needed protection, and so said their farewells, promising to come and visit in a few days.

Edward was a sensible man, tall and friendly, with a great knowledge of law and business. He unrolled a large map and pinned it to the wall for all to see. "So, these boundaries here," he began, tracing an area on the map, "are three homesteads that belonged to the same family, the Maxwells. The original settlement was below, and then they moved up here. There's another house, belonging to their son, out here as well."

Rune frowned. "Guess we missed that one."

"The land is a large plot, so you might not have gone far enough. Their deed runs from this road, all the way out to these mountains here, and then back up to this creek boundary, and then over here to this lake, and then back down here. Quite a nice area. I believe there are other Maxwells off in this direction." He waved his hand over the map. "Not a lot of roads, but good grazing for cattle or sheep and some very nice farmland. From what I heard in town, once the Uprising got underway, the Maxwells sold off their cattle and went to join it. Apparently the elder Maxwell had quite a bit of military experience and was among Charles Stuart's more trusted advisors. But...well, we all know what happened."

Saorsa cleared her throat. "Alex might have known Mr. Maxwell. We'll have to ask him."

"Mr. Maxwell died in combat, as did his son. Mrs. Maxwell returned, but took ill shortly after her husband's death and did not survive. The land passed to Mr. Maxwell's youngest brother, a blacksmith who lives in Fenwick. I went to see him. He has his hands full with five little ones under the age of ten, a rapidly growing business, and a very social young wife." Edward grinned. "And I asked him if he'd be willing to sell."

Saorsa sat forward on the chair. "And?"

Edward reached inside his coat and removed a stack of papers. "Laird Edan Scott of Buccleuch is now the legal owner of this place you call Wolfcroft." The occupants of the house voiced their enthusiasm with enough gusto that Oona began screeching and clapping her hands, wanting to join in.

"We can stay here? It's ours?" Saorsa grinned.

Edward smiled. "As long as you stay on Laird Scott's good side, I imagine so."

"Oh, I intend to!" Saorsa breathed a sigh of relief. *One less worry, then. This is Scott territory now. No one is going to show up and demand we leave. We can start preparing in earnest.*

"I intend to find that third house tomorrow," declared Eske.

"And we need to investigate that cave, as well," Willow chimed in.

"First things first," Saorsa smiled, standing up and hunting for her apron. "Let's get dinner in motion, and get Edward and Oona settled so when they feel like falling asleep, they can. We're crofters now, friends. I can't wait to tell Alex!"

....

Dinner had been merry. Saorsa felt terrifically cozy in the cabin. They had plenty of supplies, Oona safe and sound here with them, and Wolfcroft was, essentially, *hers. It's a good beginning. And now, it's time to do what I came here to do.*

Once everything had been tidied and the group was nodding by the fireside with wine in their hands, Saorsa pulled Willow and Rune aside. "It's time," she said. "The croft is ours and Oona is here. And I need to tell you both what I am about to do so you can be ready."

Willow cradled a nearly-asleep Oona in her arms. "Go ahead."

"Willow, I need you to have Oona in your room tonight. Because...I'm going to attempt to speak with someone in Faerie in mine. And I have no idea how this is going to go."

Rune looked concerned. "Explain, please."

Saorsa took a deep breath. "I am going to attempt to communicate with Thomas Scott. Alex's father."

Willow's eyebrows went straight up. "The *Magician?* The one you described earlier? If he hasn't put in an appearance yet, why do you think he will?"

"Mother Agnes seemed convinced that he is moving around here on earth. And *someone* got Adamina out of Carlisle. I think it's him. I think something is going on that is preventing him from helping Alex directly. Maybe he doesn't know Alex is in trouble."

"Or maybe he's the one who planted that awful knife, and he isn't helping Alex *on purpose,*" Willow suggested.

"Possibly. He's Fae. And...they seem to have a different perspective on things. And he's a very powerful one," Saorsa mused. "But from what I saw of his letters and the recordings at Buccleuch, he loves Alex very much. So, I want to get his attention, if I can. We're at a place of power for The Morrigan, Queen of his House. We have Oona, who belongs to his Deck. I'm pretty certain Malphus is friendly with him. I'm apparently wearing a magickal protection symbol from his son on my back. And I...may have something that belongs to him that might interest him."

"What's that?" Rune looked at Saorsa closely.

"His spells."

Willow frowned. "I don't follow. You said the Fae took his spellbook when they took Alex."

Saorsa nodded. "They did. But Mother Agnes and I...*altered* it significantly first." She spread her hands. "When Alex brought the book out of the tomb, we all read through it. There was the spell in there that Thomas used to separate Alex's soul. Mother Agnes and I discussed it later that night at Melrose. We thought it wasn't a good idea to leave that ritual lying around. I mean...if the ritual is how you split him, couldn't it be used to figure out how to put him back together? And a united *leth dhia* is illegal in Faerie because he's dangerous. So...Mother Agnes and I decided to cut that spell out of the book and sew in a fake one. Keep that we'd done it just between us. Alex saw the book, and we were afraid that meant the Violet Woman might be able to find out about it, too. We did it with a few other important-looking spells as well." She paused. "And Mother Agnes kept them safe and passed them to me at Branxholme."

Willow's eyes widened. "And then the Violet Woman and friends took the book. When they took Alex."

Saorsa nodded again. "I have a theory, see. My theory is that someone wants to put Fae Alex and human Alex back together for some reason. To command an army, or use as a weapon. I think the Violet Woman possesses Alex to practice controlling him. I think they took Alex and the book so they could put the big bad *leth dhia* back together, and then the Violet Woman could, in theory, take control and drive the weapon where she wants him. The problem is, the half she had safely locked up in Faerie is now *loose.*"

Rune started to laugh. "And if you're right, now the spell in the book they want to use to unite him is a forgery. Clever."

Saorsa grinned. "If they try to follow that spell, they are going to be *very* disappointed with its results." She looked up at the ceiling. "I may or may not have replaced a half page of alchemical ingredients with what is essentially the recipe for a nice spicy marinara sauce."

Willow was laughing so hard Oona woke up. "Oh! This is the *best* thing I have heard in a *long* time!"

"Wait, wait," Rune said. "You think the Violet Woman and company want to control the *leth dhia* so they can defeat...who? And what do your mother and Adamina have to do with it?"

"I don't know that," Saorsa said. "But I'm hoping the Magician might." She sighed. "I know it's hard for the Fae to communicate between realms, so I might not understand much from Thomas. He might also be hesitant because Alex's Faerie half told me Thomas isn't supposed to have contact with Alex here on earth, and I might be close enough to Alex that talking to me would violate that rule. Thomas might not even deign to speak to a lowly human witch he doesn't know. He might just smite me and go on his way. I have no real proof that he's one of the good guys here. For all I know, he could be the Violet Woman's boss. There are *a lot* of ways this could go wrong tonight." She put a hand to her forehead. "And to make it all even *more* awkward, I'll also be meeting my boyfriend's dad for the first time."

Realm of The Morrigan, Among the Fae

Thomas had been asleep for a very long time. The spell he'd worked on Adamina, and all of the supporting magick he'd prepared for it, had worn him completely out. Days passed and he stayed isolated in his chambers, rising only to eat, drink, or bathe before falling asleep again. Whenever he awakened, his first thoughts were always of Adamina. *Her ring has been mostly blue for days and days,* he thought. *She's probably wondering why I've been asleep so much.*

It was time to get moving again. He needed a brief audience with the Queen, and then he needed to see Alex. Thomas smiled. Alex would be thrilled to hear about the wedding and even more excited about the idea that Adamina might come to reside in Faerie. *He so wants to speak with her, to spend time with her.* And then, of course, he needed to head back to the front.

He used the entrance to the Queen's family audience chamber, accessible from the palace wing in which his chambers lay. While he knew from The Morrigan's response at the wedding that she approved of Adamina, he was most likely going to catch hell for the way he'd gone about it. Certain members of the Council would be livid once they heard he'd married a human and the mother of the *leth dhia* without having been informed first. And that anger could make things politically challenging for the House of Corvids and Wolves at a time when things were already quite rocky indeed.

He entered the room, which was pitch black save for a light shining from behind her throne. He couldn't see her face at all, which might have been disconcerting to others. But Thomas had never used sight as his primary method of observing The Morrigan; he read her magick instead.

Even though they were alone, he genuflected to her, going down on one knee briefly before rising. He smiled as he felt a distinct vibration of *humor* emanating from her. Very few beings amused The Morrigan; Thomas seemed to do so nearly every time he saw her.

"*Mar sin, tá tú ar ais,*" she said in Irish. *So, you have returned.*

"Aye." He smiled at her shadowy, veiled form. "I wanted to see if ye had given any thought to my suggestion before I return to the front."

She gestured with the fingers of her right hand without raising it from the arm of the throne. "That time has passed."

He scowled. "What do ye mean by that? Has something changed while I've been gone?"

The Morrigan did not answer. Thomas was used to this. The Morrigan often fell silent for long periods of time, her attention drawn elsewhere. It was also a trait she employed when she did not wish to answer. She'd passed it on to certain offspring as well. He'd seen Alex employ it often. *They are much alike, my son and my mother. Full of passion and constructed out of mysteries and many faces. Calm on the outside, with a chaotic interior.* He loved them both fiercely.

"Let me bring him to you," Thomas said, taking a step closer. "You will see. He is no as they say he is. He can be reasoned with, and has loyalty. The others are just afraid."

The Morrigan was silent. *Something has happened,* Thomas thought. *I had her ear on this subject last time, and she was willing to listen. But the energy from her now on this has completely shut down.* He ventured a guess. "You have decided against it, based on the position I have put ye in with the Council."

He thought he detected a slight shake of her head. "He is as he was made."

What the hell? Whatever she meant, it was clear to Thomas that his previous suggestion had gained no traction since his last visit, and might in fact be completely off the table. There was no point in continuing the conversation on this topic at this time. Thomas was disappointed. "Thank you, my Queen."

He began walking back toward the exit, his black boots reflecting in the highly polished floor, his footsteps echoing through the hall that held nothing save for The Morrigan's throne. With each step he felt his anger rising. *No one is listening. I'm being shut down at every turn.*

He knew her. He knew snapping at her would do no good, would not further his cause in the slightest. But his emotion was running high, and he felt the need to speak again before he left, if only for his own benefit. He turned and looked back to where she sat on the throne.

"We're going to lose it, ye ken," he said. "The war. I expected some on the Council to want to live in denial of that fact, but no *all* of them. And never *you.*"

She sat, unmoving. Thomas strode back toward her. "The Council isn't *there*. I am no exaggerating when I say the gods are dying. I am no exaggerating when I say we are about to lose that front." His voice rose, buoyed by frustration. "*I am no exaggerating when I tell the Council the Fae are in danger!*"

She sat immobile, still as a stone, calm as a dead sea.

Thomas found himself flying into a rage, his normally composed demeanor cracking after a year and a half of pressure. "If we lose that front, realms will start to fall. Our communication will be corrupted. We have, in this very house, the answer to this issue. And the only reason the Council will no listen to me on this is *fear!* The Council is afraid of something that will *never come to pass,* when it should be *terrified of what is already happening!* If we dinnae use every resource at our disposal, and *quickly,* there willnae be a Fae for the Council to rule!"

The Morrigan shifted slightly in her chair. "Your greatest weakness, Thomas, has always been the illusion of control."

Thomas was beside himself now. "It's *not an illusion!*" he thundered. "He's *my son!*"

He saw the index finger of her left hand twitch, and found himself back in his chambers, standing next to the bed. She had ended the audience. He'd been dismissed.

He cleared everything off the top of the dresser with a sweep of his arm, roaring in exasperation and resentment, sending boxes and candleholders crashing to the floor. A burst of magick from his fingers shattered a huge mirror by the fireplace, and then he began lifting small pieces of furniture telekinetically and flinging them into the walls. Seeing his emotion manifested made him feel better, and so he kept slamming objects around until the room was a shambles and most of the furniture lay in splinters on the carpet or impaled the hand-painted wallpapers. But telekinesis was not a magick native to the Fae, and in employing it he'd nearly worn himself out again.

He stood, panting, in the middle of the mess. And then...*what the hell?* He stood very still, listening. Feeling. *There it was again.* A strange sensation inside of his brain. His eyes widened. *Some fool is attempting to summon me!*

Lesser magickal creatures could be summoned against their will. But Thomas was the opposite of a lesser magickal creature. Any practitioner of magick in Faerie knew who he was; so did any powerful magick user in pretty much any other non-human realm. There were almost no entities in existence who were strong enough to compel him to do anything. And no one else would be stupid enough to attempt to summon him without his permission. It was *insulting.*

There it was again! He couldn't fathom who it could be. Alex was inside a prison that prevented summoning, and the rest of his children had better means of contacting him. He frowned, focusing. *Someone on earth. A human.* The magick was *human.* It couldn't be Adamina; she didn't know how to summon, and from what he understood Alex's Human aspect was deeply, immovably Catholic. Adamina had raised him that way to help prevent him from becoming curious about magick and endangering himself. *Even though I split him, he's most likely still highly attracted to magick and probably has more abilities than anyone here is aware of. Great Goddess, I can't imagine the disaster it would be if he ever discovered how to split himself in pieces on Earth!*

Certain overconfident humans had tried to summon Thomas before without invitation, but not for centuries. Those who had had quickly learned the definition of the word *combust.* And he'd become stronger these past centuries. *This human must have remarkable magickal capacity to even make me sense them, or be using a strongly infused magickal device, like one of Nyx's mirrors. And they must also have an insane amount of nerve.*

But if Thomas' greatest weakness was giving in to the illusion of control, his second was unbridled curiosity. Anything scientific or magickal that crossed his path that he didn't understand had to be investigated immediately and to its fullest extent. He thought back to particularly powerful humans in the last century that he'd interacted with, trying to recall their magickal fingerprints. *The Lovers.* Maria Stuart had called for him in Rothesay, and he'd taken the opportunity to shift The Lovers into another realm briefly where he could study them further. Not for long, of course, just long enough to observe them and collect some energy, and he'd given them the key Maria had been looking for in trade. And Maria was in a prison now, a fact he'd discovered by accident while chasing after a different goal. He shook his head sadly. He felt bad for Maria. Magick had overwhelmed her, and she was clearly no longer quite sane. She'd told him a disjointed story about a daughter he was fairly certain didn't exist.

He thought further back. The MacDonald girl. *Birdie*, they had called her. It had been a long time. William MacDonald's mother. But he remembered Birdie well; this wasn't her either. He'd been off at war for eighteen months; he was out of touch with the Fae gossip about the human realm. He'd had no recent dealings with either Birdie or William MacDonald. He didn't even know if they were still alive.

There was that green-coated mage that had appeared once, back when he was in prison. Before Alex had taken his place. But that mage wouldn't be stupid enough to approach him outside of the prison, where he had access to power. The mage had wisely stayed hidden since that first meeting.

The sensation returned, slightly more intense and insistent. Now he *had* to know. And if it wasn't someone interesting, he'd just flambé them for wasting his time and move on. And then, a *different* sort of tug. *The summoning was coming from a place of power. And one he was familiar with.* He made a quick, upwards sweeping motion with his hand, and disappeared from Faerie, accepting the summons.

Wolfcroft, Scotland

Everyone had gone to bed, and Saorsa was alone in her room. She took a deep breath in to steel herself. *What the hell are you doing?* The cautious part of her mind scolded her. *You could get killed doing this. Sucked into Faerie. Turned into a dark mage's familiar for all eternity. Imprisoned in a ...a jar or something.* But it was the best idea she had.

Saorsa sat quietly at the center of the circle she had cast on the floor. Mother Agnes had supplied her with some examples of summoning spells when she'd passed off the spell book pages at Branxholme, and she'd participated in a summoning before when they'd called for Elen. But Mother Agnes had been fairly certain Elen was a friend, and Saorsa was not certain Thomas Scott was friendly at all. She'd also seen his familiar, the memory of which sent chills down her spine. *If he hears me, please don't let him bring that thing. I may start screaming and never stop.* She shook her head. *Focus. Listen.*

This is for Alex. "I call to you, Michael Scot," she whispered. "Or Thomas, if that's what you prefer. Great Magician of the Fae, Father of My Beloved, Son of the Great Goddess Morrigan, Commander of the Dead, hear my cry. I ask you to appear not to enrich myself, but to learn what I need to protect the children of your Deck. The bearers of your blood. Grant me the favor of an audience." She paused, and then whispered, "Thomas Scott, Thomas Scott, Thomas Scott. *An Draoidh, An Draoidh, An Draoidh." The Magician, The Magician, The Magician.*

She waited. There was a cold draft coming from somewhere in the room, but that was not unusual. She could hear her heart pounding in her ears, although she did not move. She heard Malphas shift slightly on his perch.

Silence. And then...the room *shifted.* Everything in her view seemed to slide sideways, yet somehow stay the same. And then it was gone, simply *gone,* and Saorsa was no longer sitting in her room, but in a different, pitch-black space that felt larger. In front of her, on the floor, burned a single violet pillar candle.

Saorsa felt queasy. She hadn't planned on the fact that *she* might be the one doing the moving; every summoning she'd ever heard of brought the summoned to the location of the summoner. She'd coated her room in protection spells to try to keep anything that arrived from getting out to interact with the other inhabitants of the cabin; the idea that her meeting with Thomas wouldn't take place in the cabin at all was jarring. *But of course. Why meet in my territory when he's strong enough to move me to his?*

She was, she had to admit, terrified of the candle in front of her. *Violet. Like the Violet Woman. What if Thomas isn't here at all, and someone else has taken advantage of the fact that I was sitting alone in a place of power, open and receptive?* She swallowed, and saw her hands were shaking.

And then she heard the footsteps, echoing in the dark, cavernous space. *Someone is walking toward me. A man's footsteps.*

She wanted to rise to meet whomever it was, but her legs were shaking so badly she wasn't certain she could stand. The footsteps stopped. And a figure towered there in the darkness ahead of her, just out of reach of the candle flame. The might of his presence was nearly crushing. Had Saorsa been able to move, she would have been compelled to lay face down on her belly on the stone floor, prostrating herself in submission. *My body is not my own right now.*

And then, the pressure lessened somewhat. As if in making himself known to her in that overwhelming way the presence had been saying, *see what I can do. I will give you a brief reprieve. But do not forget.*

Saorsa found her voice. "Is it you?" she managed weakly. "Are you...Thomas?" She could only see the rough form of him, a blackness that was somehow darker than the rest of the room around him. Very tall, and radiating strength. He made no sound.

Saorsa heard Willow's voice in her head. *Call in the light,* Willow had instructed her. *If you ever find yourself in a nightmare, or with a presence that wishes to be hidden, try saying, "I call in the light."* Saorsa felt like she was in a nightmare now.

But there was a source of light right here. She thought of Alex, and found the energy to launch herself forward, grasp the candle, and hold it out and up in front of her. The hot wax near the wick spilled over and briefly scalded the skin on her hand, but she saw him. For a short, glorious moment, she *saw* him.

The candle went out. "Oh," Saorsa breathed in wonder. "Oh. It *is* you! You're...so beautiful." She paused. "And he looks so much like you! My Alex. He looks *so* much like you."

She thought back to those first few days traveling with Alexander Scott. "You look like a painting I once saw of the King of the Fairies," she had told him. She had no idea at the time how right she was.

There was no light at all, now. But he hadn't gone; Saorsa could still feel him in this place. And knowing that this *was* Thomas, the being she wished to speak with, made hope spark in her heart, even if he wasn't yet speaking. *But we are here together. And he hasn't hurt me or walked away. I suppose that is a kind of victory.*

Suddenly, four candles flamed to life around her at four cardinal points, and the violet pillar vanished from her hand. Saorsa found herself kneeling inside a chalked circle with a star inside it. A pentagram, approximately eight feet in diameter. She sat down in the center and waited, and heard the Magician begin to walk.

He was pacing around the perimeter of the circle, counterclockwise. *Widdershins,* thought Saorsa. *He's raising power with his movement, but keeping me here and lowering my energy. Banishing me to the interior of the circle while he observes me. And I'm fine with that.*

She looked up. She could see his clothing from the waist down. Black boots and trousers. A long, black coat with a violet lining. Every now and then, the cuff of his sleeve and the flash of his hand. His fingers were moving. *Magick.*

"Speak." It was all he said, his voice a low growl. Saorsa couldn't help but smile inside. *He's curious.* Now that she had seen his face, a face that looked so much like one she loved, she felt much braver. *This is Alex's father. Here, in the same room.* She focused on that connection. *Think of the ways he's familiar, not the ways he is foreign.*

Saorsa took a deep breath. "I thank you for this audience. I am Saorsa Stuart, the Flower of the West, the child of The Lovers. I am under the protection of the Knight of the Deck of Crows, as I'm sure you can see. And the aspect of the *leth dhia* that walks on earth, your son Alex, is under *my* protection as well. I have taken a vow to assist him."

The mage paused briefly in his walking at this statement, and then resumed.

"The daemon Malphas has befriended me. I am guarding Oona, a Child of the Stones who is of your Deck. I have arranged for the protection of another unborn child who is *also* of your Deck, and who may have been fathered by your son. I have heard the call of The Morrigan, and reside in a place of power dedicated to her. And I am keeping safe certain pages of the spellbook that you used to separate Alex as a child." Saorsa raised her eyes. "Thomas the Rhymer found me worthy of assistance. I ask that you do so, as well."

"And why do ye do these things?" The Magician had stopped moving.

"Because I love him. Your son. Alex. And he loves me. On earth, he has been imprisoned by some Fae. I'm trying to set him free. And I visited his aspect in Faerie, as well. Before he broke out of prison."

"You lie," Thomas' voice was quiet. "Ye didnae see my son in prison."

"I *did*," Saorsa countered. "I received a gift at the Court of The Morrigan in trade for returning your knife that let me in. And I...gave Alex enough magick that he broke out of prison. I didn't know he was using it that way. He made a touchstone and put it in my things."

She sensed a difference in the room, and Saorsa's eyebrows went up. "You didn't know, did you?" she asked. "You didn't know his Fae aspect is free. Or that his Human aspect is threatened on earth. You have no idea at all who I am, or that Alex is in danger, do you?" *I was right. He wasn't choosing not to come; he didn't know. But how could he not know?* "Where have you been, that you didn't know these things?"

He didn't answer. *He's hiding things. Or, he's uncertain. Maybe he needs verification that what I say is true. But I was able to summon him, and I bear the Knight's mark, and how else could I have gotten that?*

"Time is short," Thomas said, and Saorsa thought she detected a softening in his voice. "What do ye want, *bana-bhuidseach bhig*?"

Saorsa took a deep breath. *A nickname.* He'd called her *little witch*. It was the first indication that he felt friendly toward her.

"Teach me," she blurted out, rising to her feet. "Something is happening. Someone is after your spells, and after Alex. After the Children of your Deck. There are humans employed by the Crown working with some Fae on earth. I don't know what they are up to, but it's not good. I can't protect Alex and the others with human magick alone. Adamina wasn't arrested for political reasons; they wanted her *magick*. And if you can't be here to watch over the Scott family, teach me magick powerful enough that *I can*." She took a step toward him. "You have to give me something to fight with, sir. That's what I need."

There was suddenly a bit more light in the room. She could see his face now, although it was still much in shadow. He was looking at her, the silver of his eyes a shock in the dark. He was staring at her, with those eyes so like the ones belonging to her beloved, that Saorsa couldn't help but think of Alex. Saorsa's entire being missed Alex constantly; her ears searched for his voice or name in any conversation she heard, and her eyes hunted for similar features to his on the faces of every man she saw. Just the scent of cedar or leather or whisky was nearly enough to bring her to her knees with longing for him. And here, just a few feet away, was a man, or, rather, a Fae, who not only looked very much like Alex but was *related*. Who held secrets about Alex's past. Who *loved* him. *Don't leave!* Saorsa thought desperately, her energy straining toward him. *Please don't leave. You are the closest thing I have to him. And most days, I feel I might go mad from the loss of him.*

The Magician suddenly turned and looked over his shoulder, as though becoming aware of another presence. "I must go," he said quietly as he turned back toward her. "I will think on your request."

"No." Saorsa cried, looking up at him, her gaze full of steel. "I understand that the Fae think they have all the time in the world, and in most cases, *they do*. But in this instance, things are happening quickly. There's a very good chance that while you are thinking, Alex ends up hanged, Adamina ends up back in prison, two children of the Deck of Crows may be sold on the black market as scientific specimens, and a certain *leth dhia* gets put back together. And I end up dead right along with them. I need your help and I need it *now*."

He raised an eyebrow at that. She'd surprised him again. "Please," Saorsa begged. "I saw your letters. I saw the records in the spheres at Buccleuch. I know you love Adamina and Alex. And I do, too. You might not see it now, but I think soon you're going to discover you're going to need all the help you can get. To protect your family." And then, she dared. "*Our* family."

He looked over his shoulder again. *He's hearing something I can't hear.* And then, The Magician was in the circle with her, grasping her left hand in his own, and pressing her palm to his. He interlaced her fingers with his, and with his other hand he cradled the back of her head, an intimate gesture for someone he did not know.

"Ye will find your way now, Flower of the West," he whispered, "down the Path of Bones. Listen, Child, when the Dead speak. In their voices, you will hear my own." And then he began speaking in a different language, one that sounded like what she'd heard Alex speak at Melrose. There were moments where it sounded like Irish, and thought she heard him say *Realm of Ghosts*. And then the heat between their closed hands began to grow.

Saorsa felt like her hand was on fire. She cried out, her body instinctively trying to pull away from him, but she *couldn't*. He was holding her tightly, his hand almost twice the size of hers, his arms like iron. It felt like her skin had melted, her blood was boiling with his, and she swore she felt the bones in their hands stretching and twisting together. She sobbed in pain, and he pulled her close against him, offering her his strength to help her endure, even as he kept whispering the words of the invocation. Saorsa cried and gripped his arm with her right hand, their left hands crushed between them as they stood locked in their embrace. Saorsa was convinced, utterly convinced, that when whatever he was doing to her was over, she would be missing her hand and entire forearm. For how could it feel this way and then be anything other than ash?

He was holding her tightly, protectively, and now his words were in English again, soothing in her ear. "I am sorry for your pain, child," he said gently, "but often learning *is* pain." He was holding her head against his chest and patting her hair, like a father might comfort his daughter, and Saorsa found herself holding onto him as hard as she could. Saorsa realized with a start she felt *safe* here with him, a strange feeling after how terrified by him she'd been just minutes before. He had a solidness, a strong *grounding* that made Saorsa feel more balanced. *Like a tree. Like putting my arms around an oak.* Saorsa felt Thomas' grip on her hand loosen slowly and, to her shock, discovered that her hand was intact. She heard Thomas chuckle. "Ah, *bana-bhuidseach bhig,* ye lived. Well, that is good." Saorsa's eyes widened. *Had he not expected her to?*

He let her go, and Saorsa discovered that despite the fact that she'd been hurt by touching him she didn't want him to move away. *I need more. I miss feeling safe, and he can make me feel that way. I need more connection to him. More understanding. More information. And, oh Goddess, what did he just do to me?* Her hand was both numb and throbbing at the same time. He looked over his shoulder again. "I must go."

"Will I see you again?" Saorsa called as he turned away. "What...what was that? What do I do now?" But the darkness was falling on the room again, and he did not look back. The candles snuffed out as he waved his hand.

Thomas' consciousness returned to his rooms at the Court of The Morrigan, his mind reeling. *Out of prison. My son is out of prison. How can that be?*

Standing in his private chambers were a castle attendant, and four rather heavily armed Council guards. Thomas frowned. These were his private rooms. Why had the attendant let them in?

A white-haired Fae, strong and serious, cleared his throat."*An Draíochta*. The High Council requests your presence immediately. Please, come with us."

An armed escort. This wasn't a good sign. Thomas didn't need protection from other Fae; these guards were there to protect others from *him*. Thomas nodded, showing he had no intention of resisting. "Of course. Shall we go?"

Back at Wolfcroft, Saorsa Stuart awakened, and found herself curled in a ball on the floor in her room. She raised her red, raw hand in front of her. There was a spiral on the back of the mount of her thumb now and four blue dots. The symbol had been etched into her skin.

And on her thumb, middle finger, and little finger gleamed three engraved silver rings. Three rings she'd never seen before. Saorsa took a deep breath and looked up at the ceiling. He'd given her something. The Magician. Now she just had to figure out what.
She stumbled to bed and barely managed to pull back the covers before falling asleep. Her hand ached, and she worried if her fingers were swollen that the rings might not come off.

………

She opened her eyes an hour later at the end of a strange dream. Her hand hurt much less, and its proportions appeared normal. She was able to rotate each ring around the finger it adorned without pain or issue. *I'm not going to try and take them off yet, however. Not until I've studied them.*

She wondered if the fingers they were on held any significance. One of the women at the abbey had taught her a bit about palmistry. *Let's see...the little finger is the finger representing Mercury and communication.* So there was a chance this ring had something to do with communication. But then again, maybe not.

The middle finger was ruled by Saturn and associated with responsibility, wisdom, and discipline. Her friend at the abbey had pointed out that Saorsa's middle fingers were slightly curved toward her ring fingers. *You enjoy creative pursuits.* Saorsa had agreed, thinking of her paintings. And as for the ring on her thumb - she remembered that the thumb revealed a lot of things, but that it was primarily about *will*. "You're headstrong," her friend had laughed. "Stubborn, even."

"Welcome to Scotland," Saorsa had replied. "That's hardly unique here."

Thinking about that she grinned. If the angle of the thumb showed how stubborn you might be, she bet Alex's was much more severe than hers. She tried to remember what his fingers looked like when they were still, but they almost never were. *But maybe I just think he's being pig-headed when I'm being pig-headed too.* She grinned, picturing the skeptical look he often gave her right before he refused to budge about something. One arched brow, a frown, and an adorable little *twitch* that happened once at the corner of his mouth.

There were etchings on the rings. On the little finger, a strange design that looked like...bones. *Bones on the communication finger. What could that mean?*

The ring circling her middle finger had a crow etched onto it on one side, wings outstretched. When she turned her hand over, the other half of the band depicted a primitive human skeleton. *I'm...assuming it's human.* She squinted at the design. *Wait...does the skeleton have a tail?*

The ring at the base of her thumb had words on it. *Ardaigh agus ardaigh.* It was Irish. *Rise and rise.* Or, *raise and rise.* They were the same words in both Irish and Scots Gaelic. *Hmm. Interesting.* At the end of the inscription was a tiny skull and crossbones, such as one might see on a tombstone. Saorsa felt a shiver run down her spine. *Three rings. All containing imagery of bones.* Well, she'd asked a necromancer for magick, so she shouldn't be surprised. *But what sort of magick, exactly, do these rings contain?*

And then there was the blue spiral imprinted on the back of her thumb on the skin itself. *A Celtic blue spiral and four dots. One at the base on the spiral and three above. Four in total.* Four was the number of the Emperor in Tarot. Vika had taught her about Tarot as they'd traveled. *The Emperor is protection, authority, wisdom. Exactly the things I hope to be able to provide for others here. Leadership.*

Four was the number of the seasons and of the directions. A number of balances. From the outside in, the spiral began in what would be the north and continued clockwise. *A symbol of raising power. The power of earth and stone.* She thought of the amulet shards buried in her skin. *Was it related?*

She looked up upon hearing a soft knock on the door. "Come in," she called, and watched Willow open the door and peek inside.

"Oh, thank goodness," Willow sighed as she entered the room. "I just couldn't sleep until I knew you'd made it out of your summoning spell in one piece. I could sense a new energy coming from you while sitting in the next room. Rune's out here pacing, worried about you."

Saorsa sat up excitedly. "I talked to him," she said excitedly. "*I met Alex's father.*"

"And?"

Rune appeared in the doorway. "May I hear this too?"

Saorsa waved him in. "Of *course*." Willow sat at the foot of Saorsa's bed while Rune quickly built up the fire and then took up residence in a chair he pulled near the bed. Saorsa described her encounter with Thomas. "He didn't know. He didn't know Alex is in trouble here, *or* that he was out of prison in Faerie!"

"Where has he been?" Rune asked. "I imagine his son breaking out of prison would be rather big news among the Fae."

"He didn't say. But after he held my hand...I had *these*." Saorsa held up her hand. "He marked me here, on my thumb. And gave me these rings."

Willow frowned. "Where's the High Priestess ring Alex gave you?"

"I lost too much weight. It keeps falling off. I have it in this box on my nightstand so I don't lose it."

Rune shook his head. "You need to eat more, *min dame*."

Saorsa grinned. "You already stuffed nearly half a loaf of bread in me at dinner tonight, Rune. And Willow keeps adding cheese to everything she hands me." She shook her head. "I just...this is the way I am right now. Alex told me once that animals only eat when they feel safe. And without him here...I just don't ever quite feel that everything is right."

Willow patted Saorsa's leg. "We need a big bowl of whipped cream. That'll do the trick."

Saorsa laughed and then wiggled her fingers, the rings gleaming in the firelight. "These rings activate something, I think. Whether it's in me or around me, I don't know. Thomas seemed completely unmotivated to give me any instructions."

Rune raised an eyebrow. "You asked for his magick. Perhaps he thinks you need to prove yourself worthy of it by figuring it out yourself."

Saorsa nodded. "I was thinking that too. We need to investigate that cave and find the missing house tomorrow. We need to know the extent of Wolfcroft and what it contains. I have a feeling that the cave may be the center of power in this place. And if it is, I'm going into it and trying to activate one of these rings."

She looked at Willow. "I was thinking maybe we could finish working the spells into my hair tomorrow if you didn't mind. I'm going to paint some protective designs onto my clothing as well. If there's something in that cave, I need to carry protection with me." She wrinkled her nose and gestured at her left hand and throat. "The men of the Fae Scott Clan seem fond of drawing symbols on me lately and then forgetting to tell me what they mean. If anyone's going to do magickal doodling on me from now on, I want it to be *me*." She paused for a moment. "What time is it?"

Rune walked out to the main room to look at the clock. "Half past eleven."

"Still time for a good night's sleep, then," Saorsa smiled. "Thank you for looking in on me."

"See you in the morning," Rune called as he left, and Willow gave a little wave as she headed back to the room where Oona was sleeping.

Malphas tucked his head under his wing as Saorsa settled down. *Tomorrow. We learn more tomorrow. And then I learn enough magick that the Violet Woman is forced to deal with me.* She tried not to think about the debt she owed the Violet Woman as she fell asleep.

………

It was just after one in the morning when Malphas let out a low, soft croak from his perch. A moment later, he repeated the sound.

Saorsa rolled over, half asleep. She was starting to be able to understand Malphas' sounds during her waking hours. A certain quiet rumble was *thank you*. A loud squawk, *look at me. I'm showing you something*. A clicking, chattering sound meant *I don't want that*. Two short cackles was *I'm interested* or *that's funny*. He often had that response while watching Oona, his new favorite companion.

The sound she had just heard twice was a greeting. She thought she heard someone adding logs to the fire, but it was probably just part of a dream. Wasn't it? Saorsa opened her eyes just as she felt the mattress shift, and felt a hand on her shoulder. She drew in a sharp breath, startled, and then she knew.

"I'm here," Alex said quietly. "I didnae mean to scare you."

Her heart rate quickened. *Alex is here! He's come to see me again!* "You found me!" she gasped, tears of relief welling in her eyes. She struggled up to sit in the bed, partially pinned down by the quilt he was sitting on. Alex laughed and stood up to move the blanket, then sat down again as she threw her arms around him.

"I'm sorry it was so long," he whispered, putting his arms around Saorsa and returning her embrace. He kissed the top of her head. "It's good to see you, *eun beag!*"

Saorsa nodded, but was too busy crying into his chest to answer. Alex put his hands on her upper arms and pushed her gently away. "Oh no, sweet one, are ye cryin'?"

"Yes," Saorsa gulped. "I've...I just miss you, and I worry about you all the time, and...are you alright? Are you hurt?"

He pulled her close again. "I'm well enough. I've been thinking' of you too, Saorsa. All the time." He rubbed her back gently. "I'm so glad to be with ye here now, even if it's just for a short time."

Saorsa attempted to compose herself, wiping her eyes with the back of her hand. Alex grinned and handed her a handkerchief from his pocket. "Thank you," she said. The handkerchief smelled of cedar and soap, and Saorsa was glad for the familiar scent.

She thought of their conversation last time he had visited. She'd asked him to come to bed with her, and he'd turned her down. *Twice.* She was at a loss now about how to interact with him. *Has he figured things out? Does he have any suggestions for how we're supposed to function together when there's more than one of him?*

He was looking at her intently, concerned. "What is it?"

Saorsa looked up at him in the dim light. *There's that face I know so well.* "I just...I'm not quite sure what to do."

He smiled at her and ran his fingers through the curls over her left ear. "I ken what to do," he said softly, smiling, and bent to kiss her gently on the mouth.

Oh, sweet merciful Goddess, how I've missed him! Saorsa felt her entire being turn to focus on Alex. It was as if he'd poured a warm, delicious, bubbling substance into all of her veins. *My blood has turned to fire cider, hot, sweet, and spiced. How does he do this to me every time?*

She was glad. *So* glad. *If he's kissing me...he thinks we'll be fine. He still wants me.* She thought she might begin to cry all over again. *I'm such a mess.* She kissed him back, then climbed to her knees and threw her arms around his neck. He chuckled and held her tight. "Are ye alright, sweetheart?"

"I don't want you to leave again," she gasped, trying not to sob. "I know you will have to, but...it's so *awful* when you do!"

"Ah, Saorsa," he said quietly, his deep voice husky in her ear, "dinnae think about that. Just think on what you want from the time we *have*."

"I don't want to talk," Saorsa said, holding him so tightly her arms ached. "I just want to hold you, and for you to hold me." *I want just a few moments of happiness, without having to tell you anything that upsets you.*

He kissed her temple. "That's what we'll do, then." He laughed quietly as he patted her back. "You're squeezin' the life from me, precious one."

She didn't relent, so he tickled her under the arm and Saorsa gave a little screech and released him. He laughed again and stretched out on his side on the bed. "Come here, my beauty. Just dinnae break my ribs, aye?"

Saorsa grinned. "I can be good." She lay down on her back next to him, looking up at him as he gazed at her, his head propped on his hand. Her mind began to spin; she didn't want to talk, but they probably *should*. Was he still in London? Did he have any hope of escape? She wanted to tell him Oona was here. And she *needed* to tell him she'd met Thomas. *I think Thomas gave me something that will help us. That will aid me in drawing the Violet Woman here. So we can get some answers, and I can find a way for us out of this mess.*

But all these thoughts were swept away when he kissed her again. She thought of that time he'd taken her swimming in the hot springs, back before they'd gone into Hermitage together. *How do I float, Alex?* she'd asked. And he'd told her to raise up her body in the water like she was making love to the sky. She felt like that now. Floating in his arms as he kissed her, raising up her hips and chin and arching her back to be closer to him. Warm and supported. *Open.*

"I love you, Alex," she said, stroking his cheek. "I love you like the earth loves the sea. Like Sadhbh loved Fionn mac Cumhail. Like Deirdre loved Naoise. I want to touch you, have you consume me, and watch the borders between us melt away."

He kissed her again. And then the kisses became hungrier, deeper. He was adding a gentle pressure to his touches, running his hands over her body, and it made Saorsa shiver in excitement. *This is very different from our last conversation. He must have decided making love is fine with him now, or he wouldn't be doing these things. I shouldn't question it, or he might stop.* And she never, ever wanted him to stop. *Everything is right when he's here.*

He had pulled her toward him, his hands moving over her thighs and her backside. Saorsa pressed herself against him. *He's here, and he's wanting to be close.* It was all she desired in the world.

You need to talk first, she heard something in her mind say. *If he's decided this is how it can be between you, you need to hear him say it before you do anything. Because if he came through the portal...this is another aspect. Not the Alex you traveled with. You know this.*

He was lying on top of her now, holding her down and kissing her throat. She could feel him pressed up against her, and all the familiar firm shapes of him. Saorsa smiled and closed her eyes. *Goddess, how I need him!*

But the voice in her head didn't go away. *You need to hear him say it. If his original earthly form can't be here, you need to hear that he gives consent for this to happen with another aspect. You don't know how he thinks this will work. You don't know how ANY of this should work.*

"Oh...that feels *good*," Saorsa murmured, and heard Alex laugh. He'd untied the ribbon on the front of her shift and was running his lips and tongue over her breasts. "Oh, Alex, please do not *ever* stop doing that!"

He kissed his way up to her collarbone and then her throat, and now his breath was hot in her ear. "I want ye, Saorsa," he whispered. "All I've done is think of you since the last time. *Feuch gum bi mi agad a-rithist.*" *Please say you'll have me again.*

"Oh Goddess, *yes*," she breathed. "*Always.*"

But there was that *voice* again, echoing in her head. *He hasn't told you how he wants this to work. Last time he turned you down and wanted to think. And now he wants to be in your bed without saying a word of resolution?*

Well, I did say I didn't want to talk, she argued with herself. *I did say....*

Alex sat up and pulled his shirt off over his head. And Saorsa's jaw dropped in shock. *Tattoos.* His arms and chest were covered in beautiful blue and black Celtic designs. Wolves. Ravens. Spells and symbols. He tossed his shirt aside on the bed, and moved to be with her again.

"Wa-wait," Saorsa stammered. "You're...you're...oh, *Goddess,* you're...Alex *from Faerie!*"

He smiled at her curiously. "Aye." His eyes widened, then he froze. "You...you didnae ken?"

Oh. Oh shite. Oh holy SHITE. Saorsa put her hand to her head. "I...oh, Alex, *we need to stop and talk."*

He looked puzzled. "I thought ye didnae *want* to talk, *eun beag."*

"Alex...you're not supposed to be here! It's dangerous for you!"

He frowned. "I ken that verra well. I came to see *you."*

Saorsa's head was spinning. Her body was still crying out for him, but they couldn't...she just *couldn't* go to bed with him. She couldn't imagine telling the Alex in London that she had. *I think...no, I KNOW that would end things between us. We're waiting and thinking, no matter how badly I want to be with ANY version of him.*

"I...," Saorsa stammered, "did you...were you there for the conversation I had with your other half at Willow's house? About...figuring things out?"

He looked at her blankly. "What conversation?"

"The last time I spoke to your Human side here. He sent...." *Oh. Oh my. I think he might not be able to see through all of the other aspects. He might have missed....*

"Saorsa," Alex said, sitting back and running a hand over his head. "I am havin' some trouble whenever I leave Faerie. I cannae see through his eyes all the time now. There's interference when I dream. I can see some things, but at other times...it's just blank. I dinnae ken what's happening."

I need to be careful with him. Understanding. "I'm sorry, Alex. Your earthly aspect is designed to be here, and you're not. I think the interference might have to do with you not being in Faerie. Have you ever been to earth before? Since you were...separated?"

He shook his head. "Just a few times. An' for only a few minutes each. An' it feels wrong to be here this long. I'm...unsettled."

"Alex," Saorsa said, taking his hands. "I'm worried for you. I'm worried that being here for a long time might hurt you. You weren't made for this. Is there another world where you could go? Not here, not Faerie? Where you will be safe?"

"I've been to some of those places, *eun beag,"* he said quietly. "But I'm afraid that to be beyond the Council's reach, I may need to go far. Farther than I've ever been before. I dinnae ken if I'll be able to see you from there. An'...," his eyes met hers, "I *need* to be able to see you."

His eyes suddenly changed color, and Saorsa saw a new realization surfacing in his mind. He pulled her closer. "You could come with me, Saorsa," he said, his eyes full of longing for her. "It's dangerous for you here too. We could go far away. Somewhere safe. You an' I could have a life together. It might be a different sort of life, but...I think it would be a good one."

Saorsa forgot to breathe.

He ran his fingers lightly over her shoulders. "The Fae want to be rid of me. An' that's fine by me. I'll leave, an' they'll never have to deal with what I am again. If you come...if we go far enough away, I think they'll leave us alone." Saorsa watched his gray eyes sparkle in the firelight. "So many of your problems would go. The Crown couldnae find ye. You wouldnae have to deal with Fia, or have monsters and ghosts chase after you. There'd just be you and me. Wakin' up together, fallin' asleep together, an' doin' what we like in between. An' if we're no here...wouldnae everyone's life be easier?" He touched his forehead gently to hers. "That's what we both want, aye? A simple life. To be together. And we could have that. Startin' *right now*."

Saorsa took a deep breath. And in that breath, felt how utterly *exhausted* she was. *A simple life.* There were other worlds out there. Maybe there would be one with a quiet cottage by the sea. She thought of what it would be like to sleep late and wake up in a sun-filled room and look into Alex's eyes and see nothing but love there.

Every morning. Every beautiful morning. Didn't they both deserve that? They'd both spent their lives in prisons. And this...was *freedom*.

"Oona," she said, finding her voice. "What about...?"

"We'll take her with us," Alex said. "She can be our daughter. We'll be a family, *eun beag*. An' then, once we're settled...," he took her hand and tenderly kissed the back of it, "maybe a little sister or brother for her to play with comes along, aye?"

Saorsa felt her insides flip over. *I want this. More than anything else. To be with Alex.* Saorsa's voice was shaking. "Right...now?"

He nodded, and then looked straight into her eyes. "Aye. *Right now*." He smiled at her. "We'd be happy, Saorsa. An' I'd never have to leave again."

Time stopped. And Saorsa slowly came to the realization that Alex here on earth had been right. They were two different men. With two different lives. Separated for a quarter century, they shared common parents and common looks, common gestures, and common voices. They were both hunted. But their futures and options were different. Their worlds were different. One was human, and one was Fae.

One had the option of leaving now. Something Alex in London didn't have. *What if I can't get him out? What if my plan isn't good enough? What if I'm too late? What if I'm not strong enough?* She had promised him. Sworn a vow to see this through to the end. He had found her in the woods and protected her when she had no one and nothing. He'd taught her and brought her to Vika. He'd turned around and gone into harm's way to try and save her mother. He'd gone into Hermitage with her. He'd carried her away from the ghosts. He'd sat by her bed when she was sick. He'd loved her even when she pushed him away. If she left with this Alex right now, she'd be leaving the man she had fallen in love with behind.

She had to make a choice.

"I...can't," Saorsa choked. "I can't leave him. I told you I'd try to get you out of prison. So I can't leave him in one either." She took a deep breath that felt almost painful. "What you are saying...I *do* want that kind of life. But I can't abandon him. Or my mother. Or...even Fia. It's not who I am."

He frowned. "Ye feel bad for him. You pity him."

She had to tell the truth. "It's not pity. I'm in love with him."

He moved slightly away and looked at her. "But ye said ye loved *me*."

"I *do* love you. I...," Saorsa swallowed hard. "You're both *Alex*."

"But he's stuck here and I'm not," Alex countered. "An' *you're* not. You cannae have the life ye hope for with him, Saorsa! They're goin' to *kill him*. You *do* ken that, aye?" He moved away and began pacing by the fireplace. "If I go, there's a good chance I *cannae come back!* You'd throw away what we have, what we *could have*, because of a vow to a dead man? You'd be here *alone*. It makes *no sense!*"

"I can't do it!" Saorsa said through gritted teeth. "I don't want to hurt you, but I love him and I swore. I *promised*. And my word is who I am!"

She saw his face change. An expression she hadn't ever seen before. And she knew why immediately. *It's like when the Faerie knife was here.* His Fae side was starting to show. His true form. *He's forgetting to disguise it.* She saw a muscle move near his eye that humans didn't have. And she saw something else, a sharp slope to his ear that wasn't there before. And a different angle of his eyebrow.

"I see," he spat. "As long as he's alive, you'll choose him over me. You only want me when ye *cannae have him*. As long as there's any chance of him returnin' to ye, he holds your favor." His lip curled into a slight snarl. "That's how it is. Ye only want the way I remind you of *him*."

"Alex, *no*," Saorsa said, moving toward him. "I care for you *both!* You were born in the same body! I want both of you safe and well!"

"But if he says not to take me to your bed, *ye listen*," Alex snapped. "If I told ye not to bed *him*, would you give my words the same consideration?"

"We need to work this out *together,*" Saorsa pleaded. "The two of you...you can't go on like this! Split, yet connected! You've been living another man's life, Alex!"

"That's why I want one of my own!" he cried. "With you! An' Oona! Why can't I have that? Why can't we be happy?" He pressed his hands to his forehead. "Leavin' him an' me alive like this was a cruel thing!"

She wanted to comfort him, but was sure touching him would make things worse. "Alex...we just need some time. Time for me to try and free him. Time to figure out what the Violet Woman's plan is. Time for you and him to talk...."

"I dinnae *have* time," Alex said firmly. "An' I dinnae *want* to talk to him. He's taken the woman I love from me!"

"This is not a competition!" Saorsa stated. "I want to help *both* of you! To find a way forward where you can *both* be free and happy!"

"Well, I'll only be happy with *you,*" Alex said, "an' I imagine he feels the same way." He turned away. "If he dies, you'll be sorry that you sent me...," he paused. "If he *dies,*" he repeated quietly. "*Yes. If he dies.*"

And Saorsa saw a shadow moving on the wall. A shadow of wings, extending menacingly up to block out the light. "No," she whispered, shaking. "Oh, Alex, *no.*"

He looked up at her, a faint glow emanating from his gray irises. "That's the answer, then. Our enemies want both him and me in prison. So they can use us as they like. But if he was gone, I think they'd no longer be interested in me so much. They need us *both,* for some reason." A smile spread across his face. "He's a mortal. He'll die anyway in what, less than half a century or so? Goin' a few years early, it doesnae make much of a difference." He paused. "If I kill him, they might leave me be. An' if ye dinnae need to defend him, you'll be released from your vow an' can come with me."

He was ignoring Saorsa now and talking to himself. She could see his Fae traits becoming more evident. *The ears are sharper and there's no longer just a suggestion of fangs, they're obvious. And he's getting taller.* For the first time Saorsa saw clearly how *different* the Fae and human sides of Alex were. One saw the world as she did; and one saw it from the standpoint of a powerful, immortal being who had a very different perspective on the value of a human life.

I saw what I wanted to see, she thought, staring as she watched him moving and growing. He was now approaching seven feet tall, and his wings began to materialize behind him. *I wanted them to be the same, and they aren't. This is not the Alex I love. This one showed me what I wanted, because he wanted me. And I let him in.*

"No," Saorsa said again, louder this time. "Don't hurt him! You are *part of each other.* You can't just kill off a part of yourself!"

"Watch me!" he said, turning quickly toward her. "Watch me, Saorsa Stuart! His end will be the end of my troubles. And then you...you will see. You're in his thrall now, but when he's gone, your eyes will be opened an' you will understand that I did the right thing. It will set us both free!" A delighted smile appeared on his face, and he moved toward the back door of her room that led outside toward the burn.

"Wait!" Saorsa cried, trying to stop him. "Don't go! We have to talk; there are better options than this! We need to think things through! Please hear me out! *Please!*" But she saw that he wasn't listening. Her thoughts were coming out in a tumble. "And I need to know, how did you get out of prison? What is this symbol on my neck? Did you do something to me? *Am I going to have your child?*"

But he had thrown open the door to the outside, and a blast of cold air surged into the room. On the other side of the door, Saorsa saw a portal just a few steps away. It was edged in violet and tiny, reflective motes circled around it in the air.

"I'll be back for ye Saorsa," he said, turning to look at her with a smile on his face. "We can talk then." He gave her a grin that chilled her blood. "All will be well then, *eun beag*. You'll see." And before Saorsa could say anything else, he disappeared, and the portal went dark.

………

Saorsa didn't sleep the rest of the night. The others needed their rest, so she didn't want to wake them, even though her unexpected visit from Alex's counterpart in Faerie unnerved her greatly. *Will he really try to kill Alex? Can he even get into the prison in London?* It seemed a *profoundly* stupid move to go right to a Fae stronghold if he was trying to evade capture. *Does he know something I don't know?*

Of course he does, Saorsa thought bitterly. *He knows A LOT of things I don't know. Such as if he impregnated me or not. He knows how he got out of prison. He might know where my mother's spirit is. He knows what this magickal symbol on me does.*

She looked at the rings on her hand. *Strange. He either didn't notice them and the tattoo, which I find hard to believe, or found them unremarkable.* Saorsa thought for a moment. *Well, if I can't sleep, I might as well move forward with something I can do.* She looked at Malphas, who was watching her from his perch.

"All right, Mr. Malphus," she said softly, moving to stand in front of him, "you are a piece that doesn't fit. You're here for a reason, and I don't think it was just to fetch rosary beads and then return them. The Aunties sent information on you. It says that you are a daemon that commands forty legions in Hell. You are supposed to help good familiars and build towers, houses, and citadels. It says you can reveal an enemy's thoughts, which I *desperately* need. I think you used the rosary to help get Adamina out of prison. So I'm guessing that a big, powerful being like yourself wouldn't be spending his time sitting on a perch in my bedroom and eating bread crumbs unless there was a *reason* for it. What are you doing here? If you were sent for Alex, *why did you return to me?*"

Malphas cocked his head and shook his wings. Saorsa held up her hand and showed him the rings. "You know what these are, don't you? Are you the teacher that shows me what to do to save Alex? And if so...how does it begin?" She looked intently at him. "They say you stay in crow form *unless requested*. But it's not as simple as that, is it? Like all magick here on earth, I bet you need a power source, not just a request. And more power than just one witch casting or singing."

She started to pace. *I'm thinking out loud and pacing, I'm turning into Alex.* "There's something here at Wolfcroft we haven't found yet, isn't there? And it's not another crofter's house. Alex could sense a different power when just he and I were here. It elevated his mood. It draws the wolves. The wolves know where it is, don't they? And I bet you do, too." Malphas made a soft noise that sounded eerily like a hoarse man's voice chuckling.

"But you're not going to just show me, are you? I need to figure it out myself. To prove I'm worthy of an audience." She thought for a moment. "A dragon line *has* to go through this place. Willow's noticed that the plants in the area are bigger than most. The animals have some odd behaviors, too. And there was that *singing* that came out of nowhere the other night." She paused. "There are acres and acres out there I could look at...but I think the source is either at the broch or the cave with the carvings." She shivered. "Except it's pitch dark and freezing out there, and the cave might be full of wolves."

Malphas bobbed his head and chuckled. "If I wait until morning and take Rune and Willow with me, will I get the same result as if I go now? Or do you and Thomas need to witness me doing something *profoundly stupid* to earn my instructions?"

She knew the answer already. *Every story, every myth, every vision quest starts with a hardship. A test of bravery. A willingness to dare. I think Malphas is here to help me with the magick I will need to help Alex. But he's not going to reveal his secrets until I sacrifice something. Malphas is here to witness a trade. A trade of my effort for the instructions. He's here to tell Thomas I'm worthy of the knowledge that has been locked in these rings. That's how it always is among the Fae, isn't it? A trade?* She thought back to her training at Wyldwood. *Vika made me prove I was ready. This is no different.*

Malphas cackled. Saorsa took a deep breath and started to get dressed. "Let's go. I've seen the broch and though it may have its secrets...I think the cave holds more of them." A few minutes later she had her boots on and was layered clothes, her coat, scarf, gloves, and hat. In her belt she put fire starting supplies and several candles, as well as a knife of Alex's. She tucked his rosary into a leather pouch on her belt. *For luck.*

She opened the door that Alex's Fae side had gone through just a short time before, and stepped out into the bitter cold of the night with her lantern. Malphas took wing and flew out beside her.

………

It was *very* dark. Clouds covered most of the sky. After Saorsa's eyes adjusted, she could see her breath billowing in vapor clouds around her. *I'm a fire-breathing dragon tonight.*

She smiled. Everyone had been working incredibly hard. All the outbuildings near the cabin had been cleared of dead brush and repaired, and pathways had been cut. Even better, Rune knew the formula Vika used to make her glow-in-the-dark paint. He'd made some and clearly marked the trees on the paths with various runes to show the way to the stable, the broch, the burn, and the cave. *He's helping me build another Wyldwood here. They all are.*

She set out toward the cave. *When they find out I went to the cave by myself, they're going to question my intelligence.* But it was Malphas she needed to impress right now.
It wasn't very far; it just felt farther in the dark. Soon Saorsa could see the outline of the massive cave against the sky. *Goddess Morrigan, this is your place. I am trying to help your family, and you have shown me signs of welcome. Guide my steps.*

She could hear Vika's voice in her head. *Your eyes should be up. Be the most dangerous thing in this forest.* She took Alex's knife from her belt and held it in her hand. *I am the Darkflower. I am the Child of The Lovers. I am the defender of the children of the Deck of Crows.*

She was getting closer. *Thomas the Rhymer sees me as worthy. I received magick from the White Wizard, Michael Scot. I am being escorted by Malphas of the Legions of Hell.*
The cave entrance yawned in front of her, a black and gaping thing that felt alive. *I am the Champion of the Earthly aspect of the leth dhia. The Morrigan herself has welcomed me here.* She thought of how far she'd come from being nothing but a prisoner at Hermitage Abbey. She was at the entrance of the cave now. *I am a Witch of great power. I am Saorsa Stuart.*

She raised her lantern to look at the carvings. They were hard to see, as the cave face itself had not been cleared. But she could see through the vines: drawings of animals and language scratched into the stone. She could feel energy radiating from the stone. *This is a holy place.*

Malphas perched on a small, decorated standing stone near the entrance, watching. Saorsa pushed the ropes of dead vegetation aside and walked into the cave.

………

The darkness inside the cave was its own presence, and its breath blew out the candle in Saorsa's lamp. A moment of panic filled Saorsa's heart, but she managed a breath that brought a moment of clarity. She thought of Thomas' words: *I am Darkness.* Erebus. That was the Greek word for it, wasn't it? Darkness personified. So it made sense, didn't it, that darkness had been sent to greet her?

She took a deep breath. *I will not fight the darkness. I will let it in. And then, maybe, I will be granted the ability to see.* She grounded herself, reaching out to feel energy flowing up from the earth. *Darkness is a natural thing. There is darkness in the womb and in the tomb, at our beginning and end. It is not outside of us, but part of us.* She tried to open her heart to embrace it.

Her mind wanted something to process, something to focus on. It reached out into the space, groping, looking for something to center itself around. And Saorsa couldn't tell if her next experience was somehow real, or a fantasy generated by her mind.

She heard footsteps behind her. A man's stride. And then Saorsa felt a warm, solid presence she knew very well touch her, moving his arm around her right shoulder and spreading his strong fingers gently on her throat before pressing her back firmly against the front of his body.

His other hand pressed on her lower belly, restraining her, just inches above her sex. *Cedar. Leather. A warm breeze on an early autumn night. Pine and whisky, rosemary and amber. The scent in the air before a breaking storm. Alex.*

"Oh, *mo ròs Albannach fiadhaich*," he whispered in her ear, "*theid thu a nis far am bheil an t-eagal a's mo a' saltairt. Mar so luidh am Bàs. Bidh thu air do atharrachadh gu bràth. Thig thugam, a Bhan-phrionnsa nan sgriachail agus a' caoineadh. Bi air do dhalladh le gile na cnàmha, agus air do bhlàthachadh le sgoltadh na fola.*"

My wild Scottish rose, you will go now where the greatest fear treads. This way is Death. You will be forever changed. Come to me, Princess of Screams and Wailing. Be blinded by the whiteness of the bone, and warmed by the pulsing of the blood.

It sounded like him, and *felt* like Alex. Shirtless and in black trousers and boots, he was holding her, his presence comforting. But also unnerving since he didn't belong in this scenario. Whether he was protecting her or holding her in place, she couldn't tell. She felt a strange mix of arousal and trepidation in his embrace.

And then the cave was filled with eyes. Eyes, glowing in the dark. The eyes of wolves. Saorsa shivered. Alex wasn't real, but the wolves most definitely *were*. She could hear them breathing and could smell the animal scent of them. Her lantern, well out of reach on the ground, suddenly flamed to life again, and Saorsa could see the pack clearly. They were around her, watching, their eyes hungry.

And Saorsa could see that the floor was littered with bones. Four more fires burst to life. Huge torches at the east, west, north, and south: and Saorsa realized she was being held by Alex in the middle of a circle of low standing stones *inside* the cave. The stones were covered in designs Saorsa couldn't make out. And now Alex was moving her toward the center of the circle, where an enormous stone table lay.

The wolves began to pace around the perimeter of the circle, moving clockwise, raising power. And Saorsa was paralyzed with terror as a few truths became evident. *I am being moved without my participation toward what looks like an altar. Which means the being holding me is not a figment of my imagination. Something has its hands on me. But it feels so much like Alex. Could this be another aspect?*

Also, I am utterly convinced the wolves are real and there are at least twenty of them, and I am here alone. And the bones on the floor...many of them are human. She realized she no longer had her knife.

He had her at the table now. And now Saorsa could hear whispers in the darkness. *There were other beings here!*

Saorsa knew from the cold, static feeling in the air that the cave was filling with ghosts. *No. No.* She remembered how they had drained her of life and will at Hermitage; she wanted nothing to do with them. "Let me go," she gasped. "Let me go!"

"No, my beauty," he said, "this is the path you asked for. This is where the magick is born." He released her briefly and turned her roughly toward him, before imprisoning her in his arms once more. "Ye must choose," he rasped in her ear. "It will only be offered once. Say no, fight your way out, and you may have a chance at a normal human life. Or say *yes* and face your terror, and be rewarded with the first step on the Path of Bones!"

Saorsa could feel fear dominating her thoughts. She could hear the breathing of wolves and murmurs of ghosts, and this...*shade* of Alex had dragged her to a stone table where she could see ancient bloodstains patterning its surface. She couldn't process what he was saying; just the words *bones, Death, screams,* and *wailing.* She was fighting him in earnest now, but he was too strong; and then there was a blazing flash of light, and in that moment, she couldn't see.

She was going to die here. She had attempted to know what a human shouldn't know; she had gone where she shouldn't have. Thomas never intended to teach her *anything;* and now his daemon servant led her here to end her life in a dark pit of fear in trade for her hubris.

"Sacrifice," she heard Alex hiss. "Sacrifice what you have on the Altar of the Dead!" The ghostly voices were growing louder now. A fog covered Saorsa's vision as her eyes fought to recover from the shock of the burst of light. And then, Saorsa remembered something. *Thomas is Fae.*

She recalled her time in Faerie. A memory from the Court of The Morrigan, when she'd gone to return the knife. She'd entered the gates of the realm and woken up on the floor, with the exquisitely dressed Fae attendant calling her "Darkflower" and towering over her. The Fae attendant had wanted to begin by *dominating* the visiting human. To make her feel small. To put her in her place.

But she hadn't accepted that *place.* She had stood up to the attendant. And walked away with the key to a prison. *Eyes up. Like a Queen.* She heard Vika's voice in her head. *You are the daughter of Kings!*

She was being manhandled onto the altar now. Thomas was trying to see if she'd bow down to fear, to force, to domination. To see if she accepted *her place.* She took a deep breath and power flowed into her limbs.

"Enough!" Saorsa roared. "Enough with the games! I am here to *do what must be done!* Give me the test and find me worthy or not, but don't *waste my time* trying to frighten me with foolish tricks!" She ceased her struggle and looked Alex's doppelganger right in the eyes. "I don't stay down for *anyone.* Get your hands off me. The Morrigan has welcomed me, and I am here *with her blessing.* I accept your challenge! I have a clan to protect, and I intend to succeed, *no matter the cost!*"

The muttering ghosts faded, and the being before her that moved like the man she loved let her go and then gently stroked her upper arms. *Why am I being shown Alex? There's a reason for this, isn't there?*

"Verra well, then, my love," he said gently. "You would trade the lightness I love so much to become a Bride of the Shadows?" His eyes searched her face. "You would throw who you are away?"

"You've had to," Saorsa responded. "Everything you thought you were has been taken from you. I am happy to follow you down that path, if it means I might save you."

A smile on his face. "And so...the test begins." He raised his hand in the flickering torchlight, snapped his fingers, and the world went black.

………

Saorsa didn't remember anything about the cave. In fact, any attempt to recall what had come immediately before this moment seemed to drift from her mind when she tried to focus on it.

She was standing in her room at Hermitage, the paintings of her dreams covering the walls of the old chapel. Sunlight streamed through the window and played with the colors on the remaining stained-glass panel high up over where the altar used to lie.

He was sitting on her bed, smiling at her, his gray eyes full of adoration, the sunlight bringing out the auburn highlights in his dark hair. "There you are, *eun beag,*" he laughed. "Come here an' love me, my wee clootie dumplin'!"

Saorsa put her hands on her hips and pretended to be stern. "I thought you'd *never* run out of animal nicknames. But do I have to be a Daft Days pudding instead?"

He rose from the bed and walked to her, beaming. "Would ye rather be porridge? Or Cullen Skink?"

"No!" Saorsa giggled as he put his arms around her. "No woman wants to be called Cullen Skink, Alex!"

"Give me a kiss, my Cullen Skink," he teased her, tickling her and grabbing her backside at the same time. "I cannae stop thinkin' of your finnan haddie an' your onions!"

She tickled him back and he jumped, and she took the opportunity to untangle herself from him and raced toward the door. He caught her quickly and scooped her up in his arms, and carried her toward the bed, humming happily, while she pretended to protest, one arm around his neck. "Don't throw me down!" she squealed. "The slats on the bed don't fit right! We'll end up on the floor!"

"Fine by me," he smiled. "I'm hungry for ye. I dinnae care as long as I get to *mash your potatoes!*"

This sent Saorsa into peals of laughter. "Why are you *so absurd?*"

He put her down gently on the bed and climbed slowly onto the mattress next to her, heeding her warning. "Love, I think," he whispered to her, pulling her close. "Makes a man lose his damn mind."

She kissed him. "Mmm, I like that," Alex smiled. "I'll have seconds, please." She kissed him again, and ran her fingers along his cheek, marveling at how she felt in his arms.

"Do ye love me, Saorsa?" he asked.

"I do," she answered. "More than life itself."

"What if," he said, becoming serious, "I needed you in a way I'd never needed you before?"

Saorsa frowned. "What? I don't understand what you mean."

He took hold of her hand. "Love isn't all kisses, Saorsa. It isnae all sweetness and light. You're young, ye dinnae see the full truth of it yet. Love can be a terrifying thing."

A feeling of dread was creeping into her stomach. "Alex...what do you mean? What are you talking about?"

"Do ye have the strength to do what must be done?" he asked her. "Can ye face what others can't? Could you be there for those you love, no matter how little was left of them? No matter how afraid you were?"

"Alex?" Saorsa pushed him away. "You're scaring me."

"It's just the beginning, *eun beag,*" he said. And then he vanished.

Saorsa bolted upright in the bed and let out a yell. "Alex? *Alex?*"

"Saorsa!" she heard his voice calling for her out in the hall. "Oh, God...*Saorsa!*"

She was on her feet, tearing toward the bedroom door. "Alex! Where are you? *Alex!*" She heard him scream. She had *never* heard that before. She went racing toward the sound, her bare feet cold and painful on the chilled stone abbey floor. *"Alex! WHERE ARE YOU?"*

"God, *NO!*" she heard him cry. "NO! Oh God, *help me!*"

The sound was coming from another corridor. Saorsa rounded the corner and ran toward Mother Agnes' office. "Alex! I'm coming! *ALEX!*"

She threw open the door. Alex was on the floor, shirtless, the moon-shaped scar on his abdomen torn and gaping, blood pouring from the wound. And standing next to him, holding a large, strange gemstone that seemed somehow *alive* on its chain as it dangled from her hand, was the Violet Woman.

Alex writhed in pain on the floor, clutching at his stomach, but the blood poured from between his fingers; he couldn't contain the flow. The Violet Woman was motionless, as if she'd been turned to stone, but the amulet in her care wasn't. It strained on its tether, extending its chain at an unnatural angle toward the spot where Alex lay.

Saorsa fell to her knees next to him, pulling off her jumper and pressing it against the wound. "I'm here, Alex, it's going to be alright, I'm here, we're going to fix this, we're going to...."

He unleashed a howl of pain. "No, Saorsa! She's taking me! That stone is *taking my soul!*"

"No! *No!*" Saorsa cried, as she tried to control the bleeding that wouldn't stop. Then she realized why: he was bleeding from the scar on his back as well.

"It hurts, Saorsa! *It hurts!*" Alex sobbed. "Dinnae let her take me! *Dinnae let her take me!*"

Saorsa was at a loss. She didn't know what to do. The Violet Woman wasn't moving or interacting with them in any way; the only movement near her was the amulet on the chain. *"What do I do?"*

"Kill me," Alex rasped. "If *she* kills my body, she can take my soul! But if you do it...."

"NO!" Saorsa cried. "No, I'm going to heal you! I'm going to get you out of here! I'm...."

"There's...no time," he choked, and Saorsa saw blood trickle from his mouth. "You need to do what must be done!"

Saorsa couldn't fathom it. *No. There has to be another way.* But he was suffering; and Saorsa wanted to stop it with all her heart. *Some things are worse than death.*

"*Please,*" he gasped. *"Please!"* The amulet on the chain began to shake violently. Alex's back arched in pain.

"I love you," Saorsa cried, pulling the knife from her belt. "I love you! Oh, Goddess, *give me the strength to help him!*"

She had structured herself around hope at a young age. The face she showed the world was one of smiles, unguarded honesty, songs, and light. Even when times were darkest, like when Iain Burn and his men had tried to take her east, she had somehow found her way back to hope. To give up hope wasn't in her nature. If she gave it up now, if she admitted Alex couldn't be saved...who was she?

The knife shook in her hand. Her lover's blood covered the floor. She had to decide now. Push forward with who she had always been, or face the fact that sometimes, sweetness and light could not save you. Sometimes, you had to find peace in the darkness. Sometimes in this life, what was required was to midwife someone into death. And Saorsa realized that doing so was a most profound, intimate, and brutal act of love.

She took his hand. "I will protect you. *Always.*" And she drove the knife between his ribs, ending his pain, and severing their life together.

.....

The wind howled outside the cave at Wolfcroft as dawn broke. And Saorsa Stuart found herself weeping next to a stone table, upon which a half-god's skeleton lay. She was frozen, exhausted, and beyond despondent. *Alex is dead. My beautiful Alex is dead.* There were no words for the emptiness inside her. Just a cruel numbness that had eaten all of her joy and warmth.

The loss was too much to bear. She climbed painfully to her feet and reached to caress the skeleton's forehead. The ghosts of skeletal wings penetrated the top of the stone table and emerged on the other side, hanging like a shroud over a large invisible form. One passed straight through Saorsa's calves. She didn't think about it. She couldn't think at all.

And then, unbidden, came a new sensation to join the loss. A quiet. A calm. An understanding. *A presence.* She'd always spoken of love. Wanted it, revered it. Repeated in her head time and time again what Thomas the Rhymer had said: *Our greatest ally in this fight is love.* But she had not ever truly understood love until now.

You could not take just the easy parts or the enjoyable parts of life for your own and say you had loved. That was blasphemy. Love was different than that. The Morrigan stories had seemed bloody and terrifying to her when she had first learned of them. *A battle Goddess. Decider of men's fates. Her ravens and crows tear the bodies apart on the field after the battle and devour them.* But what she had missed was where the Morrigan had been *love.*

As a battle Goddess, she was there to witness fear, pain, and weakness, but it did not drive her away. She did not leave when beauty fled. Men would always go to war. The Morrigan accompanied them, and her magick carried their souls back to the Cauldron of Rebirth. And the winged carnivores who did her bidding returned the bodies to the cycle of life. Without them, disease would spread. They helped the bodies return to the earth. *The crows and ravens, they heal the battlefields.*

Blood and death were a part of life, a part everyone feared and tried to ignore. Woefully unprepared when death arrived, the shock of loss could drive a person mad. *Look at Fia. Her inability to process her husband's passing had turned a beautiful young woman into a being who betrays and lives in a state of desperation. And Alex. Losing Morag and the baby haunted him for years.*

The Ancestors understood this. Maiden. Mother. Crone. But these days, everyone tried to forget that the Crone existed. *We only chase after the Maiden and honor the Mother. And so, we never come to understand the true power of a woman.* The Crone was the wisest of the bunch.

Saorsa wiped away her tears as her mind began to settle. *Wait. Alex isn't dead. He's not even here! This was....*

But she had another series of thoughts to finish first. *We are woefully out of balance, we humans. The farther we move from an understanding of death, the more we lose our way. If I really want to be a beacon of love in this world, I have to make peace with death. Then I can show others and help them find peace.*

It is the most healing, compassionate, loving thing I can do. Just as we deserve a good birth, we deserve a good death. And those we love deserve to be at peace with our mortality.

She sensed a shift inside herself. Something fundamental had moved. Up until now, her path forward had been *go west. Try things and see what happens.* It was a plan of a woman who hadn't found her calling.

The bones on the table before her suddenly moved, and crumbled to a fine powder, the remnants of the wings falling to the floor. *How are bones related to the soul?* Saorsa thought. *There are many things I must find out.*

The light of a new day crept into the cave, and Saorsa looked up to see a stranger standing there. At his left heel was a large red wolf. The light coming in the cave entrance from behind the stranger hid his face in shadow.

"I am the Daemon Malphas, here to witness you this night," said the man, his voice deep and musical. "You have been given a great gift, Saorsa Stuart. The Wytches of the Bone bid you welcome."

·········

Saorsa stumbled down the path back to the cabin, the crow Malphas flying overhead. In one night she had had an audience with Thomas, been visited by Alex's Faerie aspect, and gone through a trial at the cave before speaking with the daemon who would be her guide. The red wolf trailed behind her, padding along a few paces behind.

Sleep. Saorsa tried to be aware of the woods around her, but she was chilled to the bone, and wanted nothing more than to lie down where she was. *Come back,* Malphas had said. *Come back when night falls, and begin again.*

She stopped walking, her mind spinning. *So much to think on. And not enough in me to do it now.* The big red wolf with the yellow eyes nudged Saorsa's leg. *Keep moving, Little Witch.*

Macha. Malphas had referred to the wolf as *Macha.* Two syllables that sounded like a child calling its mother and laughter put together. Saorsa shook her head. *My mind feels drunk.*

She heard activity on the trail ahead. Rune was there. *"I found her!"* he shouted back over his shoulder. "She's here!" He ran toward Saorsa, then slowed and stopped when he saw the wolf. *"Min dame!"*

"She's a friend, Rune," Saorsa called wearily. "She's coming inside with me."

He moved forward to her side, still wary of the wolf. "Where have you *been?*"

"The cave," Saorsa said quietly, nearly stumbling into him.

"Eske!" Rune shouted. *"En av hulestien! Du trengs!" On the cave path! You are needed!*

Saorsa felt her knees begin to give out. She sagged toward Rune, who scooped her up in his arms. "What happened to you?" he asked. "Why did you go to the cave alone?"

Eske appeared, barreling down the pathway, with Willow right behind him. "Whoa!" Willow put up her hands as if to ward off an attack. "Spirits above, *what happened?* The energy coming off her...it's like nothing I've ever seen!"

"Eske, take her inside," Rune said, carefully passing Saorsa to the big man. "Willow, there's a wolf here...."

Willow's eyes met the amber eyes of the red wolf. "A Spirit Companion," she breathed. "Familiar." She crouched down to look closer at the she-wolf. "I greet you, most beautiful one. You are welcome in our home. Please tell me if there is anything you require."

Macha moved closer to Willow and brushed against her as if to say, *I greet you and recognize a companion in you.* Then she trotted off, following Eske down the path toward the cabin.

"What has happened?" Rune watched them depart.

"I think," said Willow, "that Malphas is making himself known."

Wolfcroft, Scotland

Saorsa opened her eyes. Malphas was resting on his perch, and the red wolf Macha lay on the rug near the fire. Willow was sitting quietly in a chair next to her bed. "There you are," she said quietly. "How do you feel?"

"Shaken," Saorsa said, sitting up. "There's a stone circle in the cave, Willow. And an altar. And...I had to pass a test last night where...," she couldn't say the words *I killed Alex.* "Where's Oona? I...need to hold her."

"I'll get her." Willow disappeared into the front room and had a hushed conversation with someone, and then returned with Oona in her arms. "Here she is." Saorsa took the little girl into her lap. The little girl with the gray eyes, and the dark hair with auburn highlights. It was getting longer and starting to curl more. *Just like Alex's.* She folded the child into her arms. *Who had left this little girl alone at the Stones? How could anyone not want her?*

Saorsa began to cry. "I love you, Oona," she wept, "and *I* want you."

"Oh my," Willow breathed. "Saorsa...what can I do for you?"

"I need a quiet day," Saorsa cried. "With you. And Oona. I was shown something. Given something. And everything I see looks...different." She looked over at Willow's kind face, her warm eyes, and felt the calm energy that flowed through her. "Oh, Goddess," she whispered, "I don't deserve you! I was just a stranger, and you healed me, and have supported me, and you never ask for *anything* in return! You are just...*goodness.* And *light.* And now I...," her voice broke, "I'll never *be* you now!"

Willow looked at her for a moment, her arms on the arm rests of the chair, and sat perfectly still. *It's...almost as if she is calling on someone. Reaching somewhere else, and opening a door.* She watched Willow breathe. And then Willow stood and moved to the bed, sitting down next to Saorsa, and laying a comforting hand on Saorsa's arm. "What do you mean, *you'll never be me*?"

"I...I just thought...," Saorsa began, "that I'd turn out like you some day. You and Mother Agnes. You both are so comforting and radiate such *light.* Everything is all right when either of you are in the room. You're like...," she paused, "the perfect mothers. Animals and children are just *drawn* to you. And you give and give selflessly, and sing the entire time! And...," she fell silent for a moment, "*that's* the kind of woman I always thought I'd be. A sunny smile on her face, a baby on her hip, and a kind, comforting word for anyone who needs it."

Willow threw back her head and laughed. "You think I'm like that *all the time?* I curse just as much as the next person! And I bet Mother Agnes does too!"

"Willow," Saorsa continued, shifting Oona in her lap, "I was set on a path last night. A magic not born of light, but of *dark.* I've been called upon to walk in a different sort of place. I don't think...I don't know where I'm going now."

"Saorsa," Willow said gently, "perhaps you were chosen to do so *because* of your inherent light. To bring balance. Elen walks the dark Ways Between holding a light. Maybe you've been entrusted with this darkness because *your light is so strong.*" She regarded Saorsa for a moment. "When I work with spirits, do you think I let them consume me? That I disappear, and they just use me as they see fit?"

Saorsa thought for a moment. "No," she said slowly. "You...provide a way for their knowledge to come through and help. But they are still passing it through *you.*"

"You will be no different, Saorsa," Willow explained. "If Thomas' magick is practiced by you, it will be filtered *through* you. It will be changed by who you are. And you are a warm, funny, loving woman. You're not going to become some sort of necromancer's wraith. Your will is going to take the magick and make things manifest *through your hands."*

"Willow, in that cave...the magick said *this way lies Death.* And *come to me, Princess of Screams and Wailing*! That's...how do I...."

"Reconcile it with who you are? Saorsa, you do realize that you aren't required to be one extreme or another? That you can find a place for both?" She looked at Saorsa with interest. "What if your work is to *be* both? To help bring everything to center? To help others see that they don't have to be scared of the dark?"

Saorsa recognized in Willow's words thoughts similar to those she'd had right after the test in the cave. *I can bring balance. I can help people walk with death. And maybe I don't need to lose my self to do it.* "I...I have to think about this. I don't have to be one or the other. I can be *and.*"

Willow smiled. "You need quiet. What about this? Let me spend the day finishing your hair, and Oona can stay with us. We can take a walk and get to know Macha. I believe she was sent to help you. We'll sing, rest, and let your mind settle." She paused. "But before we begin...I think there's something you need to see." She rose and went to the dresser and returned with a hand mirror. "You were so tired when we found you that none of us wanted to say anything. But...look."

Saorsa held up the mirror and gasped. The colors in her hazel eyes had been *magnified.* The green was now a nearly unnatural hue, brilliant and instantly noticeable even across a room. And the light brown had turned a vibrant, buttery amber. *Like Macha's eyes. Like a wolf.*

And Saorsa's blond hair was streaked through with black. "Oh, *Goddess!*" Saorsa cried. "What...*what has happened to me?*"

"I believe," Willow said calmly, "that the shift in perspective you felt caused a physical shift, as well." She smiled. "Your eyes are *gorgeous,* if slightly disturbing at first. And...well, when I finish twisting your hair, you're going to have some blonde and some black tendrils. It's going to be quite striking." She took a breath. "These might not be the only physical effects, Saorsa. You need to be on the lookout for other changes."

Saorsa ran her hands through her hair. "Willow! The dark parts...they have *blue* in them!"

Willow looked closer. "So they do! That's pretty."

Saorsa laughed. "How can you be so *calm* about this? And so *positive?*"

Willow shrugged and grinned. "Well, what's the alternative?" And Saorsa felt much better.

....

Dusk fell at Wolfcroft. Willow had worked for hours, singing blessings as she twisted Saorsa's hair in knots. Oona had tried to join in, raising her surprisingly powerful voice to wordlessly accompany the song. And Saorsa had sung, too. Songs from the abbey. Songs her mother had hummed. Songs she'd heard Vika and her men sing as they rode through the forest, laughing. Songs her friends had sung at Ramsay House, and ballads from the inns and dance halls in the Borders. Songs she heard Alex sing to Oona on the road to Fenwick, and songs he sang to Saorsa when she curled up next to him at night. All of this music was sacred to her. The music of her family. The hymns of her life. The language of her soul.

Saorsa's hair twisted like tree roots, like lightning, like strands of coral under the sea. It stood out like sculpture, its alternating dark and light knotted texture framing her face like strands of moonlight slicing across a dark-glass lake. She looked at herself in a mirror. Her eyes. Her eyes were now just as arresting as Alex's, but in a different way. *His are ice and sky, mine fire on a field.* She wondered what he would say when he saw her.

Willow and she had been working on her clothes with thread and needle and the hand-me-down clothes fit her perfectly. They were working pictures and poems into them, painting with a needle. Now Saorsa was dressed in layered clothing with spells sewn into every hem. For the first time in her life, she felt like a work of art.

The silver rings gleamed on her left hand. *It's time for the cave again.* And Saorsa went out the door, singing, with Macha at her side.

....

She'd told the others about Alex's Faerie side visiting and his threats. It was a problem she'd have to think on. In the meantime, she was on her way to her first ever in-depth conversation with a daemon. She stopped for a moment and looked around. *Am I...imagining this? I can see much better in the dark tonight than I could last night. MUCH better.*

So the change in eye color wasn't just cosmetic. *I can see in the dark. I mean, maybe not if it's pitch black, but if there's any light in the area, my vision is greatly improved.* Saorsa grinned. *This will come in handy.* She passed Aeric coming from the stable and asked him to take her lantern with him back to the cabin, then continued on her way.

Eske had found the second house on the property this morning. He had come back, looking embarrassed; he'd walked ridiculously close to its location the first day they'd been here and hadn't seen it. "About the size of this one," he said. "Three small bedrooms, and a loft. There's a woodshed but no stable yet. Could use some more furniture." He and Rune had headed back there after lunch to start clearing a path to it.

They'd left a message for Willow's husband, Svend, with the cabin's location and were expecting his arrival any day. Keena and Donovan should be arriving soon to visit Oona as well. *There's so much happening, and it's happening so quickly.* Saorsa continued toward the cave, deep in thought. *And whatever happens to me in this cave tonight, I'm sure it won't make things calmer or simpler.*

She entered the cave with the wolf and saw that the stone table in the center of the circle of stones had disappeared. In its place, a small fire was burning merrily, with two large carved wooden chairs and a small table set nearby, as if for a pair of friends to occupy and converse. A jug of wine and two glasses were set upon the table.

What is this? Saorsa thought. The stone table hadn't been real? Or had it been, and then moved by magick? Macha wandered off into the darkness. There was no one else in the cave, so Saorsa took a seat in one of the chairs. There were beautiful painted carvings on the arms and legs that seemed to come alive in the firelight. Crows and wolves. Ravens and bones and roses.

"Malphas?" Saorsa said aloud. She realized she hadn't seen the crow all day. "Are you here?" When he didn't appear, she looked at the jug and the glasses. *Maybe I'm supposed to drink.* She poured herself a half-glass of the wine and took a sip.

It was unlike anything she'd ever tasted. It flowed like wine, but the flavor gave her brain the distinct impression that she was eating sweets instead. *I'm tasting chocolate. And nuts. And honey. And cream. And...cinnamon, I think.* The beverage was very enjoyable, but also confusing. *I feel like I should be chewing this.*

The walls of the cave suddenly began to emit light. Outlines of crudely drawn pictures and letters in a language she didn't understand. *Like runes or hieroglyphs, pictures and letters all at once.* But she couldn't read them. It was a script she had never encountered. She blinked and looked up, to see if the glowing figures covered the ceiling too. They did. *Is this...wine making me hallucinate?*

"You know," said an impossibly deep voice from next to her in a rather friendly tone, "I find it helpful to remember when encountering something new that if we understood everything the first moment we saw it, our lives would be profoundly boring. I revel in the *not-knowing* sometimes. Just sort of let it all...slide over your brain and drip off."

Saorsa turned, eyes wide. Sitting in the chair next to her, glass in hand, was a daemon. She knew immediately that it was Malphas.

He stretched out in the chair and sighed. He reminded Saorsa somewhat of a man, and somewhat of an ox. Close to seven feet tall, he moved like a man and gestured like a human, but where she expected to see feet were sharp hooves. He had human-shaped hands, arms, and legs and a human-shaped male chest, but his musculature was so overdeveloped that he looked like he could pull a sizable wagon all by himself. His entire body was covered in short, black hair, like one might find on the flank of a horse. He had human expressions, yet his face was shaped much like that of a bull. And he had horns which, upon closer inspection, Saorsa realized were not horns at all, but tree branches growing from his skull. His dark, wavy head of human hair thick and long, cascading well past his shoulders. And he didn't appear to be wearing any clothes.

"Oh," Saorsa said in surprise, being careful to divert her gaze away from his lower torso, "when did you get here?" *After last night, nothing in this cave is a surprise.*

Malphas grinned, and Saorsa saw that inside the bullish mouth were rather perfect, if oversized, human teeth. "I've been here since you came in. Just busy working on a form you could tolerate."

Saorsa looked up at the ceiling. "I think...you forgot your clothes."

Malphas snorted. "There. Fixed. But a loincloth is all you're getting, because magick in this area is a *disaster* right now." He shook his head. "Never understood why humans are *so fond* of clothes these days. You didn't used to be, back in the beginning. It's not practical. How can the females see who they want to mate with if they can't see what's on offer?"

Saorsa's head was spinning. *I'm talking to a daemon. An actual daemon. And he seems rather casual for a creature who was a participant in one of the worst moments of my life last night, even if it wasn't real. And...he knows everything my group here has said since we've arrived. So he knows everything we know.*

Saorsa decided to get to the point. "Thank you for that. Do you know what these rings do?" She spread out the fingers of her left hand.

He didn't even look at them. "Yes." Then he fell silent, and took a long drink from his cup.

"Well...*what do they do?*" Saorsa asked.

He chuckled. "Not my job."

Saorsa shook her head. "What do you mean, *not your job?* Aren't we sitting here because I passed your test, which was *awful,* and so now...."

"Not my test."

"*Not your test?* You *led* me here! You...."

Malphas sighed. "So like a human, wanting answers for nothing." He extended his hand toward her, palm up, and wiggled his fingers. "Pay."

Saorsa scowled at him. "With *what?* What kind of currency do daemons *use?*"

Malphas shook his head. "Look, either you pay and we move on, or I leave. I'll miss Oona, though. Reminds me of Alex."

Saorsa looked at the rings on her hand. *The thumb is will. The middle finger, identity. The little finger is communication. Could Malphas want the communication ring in trade for answering questions?* She slipped the ring off her finger. "Is *this* what you want?"

He grinned. "That's the traditional way. But just in case you're interested, I accept carnal forms of payment as well."

"What?" Saorsa spluttered. "I...*I am not sleeping with you to get answers!*"

Malphas waved his hand. "The ring will do, then. It's probably for the best. You and I are a bit...*disproportionate.* There might not be much left of you after."

"Ugh." Saorsa made a disgusted face. "Not the most gentlemanly of conversationalists, are you?"

"I'm rather polite, compared to most. Daemons aren't nearly as...*delicate* as humans. We're much more direct, most of the time."

Saorsa paused before putting the ring into Malphas' hand. "Wait...if this ring gets me communication, maybe I should...save it for someone who has more answers? Like a deity? I mean you no offense."

Malphas raised an area that looked like an eyebrow. "None taken. But do you have any deities on hand?" He laughed. "And what if I *am* one, but you just don't know?"

"I only have one of these communication rings."

"And very little time to save Alex."

"What did you mean when you said Oona reminded you of Alex?"

Malphas waggled a finger at her. "Pay."

"Oh, all right." Saorsa placed the ring on his enormous palm. "I suppose you were sent here from the Court of the Morrigan. And you've been sweet to everyone here so far. I imagine that's because you're the one I'm supposed to talk to."

The ring disappeared from Malphas' hand. "Ahh. *Tasty.*"

"Wait...did you *eat that?*"

Malphas grinned. "From your perspective, yes."

"So you'll answer my questions now?" Saorsa took another drink of her wine.

"If I know the answer. And if I'm allowed to."

Saorsa sighed. "You said you didn't make my test. Did Thomas make it?"

"No. The cave itself *reveals*. Reveals what is already there. The test was born of *you*." He waved a hand.

"Alex said *leth dhia* can do something similar. When I was in Faerie, he watched a nightmare of mine to discover my identity. Is it the same thing?"

Malphas nodded. "Similar. Yes."

"So, once I passed the test, using the rings became possible. Could Thomas see my test?"

"I don't think so. I am with you instead. When I saw you with the rings after you said you were going to summon him, I knew I must escort you and watch."

"So, does he know I passed?"

Malphas frowned. "Witch, you misunderstand. Thomas will not *teach* you with these rings. They are *tools* so that you may set out on a path. Sink or swim, succeed or fail, that is up to you. He is not *watching*. He will not *help*. This is your walk, your path. Otherwise, it will not be *your* magick. Your teachers will be many, but they are not invested in the outcome. The Magician has simply tipped the scales in your favor by giving you three tools that will enable you to get the fastest possible start out of the gate." He paused. "Most human magick-users would trade their souls for just *one* of these rings. He has given you three. You must have impressed him." Malphas laughed. "Or, he is desperate."

"And what do you have to do with this? Why are you here, and not someone else?"

Malphas shifted in his chair. "I owe the Magician a debt. He held a magick I needed. I traded him service for that magick."

"The same magick I'm going to learn?"

Malphas cackled. "Great Pazuzu, *no!*" He shook his head. "You'd *explode,* little one."

Saorsa thought for a moment. "You said Oona reminded you of Alex. And the Fae attendant who gave me the orb you were in said you were for Alex. You've met him?"

Malphas smiled. "Yes."

"When?"

Malphas looked off into the darkness. "Shortly after he was born. The Magician could not stay on earth. He would send me to look in on the child and his mother in my crow form. When I was near...it soothed the child. He was less likely to show his Fae side." He laughed. "Once, however, when I went to visit, I landed a few feet from where Alex sat in the garden. He was maybe sixteen months or so in earth time, before he was split apart. There was a woman with him, not his mother, a nanny or female relative of some sort. When I landed, Alexander clearly recognized me and clapped his hands. So I extended my wings in greeting. And then he," Malphas laughed, "extended *his*. He looked positively delighted with himself. I don't think he'd done it before. These lovely black wings with ripples of Celtic blue, arching *way* up and out from where he sat, and he just giggled and cooed and was...I think you call it *adorable*." Malphas smiled. "And then the woman looked up, saw the babe had wings, and passed out cold." Malphas turned back to Saorsa. "I've always been fond of Alex."

"If you are supposed to be for him, why aren't you with him? Why aren't you in London now? Why are you here with me?"

Malphas gave her a half-smile. "You are *for him,* yes? So by being with you, I am *for him,* too. The good I can do him here outweighs the good I can do circling over a prison."

"But you're a *daemon.* Can't you help him get out?"

Malphas smiled. "You don't understand how this works, witch. I am Thomas' representative. To seek out Alexander on earth now that he has been split would result in a *very* serious situation. Very serious indeed. I cannot approach him."

"Can he approach you?"

Malphas looked thoughtful. "Not...certain."

"Do you know who the Violet Woman is?"

Malphas smiled. "I...suspect. But who she is isn't nearly as important as what she is *doing*. You must remember that. The label isn't nearly as important as what's in the bottle."

"I want to lure her here. Question her and find out what she wants. And then *stop her*. Make her leave us alone, somehow."

"I think what she wants is evident. Two sides of a split *leth-dhia*. The amulet that is embedded in your skin, and your mother's. Adamina Scott's magick. Your enemy is a maker of prisons, and wishes to keep you all in one until such time as she obtains *the rest* of her ingredients, so she can begin her work." He laughed. "But her ingredients keep escaping."

"Malphas...Thomas' spellbook said he split Alex not in two, but *three*."

Malphas roared with laughter. "Oh, my! Debt or no, that Fae-King *amuses me!*"

Saorsa sat up in her chair. "What? *What?* Did you know about this? Do you know where the third part of the *leth-dhia* is?"

Malphas gave Saorsa a look of affectionate pity, no mean feat for someone with bovine features. "Oh, you sweet thing. Do you really think a mage of Thomas' skill and power would write down *exactly* what he did and leave it lying around on earth if he didn't *want* someone to find it?"

Saorsa sat back, stunned. "So...there's no third aspect?"

Malphas shrugged. "Who knows? But he wants someone *to think* there is. If the book was meant for you, maybe it's a clue. If it was meant for someone else...maybe it's a trap."

"Thomas the Rhymer *directed us to it!*"

Malphas grinned. "Who read the book?"

Saorsa paused. "Alex. Me. Mother Agnes. Annag. And...," her eyes widened, "...*Fia!*"

Malphas laughed. "I'm guessing this Fia is not trustworthy?"

"No, but I don't think the Magician has any idea she even exists!"

Malphas nodded. "He might not have known *who* was coming to help the Fae. But he may have suspected *someone would*." He spread his hands. "Thomas has an incredible memory. Anything valuable is *in his head*. He doesn't write his magick down. I find it hard to believe he left a book with some of the most valuable information in all the realms in an old churchyard unguarded. He might not even be the one who put it there, you know."

Saorsa hadn't thought of that. "Things do seem to be left by him a lot. The knife on the tomb. The spellbook."

Malphas nodded. "Thomas uses books a bit differently than humans do. For humans, books are repositories of knowledge. For Thomas, they are more like...*bait*. He becomes interested in certain humans and drops books in their path to catch them. Sometimes to help, sometimes to hurt, sometimes to gain a mouse to run in his maze. I once saw him drop two books in a study for The Lovers to find. He wanted to see what would happen if he put them in a world he was building - to test it out. And they dutifully summoned him, got stuck in the world, and gave him no small degree of merriment." He smiled. "He did give them a key they wanted in trade, though."

Saorsa gasped, outraged. "You're talking about *my parents!*"

"I said he gave them a key. They were happy with it, I imagine."

"So the books...the spellbook was bait?"

"Perhaps. I can *guarantee,* however, that there aren't three *leth-dhia* if that's what he wrote. Or there are, but the third is not what *anyone* is expecting."

Saorsa sighed. "Right. Like you said, if I had all the answers, life would be boring. I'm going to let the spellbook puzzle slide over my brain and drip off for now." She looked at her hand again. "What's this tattoo for? The spiral?"

Malphas poured himself some more wine. "Come now, that's just basic."

"I mean, it's on my left hand, so I imagine it's to increase power when I cast. Help me pull magick up from hidden places. It's a Spiral Path. Spirals are symbols of creation and energy. And at a lot of the old worship sites, witches going up hills and mountains to commune with the moon would walk spiral pathways around the mountain to get there." She paused. "It's also representative of the soul's journey. Even as you progress, you often feel you are circling around to about the same spot."

Malphas nodded. "Magickal energy is in very short supply in this place. And it is becoming scarcer. The Fae are at war, little human; they are pulling power from other worlds to defend themselves. To deal with your enemies, you are going to need to pick up every *scrap* of magick left in the vicinity. That symbol will help you to do that."

Saorsa nodded. "Two more rings, then. One for identity. And one for will." She looked up at the daemon. "Am I correct?"

Malphas nodded. "Yes."

"I gave you one ring and you communicated. Do the other two work through you as well?"

Malphas had a glimmer in his eye. "Yes."

"What do they do?"

Malphas sighed wearily. "Pay me a ring *and see.*"

Saorsa slowly slipped the ring from her middle finger. "Am I...about to hand a daemon my identity?"

Malphas licked his lips. "Who you are is in your *soul.* Your soul found its path once again last night. No ring will change that. *Pay.*" Saorsa dropped the ring into his strangely beautiful dark hand. It disappeared, and Malphas' laughed. "Such a *feast!*"
Saorsa sat back in the chair and waited. He smiled and drained his cup. "*Delicious.* Really." Nothing happened.

"Malphas...why isn't anything happening?"

He smiled. "Oh, something *is* happening. Just not *here.* In the forest, all around us."

"What is it?"

He gave her a half-smile. "They are bringing you your bones."

Saorsa looked down at herself. "Who? I mean...I'm fairly certain I *have* my bones."

He laughed again. "Not these bones. Wait."

"Wait *for how long?*"

He shrugged. "Until they arrive. And in between."

Saorsa pulled off the ring from her thumb. "All right, if you're determined to be cryptic, let's just go for the next one. *Will*. Give me your hand, daemon."

Malphas shook his head and waved her off. "To do that here would be a *very* poor idea."

"Then *where?*"

He grinned. "Bring Macha and come." He rose from his chair and wandered lazily toward the mouth of the cave. Macha appeared out if the darkness and padded after him, with Saorsa bringing up the rear. Once outside, Malphas began walking down the path to the cabin.

"Where are we going?" Saorsa demanded. "What are you going to do?"

Malphas stopped well away from the cave and turned. "What do you know of me?" He held out his hand, and Saorsa gave him the third ring. He smiled happily as it disappeared.

Saorsa thought back to the information the Aunties had sent. "Well, you command forty legions in Hell, you accept sacrifices but then will deceive the conjurer, you appear as a crow unless requested..."

He waved at her. "Old news."

"You...," she looked up at him, "help good familiars, which is how Macha is here, I think. And it said..." she squinted, remembering, "that you *buildeth houses and high towres wonderfullie.*"

"Don't move," Malphas said, raising his hands in front of him, "and *don't say anything.*" He closed his eyes. At first Saorsa thought she was imagining it. But then it became obvious. *The ground was moving.*

Malphas' hands gestured in the air before him, and Saorsa gasped as she saw stones begin to tumble from the front face of the cave. Dust began to rise. The earth *shook*. She stumbled sideways as she saw the mouth of the cave crack in half, and then there was a tremendous *roar*. She fell to her knees and threw her arms around Macha, squeezing the red wolf in terror. A pit opened up before her and swallowed the cave whole.

Saorsa tried not to say anything, but the scream that came from her throat was involuntary. Nature herself seemed to be delivering the full force of her destructive power, just a short distance before her. Whole trees were consumed alongside massive boulders. Everything strong and stable in the world was disintegrating, and it frightened Saorsa terribly.

Something *huge* shot up and out of the ground from the pit, rocketing up toward the sky, like a giant stone spike piercing the night. The wood was full of violence as stone became dust and then stone again, and the environment refashioned in a matter of seconds. *I should be choking on dust,* Saorsa thought. *I should be dead. I have never witnessed power like this before in my life. Ever.* Saorsa couldn't hear anything, just the crashing and smashing of stone and timber as *something* birthed into this world. It stood higher than what had proceeded it by far, but there was so much soil streaming off of it and dust in the air that Saorsa couldn't see what it was.

And then, it began to storm. Piercing, freezing winds howled down from the sky to rinse the earth's issue of soil and sand, just as an extremely warm rain began to fall. Saorsa felt alternately frozen and rinsed warm as two conflicting weathers that *could not* exist in the same place at the same time did just that. And then as suddenly as it had started, it stopped. The cold winds and hot rain disappeared, leaving something freshly scoured and bathed looming far over them in the night.

A warm breeze blew. It felt like May. *December,* Saorsa thought. *It's supposed to be December.* The ground had ceased shaking, and the wood was silent. Malphas lowered his hands. The warm breeze was lifting the damp from Saorsa clothes and ruffling Macha's fur.

"You can speak now," Malphas said quietly. "And move."

It took a long time for Saorsa to let go of Macha and stand. "What...what is it, Malphas?"

He offered her his hand. "A place from which to exert your will, Darkflower. And I mean that name affectionately."

....

Saorsa's legs felt a bit weak after that display of power. *Pure nature. Devouring and raising again.* She'd read of earthquakes, floods, volcanoes, and other earth- changing events, but had never *seen* one. *Never again will I take a peaceful wood for granted, now that I know what it might become.*

Her eyes picked up the little light that there was. *It's only a few days until the new moon.* What she was seeing was starting to come together in her brain.

He buildeth houses and high towres wonderfullie.

It was a massive tower, jutting high above the landscape, several stories above the trees. Jet black and gleaming from some inner power. *It looks like hematite. Hematite is associated with protection and balance.* Saorsa remembered a story of soldiers carrying bits of hematite to war to prevent bleeding to death on the battlefield. *Magnetism. Focus. Grounding. Bravery. From a Greek word meaning 'blood'.* Its mirror-like surface reminded her of armor.

She tried to count the stories. *Nine floors. Some of those windows are extremely tall.* And there was something jutting out of the top of the tower, up toward the sky.

"Our time together this night is done," said Malphas. "I will remain here, but as a crow. I will be...observing. I wish you much fortune on your path. May you take your rightful place among the bones." He gave her a lopsided smile. "And when the Violet Woman comes...give her hell." Before Saorsa could say anything more, there was a particularly strong gust of hot wind, and Malphas the crow flew off toward the cabin.

Saorsa walked toward the base of the tower, staring. She felt very small. *This is for me. This huge thing is supposed to help me. To be mine.* She wondered what was inside. Floors filled with trials and terror? Levels of refuges and protection? She had no idea. But whatever was in there, she knew she was going in, and she was going to the top. *And I will claim it as my own. A fortress to protect my clan.*

For she had a clan now. In the weeks since she'd left Hermitage, she'd been building one. Some of them needed protecting, and others came to defend. She'd started in the first group. Now she, too, would defend.

A witch's tower. Here is where I will begin to leave my mark. She heard voices and running footsteps. Rune appeared on the path, followed by the other men, racing toward the sounds of destruction they had heard in the woods, swords at the ready.

"We're not under attack!" Saorsa called, holding up her hands. "I'm fine! Malphas worked magic here!"

The men slowed as they heard her voice and saw the Tower. "What...where's the *cave?*" Rune gasped, gesturing at the mammoth structure before them. "Did he...*make that?*"

"He called it up from the earth," Saorsa said, turning to look at the tower once more. "It's...he says it's to help me."

Rune said, awestruck, "I've never seen anything like it!"

"In the morning," Saorsa said looking at the darkened windows rising before her, "we'll enter together in the morning. And hopefully, it will be our stronghold."

....

The strange, warm wind had disappeared by morning, and the party at Wolfcroft awakened, eager for more details of Saorsa's story and anticipating their entrance to the tower.

Saorsa was feeling apprehensive as they rounded the corner and saw the tower. She noticed the men were now walking with their hands on their swords. The tower dominated the landscape around it, and for the first time Saorsa wondered if others might see it and come to investigate. *Can it be seen from the nearest road? From the nearest croft?* Saorsa heard Willow draw in her breath sharply as she saw the structure for the first time.

Oona, who was riding along on Saorsa's back, babbled happily in her ear, her tiny hands patting the textured locs. *Maybe we should have left her behind with one of the men.* But the thought of Faerie Alex showing up unannounced such a short time ago made Saorsa want to keep Oona close whenever possible. The details of the tower were now coming into view, and Saorsa suddenly stopped walking.

Rune had seen the same thing. "Those...weren't here last night."

The exterior of the tower was covered in snaking, spiraling rose vines. They climbed from the base to almost the top of the tower but left the balconies and windows clear. The flowers simultaneously decorated the black sides of the building with their blooms and protected it with their thorns. The scent of roses wafted through the air, fresh and sweet.

The roses themselves were not colors found on earth. Deep black and violet petals edged with a brilliant Celtic blue. And some held random splashes of brilliant red, as though blood had been splattered on the flowers during some unseen battle. They appeared at once both seductive and dangerous.

"Darkflowers," Willow breathed. "That's what they must be. A gift for you, Saorsa. I've never seen coloring on a plant like that. They smell heavenly." She paused. "And yet, they look like a warning as well."

The group's eyes traveled upward to take in the entirety of the structure. A post about six feet high stood alone about thirty feet from the steps to the doors, as though marking a boundary. Malphas flew to the post and perched on it, letting out a loud *caw*.

"Maybe he's announcing your arrival," Willow suggested, twisting her hair back and up away from her face into a bun. "Do you want me to take Oona while you go in?"

"There's the image of a skull carved into the post, Saorsa," Rune called back. "A crow's skull. With a rose."

Saorsa reached out and took Willow's hand and squeezed it. "I'd like you to come in with me," she smiled. "You're much more sensitive to energy than I am. I think you, Oona and I should go in together." Willow nodded and they walked forward, hand in hand, to look at the post.

"Is this a symbol for you now?" Rune asked. "A crow skull and a rose? A banner of sorts?"

Saorsa looked closely at the post and thought of her trip to Faerie and her conversation with Alex there. *See the crow? That's my banner. When you're born in a royal house, they make a symbol for you. Even if you're leth dhia. If I fight, that symbol is raised before my army. If I wed, it goes on her ring. Any male children I sired here would have it worked into their skin to show their lineage. Any weapons I owned would be impressed with it, and my house in my father's realm has it carved on the gatepost. An' when I die, it will go on the stones of the mound that marks where I lie.*

This was *her* gatepost. Thomas had given her a symbol. *A darkflower, bones, and a crow. The symbols of the path I am on.* This was something that the Fae would *notice*. She was in their books now; part of their history. It was the crow that shocked her. *As if he is recognizing me as a member of his Deck.*

"Let's go," she said to the group, and walked with Willow and Oona up the steps, Rune and his men just a pace or two behind.

………

The tall doors swung open, untouched, as Saorsa approached. Everyone fell silent, and paused. "It's...strange," Willow said. "But it doesn't feel *bad*. It feels..."

"...welcoming," Saorsa finished.

"Yes. Like it *recognizes* us." Malphas sailed overhead through the doors, disappearing into the dark interior, followed a moment later by Macha. Saorsa smiled, and they followed the wolf and crow inside.

The tower was circular with windows twice as tall as Saorsa. The light they let in helped to see, but not nearly as much as the flame that jumped to life on the south side of the room inside an enormous stone fireplace. The advent of light was so sudden that Rune had his sword halfway drawn before he understood there was no threat. "Loki's daggers, that startled me!"

They could see the room clearly now. Saorsa could scarcely believe her eyes. It was enormous, around ninety feet in diameter, and its ceiling was thirty feet up. The fireplace was so large that the entire group could have stood comfortably inside it with room to spare. Willow was already orienting herself.

"South," she said, pointing to the fireplace. "And we came in the door, entering this circle from the east. So in the west will be..."

A waterfall cascaded down the wall to the west, ending in a large indoor pool surrounded by a low wall. Eske moved over and put his hand into the water, and then tasted it. "Fresh," he proclaimed. "You could survive an attack in here for quite some time." The water flowed over quartz crystals which jutted out of the wall, floor to ceiling, and seemed to line the bottom of the basin as well.

"South has fire, west has water, east is where the air comes in. It's a casting circle," Saorsa exclaimed delightedly. "And in the north...." On the north side of the room was an enormous stone table, inlaid with crystals and stones. A staircase began behind the table and curved its way up to the next level. "That's the biggest table I've ever seen," declared Saorsa.

Rune laughed. "I think it's a platform, not a table. There are steps on one side. I think it's a dais to hold a throne, Saorsa."

Saorsa looked scandalized. "No! Why would I need *that?* We'll just...we'll put offerings to the Lord and Lady on it. It will be a holy space."

"There are roses growing on the walls inside too," Willow pointed out. "And look at the floor." Fresh rose petals littered the floor near the walls. Underneath them was a mosaic floor in blue and black. A giant spiral. A spiral pathway.

"This place is like a temple," Rune said. "An audience room. A throne room. This is...incredible."

Willow was touching one of the roses. "There is a *very* strong grounding energy coming from these. Protective and balancing." Her eyes lit up. "Oh, I just had a thought! I know *exactly* what to do with these!" She winked at Saorsa. "I'll explain when we're done here."

"Let's look at the next floor," Rune suggested.

"This is magnificent," Eske said in awe.

"What are you going to name it?" Rune asked.

"I think it named itself," Saorsa grinned. "*Tùr nan Ròsan. Tower of Roses*." Oona laughed and gave Saorsa's hair a little tug.

They moved to the stairwell, then up to the second floor. They came to an abrupt stop on the platform when the stairs stopped. "Where...are the stairs to the upper floors?" Saorsa said, puzzled. The stone spiral staircase simply ended at the outline of an arch on the wall.

Rune cautiously reached out and touched the blank wall inside the arch. "Perhaps...this is a form of security. If the tower is invaded, the aggressors will be stopped here."

Saorsa looked at the room on the second floor. They were standing next to a massive kitchen and workspace. Multiple fireplaces lined the walls, and the waterfall fell through this room as well. Huge oak tables for cooking were set in various places throughout and built-in shelves lined the walls. *I cannot wait to explore this kitchen.* Fires were burning in two of the fireplaces, as though someone had just lit them. *I think this is built like a broch. Two circular walls, one inside the other. The chimneys are in the space between.*

There were no other sets of stairs on the floor. "So, if the archway is the way up, how does it work?" Saorsa walked up to it and put out her hand. A slight breeze blew across her face, and she found herself standing in a different place.

"*Min dame!*" she could hear Rune shouting from somewhere else in the tower.

"I'm alright!" Saorsa bellowed as loud as she could. There was an archway on the wall both behind and in front of her. *It let me through. And Oona.* Oona giggled.

Saorsa looked to her left to see a hallway that bisected the tower with doors leading to rooms on either side. *I'm not exploring those by myself. I need to get the others through.* Suddenly Macha materialized next to her. "So *you* can make it through," Saorsa said to her. "Shall we go back and try to bring the others?" Macha turned around and vanished back through the archway. Saorsa raised her hand, and soon she and Oona were back on the landing with the others.

"Try touching me," Saorsa said. "Or Macha. The tower...seems to understand she's working with me." She looked at Macha. "I really wished Malphas had told me more about you. But I suppose we'll figure it out." Willow bent over and put her hand on Macha's back, and the two passed through the solid-seeming wall together.

"Come on, gentlemen," Saorsa smiled. Her burly companions each took hold of a shoulder or an arm, save for Eske, who planted his mammoth hand right on top of Saorsa's head. Then they stepped through the wall together.

"So you or Macha must bring us through," Eske mused once they were on the other side. "Oh look, another archway. I suppose we just repeat the process to continue up."

"No one can really utilize the tower if Saorsa or Macha isn't here," Rune said, thinking. "There must be a way around this. This tower is enormous. You'll have others with you here, and I can't imagine you're supposed to spend all your time aiding them in moving between floors."

"We'll figure it out," Saorsa grinned, eager to explore the rooms. "I wonder what's on this floor?" The first door on the left led to a room half as big as the tower. A bedroom. Saorsa's breath caught in her throat.

The furniture was gorgeous. Soft blues and grays were repeated throughout the rugs, upholstery, and fabrics and all the wood in the room had been left with as many live, organic edges as possible. The high ceiling had an intertwined forest of white and gray branches decorating it, giving one the impression of being in a giant nest. And behind the branches, against the impression of a dark blue sky, tiny lights sparkled like stars.

"Ohh," Willow breathed. "The white branches are birch. In Ogham, they represent renewal and new life." She paused and smiled. "And the gray...that's rowan. It's always been my favorite. I have often thought that if I ever have a daughter, I might name her that. Rowan, symbolizing beauty and hardiness all at once." She looked at Saorsa. "When Malphas made this place, he was sending you good tidings. Blessing you."

Saorsa thought she might cry. This room...from the soft carpets to the curtained bed to the balcony doors to the fire burning merrily in the intricately-mosaicked fireplace all felt like *too much.* This had been made for *her. I don't deserve this,* she thought. *This place is...incredible. It's for someone with real standing. Real power. Not someone like me.*

Rune saw her face change. "What is it?"

"I...," Saorsa said, choking back tears, "it's too beautiful. I don't deserve it. I'm...I'm just a novice witch in hand-me-down clothes. I don't *know* anything. At least, not the things someone with a tower like *this* should know."

"Saorsa," Willow said, reaching for her friend's hand, "you've had a lot of change recently. You were in *prison* three months ago. But...look at yourself. We've taken those hand-me-down clothes and refashioned them to be those of a woman of power. You might have been a novice witch a few months ago, but now you are *leading.* And most importantly...you *love,* Saorsa. You love and that love is magick. It transforms. Everyone who meets you feels that determination and love. You get knocked down, and you get up again and keep loving. And if a person like that doesn't deserve a tower, I don't know who does."

"You do," Saorsa blurted. "*All* of you deserve a tower. You could lose your lives when the Fae come. Because they will. They can't ignore this place now. It's got magick pulsing through it. So much that it feels *alive* to me. And you are risking everything for someone who very recently was just a stranger."

"No," Rune said gently. "We do it for ourselves as much as you. Because we too, are each on a spiritual path. And our hearts tell us that there are lessons to be learned here. A clan to belong to. That comes from *you.*"

Macha moved up to Saorsa's side and nuzzled her hand. Oona clapped her hands. "Saorsa," Willow said, noticing something on the far wall, "look at that. What is it?" The walls in the room were painted white. But over on the north wall, there was a picture painted on part of the plaster. Or, *pictures*.

"Oh, my Goddess," Saorsa said as she recognized it. "It can't be." She drew closer and put out her hand. "It...*is*." The paintings from her room in Hermitage Abbey were there. All of them. Every scene, every animal, every shape. Reduced in size, but otherwise, *exact copies*. They filled a section of wall with their brushstrokes. Nothing was missing. Everything, every hope and dream she'd had as a child, was rendered in perfect detail. "They're from my room," Saorsa gasped. "My paintings. From Hermitage."

"The beginning of your journey," Willow said, moving closer. "But now they are just part of a bigger picture yet to be painted." She pointed to a table nearby, full of brushes and small bottles of pigment. "With those."

And Saorsa knew. Knew that her world had expanded, and would continue to expand, further than the young girl in Hermitage could ever have dreamed. She had much to add to these walls. *The stone circle. The Healer's Cottage. Holy Cross Church. Wyldwood. Seven Hills. Motherwell. Morrigan's Cave. Ramsay House. Melrose Abbey. Buccleuch. Branxholme. Wild Willow Ridge. Faerie. The Ways. The Court of the Morrigan.*

But her new paintings would be different. In Hermitage her fantasy had been populated solely by the ghost of a dark angel. In these new paintings, he would have a name. *Alex*. And with him he brought Vika, Duncan, Oona, Fia, Adamina, Thomas, Edan, Keena, Donovan and so many, many more. Willow, Rune and her friends here, they'd be on the walls too. She'd add her mother, Annag, and Mother Agnes. Perhaps her father would be here one day, too. She had a future to step into. White spaces to paint as her story continued.

"I'm...needing a break. This is a lot," Saorsa said. "Do you mind if we head back to the cabin for a bit? And...think about what we've seen?"

"Of course," said Rune. "Shall we look on the other side of this floor first?" Saorsa nodded, and they went out into the hall. There were three doors on the opposite wall. Saorsa led the way to the one on the left. It was already open with Malphas was inside.

He was perched on the post of a beautifully carved child's bed. Floor-to-ceiling windows let in the sun. There was an exquisite patterned Turkish carpet and hand-stitched animal toys with delicate embroidery, with a mobile of flying crows over the bed. A rocking chair and a child-sized table with a little tea set. And a toy sword set near a rocking horse that looked remarkably like Thor. Bookshelves full of folk and faerie tales. And carved into the post of the bed in Ogham: *Oona*.

Saorsa wasn't the only one crying now. Even Eske was blinking back tears. An enormous fluffy stuffed wolf toy, the same color and nearly the same size as Macha herself, sat propped in the corner near a little porcelain bathing tub by the fire. A huge mural covered the entire ceiling: a pack of wolves frolicking joyfully under the light of a full moon.

And flowers. Roses on the tea table, in a vase by the bedside, and on the mantle. Bright yellow roses. Welcoming Oona home. The little girl who had been abandoned had a room of her own.

Willow lifted Oona from her seat in the backpack and handed her to Saorsa. "Look, Oona," Saorsa said softly. "Malphas made it for you. It's for you. A room of your own." She put the little girl down on the rug, and watched as Oona let out a shriek of delight before rolling over and grabbing both sets of her toes.

Rune gestured to his men. "We'll give you a moment," he said. "We'll go look at the other two rooms."

Willow and Saorsa sat with Oona in the sun, and watched the light bring out the red in her dark hair. "Thank you," Saorsa said to Malphas. "I am more grateful than I have the words to express." The crow chuckled softly.

....

They were headed back to the cabin, each of them lost in thought. Seeing Oona's room had made each of them think of their own childhood and dreams. They were weighing those against who they were now.

Rune saw the cabin first and put out his hand to stop them. "*Horses,*" he whispered. "*Seven of them.*" A few hand signals were exchanged, and Saorsa and Willow moved to the side of the path with Oona. Trig and Aeric moved silently off into the woods in opposite directions, while Rune and Eske continued forward on the path. Willow and Saorsa stayed still, tense and listening. Then they heard a joyous shout and an *all-clear* bird whistle from Eske.

Saorsa knew the whistle because Vika used the same call. *All clear.* Had Willow's husband Svend arrived? *But seven horses. The man didn't bring seven horses.* Willow went down the path, spotted one of the horses, let out a happy scream of joy not unlike Oona's and charged forward. Saorsa followed, watching as Willow leapt into the arms of a man dressed very much like Rune but with a mischievous and loving twinkle in his eye. Svend had arrived at Wolfcroft.

And then Saorsa heard a voice she knew. "Where's that fiend Saorsa Stuart?"

"*Edan!*" Saorsa shrieked, bolting forward, completely forgetting she was wearing a baby. Oona screamed joyfully, imitating Saorsa, and threw her hands in the air as her human mount bumped down the path.

"Whoa, whoa, *you're wearin' a wean!*" Edan shouted, slowing Saorsa with his hands before she grabbed him. Rune hastily plucked Oona from her pack, before Saorsa squeezed Edan with all her might.

And *Annag!* She let go of Edan and hugged Annag, talking all the while, before spying Toran and hurling herself into his arms as well.

"Saorsa." A voice from behind her. A voice she knew. But she didn't dare believe her ears. She turned around, and standing between two unknown beautiful, tall, brunette women was *her mother*. Maria looked thin. Tired. But there was that *light* in her eyes. The light that appeared at two times: when she spoke of her husband and when she looked at her daughter.

Saorsa didn't remember covering the ground between them. They were just suddenly in each other's arms, clutching at each other, gasping with relief. Saorsa heard voices around her, but they didn't matter; her mother was here, and whole. She'd never seen her anywhere but inside a prison before. *We're out, Mum. We got out. Both of us. And I swear to the Goddess, neither of us is going back in. They will never take us alive.*

Her brain couldn't process anything. *How was her mother here?* Her mother had been living with her mind half in Faerie due to the amulet buried in her skin for most of Saorsa's life, but Saorsa felt fiercely protective of her. *Mother Agnes had to raise me. But even though my mother and I have never been able to speak much, she did the best she could. And she loves me.* In truth, there had been times growing up where Maria had felt more like *Saorsa's* child, but her mother was here now. *How?*

She felt Willow's hand on her shoulder. "It's starting to snow, my friend. Let's go inside." Dazed and clutching her mother's hand, Saorsa followed the others into the cabin.

………

"We're going to need *a lot* more dinner," Willow grinned, swinging into action once she saw Saorsa was completely overwhelmed. "Aeric and Trig, would you mind handling the horses? Eske, we're going to need more wood." She smiled as Rune started pulling chairs and benches near the fire and put on the kettle for tea. "Please, sit down everyone and warm yourselves."

Saorsa was still standing, clutching her mother's hand. She watched as the new arrivals settled in and barely noticed when Oona was handed back to her. She heard Edan speaking, but it took her a moment to begin to process his words. Between the tower and her mother's arrival, she felt as if she was living in a dream.

"Saorsa," Edan said quietly again, gesturing toward a brunette woman with intelligent, sparkling eyes, "I'd like you to meet my mother, Lady Adamina Scott of Buccleuch." Saorsa was now *convinced* she was in a dream. Adamina Scott looked to be no more than twenty-five. And then it hit her: Adamina was *Alex's* mother as well. She was meeting Alex's mother.

Adamina smiled at Saorsa, a calm smile full of affection. "I'm *so* pleased to meet you, Miss Stuart. For many reasons." Her voice softened. "I hear you take good care of my Alexander."

Saorsa felt a lump rise in her throat at the mention of Alex's name. "I'm trying," she whispered. "I'm not sure...."

Adamina reached out and touched Saorsa's arm. "I cannot tell you how grateful I am. And I hope to be a help here." Her eyes darted away. "I know the way I look is a bit confusing. It's a spell. Thomas and I...worked a spell." She laughed then, and Saorsa instantly fell in love with that laugh. Adamina leaned conspiratorially toward Saorsa. "As you know, having a man from the Deck of Crows in your life can be quite complicated."

Saorsa felt warm all over. *Alex's mother likes me. Accepts me. She thinks I'm good enough for Alex. Oh, sweet Goddess, this is a wonderful thing.* Then she remembered that Adamina and Alex were going to have a very uncomfortable conversation once they were reunited. *Adamina didn't tell him what he was.* But she could hear the love Adamina had for her son in her voice, and became determined to help them reconcile any way she could.

"I'm so glad to meet you too," Saorsa said with a full heart. "This is Oona." She shifted the little girl in her arms to face Adamina, whose eyes widened as she saw the little girl's storm-cloud eyes and the red highlights in her dark, wavy hair.

"Is...," Adamina stuttered, "is she...?" Adamina did not usually lose her train of thought, but she was losing it now. Oona raised an eyebrow and gave her a mischievous half-smile that a human child her age *definitely* shouldn't have the muscle control for. "Oh," gasped Adamina. "She looks *so like...*!"

"Like Alex," Saorsa finished.

Adamina's eyes widened. "Is...she your child? Are you her mother?"

Oh my goodness, she thinks Alex and I have been together long enough for us to have an eight-month old child together! Saorsa realized how long it must have been since mother and son had spoken, and how little Alex must share about his private life with his mother. At the same time, Saorsa felt a strange longing in her heart to make the very situation Adamina *thought* had happened a reality. *Goddess, I want a family with him. I wish I could say yes to her question.* "No," Saorsa said. "She was an orphan."

Adamina was very confused. "She's...*not* my grandchild? I mean...," she smiled affectionately at the little girl, "Alex had that same smile when he was little." Saorsa could see Adamina wasn't convinced that Oona wasn't Alex's child.

"We're not sure who her father or mother are," Saorsa said softly. "All we know for certain is that she's from the Deck of Crows."

"You and I have *much* to discuss," Adamina said, shaking her head. "I think we may be both holding halves of the same puzzle." She gestured to the tall woman next to her. "But before we do, I'd like to introduce you to Laoise." She turned to the woman next to her, who had one of the most magnetic smiles Saorsa had ever witnessed. She watched as Laoise tucked her hair behind her ear. Saorsa saw the shape of that ear. *She's Fae!*

"Just half, actually," Laoise laughed, reading Saorsa's thoughts. "I can't tell you how nice it is to meet you. I was Alex's healer. In the Tower of London."

"She got me out, Saorsa," Maria said softly. "I'm standing here because of her."

Laoise put out her hand in greeting and was surprised when Saorsa abruptly handed Oona to Adamina and threw her arms around her and began to weep. "You brought me my mother," she cried, mortified by her own behavior even as she was squeezing the daylights out of her half-Fae guest. "You *brought me my mother.* And you helped him...you *helped him....*"

"I don't know where Alex is right now," Laoise said quietly, embracing Saorsa in return, "but I can tell you that he *loves you*."

Saorsa stayed with her arms around the healer for several moments, and then began to laugh. "Oh, *I'm sorry!* I'm a little overwhelmed!"

Adamina laughed. "I think we're *all* overwhelmed! The things that people told me on the way here...about Fia, about Alex, about *you*...so much has happened in such a short time!" She smiled down at Oona, who was happy as a clam in Adamina's arms and cooing softly. "And you, little one...I could hold you *forever*." Saorsa released Laoise and wiped her eyes.

"I'm just glad...I'm just *so* grateful...," Saorsa covered her face with her hands. "You must think I'm a lunatic."

Laoise laughed. "Not at all. As a matter of fact, now I can see clearly why Alex is so mad about you." She patted Saorsa's arm. "Your love sits right on the surface."

"Do you know how he is?" Saorsa said quietly.

Laoise shook her head. "I'm so sorry. I last saw him a week ago today. His Fae captors, my former employers, were concerned that he was about to escape. Little did they know he'd already split himself and been to see you twice. They moved him to a place with more magickal security, I think, so he couldn't do it again." *That's why he hasn't been back,* Saorsa thought, a sinking feeling in her stomach.

"Saorsa," Laoise continued, "there's this Fae woman in charge at the Tower of London. I thought the woman running things was a blonde with bright blue eyes. But the night we escaped I saw her," Laoise waved her hand, "her face and hair looked *completely* different. She looked like she could be related to Alex."

"The Violet Woman," Saorsa breathed. "She seems to be involved with anything related to the *leth dhia*."

"Have you ever seen her face?"

Saorsa shook her head. "She possesses him, so I've seen her work *through* him. Alex claimed her face changed while he looked at her and that she looked like many women at once." She paused. "Wait. Fia's seen her too and saw a sort of family resemblance. But Fia may not be a reliable witness."

"I think," Laoise said slowly, "that Alex and his torturer are related." She paused. "And...once, when Alex went to find you...another *leth dhia* aspect animated the body he left behind. It said he was trapped *in the blue* and asked why he was being moved."

"There's one blue magickal object I can think of that's on the move. Edan says Alex sent the Scott sapphire east with a messenger, but we don't know why," Adamina stated. "There's a property near the Isle of Skye that Thomas instructed me to buy some time ago. I've never been there. Mother Agnes thinks Alex is sending the sapphire *there*."

"The sapphire is the gem Fia wanted as her wedding ring," Saorsa said.

"Alex didn't say anything about a sapphire to me," Laoise said. "But he was cautious about sharing lots of things. For good reason, I suppose. He wasn't sure who to trust."

"That is just part of what is happening. I think," said Saorsa, looking around the group, "once we have time to really put our heads together, we're going to finally have some answers."

....

The population of the cabin had doubled, and over dinner it was decided that half the occupants would move to the second house Eske had discovered. Soon everyone was referring to the two dwellings as *the Cabin* and *Eske House*, a fact that pleased Eske to no end. Eske House was a bit short on furniture, but did have three bedrooms with large beds. It was decided that Willow and Svend would take one room, while Adamina and Laoise would each have one of the other two. Trig, Eske, and Edan would sleep in the common room. Saorsa, Annag and Oona would stay in the cabin and Maria would take the other room there. Rune, Aeric, and Toran would sleep in the cabin's loft.

"We haven't fully explored the tower yet," Saorsa explained as they gathered in the common room, "but once we have, if everything looks safe...we could move some or all of us there tomorrow and make everyone more comfortable."

"Yes, what *is* that thing?" Edan asked. "We saw it from a hilltop on our way here. Who built it?"

"Malphas did," Saorsa said, gesturing at the crow perched on Else's shoulder.

"A crow built that." Edan looked at her skeptically.

"He's a daemon in crow form, Edan," Willow said, interlacing her fingers with Svend's.

Edan raised his eyebrows. "And...when did daemons come into this?"

"He's a friend of Thomas'. I summoned Thomas to ask for help. He gave me three rings, and one of them paid Malphas to make that tower."

"You've seen Thomas?" Adamina said excitedly. "*When?*"

"Maybe we should start at the beginning," Svend suggested good-naturedly. "And when we're all caught up...well, I have something to add that I think you should know about."

And so Saorsa began.

....

The rest of the day passed swiftly, as everyone shared the information they had. There were maddeningly big holes in their understanding, and at times it seemed more mysteries were introduced as soon as they had a possible solution for one. They took breaks to get people settled into Eske house and to cook, eat, and tend to the animals.

Saorsa found herself the leader of a very large tribe. *I have a daemon and a wolf familiar, an energy healer, a gaggle of Norse pagans, and a dragon line expert. One of Vika's trainers, a witch, a half-Fae healer, my mother and half of The Lovers, the new Queen of the Deck of Crows, the Laird of the Scott Clan of Buccleuch, and a half-Fae infant who looks more and more like she's my lover's child by the day. And they all want to help. Goddess, let me know what I am doing.*

They had finished dinner and settled the horses for the night. There were two things left to be told: Svend's story and Saorsa's plan. Svend sat back, his arm around Willow, and began.

Saorsa had never seen a couple so much in love. If her parents hadn't already held the title of The Lovers, she would have nominated Willow and Svend for it. Svend was broad-shouldered and strong, and gave the impression that he straddled the line between warrior and mystic. "I'm a scientist," he had explained. "But the things I research have incredible power; I have to bring together many skills to attempt to understand them."

There was a knowing and an openness to Svend's countenance that Saorsa trusted. His was a highly intelligent mind and he had the grace of movement of an experienced battle master as well. He had arrived not just with throwing axes strapped to his body, but with a staff as well. Saorsa wondered if it was for moving energy or fighting. Probably both.

His style was very much like Rune's, with the sides of his head shaved down to the skin and braided in the center. Saorsa saw a tattoo on the side that faced her, although it was difficult to make out in the firelight. In addition to the light armor he wore, he had a multitude of amulets and charms tucked about his person. Saorsa found him fascinating, and adored the way Svend tended to and obviously adored his wife. *They are beautiful together.* She paused and felt a twist of loneliness in her gut. *I hope Alex and I end up like them. Someday.*

"So," Svend began, after clearing his throat, "this is what I have to share. It may have nothing to do with this situation. It may have *everything* to do with it. I'll let you decide." He spread his hands. "I study a phenomenon that really doesn't have a name in these parts anymore. In the far East, it is called *dragon lines.* This is the concept that there are great paths of energy that crisscross the earth's surface like a giant net." Saorsa saw Adamina sit forward in her seat, rapt with attention.

"Where these lines flow, great energy follows. For those of you who practice magick, it would be thought of as magickal energy. The places where these lines meet are places of great power. Animals and humans both can sense these energies. Even plants can. In ancient times, when people were more sensitive to these energies, they built places of worship and strongholds on them. They are special places.

"*Hermitage,*" Saorsa interrupted. "Some of them meet at Hermitage."

Svend looked pleasantly surprised. "Yes. That is correct. But here's the thing; the dragon lines meeting at Hermitage is a fairly *recent phenomenon.*"

"What?" Adamina blurted. "Thomas...he spoke of these. Challenged me to find information on them. Said dragons are powerful forces that move. Just as a halo is a painting of a force we can't see, dragons in myth represent a force we can't see." She paused. "I've read some on this. The forces move along the paths...but the paths *don't change their orientation.*"

Svend pointed at her. "*Correct.* Until about a quarter century ago."

Saorsa heard Maria give a quiet gasp and turned to see her mother had gone white as a sheet. "Mum, are you alright?"

"William," her mother said, her voice shaky. "On the...on the night you were conceived, Saorsa. He woke me from a dream in which I was speaking Gaelic. I didn't know any Gaelic before that night, however. And he claimed I kept saying...," she looked at Svend, "*the dragon lines are moving.*"

Svend stared at her. "You're saying that in a dream you spoke a language you didn't know *warning of this?*"

Maria nodded. "Afterwards, I often heard voices. Saw spirits. Many of them spoke Gaelic to me. And when they did, I could understand and do it too." She touched her neck. "It happened much, *much* more often once the amulet was inside me."

Laoise spoke, "I can confirm that not only do dragon lines run across the earth, but they are in other worlds as well. Slightly different based on the environment, of course. But they don't relocate."

"There are conscious beings inside the dragon lines as well," Svend added. "They have a home, a source world, I suppose. Although it may be more...*void-like* than I imagine. Some venture out to travel along the lines. To explore. To learn. And over the years...I've been able to speak with a few."

"Holy *crap,*" said Toran. "You've *got* to be kidding."

Svend grinned at him. "No. Not kidding at all." He turned back to the group. "Without going into painstaking detail, one of these...well, *dragons,* hinted to me that something was amiss. One of the great achievements of my life has been the construction of a device invented and described by an advisor of Zhuge Liang in China around 200 A.D. that allows you, in the right conditions, to *see* dragon lines."

Adamina put her beautiful head in her hands and groaned. *"What?"* Annag asked.

"Thomas," Adamina said. "That was *Thomas.* He told me he was in Zhuge Liang's court."

Rune laughed. "He wasn't just Michael Scot, eh?"

"No," Adamina said. "He's been here many times under different names." She shook her head.

"Well then," Svend smiled, "I decided to take the device and travel to a few places where I know dragon lines cross. That's where I was when you all arrived to collect Willow." He looked more serious now. "And they are *moving*. Some, by just a small amount. By inches. But two in particular have moved by *miles*. They now, according to my calculations, run right through Hermitage."

"Why?" Saorsa interrupted. "*How?* How can powers that haven't wavered for millennia suddenly just *move*?"

"I don't know how," Svend continued. "And obviously I'm just observing things close to me and using maps to calculate angles. There may be others that have moved, or are about to, elsewhere. I found a journal while doing research on another dragon talker who claims he noticed slight movement twenty-two years ago. I think this has been happening over time. I'm not generally a nervous fellow, but I will tell you, *this* makes me nervous."

"Can you tell if it's a natural occurrence?" Laoise asked. "Something that happens in nature? As in, every so often they move? The same way locusts hatch or storms run in cycles?"

"Maybe," Svend said. "But if it was an expected occurrence, I doubt my dragon companion would have found it worthy of a warning."

"Why would someone want the lines moved?" Saorsa looked at Laoise, who was holding a dozing Oona.

"Faerie is at war, as I've said," Laoise reminded them. "The Fae need magickal power. It could be something the generals are doing to try to power their forces." She shook her head. "But...we've been at war before. This seems on a *completely* different scale. I don't know of any Fae powerful enough to move a *dragon line*. That'd be like me moving an ocean by myself."

Svend nodded. "These are *massive* energies. I don't know how you would even *begin* to move them. These lines moving...if it continues, it can completely restructure the power centers of a world. Remake how magick flows. Make deserts out of jungles and jungles out of deserts."

"This seems more than coincidence, though, that *Hermitage* is now a power center," Saorsa said. "I mean...doesn't it?" The room fell silent.

"Maybe the lines aren't finished," Annag suggested. "Maybe they just happen to cross there as they are moving to their final orientation."

"Perhaps," Maria said thoughtfully. "And perhaps not."

………

"When Alex was taken from Morrigan's Cave," Saorsa told the group before they turned in for the night, "I had no idea where they might take him. Somewhere here on earth. Faerie. Another world entirely." She looked around the room. "If they wanted him dead, they would have done it at the cave. They went to great trouble to enlist Fia to make certain he was *subdued*. They were saving him for something."

"Not knowing where he was, I couldn't mount a rescue mission. And once I found he was in London, I didn't see how we'd be able to pull one off. I had no information. Our resources were scattered. And just making it to the prison seemed impossible, let alone getting him out when he was injured. He was sitting in the middle of the greatest concentration of British soldiers in the world. My only idea to free him was to try and draw the enemy out of London. To try and bring the Violet Woman to me, so that I might discover her purpose and find a way to free Alex. Or...," Saorsa looked at the floor, "to see if I could trade myself for him somehow. Even being in the same prison with him would have been better than being without him." She blinked back tears. Adamina put a steadying hand on Saorsa's back.

"But to fight a Fae I needed better magick. And the only Fae I knew who might give it to me was Thomas. But he had never met me. So I came here, using Thomas' spellbook in a place special to Alex and with Oona, a child from his Deck. I was hoping to attract his attention. It worked."

"Malphas gave me three gifts in trade for the rings Thomas bestowed on me. Information. A warning about something to do with bones that hasn't happened yet. And the Tower of Roses. A stronghold that seems to have enough magick that it will draw the attention of the Fae. I am hoping that those top floors contain something that will help us fight the Violet Woman. Take her out of the picture so that if she *isn't* the puppet master in this scheme, the real one will be forced to appear. I hope to be able to capture her, or at least break her rhythm badly enough that we can reveal her plan. And maybe make Fae allies who can stop all this once and for all."

Laoise raised her hand. "If I may interject here...in giving you access to the magick he has through those rings, Thomas has violated Fae law. *Severely.* He already went to prison once for fathering a *leth dhia*. If the Council discovers ...."

"What do you mean, *went to prison?*" Adamina said, stunned.

"He went to prison. Until Alex offered himself in his place. You didn't know?"

"No," Adamina said quietly. "I didn't."

"I can tell you the story later," Saorsa said. "But at least both Thomas and Alex are out now. Well, the Alex who was being held in Faerie."

"I thought the Violet Woman had imprisoned Alex in Faerie," Adamina said quietly. "Not the Council. And not that...it had anything to do with Thomas." She looked at the floor.

Maria moved to sit next to Adamina and held her hand. "Go on," she said to Laoise.

"What I am saying is...the Council is rather distracted because of the war. If they notice Thomas gave a human magick, and a *fortress* right out in the open with which to wield it...well, we should expect more visitors than just the Violet Woman. The Council members are going to *lose their minds.*"

"Why doesn't Thomas just free Alex here on earth if he's so powerful?" Toran asked. "Why equip Saorsa instead?"

"He's not allowed to have contact with Alex's Human side," Adamina said softly. "Part of the deal to keep Alex alive is that he can't interact with Alex's Human side in any way. He made a Deck pact. If he aids or visits Alex here on earth, *all* of Thomas' children in Faerie will be killed."

"Damn," Eske swore. "They're *serious*."

Adamina looked up. "Yes. They are."

"How many children in Faerie does he have?" Rune asked.

"So, you know how the royal families of Europe intermarry to cement power and form alliances? Well, Thomas is a High Fae; he belongs to a royal family. Apparently they don't *marry* for alliance among the Fae; they just *mate*. The existence of the child is what is supposed to cement the union. Thomas has several Fae children and has alluded to having children in other worlds as well. His wife is supposed to outrank all of the children's mothers." She looked around the room. "We were married nine days ago. I'm the only wife he's ever had."

Laoise groaned. "Oh *shite*. I mean...congratulations on your wedding." She put her hand to her head. "I would *very much* watch my back if I were you."

"So in addition to the Violet Woman, we could have a High Council visit and a hoard of angry goddesses who don't like being outranked by a human," Annag said. "Got it."

Saorsa looked around the room. "There are two problems with my *get the attention of the Fae* plan. One...I don't know what the Tower of Roses contains. It might not be enough to protect us, or it might have magick I won't be able to learn fast enough to deal with the Violet Woman. I am certain she *will* come. We have the amulet shards she wants. We have information that can damage her. And we are growing in power."

"What's the second problem?" Laoise was listening closely.

"I owe her a debt."

"*What?*" Edan asked, flabbergasted. "You owe the Violet Woman a *debt*?"

"At Buccleuch Church, over a hundred redcoats came after Fia, Alex, and me. We were surrounded. I made a deal with her. It was either that or die." Saorsa paused. "I promised her to do any one chore she required of me here on this plane, as long as it does not require the injury or death of a human being or Alex."

There was silence in the room. "She could ask for the tower," Toran said. "She could ask for *Oona*."

"She could ask for her freedom if we capture her," Rune stated. "Or if Alex ends up freed...she could ask for him *back*."

"I know," Saorsa said. "And...I'm sorry. I was desperate. It makes our job harder. But I wouldn't be standing here right now with a chance to make things right if I hadn't done it. I'd be in a prison, right alongside Alex, or dead."

Edan stood up. "We have our information. I mean, there are more details to be sure, but what we know is this: dragon lines are moving, and the Violet Woman has my brother and a yet unknown plan. But we have things she wants, and possibly enough power to bargain with or fight her, or at the very least draw the attention of others among the Fae, attention which the Violet Woman is probably trying to avoid. We have a troublesome deal that must be honored and a tower of unknown abilities and power. So, what's the plan from here?"

Saorsa took a breath. "Tomorrow, first thing, we head into that tower. We make sure it's safe for all of us and then anyone with magickal or energetic experience will be needed to help me understand what we find. Adamina, Svend, Willow, Annag and Laoise, you are probably going to be the most help. I think the safest thing would be to move our sleeping quarters and our food supply to the tower so we're ready for whomever comes. Rune, can you oversee that once the tower gets the all-clear?" Rune nodded.

Saorsa looked around the room. "I can't express the depth of my gratitude for you. All of you." She paused. "This woman and her associates have imprisoned, violated, and used more than one of us. Starting tomorrow, we move to stop her plan. Or at least cause so much chaos that the Fae can't help but turn their gaze toward us...and her."

Annag cackled. "Miss Purple messed with the wrong humans this time."

England

It would be dark soon, and Alexander Scott had been on the road for four days. He was making progress north, but the freezing temperatures combined with a few days of steady snow and rain was slowing him down. And no matter how fast he went, Saorsa still seemed an impossible distance away.

He tortured himself thinking of what might be happening to her. *They want the amulet in her skin. And all they plan to do afterwards is execute her.* And he couldn't see her. *She probably thinks I'm dead.* Dark, intrusive, repetitive thoughts fed something new that had taken up residence in his stomach: *panic.* He pictured her, hopeless and alone, in pain and bleeding. He couldn't sleep. He just kept pushing north, frozen down to his bones, plodding endlessly through a nightmare that was real.

He had abandoned his exhausted horse in a tavern stable. It would take a few days for the tavern to realize they'd been gifted a horse. He had decided to hire a carriage, hoping to stay relatively dry for a few hours as his path north continued. He needed sleep and might be able to get some with someone else driving.

Then he saw it, on a steep rise to his left in the dying light. An option he hadn't thought of before. A stone circle. *Could there be a portal there?* He thought back to the night he and Saorsa had been at the safe house after pulling Edan out of Branxholme. *After Edan saved my life.* He and Saorsa had opened a portal in the room by raising energy together. He smiled at the memory.

But I didn't go through that portal. I don't know if I can and stay whole. He'd gone through a portal at Buccleuch tower with Saorsa when she'd spoken to the Silver Man but had been unconscious the entire time. And when Saorsa had had him sleep in a stone circle once, his body stayed in this realm while his consciousness had gone to Hermitage. *And I didn't know who I was in there. Saorsa had to pull me out when the Violet Woman appeared.*

So, there *could* be a portal on that hill. A portal he *might* have the ability to use if he raised his energy enough. *But once I go through, I could fall unconscious or forget who I am, and be at the mercy of whatever finds me.* He called for the driver to stop.

And once I go through...how does it work? How do I find an exit? He thought for a moment. *Perhaps I could split myself and investigate multiple exits. Leth dhia aspects are supposed to be able to communicate across worlds. I could make multiples of myself and go out multiple exits if that is an option. Then, pick the best one. Pick anything in Scotland.* He remembered Saorsa saying that the more frequently portals were used, the easier they were to open. *Morrigan's Cave, near the Aunties. Buccleuch Tower.* Anything in Scotland would be a damn sight better than freezing his ass off in England. *And the Fae have been using portals to move around.* He just needed to make certain he didn't accidentally walk into someplace like Carlisle. *They might even have opened a portal to move Saorsa. Maybe there's one in Glasgow.*

"Can you go up that hill?" he asked the driver.

The driver shook his head. "It's nothin' but ice an' mud up the side. We'll be stuck."

Alex leaned forward and handed the man a small bag of coins. "For the trip so far, an' I've doubled it if you'll wait here half a bell."

The man stared at him. "If you're no back in half a bell, ye want me to *leave* ye here? It's freezin'! As it is, I'll have to pace the road to keep the horse warm."

Alex nodded. "If I'm no back, move on." The man nodded and Alex put his rucksack on his back, climbed out of the carriage and started up the hill. The man had been right. Ice covered the hill, and days of alternate freezing and brief thawing had turned things to mud. Alex moved as quickly as he could, bundled up to his eyes and with his gloved hands in his pockets whenever he could.

The weak sun was barely visible as he approached the circle. He could feel a strange invasive sensation, humming in his ears and pricking his skin. *I don't like these places.* He didn't feel like this when using *leth dhia* portals; perhaps it was a way of warding him away from using portals to move around. *So Human me stays put.*

Saorsa and I raised power together at that safe house, and a portal opened. But ever since I had that knife for so long, there seems to be more magickal energy riding around on me. Can I open this one by myself? Is there even a portal here? He forced himself to walk inside the circle. He was feeling nauseous now, and the biting wind on this hilltop didn't help. The humming in his ears escalated to a piercing ring. *Saorsa talks to the stones. Can I do that, too?*

He pushed himself toward the center of the circle and despair overcame him. He was miles and miles from friends, alone in a hostile place, exhausted and sick and panicked. *What would Saorsa do?* She saw these places as healing, but he felt anything but healed.

Ancestors, he thought, copying the format he'd heard Saorsa use, *please hear me. I ask not for myself, but for the witch Saorsa Stuart and her mother Maria, who need help. If you can hear me, if my leth dhia or House of Corvids ancestors can hear me, help me travel. Power is changing hands, and if I am not there to help stop it, I fear there will be less light in the world.*

Light. *That's what Saorsa is to me. Light. She balances the dark. Brings hope. She is the moon in my night, the stars in my abyss. Let my love and need for her open the way. Open the way.*

The driver of the carriage on the road below shielded his eyes and clutched at the reins as a tremendous flash of light burst from the hilltop, spooking his horse. The stone circle settled back into darkness, and twelve minutes later the driver sighed and turned the carriage toward the nearest tavern.

Between

Alex was standing in a grove. It was early morning, although he couldn't see the sun. Trees spread out from where he stood in all directions. It was warm, and a soft breeze blew. And Alex slowly realized he was *inside a tree.* Roots spread out from his feet. Above, branches full of leaves extended up and outward. He could feel a gentle pulsing in his veins. *I...is that my blood? Or the tree's sap, moving?*

He was warm, and it felt *so good* to be warm. Whatever this place was, it made him feel hopeful. His nausea was receding and being replaced with a sense of peace. He drew in a deep breath and felt his lungs thawing. *I could sleep here. Aye, that's a grand idea. Close my eyes for a moment.*

He shook himself awake. *Shite.* He was being lulled, forgetting his purpose. *But I'm not unconscious. And I think my actual body is here. But something wants me to slip into forgetting and inaction. I need to move. I need to stay awake.* He stepped forward and out of the tree.

These other trees...are they all portals? He could feel his body wanting to relax. *There's that heavy, lazy feeling - the sort that settles in after a long swim.* He pulled a knife from his belt and pressed the blade lightly against the palm of his hand to keep himself awake, and split himself into thirteen.

His counterparts looked at him, waiting for instructions. *Divide into four groups, one for each direction. Orient yourselves off of me. Pick a tree and slip through. Return to me. See if you can figure out which way is north.*

He hoped that was how this worked. *But maybe all the portals for all the worlds are jumbled together haphazardly. Maybe you have to know where you are going.*

Most of the trees wouldn't let an aspect in. But one at a time, each slipped through to somewhere. Slipped through and returned a short time later.

"Random hilltop. No landmarks I recognize."

"Same."

"Same. Big house at the bottom of the hill, though. Dinnae recognize it."

"Found a road sign. Says Norwich."

That's east, Alex thought, and adjusted himself to face possible north.

Another aspect to his northwest stepped from a tree. "Fucking' *Carlisle.* Looked right into Caroline Scott's quarters. A man was there drinkin' and *ravin'.* Not him, though."

Alex's eyebrows went up. *Maybe Caroline Scott is nearby. I could pop through and kill him.* He took a deep breath. *You don't have information. Focus on Saorsa, not revenge. You can come back later. You know where Saorsa is and she's in trouble now.*

"Anyone else from the northern area? Everyone focus up there."

"Hilltop."

"Cemetery. Names on tombstones are Collingwood and Forester. North, but too far east."

Another aspect stepped out of a tree. "Found Morrigan's Cave. But that's still fairly far east of Glasgow. The Aunties might know where Vika and Duncan are, though."

"I think I've got Hermitage. Nearly unrecognizable. The only thing not completely torn apart is the abbey, an' the bell tower's at a fearsome angle."

An aspect emerged from a tree. "Oh God. Ended up in a *church.* These poor folks, they were sittin' up with the body of a dead man before the funeral. A whole family. An' I landed right on top of the altar! They screamed, an' I tipped my hat an' left. Didnae get a location. They must think I'm a ghost. Feel *terrible* about it."

"Found Branxholme!" another aspect chimed in excitedly. "But there's some sort of field on the other side. I could see the castle, but...I think there's some sort of security on the portal."

Could be friendly. Might not be, though. Alex looked around. "Anyone else got anything better? Branxholme is our best bet now, but there could be problems."

A smiling aspect wandered into view. "Motherwell."

Alex's eyes widened. "There's a portal at Motherwell? Where we met Oona?"

"Aye. On a hill by the holy well."

"That's it! Half a day's ride to Glasgow. And an inn we know well from which to procure a horse." Alex put his blade back on his belt. "Looks safe?"

"Aye, quiet. Whole town looks quiet. Snowin' a wee bit." Alex high-fived his aspects back into his body and took off at a run for the portal.

....

Alex could scarcely believe his luck as he stepped out of the portal on a hill overlooking Motherwell. *There was a portal. I was able to open it. And I have my body with me, am still conscious, and remember who I am. Maybe as long as I only move around on earth, I'm alright. Maybe it's just going to Faerie, where I'm not supposed to be, that damages me.*

He could see the inn from here. As relief flooded his body, he realized how numb he felt. *I can't go into Hagg Castle like this. I need to rest.* He'd give himself tonight, then. *A hot meal. A hot bath. A warm bed. Then I ride to Glasgow early tomorrow and be at my best to find Saorsa.*

I'm in Scotland. He was nearly weeping with relief. *The Borders. Scotland.* He headed down the hill, a smile on his face. *Finally. Some good luck.*

Wolfcroft, Scotland

Everyone was up early the next morning and gathered in the cabin for breakfast. Saorsa, Annag, and Rune had been up before the others, mixing dough for bannocks, whipping eggs to bake with cheese, and piling firewood next to the fireplaces.

Aeric, Trig, Eske, and Toran were going to set out at first light with the wagon and a few horses to return the borrowed one to Keena and Donovan, and purchase a wagon for Wolfcroft to fill with supplies in Fenwick. If the weather held and they were quick, they'd be back not too long after nightfall. Saorsa was glad someone was going to look in on Donovan and Keena. "Please tell them we're fine, and Oona is doing well," she told the men. "And that we'll see them after Yule."

Everyone else would head to the tower after breakfast. Adamina, Maria, and Laoise seemed to each be falling in love with Oona. Laoise in particular seemed to charm Oona; she sang her songs in a Fae language that seemed to transfix the little girl. At one point in the morning when Edan picked up the child she giggled at him and disappeared, only to appear in Laoise's lap.

"Ooh! My goodness!" Laoise laughed.

"I guess we know how she feels about me," Edan grumbled good-naturedly.

"Oh, Edan," Laoise laughed, "it's just that she likes the songs. I'll teach some to you if you like." She smiled. "When we get Alex back...I wonder if his Human half can trill. She'll like that even more."

"I witnessed Thomas doing it," Adamina chimed in. "It's very soothing."

Saorsa smiled. "When the knife was around, I saw Alex do it as well," she explained. "I was in a panic once, and he did it then I was able to breathe. It's like a big cat purring." It was the first time Saorsa had seen Oona move about on her own. *I'm going to have to learn those songs too. And quickly.*

With the breakfast dishes done and the animals fed, they headed to the stables to see the supply team off. Then the rest followed Malphas and Macha down the path toward the tower. When they rounded the bend, they came to an abrupt stop. Sitting on the path in front of the tower was an enormous pack of wolves, all looking in their direction as if they had been waiting for them.

"Oh," Saorsa said quietly, "I wonder if their den was in another part of that cave. The one that was...destroyed when the tower was built." She put her hand to her head. "Oh, I feel *awful* about this!"

Willow took Saorsa's hand. "Let's you, Macha, and me go and try and speak with them." She looked at her husband. "Svend, will you come to help as well?"

"Careful," Rune said, his voice tight. "I don't like this."

Svend, Willow, and Saorsa moved closer to the pack, with Macha in front. The three humans crouched down before the wolves. All three closed their eyes. *I need to slow myself way down*, Saorsa thought. *Like Willow showed me with Thor.* For a few moments, she heard *lots* of thoughts, and couldn't sort one from the next. *It's too much. There's too many.* And then cutting through the soft murmur of mingled impressions was one louder and clearer than the rest.

Greetings. I am the Wolf Macha. We wish to be friends. What troubles you this day? Saorsa's breath caught. *I'm hearing Macha!*

A distinctly lower voice answered Macha. *The pack leader.* His voice boomed through Saorsa's consciousness. *Greetings, Macha. I am the Wolf Ullr. I bear the name of one passed down. Our den has been destroyed, and this dwelling constructed from its stones.* Saorsa sighed with regret.

How can we aid you and your pack, Great Hunter? Macha continued. *We do not wish you harm, but comfort.*

There is a cave under this place, Ullr said, pawing at the ground. *We wish to live below. We have hunted these lands for a long time. We wish to continue. If you will watch for us, we will watch for you.*

"Of *course*," Saorsa blurted out, forgetting the response only needed to be in her mind.

The men here. They will not hunt us?

"No," said Saorsa, both aloud and in thought. "You were here first. We wish ongoing cooperation and communication."

Ullr pointed his nose toward Saorsa. *They will bring you the bones. And we will help.* He suddenly turned and trotted off, headed for the back of the tower. Macha followed the pack at a short distance as they trailed after their leader, observing them, and then returned to Saorsa's side.

"There's a cave under the tower," Svend smiled. "It looks like we have roommates. The entrance must be around the back somewhere."

"I bet the waterfall continues down there," Willow mused. "There may be an underground lake or river."

"I'm just glad they aren't furious," Saorsa said, standing. "Thank you for helping me to hear them. For coming forward with me. They're a bit intimidating!"

Svend laughed. "They probably feel the same about us." The group moved forward again and climbed the stairs into the tower.

"This is *incredible*," Edan said, his voice echoing around the first floor. "This is *magnificent*. Look at the carvings in the stone on the ceiling!"

"The roses," Laoise said. "They have a *very* strong energy coming from them."

"I was thinking," said Willow, looking at the floor, "of trying to make rose clay from these spent petals. If we made beads from the clay and strung them, they might serve as protective amulets of great power."

"What's rose clay?" Annag asked.

"Long ago, people discovered that if you cooked slightly-faded rose petals down after shredding them over a period of three days or so, you end up with a moldable substance you can form and dry into beads. Since roses are sacred to the Virgin Mary, Catholics used to make these beads and use them to construct rosaries. That's where they get their name. They're not waterproof, obviously, but they retain the rose scent and I've seen examples nearly half a century old." Willow gestured at the walls. "I thought we might do the same. Wearing a necklace or bracelet of these protective beads might be helpful when the Fae come."

"Wait, *wait*," Laoise said, holding up her hands. "Didn't you say only Macha and Saorsa can move through the archways on floor two and above?"

"Malphas seems to move around fine too," Saorsa said. "Probably because he made the place."

"Yes. And it's going to be a pain in the ass," Rune answered.

"I wonder if...if we added something of Saorsa, Macha, or Malphas to the beads if the tower might let *us* through with an amulet. Some of Saorsa's hair, a clipping of one of Macha's claws or maybe a feather from Malphas mixed in. There's a chance the tower could think they were with us. Then we can go where we need to go if we're under attack without having to find Saorsa or Macha."

"Let's try it," Saorsa said. "At this point, I'm willing to try just about *anything*."

....

They explored the kitchen a bit more. "Fresh water, fires that light themselves and don't consume the wood, and plenty of room to work," Adamina gushed. "It's the perfect kitchen!" Saorsa's and Oona's rooms on the third floor appeared exactly the same, with fires sparking to life in the fireplaces. "The two doors next to Oona's are guest rooms," Rune explained. "Ready and set, as though waiting for us. And there's an alcove here we missed last time with a fountain. Fresh water there, too."

"Maybe these two rooms would be a good place for myself and Maria," Adamina suggested. "We can help keep an eye on the baby."

The next two archways led to more guest rooms on the fourth and fifth floors. A large round common room sat in the middle of each floor, with sumptuous guest rooms arranged around it in a circle. To Saorsa's delight, there were freshwater fountains on these floors in line with the waterfall as well, so water for cleaning and bathing wouldn't have to be hauled up from below.

"There's enough space here for us all to have our own rooms," Annag remarked. "Goddess, that's a nice thing!"

"No monsters or cursed objects yet," Rune noted. His concern was danger first, canopy colors and comfort a distant second.

"Four more floors and the roof," Saorsa stated. "While the rooms are lovely, my goal isn't to tuck the Violet Woman in with a bedtime story. We need something that will *help*."

"There's got to be a way to go from floor one right to the roof," Rune thought. "Otherwise climbing this thing takes too much time and energy. Too bad Malphas didn't leave instructions." The bird squawked.

Floor six contained a spacious library and a laboratory, and what looked like a small area for meeting. "Now, *this is more like it,*" Adamina said, rubbing her hands together and racing to look at the titles. "Maps. Mythology. Folklore. History. Mathematics. Medicine. Philosophy. Metaphysics. All human authors, I think. All the basics you need are here." She looked at the instruments. "Lots of tools for experimentation. Thomas would *love* this!"

"For all we know, he designed it," Edan pointed out. "I'm a little fuzzy on how much of this tower is Thomas' doing and how much is Malphas'."

The waterfall in this room cascaded not over stone, but over earthenware tiles depicting constellations and alchemical symbols. "Maybe I'll just sleep *up here,*" Adamina grinned. "It's *so* lovely. The candles and mirrors remind me of my Tower of Stars."

"I've never been much of a scientist," Saorsa said slowly. "I don't know what to *do* with all this."

Adamina took Saorsa's hand. "Thomas is fond of saying that all science is born of magick. And you are about to learn an entirely new form of magick, I think. So, the science will follow."

Floor seven stopped them in their tracks. "Are we..." Edan looked around, "in some sort of strange lighthouse?"

Floor seven was at least two and a half stories tall. There was no waterfall on this floor; the four cardinal points each held what appeared to be enormous copper cylinders. And at the center of the room, dominating everything, was a massive ball made of quartz crystal. Rising almost a story high, it broke the light coming in from the floor-to-ceiling windows into random patterns of multi-hued light. A swirl of smoky quartz resided motionless in the center of the ball. The entire group stood motionless.

"What is it?" Maria asked. "I've never seen..."

Saorsa realized Laoise had turned extremely pale. "Laoise, do you know what this is?" She moved to stand next to the healer.

"I...I...think so," Laoise stammered. "But this *shouldn't be here*."

"It's not a sacred object like the knife from Hermitage was, is it?" Saorsa said quickly. "It's not going to...corrupt anyone?"

Laoise shook her head. "I'm not *completely* certain it is what I think it is. I've never seen one in person. I...I could be wrong."

"What do you *think* it is?" Maria said gently. Oona parroted her tone of voice.

"My uncle," Laoise said, shaken, "he's a high-ranking officer in the Fae military. He's described it to me. And I've seen pictures in books. This...," Laoise shook her head, "this looks like a Siphon Globe."

"And that is...?" Svend looked concerned.

"Well, Siphon Globe is just the nickname. I don't know the actual term. This is...a piece of military equipment. A very *secret* and impossible to obtain piece of military equipment. They are used to power siege equipment and the like."

"You're saying there's no way Thomas should have this. Or Malphas."

"Definitely *not*," Laoise answered. "I'm sure just having *the plans* could get you executed for high treason. And how anyone outside the military would have the resources to *build* one...but it's the right size and the copper cylinders are correct." She paused. "When it's on, it pulls magickal energy to it and stores it. I think that's what the cylinders are for. It will suck up *all* the magickal energy in an area so it can be used to power weapons and shields and such."

"That sounds promising," said Edan. "If there's something to generate protection for this place...that sounds wonderful."

"Thomas said magickal energy is in short supply because of the war," Adamina said, thinking. "If we turn this on to protect ourselves...are we pulling energy used to protect those at the front?"

"No one *owns* magickal energy when it's loose," Laoise stated. "If someone has gone to the trouble to store it and you take it, *that* would be stealing. But the Council wouldn't be happy if they knew we had this, that's for certain." She thought for a moment. "If we do turn this on...well the notion that the Violet Woman has something more powerful than it here on earth would be laughable. If we do turn this on, I think it will suck the magick out of the countryside for miles around for at least half a day. Earth doesn't have high amounts of uncorrupted magick."

"Would it drop the magickal protections Mother Agnes has for her and Fia at Branxholme?" Saorsa asked.

"I don't think so. Branxholme is several days away. But from the map you showed me...I'd guess anything within forty miles or so of here might be affected."

The group looked at the sphere in wonder. "That's all one solid piece of quartz," Svend mused. "Impressive."

"But what does it power?" Willow looked up at the ceiling. "Two more floors to go, and the roof."

. . . .

Floor eight held more mysteries. Set equidistant from each other, forming a square, were four raised platforms, marking the cardinal directions. There were large windows in this room as well, reminding Saorsa of stained glass. But silver had been used instead of lead, and the various shapes that made up the designs were made of multifaceted glass. Each of the windows pictured a large blooming rose on a straight stem. At the base of the stem was glass cut into the shape of a crow's skull.

"Reminiscent of the symbols on the post," said Rune, "beautiful."

"What are the platforms for?" Each was the size of a large square kitchen table. A circle of white tiles connected them. Saorsa walked up and touched a platform. Nothing happened.

"It might be," Maria suggested, "that you have to have the sphere running first. Perhaps that helps the things in this room reveal themselves."

"Or you have to be casting with intention," Annag added. "Looks like a circle for spell casting between them."

"Those are both excellent ideas," Saorsa agreed. "Once our team is back from Fenwick tonight, and we're all together...I'll come up here and we'll try it."

They moved on to floor nine. "Oh, *goodness,* Willow said, looking around, " what is this space for?"

There was one large square table sitting directly in the center of the room. All of the windows could be opened, but it was such a cold day that no one tried them. The surface of the table was remarkable: a black marble with a large, iridescent spiral set in the center. The table had a raised lip around the edge, as though it had been designed to prevent things from sliding off. In concentric circles around the table on the floor was writing in a language Saorsa couldn't read. "Does anyone know what this says? It looks similar to Irish...."

I think it's Fae," Adamina said. "Thomas writes in it sometimes. There are *lots* of Fae languages. But this inscription in silver in the marble...it looks like his handwriting."

"Can you read it?" Saorsa turned.

"I might be able to figure out words here and there that look like old Irish. But I wouldn't completely trust my translation, no. Perhaps Laoise could translate it for you."

"Look up," Willow said softly. On the ceiling above the table was a huge mural of three crows, surrounded by painted roses.

"It reminds me of Morrigan's Cave," Edan said quietly. "The three ravens there."

"It's beautiful," Maria sighed. Oona clapped her hands in Maria's arms.

"See all the mirrors on the walls? And the candles on the ceiling? I bet they light when it grows dark," Adamina said. "I used to light my laboratory the same way."

"But the laboratory is downstairs. What is this *for*? Loads of shelves and mirrors on the walls. Four fireplaces at the cardinal points. And it's the highest floor in the tower, other than the roof."

"Let's look on the roof and see if it reveals anything," Maria suggested. Suddenly Macha turned and trotted out through the archway.

"Where is *she* going?" Annag asked. There was a ramp from the ninth floor directly to the roof. They followed it up, and Saorsa laughed.

"It's the *exact same* stone circle from inside the cave! And the table is back!" she smiled. "It's just on the roof now!"

"I think there's something here we can't see," Maria said, frowning. "I can hear...singing." She handed Oona to Adamina. "There are...definitely voices."

Malphas' flapped into view and perched on the northernmost stone. And following him from the sky were four crows. Each swooped down in turn and dropped something from their claws onto the table before taking to the skies once more. Saorsa moved closer to look.

A spiral seashell.

A tiny wooden doll's hand, worn with age.

A small replica crow's skull, carved from lapis.

An astragalus bone.

"Gifts," Willow breathed. "They are gifts." Saorsa picked them up and held the objects in her hands. Understanding blossomed; she didn't know where the clarity suddenly came from. But she knew, without question, that these items were for her, a part of her. Part of a *collection*.

What had Malphas said after she'd given him the second ring? *They are bringing you your bones.* A long-forgotten memory rose into her consciousness, hidden away for almost two decades. Sister Elen, sitting by the fish pond at the abbey. Laughing. *We'll have to find you a bag for your treasures, sweet Saorsa. Look at all these twigs and stones you've collected! And the seeds...and what's this? Why, it's a little bone. Part of a skull, I think. You're going to be a bone-thrower, perhaps. From the time the very first human tribes walked the earth, they have called on the magick of the bones. Would you like to hear a story?*

"I know what these are," she said, a smile spreading across her face. "Oh, Goddess, *I know what these are!*" The items felt warm in her hand, like the touch of an old friend. She felt like she'd been missing them all her life. Something in her mind, heart, and belly suddenly shifted and clicked into place. She'd never been a material person; but these four items were somehow now the most important items she owned next to Alex's ring.

"What?" Rune said. "Tell us!"

The Bone Wytches welcome you. Malphas has said something like that the night she'd had the vision in the cave. It had sounded familiar, but she hadn't been able to place it.

"It's my oracle," she whispered. "*My oracle.* We don't need Malphas to give us instructions. *They are coming to me.* They are traveling here now!"

"Saorsa? You're not making a lot of sense," Edan said, frowning.

Saorsa felt an overwhelming sense of joy bloom in her. *Yes. That's it.* "When I was little, Sister Elen told me a story. I loved it and made her tell it over and over." The memory was out now. It had been buried for years. "Mother Agnes knows the story! Mama, Annag, you might remember too." She began pacing excitedly. She turned to Svend. "It was a story about a seer in China who heated bones with script on them and read the cracks to see the future. They were later called *dragon bones.*"

"Yes, I remember," Annag said. "You asked for that story every day until she left."

Saorsa turned toward Rune. "And Sister Elen said the game of dice came from tossing astragalus bones to divine the future. That the Norsemen used to do it. And here in Scotland, people used to read patterns on bones to foretell events and answer questions. And in Africa they would toss bones and read the relationships. People around the world have used shells, curios, or bones for sacred practice since before the beginning of time. These...," she smiled, "are my *bones.* The beginning of a set. To *divine with.* To get us *answers.*" She looked around at the gathered group. "And that table downstairs is where I will cast them!" They went down the ramp and through the door to the room below.

"The raised edge will keep them from flying off the table." Saorsa placed her items carefully in the center of the spiral. "These are going to teach me. Guide me. Help me get in touch with my path, and help me become what was shown to me in the cave!"

At that moment Macha reappeared, part of a deer leg bone in her mouth. She trotted over to Rune and looked at him expectedly. "Am I supposed to take this?" Rune asked the wolf, confused. "Is it for me? Or Saorsa?" He put out his hand, and Macha deposited the bone in it and walked off.

"They're coming to you, Saorsa," Willow said excitedly. "The animals are *bringing* you the things you need! It's what the second ring does! The animals are bringing you your holy objects!"

"This is sun-bleached, hollow, and clean," Rune said. "I have experience working bone. Perhaps I will dream tonight and ask what it is to be used for. I've done that before."

"The Morrigan rules over the dead," Adamina said. "It makes sense that Thomas' magick might involve working with bones."

"I'll leave them here on the table and come up after lunch and sing to them, honor them, and ask them if they want to work with me," Saorsa said excitedly. "It feels like the right thing to do." *I know what to do. My Goddess, never in my life have I been so certain about what to do! Where has this come from? Is it Thomas? Malphas? Elen? Or have I discovered the magick in myself, MY form of magick, at last?*

"Will you do the same with this one?" Rune said, handing her the leg bone. "I will leave it here in the tower for a time, and if you say it wants to be fashioned by my hands to aid you, I will be honored to do it."

"Tonight, then," Saorsa said. "We begin moving into the tower after lunch, and then tonight we'll try the sphere and see what happens." She traced the edge of the table with her fingertips. "And I'll come sing to the bones!"

Glasgow, Scotland

The Queen Maeve Inn was a whorehouse in central Glasgow. Alex hadn't been there in a long time.

It was late afternoon, and the sky was covered with clouds. Alex tipped his tricorn hat forward to shade his eyes as he walked to the inn. He went through the front door, then through the large but crowded front room, ignoring the working girls who called out to him in greeting. He passed the bar and went through a swinging door behind it to a narrow hallway with multiple doors leading to rooms on either side. It was much quieter here, although the faint sounds of the whores tending to their clients reached his ears through the walls. He strode down the red carpet that lined the hallway to a desk at the end of the hall. A petite woman with fair skin and round, ample breasts in a black low-cut dress was sitting there looking at him with interest. Her eyes were an alert and captivating green, and her red hair was a mass of strawberry-colored ringlets.

Alex took off his hat and loosened his scarf so she could see his face, holding the rucksack in his hand. The woman sat up straighter and smiled. "*Thought* I recognized that walk. Like ye cannae put a foot wrong. Where've you been all this time, me darlin'?"

He gave her a smile. "Polly, it's good to see you."

Polly grinned and twisted a red curl around her finger flirtatiously. "I hope you're comin' straight to me for a bit o' fun, an' not 'cause ye want...."

Alex looked at her apologetically. "*Clíodhna.*"

"Och," Polly said, looking disappointed. "Ye ken the password." She reached into a drawer on the writing desk and produced a room key. "Sorry, Polly," Alex said to her with affection in his voice. "I hope ye have a good night, though, lass." He put a stack of coins on the desktop. "For your trouble."

Polly's eyes lit up at the sight of the coins, and she was on her feet in front of Alex in an instant. "Come now," she purred, "surely you've time for somethin' quick to warm ye before ye head to your room upstairs." She batted her eyelashes at him and slipped her hands around his waist, pulling him close. "Gwen an' Jenna are workin' tonight, they'll be free soon, ye could have the three of us again." She flashed her jade eyes up at him. "You always were our favorite."

Alex laughed. "I tip well, that's what it is, an' ye ken it." He patted her on the shoulder. "Thank ye kindly but no, Polly. No tonight."

Polly wasn't giving up that easily, however. "Ye dinnae have to wait, then. How about just you an' me? Got a free room right here." She stroked his thigh gently. "I ken just what ye like, *an' ye ken it*. Come an' get warm, an' I'll be on my knees before ye in no time. Ye want to put your fingers in these curls again, aye?"

Alex grinned. He admired her tenacity. "Polly, I'm *knackered*. Been travelin' for a long time. Besides, I'm no in the market anymore."

Polly stepped away. "No!" she cried. "Tell me you're lyin'!"

He shook his head and smiled. "Aye, Polly, I've fallen in love."
Polly sat down again in a huff. "Och, *so what?* Lots o' men fall in love. It doesnae mean they dinnae still need my services. Verra few wives ken how to do what *I* do. I bet your hen doesnae ken...."

"Her name is..."

Polly waved him off. "No, *dinnae tell me her name,* Alex! I'll just be tempted to curse it. She's snatched one of my favorite clients. You pay well an' you're sweet an' right easy on the eyes, an' that's a rare thing."

Alex threw back his head and laughed. "You think I'm *sweet,* eh? After that time with you an' Erin an' the lot of them?"

Polly rolled her eyes. "Aye, *sweet.* Ye never touch a girl to hurt. Ye just like things a wee bit rough sometimes. You've never left a mark on me, Alexander, so you're fine." She grumbled down at the desk. "*In love. Bollocks.* Well, come back when ye ask your lover girl for that thing we did on your birthday four years ago. She'll throw your filthy arse out in the street an' I'll be waitin' for ye with *open arms.*"

Alex slung his rucksack over his shoulder. "Thank ye, Polly. I'll keep that in mind."

"Hmph. Room 33."

"Good night, Polly." Alex turned away.

"It isn't a good night anymore!" she called after him. "*In love, my arse!*"

....

Alex made his way upstairs. He'd set up a safe house here a few years ago after handling a bit of illegal business for the owner. The room number changed, but a room was always available. Duncan used it on occasion, and Vika and her trainers did as well. Its only drawback was its location in a highly populated area. Luckily, Glasgow was quickly becoming a town where it was easy to disappear into a crowd.

He was fitting the key into the lock when the door unexpectedly opened from the inside. A dying fire inside the room left most of the interior space in an early evening gloom.

Someone was already here.

"*Am madadh-allaidh agus an fheannag...,*" a voice inside the room whispered. *The wolf and crow...*

"*...na fàg ni sam bith de'n mharbh,*" Alex answered, his hand on his knife. *Leave nothing of the kill.*

Two lanterns suddenly flamed to life, illuminating the room, and two people stepped into the doorway. "I can't fucking believe it," said an incredulous Vika MacLeod.

"Get yer arse in here, kid," rasped Duncan. Alex's knees nearly buckled with relief as he stepped forward, and the door shut behind him.

………

"The Violet Woman said Haggs Castle," Alex finished after telling Duncan and Vika a very abbreviated version of his journey north, running his hand over his head. "Have ye heard anythin' about this?"

"Aye, that's why we're here," Duncan replied. "Do ye remember a man named Tobias Greene?"

Alex nodded. "A bit. You helped his brother, aye?"

Duncan nodded. "Sprung the brother from a transport just before the Uprising an' got him on a boat to America. Tobias has been a valuable informant ever since. He works the military ships now on the west coast of England. Brings news up from London, leaves it in drops for us when he's in port. After Vika an' I met up at Morrigan's Cave, we stopped what we thought was a Crown carriage with a tax man inside for a bit o' ready cash. Turned out to have Jacobite prisoners bein' taken south inside as well. Man an' wife. Clan Stuart, too."

"We decided to escort them this way," Vika chimed in. "See if we could find them a ship to France. And on the way, we find the message from Tobias. His ship was bringing some Crown dignitaries to Glasgow to oversee the execution of Saorsa Stuart at Haggs Castle. He didn't know the date it would be set for, but it would be soon. This was the day before yesterday."

"I didnae believe it," Duncan said. "I mean, Edan sent Saorsa west with Rune MacAskill an' his men. They're *verra* capable. That one man he has, Eske, I've seen him kill men with his bare hands. An' Rune'll have ye in pieces before ye realize you're dead with those axes of his. But Saorsa didnae say where she was headed after Fenwick. I think she was worried Fia would ken it somehow. Saorsa an' Edan, they kept the plans verra close. So since we were already here, an' we didnae want to take the chance that she *was* here...."

"We thought we'd check it out," Vika finished. "The madame here had no new information about Saorsa but *has* had a few rather wealthy English clients in the building in the last day or so. Including a judge."

"We spent a good part of the day lookin' into the castle itself," Duncan offered. "Even managed to get a map. There are a lot of guards on the grounds for nothin' to be goin' on." He stroked his salt-and-pepper beard thoughtfully. "I'm startin' to think Saorsa's in there."

"Did anyone say anythin' about Maria?" Alex asked.

"No," Vika said. "You said she was at the Tower of London?"

"Aye. An' I thought they were plannin' to bring Maria here an' hang Maria and Saorsa together."

"Shite," Vika said, sitting back in her chair. "So, *both* of them could be in there." She raised her eyebrows and looked at Alex. "We could use more help. Too bad you didn't show up with a bunch of friends."

"Vika," grinned Alex, "I have somethin' I think you'll like." He stood and walked to the center of the room, and a moment later Vika and Duncan MacLeod were looking at five Alexander Scotts, who simultaneously folded their arms and gave Vika a sly grin.

Vika sighed. "Jesus *Christ.* This is simultaneously good news *and my worst nightmare.* I can barely tolerate *one* of you. Tell me some of these duplicates are *less* of an arsehole."

"Figured if other *leth dhia* could do it, I could, too," Alex explained. "An'...*voila!*"

Duncan just sat absolutely still, eyes wide. Vika noticed and smiled at her brother. "You alright, *bràthair mòr?*"

"I dinnae ken," he said slowly. "I...*sweet Mother o' God.*"

"How many can you make?" Vika was beginning to get excited about the possibilities.

Primary Alex shrugged. "Dinnae ken. Been into the low teens before, I think. After that, my head gets kind o' full." He closed his eyes for a moment, and three more Alexes appeared and began wandering around the room, doing Alex-y things. "Each of us can think for themselves. But if one sees somethin' the others should know of, we can share the thought."

"Well, I'll be a possum's twelfth tit," Vika grinned, watching one Alex build up the fire while another locked the door. "This will work *very* nicely."

Duncan had recovered somewhat. "Aye, V, except that if they're all Alex, not a single one of them will listen to a damn thing ye have to say." Vika smirked and threw a pillow at her brother.

………

"Can we go in tonight?" Alex asked, after the three of them had eaten and Vika and Duncan had gone over all the information on Haggs Castle that they had. "We have two uniforms. You seem to know when patrols change. This unused chimney in the old section seems a way in. Can we go?"

Vika looked appraisingly at Alex. "You're *exhausted.*"

"I slept last night, MacLeod. An' if ye think I'll be dreamin' like a bairn when Saorsa might be ten streets over awaitin' her execution...."

Duncan patted Alex on the back. "I understand. But we're plannin' on doin' this with twelve people, an' ten o' them are *you.* It's nearly seven already."

"Can you get the cart?" Alex asked, undeterred. Duncan could see the desperation in Alex's eyes. "They could be *hurtin'* her. I cannae take that."

Vika took a deep breath. *If we don't go tonight, he'll be in a worse place tomorrow. He might even try to go in on his own.* "Alex. I'm willing to go tonight if you follow the plan I've set out."

Alex shook his head. "There's no need for ye to go in with me. Why risk yourself when I can do it alone? Ye can stay on the perimeter."

Vika added a sterner note to her voice. "No. You are emotional about this, Alex. That's when things go wrong. Now, I want Saorsa out too, but I think my head's a bit clearer than yours. Duncan will handle the cart and I'll be on the roof. Close by in case something goes wrong."

Alex looked at Duncan. "I'm in for tonight too, if ye listen to Vika. Her plan's the best one," he said calmly.

"All right," Alex said. "How long?"

"I'll go fetch the cart now," Duncan said. "When I get back, we can go." Alex nodded and looked down, his gray eyes trained on the floor. *Please let Saorsa be alright.*

Wolfcroft, Scotland

Toran, Aeric, Eske, and Trig returned after nightfall. Once the animals were settled for the night, everyone returned to the Tower of Roses to eat supper in the kitchen. Everything felt new in the tower, full of possibility. They had brought all their food and clothing, and Malphas' perch. Each room had fresh bed linens and the kitchen came equipped with beautiful earthenware dishes and iron pots and pans. Eske rejoiced in the self-lighting fireplaces that never ran out of wood, and the candles that never seemed to lose their height. Even the pantry and supply room off the kitchen was a wonder, full of fresh brooms with colored broom straw and a multitude of beautiful baskets.

They carried baskets of rose petals to the kitchen to shred and set in the cast iron pots to boil after dinner. The room soon smelled of roses, and everyone took turns stirring the pots as the petals boiled down.

"I'm going up to talk to the bones," Saorsa announced. "Macha, will you stay here to help people use the archways? I won't be long." The wolf moved closer to the staircase in response.

Saorsa passed through archway after archway in the quiet tower until she came to the bone room, her spiral progress reminiscent of priestesses of old following a path up a mountain to worship. She stood by the table for a time, looking at the deer bone and the items the crows had brought. After she felt her mind settle, she lifted her voice and began to sing a song of welcome.

At first, the song didn't have words. Just clear notes, echoing through the room. And then the words came. She lifted her voice in gratitude for this place. For the freedom of her mother, Duncan, and Adamina. For her own freedom, and the freedom she hoped Alex would soon have. She sang over the bones and to them. A song of a woman putting down roots. A song of a woman who was following her calling, no matter what others might think.

She sang for blessings for Mother Agnes and Vika. A song of thankfulness for Thomas. A melody for Edan, Willow, and Rune, and everyone who lifted her up and believed in her, even when she didn't believe in herself. She sang for Oona and for Fia's unborn child. And for the child she might yet bear herself.

And she sang to Alex. *No matter where you are, know that I love you.* Tears flowed down her cheeks, but she didn't wipe them away. *I am becoming something else now. Something more. Something not everyone will understand. I am becoming unashamed.*

It was what she had sensed in Vika. What she had wanted but couldn't put her finger on. *People tell women we are not supposed to enjoy ourselves, not supposed to desire, not supposed to chase our own dreams,* Vika had said on more than one occasion. *And that, my sister, is a lie.* Vika lived without shame. She was strong. Opinionated. Outspoken. Traveled. Enjoyed her lovers and didn't hide it. *I think I am finally walking that same path.*

I will be the witch I was meant to be. Do the work I was meant to do. Lead my clan and protect it. I will keep the old ways alive, where the Goddess of Battle is a woman.

Thomas has given me an opportunity humans aren't supposed to have, and tools we aren't supposed to touch. I will take it all and rejoice.

She heard the bones speak to her from the table in the candle-lit room. *We have traveled far to fulfill the next step in our path. Let us be allies.*

She could sense the energy of the wolves in the cave far below under the base of the Tower of Roses, as they moved into the evening to hunt. *Let us be good neighbors. For we are both wild things now.*

She was ready. It was time to pull magick into the tower, her tower.

She went downstairs to tell the others to be prepared. She was going to activate the Sphere.

Glasgow, Scotland

Duncan returned. The siblings made a habit of carrying British army uniforms with them when they traveled. People often didn't notice faces, but they respected uniforms. Alex and Vika changed into the uniforms. Alex was lucky that Duncan was only an inch shorter than he was. "Tight in the shoulders," Alex grumbled. "Cut's all wrong."

"If you split yourself in that, they'll all be dressed accordingly, right?" Vika verified.

"Aye."

They went over the plan one more time. Duncan would go ahead with the wagon to be near Haggs Castle. In the center of the bed of the cart he'd placed a long, low shipping crate, big enough for two people to lie in. Around the box went bags of refuse, and a tarp covered the whole thing. Vika and Duncan had witnessed carts making deliveries and carting away trash from Haggs Castle until ten the night before; half of the estate was in working order and the other half was being renovated. If Maria or Saorsa weren't in physical condition to walk far, they could be hidden in the crate and driven off the property. Duncan was counting on no redcoat wanting to dig through trash.

Vika and Alex would move into position during the upcoming patrol change. Alex would send four duplicates to various positions to keep watch on Duncan's route while he and Vika made their way to the roof above the renovations. There were several very tall old trees right near the building and almost no moon. Alex, who was a talented climber, would go up the trees to the roof first and secure a rope for Vika. Once on the roof they'd send Alex down the very large, crumbling chimney with Vika and a duplicate to guard the way out. Once he was inside, Alex would generate four more of himself and they'd fan out to hunt for Maria and Saorsa.

"You can skip the basement," Duncan pointed out. "I think that's where the soldiers are housed. They go in an' out that basement door all day. Way too much activity to have a prisoner there. An' there's almost no guards on the part bein' renovated. My guess is that if mother an' daughter are there, they're in the new building, up high."

"If they are trying to get amulet shards out of the Stuarts, they'll need a lot of light for surgery," Vika suggested. "Head for rooms with east-facing windows first."

It was time to go. "Ah, feels like old times," Vika grinned, jamming a knife into the holder on her belt. "No moon. Stolen clothes. And way too many redcoats." Duncan said a brief prayer for success and safety, and they headed to Haggs Castle. Everyone they passed was bundled up in scarves, as they were. It would go a long way toward keeping them disguised.

Alex followed Vika through the cobblestone streets silently. No ice. A dry night. Good for climbing. He couldn't help but smile watching Vika walk the crowded Glasgow streets; she had such a commanding stride and focus that most nearly threw themselves out of her way to avoid being run over. She knew where she was going and walked like it. It was one of the many things he had learned from her.

He felt better, following in Vika's wake. He was tired of cutting through the currents of his life on his own; it was soothing to let someone else do the pushing aside. *If Saorsa and Maria are here and we can get them out, I will sleep for days. Perhaps weeks.*

He had slept barely at all since London. Part of it was his rush to get to Saorsa; but part of it was the nightmares that plagued him. He'd never felt such evil in his life as he'd felt on Tower Hill; thousands of people crying for the death of a man they didn't know, and didn't care to know. In Alex's mind, compassion for others was the quality that made one human. If you lacked it, you were little more than a monster. He'd stood in front of a mob of monsters that day. He'd had nightmares about it ever since.

A high brick wall surrounded the spacious grounds of the castle. Vika continued right past the front gates and followed the perimeter of the wall along a service road that led to the rear of the property. The 16th century tower house had additions from recent years, and this large, more modern addition seemed to be the focus of most of the activity. The old section of the castle, steep-roofed and four stories tall, boasted a massive chimney that went all the way down to the kitchen on the ground floor. The old section was either in limited use or unused completely, and parts of it had fallen into disrepair. They'd have to be very careful on the pitch of that roof. There was no flat area on which to stand.

They rounded the corner of the wall and continued to follow it into the shade of the pine trees near a service entrance. A wagon rolled past, delivering firewood. Duncan would come this way with his wagon later. For now, they needed to focus on going *up*. Once the wagon was gone, Alex tapped Vika on the shoulder, and she paused for a moment. She moved on again when she saw four additional Alexander Scotts move off into the darkness.

They passed through the service entrance. A guard glanced at them but said nothing. In their hats and long uniform coats, their profile fit that of two soldiers returning from town. When a carriage clattered out on the gravel path, Vika and Alex ducked behind an old tool shed that provided cover from prying eyes. They rounded the shed and headed toward the trees on the inside of the wall that bordered the house.

Alex's eyes had adjusted to the dark by now. Still, it was a struggle to remove his climbing equipment from under his coat and get himself safely anchored to the tree. The pine was around eighty feet tall, and the branches didn't start for quite a long way up; it was going to be slow going, using the ropes to go up in stages until he hit the lowest branch. He grinned. *Imagine if I survived being hung on Tower Hill only to fall to death from a Scots pine because I didn't tie my rope correctly.*

He started up. Soon he couldn't see Vika below at all in the darkness. He got into a rhythm of activity. One rope. Move. Then the other. Move. The light background noise of his duplicates' thoughts was comforting. *All well here. Nothing but wagons. No one headed toward the back of the house.* He was almost startled when he found himself among the branches of the tree.

He could move faster now, much faster, and soon he saw the roof's edge. It was full of various steeples, decorative sculptures, and three chimneys. There were lots of options to tie on to. The only problem was he couldn't get a good look at them in the dark to see which ones were *stable*. He threw his rope around a massive decoration at the apex of one point, only to feel it move when he tugged on it. He climbed a bit higher. There was a smaller chimney close by. After a few tries, he was able to secure the rope.

He dropped a rope for Vika to climb. She made several bird calls to communicate with him: *ready*. A short time later, *wait*. Then *ready* again. Before he knew it, she was perched in the tree near him. He made the jump to the roof first; then she made her way across. They were going to need lots of ropes up here to keep Vika and a duplicate on the roof, and to get Alex down the main chimney. He prayed Maria and Saorsa were conscious and able-bodied. Trying to get them off this roof would be next to impossible if they weren't – and an incredible challenge even if they were. *I'll need to be looking for another way out.* While the guards they'd passed weren't terribly aware of what was going on around them, there *were* a lot of them. Trying to fight their way out and then disappear would be impossible. They were only going to be successful here through stealth.

"Get close," Alex whispered to Vika once they were both safely anchored. "I may slip out of this rope when I make a copy o' me, an' the new man willnae have anythin' to hold onto."

"Got it," Vika answered. Alex loosened his harness a bit, and thus was able to stay inside the rope even when duplicating. He looked over to find her holding his copy firmly by the arm.

"To avoid confusion when we're together," Vika whispered, "you, original Alex, are *Alex*. And you," she said, handing a rope to Alex's duplicate, "are now called *Doug*."

"No," both Alexes whispered in unison.

"I dinnae like *Doug*," the copy complained.

"It's either that or Susan," Vika said, making her way to the large chimney and getting the ropes in place. "Your choice, Doug."

Doug sighed. "Why do you always have to make things *harder?*"

"'Cause it's fun. Okay, Alex, we have a secure rope. Doug, are you locked in place? Hopefully Alex won't have to bring anyone out this way, but if he does, your main job is to help anyone coming out of this chimney to make sure they don't fall." She turned to Alex. "Whenever you're ready."

He nearly lost his footing climbing into the crumbling chimney, and they all froze as a few bricks clattered down the roof and fell to the earth below. Alex promoted a thought. *Anyone down there hear that? Any guards coming to investigate?*

No, came the answer. *You're in the clear.* He began his descent.

………

The old section of the castle was, indeed, abandoned, save for storing piles of military provisions and decaying furniture. Alex emerged from the fireplace on the fourth floor. He duplicated himself and sent the copies on their way down the main stairwell. *One on the first floor, new section. One on the second, new. One on the third, new. One to look around here in the old section to find a way out that doesn't entail using the roof.* There was a good chance a lot of the doors would be chained to prevent theft of government property, but if he could pick a lock on a quiet side of the building it would make everything easier.

He would take the fourth floor in the new section for himself. He had a feeling he'd find any prisoners there. He set off to find a way into the new section of the building. There were four corner towers, two of which had east-facing windows: *that's where I'll begin.*

He picked his way through the room, looking for a door that would take him to the more recently built section of the castle. *There might not be one. Might have to go down a floor.* The front wall of the building was large, and he lit a candle to help him see. *There could be a door here, but there's so much shite stacked in the way it's hard to see it.*

He heard a thought from his duplicate on the first floor: *I have a prisoner roster. A guard just signed it after finishing his rounds! Left it right here. Give me a moment.* Alex froze, and listened, barely able to breathe. His duplicate was reading rapidly.

James MacDonald-transferred.
Alexander MacLea-transferred.
Brian Ogilvy.
Jack Hay.
Lyall MacInnes.
Sophie Stuart.

Not Saorsa Stuart? You're sure? Alex's heart was in his mouth.

Sophie. And says 'transferred'. Alexander Oliphant. Harris MacIver. A pause. Then, *she's here. Saorsa Stuart.*

Alex had a visceral reaction to the news. He was, at the same time, triumphant and terrified; enraged and overcome with longing. For a moment he felt horrifically dizzy. His duplicate kept reading, and finally he realized what was being said. *There's no Maria. No Maria Stuart. She's not here.*

The feeling of gratitude nearly knocked Alex sideways. *Only one to get out. Just one.* He'd worried about moving Maria; the fact that she'd recently sustained multiple surgeries while her body and soul were separated for weeks meant she might be impossibly weak or comatose, to say nothing of her mental state. *Where the hell is she, then? Still en route? Had Laoise somehow gotten her out? Was she even alive?*

There was nothing he could do in this moment. *Worry later. You've got to find your lass now.* His other aspects were hearing his thoughts, trying to encourage him and keep him sane. He kept moving, hunting for the door. At last, he found it. He had to move an old sofa, dresser, and three heavy crates, but there it was. *Locked.* He put the candle back down and pulled his lock picking tools from his belt.

His hands were shaking. *She could be right on the other side of this wall.* He heard the aspect exploring the old section of the castle say something about a window, but he was too focused on the task at hand.

Click. He turned the door handle and found himself near the end of a long hallway full of doors. *East side, maybe. If they were trying to take the amulet shards out, her room might be on the east side.*

A guard appeared at the end of the hall, patrolling. *So, not officer's rooms up here. Prisoners.* He shut the door most of the way, and waited until the guard moved past. There were candles lit on the wall sconces in the hallway. Alex could see a ring of keys on the man's belt.

A grandfather clock in the hallway began to chime out the hour, and Alex grinned. *Lucky timing.* He moved quickly behind the guard, grabbed him by the neck, and slammed his head into a marble pillar hard enough to knock him unconscious. The chiming clock masked any sounds. A few minutes later he'd dragged the man through the door to the old castle attic and had tied his hands and feet, gagging him with a strip from one of the sheets that had been used to cover the sofa and keep the dust off. Key ring safely in hand, he went back into the new section of the castle and checked for evidence of his deeds.

There was some blood on the carpet, but the carpet was red. *The odds of someone noticing are slim.* He promoted a thought to his compatriots. *Everyone from the new section to the top two floors. Start picking locks. If you find a prisoner you can get to the old castle without letting on we're here, do so. The names on that list are all from clans that participated in the Uprising. This is a Jacobite holding area.*

And if you run across Caroline Frederick Scott and can do so safely, send him to meet his maker.

Alex was trying keys on all the rooms on the east side. The first one was locked but empty. The second, unlocked. In the third he found a young man, no older than eighteen, with bruises on his face.

"What's your name?"

"Jack Hay, sir."

"I'm no a British officer. My name is Alexander Scott. I have a way out. Follow me." The young man did so without question. Alex took him to the door to the old castle. "Through here, go straight. You'll find a verra big fireplace at the far end in the center with a rope. Pull on the rope when you are there. People at the top will help." The lad looked strong. The young man nodded, eyes wide, and took off.

Alex promoted a thought to his counterpart on the roof with Vika. *Tell Vika a young man is coming. Jack Hay. Help him out.* Back to try the next door. No one inside.

He saw a shadow at the other end of the hall and started, then realized it was one of his duplicates with another ring of keys, opening rooms on the north side of the building. Alex continued down the east side. The next room one held an older man named Harris MacIver. A man who recognized him from their time marching with the Bonnie Prince, even though Alex didn't remember him.

"Dear God! You're the Quartermaster! I don't understand." He stared at Alex, trying to reconcile the Crown uniform with who he knew him to be.

"Long live the King Over the Water. Come with me. *Sending Harris McIver to the roof exit. Tell Vika.* The man rose and followed Alex with great haste. Alex showed him the door and repeated the directions, and the man moved into the gloom of the old castle's attic.

He could hear his other aspects promoting thoughts. *Two soldiers unconscious on floor three.*

Got window exit on floor one open! Good cover. Send any other liberated prisoners here.

Found Lyall MacInnes. Taking him to window exit in old castle, floor one.

Guard down on floor four. Unconscious. Locked in room.

Jack Hay is on the roof.

Tell Vika we have another way out. After MacIver, get the hell off that roof!

We have a guard walking into the old castle on floor three! Down. He's down.

We have an unusual patrol circling near the old castle outside.

MacIver can't go down the rope. He's panicking. Might need to send him back down the chimney.

Found Alexander Oliphant! Floor four.

Jack Hay halfway down.

I'll meet him under the trees!

A prisoner here. Badly beaten. Not conscious.

Alex's emotions were running high. *Get that prisoner out if you can. There's room in Duncan's cart.*

Aye. Splitting myself to carry.

Alex was running back to the last room on the east side, the corner room. He found the key, slammed it into the lock, and turned it. Alex threw open the door and raced into the room.

Two more men here. Sending them down.

A man and his wife. Sending them down.

The room was dark, save for a single candle on the floor by the window. The glow illuminated a young woman sitting next to it with her back turned to Alex. Sitting and sobbing. A young woman with a mop of beautiful blonde curls.

"Saorsa?" Alex gasped. *"Saorsa?"* He knew immediately in his heart something was wrong.

Wolfcroft, Scotland

Saorsa Stuart looked at the Siphon Globe and then at Laoise and Adamina. "Any idea how I turn it on?"

Adamina smiled. "Try using your *will*. That's what a certain Fae general I know would do."

Laoise nodded. "Touch it, and try to send your emotions into it. It's worth a try."

Saorsa took a deep breath, closed her eyes, and grounded herself. And thought of her desire to raise power. Nothing.

"Try again," Laoise said hopefully. "There's no levers or weights that I can see. No mechanism to get it to start. I think it has to come from *you*."

"Maybe I'm not strong enough," Saorsa said. "Maybe I have to learn more first."

Adamina put her hand on Saorsa's back. "Although I don't have much firsthand knowledge of magick, I have read enough to know that much of it is driven not by knowledge, but by feeling." She took a step forward and put her arm around Saorsa's shoulders. "Saorsa Stuart, do you love my son?"

Saorsa's eyes welled with tears. "Yes," she whispered.

"What would you do for him?"

Saorsa swallowed hard. *"Anything."*

"And what is your greatest fear where he is concerned?"

Laoise stepped forward, listening. Saorsa could barely bring herself to confess it. Especially not to Alex's *mother*. "Things went...things went *wrong*. Things were perfect. *So* perfect. And then they weren't. He lost himself. I lost *myself*. We hurt each other, but we were just doing the best we could." She took a deep breath. "I'm afraid we won't make it back there. To the place where we hoped and trusted, and... just *loved*. I can forgive. I'm already there. But when we last spoke, he needed *time*. He wouldn't come to me. Let himself just *be* with me. My greatest fear is that...," she shuddered, "he'll never feel safe with me again."

"Raise your hands," Adamina said. Saorsa lifted her hands toward the sphere. And a spark shot out from her hands toward the smooth quartz surface. Laoise's eyes widened.

"Keep talking about him," Adamina instructed. "Tell me what you want if he *does* return."

"I want...," said Saorsa, as another bolt of electricity shot from her palm, "I want *a life* together. I want to *stop running*. I want a home by the sea, Alex in my arms, and to just do *nothing* with him. Sit by the shore and watch the clouds and laugh." Another bolt of lightning moved into the quartz, this time colored blue. "I want the Fae to *leave us alone!*"

Laoise stepped closer. "Keep going!" she whispered.

"They take *everything!*" Saorsa howled, as the entire sphere suddenly began to glow with an eerie blue light, and the energy bolts from Saorsa's hands became more frequent. "My freedom! My childhood! My dignity! My mother! My friends! I *won't let them take him too!*"

The sphere began to rotate slowly, and began gaining momentum, and a humming noise filled the room. "Tell me of the Violet Woman!" Adamina cried.

The sphere gained momentum, and the entire room was filled with sound and light. "Let her come here!" Saorsa bellowed above the din. "*Let her come here, and be devoured by wolves when I crush her and hurl her body to the base of the Tower of Roses!*"

The four massive copper cylinders with the inset strips of glass in the corners of the room suddenly seemed to be filling with a strange substance. It bubbled and frothed, drifted and dripped, in a mix of black, blue, and silver hues.

"You've done it!" Laoise shouted. "It's *working*! Keep your hands up! Keep them up until the chambers are filled! The magick is *flowing this way!*"

Glasgow, Scotland

"Saorsa?" Alex said softly as he crossed the room. His mind didn't want to believe it. But his heart *knew*. He crouched next to the young woman on the floor who turned at his approach. The same height. The head of golden ringlets. The same fair skin. Eyes of a stunning *blue*.

Not Saorsa.

The woman, not much more than a girl, whimpered and recoiled in terror. He saw a dark bruise along her cheekbone. "Oh, lass, I'm no here to harm ye," he said softly. "What's your name?"

She just stared. He didn't want to think about what they might have done to this girl. "My name is Alex," he said, putting out his hand. She winced and moved further away. "Have ye seen a woman named Saorsa Stuart? Blonde hair like yours. Hazel eyes. I'm here to get her out, and I can get ye out too. Tell me where she is."

"I'm not Saorsa," mumbled the girl. "I'm not Saorsa."

Alex took a breath. "Tell me your name, then."

"Elphinstone."

Alex ran a hand over his head. "Do ye ken an Arthur Elphinstone? He was a good friend of mine. Was a colonel in the Jacobite army."

The girl began to sob. "They killed him. On Tower Hill. My uncle. They...."

Alex sighed. "Aye. I know. On Tower Hill. Four months past." *Beheaded,* Alex thought. *And from what they say, a gentleman to the end.*

"I'm Alexander Scott. I was the Bonnie Prince's Quartermaster. Come with me. I'll help you." The girl blinked. *She thinks every man is a threat.* "Your uncle would want ye to come with me an' help, lass. Saorsa is the Bonnie Prince's niece. An' she's here, somewhere." *Time is short. She needs to decide to come soon, or I'll have to leave her. My God, where is Saorsa?*

Thirty-one miles away, unbeknownst to Alex, the subject of his inquiry and affection had just activated a process that was leeching all of the magickal energy from the area to store at the top of a dark tower.

An absolutely horrifying sensation shot through Alex's brain. The voices of his duplicates - *all of his duplicates* - who had been thinking in the background, keeping him informed, suddenly went dead silent. The silence in his head was so unexpected he jumped. *What the hell?*

"Maggie," the girl cried. "My name is Maggie. But the guards call me Saorsa. They *think I'm Saorsa!*" The girl's voice was raising, heading for hysterics. "They're going to kill me! In one week! *Saturday!*"

Alex looked at her sharply. "The guards think *you're* Saorsa Stuart?" *What the hell was going on? Where were his duplicates? What was this girl talking about?* He suddenly had the chilling sensation he was inside a nightmare.

Duncan got out. Adamina got out. Maybe Maria has escaped as well. They don't have my Fae side, and they don't have Saorsa.

Saorsa had never been here at all. Caroline Scott, or the Violet Woman, or both, were going to execute this poor girl and pretend that they had executed Saorsa Stuart. As a show of strength. To try and convince someone higher up the food chain that the plans they had in place were working; to buy them time to right the ship. A lie to save face after other defeats. And all the underlings believed the lie, and called this poor girl *Saorsa.*

"You're *sure* she's not here?" Alex said shakily, disconcerted by the silence in his own head. "You're *sure?* She wasn't here and they... moved her?" He wanted to see her so badly it pained him.

"They think I'm her! They think I'm her! But I'm not! *I'm Maggie!*"

....

On the roof, Vika breathed a sigh of relief as the rope went slack. *MacIver is on the ground. Jesus, that was hard.* "My turn, I guess," Vika said, turning to the duplicate she called Doug.

He started to say something, and then vanished in front of her eyes.

"Doug?" Vika looked around. *Maybe this was some sort of skill the duplicates had she didn't know about.* "Doug?" She paused for a moment. "*Susan?*"

She looked down at the field below. Another duplicate had been pacing a track near the wall, keeping watch. He was gone as well. Something must have happened to Alex.

"Oh *shite*," Vika muttered. Alex and Saorsa could be injured inside. She stood still for a moment, thinking, then checked her ropes and began lowering herself down the inside of the chimney, praying the crumbling masonry she was anchored to would hold.

....

Nigel Cook was going places. He hadn't been in the British military for long. He'd been transferred to Haggs Castle as part of a group of soldiers who would help prepare the castle grounds for the hanging of Saorsa Stuart and several other Jacobites in a week's time. Nigel was eighteen years old, full of energy and eager, with a quick mind that never forgot a detail or a face. He often noticed things his fellow soldiers didn't.

He was crossing the castle lawn, returning from town, when he noticed something in the dim winter night. A figure, running in the distance, and disappearing out the service entrance. The figure moved like a middle-aged *woman*. He was certain he saw the outline of skirts. And the figure didn't move like someone bundled in outwear. No fullness around the head and torso.

His mind went to the guard he'd shadowed that morning. *Two women here. One is Saorsa Stuart. She's the most important one. Charles Stuart's niece. Wanted on her own, as well. Runs with the MacLeods. Never enter her room without at least three others with you. She's a witch. And you know what I say? That Alexander Scott, he's the demon that works for her. That's what I say. An unholy union if there ever was one.*

The second woman, she's in with her husband. Silent, those two. Older. They willnae give you any trouble. Last name is Murray. The guard had opened the door to the Murrays' room, and he'd had a look at them. Nigel was absolutely certain he'd just seen Mrs. Murray fleeing the old castle. And then he saw *more* movement. At the base of the east wall of the old castle, near the pine trees.

He raced toward the closest patrol. "Whistle!" he yelled, his mind moving so fast he didn't even think to explain. The startled guard handed his whistle to Cook. And young Nigel Cook blew three long bursts into it. *Escaped prisoner! Escaped prisoner!*

An officer on duty nearby came tearing over toward the sound. *"What? Where?"*

"Old castle!" Nigel shouted. "East wall, sir!"

More men were moving, awaiting instructions from the officer. Other patrols took out their whistles and sounded the alarm. *Escaped prisoner! Lock down the grounds!* The lawns outside of the castle suddenly came alive with soldiers shouting and running in all directions.

Reinforcements moved quickly toward the walls and gates. A bell began to clamor, and halfway down the chimney Vika heard the noise and looked up at the sound. "Oh, *come on*," she sighed, just before the bricks her rope was tethered to on the roof crumbled and gave way, and she started to fall.

·········

What had his other aspect in the old castle said? A window. First floor. The way out. "Come," said Alex, putting out his hand toward Maggie. "It's time to go."

"They're going to kill me." Maggie gasped, and began looking around the room as though Alex wasn't there. "Kill me. Kill me. Kill me."

She's mad, Alex thought. *Lost her mind with fear and worry.*

"I'm not Saorsa. I'm not Saorsa," the girl babbled.

Alex heard a whistle blast outside. And another. And another. And then voices, and more whistles. He stood up. "Lass, ye need to come with me *now* if ye want to keep breathin'!" He pulled a knife from his belt. "Come *on!*" The girl stood up, and he realized how thin she was. She was smaller than he'd realized, too. *She can't be more than fifteen. Christ Almighty.*

"Everyone thinks they're looking at *her,*" the girl said, her voice rising to a wail, her eyes unseeing. "But I'm not her, I'm *me!*"

Lucid one minute, gone the next. If he dragged her out the door, he was fairly certain she'd scream. And this room would be the first one her jailers would run to now that the alarm had been sounded. *They're already on their way.*

He needed to go. *Now.* He and Vika might be able to fight their way out somehow. This girl...she was already gone. Taking her would only make their retreat harder.

Go! a part of his mind screamed. *You can't save her!* But he couldn't let a girl suffer and die in Saorsa's place on the gallows, either. He knew all too well the terror of standing on the platform, staring the worst of humanity right in the eyes and watching the noose sway in the breeze. He couldn't let that happen to this girl. It would be inhumane. There was no peace in that sort of death.

He swore under his breath and returned the knife to his belt, then grabbed Maggie roughly by the arm, pulling her back against his chest. She began screaming and flailing, beside herself with fear. "I'm so sorry, lass," he whispered, as his strong hand closed around her neck. "I'm *so sorry*."

………

Vika managed to catch herself on the base of the fourth-floor fireplace before almost plummeting straight down the back of the cavernous chimney into the basement below. *Holy shite. Shite, shite, shite.* She pulled herself up painfully over the massive iron log holder on the floor of the fireplace, out through the fireplace and into the attic. The rope around her waist was no longer attached to the roof. *Well, that way out was a pain in the ass anyway.*

Once on her feet again she untied the rope, coiled it, and threw it over her arm. *Might still need it.* She pulled two throwing knives out of her belt. *Right, time to get down to business. Find Alex.*

She wasn't sure how Duncan would handle this turn of events, but didn't let herself think that far ahead. *In the moment. Focus. This floor first.* She moved forward, pulling up the map of the castle in her mind. *Check the east side first.*

She heard the men outside now, shouting, but put it out of her mind. She found her breath and followed it, her chin up, her mind alert. *I am one with my environment. I am the predator here. I move in my own time.* Everything else in her mind fell away. She moved forward, silent and catlike, toward the north wall of the old castle.

She saw the door Alex had gone through and the bound man on the floor. She paused as she listened at the door to the hallway. She heard footsteps and pivoted, back to the wall, knives at the ready. *The man on the other side of the door was moving with haste and effort, and wasn't keeping quiet.* She raised her knives.

The man opened the door with a light kick, and Vika nearly let her knives fly before she realized who she was looking at: Alex with a knife in one hand and an unconscious teenage girl over his shoulder.

Via lowered her knives. "Alex! Are you alright?"

"No!" Alex spat. "Saorsa's no here! An' this lass is heavier than she looks! Had to choke her out!"

Vika grinned in the dark. This was not the first time she'd seen Alex mad at himself for having a conscience. *His brain wants him to run on pure logic, but his heart's just too damn big.* The girl was going to be a liability, but Vika was on board. "We can't go out the roof. Things crumbled."

"Window on the first floor is how the others went," Alex said, holstering his knife in his belt. "But I imagine that will get blocked right quick. Is Duncan here?"

Vika was busy barricading the door with furniture and small supply crates and barrels. *These little casks are full of whisky. The strong stuff. Gods above, I could use a good shot of this now.* "No idea. Where'd your other selves go?"

Alex sighed. "No idea." He looked at Vika. "Got a plan?"

I need to get my team out of this. Vika's mind snapped into action. "Supplies. What do you have?"

"Four throwing knives. Lockpick. Dirk. Fire startin' supplies."

Vika frowned, thinking. "Bring the girl. Follow me." *We need to go down. Any way we can, we need to go down. If they catch us up here, we're done for.*

Alex repositioned Maggie across his shoulders and began to follow, being as quiet as he could. Vika began walking back toward the fireplace, then changed her mind and took a sharp right toward the west side of the castle. *What do I have? Rope. Lockpick. Eight knives. Fire starting supplies. Basic first aid kit. What's around?*

Furniture. Crates. Tools. They're using this floor for wine, beer, and whisky storage. So it's not easily accessible to the men, and they can ration it.

It's freezing outside. Will that help? Soldiers. What do they have? Swords. Disguises. Pistols....

"Who's the girl?" Vika asked, her mind looking for an option.

"Maggie Elphinstone. But everyone thinks she's Saorsa."

Via stopped walking. *"Everyone?"*

"She's set to be executed in a week. A big show. They dinnae have Saorsa, so they are *pretendin'* they have a Stuart in hand." They ducked into an old bedroom. Many more casks of beverages in here and small barrels of flour. There was an oversize dumbwaiter on the north wall of the bedroom of the old castle.

Vika had an idea. "Put the girl down in another room and help me, quick!" she urged Alex.

....

The gated exits of the grounds were well guarded now, and all wagons had been stopped from entering or leaving. Albert Fisher, the highest-ranking officer on duty, had sent the majority of his men to scour the grounds to look for escaped prisoners. He had sent another group of men, some of his best, up to the third and fourth floors to ascertain exactly *which* prisoners they were hunting for.

The men returned to his office on the first floor as fast as they could. The news wasn't good. "Gone, sir. All of them."

"All of them?" Fisher stared at his men. "Not Saorsa Stuart!"

"Yes, sir."

He was on his feet. "We just did rounds! Some of those prisoners were injured! They can't *all* be gone. Some of them are here *somewhere!* " *My God. If we've lost Saorsa Stuart....* "You three, top floor. You three, third floor. You lot are the second floor. You there, take these two men and do this floor. I'll head to the basement...."

There was an ominous rumbling sound from the wall. "What the hell is *that?*" said one of the men. It was the last phrase spoken in the room before the explosion.

......

Three stories up, Vika and Alex had just finished tossing several stacks of sheets and as many casks of whisky as they could into the dumb waiter, prying off the lids with a crowbar as they went. Alex had taken hold of the rope on the pulley system and as soon as Vika had made a flame to ignite a chunk of alcohol-dipped wood from an old rocking chair, they were in business.

Vika tossed the flame into the dumbwaiter, making sure not to hit fluid, and Alex yanked on the rope to get things moving, sending the overloaded box of alcohol fumes and flammable materials plummeting along its tracks toward the basement far below. Then they ran, and threw themselves as far away from the dumbwaiter as possible. They had just sent an alcohol bomb straight into the soldier's quarters in the cellar.

And after a night full of the worst luck, Vika and Alex finally found some: the dumbwaiter combusted near a delivery door, where five additional full-size barrels of whisky had just been unloaded and a barrel full of nails for the castle restoration. The explosion ripped open the larger supply barrels, which quickly ignited and became a *second* explosion.

The first blast shook the building, shooting wood, bricks, and fire over everything in the basement and compromising the structural integrity of the old building. When the large barrels ignited a few moments later, nails filled the air. Men couldn't see, and many now had nails stuck through their skin. The exit through the service door was blocked by a magnificent ball of flame so soldiers went scrambling for the only other exit, trampling each other in the process, howling and trying to pull the injured with them.

On the first floor, Fisher and his crew hadn't fared much better than their counterparts. Fisher had a rather large bar positioned against the wall next to the dumbwaiter, so when the blasts went off every glass item shattered and became airborne, sending glass projectiles across the room. The wall behind the captain exploded outward and the floor under him collapsed completely, sending his chair straight into the basement with his heavy oak desk toppling after him. It was the last time his men saw him.

The men beat a hasty retreat, in shock and bleeding as they tried to carry out three injured men. Other soldiers went running toward the sound of the blast, trying to determine what had happened, the escaped prisoners rapidly falling in priority.

It was at this moment that the renovation scaffolding on the west side of the building between the old and new sections gave up the ghost. Shaken by the blast and knocked about as parts of the wall near the dumbwaiter caved in, the four-story tall scaffolding began a slow-motion descent to the earth below, sending men running away from the castle walls.

The sound of the blast and the shadowy scaffolding collapsing on a night with almost no moon made it appear the entire building was about to come down. The soldiers fleeing the destruction only added to the chaos. While the old castle was made of brick and stone, the new addition contained significant amounts of wood. Fire began to spread.

On the third floor, Vika ran back to an unconscious soldier, untied the man's boots, pulled them off and after a moment of wrestling in the dark, got his trousers off too. Clutching them, she raced back and they dressed Maggie in them. "Pick her up!" Vika shouted, and she tossed an old sheet over Alex's shoulders, covering the girl's upper body and bright gold curls. Then she began coating both herself and Alex with flour from one of the remaining barrels. It wasn't ash but it might look like it to others in the chaos outside; she hoped it would help hide their identities.

"Let's move!" she said to Alex and took the lead, hands close to her knives. Alex followed with his unconscious burden, who now looked like an injured British soldier being carried out of a burning building by one of his brothers in arms. Down the stairs to the second floor. Soldiers were rushing into the building now, and looked at Vika and Alex. Vika turned her face away so they couldn't see her clearly.

"It's bad up there!" Alex blurted, and Vika was shocked to hear a very convincing midlands English accent come flying out with his words. "There's more injured on the top floor! The fire is spreading! Go! *Go!*" The soldiers, who couldn't see much between the flour and the darkness, took him at his word and charged up the stairs. Vika and Alex moved as fast as they could in the opposite direction.

Outside, several soldiers approached Duncan's cart. "We have injured to move!" They pulled the tarp off the cart and began hurling the burlap bags of refuse to the ground. "When we're done, drive over there to the east side!"

One man had found the large box. "What's in here?"

"Nothin'," Duncan answered. "It's got rot. Some of your lot wanted it hauled away." The soldiers shoved the box out of the cart onto the ground. *So much for a place to hide Maria and Saorsa,* Duncan thought. From the look of the castle, however, he doubted the original plan was still being followed. He'd bet money the explosions he'd heard were made by his sister; she always liked her distractions to take center stage. He moved his cart into position with the others, and waited.

………

Vika and Alex made it to the ground floor. The bucket brigade wasn't working; the fire was spreading along the west wall, and the breeze blowing through Glasgow was only encouraging it. They made it out and turned into the shade of the pine trees, just feet from where they'd entered the castle. To Vika, it felt like they'd been here for days; in truth less than two hours had passed.

"Where's Duncan?" Alex said, putting Maggie down briefly on the frozen ground.

"Wait here," Vika said, and darted out to look at the east side of the building. A line of wagons...*there!* She saw Duncan and then grinned as she noticed nearly everyone else exiting the building was covered in flour too. *We'll fit right in.* She ran back to the trees.

"Let's go!" she whispered to Alex. The five wagons were full of injured men, and the drivers were being instructed to move the injured away from the castle proper and take them to a small church on the other side of the property, which was being converted to a makeshift hospital.

Alex hoisted his young charge up over his shoulder once again, and followed Vika toward the wagons. The fire had made it almost to the roof of the castle; there was no stopping it now. Alex jogged toward the wagons, trying to catch up to Duncan, who was fourth in the line. "One more!" he called. "Hey! Wait!"

Duncan slowed, and Alex put Maggie in the back of the wagon, being certain the blanket covered her head. An officer glanced at Vika and Alex curiously as they continued to jog next to the wagon as the train moved on. "We're medics," Alex said to the man. The officer nodded and looked away.

The wagons rolled away from the castle, down the path to the edge of the property on the south side where the church lay. Duncan didn't acknowledge Vika or Alex, nor they him; but all three were thinking how to get outside the six-foot perimeter wall unnoticed with an unconscious body.

Duncan kept his wagon in line and followed the others. The wagons circled the church, with the first wagon drawing up to the church's doors and the others waiting behind. Vika shot Alex a look. *How do we get Maggie out of the cart and over the wall without arousing suspicion?*

Someone lit a torch on the wall outside the church. Vika saw Alex stare at the church for a minute, his mind working. Then he looked down at his hand. Vika looked too, and saw he was signing to her. *Stay. No talk. Follow along.* He had a plan. Vika nodded and repeated the signs to Duncan as Alex turned and walked away from the wagon.

Alex rounded the corner of the church out of sight of the wagons, heading for a door on the other side of the building, pulling his lockpicks from his belt as he went. He'd seen enough small churches in his time to guess where the door led. The door was locked but it was a simple one; less than twenty seconds later he had it open and pushed the door ajar to look inside.

He'd been correct. It was the sacristy: the room where the priests' vestments and other items needed for services were stored. There was no one here, so Alex stepped inside and headed straight for the wardrobe.

Candles were lit; a priest must have been in here a short time ago. Alex tore the flour-covered hat and uniform coat off, stuffed them in the back of the wardrobe and began looking through the vestments. He found a black priest's cassock that looked to be about the right size and smiled, then pulled it on over his linen shirt and his trousers. It would do. He spied a mirror and brushed the rest of the flour out of his hair, grabbing a shirt from the wardrobe to try and scrub the flour from his face. He used a pitcher of water on the table to wet the shirt and get the traces of the flour off; what he'd done would have to do, as he didn't have much time.

He exited the way he'd come in, and continued around to the front doors where a few soldiers were unloading the injured from the second wagon. He stepped inside the church as the first wagon rolled back to the castle for more wounded. There was a priest inside the church, lighting candles. A smallish, older man, he looked completely overwhelmed as military soldiers rearranged the pews to convert the church into a triage unit. Alex headed straight for the priest.

"Hello!" he smiled, greeting the older man. "I'm Father Alexander, from Saint Mary's. The commanding officer at the castle sent a messenger to us to ask for assistance. I'm new there, but thought I'd come over an' help. We're sendin' some healers over straight away."

The priest looked relieved. Saint Mary's was a cathedral just a few blocks away; Alex and Vika had walked past it on their way here. "Oh, that's *verra* kind. These men are takin' my church apart!"

"How can I help?" Alex said, smiling kindly.

"I've...not had anything happen like this before!" The older man looked unmoored.

Alex took charge. "Come with me, father...."

"Frederick. They call me Father Fred."

"Come with me, Father Fred. We'll get this sorted." He walked toward the wagons. "You there! Wagon master!" he called to the driver of the second wagon, which had just finished unloading. "Back to the castle! We need blankets. Bandages. Medical supplies. Anyone with first aid trainin'. Understand?" The man nodded, and drove off.

The four soldiers who had escorted the wagons were now unloading the third. Alex kept giving orders, and the soldiers seemed only too happy to have someone in charge. It had been a long night. Alex gave the third wagon a different set of directions. "We'll need more firewood down here to keep the injured warm. An' fresh water. Take two of these soldiers with ye to fetch it."

The third wagon rolled off, taking two soldiers with it. The two remaining soldiers followed Alex to Duncan's wagon, which was now at the front doors. Vika moved slightly off into the darkness. Alex went around to the far side where Maggie lay, her head covered. As soon as the guards had begun helping two conscious wounded men inside, Alex made a show of looking under Maggie's sheet.

"Oh," he said solemnly. "This one's gone, Father. We shouldnae let the wounded see this. It may break their spirits." He covered Maggie's face. "Where...where would ye like the dead to be kept?"

The priest looked sad. "Oh, my goodness. Oh, bless that poor soul." He thought for a moment. "There's an old guest house on the adjoining lot, past the wall. I'll get the key." He fumbled with the keys on his belt.

"How about this, then?" Alex said in a calm voice. "I'll go with this driver, and take a man to help move the deceased into the guest house. I'll administer the Last Rites, an' we'll be back to help ye straight away. That way ye can oversee things here."

"Oh, that would be *verra* helpful," Father Fred replied, elated. Duncan moved the wagon forward to make room for the soldiers to unload the wounded from the fifth wagon behind him, and Vika jumped up into the bed of the wagon next to Maggie. "Is there anythin' ye need, Father Alexander? Anything' at all?" the older priest said, handing Alex the guest house key.

"No, I've everythin' I need with me,"Alex smiled, patting his empty coat pockets. "I like to be prepared."

"Bless you," Father Fred called, as Alex climbed up next to Duncan at the front of the wagon. "Just go through the wall over there. If the guards give ye any trouble gettin' to the guest house, just show them the key. An' the password this week is 'Prince William'."

"Thank ye kindly. We'll be back soon," Alex called, as Duncan moved the horses forward.

Alex held up the key as they passed the guards several minutes later. "We're movin' the dead! Prince William!" he called to them, and they nodded and waved them through. Duncan turned the corner and headed toward the guest house, but did not stop. Ten minutes later Haggs Castle was well behind them, and Glasgow opened before them.

Wolfcroft, Scotland

Saorsa Stuart walked toward the stables to visit the horses in the early afternoon light, Macha at her heels. She was feeling more hopeful now. The group was settling into the tower, and she had four gigantic copper cylinders full of stored magickal power. And in the last day and a half, Saorsa had learned more about how the Tower of Roses worked.

She'd discovered that putting her hands on an archway wall and directing it to let everyone pass opened the way for her friends, and that she could close the passageways the same way. They were now using all the tower floors without her or Macha. And putting your hands on an archway and picturing a different floor in your mind allowed instant transport between the floors the next time you blinked, meaning one could go to the roof from the ground floor instantly.

And once there was magick stored in the tower, the purpose of the empty platforms on floor eight above the Siphon Globe became apparent. Above each of the platforms a large rough, smoky quartz crystal had appeared, seemingly suspended in the air by nothing but magickal force. Each was about two feet tall and approximately a foot wide, although each of the four was shaped slightly differently from the others. They emitted a soft whispering sound that at times sounded like singing or chanting.

"What are they for?" Saorsa had wondered aloud when she, Adamina, and Laoise had discovered them the morning after filling the cylinders. "Smokey quartz is supposed to draw things out. Relieve anxiety and depression." She laughed. "The only thing that would relieve *my* anxiety is if I could put up some sort of protective field around this place!" She paused. "Wait...."

Saorsa walked to the circle between the platforms. "What if this is a casting circle, and each of those crystals can hold an intention or a spell? Maybe the magick in the Siphon then powers them so I don't have to, leaving me with less to worry about!"

"Couldn't hurt to try," Laoise grinned. "Do you want us here, or...?"

"Would you mind going to the Siphon to see if anything happens there while I cast here?" Saorsa asked. "I'd like to know what happens." Laoise nodded and she and Adamina headed for the Siphon room.

Saorsa closed her eyes and grounded herself, facing north in the center of the circle between the platforms. *An intention.* She took a deep breath, and felt energy begin to travel up through her body. A peaceful, humming light. *I don't know how far these spells will reach. I don't know if they will lose power over distance. I don't know how my requests will be answered. So let me start close, with effects I can see.*

Saorsa greeted the four directions and called for her ancestors. *In this place sacred to The Morrigan, where I have been gifted so much, I humbly ask for protection. May this tower and any I welcome to it be guarded against attack in this place.*

The crystal in the north began to rotate, and a bright light filled its core. Saorsa's heart began to race. *Something is happening! If we must endure an attack, may the spirits of these woods come to our aid!*

The eastern crystal began to glow. *This is it! This is how this works!* Saorsa raised her hands, and felt power surge up through the soles of her feet. *May any enemies who come be weakened and filled with doubt!* The southern crystal brightened and began to spin.

One request left. *May those who love us and seek us find their way safely to our door!* That one was for Alex. She watched as a light like a rising sun filled the western crystal and began a sunrise rotation.

Four spinning crystals. Four standing spells. *Protection. Aid. Advantage. Reunion.* She lowered her hands and cautiously closed her ritual, and the crystals spun on.

………

Laoise and Adamina monitored the movement of the magickal energy in the cylinders the rest of the day. "The crystals *are* using some of the stored magick, but very little," Adamina announced at dinner. "It's like the spells are *ready*. The one to bring loved ones close seems active and its cylinder is draining a bit faster than the others. But even so, we seem to have *plenty* of energy. I estimate we could go several weeks at this rate."

After dinner, Svend and Willow brought trays to the tables. "After shredding and grinding thousands of darkflower petals and boiling them down three times, we were able to make the rose clay," Willow explained. "We don't need for them for the archways now, but there *is* tremendous protective energy coming off of them. And Saorsa did donate some of her hair to the recipe, just for good measure." She smiled. "Rune, Svend, and Eske used that leg bone Macha brought to make a bone bead for each."

On the trays were several dozen rose bead bracelets, strung on black cord, the ends crossed through a bone bead on which was carved the rune Algiz for protection. "Annag worked the knots in her circle," Willow added, "and Svend and I worked some light energy into the beads as we rolled them as well. So: the petals are protective, the knots are spells, the bone bead is protective, we called in the light, and Saorsa's added a piece of herself to them too."

"They're beautiful," Adamina smiled. "And you can *feel* the energy coming off of them. I feel...calmer. Safe."

Edan slipped one over his wrist and next to him, after a moment's hesitation, Toran did as well. "Oh my," Edan said. "I mean...I'm probably going to have to say a lot of Hail Marys for wearing this, but it feels *amazing*. I feel clear-headed now."

"Thank you," Aeric said, smiling at the group, and Trig nodded. Many softly spoken and reverent words of gratitude filled the room. A string of larger beads was offered to Macha, who stayed still as the strand was tied around her neck. Oona received a little hat with a patch on it where a rose clay amulet had been sewn underneath.

"So it's on her but she can't put it in her mouth," Willow explained, as everyone grinned at Oona charming the room with her mischievous smile in her brand-new hat. Malphas landed nearby and gave an approving *caw*. Svend, who was holding Oona, nodded to the bird.

Saorsa felt a lump in her throat watching Willow and Svend with Oona. The couple was so beautiful and affectionate together, and Svend had pitched in on the Oona-tending duties readily. Oona had been in the backpack with Svend on and off all day, watching the world around her. *They'd be amazing parents,* Saorsa thought. *Just amazing.*

She had wondered if Oona would remember Alex. *You're just lonely for him. Keep moving forward.* Saorsa thought about the note Keena and Donovan had sent back with the supply team.

> *Dear Saorsa,*
>
> *We had hoped to come visit by now, but the day after you and Oona left a wagon arrived with six infants, Children of the Stones who will go west in a few weeks. Two of the infants need medical care, and more are expected, so we cannot come now. We miss you and Oona and think of Alex every day. We will come once the children head west. Please tell Oona we love her.*
>
> *All our love,*
> *K & D*

Yes, it had been a very eventful day and a half. Full of learning, bonding, and even some gifts.

"*Min Dame,*" Rune had said, pulling her aside as everyone put on their bracelets, "there was a bit of bone left over. I made you something." He opened his strong, weathered hand. On his palm were four very large beads. "In Norway, many of the men and women who follow the old ways put beads in their hair," he smiled. "And as you are on the path of *bein heks* now, I thought you could use them."

Saorsa smiled. "What does *bein heks* mean?"

"*Bone witch.*" He smiled at her affectionately. "Do you like them?"

They were stunning. He had formed the bone Macha had brought him into thick, organically shaped beads, which felt beautifully smooth and were large enough to ornament the hair. On each there was a symbol. *Fire. Water. Earth. Air.* Saorsa loved them instantly. Other than Alex's ring, which she had begun wearing again after her conversation with Malphas, she couldn't think of anything she owned that she liked better.

"I don't know how to thank you," Saorsa whispered. She looked up into Rune's eyes. "You and Willow...how is it you always already see me the way I'm struggling to see myself?"

"Love, *min dame,*" he said in his rich, deep tone. "We have great love for you. You are part of us now."

"Help me put them in?" she asked Rune. He smiled and selected a few of her rosemary-scented locs to adorn, and slid them onto the twisting tendrils, where they stayed.

Saorsa thought of all of these things as she entered the stable. Her friends. Her spells. Her tower. Her bones.

More of her collection had arrived. An old Roman coin sitting on the railing of her bedroom balcony that morning. A small chunk of highly polished tiger's eye right in the middle of the path. She'd found an old bronze Celtic ring on the front steps of the tower, and Svend had nearly split his sides laughing that morning when she'd cracked an egg open and a wolf's tooth fell out.

Magick was all around her now. It was stitched into her clothing and inked into her hair, an ingredient in her food and drink, and it crept into her home. It had changed the color of her eyes and adorned her limbs and skin. And it was changing her, too. Magick was no longer something she summoned; it was becoming *who she was.*

"Svend," she had said yesterday morning, looking at the tattoo on the side of his head, "have you ever done that to anyone?"

"Marked them?" His eyes twinkled. "Yes." He ran his hand over the intricate Nordic design on his head. "Rune did this, actually. Hurt like hell."

"He *did?*"

"Yes." Svend laughed. He had the most delighted-sounding chuckle she'd ever heard and he always seemed to be smiling. "And I returned the favor. For a while, every time Rune came to visit, Willow would sigh and say, 'I'll go get the ink and the poke stick.' He always left with more art than he came with."

"Could you two...do it to me?" Saorsa said hopefully. "I want more designs on my arms. Mother Agnes did the ones I have, with some help from others in my coven. I'd be so honored if the two of you would continue them. And maybe others who are here could help a bit. I'd love to say that...well, that the family I have here had a hand in it. To remember you all by."

Svend's face lit up. "I think that is a beautiful idea."

They set up a space in Saorsa's room where the light was good, and Annag blessed and cleared the space for them and closed the circle afterwards. Throughout the day, Rune and Svend worked on Saorsa, and the women sat and sung blessings and stories to her. They worked slowly, with plenty of breaks, with Laoise supervising the process from a medical standpoint, making certain Saorsa felt well and that her skin would heal properly. Everyone came in for at least one gentle tap to push the ink into the skin; Willow had even assisted Oona in taking part. Edan was fascinated by the process; he'd always been a gifted illustrator, and by the end of the day was wanting to help. Toran was interested as well, and Annag began speaking of adding to her designs. Saorsa had the feeling that she wasn't going to be the only one with new artwork over the next week or so.

Her arms ached a bit as she raised up her hands to greet Thor in his stall. She'd just bathed and still couldn't get over the beautiful work that had been done. She'd stayed in the bath a long time, looking at her arms. *Spirals and ravens. Crow feathers and wolves. Roses and bones.*

She walked up to Thor's stall. *Hello, my friend.* Macha settled down outside, giving the horses their space. Saorsa had come to speak to Thor every day since their first conversation. He was a steadying grace in her life, hopeful and strong; she shared how she was feeling, and his large, warm presence always made her feel better. She'd tried to talk to Brigit the same way, but she was more inclined to use the interaction to try and convince Saorsa to give her more treats.

As she finished her conversation with Thor, she heard voices outside that sounded like a greeting. She went into an empty stall and opened the shutters to the outside, where she could see the clearing near the cabin. She saw Rune and Eske talking to someone, but she couldn't see who. They seemed relaxed, even *joyful*. Then one of the horses moved, and she saw a girl she didn't recognize. *Had Donovan and Keena sent one of their helpers here...? Did they need something?*

And then she recognized one of the horses. *Moose.* Another person rode up, and Saorsa couldn't believe her eyes; Duncan MacLeod, astride the horse Edan had given him at Branxholme. *Duncan and Vika are here! VIKA IS HERE!* She couldn't believe it. How could this be? Had they gone to Branxholme? Had they seen Mother Agnes?

She didn't think any further. She whooped with joy, turned and charged out of the stall, eager to greet them, just as Thor's head shot straight up as he scented something familiar. *Moose! He must sense Moose!* But then Thor began pawing the ground, wanting out of the stall, and began vocalizing excitedly. She'd never heard him make this much noise.

"Thor?" she said, stopping. "What's...?" And then she heard a voice.

"Saorsa! *Saorsa! Where are ye?*" A voice she knew. A voice she had been praying to hear. Calling for her, a desperate note in the delivery. She stopped dead in her tracks.

It was a fantasy. A hallucination. It had to be. She'd imagined him so many times over the last weeks that it had become part of her routine. *Wake up, and imagine him beside you.* She'd pictured him holding Oona, feeding the fire, leaning on the stall door next to Thor. She thought she'd heard his voice a hundred times in the wind. She dreamed of him at night, and cried herself to sleep trying to imagine he was there beside her. She scattered the scents he wore in her bed and sang his songs to the child they both loved so she wouldn't forget the words. And she wore the rosary she'd mended under her blouse around her neck, next to the flower amulet that protected her. *His* rosary. Every day, a little hope for his return faded. Every day, she became a little more accustomed to loving a ghost.

"Saorsa!" She couldn't breathe, couldn't move as she heard his footsteps on the wooden floor outside. And then he was there.

Alexander Scott stopped in the doorway of the stable.

Here in Wolfcroft. Here in *Scotland.* He began to turn away again to continue his search. And Saorsa realized *he hadn't recognized her.*

Gone were her golden curls. Gone were the light hazel eyes. Gone was the young woman in safehouse men's clothing. The boots Saorsa wore now made her three inches taller; the cut of her clothing wrapped her hips and breasts in words and pictures. Her eyes were a supernatural green and gold, like sunlight filtering through leaves on a summer afternoon. Her spells extended to her wrists now. And her hair was that of a wild forest spirit, black and gold and twisted through bones.

And most importantly, she now stood like a woman standing on her own land. But she still had his ring.

She watched as he went absolutely still, his mind trying to process what he'd just seen. Then he turned back in her direction. *"Saorsa?"*

She took a breath, and took him in. He looked much the same as the day she'd met him. Almost exactly the same, in fact. Dressed in black clothes, with a black coat and tricorn hat, his dark, wavy hair fastened at the nape of his neck. Alert, broad-shouldered, and radiating a hypnotic *presence.* She hadn't known what caused it when she first met him; she knew it all too well now. His grace and balance, his startling gray eyes, his arresting and beautiful bone structure all came from *the Fae.* She was under a spell he had never intended to cast. Every inch of his six-foot-three frame enchanted her. She would never understand the way he moved, the way he spoke. And she would never fail to be captivated by him.

She felt blood rush to her head and her pulse race, even as she admonished herself. *Don't hope. It can't be him. It's a dream, a shade, an aspect. If you hope, you'll just be destroyed again when the truth is revealed. It can't be him. Alexander Scott is in the Tower of London. And you know, YOU KNOW, that he may die there, if he isn't dead already. You're just pretending he's made it here somehow so that you don't want to die as well.* Her knees locked. Her vision began to go dark at the edges.

He was moving toward her now. Not fading, not dissipating, not settling like a crow's feather shed and drifting toward the ground. He was crossing the stable and she heard Thor whinny in greeting, and then she felt Alex's hands on her upper arms.

His hands. He was touching her. He was *right there.*

"Saorsa," he breathed, looking at her, and she saw relief flood his face. There was something else there too. A weariness. A glimpse of the dead gray of a bitter winter's forest in his eyes. "Saorsa."

She opened her mouth to speak, but no words came. "My God," he whispered. "What...what has happened?" And then, "You are *so beautiful.*" He folded her into his arms.

She let herself believe then. He was warm and his arms were strong around her. She could smell wood smoke, cedar, and pine on his coat and the scent of his skin. And when she felt his hand cradling her head gently against his chest the whole world fell into place. *Alex had come back to her.*

"I'm here, *eun beag,*" he said to her softly. "It's been a long way, but I'm here." And Saorsa began to cry.

....

They stood in the stable, holding each other, as Saorsa wept in gratitude. Alex shed some tears of his own, and eventually they both settled and began to breathe together. They didn't speak. They just *were.*

Until Thor, who wanted a greeting from Alex of his own, shoved his nose into the side of Alex's neck and snorted. Alex started laughing. "Oh," he said, keeping his arm around her as he wiped tears from his eyes with the back of his hand, "how are ye, old man?"

Thor nodded his head up and down three times, and Alex and Saorsa both laughed. "He's been such a good friend to me, Alex," Saorsa said. "He keeps me sane."

Alex smiled at the horse and stroked Thor's face. "Aye, he's always been a good one," he said fondly. He looked back to Saorsa. "We saw...a tower. From the hill. I went to Glasgow lookin' for ye, an' when ye werenae there we went on to Donovan and Keena's...."

"And they sent you here." *The supply team must have just missed them.*

Alex nodded. "You...ye look...," he paused, searching for the words. "Well...like a lot has happened, Saorsa. Your hair, an'...," he grinned. "Ye look *wild.*"

Saorsa raised her eyebrows and smiled up at him. "Too wild for you?" she said, teasing. *I hope not. Because I think I'm finding out who I am.*

"Oh, *no,*" he said, slightly breathless, pulling her close again. "Ye cannae be too wild for me, Saorsa Stuart." He was smiling, the exhaustion falling away. "I think you're *lovely.*" He stopped, looking at her, his eyes searching her face for something.

He said he needed time to think. He said we needed time *to try and build trust in each other again. He said he wanted to be comfortable with his choices.* He was relieved to see her, he had missed her, and he had love in his heart for her. *But I don't know what he's thinking, what he's comfortable with, or where we stand. Time. Not everything needs to happen at once.*

"Saorsa!" She looked up as Vika strode into the stable, followed by Duncan. Vika held out her arms. "Get over here, you... *whoa!* Oh my God you look *phenomenal!*" Saorsa ran toward Vika, laughing, and embraced her. *Wait until you see the tower, Vika! Wait until you see it all!*

"Now *this,*" Vika said, stepping back to look at Saorsa, "*this* is what I'm talkin' about. You look ready to slay dragons, beautiful!"

"Actually, there's someone here who *talks* to them," Saorsa grinned. "I can't wait to introduce you!"

Vika pulled Saorsa close again. "Alex hasn't slept in *days,*" she whispered. "He's falling apart. He needs you." She stepped back and raised her voice again. "It's so wonderful to see you!"

Saorsa nodded and threw her arms around Duncan next, who laughed. "Settin' up your own fortress out here, eh?" Duncan chuckled. "Rune told us a bit of it."

"We have a girl with us. Her name is Maggie. She's not well," Vika said quietly once the greetings were done. "She's going to need some healing. Head, heart, and belly. Skinny as a rail."

"Luckily for you, I have *several* healers here," Saorsa grinned. "Where is she?"

"Just outside. Rune said he and his boys would take care of the horses and bring our packs up. I'll get her." She returned a moment later with Maggie, who stared at the ground. She looked exhausted and terrified.

"Hello, Maggie," said Saorsa quietly. "We're going to take care of you. There are kind people and healers here. My name is Saorsa. Can you follow me?" Maggie didn't respond for almost half a minute. Then she managed a slow nod, but didn't look up.

This girl Maggie needs help. Vika and Duncan are tired. And Alex is a mess. I can wonder about my relationship status later. I need to take care of my clan. "Come with me," Saorsa said, taking Alex's hand as Vika took Maggie's. Macha rose from her spot, and Duncan started as he noticed the wolf for the first time.

"Is that...?" Alex began, staring at the wolf in wonder.

"A friend," Saorsa said. "She's...a spirit companion of mine. She'll lead the way."

"A familiar?" Vika asked.

"She aids me with magick so...yes," Saorsa said, guiding Alex down the path. "And she helps us speak to the other wolves."

"They're still here?" Alex said, his face lighting up. "You've seen them again?"

Saorsa grinned. "They're living in a cave under the tower. A huge pack of them." They rounded the corner of the path, and the Tower of Roses came into view. Everyone stopped.

"Oh...my...God," Duncan said quietly.

"Well," said Vika, who found herself without words for a moment, a condition that was extremely rare for her. "Isn't that...something."

Saorsa looked back at Alex, who was simply looking up at the tower in stunned silence. "It *is* big," Saorsa admitted.

"It looked grand on the hill, but...," Vika shook her head. "This is like something from a myth."

Suddenly Saorsa remembered who was inside the tower. "There's quite a crowd in there," she said, turning to them. "Vika, Edan's here."

"He *is?*" A huge grin spread across all their faces. "Well, *that* certainly makes this dark tower *infinitely* more appealing!"

"And...," Saorsa squeezed Alex's hand, "Adamina is here too."

A series of conflicting emotions crossed Alex's face. Relief. Anger. Affection. Exhaustion. "Saorsa, I...I dinnae ken that I'm ready to see her." He squeezed Saorsa's hand tight. It would be the first time he'd seen his mother in months. In the meantime, he'd discovered Adamina had been lying to him his entire life about who and what he was.

"You should know," Saorsa said to the group, "that she has had a Fae spell worked on her. She looks about twenty years old." Alex looked sharply at Saorsa, and Duncan and Vika both raised their eyebrows.

"Let's just...," Saorsa sighed, "not rush things. There's plenty of time to explain. Things are going well here. I believe us to actually be *safe*. Tomorrow at noon, when everyone is fed and rested, we'll come together and trade stories. Sort everything out." She looked up at the tower. "But for today, let's just *heal*. Let us take you in and take care of you."

Vika nodded. "A wise plan." She moved forward, bringing Maggie with her. "Come on, Duncan!" Vika moved down the path and up the steps of the tower, and disappeared inside.

Alex looked at Saorsa. "Saorsa. About my mum. I...," He ran his free hand over his head, "I just *cannae do it now*." He sighed. And Saorsa saw that he wasn't just exhausted; he was beyond feeling. Being reunited with her had briefly brought Alex back to life, but now the color was draining from his face, and looking at him brought one word to mind: *hollow*.

He's shutting down. The strain of all the change he's endured is breaking him. Saorsa experienced a moment of panic. *Vika says he needs me. I have to heal him.* "Your mother will listen," Saorsa reassured him. "Everything will be fine. We'll tell her you need space. This is *my* tower, Alex. It's a good place. I promise." Alex nodded, looking numb, and she led him up the steps and into the Great Hall.

………

Vika and Duncan were just finishing taking the room in. "Sweet Habonde's dancing shoes, doesn't *this* just kick ass?" Vika chuckled. "No one down here, though." She crossed to the center of the room and took a deep breath, and then bellowed up the stairs at the top of her lungs.

"Edan Malcolm Devlan Scott, Laird of Buccleuch, you'd best GIRD THY LOINS! The bandit Vika MacLeod is AT YOUR DOOR!" She released Maggie's hand and raised her arms in triumph. "Ready or not, *here I come!*"

Her voice carried up the stairs to the kitchen of the tower. There was a brief period of silence, and then Edan appeared at the top of the staircase. He stood utterly still, his eyes trained on Vika. And then he noticed Duncan. And then he saw his younger brother walking in the door.

Edan Scott had been raised to be dignified. Polite. Graceful under pressure. A gentleman. All of that was forgotten as he unleashed a tremendous sound somewhere between a scream of disbelief and a cheer as he went tearing down the stairs. He headed for his brother first, and threw his arms around Alex, babbling incoherently as a mass of people rushed to take his place at the top of the stairs.

By the time Edan had launched himself at Vika, the hall was full of the sounds of running footsteps and the sound of people calling for one another and exchanging names.

"Duncan!"

"Toran!"

"Holy shite, *Vika!*"

"Annag!"

"*Alex!*"

"Maria!" Alex shouted, eyes wide. "My God, how did…?"

And then he saw Laoise and his mouth fell open in disbelief. She walked up to him, her eyes bright, grinning. "Hello, Alexander Scott," she laughed. "You have no idea how glad I am to see you."

He grabbed her roughly and pulled her into a hug, nearly squeezing the life from her. "I was worried! *So worried!* Thank God!"

Duncan was introducing Maggie to Annag. "She needs quiet, Annag. Some food. A room. Dinnae leave her alone." Maggie looked up at Annag's face. *A good sign,* Duncan thought.

"I'll help you," Annag said. "I bet you'd like a warm bath." She waved at Willow and Laoise from across the room. *This one needs help.*

Toran was hugging Alex and Duncan, then began hauling bags up the stairs as Rune and Eske came in the door, joking with Vika. "I'll get rooms ready!"

Laoise excused herself to follow Maggie and Annag up the stairs. "I'll find you later!" she called to Alex.

"Alex, this is Svend and Willow. They are...," Saorsa breathed, fighting back tears, "two of the kindest, most talented people I have ever met. Willow made my ghosts go away. I don't know...," her voice broke, "I don't think I'd be standing here without her."

"Thank you," Alex said, shaking Svend's hand and squeezing Willow's. "I...I dinnae ken how to tell you how much..." He stopped, overcome with emotion.

Willow and Svend exchanged a look. "We're healers," Willow said softly. "Once you've settled, you tell Saorsa if you want us. We'd be happy to help bring you some light."

Alex covered his eyes with his hand and nodded, and Willow patted him reassuringly on the arm. "Take your time."

At that moment, Maria walked up with a child in her arms. Alex turned, and Saorsa saw his breath catch and his hands tremble as he saw Oona. And Oona saw Alex. *Blood knows blood.* Oona had never really cried. She'd grumble sometimes if she was frustrated, but never raised her voice much, and tears never fell. But as soon as she saw Alex she let out a wail and burst into tears, holding out her arms toward him. And then she disappeared from Maria's grasp, and Alex was shocked to find himself suddenly holding a small child positively *screeching* with joy and need.

And now Alex was weeping too. "Oh *God,*" he gasped. "*Oona!*" The little one had hold of his shirt and buried her face in his neck, laughing and sobbing, nearly hysterical. "It's alright, *mo ghràdh,*" he soothed her, rocking her slowly. "*Tha sinn uile còmhla a-nis." We're all together now.* "I'm here. Oh, how I missed you!"

Seeing Alex actually *holding* Oona after she'd imagined it every day since arriving at Wolfcroft made Saorsa start to cry again. Svend handed her a handkerchief and Alex laughed through his own tears and patted her on the shoulder. "I'm worse than the bairn!" Saorsa hiccupped, as Maria took Saorsa in her arms. "Oh, my Goddess, I'm such a mess!" Oona giggled and babbled.

Willow noticed something over Alex's shoulder. "Maria...why don't you, Svend, and I head upstairs and help get some food on the table for our travelers?" Maria glanced at what Willow was looking at, nodded, and the three excused themselves. Saorsa realized everyone had left to give them privacy.

"Alex?" Adamina was standing about ten feet behind Alex. When he heard his mother's voice, he swallowed hard. He held Oona tight and didn't turn toward Adamina.

Saorsa wiped her tears and moved quickly to Adamina's side. Everyone else had gone upstairs. "Adamina," she said in a hushed tone, "he hasn't slept in several days." Adamina nodded. She understood. She took a deep breath, and Saorsa moved back to stand closer to Alex.

"I'll give you space to rest and heal," Adamina said, looking at Alex. He still wouldn't turn toward her. "I will stay away from you unless you say you want to talk. And if you don't...," Saorsa saw Adamina twist her wedding ring on her finger, trying to release an incredible tension, "I understand. I do. I will leave if you want me to. Just tell Saorsa you want me gone and," she looked at the ground, "I'll go to Paris."

A heavy silence descended on the room. Alex gave no indication that he had even heard Adamina. He shifted Oona's position in his arms, and Saorsa could see from where she stood that his eyes were tightly closed. *He's in pain. Shutting her out.*

She looked at Adamina and shook her head. *He's not going to talk now.* Adamina swallowed hard, turned and walked toward the stairs. Alex adjusted his stance with Oona as she passed so his mother couldn't see his face.

At the foot of the staircase Adamina stopped. "Your daughter, Alex," she said, gesturing toward Oona, her voice catching, "she's ...*so beautiful.*" She turned, and started up the stairs.

Saorsa caught the unspoken meaning between mother and son. *Oona reminds me of you, Alex. When you were little. When we were each other's world.* On the fifth step Adamina heard her son's voice behind her and stopped.

"Wait," Alex said, his voice choked with tears. "I want...we *will* talk. I just...I cannae do it now." He still wasn't looking at Adamina. "*Please.* Ye dinnae have to go. I just...I can't...," his voice broke completely, and Saorsa saw his breathing was disordered. She moved quickly to his side.

"Thank you," Adamina whispered. "I...*thank you,* Alexander." She turned and picked up her skirts, and raced up the stairs.

Saorsa put her arms around Alex. *He has nothing left.* "Come with me," she said to him. "It's time to rest."

....

She took Alex past the din of people talking and laughing in the kitchen and through the archway to the third floor. She found Laoise there, who looked concerned when she saw Alex's face. "Do you need help?"

"Could you take Oona please? I think she'll stay with you. She might need a nap," Saorsa said. Laoise nodded. Alex started to hand her over, but paused. "She'll be right across the hall," Saorsa told him. "See that door? That's her room." Alex nodded.

The little girl babbled brightly at Laoise, who updated Saorsa quickly. "Willow and Annag are with the girl, Maggie, getting her food and a bath. And she is drowning in dark energy. Willow and Svend are going to try and release as much of that as they can. Hopefully then Maggie will rest." Saorsa nodded and Laoise started with Oona toward the little girl's room.

Saorsa led Alex through the door to hers. He stopped just inside, dazed. "What is this?"

"It's my room," Saorsa said calmly. "Come here. Over near the fire." *His mind seems to be shutting off.* He took off his coat and hat when she told him to, and she hung them in the wardrobe. "Boots next," she told him, and he sat down on the sofa. She bent and pulled them off for him before he could, and took them away as well before returning to sit next to him. "Do you want to eat something?"

He looked around the room. "Alex," she said, trying to get his attention, "do you want to eat?"

"No thank you," he said softly. "Ate this mornin'."

"It's three in the afternoon. It will be dark soon."

"Oh," he said. "No, thank you."

"How about a hot bath?"

"No, thank you. This room...it looks verra much like you."

"Why don't you try to sleep?"

He sighed. "I cannae sleep. I need to get there."

Saorsa was growing alarmed. "Alex," she said, picking up his hand, "you're *here*. In Wolfcroft. I'm *here*. You just saw Oona. Where else do you need to go?"

He smiled at her sadly. "The portals dinnae work, Saorsa. How will I see you?"

Oh, my Goddess, Saorsa thought. *I'm not the only one who's been talking to my lover's ghost.* The scene downstairs had been too much; he was now so physically and emotionally tired he thought he was hallucinating her. She moved to the far end of the sofa and put a pillow in her lap. "Come here, my love," she said. "Lie down."

He stretched out on the sofa, put his head in her lap, and sighed. "Close your eyes," she said to him.

"Hold my hand," he answered back. She took one of his hands in hers, intertwining her fingers with his. "I cannae sleep, Saorsa," Alex said.

"Just look at the fire." She used her free hand to begin to run her fingers through his hair. *This should soothe him.*

"I cannae sleep, Saorsa," he said again. "I have to get to Glasgow."

"That's fine," she said, humming one of the Fae lullabies Laoise had taught her for Oona, "just breathe." *Song and touch. Song and touch will help him.* She grounded her feet on the floor and felt the energy of the earth. *Great Morrigan, this place is sacred to your children. This one needs healing. And rest. May your blessings flow to him.*

She heard the door open, and Macha padded into the room and lay by the fire. *I must not have closed it all the way.* A moment later Malphas was there, perched on the back of the sofa. He looked at Alex with interest and settled down to watch. And Alex lay and stared at the fire, halfway in the waking world, and half in a dream.

………

Finally, Alex fell asleep. But he never relaxed. He tossed and turned, waking frequently. And Saorsa spoke to the tower and the ancestors, asking for release for him. When he awoke two hours later, he was lucid. Conversational. His energy had coming back, but he wasn't truly at *peace.*

There's chaos in him. Of course there is. But there *was* improvement; he was hungry and interested in a bath. Saorsa went down to the kitchen where a lively dinner and conversation were underway; everyone was sharing stories with Vika and Duncan, who were telling their own tales of Carlisle and Glasgow.

Willow and Svend had stepped in to run things while Saorsa tended to Alex. "Maggie ate and is sleeping," Willow smiled. "We moved another bed into Annag's room for her. She responds to Annag well." She handed another loaf of bread to Svend for the cutting board. "How's Alex?"

"A bit better. And *hungry,*" Saorsa smiled. "I thought I'd fetch us some food to take upstairs. He needs more rest."

"We can bring it up," Rune offered.

"That would be lovely," Saorsa thanked them and returned upstairs.

Rune and Eske brought heaping bowls of chicken stew, bread, cheese, wine, and a pitcher of water to Saorsa's room a short time later. Saorsa saw Alex blink as if trying to place them, and thanked the big warriors as they left the room. "Saorsa," he said slowly, "tell me again where the Vikings are from."

"Rune has been your mother's bodyguard off and on the last few years. They're family friends of Duncan and Vika. You saw them when you got here."

"That's right," he said, remembering. "I was a bit tired, Saorsa. I'm sorry."

"And you think you're fine now?"

He smiled. "Aye. I think so." She was glad to see him eat, and noticed he was becoming more alert. *The food helped. But I think the tower is helping too.*

"Ye dinnae have to feed the fires here, eh?" He gestured at the fireplace.

"No. *And*...the bathtub fills and empties itself too."

He scowled at her. "Saorsa Stuart, *you're lyin'.*"

"No, I swear! Come here, I'll show you how it works." He was impressed, and she took the dishes downstairs to give him time to bathe and change his clothes. Down in the kitchen, she kissed Oona good night, and took a few moments to tell Adamina that Alex was feeling a bit better. Her mind just kept rejoicing. *Alex is upstairs! In my room!*

She paused. *But I need to talk to him.* She said goodnight to everyone and went up the stairs. He had finished his bath and came out from behind the dressing screen scrubbed and refreshed, dressed more casually in loose, linen trousers and a dark shirt. Saorsa closed the door and walked over toward him near the foot of the bed. "Alex. I should...probably ask you a question now. Just so we're clear."

He smiled and gestured at her to continue. "Go ahead."

"Well...we have plenty of space here in the tower. Everyone has their own room." He looked at her patiently, waiting for her to continue. And in that pause, Saorsa momentarily forgot herself. *Goddess, look at those eyes.*

"I...umm," Saorsa suddenly wished she hadn't eaten. Her stomach was nothing but waves of acid. "Do you want me to show you to another room? So you can...get some rest, and have some time alone?" He briefly raised his eyebrows, but said nothing and just kept looking at her.

"I mean, I just didn't want to assume..." Saorsa didn't know what to do with her hands, so she twisted her ring around. *Ugh. This is so awkward.* "I didn't want to assume, with all that's happened, that you would be comfortable...," she tried to breathe, "...staying in here."

He moved to stand right in front of her. "What do you want to know, *eun beag*?" he said softly. "Just say it plain."

"I..." *I want to fall asleep with you tonight, and wake up with you tomorrow. And have it be real.* "I want to know if you want your own space to sleep tonight. If you need that. Or...if...," she looked up at him, the iridescent hue of her eyes meeting the stormy ocean of his. "Or...if you want something *else*."

Neither one of them looked away. "What do *you* want?" Alex asked her softly.

"I want you to be well. I want you to *rest*." He gave her a crooked smile, and waited. *Oh, my God. I hadn't forgotten that smile. But when he's here, it's my undoing.* "Do you want to kiss me?" she blurted. *I shouldn't have said that. Oh Goddess, please let me take that back! I was going to be patient! TAKE MY TIME!*

His smile reached into his eyes. "Ye ken, Saorsa Stuart," he said, moving closer still, "I was lookin' at ye just now, in this tower of yours. Ye move different. Ye look different. Ye act different. Like...like the strong woman I've always known ye to be. But now I'm seen' it on the *outside*. An' I was just thinkin'..." he moved a bit closer, "maybe now that she sees herself the way *I* see her, maybe now that she defends her own an' rules her own house, maybe now that she has her own clan...maybe she feels *different* about me, too. Maybe she...," he looked away, "doesnae need me the same."

She looked up at him, her eyes mesmerizing in the firelight. "I need you, Alexander Scott," she said. "I will *always* need you." He looked as if he wanted to say something, and then stopped himself. She noticed he was breathing a bit faster. But his statement made Saorsa bold. "Are you going to stand there thinking about it?" she said softly. "Or are you going to come over here and let me touch you?"

A moment of wonder in his eyes. And then she found herself breathless as he moved to her and pulled her roughly against him as she saw an indigo spark flame to life in his eyes. "I've wanted this a long time," he said, his voice almost a growl. And he kissed her.

Saorsa felt something slam open inside her. She was a whirling dervish of desire, an absolute *cyclone* of emotion. *Yes. YES! He wants me! He still WANTS ME!* She felt *completely* out of control. She wanted to throw him to the floor and pounce on him. She wanted to kiss him until she stopped breathing. Her head was spinning with love and relief. She couldn't think straight. She kissed him back, again and again, and the next thing she knew she had turned him around and shoved *him* against the wall.

She felt his hands on her, trying to slow her, trying to soothe her. "Oh, sweetheart," he said, "it's all right. Easy there." He laughed. "I'm no gonna run from ye, Saorsa."

"I *missed you,*" she gasped. "I want to hold you, hear you, and watch you do *everything*. I don't...oh Alex, *don't go away again!*" He held her close until she calmed a bit, his hands stroking her back.

"I want to turn the lights down now, Saorsa," he murmured in her ear. "An' I'd like to get ye out of these clothes, too." He smiled down at her. "An' maybe...just see where things go."

"Yes," she said, running her hands over his chest, "see where things go." *I feel like I'm starving for him. But at the very least...he might sleep in my bed tonight. And that alone will fulfill me. Just to have him close.* She took off her boots, trying to slow herself down. She slid the bone beads from her hair and began to undress for bed as he turned out the lamps. Finally they found themselves standing next to the bed in their nightclothes, she in her shift and he shirtless in his linen trousers, gazing at each other.

She let her eyes wander over the muscles on his arms and shoulders, and lost her breath looking at his stomach and hips. *Goddess, this man is everything I desire.* She wanted to touch every part of him and rediscover his design. She moved quickly to stand closer to him.

"Slowly, *eun beag,*" he whispered to her, smiling. "Slow, please." He moved away from her and climbed onto the bed, settling back on the pillows. His eyes were soft as he looked at her. "I dinnae want to miss anythin' about finally bein' alone with you. Let's take our time." She watched him as he closed his eyes and raised his arms up over his head, wrists crossed on the pillow. "Ahhh," he sighed, breathing out, stretching and extending his back and arms. "*Yes. Finally.* God, just bein' here in your bed feels fine."

She moved to sit next to him and stroked his stomach with two fingers, then bent to kiss him gently on the cheek. She heard him take a deep breath. He was quiet for a long moment, watching the firelight play on the walls before he spoke.

"For a long time now," he said, "I've had to *remember* what ye were like. How ye touched me that night at Hermitage. How you told me you loved me. What ye looked like underneath me as I moved my body into yours." He turned his head to look up at her face, his eyes liquid. "An' then there was twice we were together at Deadwater, an' then Melrose, when I wasnae myself." He reached out and took her hand. "Just four times between us, Saorsa Stuart. Four times. An' in half of them, I was becomin' a monster."

"So, here we are again," Saorsa said, raising his hand to her lips and kissing him on the back of it. "We're here. We're safe for now. This is time number five. Or, it could be."

He smiled at her. "I want to start all over again, Saorsa." He sat up, moving close to her and touching her cheek. "I want it like it was at Hermitage. When we were just...possibility. Hope. Before the knife. Before Faerie. Before London. When...," he kissed her gently on the cheek, "when ye didnae yet know what a liar I was, or what a brute I could be. Back when you trusted me to love ye right."

She touched his shoulder and looked into his eyes. "I *still* trust you, Alex," she said. "More than anyone else in the world. And I know you're working to trust me again too." He searched her face with his eyes.

"I would give anything to be back at Hermitage with you," she continued. "Before you saw my cowardice, and my desperation. Before I went to Faerie and the other Alex's bed. When it was just...," her voice lowered to where it could barely be heard. "Just you, and me."

Something in his face changed. "I dinnae like that you blame everythin' on yourself, *eun beag*. Ye dinnae deserve that."

"Well," she said softly, "neither do you."

He thought about that for a moment. "Come here," he said quietly. "Come here, my dearest, my most adored, the queen of my heart. Come here and let me love you like it is our first time, but without any forgetting. Let us just try to accept each other, and ourselves, for who we are. Imperfect, and yet we endure."

He kissed her slowly, full of longing and anticipation. She smiled and watched as he stood and pulled off the rest of his clothing, leaving him standing naked before her. Her breath caught at the sight of him. She followed suit, her white shift joining his cast-off clothing on the carpet.

She moved slowly to stand before him. "I want you," he said, brushing the side of her face gently with the backs of his fingers. "I want ye *so much*." He looked down at her arms. "This is new, aye?" he said, looking at the designs.

"Yes," she said. "They're...part of who I'm meant to be."

"I'll be careful," he said softly. "I know I wasn't before, at Melrose. And I'm sorry. But I'll be careful this time." She kissed him on the chest.

He moved and sat on the edge of the bed, his feet flat on the floor, the backs of his knees against the edge of the mattress. "Can we start like this then, sweetheart?" he asked, looking up at her. "I want ye facing me, in my lap. So I can see you, an' hold you.

She nodded and moved to kneel on the mattress facing him, straddling his thighs. *I'm so nervous. More nervous by far than our first time at Hermitage. I want...I want us both to be happy. To be able to connect again.* She paused, raised up over his lap, gazing down at him. He looked up at her the way he'd looked at her on the dock the first time he'd told her he loved her. And Saorsa returned the look, her eyes full of light. *It feels like forever since we've been like this together.*

She felt his fingers gently brush the tender skin of her thigh, high on the inside of her leg, and her body begin to quiver. And then his fingers brushed her again, slowly, revealing to him the damp eagerness of her sex. "Oh," he said, smiling, "you're...you're so *perfect,* my Saorsa."

"I love you," she breathed, her voice shaking. "*I love you.*"

"An' I love you," he said quietly.

She felt butterflies in her stomach. "There's so much I have to tell you."

"Maybe...let's no talk for now," he said to her. "Is...is that alright? I want to...," he looked up at her. "I want to just *be* with you." She nodded, and then he was putting a gentle pressure on her hips, guiding her body down toward his lap. *Oh, Goddess. He's going to make love to me.* She felt the head of his engorged cock pushing into her as his hand stroked her back. *Please. Please.*

They both gasped in unison as he entered her, their eyes never leaving each other's faces. "Ohhh," Saorsa breathed. "*Ohhh.*" She looked right into his eyes as she felt him slowly push himself deeper into her body. *Oh, he feels...so right. So essential. So true. Sweet starry nights, I love how he fills me. How he pulls everything into alignment!*

"Ahhh," Alex groaned softly, closing his eyes, his exhale a vocalized deep baritone. He took a deep breath in, sinking the bulk of his long phallus still deeper into her. "Ahhh." He was breathing deeply and slowly, enjoying being welcomed into her body. She had become his refuge.

He pushed himself all the way into her, his entire shaft buried in the soft, warm, tight wetness of her, and she felt a convulsion of pleasure traverse his spine. He gazed up at her with adoration, lips parted, breath slightly quickening, and she ran her fingers slowly through his dark hair, then kissed him lovingly on the forehead. For several breaths they stayed nearly still, and then he circled her waist with his strong, well-muscled arms and pulled her closer. The gray of his eyes changed, questioning; and Saorsa looked at him and nodded. Without words, she knew what he was asking. *Will you move with me?*

She rested her hands gently on his shoulders, and began to undulate herself against him. She pivoted her hips forward and back, rising gently up on her knees and then down, beginning the motion they would build together. She rocked against him, a slow and intimate dance, sliding herself up and down on him, stroking his sensitive and swollen member with her body with each motion.

Saorsa had always been excited by Alex's voice. Her ears were tuned to pick it out of a crowd, to give it priority over every other sound in her life. It was, at different times, a balm for her soul and mind, or a stimulant for her heart and loins. But there was something in this near-silence now, in *their* near-silence, that revealed a brand-new path of arousal for Saorsa. She was listening for the sounds he made *beyond* the words.

"Ahhh," Alex exhaled each time she moved down onto him, vocalizing each breath slightly. She kissed him, slowly and deeply. He pushed himself repeatedly as far as he could each time she lowered herself to him, emotion swelling in his heart as he did so.

After the kiss, she moved her mouth near his ear, and began softly vocalizing her own sighs of pleasure, with just enough sound that she knew he could hear it. "Ohhh."

He was guiding her rhythm, his feet planted firmly in the floor, his arms tight around her waist as she moved gently in his lap. Thrilling shivers of pleasurable sensation traveled through Saorsa's entire body, brought on by the feeling of his body inside her, the sound of his sighs, and the determination with which he held her.

And his eyes. Those gray eyes, which looked at her as though she'd painted the stars in the sky herself. Those eyes, hungry and hypnotized as they followed the motion of her full breasts as she bounced slowly up and down on his lap. "Ohhh," she gasped, a sweet contentment settling in her soul. He answered her with his breath, one hand moving to tenderly stroke her back.

Saorsa tilted her head back and smiled, overcome with happiness. *Goddess, he feels glorious! He's so deep in my body, so connected to me. His hands are soothing me and exciting me at the same time.* Alex was using the lightest of touches, his fingertips on her skin, and then after a time he would press his whole hand, warm and strong, against her flesh and the change in touch and temperature would cause a delicious shiver Saorsa felt down to her bones. *I...this is what making love is supposed to feel like. It's...he's...perfect.*

She forgot all the things that had gone wrong, all the mistakes that either one of them had made. She felt safe and free, here in his arms. *This is the most beautiful thing. This.*

But Alex seemed to be having more difficulty going slow now. She watched him squeeze his eyes shut, trying to keep control, but he had been gone from her bed for too long to withstand this stimulation as long as he might have wanted. She noticed his breathing becoming irregular, and he closed his eyes more. The little line between his beautiful dark arched brows that arrived when he focused appeared. He was starting to get lost in his own pleasure; his body wanted to move more quickly.

And Saorsa *loved* that. Loved that when he was with her, he wasn't in complete control. Loved that the things she did to him drove him out of his mind with need. Loved that his desire for her overpowered his thoughts, and sent him chasing after release and ecstasy. She saw him fighting and knew he would lose. And it was going to be a thing of beauty.

She took his head in her hands, and he looked at her, beseeching. He wanted to please her, but he was being overwhelmed by his own arousal. She smiled at him and nodded, letting him know she knew what he was feeling. *I give you permission. You don't have to hold back. Lose yourself between my thighs.*

As soon as he saw her nod, the pace of his thrusts began to increase. His touches became deeper; he gripped both of her buttocks in his hands, encouraging her to bounce on him a bit harder, pulling her up just a bit higher. And Saorsa responded, her voice a whisper near her lover's ear. His excitement became her excitement.

He was rapidly losing himself, burying himself in her scent and motion, and then he stopped her movement with a firm hand on her lower back. His mouth found her breasts. She paused and closed her eyes, letting out her breath in a staccato rhythm to show him how high he was driving her with his lips and tongue and teeth on her nipples.

"Ohhh-oh-oh-oh-ohhhhhh!" She felt him thrust into her again, a savage motion as his mouth left her and he looked up at her, and it made her insides shake with desire. *The way he looks at me!*

He bit her gently on the neck, and then kissed her lovingly in the same spot, and she felt a warm flush all over, just before her body created a hot wave of excitement between her legs. He growled, deep in his throat, answering to her body's response to him, and repositioned his feet slightly. And Saorsa wanted him to take her *harder*.

Their eyes met. He was staring at her intently, focused, every scrap of his attention trained on her face. And then he spanked her.

It was such a different sensation from the way he'd been touching her that it commanded her attention. He hadn't hurt her, but there was no mistaking that he had *spanked* her. *Well, so much for 'I'll be gentle, Saorsa'!* She thought for a moment, and decided she rather liked it. She took a deep, quivering breath in, the air in the room cold in her lungs, and bent to bite him gently on the shoulder. She heard him exhale as he absorbed the sensation of her teeth putting pressure on his skin. Alex stroked her gently on the bottom where he'd smacked her with a light touch, showing her he wanted to be not just rough, but sweet as well. "Mmmm," she breathed happily into his neck, and then he kissed her again.

"Mmmm," he laughed into her chest as she stroked the back of his neck. He was happy, *so* happy. She wasn't sure where the spanking had suddenly come from, but he seemed profoundly satisfied by the outcome, his eyes full of lust and worship. She kissed him on the top of his head, and he put his hands on her hips. And she realized that this little interlude of spanking and biting had broken the deep rhythm of his thrusts. *He's trying to last longer. He was losing control and didn't want to stop, didn't want to climax yet. So he played rough with me for a bit to slow himself down. Gave me a hard sensation in a different way.*

This endeared him to her for a reason that was difficult to articulate. She also found it thrilling. *He has to manage himself with me. I drive him too high. Have him too much in my power.* Saorsa wrinkled her nose at Alex playfully and moved to touch her forehead lightly to his. He stayed still a moment, enjoying the touch; and then he was moving, exiting her body for a bit, rolling and taking her with him. They ended up with Saorsa pinned underneath him on the bed. Saorsa's eyes widened in delight.

He smiled, pushed her hair back from her face, and kissed her slowly. Then again. Then again. And then he kissed her neck and her breasts, while she uttered about thirty tiny "oh!"s as he did so. He laughed, the sound rumbling deep in his chest.

He shifted his weight from her, and his fingers gently found their way inside her. He was watching her face closely. "Ohhh," Saorsa sighed, nestling closer to him. She raised her hips toward him, and he kissed her again, biting her gently on her bottom lip at the end of the kiss. Saorsa could feel a pleasurable electricity in her limbs.

He looked deep into her eyes, and began to move his hand, his fingers penetrating her, wet from her arousal. Saorsa breathed deep. This bed was full of their scents now, mingled together. Cedar and rose, leather and sandalwood. Fresh air, and warm skin. He kissed her neck. He could scent her sex, a primitive, deep note that was like rain, and wind, and deep moving water. It was his favorite scent in the world, and it was lighting up the animal parts of his brain. Alexander breathed his beloved in. "Ahhh."

He curved his strong fingers, sliding them in and out of her, finding a rhythm and pressure she liked. He watched her face closely. There it was. That first little frown she gave as she met the beginnings of sensation. A brief fluttering of her eyelids as she processed it. And then a tightening in the vicinity of her thighs and belly. Her want was growing. Her breathing was a soft question. *How do you...how do you always know how to touch me? How to make my body respond? How to hold me just right, so that I feel safe, and centered, and loved, and...free? So that I know you adore me, and the shame and doubt I carry just ebbs away? Ohhh. Alex.*

A quivering in her thighs, in her hips. She bit her lip and looked at him, and he understood. His fingers were stroking her, sliding rhythmically in and out of her, and now he was moving his hand harder against her. He was learning each time he was with her, learning what she liked and when. And he had learned that penetration, deep, rough penetration, was a huge contributor to Saorsa's arousal. He slid his fingers deeper into her body, increasing the tempo of his movements. *Come for me, sweetheart. I want to watch you.*

"OHHH!" This breath was fully vocalized, and she thrust her hips forward and clutched at him. "Mmmm," he murmured in her ear, appreciating her response and encouraging her.

"Oh...oh...oh...," she was squirming now, trying to get closer to him as he lay on his side against her, holding her and increasing the rhythm of his strokes between her legs. "Ohh..oh..ahh! Oh! Oh!"

She was looking at him desperately, and he was holding her tight, bringing her to the edge. Her cries were soft sobs now; she was bucking against him, wanting him to touch her harder, more violently, and faster. "Oh! Oh! Mmmm! Ohhhhh!" Her voice had gone up nearly an octave in pitch. She was his, at his mercy, pleading with him for release. She had missed him desperately, holding herself together, fighting her misery at being without him every day, and now her body wanted *release* from it all. Her fingernails clawed his arm. He felt like the most powerful being in the world. She was his *everything*. She was passion incarnate. He was fighting not to climax himself just watching her.

He moved his hand a bit faster, and added a slight twist to its orientation. He watched as her knees bent, and she braced her feet on the bed, and then Saorsa's entire lower body thrust violently toward Alex, shaking, her thighs clamping hard around his arm. She nearly screamed. Screamed with joy at the feeling of release. Actual, pure, *release*. Abandoning worry. Throwing off loneliness. Casting aside frustration, grief, guilt, and longing. The physical release was letting loose the emotion in her as well.

He was *here*. He had come back. And he was with her, trying again, showing his desire, wanting her. Alex was *loving her*. He had fought his way back to be here, touching her, holding her, *right now*. Everything in her body became a wave of freedom and joy. Her back was arching; she wanted to pull him *inside her soul*. Everything in her body *reached*.

He suddenly found his hand and the entire lower half of his forearm covered in little trickling rivers of water from her. She was crying out wordlessly, over and over and over, as though a dam had broken and she was drowning, but in between her gasps was nothing but ongoing euphoria. "Oh-oh-oh-oh-OH! Oh, ahh....oh!"

Alex let out a startled laugh. He'd never seen a woman this aroused before, this intense, this...*explosive* during an orgasm. She was damp halfway down to her knees, and *he* was damp well past his wrist, and now she appeared to be laughing and crying at the same time, and there was a good possibility she had momentarily lost her mind. *What the hell just happened?*

He moved his hand from between her legs, pulled her against him and rubbed her lower back. He kissed her cheek and forehead, soothing her, rocking her gently, smiling and laughing quietly in amazement at the miracle that was Saorsa. *I've never seen a woman's body respond like that*, he thought. *Like something flowed through her. A drenching tide.* He was overjoyed, his heart pounding. *He* had brought out that response in her.

She sobbed into his chest, her breathing ragged, her hands clutching at him as though she couldn't believe he was actually there. He kissed her eyelids and her cheekbones, her chin and her forehead, and then gave her a long, lingering kiss on the mouth. He couldn't stop kissing her. Every time he did it, he thought he'd die if it wasn't followed by another.

I haven't been here for her. He wanted to make up for every second he'd been away a thousand times over. *I love you. I love you. I love you.* Her hand found his shoulder, and she gave him a little push. He understood, and rolled onto his back, and she moved onto her side to face him.

Her eyes took him all in, lying there. He was built so differently than she was. He was so much...bigger. So *solid*. The width of his biceps was double that of hers; his shoulders and upper chest dwarfed hers by comparison, and his legs looked impossibly long. Saorsa considered herself strong, but her strength had a certain roundness to it. It was molded around tinier bones. Alex was another type of creature entirely. Where she was water and young vines and the fertile earth, he was stone and tree trunks and flames. Iron and steel. She wondered how it felt to be in a body like his. One that took up so much space, and had so many angles. One that was such a large presence. Had such...impact. One that was *hard*.

Saorsa let her fingertips wander over his chest and down Alex's abdomen. He shifted himself slightly on the bed and watched her. Watching her climax had kept his excitement very high, and he closed his eyes and took a deep breath in as Saorsa lightly ran her fingers along the length of his arousal. "Ahhhhh." Then she kissed him there, her lips soft against the taut skin of his cock. A sweet, adoring kiss. He moaned a bit, and involuntarily shifted his hips. He wanted her.

Saorsa smiled. They were still new to making love with each other, and she wanted to touch him, to discover more. She wanted to know all about him. She was already in love with the slight curve of his erect penis, the pattern of veins in his erection, with the heat and definition of his thigh muscles, and the texture of dark hair on his legs. She reached down and let her fingers wander over his scrotum, already tight as his body moved closer to ejaculation. He shuddered and let out a soft gasp at her touch; she'd never stroked him there before, and he *loved* it. *I love you, Alex,* she thought. *You are so wonderfully made. A miracle. I love you.*

She got on to her hands and knees, and straddled his hips. He was panting, his hands gripping the sheets, his face revealing the depths of his desire. He was hopelessly in love with her. He knew he always would be.

I'm not going to let him stop this time, thought Saorsa. *I want to watch him, the way he watched me. I want to tend to his needs and give him total release. To bond him to me once more and remind him that he belongs here, with me.*

Her eyes held a question for him. He understood, and nodded. She reached down and gently wrapped her hand around the thick, heavy shaft of his very substantial member, and guided him to enter her. And then she saw the look on his face. *Fear.* The emotion was quick, but it *had* been there. And he knew she'd seen it. Saorsa knew its cause immediately.

He didn't want to feel this way. But he did. Between the last time they'd been in bed together and now she'd gone to Faerie. Met his Fae side. And in his heart, he felt she'd gone to bed with another man. He was afraid. Afraid to let himself go completely with her, to trust her to hold him while he lost control. He was afraid that if he did that, there'd be nothing of him left when she abandoned him for his rival. He thought it was a possibility, a very likely one.

But she knew that would never happen. She knew now that the entire reason she'd loved *that* Alex was because it was the closest she could get to *this* Alex. This Alexander Scott, this one right here, was first in her heart. It was to him she was bonded. She knew that now, without question. She would have to try and show him. Guide him to that place. Make love to him so many times that he understood it could be no other way.

She gave him an understanding smile. She reached up and tenderly stroked his cheek. He hadn't shaved in a few days, and she adored the roughness she found there. Everything was dear to her. She looked at him and waited. He looked back into her eyes. He wanted to be with her. He took a deep breath, and nodded *yes* despite his fears.

She finished what she'd started, guiding him into her body. *Your head and heart are cautious, Alex. You've been through a lot. Let's see if the drive in your belly can help.* She was grateful when he didn't hesitate. She closed her eyes as she felt him inside her body once more. She began to move slowly.

"Ah," she heard him respond. "Oh..ah, ah, ah, ahhh." His hips were moving. "Mmmm." He looked up at her. *My Saorsa. My beautiful Saorsa. Oh God, please don't leave me. Please. It would be the end of me. I know this.*

So much had happened between them. The knife. Ghosts. Separation. Fia. Betrayal. Illness. Desperation. Secrets. Abandonment. Fatigue. Worry. Loneliness. Frustration. Many walls had been built since they'd left Hermitage. Walls that needed to come down if they were to truly find each other again. Saorsa had already dismantled almost all of hers. But Alex, who had been trying to hold himself together since he'd picked up that knife in the tomb, hadn't let much of anything go. He was now constructed nearly entirely of a swirling, chaotic *tension*. Saorsa hoped to use his desire for her as the sledgehammer on those walls. If he could trust her here...truly come back to her bed...and *let go* in her presence....

He looked at her, and she could see he was resolute in his decision to try to have faith in her. He began thrusting into her harder. "Ahhh!" He had his hands firmly on her hips now. She watched him frown in intense concentration and close his eyes. She could feel his body gathering. *Come to me, Alex. Come home to me. Trust me.*

She watched the line appear between his brows once more as his focus narrowed to the sensations in his body, the feeling of her surrounding him, and Saorsa realized his thrusts were becoming less voluntary and more automatic. *Not long for you now, sweetheart,* Saorsa thought, watching him tense all over. She loved watching him like this and feeling him inside her. *I love you, Alex. You're almost there, darling. You're in thrall to your want. It's all right to be that way.* She moved her hips with him, and bliss flowed in her veins. *Come with me. Let go. Let it all go.*

He threw back his head, and squeezed his eyes shut tighter, as if fighting to hold something back. And then...tears. Tears were trickling out of his eyes, leaving lightning-shaped trails of wetness down the sides of his face. Tears he couldn't help. Those silver waterways were the first sign that the walls were about to come down inside him, and Saorsa had never been so glad to see someone cry.

He let out a sound, somewhere between a gasp and a sob, straining inside her body. He was chasing after something inside himself. And Saorsa was going to help him catch it, with the first words they'd spoken since this encounter began.

"I'm yours," she whispered, "just yours. I love you. It's alright. Don't be afraid. Come home to me. I'm a safe place for you, Alex. I'm safe."

Alex opened his eyes, looked up at her desperately, and found his way. "Ahh-ah-ah-oh....oh god! God! *GOD*!" he cried, as an extremely powerful, nearly minute-long orgasm began tearing its way through his body. He arched his back and let loose a sound, more of a soft, low howl, moving as though his spine itself was coming apart in explosions of rapture. Saorsa was shocked to discover that she wasn't yet feeling the expected convulsions of his penis inside her. He was shaking everywhere else though, even as he kept thrusting; clutching at her desperately and crying out quietly, over and over, as the muscles all over his body trembled and tears flowed from the corners of his eyes. He seemed to be collapsing in stages, and Saorsa watched in absolute wonder as it happened. She had had no idea that a man could orgasm without ejaculating, but apparently Alex was doing that *now*. She lay down to touch her chest to his, and held him tightly. "*Tha agam thu, agus cha leig mi as,*" she whispered to him. *I've got you, and I won't let you go.*

And then came the final physical release. She felt it inside her when it happened, his body seizing and releasing yet again, his back arching and his arms tight around her as he let the last of his defenses down. Saorsa sighed with happiness as she felt his cock jerk involuntarily and repeatedly inside her, and heard him gasping as each spasm of earth-shaking pleasure coursed its way through his body. His walls were about to turn to dust in her arms. He was *trusting* her.

She could see the barriers that had kept them apart crumbling. She had wrenched his soul from the defenses that had been constructed around it in the last few weeks, leaving him exposed and vulnerable. He had no will to guard his borders any more from her. He just wanted to be close. *Thank the Goddess!*

Every scrap of tension flowed out of Alex in shuddering waves, and every time Saorsa thought he had begun to settle there was another series of tremors. But gradually they began to subside as every part of his body and mind shook off its armor. Saorsa waited, and held him tight.

After a time she rubbed Alex's shoulder slowly and sang softly to him, a little Scots Gaelic song about the moon, as a stillness flooded his body and his breathing slowed, like a calm sea settling back into itself after a storm. She smiled in the dark as she felt his hand rest heavily on her back as she lay atop him with his spent manhood still inside her. *This is how we were meant to be. Close. Safe. Trusting. And healing each other through touch. He's finally going to find some peace.*

She giggled in surprise a moment later when he let loose a deep, cleansing yawn, followed nearly immediately by a soft, contented snore. She raised her head to see the dark lashes of his eyes closed. *Sound asleep. Relaxed. And...with me.* She was so, so thankful. She pulled the covers up a bit closer around them. "Goodnight, Alex," she whispered. "And welcome home."

....

They slept deeply that night, entwined in the bed, a much-needed sense of peace settling over them. They shifted positions a few times, their bodies instinctively moving in response to each other. Saorsa was awakened twice during the night. The first time was around midnight when she heard Alex whisper her name in his sleep. "Saorsa?" A pause. "Saorsa?" There was a forlorn note in his voice.

"I'm here," she whispered back to him, and moved to stroke his chest. "I'm right here." His eyes fluttered open for a moment, and he looked at her as though uncertain whether she was real or part of a dream. "I'm here with you," she reassured him, brushing his hair back from his forehead with her fingers. "You can feel me, aye?"

He smiled. "I can feel you." He sighed. "You're well?"

Saorsa grinned. "Yes, silly. Go back to sleep." She kissed him on the cheek and then put her head on his chest, and they both fell asleep again.

"I love you," she heard him breathe just before she drifted off in his arms.

She heard his voice again, about two hours later. This time his speech wasn't as clear, but Saorsa could tell he was distressed. His breathing was shallow and hurried, and he was shaking while he slept. Saorsa thought back to their time at Holy Cross Church. *After he trusted me and told me about losing Morag and the baby, he had nightmares. And tonight he let go and trusted me again, and now here we are.* It seemed that once Alex decided to let his guard down, all manner of bottled-up emotions came pouring out; some while he was awake, and others forcing their way back into his mind while he slept. Last time this had happened he'd started sleepwalking and had hurt himself; Saorsa didn't intend to let things progress that far this time.

"Alex," she said, shaking his arm. "Alex, you're having a nightmare. *Wake up,* my love."

When he didn't respond, she gave him a good thump on the chest and his eyes flew open. "*What?*"

"Alex," Saorsa said calmly, "you were having a nightmare. You're at Wolfcroft. Everything is fine."

"Oh, *Saorsa,*" he breathed, and put one arm around her and held her tight. "Christ, that was bad."

She gave him a squeeze. "What were you dreaming about?"

He ran his free hand over his head. "I...I havenae had the time to tell you. It happened while I was in London. They tried to execute me. Read the charges. King George was *right there.* A horrid big, monstrous crowd, cryin' for my death. Got my neck in the noose and pulled the lever an' everythin'...and God Almighty, I dream of it most every night."

Saorsa felt as if the blood had been drained from her body in an instant. *"What?* They...*they actually hanged you in London?"*

"Tower Hill," he whispered. "I was in the White Tower before that."

Saorsa held him as tight as she could. "Laoise told us you were in the White Tower, but *not about the hanging!"*

"I dinnae ken that she knows. It was three days after I saw her last. She was most likely runnin' with Maria by that time."

"How did you escape?" Saorsa was nearly beside herself with displaced fear. *"How are you here?"*

"I split myself an' got out if the noose. Fought my way out. I can show you tomorrow. Saorsa," he said, "I'm sorry I woke ye, but now since you're awake, I have somethin' I need to say."

She loosened her embrace a bit and he did the same, so that they could see each other's faces. "Go on. I'm listening."

He took a deep breath. "If the Fae come here...well, if we're still both alive after that, I want us to take Oona and go east. Once we ken everyone else here is safe."

"East?" Saorsa was confused. "Why?"

"I'd like us to go to Holy Cross."

"What's at Holy Cross?" Saorsa thought for a moment. *Does he want to get Oona baptized? And have Father Andrew do it? But...I thought his views on Catholicism had changed. Maybe having that experience on the gallows reignited the faith he was raised in?*

"You...you want to have Oona baptized? With Father Andrew?"

"No...no," Alex said softly. "I was thinkin'...well, I was hopin' maybe he could marry us, Saorsa." Alex was tense and seemed to be holding his breath.

Saorsa stared at him. "What?"

Alex's words came tumbling out. "I didnae mean...I didnae mean we should *only* get married in the church. I dinnae ken how witches get married, or who does the ceremony...."

"Handfasting," a stunned Saorsa blurted. "It's called *handfasting.*"

"If Mother Agnes can do it, then we could be wed that way too. I ken we've had a hard time. I ken that I wasnae honest wit' ye about Fia an' the others, an' that I hadnae been kind to you while the knife was here, an' that...."

"Wait," Saorsa said, her mind reeling, "are you proposing to me? *Right now? In this bed?*"

"No," Alex said, and stopped talking.

Saorsa's eyes widened. "What do you mean, *no?* You *just said* you wanted to go east so Father Andrew could marry us!"

Alex shifted in the bed. "Saorsa, proposals should be done right an' proper. I cannae propose to you *here*. We're naked in a bed in the woods an' it's the middle of the night! An' I must speak to your mother of it, as your father isnae here. You're the King Over the Water's *granddaughter*! When I propose it'll be in daylight, we'll be *dressed*, I'll have a ring for ye, an' we'll do it *properly.*"

Saorsa gave a short laugh. "Then what *are* you doing right now?"

He gave a slight shrug. "Tellin' ye that I want to go east."

Saorsa was fighting the urge to laugh. "Alex, how can you be such an absolute rebel in ninety percent of your life, and so fixated on what is proper in the other ten percent?"

He shrugged again. "I dinnae ken. I just am."

She kissed him on the forehead. "I love what you *just are.*"

"So...," he said, and went quiet.

"So...what, Alexander?" she said, smiling at him. *Oh, Goddess! He wants to MARRY me!*

"So...," Alex seemed nervous again, squirming a bit in the bed next to her, "what I said before." He lowered his voice. "That I ken we've had a hard time. I didnae tell ye of Fia or the others I've been with in the past. There were times when I was too rough with ye. I'm hard to be around at times, an' I'm not all human like you are, an' you're *royalty*, Saorsa, an'...."

She realized what he was trying to ask and put her hand to her heart, overcome with feeling for him. "Oh *Alex*. Are you trying to ask me...are you asking me what I'd say if you *did* propose?" He nodded and looked away, and she felt how nervous he was.

He's actually worried. He isn't certain I'd accept his proposal. How can he begin to think I wouldn't say yes? She smiled and put her hand on his cheek to gently turn his head back toward her so he could see her face. "I'd say *yes*," she told him quietly. "*Of course* I would say yes. Without a moment's hesitation. What else could I *possibly* do?"

He beamed at her, relieved, and she felt him begin to relax. Saorsa kissed him gently on the mouth, and he pulled her close.

"Walkin' up the steps to the gallows, I was thinkin' of only one thing," he whispered after kissing her forehead. "That my greatest regret in life was that I'd thought of marryin' ye hundreds o' times, but had no ever asked. And I was about to die without ever askin' ye to be my wife." He took a slow, deep breath. "The idea of bein' without you...it scares me more than death, Saorsa. Scares me more than pain. These nightmares I have...they're no so much about the noose, the crowd, or the evil I saw on the faces on the platform. My nightmares are all about bein' away from *you*."

"Never again," Saorsa whispered to him. "Never again will I trust someone else's word over yours. Never again will I let someone drive us apart. Never again will I keep my fears to myself. We walk forward *together*." She paused. "This does bring up the question, though...when you *do* propose, what are you going to do about the fact that you're already engaged?"

"I'm no going to marry Fia. I'll tell her."

"Yes, but...Alex, she's *not well*. She seems to function in a state of desperation. And I am absolutely certain she is obsessed with you. If you tell her the engagement is off...what if she throws herself down the stairs? Or finds a way to run off to Faerie? We have to think about her child. And...," Saorsa paused. "We have to think about *her*, Alex. She needs someone. Someone who can be *hers*. If it's not you and it's not me...what will become of her?" She took a deep breath. "I'm angry with her. I've never *been* so angry. But...there are things about her that I loved once, too. And I don't know that I'm ready to lock those parts up and throw away the key."

Alex nodded. "We willnae tell her until after her bairn is born. You and I, we willnae tell anyone we're to be wed. It'll just be for the two of us. We go an' see Father Andrew an' we wait until Fia's bairn is here. Then I'll tell her you and I are married. That way if she runs off or tries to hurt herself, at least we can keep the child safe."

"But what about *her?*"

"I dinnae ken that yet, Saorsa. I think...I'll have to talk with her to figure that out." He sighed. "Once she knows the truth, we'll see what she wants to do. An' what is the safest thing for the babe." He paused. "I dinnae ken what was true an' what wasn't in all she said. Maybe she doesnae even want to keep the child. I dinnae ken."

"If she *doesn't*," Saorsa said slowly, "what are you going to do? If you consider your Fae side a different person, then it's his baby, isn't it? Will you...what will you...."

Alex looked at her intently. "Well, part of that will depend on *you*. What would you do?"

"Alex, that baby will be a *leth dhia* crossed with a non-magickal human in a ritual. Mother Agnes says the baby might be a daemon. Or even an entirely new form of Fae."

There was a long pause as Alex digested the information. "Well, it hasnae happened yet. But my first thought is, if Fia cannae care for the child, an' its father doesnae come for it...."

"Then...we care for the baby." Saorsa paused. "That's what you are thinking, right?"

"Aye. Until such time as we can contact someone from the Deck of Crows, an' ask them what to do." Saorsa knew he was thinking of Thomas. And she was thinking of something else as well. Something she hadn't brought up. *Never again will I keep my fears to myself. We walk forward together.*

"Alex. I need to say this. It's a fear I have. I know you don't want to talk about him but...," she struggled to find the words. "When I went to Faerie, your Fae side worked magick on me. Elen says there's a magickal symbol on my chest and no one seems to know what it is. Apparently *leth dhia* can...well, they can *choose* to impregnate someone. It's not mostly chance like it is among humans. And I don't know if your Fae side chose to do that to me or not. He said he wouldn't but...ever since this mark was put on me, I've worried that it has something to do with my being pregnant. I could be carrying his child. Or have his seed in my bloodstream for the next time my moon cycle is ready for it. Apparently *leth dhia* can do that."

Alex had gone tense again. He let Saorsa go and sat up in the bed and moved away. Saorsa was afraid to move or speak. *This is too much for him to handle. If I do anything, it might upset the balance of his emotions and bring things crashing down.* She tried not to breathe.

"I just...need a moment," he said hoarsely, covering his face with his hands. "Just...a moment. *Please.*"

I will stay still for years, Saorsa thought. *If it means you don't get out of this bed, get dressed, and leave.* But he didn't. She noticed with a sinking feeling that his breathing was ragged. He was either furious and trying to keep control of himself, or weeping. *Probably both.* The silence seemed to go on forever. Saorsa couldn't stand it.

"I'm sorry," she gulped, fighting tears. "I'm sorry. And I'm *scared*."

She heard him take a deep breath. "Is there," he said through his hands, "anythin' else?"

"No, that's the worst thing," she whispered. "I have other things to tell you, but that's the hardest thing, by far."

He moved his hands from his face and looked at her. "I'm no going to leave," he said upon seeing the expression on her face. "I just need to...get up and walk a bit. All right?"

Saorsa nodded. *He's communicating. He's trying.* She watched as he got up and picked up his trousers and put them on before going to stand by the fire. And then he started to pace. *He's processing this. Or trying to. In one conversation we've gone from him being hanged to getting married to Fia and her baby and to...oh Goddess, the possibility of my being pregnant. With another man's child.*

He'd look after that baby too. She knew it. *Suddenly he might be a father of three, and quite possibly none of them are his. Or, depending on what else we find out and how you look at it...they all are.* She watched him walk. Back and forth. Thinking. Thinking.

Finally, he stopped. "Will ye come here to me, sweetheart?" he said quietly. Saorsa climbed out of bed and picked up her shift from where it lay on the floor. She felt...exposed. Raw. She wanted the feelings she'd had while making love to him back. Not this knowledge that she'd most likely torn out his insides. She pulled the shift over her head and went to stand in front of him by the fire. She felt somewhat better when he took her hands in each of his.

"You dinnae ken for certain that you're to have...," he said, his voice trailing off. "Aye?"

"I don't know for certain. It's just...a worry I have."

He nodded, and seemed to pin his hopes on what she'd said. "If it's no certain, we shouldnae worry about it yet, aye? We've enough to look after." He paused. "But you said you were afraid. And I dinnae want you afraid, *eun beag*. Is it because...well, because somethin' makes you think you are...?"

He's avoiding saying the word pregnant, Saorsa noticed. *He's still processing. And having trouble.* "No, I...I just wanted you to know. In case it comes up later. And because it worries me." She took a deep breath. "And I think that if I found out I was with child, and it wasn't yours...well, that it would change things between us."

He put his arms around her and sighed wearily. "It would be hard, Saorsa. I willnae lie. But I'd still love you. I cannae help myself." She felt his arms tighten around her. "Dinnae be afraid, my Saorsa. If it comes to pass...well, I'll stay with you. An' love ye right through it."

Saorsa felt the tears come. She put her arms around him and let herself cry. "Thank you."

He rubbed her back. "We work together, aye?"

"Aye," Saorsa responded. "We work together."

Wolfcroft, Scotland

Alex was up before her the next morning, and Saorsa smiled at the familiar sounds of him moving around the room, washing and dressing, and heading out the door to tend to the horses. *Aeric and Trig will most likely have done everything at the stable already. But Alex will like to look in on Thor anyway.*

It was so quiet in the room without him. *My mind likes knowing he's nearby, tending to things.* Saorsa opened her eyes. *After last night, I will need to be careful around him. That was a lot to take in. He might talk to Adamina today about Thomas too. That will add more stress.*

She rose and headed for the washstand. She scrubbed herself clean with rosemary soap and a cloth, and brushed her teeth before putting on a clean shift. *I need to do the laundry; I'm nearly out of clothes.*

She looked at herself in the mirror, finger-combed the wild ropes of hair Willow had fashioned for her and put her beads back in. *It's like having wind and sun on my head. Like nature. Like sculpture.* The locs were even wilder than her curls, and obeyed her even less. She loved them.

She added a bit of rose oil to her palms and stroked her hair to tame everything a bit, and had fixed herself a cup of mint tea when Alex came in. He removed his outerwear after he shut the door quietly behind him, and smiled. "What are you doin' up?" he asked. *He seems to be in a wonderful mood,* Saorsa thought. *Much, much better than I expected.*

"Waiting for you," she smiled back at him. She crossed the room and put her arms around him, and jumped in surprise before pulling away. "Alex, your clothes are *freezing!*"

He laughed. "It's snowin' a bit, *eun beag.*"

Saorsa put out her hand to touch his right hip. "If you take those clothes off," she purred playfully, "I'll be happy to help warm you up." *Let's see if you're actually in a good mood, or just pretending to be for my sake.*

She thought he might say no in light of the revelation of her possible pregnancy last night. He might need time away from her to think. *We've things to do today, Saorsa.* But to her surprise and delight he stripped his clothes off, hurriedly climbed back under the covers, and looked up at her expectantly. She was beside him in the bed in a flash.

"Get over here an' be my bed warmer, ye wee rascal," he laughed, pulling her halfway across the bed under the quilts. "Where are those thighs of yours? They're hot like a desert sun." He pulled up her shift with no further preamble and shoved his right hand, which was quite cold, directly between Saorsa's thighs.

She let out a screech and started laughing, trying to pull away, but he held her tight. "Ahh, *better,*" he declared, grinning, while she tried to fight him off. "An' your ass is hot like a bread oven, I think I'll have some of that too." And he planted his other cold hand directly on the skin of her backside.

She was howling now, hysterical and protesting, trying to push him away as tears ran down her cheeks. He was laughing along with her, nuzzling her throat, and she yowled like an angry cat as his cold cheeks and nose met her warm flesh. "Alex! Alex, *NO!* Oh Goddess, you're *so cold!*"

He blew raspberries on her neck and held her tightly in place and chuckled. "Just stay still, I'll warm up eventually."

"Oh, *Carpundia's left tit,* even your legs are freezing!" Saorsa shouted as he attempted to pin her underneath him. "Is there *any* part of you that *isn't* an ice block?"

He was beside himself with laughter now. "Who the hell is Carpundia?"

"Gaelic river goddess," Saorsa panted. "How is this possible? No one can be this cold and live!" She wiggled happily underneath him. "What is this hair on your legs and arms and chest for if it doesn't keep you warm?" He bit her gently on the neck and she gasped.

"I must say, *eun beag,*" he murmured playfully in her ear, "I find ye fightin' me like this a wee bit arousin'." His hand found her breast. "I think my cock needs some heat too. Do ye have anywhere warm I could put that, *leannan?*"

She stopped thrashing and reached down to touch him. *Well, he's certainly in the mood.* "Oh my," she smiled. "Why yes, Mr. Scott, I think I *do.*"

He closed his eyes for a moment, enjoying the feeling of her touch. Then his gray eyes opened again and he kissed her hungrily. "Oh, Saorsa," he breathed a few moments later, as he pushed his way slowly into her body. "Oh God, you're good to me."

"Oh," she smiled, kissing his cheek. "You feel so *wonderful!*"

"Think I'm startin' to warm up nicely now," he whispered to her. "Maybe just...a bit more." His breath was coming faster now. "God, *sweetheart,* I love bein' with ye like this."

She wrapped her legs around his waist, and felt her desire quicken. "Alex, *right there.* Yes, my love, *don't stop.* Oh please. Please. Please, please, please!"

"I love you, Saorsa," he said quietly in her ear, as the rhythm of his thrusts increased. "I love you."

Saorsa was so happy she started giggling uncontrollably in between exclamations of pleasure. "Oh! You are so...*good at this!* You could give lessons!" She threw her hands in the air. "You make me want to yell, 'Wheee!'"

Alex started laughing too. "Stop laughing! *Stop it!* You're makin' *me* laugh! I cannae *focus...*," he paused and scolded at her, pretending to be stern. "Saorsa Stuart, the bedroom is no for giggles! We're doin' a *serious thing!*"

She gave him a saucy grin, then slid her legs up his back so that her ankles were over his shoulder blades, reached up and held onto her toes. "Oh, *sweet Hell,*" Alex moaned, moving into her again, nearly swept away by the feeling of this new position, "it isnae *fair*. It isnae fair how bad ye make me want you!"

Saorsa closed her eyes in bliss. *He is...perfect. This man is absolute sexual perfection. The way he moves inside me.* "Oh, Alex, that's so good! Right *there, right there!* Oh, I love the way you feel! You're going to make me lose...my...mind!"

"Sweet one," he panted, "you're going to make me come too." His pulse was racing. "A little more, my beauty. Yes, *fuck, just like that!*"

And then, they were both there together, calling out in happiness and delight to each other as they climaxed. Saorsa laughed all the way through hers, mostly because Alex shouted a surprised, "*Whoa,* WHOA THERE!" just before he tumbled over the edge into bliss, which Saorsa thought was the funniest thing she'd ever heard. *It sounds like he's getting tossed into rapture by a naughty horse!*

They were flushed and joyful afterwards, eyes shining; and Saorsa's cheeks hurt from smiling at Alex, who was kissing her repeatedly and playfully on the cheeks, eyelids, forehead, and mouth. *When was the last time I was this happy? I can't remember!*

"Saor-sa," Alex sang in her ear softly, "I lo-ove you!"

She gave a delighted squeak and kissed his cheek. "I love you, too!" *The wolves! The last time he was this carefree was here at Wolfcroft. The night we saw the wolves!* This place held healing magick for him. *Definitely.* There was something here, something that wasn't anywhere else which seemed to free him and help him find light. *I must figure out what it is.*

"Let's stay in bed forever," he said to her, touching his forehead lightly to hers. "Just stay here in bed. I just want to be with you, kiss you, an' talk wit' ye, an' forget everythin' else."

There was a soft knock on the door. "Saorsa," Willow called softly, "you asked me to tell you when breakfast is ready."

"Thank you!" Saorsa called. She kissed Alex on the nose. "I'm sorry, but we can't stay in bed forever today, Alex," she said softly, running her hands through his hair. "We have a clan to look after, and stories to trade. But...will you come back to my bed tonight?"

"Always," he smiled at her, kissing her forehead. "Forever an' ever. For always."

"Everyone's gathering in what we've decided to call the Great Hall," Annag told Saorsa. "Svend and Eske put a grand table in the center we can all sit around. Maggie's a bit better. She's answering questions and eating. An' Lord an' Lady, after Willow an' Svend did their energy work on her last night, the girl slept like a rock an' *snored*." She grinned. "I wish there was a way they could send away the snorin', too."

Saorsa spent the time after breakfast in the spell room at the top of the tower. Now that Alex was back and since Mother Agnes already knew where they were, the crystal she had used for the spell to guide loved ones home seemed less necessary. She cleared the crystal and tried something new. *I have no idea if it will work. And I'm uneasy about using it even if it does. But if push comes to shove....*

"I'll be right down, Annag," Saorsa told her fellow witch. "I just need to drop off something on the Bone Table first."

After Alex had risen from their bed that morning to get dressed for the second time, Saorsa had lay in the sheets, her limbs feeling heavy with bliss. She watched Alex moving around the room, her heart overflowing with feeling. *He wants to marry me. He's finding himself again, healing. And...he's here.*

Her hand brushed an object under Alex's pillow, and she closed her hand around it, and knew immediately what it was. *Another bone for my collection. Another gift.*

But this one was...unusual. It was mostly flat, and about an inch and a half high. A little girl's face. *A doll's face, I suppose. But there's no holes to sew it onto a doll.* It had the suggestion of hair, too. The eyes were closed. Saorsa had no idea what substance formed it. *It looks like bone or ceramic, but isn't nearly as brittle. It could be thrown many times without fear of damaging it.* The face had a happy, peaceful expression that reminded her of a sleeping baby. *Baby.*

Her eyes widened as she watched Alex pull his shirt over his head and turn toward where she lay to give her a smile. "Washstand's all yours, doll. I cannae find my comb. Is yours around?"

Doll. She'd heard Scottish men use the term of endearment before, but she'd never heard *Alex* use it until this very moment. She looked down at the little doll-like face on her palm. *Someone is sending me a message.* She nodded and gestured toward the dressing table. "Top drawer on the right."

Goddess...am I being told that there's a baby on the way? She put her hand tentatively on her belly. *Am I...did my moon cycle hit the right phase, and now I'm carrying a Fae's child? Or...*she looked at Alex, who had tied his hair back and was hunting through his bag for something. *Or am I being told that he fathered a child last night? Or this morning?*

"Great Heavenly *Father*, I need a haircut," Alex moaned, as a dark wave of hair escaped control and fell forward over his eyes. "Havenae gotten to tend to regular things in such a long time. Been just too sired...I mean, *tired*." Saorsa's stomach tipped at the sound of *father* and *sired*.

"What do ye have there, *eun beag*?" He was standing next to the bed, looking at her affectionately. "Is that somethin' of Oona's?"

"No," she said, climbing out of bed and holding the little face out for him to see, "it's something of mine. But I found it in the bed, and I don't know how it got there."

"Looks like a bairn," he said, taking it from her. "Maybe it's magick. Maybe we made the wee thing with our kisses." And Saorsa went weak in the knees.

………

"The good news is," Duncan laughed as the last of the group settled around the table in front of the fire, "that we're a chatty, familiar lot. We talked all last night and this mornin', so other than information Alex might have to add and any future plans, everyone's mostly caught up."

"That's wonderful!" exclaimed Saorsa. "First, I'd like to thank you all for being here. For *everything* you've done. I think we're going to get some answers soon. And it's so nice to have all of you together in one place. I can't thank you enough."

She looked at Maggie, who was watching her with interest. Annag had asked Maggie if she wanted to come to the meeting, and said it was about magick and faeries. Maggie had nodded, even though Saorsa wasn't certain the girl actually understood. She seemed much improved being with Annag and Maria. *I know what it is like to live between worlds,* Saorsa's mother had told her. *And so I will stay with Maggie as long as she needs it.*

"The purpose of this meeting," Saorsa began, "is to discuss the Violet Woman and her plans. To advance theories and see if we can predict her next move. Whatever the plot is, she seems to be in charge or high up the command chain here on earth. We know there are humans working with her in the British military, Caroline Scott most likely being one of them. If we figure *her* out, we have a better chance of protecting ourselves, and perhaps getting in a position to end this whole thing." She looked around the table. "She's going to come here. We have Alex. Oona. A spell book she might want. The amulet shards Laoise took out of Maria. The shards in *me*. And...."

Alex stood up, reached under his coat to his belt, and then tossed something on the table. Saorsa looked at him sharply. "What is *that?*"

A coiled whip sat on the table. Vika stood and bent forward for a look. "Dinnae touch it," Alex cautioned. "It works on its own once ye open it, and creates more whips that are on *fire*. And it screams somethin' fierce." He fished another object from a leather pouch on his belt and placed it on the table. "An' then there's *that*."

"Where did you get these?" Rune asked.

"Took them off o' her. When they hanged me."

There were exclamations of horror all around the table. "What do you mean, *when they hanged you?*" Adamina shrieked.

"It's a long story. Suffice to say they took me to Tower Hill, put my head in a noose, an' opened the trap door. But I got free an' took these off the Violet Woman before my escape." He looked around. "Anyone know what...."

"Oh, glorious hounds of Hecate!" Laoise cried, leaping to her feet. "*I know who the Violet Woman is!*"

There were exclamations around the table on all sides. "Who? Tell us!" Saorsa shouted.

Laoise took a deep breath. "When Alex was in the Tower of London, he sent an aspect to see you, and the body he left behind was briefly occupied, or *co-occupied,* since he was still in there but asleep, by another aspect. The aspect said he was *in the blue,* kept asking for 'his mistress', and asked why the 'Children of Rhamnousia' weren't coming for him." She looked around the table. "Rhamnousia has another name: Nemesis. She was the ancient Greek goddess who carried out retribution against those who were arrogant before the gods. She delivers her justice with a very specific whip." Laoise pointed a finger at the weapon on the table before Alex. "And *that*...is the whip of Nemesis."

Everyone began talking at once. "Wait, wait!" Laoise said. "There's more! Nemesis has disputed parentage, but the most popular tales say she is the daughter of Nyx, goddess of night, and Erebus, the personification of darkness."

"*I am Darkness*," Saorsa stated. "That's what Thomas has said on many occasions."

"It's a title," Laoise explained. "Nyx is a...particular type of creature called an *Elemental.* They are related to the Fae, but don't belong to any houses. Their magickal practices are...*different.* The Fae aren't supposed to study them. But there's a rumor that Thomas was given leave to, so that the Fae could understand the Elementals enough to figure out protections against them. I don't know if it's true, but there's a story that Thomas was given an Elemental title, that of *Darkness,* once he was among the Elementals. And as part of the...political union, I suppose, he could have fathered a child among the Elementals as well. The High Fae do that. It's sort of like royal marriage here."

"So if Thomas fathered Nemesis," Vika said slowly, "that means the daemon that's been torturing you, Alex, is your *half-sister*." The room fell silent.

"Nemesis is also supposed to be able to...change faces," Adamina said shakily. "I've read about her. There are folk tales about it."

"And we have conflicting accounts of exactly what she looks like," Saorsa said. "And when Alex saw her once, her face changed *right in front of him.*"

Alex nodded. "It makes sense," he said. "Saorsa...you told me the Fae say *blood knows blood.* When I pick up Oona, there's...a little flutter, *a feeling,* in my heart. You said we ken she's of the Deck of Crows." He paused. "On the platform, when I took this whip off the Violet Woman, there was a similar feelin'. I think...," he looked at the whip, "I think we *are* related."

"But what the hell is she *doing?*" Vika said. "This isn't just inter-sibling angst. She's manipulating things. Maria and Saorsa were in prison for *twenty-five years.* How does all this fit together?"

"I have a theory," Saorsa said. "And...keep in mind, I could be wrong." She fished a large piece of chalk from her belt and looked down at an enormous slate slab Eske had found in the storage room and had placed on the table before her. "Can everyone see?"

"Before we get goin'," Alex interrupted, "can someone tell me why this crow's in here, an' why it keeps followin' me around an' starin' at me?"

"That's a daemon, Alex," Saorsa said, not wanting to lose her train of thought. "His name is Malphas. He built this tower. And he was your babysitter, sort of, when you were one and two."

"He can't talk to you now," Adamina added. "Not since you've been split."

"Oh," Alex said, looking at the crow. "That makes *perfect* sense."

People shifted to get a better view of Saorsa's slate. "Adamina and Laoise tell us," Saorsa began, "that the Fae are at war. And that it sounds like it isn't going well. Magick, which powers a lot of their defenses, is in short supply. Rumors and prophecies are starting to spread among the Fae. Including ones about the *leth dhia*."

She paused, thinking. "Here's what we have on *leth dhia*. They are dangerous creatures who can split themselves into aspects and those aspects can communicate across realms. They can influence minds by sending dreams and visions. They are, apparently, highly charismatic and intelligent...."

"Thank you," Alex said, smiling.

"...and *insanely* dangerous. As in, they go insane and things get dangerous. World domination and tyrannical rule are their favorite pastimes."

"I dinnae think it's *so* bad as that," Alex said softly.

"*Leth dhia* are rare. Because of their inherent danger to everyone and everything around them, they are supposed to be killed at birth. *Parenting* one is illegal among the Fae. They do sometimes keep them alive for a while to study them." She looked around the table. "But, in Alex's case, he *wasn't* killed. He was, instead, split into human and Fae components, and the connection between them was severed. Mostly. Each part was to be contained in its home world."

"But if you put them together, you'd have a megalomaniacal general," Vika chimed in. "And if you *could* find a way to control him, to get him to work *for* you...you'd be damn hard to beat. You could take over a world and hold it."

"Exactly," Saorsa said. "The question is...how do you control the *leth dhia*? It has to be a magickal method, yes?" She drew a huge circle on the slate. "So, let's think about Fae magick."

"The map you got from the Aunties," Rune said. "Four tribes. Leading to how magick is worked now."

Adamina grew excited. "Thomas...he told me about four tribes!"

Saorsa looked at her. "He *did?*"

Adamina nodded enthusiastically. "Yes! There's a story. Of how the Fae lost the earth as their home."

"I'll put down what I know, and you tell me if Thomas agrees," Saorsa said, smiling.
"Long ago, all the land on earth was one mass," she began, drawing a large circle. "And the Fae lived here. There were four tribes. One in the north, one in the east, one in the south, and one in the west. Each tribe had a special kind of magick." Saorsa made notes in the four directions as she spoke. "The northern tribe specialized in earth magick. They were gifted in the ways of plants and animals, and working with stones and earth." Saorsa looked at Adamina, who nodded.

"In the east, the people became great scientists. Logic was their specialty. *Thought.* The southern tribe had a great aptitude for being able to learn the magick of other races." Saorsa looked at Svend. "Including working with the dragon lines."

"Thomas' ancestors are from that tribe," Adamina added.

"The Magician. That makes sense," Duncan stated.

"And in the west, the magick was based around love and emotion. Art. Music. Inspiration. This was represented by water. What if," Saorsa said slowly, "to control a *leth dhia*...or, maybe to reassemble him...you need a ritual?" She pointed to the four directions on the circle. "Four items. Each infused with magickal energies from one of the four original tribes. The Aunties told us certain families here on earth are thought to be associated with these tribes. These families sometimes produce magickal humans." There was a long pause. "Trying to capture *Fae* related to the four tribes might arouse suspicion. But most Fae don't *care* what happens to humans. They dislike us, even."

Laoise's eyes lit up. "The stone! Maria, the amulet shards...they're part of a magickal stone here on earth. No one among the Fae probably even knows it's here! And you're a *Stuart*. And it spent *years* in your skin! So...what if the amulet, a stone, is the item for the *north* in the ritual?"

"They wanted the amulet, but then it broke and ended up in *me*," Maria gasped. "So they held on to me, and Saorsa...."

"...for a quarter of a century," Edan said flatly. "Put you in a prison, so they'd know where the amulet was until they could collect the other ritual items!"

"Could that be *it?*" Willow said. "If so, where are the other items?"

"Oh, Thor's thunder," Svend said, standing up. "The dragon lines started moving *right around the time Maria was imprisoned.* What if they are moving them to *power the ritual?* Make it happen in a specific place?"

There was a stunned silence. "All right, *deep breath,* everyone," Saorsa said. "" There *is* a problem with my theory. The eastern tribe is extinct. So, no eastern magickal human is here. They were wiped out before the Fae left earth."

"No!" Adamina cried. "They *weren't!*" She looked at Alex. "I have eastern tribe blood! And so does Alex!"

"What?" Saorsa held on to the edge of the table.

"When Thomas did the ritual that...that makes me look young like this, the magick...well, I displayed eastern faerie traits. I did something called *striking*. I had a forked tongue. Apparently eastern Fae have *reptile* traits. Thomas says if I ever get really cold, I may go into a hibernation state where my heart shuts off...."

"Oh GOD!" Alex shouted. "*I've done that!* Saorsa...when I was shot, an' it snowed, you thought I was dead!"

Saorsa's mind was reeling. "But then why did the map say *extinct?*"

"Thomas was shocked as well," Adamina said. "He couldn't believe it. He says there is only *one* Fae left with eastern blood and that she's had no children. He can't figure out how the blood got to *me*."

"One Fae left?" Vika asked. "Where? Does only Thomas know about her?"

Adamina paused. "I think most people don't know she still exists," she said. "Or, if they do, no one goes near her. Thomas says she's mad." He took a deep breath. "He said her name is...*Medusa*."

Silence. Then Vika spoke. "You mean...like turn men to stone, snakes-for-hair...*that* Medusa?" Adamina nodded.

"Wait, wait," Saorsa said. "Back up. Adamina, if you have eastern Fae blood...."

"Oh, Goddess, then any of Alex's children do too," Annag gasped. *"Fia's bairn!"*

"So the Violet Woman is trying to keep the eastern Fae bloodline alive?"

"Wait!" Saorsa said. "I mean, the bairn is important but...Adamina, what did you have to do at Carlisle? To buy Duncan's freedom?"

"Sing," Adamina said. "In Gaelic." She put her hand to her face. *"Over a sword!"*

Saorsa pointed to her map. "Sword! Symbol of the east. Infused with your music! That's...that's another ritual object!"

"So they thought they had the stone, and now they have a sword," Edan said. "What other items do they need?"

"A wand for south. And a chalice or bowl for west," Saorsa answered. "Oh, Goddess, *we might actually be on to something*."

"They've been collecting magickal humans to get or make the ritual objects, and trying to figure out how to put the *leth dhia* back together," Toran stated. "And moving the dragon lines for power. Got it. But...does anyone actually know how many pieces of Alex there *are?*"

"The thing that tried to take me through the portal the night we got you out of Branxholme," Saorsa said, "claimed it needed *Maria, Saorsa, Adamina,* and *one more.* But the amulet is in both me *and* mum. The numbers don't add up."

"You're the Flower of the West," Rune noted. "Perhaps you are part of both north *and* west."

"On another note, does this actually have anything to do with the war?" Vika asked. "The Violet Woman doesn't strike me as the *save the world* type. Is she trying to reassemble Alex to win the war for the Fae? Or to get a world for herself, while everyone's distracted by the war?"

"She's been trying to learn to control me," Alex said. "*That's* why she comes through!"

"This is starting to make sense," Duncan said. "Toss people in prison so you know where they are...."

"Och, it's why I cannae leave the island anymore!" Alex moaned. "To keep me near the ritual site!"

"Saorsa, if Fia's baby has eastern Fae blood," Laoise said, "the Violet Woman isn't the only one who will be interested. We should move Fia *here*. Where it's safer." All eyes moved to Oona, who was happily sucking on a bit of bread in Willow's arms.

"Alright," Duncan said. "We ken Oona's Deck of Crows. So...she could be eastern Fae too." He shook his head. "We have to watch this bairn *close*."

"She has to have been fathered by some male in the Deck related to Alex, or by one of his aspects," Saorsa pointed out.

"One other thing," Edan asked. "Speaking of Fia and going back to *in the blue*...Alex, do you have any idea where the Scott sapphire is?"

"An' what's that *other* amulet belongin' to Nemesis that you've brought us?" Duncan added.

There was a distant sound, high in the air above the tower, like a boulder smashing into the ground. Everyone stood and looked up. "What was that?" Vika said, her hands on her knives.

"I dinnae ken," Alex said, "but I dinnae think it's good."

But Saorsa was ready. "Rune, bar the doors and you and your men stay here and guard this entrance," Saorsa directed. "Laoise...please go with Adamina, Maria, and Annag to the third floor. Take Oona and Maggie with you, and stay there. Everyone else...let's head up to the spell room and see what is happening." Alex grabbed the whip and Nemesis' amulet. "Let's go!"

"You've some sort of barrier up, aye?" Duncan asked.

"Yes," Saorsa said, "but I don't know how much magickal energy actually *using* it takes." She grabbed hold of Alex's hand. "You haven't been up there, you can't picture it yet. Hold my hand and I'll take you through!" Macha raced through the archway and disappeared, followed by Malphas.

"Here," said Willow, fishing in her belt pouch once they arrived in the spell room and producing one of the rose clay bracelets. "Put this on, Alex. Maggie, Duncan, and Vika got theirs last night."

"What is it?"

"Protection," Willow stated.

"Alex, is there enough magickal energy in this room for you to split? And send an aspect to the roof?" Saorsa asked.

Alex nodded. "Think so." He closed his eyes, and then there were two.

"That's a good one," Svend grinned.

"Hello, Doug, nice to see you again," Vika quipped.

"I'll take him up, so he can go faster," Saorsa said. She grabbed the aspect's hand, and they raced together through the archway before her primary Alex could protest.

They were on the roof now, and storm clouds were moving in. Saorsa left the aspect and went back through the archway. "Now you know what it looks like, so you can send aspects yourself next time," she said to Alex. "Does he see anything?"

"No yet," Alex said. "He can see the shield a bit, though." Saorsa looked out a window. Sure enough, there was a faint movement in the air, making a dome shape over Wolfcroft, barely visible against the heavy cloud cover.

"Wait!" Alex said, pointing to the west. "He says somethin' tried to come through over there!" Everyone moved to the western window. Sure enough, the shield was slightly brighter in that direction, and the shape seemed distorted.

"I need to check the cylinders," Saorsa explained, "and see how much energy it took to use the shield."

"I'm goin' to leave him up there on the roof," Alex explained, as Saorsa took his hand and led him to the Siphon room. The others followed.

"Here's the reason you were stopped from being able to split at Haggs Castle," Vika said to Alex. "Saorsa sucked all the magick out of Glasgow!"

"Sorry," Saorsa grinned. "Let bygones be bygones?" Her sense of humor faded quickly when she looked at the cylinder powering the shield crystal. It had dropped noticeably.

"She was testing the shield to see how strong it was," Vika guessed. "Or *someone* was. But they are *here,* and now they know we're ready."

"Except we don't exactly have a plan," Svend said. "Or do we?"

"So," Saorsa said, "I think *her* plan is to break in here and capture me. Doing that will lower our defenses since I run the tower. I also have the rest of the amulet shards they need in my body." Saorsa paused. "I can run four spells at a time. Right now, we have a Shield, Help from the Spirits of the Woods, an Enemy Doubt and Weakening Spell, and...," she looked at Alex, "one empty one. I was hoping to try and *catch* her with the fourth crystal. Take Nemesis off the battlefield. But...being a jailer, it feels *wrong*." She paused. "And if she's an Elemental..., do I even have the magick to hold her?"

Alex held out the amulet he'd placed on the table with the whip downstairs. "Maybe this can." He looked around at the assembled faces. "It was meant to hold my soul, after I died on the gallows. I heard Nemesis talkin' about it in the prison."

"How does it know who to hold?" Duncan asked. "Does it just take in the first soul around?"

"Can I see that?" Svend took it from Alex. He held the stone by the chain, and they all watched as the stone pivoted its largest facet in Alex's direction and swung at an unnatural angle toward him and stayed there. "It's...it seems to be attuned specifically to you."

"Can you change attunement?" Toran asked. "Wipe out the old, and put in a new?"

"We can try," Willow said, looking at Svend. "We're really good at releasing things. And I know how to attune *beings*. But this is an *object*. How do we get it to look for Nemesis?"

"Let's do what we *do* know," Svend said, "and clear whatever is in it that's looking for Alex first."

"You can use the library," Saorsa said. "It's quiet there."

"We'll be back," said Svend, taking the amulet. "Alex...can we have that whip? Since it belongs to Nemesis, the energy on it might help us." Alex handed Svend the whip, and he took Willow's hand and headed quickly for the archway.

"Next," said Saorsa. "We need to get her close. She's probably going to bring friends. And they can *fly*."

"If ye dinnae need the fourth spell crystal to hold her," Alex said slowly, "maybe ye can use it to charge me up instead."

"Oh my God," said Vika. "That makes sense! When Alex was exposed to the knife, which generated a lot of magickal power, his Fae traits appeared! Saorsa, if you can direct that power at Alex, maybe it will happen again!"

"He'd be able to fly," Edan chimed in.

"An' then...," Alex said, spreading his hands, "I can split myself. She an' most of her henchmen have wings, according to you an' Fia. So we can have just as many men with wings to fight them." He grinned. "An' they may be better at flyin', but *my team* will be able to communicate."

"This could work," said Vika. "Lure them in, and if we can get her out of the air, those of us on the ground can take out her body and trap the soul in that amulet!"

"But Alex, you *hated* the way the knife made you act! What if...what if we put in too much magick? What if you can't control yourself?" Saorsa was concerned.

"I'll send up duplicates," Alex said, "an' keep me safe in here. Vika can watch me. If she thinks I'm changin' too much, she can tell ye to power down the spell."

"Alright," Duncan said. "So...our most vulnerable are safe in the middle of the tower with Annag to protect them with magick and Laoise to help if something happens. I'll run down and tell them we've seen someone attack the shield and to sit tight. I'll tell Rune to be ready for anything trying to come in from the woods, animal or Fae. And then...," he looked around, "Saorsa changes the spell on the fourth crystal to transform Alex. Vika watches Alex. And the rest of us, we beat the shite out of anything that comes into this tower and tries to stop Saorsa from managing the magick in those crystals. With luck, we get the Violet Woman down and trap her." He headed for the archway.

"And then figure out what to do next," Vika said. "If we pull this off, it will *definitely* give the other side pause."

"One more thing," Saorsa said. "Everyone else knows this, but...Alex, Vika, Duncan...I don't think you do." She took a deep breath. "At Buccleuch Church...when we were attacked...."

"Rune told Duncan and me," Vika said quietly. "It is what it is."

"Told ye *what?*" Alex looked suspicious.

Oh, no. Here goes. "Alex...when you and Fia were attacked, and you were hurt...I called on the Violet Woman to assist. I made a deal. She worked through you, and...."

"You called her in?" Alex said, stunned. "You...*you gave me to her?*"

"You would have died if I hadn't! And I couldn't ask you for permission! You were down in the cemetery!"

Alex just stared at her in shock with pain in his eyes. "You *gave* me to her?" he said again, bewildered. "Saorsa...I killed over *a hundred men* with that knife."

Saorsa felt her blood turn to ice. "Alex...it was all I could think to do! If we'd been killed there...."

"What did ye promise her, Saorsa? What did ye give her in trade for her aid?" Alex spat angrily.

"A favor. Here on earth. As long as it doesn't injure or kill any humans or you."

Alex shook his head. "So if we *do* capture her, she could ask to be freed."

"Yes."

"She could ask for this tower!"

"I didn't know I'd *have this tower!*" Saorsa moved to Alex's side. "I didn't *want* to do it, Alex! I know letting her in hurt you. I know a hundred men were trapped in that knife. But I didn't know it would be *that bad!* The alternative was for us to be killed! And *you know* we are at the center of this thing! If we aren't here to figure it out...a lot more than a hundred people could die!"

"We dinnae know that!" Alex growled. "We dinnae have *proof!*"

"I had *moments* to make that call!"

"Wait," Toran said. "Why *did* the Violet Woman make that deal? Aren't she and the redcoats on the same side?"

"No," Vika answered. "The Violet Woman works with very *specific* members of the British military. Those soldiers would most likely not have taken Saorsa and Alex prisoner, but simply strung them up. Alex is wanted by the rank-and-file military *dead or alive*. The Violet Woman, Nemesis, wants Alex's *soul*. I'm pretty sure she can't get it if it's left his body and she wasn't around to witness it. These are two different sets of enemies here, for the most part."

"She didnae have that amulet to imprison me yet," Alex muttered. "She still needed me alive."

"I'm sorry," Saorsa said, looking at Alex. *Please don't shut me out.* "I didn't know that. I know it's awful and I violated your trust. I didn't know what else to do. I didn't know it would be that awful. I'd never seen her come through before."

She watched him close his eyes, and then he glared at her as he took a shuddering breath. "*Dinnae do it again,*" he said through bared teeth. "I'm no a slave, Saorsa. I'm no a thrall."

"I know," she said quietly. "I'm sorry." He wouldn't look at her. "I'm so sorry," Saorsa said. "I was trying to save you." He nodded. He wanted to move on, at least for now. They had more pressing concerns.

And then...another sound from the sky. At first, Saorsa thought she was hearing thunder. But then the shield gave off a huge amount of light to the west, and she saw further distortion in its shape. *A lot* of further distortion.

"What was that?" Duncan said, reappearing from the floors below.

"Here we go!" Vika said, snapping into her battle mindset. "Let's get in position! Duncan, you stay here with Edan and Toran and protect this Siphon and those storage cylinders. Saorsa, you, Alex and I will head to the casting room with your spells. Hopefully Svend and Willow figure out how to attune that amulet quickly!"

They raced for the archway and reappeared in the casting room. "I'm going to change the spell to power Alex!" Saorsa cried, grounding herself.

"You. Over here," Vika said, leading Alex to an area where she could see out a window and Saorsa clearly at the same time. "I know you want to defend her, but let me handle that first. You focus on what's happening in the skies. Give clear orders. If I go down, *then* you protect Saorsa. Got it?" Alex nodded.

"It's changed!" Saorsa said. "Tell me what's happening!"

Alex commanded his aspect still on the roof to return and rejoin. "He says the shield is taking a hit!"

"We don't want to waste all our energy on a busted shield!" Vika stated. "As soon as that amulet is attuned, we can go ahead and drop it! Use the power for something else!" She looked at Alex. "Is the new spell working? Feel anything yet?"

………

In the woods, a portal appeared. It was just outside the shield, and slightly to the west. It opened, and men in green coats swarmed out, followed by one of the Fae.

Tadhg. The Violet Woman's second-in-command here on earth. He had fifty of Lord DeSoulis' soldiers with him, all of whom were coated in spells to make them resistant to magick. Trained not only to operate on earth but in other worlds as well, they were well-disciplined fighters and operatives who followed orders ruthlessly and without question. On their last mission in Scotland they'd burned Buccleuch Castle while hunting for the Scott sapphire; it was the rare occasion where they turned up empty-handed. They didn't intend to fail on this one.

Tadhg handed a wooden box to the man next to him. "Eight seconds," he called to the troop leader. "That's all you'll have. As soon as you see the signal, you have eight seconds to place it and get clear to power it off the residual magick. After you blow the door, bring me the child. Then you can go back in for the other things."

"The child comes first."

"Yes," Tadhg answered, "the child comes first." And the green-coated men fixed their attention on the steps of the Tower of Roses.

………

The sky above the tower was filling with ravens. First there were ten, then twenty, then fifty. Vika MacLeod saw them, and knew the time had come.

"They've gotten in somewhere! Drop the shield!" she called to Saorsa. "They're in! There's no point in having it up anymore. They're here somewhere!" She looked at Alex. "Nothing yet?"

"No." He looked worried.

"Saorsa! Direct the shield resources toward Alex!"

"Vika, it'll be too much for him!"

Vika looked out the window. The storm clouds had taken on a strange violet hue, and now there were at least a hundred ravens circling above. "Saorsa, *something is coming*. A *leth dhia* may be our only defense here soon!"

"Do it!" Alex called to Saorsa. "*Do it now!*"

Saorsa took a deep breath at the sound of his voice. *He's angry about my deal with Nemesis.* She shook the worry from her head and began to cast. *What if this doesn't work?*

"DARKFLOWER!" a supernaturally loud voice rang through the top floors of the tower. "I AM HERE! I WISH TO SPEAK!" Saorsa looked up. *The roof! Nemesis was on the roof!*

"I HAVE COME FOR THE DEBT YOU OWE ME!"

"She's not attacking us yet," Vika whispered. "We should go up. She *might* be trying to avoid a giant magickal event the Fae would notice. Can you just shield *us* in place of that doubt spell you have on the Fae? Because...they don't seem that doubtful."

Duncan appeared. "What do we do?"

"You, Edan, and Toran stay put. Guard that energy. We're going to try and buy some time for the spell to work on Alex and for Willow and Svend to attune that amulet," Vika explained.

Saorsa's spells had been reset. *One for help from forest spirits if we are attacked. Two to try and transform Alex. And shields against physical harm on me, Alex, and Vika.* "All right!' Saorsa called up to Nemesis. "We're coming up to talk!"

She stepped through the archway and suddenly she was in the stone circle on the top of the Tower of Roses with Alex and Vika behind her. The forest fell away on all sides. It felt like standing on top of the world.

There were torches between each of the standing stones, and as the storm clouds blotted out the afternoon sun they flamed to life. Saorsa Stuart stood at the top of her dark tower, silhouetted against an eerie purple and gray sky. Before her stood the Violet Woman, flanked by two attendants. Saorsa recognized one: Ciannat.

"Greetings, Darkflower," Nemesis said, an expression between a sneer and a smile on her face. Saorsa watched her features slide, and then *shift*; and suddenly she saw the resemblance Laoise had seen. *Similar bone structure. The dark hair tinged with red. The tall, graceful way of holding herself.* She saw the family resemblance to Alex and Thomas.

"What do you want?" Saorsa said coldly, and surprised herself at how confident she sounded.

"I want the debt paid," Nemesis spat. "Fail to do so and...."

"Just tell me what you want," Saorsa hissed, cutting her off.

Nemesis raised an eyebrow. "Give me the Terrastone. The fragments that were taken from Maria Stuart. And, of course, the ones from *you*."

"The deal said I can't be harmed in the paying. How am I supposed to get fragments *out of my flesh* without being harmed?"

"If you have magick for that shield, you have magick for this," the Violet Woman countered. "Deliver me the Terrastone. Now. Or you will have broken our contract, and the Fae will not let that stand."

"I need a few minutes."

Nemesis smiled. "We will wait."

Saorsa turned and went back through the archway with Alex and Vika. *How long do we have? Can I even do this? Will it give Willow and Svend the time they need?*

"I need the fragments from my mother," Saorsa said to Vika. "They're in the Bone Room. I'll be back." She disappeared through the archway. She fished the pouch containing the fragments from its hiding place behind a decorative wood panel in the table. *Thank the Goddess Laoise got all of these out of my mother. Otherwise I'd have to bring her up here too, and try a process that I have no idea how to do.*

Her mind was filled with spinning thoughts. *I have minutes to get the amulet shards out of me. Will it hurt me? Can I even do it? Maybe we won't have to fight the Violet Woman and she'll leave.* But she knew that was wishful thinking. *She wants her whip. And the soul amulet. And Alex.* There was no way Nemesis was going to leave Alex alone.

On the other hand...if I can bring her the amulet, she can't ask for the tower. Or freedom. But she'd have her hands on half of the ritual items. Saorsa put her hand over her belly. *She could have asked for Oona. Or...my firstborn. Like in the faerie tales. But she didn't. That's a blessing, indeed.*

You know she isn't going to go peacefully after you give her this stone, she said to herself. *You know.* And then, a curious thing happened. Her eyes fell on the bones that had been delivered to her thus far, lying on the table.

A spiral seashell.

A tiny wooden doll's hand, worn with age.

A small replica crow's skull, carved from lapis.

An astragalus bone.

A Roman coin.

A polished tiger's eye.

A wolf's tooth.

A bronze Celtic ring.

A doll's face.

Nine bones so far. Not yet a complete set. But three times three. And she felt compelled to use them. She scooped them up and piled them into an olive wood cup she'd found sitting on the center of the table yesterday morning. *Olive wood. Symbolizing hope.* And for the first time, she cast her bones.

They bumped and scattered across the table's surface, each spinning on their own path. Each had its own meaning for her; she would read their relationship. Except instead of nine bones falling from the cup, *ten* appeared. And the tenth item landed in the center, with all the other bones framing it and pointing toward *it*. The ring, the coin, and the little doll's face were, impossibly, balanced on their edges, radiating out from the tenth object like rays from the sun.

This bone. This. This is the answer.

Saorsa picked up the new object. A large plate, triangular in shape. It curved slightly, and the shape reflected the light that hit it and showed it to be iridescent. A beautiful blend of green, purple, and blue. It felt like thick leather. *A dragon's scale.*

And Saorsa knew.

The Violet Woman was going to get her Terrastone. And then she intended to tear the tower, and everyone in it, apart. She'd take what she wanted. But she didn't know the secret in Saorsa's bones.

Saorsa whirled around and raced through the archway to the spell room. "Vika! I need Svend up here *now!* Get him!" Vika didn't argue. She saw the spark in her eyes. *Saorsa Stuart has a plan.* She nodded and headed for the archway at a run.

"Alex! Is the spell working yet? Any changes?" He crossed the room to her. "No yet." She had to take a moment for him. "Alex," she said, taking his hands. "I know you're angry at me about Buccleuch Church...."

He shook his head. "I forgive ye," he said quietly. "Just...I feel badly, is all. Killin' men who are doin' their job without mercy...it's no who I am."

"I know," she said, touching his cheek, "and we can talk more later. But I need you to do something. I'm going to keep two spells on you, and direct the other two at me to pull the shards out and reform the stone. I don't know what this is going to do to me, Alex. But *don't stop the process.*" She paused. "And later. When I tell your aspects to *get out of the sky,* I need them to do it *immediately,* and then turn all their attention to Nemesis."

"We almost have it!" Svend blurted, running into the room behind Vika. "Willow's finishing it!"

"I need to talk to you. Quickly!" Saorsa pulled Svend aside.

Saorsa stood in between two of the casting crystals. Each time she stopped a spell and cast another her energy level dropped somewhat. Soon adrenaline alone would be her fuel. Toran appeared through the archway. "We're losing energy at a much higher rate. As in, *quickly*. Just be warned."

But Saorsa had no choice. She needed to try and transform Alex and she needed to extract the shards from herself. "Can you find me a chair?" she asked Toran, who left and returned with one from the Bone Room before disappearing again.

And once more, Saorsa cast a new spell. *Help me. Pull these shards from my skin. Free me from them. Help them to be joined once more.* This was an entirely different type of spell casting. She no longer asked for something and hoped for a response; the magick in this tower was so concentrated that it was less of a request and more of an action of *will*. Each time something worked, like raising the shield, she was shocked. She also wondered how it might change her.

She sat in the chair, hands raised, bathed in light from the two crystals. Vika, Alex, and Svend watched as the light turned slightly more opaque, and then they couldn't see her at all. But they could hear her. A *whispering*. A whispering that grew to a tremendous volume. And Svend realized they were actually hearing *the stone*.

"Saorsa!" Alex cried, starting to move toward the light. "*Saorsa!*"

"No, no, *no!*" Vika yelled, trying to physically stop him from interrupting the spell. "Alex, *let her be!*"

The whispering grew louder. "Somethin's *takin' her!*" Alex shouted, and now Svend was helping hold him back. "*Saorsa!*"

Svend had managed to push Alex back a bit. "Look at me. *Look at me.* Try to breathe! She's going to be alright."

But Alex continued to keep his eyes trained on the column of light that contained Saorsa. "Let me go to her!"

"Alex!" Svend raised his voice, which got his attention. "I don't want to hurt you, friend, and I know you don't want to hurt me. So you need to stop fighting us. She's in *the light,* Alex. She's being cleared of something that was never supposed to be in her in the first place! That's a *good thing*."

"You told me those shards crack and burn her, Alex," Vika said. "I know you're not comfortable around magick. But this is *good*." She wrapped her arms around him. "Just stay here. And let her do her work."

"I want to protect her, Vika," Alex told his friend.

"I know. But you can't protect her from everything," she said, trying to calm him. "You just can't."

And suddenly the light column vanished, and Saorsa sat in her chair, gazing in wonder as the shards that had been embedded in her skin floated lazily about her in the air. "Oh, my Goddess," she breathed, her eyes lighting up. "They're *out!*"

Alex, Svend, and Vika stayed still. "You're alright?" Alex asked.

"Yes." Saorsa opened the leather pouch of shards she'd retrieved from the Bone Room and the shards inside joined the others in their slow dance in the air. "They're...out. They're *out of us*." She shook her head. "I...I can't believe it!"

The whispering began again, but much softer this time, like a mother comforting a child. The shards moved closer to each other in the air on each subsequent rotation, and then, with a burst of light, they joined themselves and a solid, oval stone the size of a palm dropped into her lap. Saorsa held it up. "Unakite," she marveled. "It looks like unakite."

"TIME ENOUGH!" the Violet Woman roared. "Bring me the stone!"

Alex was by Saorsa's side. He took the stone from her and started toward the arch. Saorsa turned back to her spell stones for one last quick cast.

....

Saorsa was the last one on the roof. "Well?" the Violet Woman said impatiently. "Where is it?" Alex tossed her the stone. Nemesis looked at it and smiled.

"Twenty-five years," she laughed. "Twenty-five years we tried to put this stone back together again. And you did it in *twenty minutes!*" She grinned, delighted. "How did you *do* that, Saorsa Stuart?" Her expression then transformed quickly to one of anger. "Why does my father's magick *listen to YOU?*"

"Well," Saorsa said with a confidence she did not feel, "maybe I'm not an arsehole." Vika stifled a laugh, and the face of the goddess Nemesis became a mask of rage.

"The debt is settled, Saorsa Stuart," she growled, "but the score *isn't.*" She held up her hand, and a burst of violet lightning lit up the sky. "*Bring me the child and the leth dhia aspect! And hang the Stuarts and Adamina Scott from the tower walls!*"

And the night came alive.

....

On the ground floor, a tremendous explosion blew the front doors of the Tower of Roses wide open, and green-coated men began to push their way into the tower through the smoke. They were unprepared for the sight of Eske wielding two full-size axes.

Rune and his men were ready. They were, however, outnumbered more than ten to one, and their opponents were not without skill. *Hold them as long as we can,* Rune thought, trying not to slip on a floor already slickening with blood. He saw Aeric a few feet away nearly lose a limb. *Give those on the roof time.*

The warriors spun and slashed, axes, swords, and shields moving the way that their ancestors had wielded them for ages before. There were many close calls, but Rune and his men were holding their own, aided by the protective rose-clay spells on their left wrists.

They were being pushed toward the stairs. *We'll hold them there, and then retreat to the third floor when we can't go on.* He wondered how long it would take for Nemesis and her team to break the magick on the archways. He thought of Oona upstairs. *Don't let them get to the bairn.*

But then, something shifted. A disturbance back by the entrance. It took Rune a moment to realize what it was. He turned and looked up the stairs. Willow was there, her hands raised. She had called the wolves of Wolfcroft.

The pack flooded into the hall, snarling and savage, and began attacking the swarm of green-coated men from the rear. The hall filled with screams as the wolves, led by Macha, threw themselves at the throats of Tadhg's men.

Rune offered up a brief thank you to the Allfather and saw Willow spin and race for the arch outside the kitchen.

·········

Saorsa had never moved so fast in her life. She saw what was happening out of the corner of her eye as she spun and raced toward the arch; ten winged Fae rising into view over the edge of the tower, armed to the teeth and ready to fight. *I need to get inside!* They were coming for Alex.

Vika went through the arch ahead of her, and she felt Alex's hand on her arm as he dragged her through. Three things needed to happen now, and they needed to happen quickly, or all would be lost and the Violet Woman would win.

Svend had stayed below, positioned in her chair. Willow came tearing through the arch. "Here! Here!" She threw the amulet to Alex, and raced to stand behind Svend. "I'll help you call!"

Vika heard glass shatter on another level. "They're coming in the windows! They're after the Siphon!" She disappeared through the archway to aid Edan and the others.

A window shattered, as a Fae broke through. He landed next to Saorsa and reached for her. And Alex's emotion boosted the magick that had been sent to him. *Rage.* The thought of that male Fae putting his hands on Saorsa flipped every switch in Alex all at once. He did not so much transform as *explode* outward. Fangs. Wings.

His hands and ears elongated, his body stretched, and his eyes began to glow. And he shot forward, too fast to be seen, and tore the Fae's wings from his body before tossing him out the window. The monster that was Alex bellowed out an unmistakable *roar*.

Willow screamed, as blood flew across the room, briefly interrupting her casting. "Oh my GOD!"

The *leth dhia* let out another roar, glanced at Saorsa cowering on the floor, and dove into the sky through the broken window, his wings shooting out to the sides and beating the air as he rose to the top of the tower.

And then...there were ten.

Vika, Edan, Toran, and Duncan were trying to defend the storage canisters from two Fae when two *leth-dhia* duplicates came in through the windows. The Face quickly realized that they were probably going to lose if they stayed, so they took to the skies to take the duplicates down with arrows. The ravens assisted, diving and tearing, to try and slow the duplicates down.

"TOO FAST!" Saorsa screeched, running for the casting stones that fed magick to Alex. "Oh Goddess, *we lost him!* He changed *all at once!* And he didn't stay here, so we could communicate!"

A pitched battle was going on all around and through the tower. Ten Fae under the Violet Woman's command were breaking windows and entering from the air, searching the tower; but they were met by Macha, Rune, Aeric, Trig, or Eske. They had left the remains of the battle below to the wolves and were standing guard outside Oona's room. Annag maintained a strong protective spell from inside the room, but she was getting tired, and though Maria was aiding her, they couldn't go on too much longer.

"I hear something!" Svend called from his seat suddenly with excitement. "Oh my God, I think I hear one!"

Saorsa looked out the window, trying to spot the Violet Woman. And saw her hovering in the shadow of the tower. Nemesis handed a small bag to another Fae, who nodded and bolted off through the air. *Crap. There went the Terrastone.* No chance of retrieving it tonight. The sky was full of winged creatures; ravens, Fae, and *leth dhia,* and every single one of them trying to kill someone else.

She saw one of Alex's aspects split into three more. She didn't know where *her* Alex was; and he was the one carrying the amulet in which to trap the Violet Woman. His body had reacted differently to the magick than it ever had before; it had been a sudden and complete transformation.

She didn't know if this level of magick might transform him for good. She didn't know if he would listen to her, or anyone else at all. *I may have unleashed a leth dhia into the worlds.* "Alex!" she called, putting her hands on one of the crystals that powered his spell. "Alex! I need to talk to you! Can you hear me? Alex!"

....

One of the Fae had gotten smart. There was a metallic sound as a metal device hit the floor inside the Siphon room. It rolled under one of the copper storage containers and let out a high-pitched sound.

"*Move!*" Vika shouted, as she and Edan, Duncan and Toran raced for the archway. "Third floor!" The device raised its pitch, and a wave of sound radiated outwards from it before it exploded. The Siphon Globe cracked, and three of the four canisters began leaking magickal energy at a high rate.

Vika, Edan, Toran and Duncan appeared on the third floor in the middle of a battle. Vika's knives were flying before her feet were even firmly on the ground.

Rune wiped his forehead with the back of his hand and smiled as another Fae fell to the ground. Just he and Eske were left; both Aeric and Trig had been wounded and were with Laoise. "Hello, friends," he grinned, his face and armor splattered with blood. "Welcome to the third floor."

....

At the top of the tower, one of the crystals sending magick to Alex suddenly went dark and disappeared from its platform. "Oh Goddess!" Saorsa shouted, and ran for the archway. She emerged in the Siphon room and took in the destruction. *Cracked Globe. Two cylinders leaking. One dark.* The cylinder that remained intact was under Alex's remaining spell. The two providing energy to Willow and Svend's work were leaking badly.

How much time do we have? Will it be enough? Half a dozen ravens swooped in the window, and Saorsa went running back through the arch. She burst into the spell room. "The Globe and cylinders are cracked," she told them. "We don't have much time."

"Our calling is done," Svend told her. "It can't be stopped now."

Saorsa nodded. "Alex. He can't hear me. I can't get him out of the sky." She looked up to see a *leth dhia* get hit with an arrow and fall, splitting himself into two as he descended and leaving a live aspect in his wake, a shower of feathers surrounding him. "I think...he might be gone."

Willow shook her head. "Saorsa. We've used what we needed. Try calling him again with what's left. Magic never works exactly as it seems." She paused. "And remember, our greatest ally in this fight is love."

Saorsa's mind suddenly became clear. *Did I tell Willow Thomas the Rhymer had said that? Or was something speaking through Willow?* It didn't matter. It was the *message* that mattered.

She ran to stand between the three-still functioning spells. She grounded her exhausted body and tried to raise power once more. *Alex. I love you. If you are still able to hear me, know that I love you. I know we've had to work separately for a long time to stay alive. But remember: you and I, we always work better together.*

Hear me. Something is coming. Something to give you the advantage up there. Listen for my call or it may kill you. She paused. *Be ready, my love.*

And just then, the sky changed. A strange light appeared. Like an illuminated tunnel, cutting through the clouds. It was growing, and heading straight for the stone circle at the top of the Tower of Roses.

A dragon line. This place, this place sacred to The Morrigan, had been constructed on a dragon line long ago. Malphas had made the cave a tower and preserved the circle. A circle that was but a stopping point on a web of energy that circled the earth, and went *beyond.* A network of pathways traveled by *dragons.*

"Get out of the sky!" Saorsa screamed, throwing her hands onto one of the crystals. "*Get out of the way!*"

She saw the Violet Woman now, in a heated battle with a *leth dhia,* right in the tunnel's path. Just to the west of the circle.

Svend shouted, grabbing Willow and diving for cover, "Saorsa, *get down!* It can take off the whole top of this tower!" A tremendous sound. The entire tower shook. Svend and Willow had called a *dragon.*

But Saorsa didn't hear. Her hands were on the crystal. Calling. *I love you. Hear me. Oh, Goddess Alex, get out of the sky!* Two of the crystals disappeared, leaving the one that rotated slowly under her hands. *I am with you, Alex. I will try and reach you. Until the end.*

There were no words for the power that roared down the tunnel along the dragon line. A massive stream of conscious *light.* It moved at a tremendous speed, and Saorsa saw ravens near its path simply disintegrate.

The power of its passing knocked even the most powerful Fae and *leth dhia* from its path as if they had no mass at all. The sky went still in the dragon's wake as the combatants fell to earth.

Saorsa saw the Violet Woman fall. She tumbled from the sky. Tumbled, her violet-edged raven's wings motionless. She was helpless against the dragon, which had simply plowed through the sky over Wolfcroft at an unfathomable speed, knocking Nemesis to the center of the stone circle before disappearing along the dragon line just as quickly as it had come to the east. And in that passing, Saorsa understood the word *awe.*

She rushed through the archway and appeared in the circle. "Alex!" Saorsa shouted. Nemesis was on the ground before her, shaken and bruised, but love was what Saorsa sought. "*Alex!*"

Blood was pouring from the Violet Woman's mouth. She looked up at Saorsa. "Mine," she said, starting to laugh. "He's *mine.*"

But the dragon had given Alexander Scott the opening he needed. The *leth dhia* struck quickly. In an instant he was on the goddess, and Saorsa saw the attuned amulet crash to the stone a foot away from the Violet Woman.

He roared and began tearing at her with fangs and claws. *Blood and bone. Water and cloth. Heart and belly and brain.* Nemesis had no form anymore. Alex was breaking her body, tearing her apart like old paper, howling and screeching as he took his revenge for being made her slave. Saorsa threw up her hands to cover her face and turned away. She could see parts of the goddess' skull. *This, this is a bitter death.* The amulet shook and bounced as it snatched up all that was left of Nemesis; *her soul.*

All of the mercy that the Violet Woman had denied others was now being denied to her. The *leth dhia* tore her apart, snapping her bones. There was no compassion in him, and no hesitation; just a screaming *drive* to dismantle the being in front of him. His torturer. His possessor. *His sister.*

Saorsa heard a voice inside the amulet *scream*. An enraged scream that turned to terror and then anguish as the Violet Woman became aware of her new prison.

The sky overhead went dark. Saorsa was huddled in a ball at the base of the easternmost standing stone. She did not see the few surviving Fae beat a hasty retreat through the skies. She did not notice the light rain that began to fall. She sat, trembling, her mind blank. All she could feel was the beating of her heart.

The Violet Woman was gone. And perhaps the Alex Saorsa knew was, too.

A long time passed. And then she heard a man weeping. Saorsa raised her eyes. Alex sat next to the carnage, human in form again save for his blue-edged crow's wings. His head was in his hands as tears of confusion, exhaustion, and shame found their way out of him. He rocked slightly back and forth in place, like a child trying to soothe himself after a brutal nightmare.

Alex. She ran the few steps to him and knelt, putting her arms around him.

"Don't look, Saorsa," he sobbed, clutching at her and trying to turn her away, "don't look at what I've done."

·········

They sat on the roof for a long time, until Vika came and helped them down below. They retreated to the mostly windowless kitchen where it was warmer, and counted their blessings.

The Nemesis gem hung around Saorsa's neck. She hated it, but it was the safest place she could think of to keep it for now. *Alive.* Everyone was alive, although both tower and team were badly hurt. Windows shattered. Covered in blood. *But we endure.*

Saorsa thought back to her training. "We're all here. We're safe. That's step one." Saorsa paused. "I love all of you." She took a deep breath. "And I know our spiritual paths are different, but they all lead to the same place: light and love. So, before we continue, I would like us to spend a moment in gratitude. For each other. For the wolves. For the dragon. For the *light.*"

She saw Vika smile approvingly. *I'm leading the way she showed me.* The room fell silent. And then Eske let out a yell.

"What?" Everyone reached for their weapons.

"Look!" Eske pointed at the small stained-glass window near the closest fireplace. It had been shattered by the Fae. And it was *healing.* Laoise ran over for a closer look. Shards of colored glass and metal were disappearing from the floor, and reappearing in the window, fusing themselves into a whole.

Everyone in the room went as quickly as they could down the stairs to the Great Hall. It was happening there, too. Windows reforming. The door slowly rebuilding. Shattered furniture growing missing limbs. The fires in the fireplaces reappeared. And the dead were fading from view before their very eyes.

"What is happening?" Maria cried, holding Oona tight. "I don't understand!"

Malphas flew into the room and perched on the arm Rune offered him. "Did you do this?" Saorsa asked him. "Did *Thomas* do this?" The raven muttered and shook his head, then flew over to the table.

"The Morrigan," Willow said. "Goddess of victory in battle. This is her place. Could it be *her?*"

"That was a *lot* of magickal power we used," Laoise said. "Not to mention, we un-bodied and imprisoned a *goddess*. Somebody out there has to have noticed."

"And either the tower is designed to do this," Duncan stated, "or someone approved of us."

The castle continued to heal, and they turned their attention to doing the same. Saorsa took an exhausted Alex to her room to bathe, and then tucked him in her bed with Oona beside him. Oona cooed and nestled into Alex's arms.

"What now?" Alex asked Saorsa softly. "We have to do somethin' with that amulet. I dinnae want to be a jailer."

"I don't, either," Saorsa said. "It feels like she should be returned to the Fae. So they can decide her fate."

"This isnae the end of it, you know," Alex told her. "Nemesis wasnae working alone. Someone out there has two ritual items now. And we know too much, we've shown we're a threat. They'll be back, Saorsa. They have to show their face now."

Saorsa thought of the Nemesis amulet locked in her dressing table. "We won the day, Alex," she said, kissing her beloved on the forehead. "And we can do it again. The way forward is clear."

Alex looked at her. "What do ye mean, *eun beag?*"

"They're never going to stop. Not until they get the ritual items and the humans to charge them. Not until they get all the pieces of the *leth dhia*. So we...," she squeezed his hand, "are going to get to all of them *first*."

"And do what?" Alex looked slightly alarmed. "Destroy them? Stick me back together? Do a ritual ourselves? Hand everythin' over to the Fae High Council?"

"I don't know yet," said Saorsa. "It depends on what we find as we go. We're not even sure what the ritual, if there is one, is *for*. But the ones who partnered with Nemesis won't make victims of us any longer. We're going to be their opponents now. We have my bones to guide us. We've shown ourselves to be strong." Her mind was picking up speed. "We have a lot to do. I need to contact Mother Agnes. We need to deal with Fia. Edan will need to head to Branxholme, and we need to send word to the Aunties and Valkyries. I need to hear about the Scott sapphire. Maybe we can try and contact Elen about the...."

She found Alex's finger on her lips, gently but firmly stopping her speech.

"Tomorrow, *eun beag*," he said softly, his gray eyes sparkling. "Tomorrow. But for tonight, your man and this child here need ye. Come to bed an' hold my hand, Saorsa Stuart. Let's fall asleep, an' be grateful for the peace." Saorsa smiled and turned out the lamp.

And the orphan, the *leth dhia,* and the fledgling bone wytch fell asleep together, safe in each other's arms.

END OF BOOK FOUR

Thank you for reading! To read more on the real-life locations and character inspirations for this series, visit
tavabaird.com

Book Five is already underway!

....

A special thank you to **Diane B.**,
who edits this adventure out of the goodness of her heart.

A big hug to **Jennifer R.**,
who watches for all the little things that slip past me.

....

Interested in learning more about working with Light? Wish to experience energy healing for yourself and/or your animal companions?

Visit Willow Ridge Reiki and Healing Arts at <u>*www.willowridgereiki.com*</u> *for a full list of classes and private session offerings, or connect directly at jennifertaylor@willowridgereiki.com*

Made in the USA
Middletown, DE
12 September 2024